Ger

An English Composer

STEPHEN BANFIELD

ff

faber and faber

LONDON · BOSTON

First published in 1997
by Faber and Faber Limited
3 Queen Square London WC1N 3AU
This paperback edition first published in 1998

Phototypeset by Intype London Ltd
Printed in England by Clays Ltd, St Ives plc

© Stephen Banfield, 1998

Stephen Banfield is hereby identified as author of this
work in accordance with Section 77 of the Copyright,
Designs and Patents Act 1988

A CIP record for this book
is available from the British Library

ISBN 0-571-19598-9

2 4 6 8 10 9 7 5 3 1

To Howard Ferguson, on the seventieth anniversary
of his first meeting with Gerald Finzi

August 1996

I'm amused to hear that a number of RCM professors are now saying 'why is this fellow Finzi talking about Parry when he never knew him'. The answer, of course, is that I'm talking about him precisely because I *didn't* know him!

Gerald Finzi to Robin Milford, 22 February 1948

Contents

Acknowledgements

This book was commissioned by the Finzi Trust, who financed its research and writing in full. I thank the Trustees, including my initial contact, Robert Gower, for this support and for their co-operation and forbearance with various delays, and apologise to them and to other readers for the fact that, since the book had nonetheless to be completed within a precise timescale, there are still many avenues of investigation requiring further research. The Finzi Trust also paid for the help of three research assistants, Stephen Newbould, Grahame Willis and Denny Lyster, to whom I am grateful for sterling work in transcribing letters and occasional inspiration in deciphering them.

Several individuals have offered assistance in less official but crucial ways. Many years ago, when I was writing about Gerald Finzi in my D.Phil. thesis, Joy Finzi and Diana McVeagh were kind with encouragement and generous with material, and I wish to record my overall debt to them. I have continued to draw heavily on Diana McVeagh's expertise, and not just from her published writings, for when I commenced this book I was presented indirectly with the fruits of her research in the form of Finzi's collected correspondence; having this to hand facilitated my work enormously, though a number of items appear to be missing. I have not, however, read any portion of Diana's own uncompleted book on Finzi, unlike one or two previous students who did have access to it, which explains why I occasionally draw on them rather than her.

Philip Thomas likewise provided the groundwork for much of my own research, and the generous loan of all his notes and manuscript material, including Finzi's sketchbooks and many other fragments, was of inestimable benefit. Andrew Burn also provided material (and encouragement at a vital stage), and Megan Prictor magnanimously shared the hard-won fruits of her research in the BBC Written Archives. On the genealogical front, Jerome Farrell, Archivist to the City of Westminster, Miriam

Rodrigues-Pereira, Archivist to the Spanish and Portuguese Jews' Congregation, and Dr Anthony Joseph contributed a good deal of information, as did Miss D. L. Lawrence and Mr Clark of J. A. Finzi, Layman, Clark & Co. Ltd. Christopher Grogan and Jonathan Cook allowed me to see and use important unpublished research. Special thanks are due to them all; to many others, including the late Iris Lemare, Anthony Scott, Ursula Vaughan Williams, Adrian Officer and Nigel and Jo Finzi, who loaned, shared or copied material; to Peggy Bendle who showed me over Beech Knoll with the kind permission of its owners; and to Rowan Armes who mined the Royal Academy of Music archives for me. I wish to record greater gratitude still to Christopher and Hilary Finzi for their excellent and friendly hospitality and to Christopher for his patient supply of information and encouragement. The greatest debt of all is to Howard Ferguson, who over six years or so has never failed to provide warm friendship, *haute cuisine* and replies to my queries by return of post in equally wondrous measure. I must thank him also for his extraordinarily sharp memory and critical sense, the latter safeguarding any over-reaching of the former with rare reliability and, most important of all, humour.

Howard also read and commented on the entire script. So did Christopher and Nigel Finzi, Megan Prictor and Jeremy Dale Roberts. I thank them heartily for this, while apologising for any stubbornness towards fact, emphasis or interpretation in response. Portions of the script have been the subject of invaluable feedback from others, notably Michael Daly, Jerome Farrell and Carole Rosen. Nigel Fortune very generously read the proofs and rescued me from numerous errors.

Liz Pooley and Ann Warner of the Finzi Trust Friends have been frequent and essential points of contact. I am sorry that I cannot similarly list and thank individually all those who have answered letters, hosted and guided my work in libraries, allowed me to interview them and supplied information or a critical perspective on an institutional or personal basis. I am grateful to them all, and to the staff at Faber and Faber, especially Belinda Matthews.

Finally, I should like to thank my colleagues at the University of Birmingham, especially Professor Colin Timms and Dr Robert Meikle, for doing without me (and a microfilm reader) for a year, perhaps to their relief but undoubtedly at their inconvenience, and Heather Espley of the School of Performance Studies for keeping all comers at bay.

Stephen Banfield

ACKNOWLEDGEMENTS

The author and the Finzi Trust wish to thank all those who, many years ago, put their letters from Gerald Finzi at the disposal of his original biographer; they are listed in the Index of Letters. Thanks are also due to the custodians of collections of Finzi letters listed at the head of the Index of Letters (p. 518) and made available to the present author more recently. Every effort has been made to trace the copyright holders of letters to Finzi and of other material quoted and we are grateful to those, listed below, who have given permission for them to be quoted. The author or the Finzi Trust would be glad to hear from those whom we were unable to locate. Grateful acknowledgement is made to the authors, publishers and periodicals listed below for permission to reprint previously published materials; if any have been inadvertently omitted, apologies are offered.

John Amis, for extracts from *Amiscellany: my life, my music*.

Banks Music Publications, for musical examples from *Requiem da camera* by Gerald Finzi.

Lady Bliss, for extracts from the correspondence and writings of Sir Arthur Bliss, including his autobiography, *As I Remember*.

Boosey & Hawkes Music Publishers Ltd., for musical examples from the various works by Gerald Finzi in their domain.

© Breitkopf & Härtel, Wiesbaden-Leipzig, for a musical example from the Serenade for strings by Edward Elgar.

Nicholas Busch, for extracts from the correspondence of William Busch.

Antony Bye and Peter Phillips, for extracts from *The Musical Times*.

Carcanet Press Ltd., on behalf of the Estate of Edmund Blunden, for extracts from the poems of Edmund Blunden.

Faber and Faber Ltd., for extracts from the poems of W. H. Auden and Walter de la Mare.

Howard Ferguson, for extracts from his correspondence and articles.

The Guardian ©, copyright owner, for an extract from a review by Colin Mason.

Paul Kildea, for extracts from his doctoral dissertation *Selling Britten: A Social and Economic History* (forthcoming, Oxford University Press).

Alfred Lengnick & Co., for a musical example from Symphony No. 7 by Edmund Rubbra.

Diana McVeagh, for extracts from articles and sleeve notes.

Michael de Navarro, for extracts from the correspondence of José Maria de Navarro.

ACKNOWLEDGEMENTS

News International Syndication, for extracts from *Times* reviews by Frank Howes.

Oxford University Press, for a musical example from *Street Corner* by Alan Rawsthorne.

Benedict Rubbra, for extracts from the correspondence of Edmund Rubbra.

Schott & Co., London, for a musical example from *A Shropshire Lad: Rhapsody for Orchestra* by George Butterworth.

Anthony Scott, for extracts from his correspondence.

Mrs Ursula Vaughan Williams, for extracts from the correspondence of Ralph Vaughan Williams, Adeline Vaughan Williams and herself, and from her book *RVW: A Biography of Ralph Vaughan Williams*, published by Oxford University Press.

Note on sources

The author–date reference system in the main text should be self-explanatory when taken in conjunction with the Bibliography or Index of Letters, as the case may be. 19151214 indicates the date 14 December 1915. Quotations from Joy Finzi's journal are indicated by 'J. Finzi [+date]'; from letters to, or conversations with, the author by 'Ferguson 1985–96' or whatever, these sources being listed in the Bibliography (rather than in the Index of Letters). I have silently corrected misspellings and added deficient punctuation and apostrophes in quotations from letters and Joy Finzi's journal, for Joy's were sufficiently idiosyncratic that a great many pedantic and obtrusive '[*sic*]'s would otherwise have been necessary. Gerald's style was more standard, though he always misspelt (thus) 'occaison' and 'buisness' and could not get the right number of 't's and 'n's in *Britannica*.

List of illustrations

Unless otherwise stated, the photographs are reproduced by permission of the Finzi Trust

CHAPTER I

From Padua to Harrogate

On 1 February 1928, in an LSO concert at the Queen's Hall conducted by Vaughan Williams, Sybil Eaton gave the first complete performance of Gerald Finzi's Violin Concerto. This was in effect Finzi's London début, and the following day the *Times* critic referred to 'a Concerto for violin and orchestra by one Finzi, who set us wondering why a composer of his name dealt so confidently in a definitely English idiom', adding, 'The fact that Mr Finzi . . . was present to bow acknowledgments at the end helped to solve the problem' (:10). Vaughan Williams sent a copy of the review to his brother-in-law, R. O. Morris, Finzi's counterpoint teacher, who replied to Finzi from Philadelphia: 'What did make me angry was the insolent personal comment in the *Times*' (19280208+?).

What did the *Times* reviewer mean? Was it simply that the composer's presence suggested British rather than overseas domicile? This alone would not have roused Morris's anger and could have been deduced from Finzi's first name, absent from the reviewer's comments. We are therefore led to assume that he or she found something significant in Finzi's appearance. Without being told what it was, we can only wonder whether on the platform he looked British or Italian, fully assimilated or conspicuously Jewish. Either way, we are now entitled to ask whether it was the question or Morris's refusal to countenance the question that was the more insolent. A year in the United States seems to have made little difference to Morris's perspective, which was that of his time, nation and class. Finzi himself emphatically shared it. While still in his teens he had rejected his heredity and chosen his environment, which he never ceased to compose alongside his music. Both music and environment were to be pursued as wholly indigenous English constructs. As we should say today, he invented himself. Perhaps he had to.

The invention worked, for Finzi still powerfully represents a restricted code of cultural nationalism, an ethos of island containment and uncompetitive self-sufficiency. Did he view this as a choice or a given? He modelled himself on the idea of the minor English poet, and we have come to see him as he probably saw himself: as an artist whose limitations were innate and whose pastoral or provincial lifestyle and aspirations would reflect those limitations while somehow invalidating them. In almost everything he undertook, be it cultivating apple trees, collecting books, reading Hardy and setting him to music, editing Gurney's songs and poems, or performing eighteenth-century English music with his amateur string orchestra, he responded to the idea of the 'mute inglorious Milton' and the possibility of its transcendence. Yet in creating this world for himself he was relying on the very cornerstone he preferred to reject, that of birth, for in his case innate limitations were in reality innate resources. There was nothing minor about the achievements, social standing and finances of the family into which he was born and which nurtured him into secure economic freedom. A cynical view would be that he had it both ways; a sympathetic one that his background gave rise to tensions in his life and work which he unconsciously suppressed. To be fair to Finzi, he recognised his privilege and was anxious not to condemn the confines of those who had not enjoyed it, though he also recognised that achievement may depend on it. 'As for the "mean-spirited" professors,' he wrote to Robin Milford in 1948, 'perhaps the pressure of life, of competition, has been too much for spirits too frail to bear it. I don't like to think of how much worse I shd have been if I had not been a comparatively free man, for I cd never have earned my living as a musician, not even as a pedagogue; and how sour that might have turned me' (19480308b).

Finzi's relatives all belonged to respectable, prosperous and distinguished Jewish families that had been settled in England for several generations, Sephardi on his father's side, Ashkenazi on his mother's. The Sephardim, worshipping at the old Spanish and Portuguese synagogue in Bevis Marks in the City of London and sometimes making use of their own language, Ladino, were largely of Hispanic origin, though many of them had already dispersed (for instance to Italy, where the Finzis were and are most firmly established) long before the expulsions from the Iberian Peninsula of the 1490s. They had come and gone in

Britain at various times according to the political climate but stayed after Cromwell gave them his blessing in 1656. Although not politically emancipated until the nineteenth century, they enjoyed, by and large, happy relations with the civic authorities in London and other mercantile cities such as Bristol, and the Bevis Marks synagogue was actually built for them by a Quaker (Jews were not allowed to join the construction guilds). The English Sephardim retained their dynastic and trading links with the continent and flourished greatly in the eighteenth century, but by the late nineteenth they represented 'old money', an easy-going and sophisticated but declining cultural aristocracy, and were a 'dwindling group' (Gartner 1960, 2/1973: 225), despite having thrown up several families and individuals who served their nation magnificently, including Disraeli (who, however, had converted to Christianity) and the Montefiores. Not that decline applied to Finzi's own family, whose wealth and status were comfortable, stable and almost certainly on the increase into his own generation.

Sephardi relations with the Ashkenazim, who originated from central and eastern Europe, were generally good, and there was plenty of intermarriage, particularly in the nineteenth century. The differences were and are primarily liturgical. However, the centrality of the synagogue and its leaders to Jewish family life and that of the whole community has meant that they have also been cultural, for example where customs in the naming of offspring are concerned. Families stayed overall within one tradition or the other, usually distinguishable by surname, and the 'Sephardi cousinhood' has remained a tight-knit group, albeit one which has long been fully assimilated into British life.

There were Ashkenazim in Britain in the eighteenth century, but it was their huge waves of immigration in the later nineteenth that overlaid the older Sephardi culture. The London Jew of Dickensian imagination and prejudice was a poor East Ender and a relative newcomer, swarming, uprooted, living very much at the city's surface intersections, liable to sink or swim, and if able to swim, becoming very quickly upwardly mobile. There were undoubtedly social tensions between the 'cousinhood' and the Ashkenazi 'new money', flashy and upstart to Sephardi thinking which became all the more assimilationist as the highly visible growth of the Ashkenazi communities in London and other European cities triggered the great wave of latent anti-Semitism in the later nineteenth century that became manifest all too soon and all too widely.

3

If the Finzis did regard Gerald's mother's relatives as in any way *arriviste* or socially inferior, it cannot have made for any serious tensions, for the two sides mingled closely, supported each other, lived in the same road during Gerald's youth, and prospered alike financially. And if they eventually became differentiated in his own mind, it was partly through the chance patterns of bereavement, though, as with all aspects of his relationship to his heritage, we really do not know how or why his views and experience were formed in the course of childhood. Nevertheless, we do know that he had no time for his maternal uncles, and it was undoubtedly this side of the family which he associated with 'a lot of infamous nonsense about banking' (19231103).

The Italian Finzis can be traced back to the fourteenth century, beginning with one Musetino del fu Museto de Finzi di Ancona 'who was concerned in establishing the first Jewish money-lending office in Padua in 1369' (Elbogen 1903: 389). Formidably learned and enterprising by turns, they make it difficult for one to ignore the more far-reaching hereditary elements in Gerald's make-up, though he may not have known anything about his continental forebears and always violently repudiated the notion that blood is thicker than water. They were rabbis, astronomers, bankers, translators and physicians and spread east to the Balkans and as far as Jerusalem. Isaac Raphael Finzi's preaching in Ferrara in the eighteenth century was outstanding enough to attract Christians as well as Jews. The nineteenth-century Finzis included poets, lawyers, an Assyriologist and two patriots, one of whom, Ciro, died at the age of sixteen defending the Roman Republic in 1849, the other, Giuseppe, becoming the confidant of Mazzini and Garibaldi and a long-standing member of parliament.

As for the English Finzis, present in London from the eighteenth century onwards, some sources state that Gerald's great-grandfather's family came from Leghorn (Livorno), whose coral trade and connections with London as a rising centre of international finance in the early nineteenth century were certainly the reason for the transplantation of a number of Sephardi families to England, including the Montefiores. Most likely, however, it was Samuel Isaac Finzi from Ferrara who was that great-grandfather (Judah)'s father. Ferrara is still the city most associated with the Italian Finzis, because of Bassani's novel *The Garden of the Finzi-Continis* and its film. Samuel Isaac arrived in London in 1768, worked in a counting house, and died in 1807. Judah, whether or not he was his son, married a Portuguese widow, Simha Carvalho, in 1808, and it was their second son, Samuel Leon, who became Gerald's grandfather.

Samuel Leon Finzi (1811–95) was a 'surgeon dentist', a common Sephardi profession in nineteenth-century Britain, and he designed a universal drill exhibited at the Great Exhibition of 1851. He was also a keen violinist and a member of the Beethoven Society. An only child from his first marriage died young, as did the mother. His second wife, whom he married in 1850, was Harriette Abraham (1821–95) from the Jewish community of Bristol, where her father was an optician. By the time she died, within a month of her husband, the couple, who produced five children, had seen three sons rise to prosperity, with all the family members living relatively near each other, evidently in some style, in substantial households in north-west London (Paddington, Maida Vale and St John's Wood).

Their first child, Haim Warburg, probably did not survive. The second was Leon (Judah) Moses Finzi, who became a well-known medical practitioner. He may have gone over to the Reform faith, for he does not feature in the Sephardi records. Third came Daniel (1853–1906), who got as close to music as publishing it for a living permitted. Evidently his business flourished, for by the time of the 1891 census he was 'living on own means' with five servants in a six-storey house in Notting Hill, and in 1897 he moved further upmarket into Hamilton Terrace, St John's Wood, where he lived at Number 32, across the road and a few houses further down from where Jack Finzi established himself in the same year. Gerald would barely have remembered him, but his second wife lived on until 1945 and their children and grand-daughter, Jean Finzi, kept within the Spanish and Portuguese congregation.

John Abraham (Jack) Finzi (1860–1909), Gerald's father, was the youngest of the five children. (There was also a girl, Esther [1855–1913], who seems to have kept a low, spinsterly profile.) A keen sportsman and naturalist – butterflies were his speciality – he had a good baritone voice. We are told that he was not a practising Jew; be that as it may, his cultural background was still firmly defined. He was educated at University College, London, founded in 1827 as 'the first great educational institution [in Britain] to admit all classes and all creeds: Catholics, Jews and Dissenters were no longer debarred from taking degrees', and there, in addition to a firm friendship with Frank Heatherly, son of Thomas Heatherly who founded the Heatherly Art School, he made 'the many and important ties between . . . individual Jews' which were still a fact of life for him. One of these associations was with Raphael Meldola, a fellow entomologist. Meldola was 'among the greatest English Jews' and, according to Henry Mond, 'the greatest in science', discovering coal-tar dyes and producing in 1879 the first aniline blue (oxazine blue) dye, known as Meldola's Blue; and in 1913 he was awarded the annual Davy Medal for the most important discovery in chemistry made in Europe or Anglo-America (Emden 1944: 117, 122, 254). He was Gerald's godfather, his first name presumably accounting for Gerald's second (though it could equally well have been added, according to Sephardi custom, if he had become seriously ill at birth). Meldola's grandfather, also called Raphael, had, perhaps like Judah Finzi, come to London from Leghorn in 1805 and became Chief Rabbi of the Spanish and Portuguese synagogue, his own grandfather having been Chief Rabbi of Pisa and his father Professor of Oriental Languages at the University of Paris. This provides an obvious parallel with the eminence of the Finzis, and that the connection should have been so strong in Gerald's father's generation is surely evidence of the continuing power of his Jewish intellectual and social ties.

Jack Finzi died of cancer of the roof of the mouth just before the eighth birthday of his youngest son, Gerald. Gerald must have been traumatised by his father's condition, for it disfigured him for two years, causing great pain and involving an unsuccessful operation to remove his right eye and part of his upper jaw. And with Jack's death, Gerald was deprived of any male role model on his paternal side, for Jack's brothers as well as his father had predeceased him. Moreover, all three of Gerald's own brothers, one of whom was highly creative, plus his first composition teacher, Ernest Farrar, were dead by the time he was scarcely seventeen, as we shall see.

Gerald's mother, Eliza Emma (Lizzie) Finzi, *née* Leverson, and her relatives accordingly loomed all too large in his upbringing. Her own mother, Kate Hyam, was one of four children of David Hyam and Hannah Moses (Marsden). David, Lizzie's grandfather, had three sisters and five brothers, two of whom founded the famous Manchester clothing firm Hyam Brothers. Their parents were Hannah Lazarus and Hyam Hyam, whose own father Simon Hyam of Ipswich was born about 1740 and came to England from Hamburg.

Lizzie, the youngest of Kate's four children, was born in 1865 in Dalston, an area of north London which already had a Jewish congregation but was not yet the important staging post it would become for Russian Jews on their rise from Whitechapel and Stepney to the northern suburbs. Here Kate lived, deserted by her husband, Montague Richard Leverson, and soon to move to her ancestral Germany to keep a girls' school in Hanover. Lizzie Leverson was brought up in Germany, spending sixteen years of her youth there, and spoke all her life with a German accent, though she returned to London at some later stage before her marriage to Jack Finzi, which took place at her home in Kensington Square Gardens under the auspices of the Bevis Marks synagogue in 1887, the year after he founded his shipbroking firm, still trading as Finzi, Layman, Clark. It is not known whether she met him in England or Germany. She had a sister, Hettie, and two brothers. Hettie married Adolph Schwabacher, a Hanoverian banker, one of whose relatives, of proud Prussian officer stock, face scars and all, visited the Finzi family home just before the Second World War, assuring Gerald that he had nothing to fear concerning Germany's intentions, and later committed suicide in shame. The two brothers became tobacco merchants, though not, apparently, in partnership. One was Louis Pianciani Leverson; he had four daughters. The other, unmarried, was the Uncle William against whose patronising attitude Gerald later railed when his music began to make its mark in the 1920s.

The Leversons were a formidable, burgeoning family. Gerald's great-grandfather, Montague Levyson (c.1793–1850; the name was changed around the time of his death), may have been the first to settle in England. He was a diamond merchant and founded the firm continued by his first son George (1826–1906), an acquaintance of Garibaldi, whose own first child Ernest (1851–1921) could afford West End premises shared with Louis Rothschild and outlets for both business and pleasure in Paris. There were two other sons, James (1828–1908) and the youngest child, Montague Richard (Lizzie's father), plus a daughter, Hester. The three sons between them produced in their turn thirteen offspring, of whom nine were male and whose combined wealth must have amounted to millions, since most of them were very good at making money or rising in the affluent professions (two of George's five sons founded a military dynasty). This was the family into which the novelist Ada Leverson (1862–1933) also married (as Ernest's wife), her own pedigree, in this case Marrano, every bit as distinguished as the Finzi one and including a pupil of Charles Burney, a councillor of Louis XIV and a friend of Spinoza. The fact is that in Spanish and Portuguese

Jewry in particular you could not take two steps without stumbling across some link with the intellectual or social nerve-centres of Europe, past and present.

Lizzie's father, Montague Richard Leverson, is nonetheless a shadowy character. Born in 1830, he claimed to have been university-trained in Germany or Switzerland, though it is difficult to see when or how this could have happened, since he was an articled clerk in London in 1850–51 at his father's grudging expense and continuously in business as a solicitor and patent agent between then and the mid-1860s. Somehow he also managed to append a doctorate and a master's degree to his name from that point on. Could he have studied political economy part-time at University College? He was certainly an out-and-out Benthamite and mirrored his hero's maverick radicalism and diversity of undertakings as the prolific and wide-ranging author and pamphleteer that he became. And was he musical? We do not know; but he came into contact with music through his initial area of expertise, copyright law, his first publication being *Copyright and Patents; or, Property in thought* . . . about the Boosey ruling of 1854. His *bête noire* was the European legal system, but having clearly failed to persuade Britain to change its ways when he published *The Reformers' Reform Bill* . . . *a* . . . *new and complete code of electoral law for the United Kingdom* in 1866, he left for the United States, minus family, and appears to have travelled steadily westwards, becoming an educationalist and publishing first in New York *On the Uses and Functions of Money* and other topics, then in Denver, where he tried to influence the Colorado state constitution but again must have failed. One senses that nothing short of an entire society run on his envisioned lines would have satisfied him. After a period in San Francisco he seems to have settled back on the east coast, lecturing at the University of Virginia on *The Science of Legislation* in 1890 and keeping his mind active on other topics such as *Thought on Institutions of the Higher Education* and *War Clouds of Europe and How to Disperse Them* (both 1893, the latter appearing in the international language Volapük as well as English).

It was probably then that he fully grasped what the land of opportunity could offer and qualified in a third discipline, medicine, complete with a Baltimore Ph.D. In 1900 he published a homoeopathic pamphlet and in 1911 a translation of Béchamp's treatise on the blood. Eventually he drew together two of his professional strands, for his last work was about ownership and plagiarism of medical discovery, published posthumously in 1923. This was described by Gerald at the time as 'not worth getting' (192309); he was doubtless more pleased with one of Leverson's material effects, a chair, reputed to be George Washington's presidential one, which is still in the library at Ashmansworth. Apparently one of Leverson's ancestors had been Washington's secretary, though it is not clear how this might link in with what else we know of his family. He did eventually return to England, where he remarried and lived (rather tamely, one might think) in Bournemouth. Did Gerald ever meet him?

Montague Leverson could have been anything from a brilliant original to a Dickensian charlatan, but by Gerald's standards, if he thought much about him at all, his career must have seemed that of a soulless Utilitarian, one of the inartistic class more proximately represented by Uncle William. At the very least, and however much of a connection we may now sense with Gerald's own (and his sons') unusual diversity of interests and activities, Leverson's cosmopolitan field of vision was something to react against, for it had involved the abandonment of his family, including Gerald's mother. To her, on the other hand, Gerald owed the security of his music. She was a fine amateur pianist and even composed, *Deux études* for piano being published by Novello in 1906 as her Op. 9. Against his and Joy Finzi's later exasperation with her as 'a simple & rather silly little woman, [in] whom lifelong deafness, & a fundamental lack of brain, had created permanent illusions about everything' must be placed his gratitude to her 'for having made him independent, in a small way, as a young man, thus enabling him to take up music' (J. Finzi 19550807–09) and, earlier, 'for allowing him down as a small child from the nursery after tea':

He was the only child with a musical interest . . . There, without speaking and with a stereoscope to look through, he would sit on a fur rug in front of the fire to listen to her playing. The seriousness of these occasions made an impression on him, and through all the stress and trials within the family after the early death of his father she continued to support and foster his musical preoccupation. (J. Finzi 1973)

Gerald may have been a lone musician, but he was not the only one of Samuel Leon Finzi's grandchildren to achieve national eminence. Leon (Judah)'s son Neville Samuel Finzi (1881–1968) – Leon also had two daughters, but none of the three married – went on to become the most eminent member of the family with the exception of Gerald (an exception perhaps doubtful during their lifetimes: Neville, not Gerald, is the Finzi in *Who's Who 1942*, though Gerald, not Neville, is the one with a *Dictionary of National Biography* entry). Neville was medically trained like his father and, like his Uncle Jack, attended University College – School, college proper and Hospital. He was a pioneer in the therapeutic use of radium, initiating his researches, and British radiology, in 1908 with the treatment of Jack Finzi's cancer and publishing on the topic in 1913. (Jack had bought radium direct from Madame Curie and told Neville, recently qualified, to do what he could with it.) He became head of the X-ray department at St Bartholomew's Hospital and 'because of his insistence against all opposition on the need for even higher voltages [he] exercised a profound influence on the development of radiotherapy throughout the world' (W. M. L. 1968), though later on he began to reverse the dosage trend. Like Gerald, who was able to turn to him for advice when his own health eventually failed, he pursued multifarious interests and abounded in nervous energy, 'a familiar figure at Barts in a very brief white coat bounding up the stairs of the outpatient block, three at a time, or racing across the square' (ibid.).

The first of Lizzie and Jack Finzi's five children, Kate (Katie), had been born in 1890. Gerald, the last, was born on 14 July 1901, according to Joy 'an unwanted addition to a bursting upper-floor nursery and not welcomed by his sister and brothers'. This may well be true enough, but any impression of straitened circumstances or family over-reaching must be firmly denied. Gerald's birthplace, 53 (now 93) Hamilton Terrace, St John's Wood, is in one of the smartest streets of one of the smartest suburbs in London, and with Daniel Finzi at Number 32, another of the Leversons, Louis George, at Number 48 (next door to Charles Mocatta), the composer and conductor Frederic Cowen about to move into Number 54 and Edward German busy writing *Merrie England* just around the corner in Hall Road, he was in excellent if perhaps overwhelming company. These are large, detached, extremely stylish houses, built around 1840 and bristling with blue plaques. The Chief Rabbi of the British Empire was the other next-door neighbour of Louis George Leverson's successor from 1913, and further down the street, towards town, lived the artist William Strang (in the house that had been George Macfarren's) and, at an earlier period, the civil engineer Sir Joseph Bazalgette. The violinist Hans Wessely was at

Number 4. Nothing short of a *Forsyte Saga* or a *Buddenbrooks* could do such a background justice (and Louis George's cupboard certainly contained at least one skeleton at this time).

Despite this solidarity of family and culture, which with a number of successful artists, including musicians, in the street could not by any stretch of the imagination be described as a philistine environment, Gerald, although fond of his father, maintained that 'he always felt a stranger' among his siblings and 'likened this feeling to a group of telegraph wires, each being able to communicate forward and backward to eternity, but never to the closely adjoining lines on either side' (J. Finzi 1973). There was certainly little love lost between him and Katie, the only one of his siblings to survive beyond the First World War. Described by Neville Finzi as 'a bounder with charm' (C. Finzi 1990–96), she married and became Kay Gilmour, and with something of her maternal grandfather's versatility she published three books, *Eighteen Months in the War Zone: the record of a woman's work on the Western front* in 1916, *Finland* in 1931 and *Committee Procedure* in 1950, this last title more or less summing up the difference between her and Gerald (though by this time he himself had learnt more than a modicum of committee expertise). Of his three brothers, Felix (1893–1913) was the eldest. A brilliant youth who submitted a design for an aircraft carrier to the Admiralty, he committed suicide in India at the age of twenty, depressed by adolescent feelings of sexual degeneracy, as was confirmed to the family decades later when the doctor who had signed his death certificate happened to be staying with one of their neighbours at Ashmansworth. Douglas, born in 1897, died of pneumonia on 7 July 1912 in the care of his school, Bradfield College near Reading (which did not prevent the Newbury String Players from performing there many years later). Edgar, born in 1898 and closest in age to Gerald, showed great talent as a teenage cartoonist – his work is supposed to have been accepted for *Punch* around 1915, though it cannot be traced in print – but died in action with the Fleet Air Arm in the Aegean, shot down on 5 September 1918.

The family flourished long enough to produce the celebrated 1904 photograph of five stepped siblings (see illus. 3) but was soon overshadowed by Jack Finzi's cancer. He was already wearing an eyepatch in family photographs dating from summer 1907, and succumbed two years later, on 1 July 1909; no less than twelve black horse-drawn coaches formed his funeral cortège, which must have been quite a sight in its progress up Hamilton Terrace. The *Times* announced the net personalty of his residual estate as £22,583 15s. 3d. (6 August 1909: 11). This was the source of Gerald's income as a young man, though since Jack left all his financial affairs in the hands of Lizzie and her two brothers as trustees, there is no precise way of telling how much he was given as an allowance or what, if any, arrangements they agreed to on his majority.

Nor do we know much about Gerald's childhood beyond his perception of it as isolated and unhappy. At first he was educated privately, and it was probably after the death of his father that he was sent to a boarding school, Kingswood, in Camberley, Surrey (now part of Collingwood College). This was a bad experience: he remained in the same form for four years and faked fainting fits in the bath in order to escape. One should probably not blame the school, which was a new establishment priding itself on 'a well-equipped gymnasium, a carpenter's shop, a dark room for amateur photographers' and a curriculum 'thoroughly up to date, and ... varied to suit individual requirements' (press advertisement, quoted in Toynbee n.d.). Nevertheless, it was preparatory 'for the Public Schools and the Royal Navy', taught physical drill and rifle-shooting, and encouraged its pupils 'to take part in all manly games' (ibid.), and Lizzie or her relatives may have thought that the children should have military careers. More likely they were simply responding to the loss of paternal discipline at home. Gerald contracted measles at Kingswood in February 1913, a lonely business – given that his mother and sister were in France, for with Douglas dead and Felix in India Mrs Finzi had sold up at Hamilton Terrace three months earlier, presumably to winter abroad – and not the only time he would have to go into a sanatorium.

Gerald, with Edgar, then went to Switzerland with a tutor for a year because of his – their? – uncertain health, real and simulated; he also spent some time in Germany: 'I'm old enough to remember a little of Germany before the war,' he later told William Busch (19381012). By this time, indeed at the age of eleven, he had decided that 'music was his job' (McVeagh 1979a) and had started composing, as we know from an undated newspaper cutting, probably from summer 1913, which powerfully evokes a world which was soon to disappear for ever with the war:

ST VALERY-EN-CAUX IS MECCA OF MANY VISITORS

Every hotel is full . . .

The weather is superb, and everyone is enjoying to the full the delight of excellent roads, charming pastoral country, or shady wood. For all these are to be found in this favoured nook of Normandy.

A concert was held last night at the Hotel de la Paix . . . the sum realised substantially assisted the funds of the 'Société de Préparation militaire'. It was, too, a great success artistically.

. . . Master Finzi, aged eleven [Gerald corrected this to 12 in pencil], played one of his own compositions on the piano. Mrs K. [corrected by Gerald to L.] J. Finzi also played some of her own compositions . . .

After the concert the large dining-room was cleared, and dancing was continued into the small hours of the morning.

Needless to say, a very fair quantity of champagne was taken to keep the animated dancers going, especially those who gave a very graceful exposition of the tango.

The boys returned from Switzerland with their mother when war broke out, but with characteristic light-mindedness she took them to Paris on the way home to see the sights, which they did within the sound of German gunfire. This was probably in early September 1914; later the same month Gerald was back in Camberley.

Next, Gerald and Edgar were sent to Mount Arlington, a private school at Hindhead, Surrey. Probably the only thing that would have endeared it to Gerald was the fact that Harold Monro, founder of the Poetry Bookshop, had been there some years earlier. The April 1915 issue of the school magazine, *The Magnet*, announced the two new boys and reported their participation in the musical play *Ali Baba* and their mother's presence in the audience. Gerald played the slave Morgiana, Edgar Ali Baba's wife Zaida, and *The Magnet*, which found most of the songs well sung, added, as though the music was so much cricket, that 'the chief credit lies with Adams, G. Finzi and Gray, who all scored successes' (anon 1915). But Gerald cannot have stayed at Mount Arlington for long, for in October his mother moved to Harrogate and he settled there with her at 22 Duchy Road, a large house in a spacious street. Edgar probably enlisted at this time, around his seventeenth birthday.

Mrs Finzi is thought to have chosen Harrogate, perhaps after the Zeppelin raids on London began in April 1915, in order to be in the centre of Britain and as far away from aerial bombardment as possible. She was, Philip Thomas points out, 'by all accounts a charming woman but a defective map reader' (1990b: 14), but her logic was probably shared by many at the time. Harrogate was in any case an obvious choice for a Jewish widow who could no longer decamp to the continent. She doubtless had connections there, and it was much more of a cultural centre then than now, modelled firmly on the German spas (it still has a *Kursaal*) and with a professional orchestra during the season. Known for its good air – it spreads breezily up towards the Pennine moorlands – which Gerald's health was thought to require, it was all in all about the most sensible place to which she could have taken a musical son during wartime. The Municipal Orchestra was conducted by Julian Clifford, who had studied in Leipzig, and it was to him that Lizzie Finzi first turned for advice about him. He recommended Ernest Farrar as a teacher.

Farrar's presence in Harrogate was fortunate, for he was a young and enthusiastic composer closely connected with the best musical talent of his generation, a generation which formed the backbone of the turn-of-the-century English musical renaissance. Born in 1885, he had studied with Stanford at the Royal College of Music from 1905 to 1909. There, as one of the 'Beloved Vagabonds' and in other circles, he was friendly with Audrey Alston (Britten's early viola teacher), Frank Bridge, Clive Carey, Ivor James, Felix Salmond, and two musicians with whom Finzi would later have separate connections, Marion Scott and Harold Samuel; indeed, Scott performed his violin pieces with him. A close Yorkshire friend was Ernest Bullock. Most important of all, he knew and admired Vaughan Williams. More than thirty-five years later, staying with the Finzis after the first performance of his *Oxford Elegy*, Vaughan Williams would eventually see the connection come full circle, as Joy Finzi described in her journal, transcribing or absorbing Gerald's thoughts and opinions as was her custom.

G[erald] referred to fact that he [Vaughan Williams] had used a quotation from the Matthew Arnold poem in a very early orchestral work Harnham Down (now a bungalow village!). VW seemed amazed that G knew about this work which had been discarded nearly 40 years ago. He had incorporated some of its material into the new work. Later he posted G the early MS of Harnham Down for G to look at. G found it all rather touching, & remembered Ernest Farrar's enthusiasm for it round about 1916. Then VW was the rising young composer & the order of the day was 'out-of-door' music, Whitman, Norfolk jackets, pastoral impressions. It all seems so far away & though the beauty of these musical counterparts of the English water-colour school will one day be re-felt, for the present it is a turned page. Harnham Down has something of the VW we know in it, but has a good deal of amorphous impressionistic harmony which has long ago been discarded from his vocabulary. (J. Finzi 19520719)

However, we might also infer Farrar's limitations from this connection. Despite his probable familiarity with *A London Symphony* through Julian Clifford's 1914 performance of it in Harrogate (see Lloyd 1996a), the evidence rather suggests that if in 1916 he was still enthusing about an unpublished, discarded work dating from 1904–7 which he must have heard during his time at college, he had not fully kept abreast of Vaughan Williams's subsequent development beginning with *On Wenlock Edge* and continuing (fitfully) with the *Sea Symphony* and more radically with the Tallis Fantasia, though this last had not yet taken root. Farrar's music bears this out, its search for the picturesque and vernacular timely but ultimately parochial, fearful of the imaginative leap into *plein air* Franco-Russian primitivism that saved Vaughan Williams, Holst, Bax, Ireland and others in the years leading up to the First World War. Heartfelt and sometimes adroit at the local level of expression, as we can appreciate from the second of his three *Vagabond Songs*, a setting of 'Silent noon' which Finzi later championed, Farrar's inspiration remained short-breathed.

Yet there was something positive in this for his pupil. Farrar's urbane and congenial spirit, with no axes to grind and no chips on his shoulder, perhaps basically unambitious behind the 'extremely reserved, well-liked', handsome exterior (Officer 1984: 24), must have made for a relaxed and fruitful relationship, satisfying Finzi's musical curiosity rather than challenging his character. If Farrar found in his young pupil a promising artist, Finzi probably found in his young teacher a friend to idolise (Thomas 1990: 14), certainly a real musician to talk to and write for. When Farrar was taken away from him and he went to Bairstow, the contrast between what a fresh practitioner had offered and what a strict pedagogue now demanded would prove at first acutely painful, and although he and Bairstow developed a respectful and productive relationship, Finzi never accepted his doctrinaire approach. Whereas Farrar in the early days could write to Mrs Finzi concerning Gerald's free composition: 'I am quite agreeable, and indeed wish him to widen his own experiments in writing, so long as the somewhat

EX. 1.1

Spartan training in Harmony etc. is not neglected' (19151214), Bairstow's initial cast of mind, two years later, was to think in terms of
'putting him through his paces' and ensuring that he was not a pupil
'who would not work' (19171202).

As for specific cases of influence, in the absence of any Finzi compositions dating from his time with Farrar we can only guess that he was
still too young and his needs were too rudimentary for real stylistic
assimilation – or reaction – to have been possible. Later points of
contact may nevertheless have been partly conscious. The writing in
Farrar's affecting part-song 'Margaritae sorori' ('A late lark') that
sounds like Finzi, who was studying with him when it was published,
did influence him nearly forty years later (see ex. 1.1 and compare ex.
11.3). 'Silent noon' affected a clarinet Bagatelle, as we shall see. Probably in 1930, Finzi began his own choral setting of 'A late lark' (see
Sketchbook W: 5), but as in so many cases pursued it no further than
the first line. Both composers set Shakespeare's 'O mistress mine' (with
vamping colloquial accompaniments) and 'It was a lover and his lass',
the latter for solo voice in Finzi's case, chorus in Farrar's. Both made a
number of Christina Rossetti settings, though not of the same poems.
This is as much as can be said, and it is not callous to observe that it
was Farrar's early death in action, not his music, that would unlock
creative inspiration in others: Bridge dedicated his seminal Piano Sonata
to his memory in 1925, a year after Finzi had done the same with his
first extended work, the *Requiem da camera*. Bridge at least shared
with Farrar a propensity for the deft salon *morceau*, however macabre
its figurations had become in the Piano Sonata; Finzi, unlike his mother
and probably because of her, steered clear of the genre altogether.

After Finzi's death, Farrar's widow Olive recalled with affection how the boy used to turn up at their home, 15 Hollins Road, 'with a huge Music case, full of music & books which almost weighted him down, & a little note book in which he entered questions to put to Ernest, concerning all sorts of queries relating to various Composers' (19570113). At other times he would 'sit on the fence opposite . . . & wait until Ernest had finished teaching & would sometimes go for a walk with Ernest, & they used to go together to the Orchestral Rehearsals at the Royal Hall on Wednesday mornings before the afternoon Symphony Concert. Ernest asked Julian Clifford's permission for G to go to the rehearsals' (19561114). Farrar was pleased with Finzi's piano playing, while commenting that 'his enthusiasm is so great that I think he would like to do 2 or 3 sonatas a week!!' (19151214). But he tried not to rush Gerald's creative ambitions, ensuring, as any sensible teacher would, that routine technical skills developed alongside free self-expression and explaining that 'one must have the patience of Job multiplied by 4 to get on as a composer' (ibid.) and that if he wanted to make a living out of music it would have to be as an instrumental teacher. But his pupil already knew his own mind: 'Gerald loathed the idea of teaching!!!' (19561204).

Farrar had enlisted as a private in the Grenadier Guards even before he first wrote to Mrs Finzi about her son's progress. How difficult he found this decision and whether Finzi was party to his conscience we do not know. We cannot even be sure that Finzi knew about it; if he did, it would have furnished an early focus for his perpetual awareness of the shortness of time as he enjoyed his brief months of study. Farrar was called to join his regiment at Caterham, Surrey, in August 1916, while the Battle of the Somme was running its desperate course. Gerald was now naturally upset at losing yet another male bond.

Thrown back on his own resources, he doubtless followed Farrar's advice to 'keep on writing & study all the music you can lay your hands on. *Devour* it' (19161016), but Farrar scarcely had time even to answer Finzi's letters with their 'innumerable queries' about music which, he said, 'make my brain reel!' (19170322). He tried not to neglect his pupil entirely, however, and met up with him on leave in Harrogate in March 1917, set him on a Charles Pearce course of species counterpoint in June, and at some point before October, when Gerald and his mother were staying with one of her brothers in London, took him to see Stanford at the RCM.

Did Mrs Finzi consider sending her son to the College? It was too late for a further attempt at general schooling, and although he was only sixteen, this was not unusually young for college entrance in those days. But unless the option of lodging him with a relative was available and considered, he was too young to leave her side, and she was presumably not willing to countenance a wartime return to London. Stanford, in any case, advised strongly against a musical career, whether because he did not rate Finzi's talent highly or for other reasons we do not know.

Something had to be done, for Finzi was determined to go against this advice and Farrar, apparently urged on by Stanford and Vaughan Williams, was on course for a regimental commission, and writing late in October from Cambridge, where he was in further training as a cadet, made it clear that he simply did not have the time to continue Gerald's counterpoint tuition by post. At this the Finzis went to Cambridge for a few days to consult him in person. He rightly said that Edward C. Bairstow (later knighted), organist of York Minster, was the only possible further choice of teacher from a Harrogate base. 'Poor G was horrified as he had heard such tales of Bairstow's strictness & at first he did not go' (19561204). Instead he went to Frederick Helmsley, organist of St Wilfrid's, an imposing church further up their street in Harrogate, but 'he soon found out his limitations . . . [and] used to call him Freddie Himsley, composer of fine Hymn-tunes!' (ibid.) Then he bit the bullet. Mrs Finzi had already written to Bairstow from Cambridge in November to enquire about terms. Bi-weekly tuition in piano and composition was agreed upon, and her son entered the awe-inspiring precincts of York Minster to meet his new master after the ten o'clock morning service on Christmas Eve 1917.

In later years Finzi 'was scarcely ever mentioned by ECB' (Jackson 1996: 128); nor did he himself say much about Bairstow, and may never have seen much virtue in his severe methods and restricted outlook. He certainly resisted them as a young man, for it is not until three months into the pupillage that we find Bairstow reporting to Mrs Finzi: 'I think your son and I are beginning to understand one another better now. He is doing much better work, and I am very interested in him' (19180403). When Finzi undertook a stylistic counterpoint course with R. O. Morris a few years later and Bairstow wrote, with characteristic imperiousness, 'I am glad you are tumbling to it at last that a little hard grind at CP won't do you any harm,' Finzi felt impelled to add at the bottom of the letter (was he already confident that posterity would read it?):

'Yes, dear old ECB, but the counterpoint is nothing to do with the rubbish you tried to teach me for a year. I showed extraordinary common sense in jibbing against it. I learnt cpt by writing it as music and that's what I'm going on doing with ROM – not your sort of cpt' (19250425).

All the same, he stayed with him for four and a half years, though in truth there was little alternative. And it was a proper apprenticeship:

Following the continental tradition, Finzi was also expected to sit in on fellow students' lessons, and because his new teacher gave instruction in singing, he learnt the repertory of English songs and heard Bairstow repeatedly insist on clear enunciation and faultless prosody. (Liley 1988: 4)

Most of his lessons were held in tandem with another pupil, George Gray, later organist of Leicester Cathedral. Turner (1987: 6) believes that Finzi even did some organ playing for Bairstow.

If the schoolmasterly aspect of Bairstow's patronage irritated him, it nevertheless had its generous side, for Bairstow took pains to perform several of Finzi's early compositions, both while he was studying with him and after Finzi had moved away. He let Mrs Finzi know how highly he regarded her son's talent, assuring her, when she was in temporary financial difficulties, 'I would do what I could for your boy if I never received a cent for it . . . one can help the real thing when there is a chance to do so' (19200808) and telling her, after the lessons had ceased, 'I shall always be very thankful for having had the opportunity of teaching him what little I could' (19220702) – even if the compliment was classically ambiguous! And he did treat him as a young fellow-professional, albeit one who had to have his inexperience brought home to him. Finzi's stubbornness about the counterpoint did not prevent them becoming good friends, though in 1918 we have to picture the shy, short seventeen-year-old (Finzi was only 5'5" tall), still looking 'very young' and still always accompanied by his mother (Eaton 1986: 13), going to lessons aching with an explosive adolescent mixture of inarticulate timidity and creative arrogance, both fearful of his teacher and determined to show him what a real artist should be like. For his part, Bairstow was probably shrewd enough to recognise that Finzi, like many a young person with overdeveloped artistic ideals, would not accommodate himself to the demands of practical music-ianship without a constant battle. Bairstow never entirely won the battle.

Meanwhile, Farrar had been granted his commission as Second Lieutenant with the Devonshire Regiment, was moved to barracks at Devonport, probably only saw Finzi once or twice more on leave in Harrogate, and embarked for France along with a new friend, J. B. Priestley, in early September. Olive wrote to Gerald from South Shields on the eleventh: 'I'm sure you would feel very miserable & upset when you heard that dear Ernest had gone to France, but I thought it best to tell you, in case you heard about it from someone else' (19180911). In this she was reflecting Finzi's strength of feeling for Ernest, but she also knew that Gerald's one remaining brother, Edgar, was now missing in action and that she must gently but doubly prepare him, as she was preparing herself, for the worst. They did not have to nurse their anxieties for long. Ernest was killed a week later, after only two days at the front; Edgar's death was confirmed by mid-October. We do not know how Gerald expressed himself in letters to Olive, but Joy Finzi later testified that he not only retained a lifelong devotion to Ernest's memory but 'was never able to get over the tragedy of Olive being left . . . so swiftly after her marriage & being tied to a querulous invalid

EX. 1.2 (voices and piano)

[mother] for her remaining life' (1974–85). For her part, Olive, who was long to outlive Gerald, shared something of her grief with him.

Edgar had been missing since early September, and Finzi's first surviving composition, which is also his shortest, eight bars long, was a setting of Herrick's 'Upon a child' written the previous month (ex. 1.2). He dedicated it to his mother when it was published with 'Time to rise' in 1922 (see Chapter 2), as though it somehow touched on her loss or on his task, as the only male left in the family – indeed the only child left at home (Katie got married in May 1918) – of comforting her. Yet its elegiac innocence scarcely fits the situation of a son, still only seventeen years old, left suddenly exposed, responsible and alone in a suffering adult world. Under these circumstances, Bairstow may have provided more support than either he or Gerald cared to acknowledge.

CHAPTER 2

Youthful indiscretions

Apart from 'Upon a child', Finzi's earliest extant compositions date from the latter part of 1919. So does the first of his friendships that enable us, through his letters, to read and interpret his creative self-construction, forceful and discursive with his correspondents as this always was. The friendship, strange perhaps for a teenager, was with Vera Somerfield, a Jewish Australian artist ten years his senior; he had met her through his sister Katie. She had money, an apparently loose marriage, and a frequent desire to escape the stultifying aspects of England and its climate to paint on the continent. But Gerald, already full of English pastoralism, would have none of it. Writing to her in April 1920 from Wiltshire, he described the village near Malmesbury in which he was holidaying with his mother:

Great Somerford is a tiny little *English* village. Pigs, fields, thatched cottages, lanes, an Inn, a parson, squire & about 200 inhabitants – no cinemas, theatres or barrel organs – Perfect quiet – heavenly! Now it quite passes my understanding that you & Mrs Henochsberg, who both need healthy surroundings and perfect peace, could not spend the summer in a place like this. I can, in a way, understand your going to Nice for the winter but I honestly believe that in remaining in France for the summer you are wasting both health & time (to say nothing of money, but that doesn't concern me). (19200406)

This is of its period but includes an admixture of youthful chauvinism that should not be blamed on the cultural formation, for it contrasts tellingly with George Bourne – admired by F. R. Leavis and an enduring influence on the 'rural England' movement – whom Finzi was reading around this time. In *William Smith, Potter and Farmer* (1919), Bourne's comments on the advent of the cinema are more ambivalent, held in balance by irony. He is recounting the village schoolmistress's moralising reaction to news of the murder of Lord William Russell in 1840:

Lest the children should miss the lesson after all, they were set to learn a hymn – the metrical version of the Penitential Psalm. Ah! why wasn't there a cinema? If only Lord Russell had been a modern Premier of England, little village children might have known enough about this affair without being plagued to learn a psalm. (:145)

Even if there was, comparably, always a bantering tone in Finzi's exchanges with Somerfield, bantering is nonetheless close to bullying, and he never dissembled strong, often arrogant opinion. 'By the way,' he continued, writing again to her a few months later, 'now that Holst is recognised I expect you'll find many people wanting to make him out German,' and he went on to quote the following passage from Vaughan Williams's article about Holst in the third issue of the periodical *Music and Letters*:

... and it may be well to add here that 'in spite of all temptations' which his name may suggest, Holst 'remains an Englishman'; on his mother's and grandmother's side he is pure English; on his father's side there is Swedish blood, but the Holst family came to England from Russia, where they had long been settled, more than a hundred years ago. There is a good deal of unclear thinking prevalent on the subject of race and nationality. Every one is to a certain extent of mixed race ... (19201124)

'You may as well learn it by heart,' Finzi wrote. No doubt he had already done so.

This was the period, immediately after the First World War, when English musical nationalism was at its height and consolidated the identity not always accurately thought of as pastoral, in league with poetry and with Vaughan Williams its figurehead as Elgar's output declined. A complex, often political web of ideas, beliefs and strategies was involved, and many of these had been gathering force for a long while, if somewhat belatedly, as musical responses to socio-economic issues – and indeed to the movements in the other arts associated with them – that stretched back as far as Ruskin and William Morris, perhaps even back to Wordsworth, though admittedly some musical manifestations such as the Tudor and early instrument revivals were already well under way by the end of the nineteenth century. Conservationist, parochial, historicist, liberal or socialist, anti-commercial, and broadly anti-modernist, this aesthetic identity, locatable in some form or another ever since in most of the arts in Britain, gathered strength as a very long-drawn-out reaction against the nation's industrial revolution, a reaction which has been charted over a period of more than a hundred years by Martin Wiener (1981) as a vector of national decline. Whether or not in the long view it has been an artistic strength is not our concern at this point, though it is a question that Finzi's music must certainly be called upon to help answer. What does matter is to grasp how naturally he fell in with it as a young man.

If becoming ardently English at this juncture seems to us like too convenient and unacknowledged a cultural release from his Jewishness, we need to accept that it may have been a largely unconscious or involuntary orientation. As Christopher Finzi testifies, his father always said that he simply did not feel Jewish. On the other hand, if he was willing to argue it out in racial terms with Vera Somerfield, he probably had to argue it out with his mother too unless, all the more indicatively, he flatly refused to do so. Would she have been able to avoid a Jewish frame of reference or at least attitude of mind? As with his father, it is difficult to guess at what point and to what extent she exchanged cultures. We know that she went on to embrace Christian Science (as did Katie), walking with a permanent limp after refusing to have a broken hip seen to. But we also know that she continued to pay her triennial subscription (*finta*) to the Spanish and Portuguese synagogue until it lapsed after 1923. There was certainly a free-thinking strain in the Leversons: George 'believed that Jews who were lucky enough to be born in England should not intermarry but should be assimilated' (Wyndham 1963: 18), and his father seems to have been one of the six original Ashkenazi secessionists to the Reform movement in 1840, along with eighteen Sephardim. At the same time, whatever they did about their religion, they did not on the whole negate their culture, to judge from their lifestyle, marriages, and legacies to Jewish charities. Gerald did. Was his mother a channel or a buffer in this?

The relationship between a Jewish boy and his mother is highly charged at the best of times – one thinks of *Torch Song Trilogy* – all the more so when the two of them are on their own and the boy has artistic career ambitions. We can only speculate as to what passed between them and on what and whose terms the decision was made to leave Harrogate for the vernacular aesthetic life in the Cotswolds. To Lizzie Finzi, used to London, the Home Counties, provincial spas and continental resorts, it must have seemed a strange way of going about a career, and we can be sure that antagonism showed between them; indeed, both Herbert Howells and Howard Ferguson said much later that they found Gerald's attitude to his mother shocking, and Anthony Scott (1996) that he was almost sadistic towards her. No doubt she was exasperating, but even Joy's remarks quoted earlier seem a little too censorious not to have been tinged with Gerald's own very deep-seated prejudice. He all but disowned her, in effect, telling Joy, not long after their marriage: 'I feel toward my Mother . . . as I feel to no one else, as a result of an enforced relationship based on kin-ship – not akin-ship. Akin-ship is more that kin-ship – why else should we marry?' (J. Finzi 19360512).

But what choice did he have when it came to cultural affiliation? As a serious-minded youth, growing up in the war years and with his particular background, he may well have been aware of the Speyer case. Edgar Speyer, a German Jew born in New York but naturalised as a British citizen, owned one of the biggest banking firms in the world, operating from Frankfurt. A friend of Elgar's and the dedicatee of Strauss's *Salome*, he was a passionate patron of music and a confidant of government; but war madness raised questions about his Privy Councillorship in 1915 and he became utterly disaffected; this led to the revoking of his naturalisation, and he went to live in the USA. Was this anti-German or anti-Semitic hounding? To the young Finzi either of these spectres now represented the alien side of the cultural equation, and his bread had to be buttered on the other side.

Today, cultural minorities and their histories play so prominent a part in our awareness that we thread our thoughts through labyrinthine chambers of dilemma, imperative and image in matters where to Finzi and his contemporaries there would probably have been no conscious issue at all. He was simply an English composer. The question is, what was going on subconsciously? Bryan Cheyette, putting it brutally, claims that difference is always a moving force in the world, whether or not we acknowledge it; that 'to be Anglicised, is *emphatically* not to be English' (1990: 98–9, quoting Bhabba 1984), and that the 'liberal fantasy' – at its height, perhaps, in Finzi's Newbury String Players project (see his letter of 30 December 1940, quoted below on p. 284) – is a 'mirage':

a minority community tends to accept the 'mirage of themselves' generated by the majority culture which necessarily results in a form of 'self-hatred'. That is, ... an 'illusionary definition of the self' is caused by minorities accepting the dominant image of the Other. This ambiguity ... results in two common definitions of racial difference which are internalized by Jews. The first ... he has called the 'liberal fantasy', where 'anyone is welcome to share the power of the [majority culture] *if* he abides by the rules that define that [culture]'. The second, contradictory definition ... excludes participation in the dominant culture. This Gilman has called the 'conservative curse': ' ... The more you are like me, the more I know the true value of my power, which you wish to share, and the more I am aware that you are but a shoddy counterfeit, an outsider.' All of this plays itself out within the fantasy of the outsider. (1990: 98–9, glossing Gilman 1986: 2)

If we are to take this theory seriously, as we surely must, we shall see Finzi steering his activity and thought strikingly if unconsciously between the two 'differences': between the fantasy of sharing in the cultural power and remaining an uncompetitive, self-dependent outsider. Evidence such as his authoritative scholarship and collections, his friendship with Vaughan Williams, and his involvement with other arts and artists on the one side, and his secluded rural lifestyle, confined output and preference for amateurs on the other, cannot resist interpretation in these terms.

A brief comparison with the imperatives of another English Jew of almost exactly his own age, the athlete Harold Abrahams, suggests itself. Abrahams, as depicted in David Puttnam's film *Chariots of Fire* (1981) based on a screenplay by Colin Welland, is, like Finzi, an 'arrogant, defensive' young man with a mercantile father. But unlike Finzi he acknowledges the dilemma of trying to be English and openly Jewish at the same time – hence his intense competitiveness. We actually see him singing 'For he is an Englishman', the lyrics quoted by Vaughan Williams and requoted by Finzi above, onstage in the university Gilbert and Sullivan Society, but he remains an outsider too, most pointedly at the end of the film, not just in marking his Olympic victory without joining in – or being invited to join in – with any communal celebration but by courting a professional musical comedy actress (though one could argue that this was an upper-class fashion at the time). Earlier in the film, by hiring a professional coach, he has outraged his Cambridge college authorities who accuse him of playing the tradesman, not the gentleman, in showing himself prepared to win at all costs. In reply he points out that they want to win just as much as he does but can afford to do so effortlessly because of their background of privilege. Before the Olympic race, however, he says that he has known the fear of losing but is now afraid of winning – for when he does win, what he has achieved is precisely to prove his difference. All in all, this depiction of the three athletes, one each from the 'effortless', nonconformist and outsider classes, offers certain parallels with, say, Vaughan Williams, Holst and Finzi, so long as it is acknowledged that one can equally well go with or against the grain of one's background.

One also has to ask to what extent Finzi's self-construction, created in the image of the liberal artist, although a painful, incomprehensible affront to at least some of his mercantile and utilitarian seniors, was simply the next stage in assimilation or even simply emblematic of the way British culture was going. If Gerald's violin-playing grandfather, irrespective of his race, was a typical Victorian who cultivated musical creativity but kept it within amateur bounds and would never have dreamt of it as a career for his children, his grandson was equally typical in rebelling against this when his turn came, though it is possible that the balance between market and cultural priorities was already beginning to tip with Jack Finzi, if we risk a comparison between him and his Jewish contemporary Marcus Samuel, founder of the Shell oil company, for whom the making of money was 'only a means to an end' whereby, via public service, 'he and his family could win acceptance' (Wiener 1981: 146–7, quoting Henriques 1960). Full acceptance would only come when they stopped making it, if enough people still felt the same way as Trollope's Miss Marrable, who

had no doubt whatever that when a man touched trade or commerce in any way he was doing that which was not the work of a gentleman. He might be very respectable, and it might be very necessary that he should do it; but brewers, bankers, and merchants were not gentlemen, and . . . the world was going astray, because people were forgetting their landmarks. (quoted in Carr-Saunders and Wilson 1933: 295)

Considerations of Jewish assimilation apart, the generational model thus far would once more be reminiscent of *Buddenbrooks*, yet Thomas Mann might have been surprised to see how suddenly the pendulum would swing back again, even though, to quote Gerald himself and to change the metaphor, 'We are, after all, only a link in a chain and each link must, of necessity, lie the opposite way to its predecessor' (1954a: 180). For Gerald's two sons, Christopher and Nigel, trained to be professional string players, have both reverted to commerce. Christopher runs a wholefood business in Newbury and Nigel, having returned for a while to his ancestral Portugal, lives in Dubai as a specialist concrete contractor and waterpark designer. All one can say is that in each generation the Finzis have been highly charged with creative enterprise of one kind or another, and that the route from the Crystal Palace to the Persian Gulf would have a certain historical resonance even without the stamp of a composer's achievement along the way.

However subliminal his agenda and unacknowledged his insecurity, Finzi honed his intellect by voluminous solitary reading and vehement epistolary discussion with Somerfield. His diet, ranging from Benvenuto Cellini and Israel Zangwill to Wells and Yeats, was catholic, though the eighteenth century received particular attention and he sent Somerfield the following:

> Hail! hapless Zephyr's wond'rous glow
> Where'er reclin'd in Sov'reigns shafts!
> Thou haste the hov'ring murmur'd snow
> The distant warblings scept'red crafts.

> When Sappho, with redoubled ray
> Thy falt'ring Caledonian springs
> Upon the empire of display
> Thro' joyous quiv'ring throbbing sings.

'It doesnt mean anything, but wdnt I have made a magnificent eighteenth cen. poet?' he added (192109). He also discussed music with her – Berlioz (an enthusiasm at this stage, though in later life he was unappreciative), Boughton and the Glastonbury Festivals, Cyril Scott – 'a second-rate mind' (19210512) – Delius, Holst, Vaughan Williams and Elgar, the last four with great admiration. As for the socialist E. Belfort Bax: '[as] I've never read anything of his ... I must confess that, in spite of my violent socialistic tendencies and aversion to uncles, he remains to me – Arnold's Uncle!' he proclaimed (19200224).

Beyond such eclecticism, his sights were already focused on a particular set of current concerns. He was and for a long while remained vegetarian, though so was his mother, so the habit may simply have been residual. He told Somerfield about folk dancing and Cecil Sharp, and urged her (19191231x) to see to it that 'any intelligent persons in London at present' should go to the inaugural concert of the English

Singers at the Aeolian Hall on 28 February 1920 (this was Steuart Wilson's group that resurrected the performance of English madrigals one voice to a part and table-wise). As a young English pastoralist, the grain of his thinking was predictable but its precocity was remarkable all the same. He found it 'amusing to see a Nation & Atheneum critic saying "I distrust romantic rustics, folk songs, folk dancing, madrigals . . . "!!', countering with 'I distrust the theatre, I distrust sonatas, I distrust symphonies' (192309). He also distrusted a classical education ('It takes off the tip of the imagination . . . Of course, when you make yr own education it's splendid. But disciplined education is foul & wicked' [19191222]); the metropolitan mentality ('Londoners think too much of themselves & imagine that because London is the centre of England the rest of England is as rotten as London' [19210512]); and outmoded foreign art, particularly when these last two were linked. 'Russian Balletitis' was by 1922 'spent' and 'in another world' (19201124, 19220527–28?). His scorn for Charpentier's opera *Louise* and Rolland's novel *Jean-Christophe* was virtuosic:

Louise is the property of arty, sentimental women . . . I am really amazed at any intelligent person being attracted by such poor, empty headed, pseudo-intellectual muck. *La Bohème*, that Bull's body for every matador critic, is superior in nearly every way. Neither the greatest artist nor the finest setting can alter the wishy-washy poverty-stricken music. If you imagine *Louise* is musically progressive you'll have a great many shocks yet. Wait until you hear Delius' opera *A Village Romeo & Juliet* in London this season. That'll wake you up. (19200224)

I've read JC 1 2 & 4 so am competent to give an opinion . . . It's a most miserable book.

I alternately laughed & blushed as I read of the tremblings, intoxications, profound emotions, the thumping of the fists against the forehead. The heroics at the end of each chapter remind one of the sensation at the end of any 'to be continued in our next'!

Oh! the lack of humour & the eternal parallels, & similes; the heavy moralising.

Thank God for Thomas Hardy & a little dignity. Of course I know that I'm judging it from the English point of view but that can't be helped.

. . . JC as an old man is rather a fine picture but the book as a whole belongs to the 'Yellow book' period in England.

It's poor stuff. (19210310)

It was the bohemian apotheosis of art and artists and their aestheticisation in the popular mind with which he took issue, not their importance, which Robin Milford would later find equally overbearing a creed with Finzi. His expression of that creed, with its adjuncts such as the indicative privileging of environment over heredity already mentioned, the denunciation of nineteenth-century capitalism, and the upholding of the artist as the truest representative of a civilisation, deserves to be quoted at length from the Somerfield correspondence because it shows him, at the age of twenty-one, already remarkably in command of it:

As usual, yr generalisations about Art are wide of the mark. Who cdnt fail to see that you lived through the decadent Franco–Victorian Yellow book period? What a pity we all seem to stay still in 'later years'! To begin with, your eyesight failed you in the vision of young students from the RCM – spectacled & weedy. What about those who are so like other people that you don't know that they are students? Musicians have a tremendous record. When your athletics are slipping into the grave at 40 with ruined hearts, Parry gets well over 70. Stanford & Elgar are nearly there: (RVW will get to 80) . . . Holst, for instance, composes in the *summer holidays*! The rest of his time is a rush between St Paul's Girls School & Morley College, the RCM & private teaching, half a dozen district choirs & lectures at the most insignificant schools all over England. This from a constitutionally delicate man.

I don't think you have the least conception as to what Art is. Art is ordinary conversation & like speech is to bring affinities into spiritual contact. This is quite straightforward. It is just the same as personality. I, for instance enjoy talking to you more than to my uncles . . .

Now, the greatest understanding being between those of the nearest affinities, it stands to reason that affinities are found in the same type. Speaking broadly, a European has more affinity with another European than with a Fiji Island savage. Speaking less broadly, but not the less vitally, an Englishman has more understanding of an Englishman than of a Frenchman, & a Yorkshireman more understanding of his fellow Yorkshiremen than of a Gloucesterian.

Now, types are caused by custom & climatic conditions. In other words, *environment*. (Heredity, in this case, is only 'rooted' environment.)

This touches nationality & Folk-art in general (which is always destroyed by disintegration).

Do you see now, how your tennis players are represented – as long as a civilisation is represented – by those they most despise?

And who is the greater value, the tennis player or the national representative?

How I have *diluted* what cd be *dilated* for volumes is a wonder & I hope you understand. It is my explanation of Art but I believe the true one.

Note. Don't talk of insularity. Art flourished in every healthy age before the cursed Victorian introduction of international communication.
Note also: if you have any arguments you may bring them out, though I don't expect they'll be any good. (19230122)

English music and its conditions were Finzi's overriding concern, more so at this still adolescent and openly chauvinistic stage than in the later 1920s when his horizons were broadened by London and the friendship with Howard Ferguson. Nowadays we expect and indulge such powerful identifications on the part of a fledgeling creative artist, be they nationalistic or cosmopolitan, progressive or reactionary. But one cannot imagine an English composer of the generation before Finzi having such a confident battery of responses to hand (and it is interesting to note how little the occupancy of the niches in the pastoral pantheon has changed since 1920); this is testimony to how well the cultural formation of the English musical renaissance had done its job by the end of the First World War. (Similar confirmation of this can be found, very slightly earlier, in the letters of Gurney.) Thus a London concert programme with 'not a single Native work on the programme' was of no interest to Finzi (19200619). He attended Boughton's Glastonbury Festival in 1919 (when Hardy was there and he heard his first Vaughan Williams – *On Wenlock Edge* [Dressler 1997: 12]) and again in 1920, and explained its aims to Somerfield:

The Glastonbury affair is in no way an attempt to compete with professional ability. The prime motive is to bring music *into the life* of the people of Glastonbury by making it themselves.

'Professionalism' is, to a large extent, *impression*. It is the set of yokels listening to the Rev Vale Owen's spirit messages. But at Glastonbury all is *expression*. They make their own spirit messages. Do you understand?

How wonderful it wd be if every village were a Glastonbury. It is bound to have a great effect on the inhabitants (2 or 3,000?) and their descendants. (19200619)

Nor was he afraid of sticking his neck out with other British composers. Butterworth's music was 'the most intimate & sweet (in the fine sense) that I know: It sums up our countryside as very little else has ever done' (19220527–28?). Vaughan Williams's *A London Symphony* belonged to his 'great period' (19201124). Gurney's insanity, when he heard about it in January 1923 (from whom?), was 'the most terrible news I have had for five years' – not a reference he would have made lightly

31

– occasioning the eulogy: 'He is quite unrecognised now, but in 50 years' time his songs will have replaced Schubert's. In his line, Gurney is supreme. I always said he wdnt live long – his work was such a consummation – & now he is in all but name, dead' (19230122). Holst, as we have seen, was his chief idol: referring to the first complete performance of *The Planets*, he wrote to Somerfield on 24 November 1920 that 'For several days now I have been dancing incessantly on account of the success of Holst's great work. He is a wonderful man.' Altogether, Finzi's letters are a useful indicator of the cultural moment around 1920 when Britain and its artists took stock of themselves after the lengthy process of demobilisation and found – particularly in the performing arts – that a lot of stones had been left lying on the ground for six years or more and there was now a unique opportunity to build with some and reject others. For many, Russian ballet and Elgar were among the rejected, as Vaughan Williams and Holst, each with works long awaiting a first or a second performance or publication, were elevated, rather abruptly, into positions carrying the weight of their own histories: before the war they had barely arrived, now they were suddenly the senior generation – an exciting telescoping of time and influence. What would their pre-war works taste like as they came out of cold storage? What would they do next? Indeed, Holst and Vaughan Williams had to ask themselves these questions, which enhanced the sense of cultural solidarity. A similar measure of the moment was the first volume or two of the new periodical *Music and Letters*, which commenced in 1920. Finzi subscribed to this, and the names and topics on the early contents pages practically write his intellectual biography: Elgar, Plunket Greene and English song, Parry, Vaughan Williams, Holst, Gurney, music in country churches, R. O. Morris, Cecil Sharp and folk dancing, Tudor counterpoint (an article by Sylvia Townsend Warner), and Bairstow.

The letters to Somerfield tell us a lot about what Finzi thought at this time, but they say nothing about the music he was writing. Given a free hand, he produced very much what one would expect, to take one of his earliest surviving efforts, *A Passer-By*, a short instrumental work in piano score – '*c.*1919: GF's only excursion into Tone Poems!', as a note on the manuscript in Howard Ferguson's hand indicates. It includes much bold, undigested Holst and Vaughan Williams, though the influence of *A Sea Symphony* could hardly have been avoided given the cast of the eponymous Bridges poem on which *A Passer-By* is based (its first line, used as a superscription, is 'Whither, O splendid ship, thy white sails crowding'). There are pointers: Finzi's 'open' form is already sensed, in that the first, vehement section, with much semi-tonal sliding of triads, subsides into a processional one which fades without any recapitulatory reference; so is a foretaste of *The Fall of the Leaf*. However, for a sustained view of his early development one looks to the vocal music and its relation to his pupillage, for he apparently took mostly songs to his twice-weekly lessons.

Bairstow himself was not a prolific composer, and a number of his more enduring pieces were yet to be written. He had published a few songs and partsongs in addition to church music, but nothing much stands out that might have influenced Finzi, except perhaps the choice of Jonson, Herrick and a metaphysical poet, George Herbert, for some of his texts and a virile, Elgarian style and bold, forthright communication of the words in his Whitman song 'When I heard the learn'd astronomer', published in 1919 while Finzi was studying with him. His published pedagogy also dates from later, though it is inviting as evidence of what may have passed between master and pupil around 1920. His approach in *Counterpoint and Harmony*, not published till 1937 but seemingly already in progress on Bairstow's summer holiday in 1922, may or may not have infiltrated Gerald's mind (given his resistance to it); if it did, it would go some way towards explaining the premium on uninflected modality in so many of his compositions from the earlier 1920s, for the book is a compendious, indeed virtuosic coverage of tonal and modal harmony and counterpoint, within two covers and as a simultaneous study. Bairstow in his Introduction credits Stanford with having suggested the book, the simultaneity and the modality, and this approach is both a strength and its ultimate weakness in that the various strands can only meet on ground which is inevitably the abiding-place of sterility and self-contradiction – 'Harmonising Modal Tunes':

In order to preserve the peculiar fragrance of these tunes they should be harmonised strictly in the mode without the use of any accidentals except perhaps an occasional sharpened third in the final triad. After harmonising them for voice they should be set as songs with a pianoforte accompaniment, using the vocal harmony as a basis . . . There should be as few notes as possible.

The accompaniments may be chordal, contrapuntal or mixed.

Rhythmic figures should be appropriate to the style of the tune. (Bairstow 1937, 2/1945: 188)

This is a very British prescription in its assumptions about the relation between musical resources and musical imagination – one wonders what Bairstow made of Bartók and *Mikrokosmos* – and in his own examples it gives results that betray the Stanford tradition of folksong presentation, an aesthetic of 'pure' tune and 'innocent' accompaniment. Vaughan Williams was often bound by this tradition, and Finzi's early compositions are stuck in it, though by the mid-1930s he had moved on sufficiently to see other sides of the matter, including Bartók (see G. Finzi 1935).

Singing Learned from Speech (Bairstow and Greene 1946) is a more intriguing matter altogether. Joint authorship with the baritone Harry Plunket Greene is attributed; he and Bairstow had been close friends over a great many years, but Greene died in 1936 before they could write together the singing primer they had planned. Bairstow edited the material Greene had left behind, adding sections of his own and indicating who had written what, though one imagines that quite a lot of Bairstow's own points originated with Greene.

How much of the book's ideology was already coherent doctrine in Bairstow's teaching in 1918? Bairstow's Foreword suggests that it was in place as early as his move to Leeds in 1906, and it is difficult to gainsay its influence on Finzi's eventual aesthetic of word-setting; once again we marvel at how effectively the English musical renaissance consolidated its ideals through linchpins such as Plunket Greene (given that he was Parry's son-in-law and Stanford's biographer and close colleague), whose influence, according to Bairstow, 'did more than anything else to revolutionise English singing, and to change it from a bad imitation of the Italian style – largely taught in this country by Italians – to a healthy, native art. This was due primarily to his perfect diction: intensely clear, absolutely natural and full of significance' (:5). The nub of the book is in the following conviction, mostly penned by Greene:

The words were written before the music and inspired it. Singing being speech beautified, the ultimate goal of every singer should be to get home to the hearts of the listeners every shade of meaning and emotion in the words. The music is a great help towards this, but not if it distracts the attention of the singer from the words.

The words should be learned first. Then they should be spoken as if to an audience ... singing slow is much harder than singing fast. Therefore the beginner should keep his ordinary speech pace as his standard pace at first ...

Your first object is to get your voice across the footlights – to get your breath to tell somebody something. Therefore fix your eyes on that audience, real or imaginary, and address them in everyday sentences, in the form of an order, a declaration, a question, a reproach, a correction, a narrative, a joke or the like. You have got to hold their attention with those sentences; they can be as short or as long as you please. They should be in the idiom of everyday intercourse with your fellows, and they cannot be too lighthearted – the nearer you are to laughter the nearer you are to song. Above all, don't be afraid of making a fool of yourself. You cannot be shy and a singer at one and the same moment. You will have to speak your sentences first and coax the note on to them afterwards . . . You may start speaking them and merge them into song as you move along. You can even go from one to the other and ring the changes . . . Don't attempt to put power into it at first – don't try to make a noise – be conversational. It must be effortless as ordinary speech, and except in the matter of the clarity of its consonants, casual in handling. Do not feel any change take place when you pass from speech to song. *Music is not put on to words; it pervades them.* (:27, 34)

This goes far beyond the common sense of a singing teacher to a remarkable vision of what vernacular song might be. It went too far for the classical tradition, and Greene would probably have been surprised to find his vision eventually coming to rest with the aid of the microphone in musical theatre and cabaret, where his point about humour can strike home with particular aptness and whither his own celebrated old-age recording of 'The hurdy-gurdy man' (*sic*) by Schubert was so clearly bound. At the same time it relied upon his period's co-option of folksong in what has now come to be seen as an unacceptable way, for the appropriation did not take on board folksingers' often very 'unnatural' vocal delivery, let alone lack of a piano or presence of anything else. But *en route* to these unforeseeable ends he surely influenced English art song for good, promoting a melopoetic ideal that reached its apogee in Finzi before being iconoclastically rejected by Britten. Transferred from singing to composition, Greene's aesthetic can be equated with the 'to every syllable a note' dictum – an unswerving 'article of faith' with Finzi (Ferguson 1985–96), who almost completely avoided casual vocal slurs in his songs and only used melismas 'affectively' and rarely – but it is also much more than this: how better can we account for not only the rustic humour of passages such as the graveyard conversation in 'Channel firing' but also the utterly casual intimacy of address in 'To Lizbie Browne' and 'For Life I had never cared greatly' than to believe that Finzi, through Bairstow, imbibed what Plunket Greene had propounded and raised it to its highest power in English song? Not that it was all panacea: there are plenty of times when one wishes that Finzi had learnt to progress beyond his 'ordinary speech pace' and conversational delivery to wilder flights of movement and invention, especially in the large-scale works (where he tends only to sustain such flights instrumentally); vocal scherzi such as Britten's were beyond him.

Most intriguing of all is the possibility that Finzi heard Plunket Greene's singing exercises, if these had already been made available to Bairstow. Some of them, with their single-hand accompaniments, are familiar enough – gruesomely familiar – as the immemorial stuff voice trainers provide for solo singers and choirs, one hand on the keys, the other coaxing and exhorting. Others, however, turn the corner into weird, almost surrealistic miniature songs. Doubtless even here some forgotten tradition of verbalising is at work, much as in Ebenezer Prout's words to the fugue subjects of the '48' (reproduced in le Fleming 1982: 188–91), but the results are striking enough in any event (see ex. 2.1.a and b), especially when we consider the possibility that Finzi's

EX. 2.1.a (voice and piano)

36

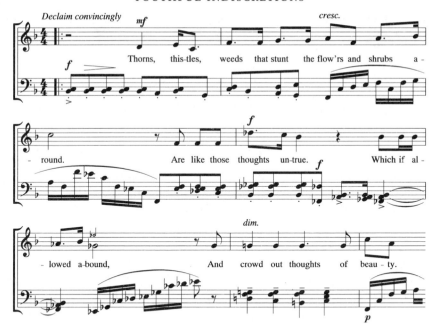

EX. 2.1.b (voice and piano)

imaginative low piano textures and between-phrase commentaries, his simple but pointed use of harmonic dissonance, age-old rhetorical 'affects' such as horn calls, chromatic chordal inflections, and above all his catchy, homespun, conversational melopoetic phrases – and all this particularly in the Hardy songs – may have owed something to them.

The possibility remains in the mind when we turn to Finzi's earliest surviving song, a setting of Fiona Macleod's 'The twilit waters' dated 13 September 1919, for although in some ways barely beyond juvenilia, in others it has individuality, and the significant pointers are the low vocal tessitura and striking speech rhythms (ex. 2.2.a), above a murky accompaniment figure reminiscent of Gurney's 'Dreams of the sea' (which at this point he cannot have known). Even at this early stage Finzi has latched onto the 'processional' ending as a resolution of musical structure, and for all its later parallels with baroque practice in his work, here its inspiration is clearly Holst or Vaughan Williams (ex. 2.2.b). But it is pretty gloomy stuff (the tempo marking, a quotation from the text, is 'forging slowly'), as is another Macleod setting, a 'song of death' completed a fortnight later: 'The reed player'. This is with

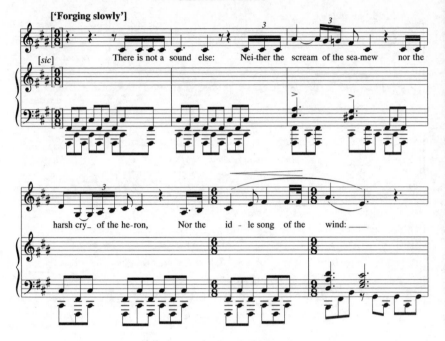

EX. 2.2.a (voice and piano)

EX. 2.2.b

EX. 2.2.c

orchestra, the instruments carefully chosen and competently if darkly scored. Again it has a low tessitura and is basically Holstian, though the influence of Boughton's and Macleod's *The Immortal Hour* is also inescapable, especially in the use of a memorable if all too spineless reflexive motif (ex. 2.2.c) to bind the song together, rather as in the first movement of the *Requiem da camera*.

Still in Celtic mood – a passing phase: he never returned to these two poets – Finzi completed a setting of Padraic Colum's 'A cradle song' ('O, men from the fields') on 3 November 1919. It was a popular lyric with composers: Howells and Rubbra made settings around 1920 and in 1923 respectively (Howells never finished his), and Bridge published one in 1919. Finzi's could hardly be simpler, just sixteen bars for the eight lines of verse, with a chordal accompaniment, most of it built bi-modally from fifths, and no ostentatious cradle-rocking effects; in fact, without an introduction, it is too simple even to be a carol. It ends effectively with its Irish melodic cadence couched on the subdominant (ex. 2.3.a). Another Colum setting, 'The terrible robber men', followed a few months later, dated 25 April 1920 (revised 17 October). This is a presto ballad, its opening rhythm, melody and harmony by way of a head-motif variant of 'A cradle song' but the ending of the second- and third-stanza refrain more enterprising, its semitonally posited C♯ and G♯ again reminiscent of Holst, bold but essentially well-mannered (ex. 2.3.b).

Around this time Finzi turned to seventeenth-century English verse; not, however, to his later speciality, the metaphysical poets with their achingly sharp and sensual imagery, but to the neatness of Herrick. Four settings were completed, and more were planned. One of them, 'Time was upon the wing', is slightly later and will be discussed below.

O, men from the fields! Soft, soft-ly come thro'. Ma-ry puts round him her man-tle of blue.

EX. 2.3.a

EX. 2.3.b

Another was 'Upon a child' (see Chapter 1). The other two, both from Herrick's *Hesperides*, are 'Ceremonies' and 'The fairies', dated 1920 and 1919 respectively. 'Ceremonies' contains faint pre-echoes of 'Rollicum-rorum', but is curiously misconceived because instead of inhabiting a genuinely ABA form it treats the first two stanzas together as a sixteen-bar musical strophe, thus ending half way through the strophe when it is brought round again for the third, final stanza. Finzi thought more of 'The fairies' – 'not much good, but it has its place' (1941, R.1951) – and slightly revised it with a view to a re-issue after he withdrew both songs from Curwen, who had published them in 1923. However, it epitomises the vapid diatonicism that is the worst part of the English pastoral style: in ex. 2.4, notes are freely added to chords (as at the words 'dairies' and 'fairies') and dominants are avoided at all costs (hence the C♯ in the second bar), but without tonal depth or contrapuntal tension these procedures fail to create explanatory contexts and, like other details (for instance, the compound fifths, triplet and tonic minor inflection in the last two bars of the example), they remain inconsequential, as does the song's ending, on a subdominant seventh, though it forces the point of some kind of neo-modality, lydian on G or mixolydian on D. It may seem unfair to belabour such an innocent song, but its problems recur on a larger scale in many of Finzi's other early compositions.

Pastoral freedom of expression is more ambitious in 'Tall nettles', Finzi's earliest extant setting of English poetry of his own time. The poem, by Edward Thomas, who died in 1917 in the First World War,

EX. 2.4 (voice and piano)

is about a rusty corner of a farmyard, and one wonders whether Finzi read a subtext of war into it, though there is nothing in his setting of May 1920 to indicate this other than that the poem seems to remind him of Butterworth, whose 'cherry tree' phrase from the Housman song 'Loveliest of trees' is echoed, for the first of many times in Finzi, at *x* in ex. 2.5. This song simply tries too hard, though it is extraordinary to think that its instrumental (possibly orchestral) rhapsodising – the imitation, metric flux, rhythmic freedom of triplets and other groupings, and long succession of six-four triads couched as a contrapuntal 'part' and giving rise to the clash of D minor and D♭ major at the end of the passage – predates Vaughan Williams's *Pastoral Symphony*.

The following month he set Walter de la Mare's poem 'O dear me!' ('Here are crocuses') as a good-humoured, pert duet for two sopranos who alternate with interjections; it is almost a carol, though this is not revealed until the end ('Snow lies thick where all night it fell: / "O dear me!" says Emmanuel'). His other early de la Mare setting, 'Some one', followed in May 1921 and already shows his remarkable feeling for

EX. 2.5 (voice and piano)

EX. 2.6 (accompaniment omitted)

vocal accentuation and intonation within the simplicity of folk-like melody (ex. 2.6), though again his accompanimental intentions are unfocused. 'Some one' was published in the 1922 'School Song' set yet seems more a solo than unison conception. Finzi returned to de la Mare's verse several times and intended a de la Mare song set, but he only completed one other setting, 'The birthnight', right at the end of his life. The rest are fragments: 'The mocking fairy', undated and consisting merely of a vocal part for the first few lines; 'All that's past', a partsong from the 1930s; and 'England', from the 1940s.

Of further songs composed around 1920 and 1921, one, 'Time to rise', its text from Robert Louis Stevenson's *A Child's Garden of Verses*, was published for unison voices with 'Some one', whose date it shares, but again seems more suited to solo singing, for it is as vivacious, wayward and small as the bird it depicts (only fifteen bars long) and uses a witty twittering figure as ritornello. Two other songs, a setting of Chaucer's 'Rondel' ('Your eyën two') written in October and 'The battle' (W. H. Davies) dating from 1921, must have been submitted to publishers after the move to the Cotswolds in 1922, for Finzi added his address to manuscript copies and scribbled the names 'Curwens/Stainer/ Winthrop' on them. Another copy of 'The battle' has 'For a set of W. H. Davies songs' in pencil at the top of the first page, but again the set never materialised: of his other Davies settings, 'Oh, sweet content' is only a fragment, probably from the 1920s, though 'Days too short' was completed in 1925. Both 'Rondel' and 'The battle' have antique touches, and one has to assume that the lumpish flatward plummeting near the end of the refrain of 'Rondel' (ex. 2.7), suggesting Vaughan Williams (who also set the poem, in 1919), and the following curious cadence on A intend mediaeval associations. 'The battle' is more of a mock lute song (the first line of the poem is 'There was a battle in her face'), in the dorian mode on G and with simple chords; one copy is dedicated 'To SS & PW', and this probably refers to Sydney Shimmin and his partner Peggy, although Finzi did not meet Shimmin until 1925, just after he had left the address given on the copy.

The poet set most extensively by Finzi at this time was Christina Rossetti, in a unison carol, 'Before the paling of the stars' (composed 25 July 1920), the Ten Children's Songs, and 'Oh fair to see' (unless its first version was later). Most of these settings, including 'Oh fair to see', are of poems from *Sing-Song: a nursery rhyme book* (1872), and many another composer at this period was broaching her lyrical,

EX. 2.7 (voice and piano)

contained children's verse, the Year Book Press publishing two anthologies of Rossetti settings, *Kookoorookoo* and *Kikirikee*, in 1916 and 1925. But as with Colum, Herrick and de la Mare, one wonders whether such obviously 'settable' poetry was worked at Bairstow's behest. If this was the case, 'Tall nettles' and perhaps the Macleod settings would represent a rather more personal programme of identification, which is what one senses from their music.

Be that as it may, the Ten Children's Songs became Finzi's Op. 1 and 'Before the paling of the stars' was probably his first work to achieve public performance. This was in York Minster on 28 December 1920, and Bairstow, who thought the carol 'quite beautiful' (19210101), later lent it to Harold Geer, organist of Vassar College in the USA, and Geer wrote to Finzi in November 1923 asking for a second part for his altos at the high climax. Finzi obliged with a couple of alternatives but did not think the piece 'worth while bothering over' (19231128). It is worth bothering over, a real tune in dorian E minor with a touch of French *rataplan* rhythm and some affecting Warlock-like touches of modal and chromatic harmony.

The other Rossetti settings have a chequered history. The canonical order of those eventually designated Ten Children's Songs is as follows:

1 The lily has a smooth stalk
2 Dancing on the hill-tops
3 Lullaby, oh lullaby!
4 Rosy maiden Winifred
5 Dead in the cold
6 Margaret has a milking pail
7 Ferry me across the water
8 There's snow on the fields
9 A linnet in a gilded cage
10 Boy Johnny

According to Finzi (1941, rev/1951), 'most of these songs were written around 1920 & 1921', and all the early publications are dated: Nos. 6 and 7 to 1921 and 1920, and Nos. 5, 4, 1, 2 and 3 to June 1920, October 1920, May 1921, May 1920 and May 1921 respectively. All are for soprano voices, and as later revised they are of three types, unison (Nos. 1–3), antiphonal with unison performance as an option (7 and 10), and two-part, imitative and predominantly in free canon at the unison (4–6, 8 and 9). Nos. 1–5 were published by Stainer & Bell in 1922 in a set of seven School Songs by Finzi, but in the order 5, 4, 1, 2, 3 and followed by 'Some one' and (as a single number, because so short) 'Time to rise' and 'Upon a child'. Nos. 6 and 7 of the Rossetti songs were published by Curwen in 1924. They were still selling in 1934 when Finzi, who regarded all the songs as 'premature publications', arranged for his royalties on these two to revert to Curwen before withdrawing them entirely at his own expense in 1935. Stainer & Bell presumably did not agree to a similar arrangement, and Nos. 1–5 must have remained in print until 1952, the other three (non-Rossetti) School Songs possibly even longer. Meanwhile, he had revised Nos. 6 and 7 and reissued them, together with the first publication of Nos. 8–10, with Oxford University Press as separate numbers in 1936. It is quite possible that Nos. 8–10 were not composed until 1934–5, added to the others to make a prospective set of ten or twelve (see below) as a kind of generic complement to *A Young Man's Exhortation* and *Earth and Air and Rain*; certainly the last two songs, 'A linnet in a gilded cage' and 'Boy Johnny', show a maturity that it is difficult to imagine any amount of rewriting of much earlier material having produced. In

1940 Finzi revised Nos. 1–3 and 5 and 'entirely rewrote' No. 4, and after Stainer & Bell had released them in 1952, Oxford, now at last in possession of all ten, issued the rewritten versions in 1954. At some later stage the entire set was taken over by Boosey & Hawkes.

A real style begins to appear in these songs, if blandly. To a certain extent this is because we know the revised versions, and comparison with the early published originals reveals a fair amount of change, always in the direction of sharpened idiom and intention, especially in 'Ferry me across the water', 'Dead in the cold' and 'Dancing on the hill-tops' (see Chapter 5 for specific discussion and illustration of Finzi's rewriting practice). 'Rosy maiden Winifred' was given a different setting altogether, the original having been a unison one with a blowsy piano part; but 'Dead in the cold' was also pretty much taken apart, being originally in unison, without the repeated first stanza and its minor-key harmonic warmth. But even in the early 1920s Rossetti's simplicity, or the sustained approach to one poet, one set of musical problems and a specific market, seems to have made all the difference. Modal and tonal planes are handled with simple competence. Four of the songs embrace major-key diatonicism, though there is still no cadencing in the dominant and there are no accidentals at all in 'There's snow on the fields' and 'Boy Johnny'. Where there is a modal bias in the others it is unambiguous or subservient to harmonic depth. As Philip Thomas has commented (1990a), frequent prefigurings of later songs occur, notably of the songs 'For Life I had never cared greatly' in 'Dead in the cold' and 'Ditty' in 'Boy Johnny', the latter particularly effective with its complementary pairs of three-line stanzas, their refrain (echoing Vaughan Williams's hymn tune 'Sine nomine'?) alternating between C and E entries and capping both with high G in the final stanza (ex. 2.8). Word-setting is regular and satisfactory; nevertheless, the texts are obscured when imitation is close, an inevitability Finzi acknowledged years later in his Crees Lectures (1955: III, 10), though it is interesting to see how he mitigated it in the later version of 'Rosy maiden Winifred', keeping the vocal phrases short (so that the imitation is active in their interstices) and clarifying the vertical space between voices by imitating at intervals other than the unison. (Unison imitation makes rather a clutter of 'Margaret has a milking pail' and 'There's snow on the fields', which is entirely canonic.)

It is quite possible that 'Oh fair to see' was originally a unison song and Finzi recast it for solo voice during his 1940 bout of revision.

EX. 2.8 (sopranos and piano)

Despite a 1929 dating by Howard Ferguson, the pencil '12' at the end of the manuscript could indicate its nominal inclusion (plus that of 'Before the paling of the stars'?) in his Op. 1 at this interim stage before eventually being fitted into a miscellaneous solo set. Finzi's description of it to Toty de Navarro suggests that he thought of it – as 'negligible' – in the same breath as the 1920–21 settings (see 19401218). In fact with the benefit of his stylistic gains from the 1930s it works rather well, cultivating candour and warmth on the simplest possible premises. One can imagine what the revision brought: the instrumental echoes of vocal phrases; a basic feeling for keyboard sonority, particularly of open-position triads and parallel sixths (see the accompaniment at 'Arrayed in sunny white'); the framing of dissonance so that it has space to sound (as at the final refrain); perhaps the vocal climax; and secondary-dominant inflection (the E♮ at the word 'delight') and momentary harmonic colouring (at 'shining' and towards the final cadence). The artless melodic line conceals its logical perfection, itself testimony to cool unified construction rather than heated piecemeal inspiration, the latter not always an overall gain in Finzi's more rhetorical solo songs.

The best song from Finzi's earliest period is 'As I lay in the early sun', composed in 1921 to a poem by Edward Shanks that had already been set by Gurney and Armstrong Gibbs, Gurney's song unpublished, Gibbs's, an attractive setting which Finzi could have known, appearing in 1920. Exceptionally, the original manuscript survives. Finzi revised the song for the projected miscellaneous set that was also to include the revised version of 'The fairies', 'Oh fair to see', 'To a poet a thousand years hence' and 'Only the wanderer', and since the handwritten list telling us this also refers to his 1956 Blunden setting, 'Harvest', we may date it and possibly the revisions themselves to that year. 'As I lay in the early sun' eventually appeared posthumously in *Oh Fair to See*.

Shanks, unlike Edward Thomas, was a 'Georgian' poet in the strict sense, represented in Edward Marsh's last two *Georgian Poetry* anthologies, and both this poem, which appears in *Georgian Poetry 1918–1919*, and Finzi's setting epitomise Georgian values. The poem does so with its Elizabethan echoes (of Sidney's 'My true love hath my heart and I have his'), nature setting and assumption of the 'pathetic fallacy' on the part of the birds, the music with its 'Butterworth' thirds representing the 'wheeling' day and its gently modal touches within the diatonic security of E major (see, for instance, some of the local approaches to G# minor). Another Georgian touch is the graceful, quin-tessentially English triple metre of sarabande-like flexibility in which three, four or five syllables cross the three beats with a variety of long and short groupings. This was nothing new in English song by the 1920s, and suggests Quilter's influence, as does the newly admitted relaxation of a pianistic accompaniment figure that of Vaughan Williams, probably from 'Silent noon'. What Finzi had not learnt by 1921 was how to build a co-operative yet distinctive persona into the piano part, as the first three bars of ex. 2.9.a demonstrate. The initial syncopation and echo of the vocal contour in the published revision (ex. 2.9.b) make all the difference. A number of other changes were made, mostly in these central reaches and generally enhancing the song's pacing and harmonic directness, as ex. 2.9 also shows. The survival of the early manuscript offers a valuable spotlight on traits Finzi only later learnt to exploit.

Finzi completed a few more songs during the Harrogate period that have survived singly or in incomplete sets. One, dated January 1922, was 'Epitaph', a unison male-voice setting of Raleigh's 'The conclusion' ('Even such is Time') and the most obviously Holstian of these early songs, full of alternating metres on a marching bass, containing apparent references to the *Dies irae* (ex. 2.10.a) and not a patch on Gurney's slightly earlier setting of the poem. It seems to have been

EX. 2.9.a and b (voice and piano)

EX. 2.10.a (voices and piano)

considered for fourth or fifth place in the projected Six Elegies, of which the only other to be completed, also labelled 'IV' and dating from 1922, was the Herrick setting 'Time was upon the wing' for baritone, five-part female voices and piano, a combination again suggesting Holst's influence (compare *Sāvitri*). These two songs are thus Finzi's first overtly to proclaim that *tempus fugit*, a preoccupation with which we associate so much of his work. 'Time was upon the wing' is also significant in that it shows Finzi beginning to place and mould his melodies rhetorically (ex. 2.10.b) and manage a dramatic shape, for it starts with a baritone solo over a marching accompaniment, the female chorus provides a central imitative section, and then the baritone returns to round the piece off – *In terra pax* anticipated in miniature.

'English hills' (John Freeman), again composed in 1922, became the first of Two Songs in 1925 when it was joined by 'Only the wanderer'. The latter is Finzi's one setting of Gurney, its poem one of the very few of

EX. 2.10.b (voice and piano)

his own that Gurney set to music. (It has sometimes been assumed that Finzi modelled his setting on Gurney's; this is possible, for although Gurney's was not published until 1927, Finzi was already becoming familiar with Gurney's *Nachlass* and its custodian, Marion Scott, about whom he had first heard from Farrar – see Chapters 3 and 10 below.) Both poems express the wayfarer's topographical yearning in the tradition of 'Kennst du das Land', Freeman with rather less subtlety than Gurney. Finzi also quoted Flecker on the songs' title page: 'Half to remember days that have gone by, / And dream the dream that I am home again' (from 'Brumana'). The musical technique in 'English hills' has gained confidence but is still modally wan. Put beside 'Only the wanderer' this limitation in both songs is all the more apparent because of the vague, semi-motivic shapes and gestures they share (see ex. 2.11.a and b).

A 1922 song that was published (though withdrawn in 1934) was 'The cupboard', projected as No. 3 of Three Dramatic Ballads for soprano and piano to poems by Robert Graves. No. 1 was to be 'Apples and water', for which no music survives, No. 2 'A frosty night', richly but incompletely sketched. All three poems are imitations of narrative folk ballads in the form of dialogues between mother and daughter with a final shocking revelation. Finzi would have found this format difficult to balance out in triplicate, especially since Nos. 2 and 3 are both in the minor, only a tone away from each other (the original key of 'The cupboard' was A minor). Nevertheless, he had later hopes of revising 'The cupboard' and completing the set and did further work on 'A frosty night', possibly in 1946 after the singer Sinclair Logan had expressed an interest in 'The cupboard'. In 'Apples and water', the mother reveals to the daughter that her father was a passing soldier. In 'A frosty night', musically more interesting than 'The cupboard', a pregnant monodic motif of the by now familiar Butterworth/'cherry tree' shape introduces the initial arioso and foils one of Finzi's baroque, motoric aria sections – probably added at the revision stage, judging from the manuscript and the style – for the mother's recognition that her daughter's frosty night was one of love. The daughter's response to this confrontation (ex. 2.12) is more compelling in its brevity than the musically bloated *fortissimo* ending of 'The cupboard', though the latter – he was right to put this one last – has the poetic edge, when the daughter finally admits what is in the cupboard:

> White clothes for an unborn baby, mother,
> But what's the truth to you?

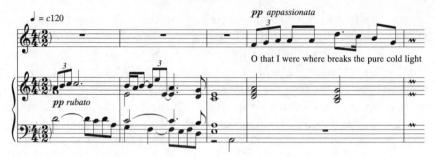

EX. 2.11.a (voice and piano)

EX. 2.11.b (voice and piano)

'Unborn' is ambiguous: the daughter may just have had an abortion, or, since she is called Mary, she may even be the guilty mother of Jesus, a blasphemous interpretation one can imagine Finzi relishing in his arrogant young days. No performance of 'The cupboard' has been chronicled, but years later Sinclair Logan recalled that 'it must be more than twenty years since I heard it, but I can only say that Gladys van Der Beeck made an unforgettable effect when she sang it' (19461025a).

EX. 2.12 (soprano and piano)

Logan liked the use of melisma for the girl's evasive replies, though it went against Finzi's mature doctrine.

Finzi's most ambitious undertaking during the Harrogate years was his first batch of Thomas Hardy settings. Over fifty Hardy songs were completed during his entire lifetime, and of sketches, fragments and pencilled notes or titles there are about as many again. Joy Finzi and Howard Ferguson dated most of the fragments to within a decade, but it is not easy to guess exactly what Finzi was working on in the early 1920s. However, enough is certain to show that he was already penetrating the centre of Hardy's poetic vision. He was more or less the first composer to attempt this, for most of the earlier settings, by Holst, Balfour Gardiner, Cyril Scott, Gurney and Vaughan Williams, are of 'diegetic' lyrics from dramatic or narrative prose works: they represent songs whose performance is part of the action or story. Bliss's 'The dark-eyed gentleman' was an exception to this – and he got into trouble for it from his teacher Stanford. Holst, who set 'In a wood' and 'Between us now' in 1903 and 'Her picture' around 1909, was another, though these settings were not published and could not have influenced Finzi. Furthermore, most of the poems Finzi set in his first batches had only been in print a short while. Of the poems used in *By Footpath and Stile* 'The master and the leaves' and 'Voices from things growing in a churchyard' are taken from the 1922 volume *Late Lyrics and Earlier*, set to music hot off the press.

Composed in 1921–2 and published in 1925 by Curwen at Finzi's expense, *By Footpath and Stile* certainly was ambitious. A cycle of six Hardy songs for baritone and string quartet, it tries to sustain an elegiac programme while already sampling, as Finzi was to continue to do in his later song cycles and sets, a broad range of Hardy's poetic types and concerns irrespective of 'settability'. The depth of Finzi's resolve to create a musical memorial, presumably to personal loss as much as anything, is not in doubt. 'The music is felt,' affirmed the friendly *Times* reviewer of the first performance, who also found 'plenty of contrast' while wishing for 'a good deal more grip' (27 October 1923: 8). But in immature work the distinction between technical grasp and feeling can be a false one, and just as much as the torn-off inscription at the end of one manuscript draft of *By Footpath and Stile* (RCM MS 4462) does the lack of musical clarity indicate an emotional inarticulacy in the young man. A further diagnosis might be the undigested influence of Vaughan Williams's *Pastoral Symphony*. Did he attend one of its first performances, in London, in early 1922? No letters from these months survive, so we do not know whether he would have included his own cycle amongst the 'pastoral whatnots by younger composers' he later identified as immediate fruits of the *Pastoral* (G. Finzi 1954: 180). Certainly the opening bars of the two works suggest the connection. So do the general cast of thought – Howells's 'complex mood' (Spicer 1992: 5) – and a number of further specific similarities, such as vanishing-trick scherzo topics towards the end of Vaughan Williams's third movement and at the close of Finzi's fourth song, and the trio episode in the same Vaughan Williams movement, comparable with the clodhopping gait of Finzi's Bachelor Bowring and Squire Audeley Grey.

In the first poem, 'Paying calls', Hardy writes a largely monosyllabic lyric very much in the style of Housman. Finzi's setting is on a different plane altogether with the string quartet's discourse (there is a long instrumental introduction), one which smothers the poem. His melody is folk-like and modal but is forced into middle reaches and does not know how to handle them, getting becalmed in an irrelevant modal dominant minor in the third stanza. The second poem, 'Where the picnic was', takes us to the core of Hardy's personal myth, for it is the last in his heart-searing sequence *Poems of 1912–13* representing the outpouring of remorse and retrospection after his first wife's death. The imagery may be a matter of charred sticks and embers, but the underlying emotional temperature is still intense, that of 'The phantom horsewoman' of a few pages earlier, Finzi's later setting of which demonstrates at a stroke what is missing in the wan looseness of 'Where the picnic was'. 'The oxen', the third song, has long been one of Hardy's most popular and frequently anthologised poems, but musical settings (by Dent, Rawsthorne, Armstrong Gibbs, Britten and Vaughan Williams among others) have never done justice to it. Perhaps the poetic conceit implies a greater underlying perspective of time and place than is consistent with its fragile, whimsical lyric, for the retrospect to distant childhood implied by 'an elder', a hearthside 'flock' and naïve faith, the reference to the First World War in 'these years', and the visit to the lonely barton which no one dares make are a strong scenario. Finzi himself was to commence two further attempts at the poem (see Thomas n.d.), one of which set the opening line to the same music as he used for the beginning of 'Fear no more the heat o' the sun'.

The fourth and fifth poems, 'The master and the leaves' and 'Voices from things growing in a churchyard', pose a shared specific problem: an image procession of the four seasons in the former, of a contrasting collection of six corpses ('maskers') from Stinsford churchyard that have turned into various plants in the latter. In both instances Finzi rightly goes for a scherzo ambience of articulated sections, complete with changes of tempo and time signature, but the musical skill in such cases is all in the strength of characterisation, which is what is lacking, the result being a great deal of overwritten activity at the expense of straightforward momentum. There is little point in burdening these songs with closer criticism, though ex. 2.13.a, from 'The master and the leaves', does display the better points of Finzi's contrapuntal style even at this early stage of its development, largely because it is tonal rather than modal. In the final song, 'Exeunt omnes', motifs and passages from the first three return timidly. One wishes they had not been so sheepish in the first place.

Finzi took his modality seriously at this time, but treating modality as a whole language rather than a compositional topic is the problem. With it in *By Footpath and Stile* goes a general tendency to overwrite and a lack of straightforward musical perspective, above all in the

EX. 2.13.a (baritone and string quartet)

matter of harmonic pacing. Comparing the succession of musical images in 'Voices from things growing in a churchyard' with that of 'In a churchyard' – the poems explore similar conceits – one misses in the early song any real communication of time's *dance*. And although the point has already been demonstrated through ex. 2.9, it is worth noting similarly that when Finzi revised *By Footpath and Stile*, in every case he simplified detail or threw it into greater relief while adding tonal depth, often of a very traditional kind. When the second stanza of 'Paying calls' was entirely rewritten (see ex. 2.13.b for the original version, ex. 2.13.c for the revision), the pizzicato cello notes pointed up the lilting beginnings of a cadence (minor-key imperfect, not modal) where none had been granted before; a short motif, in this case the two-semiquaver rhythm of 'did I call' and 'who had been' (taken from 'and by stile' in the first stanza), was echoed in an infill rather than laboured in all four instrumental parts like the two quavers at the words 'years past' in the original; the emotion of 'who had been / The oldest

EX. 2.13.b

On cer-tain ones I had not seen For years past did I call, And then on o-thers who had been The old-est friends of all.

EX. 2.13.C

friends' was realised in a cycle-of-fifths bass line; and melodic lines were far more tuneful and relaxed, spacing more open. Revisions to 'Voices from things growing in a churchyard', which Howard Ferguson did not incorporate into his 1981 edition because Finzi had not completed them, strengthened the sense that the song's entire perspective was that of promiscuous bees by adding instrumental long notes, hairpins and 'murmurous accents'.

A seventh Hardy song with string quartet, dated November 1921, was sketched at the time of *By Footpath and Stile*, doubtless with a view to possible inclusion. This was 'My spirit will not haunt the mound'. As with 'Paying calls', which it could have complemented at the other end of the cycle – it is labelled 'VI' – the modality (dorian) is oppressive and the poetic blitheness lost. Nonetheless, Finzi kept it under consideration, for a list in his hand (Bodl MS Mus.b.34) survives giving details of Hardy cycles or song sets he was planning:

[*recto*]
  string 4tet ones
      The darkling thrush.
      The self unseeing.
      Postponement.
      The night of the dance.
      In a wood
      The subalterns   } [*these last three in pencil*]
      My spirit will not haunt the mound

[*verso*]
  Ten for Tenor & Piano.
          (written)
  Twelve for Baritone & Piano
          (written)
  Eight for Tenor & Pian
  Soprano set
  By footpath & stile. (Revise)
  De senectibus   Bar Str 4tt
  Tenor set for Bar St 4tet

This is undated, but the reference to a set of twelve songs for baritone
and piano already written would suggest that it predates the publication
of *Earth and Air and Rain* (which only included ten). The reference to
a revision of *By Footpath and Stile* makes a date of 1934 probable, just
after Finzi's marriage and the year in which he withdrew the cycle from
Curwen, though the lack of a specific reference to the title *A Young
Man's Exhortation* could also indicate 1933 or earlier.

  The prospect of 'The self-unseeing' as part of a cycle with string
quartet is intriguing; its textures and gestures would suit the medium
well, but it was eventually published with piano in *Before and After
Summer*. No music survives for 'The darkling thrush', 'Postponement'
or 'In a wood'. There is no telling whether the seven songs listed might
have become a cycle entitled *De senectibus* or, if not, what that would
have consisted of; nor is there evidence (*pace* Banfield 1985: I, 288)
that they were sketched as early as 1921, or of an entire cycle called
The Mound (which is a different poem by Hardy, one never set by
Finzi). Fragments of 'The night of the dance' and 'The subalterns' for
voice and string quartet are extant, both rather promising and far more
mature than anything from the early 1920s. Possibly they would have
found their place in a new version of *By Footpath and Stile*, 'excluding

some of the songs and including other new ones, [which] has always been at the back of my mind', as Finzi wrote in *Absalom's Place* (1941), had he ever got further with this than revising 'Paying calls' – prudently re-titled 'By footpath and stile' – and 'The oxen'. But having evidently taken the bashful Butterworth of his recently-published *Love Blows as the Wind Blows* rather than the bold Vaughan Williams of *On Wenlock Edge* as the model for his chamber cycle – the very opening of 'Paying calls' seems to echo Butterworth's title motif – Finzi never subsequently found the opportunity to disprove Frank Howes's contention that the string quartet, 'contrary to expectation, hardly ever makes a good accompaniment for the solo voice' (1966: 310). He later worked miracles of vocal expression with strings, and of interpretation with Hardy, but not together.

CHAPTER 3

Arts and Crafts in the Cotswolds

Finzi's last composition written in the north of England was probably the Allegro for Toy Symphony Orchestra dated 9–10 April 1922. It was presumably occasioned by some kind of a party at which the Toy Symphony attributed to Haydn was also performed, for it is scored for almost the same combination: 'toy' nightingale, quail, cuckoo, two trumpets, triangle, drum and rattle, 'real' violins I and II and cellos, plus an apparently 'real' piano – the birds also those of Beethoven, though Finzi's and Haydn's nightingale has only one note, Finzi's the same as the quail's (G). Quite a substantial movement, it poses a structural challenge to which a combination of the fixed pitches of the toy instruments and Finzi's folk modality cannot rise, making it a curious postscript to his Harrogate period.

All his subsequent works were written in the adopted 'South Country' (see Howkins 1986: 63–4, 74–5) of a true musical renaissance man. In the summer of 1920 Gerald and his mother had taken a holiday at Churchdown, near Gloucester, lodging with a Miss Dighton of Badgeworth Road from 31 July to 24 August. They returned in March 1921, this time staying at Chosen Hill Farm in the care of a Mrs Champion who amused them by assuring them that two Lely portraits in her room, which Mrs Finzi admired (and Gerald didn't), were ''and painted' (19210404). Then they moved to the Cotswolds. This was in June 1922, and at first they stayed once again with Mrs Champion. By mid-July, however, they had taken up occupancy of King's Mill House near Painswick, though they went back to Harrogate for Gerald's twenty-first birthday party.

Was it Lizzie who precipitated the move? The decision may have been hers, for later Gerald wrote that she had 'searched for all those years [for a house] in the west' (19271221b) before settling in Suffolk, and she did eventually return to the Gloucester area – though not necessarily of her own volition – when she could no longer look after herself. Or was the driving force her son, perhaps celebrating his majority by choosing where to live? If so, what were his reasons?

Gloucestershire and the Cotswolds at that time were a magnet for three different kinds of artist, and he may have been impelled at the outset by the example of any or all of them: musicians, poets, and Arts and Crafts practitioners. Before he left the Cotswolds for London in 1926 all three communities had profoundly influenced him. But what is tantalising is that we can only guess when he first became aware of each; who, if anybody, he met while he was on holiday there; and whether the Finzis moved to the area because of its artists.

Not only were the region and its general topography a *locus* for certain aspects of contemporary culture and its myth-making, but Churchdown itself, incorporating Chosen Hill, could be said to enjoy an extraordinarily localised spirit of place, musically and poetically, one to which Finzi in turn was destined to contribute.

Below the southern slope of the hill, which is an outlier of the Cotswold escarpment, and in the parish of Hucclecote, stood Chosen House, the centuries-old manor in which Elgar's father-in-law had been born. This was a different place from Chosen Hill Farm (now Chosen Hill House) where the Finzis stayed, a mid-nineteenth-century building on the hill's eastern side. A poet, Jack Haines, lived in Hucclecote, and his friend Ivor Gurney was in April 1921 staying three miles to the west at Longford with his aunt, tramping his beloved hills, Chosen doubtless included, and catching up with his other local poet friends, F. W. Harvey – who was working in Swindon at the time – and W. H. Kerr, as well as Haines. William Kerr was one of the Georgians, and Finzi later began a setting of his poem 'In memoriam DOM', though he never got beyond the first line. Herbert Howells (1892–1983), another of Gurney's Gloucestershire friends, had the closest relation of all to Chosen. Gurney had said to him, looking at Chosen Hill, 'I wish you'd write a tune that shape' (Michael Hurd, quoted in Palmer 1992: 36), and that is more or less what he did in his 1916 Piano Quartet. Howells dedicated the Quartet 'to The Hill at Chosen and Ivor Gurney who knows it', also inscribing one copy of the score with the sentence, 'It was enchanting to be on Chosen Hill with Ivor on a clear April day looking across to the distant Malverns – and listening to his talk of the poets' (see Palmer

1992: B3). It was published in 1918 in the Carnegie Collection of British Music and the likelihood is that Finzi, who was soon to have a work of his own published in the series, already knew it in 1920.

This was just one unusually precise manifestation of the area's wealth of musical associations – a region claiming Elgar, Parry, Vaughan Williams and Holst for its own (Holst had even written an early *Cotswolds Symphony*). Gerald, who had already hitched his wagon to the star of the English musical renaissance, revelled in it on holiday, and with his 'heritage' sense fully developed went off with his mother in search of Vaughan Williams's birthplace, the vicarage at Down Ampney, a rather plain village between Cirencester and Swindon. Perhaps he should not have been surprised that at this date no one had ever done it before ('Many will make the pilgrimage but we are the first!!') and that the incumbent had never even heard of Vaughan Williams. 'I was shown over the house from top to bottom so that there cd be no chance of missing the room where our hero was born!' he reported to Somerfield (19210404).

The move to King's Mill House in 1922 meant that they were settled in before that year's Three Choirs Festival meeting at Gloucester with its propagandist programming (suggested by Elgar) of three works by young British composers – Howells, Goossens and Bliss – of which Finzi duly wrote an account to Bairstow. It would be good to know whether he had already met Howells, whose Chosen Hill connections were reinforced by his courtship, below the hill's northern slopes, of Dorothy Dawe, whom he married in another neighbouring village, Twigworth, during Finzi's 1920 holiday in the area, but by the time of Finzi's 1921 visit the couple were living in London. They had a common acquaintance in Sybil Eaton, the violinist to whom Howells had dedicated his E major Violin Sonata of 1917–18 and for whom Finzi later wrote his Violin Concerto, having met her in York. But to judge from their letters, the friendship between Howells and Finzi only ripened in the first months of 1925, by which time the Finzis had been living in the Cotswolds for nearly three years and Gurney had been confined in an institution for more than two. This supposition tallies with the date of Finzi's earliest recorded interaction with Marion Scott. By early 1925 they had met and he 'began to prod' her about getting 'an edition of Gurney's songs' published (Hurd 1978: 182; 19250225b).

Finzi got to know two other ex-RCM young musicians from the Gurney/Howells circle around the same time: Rupert Erlebach, a

Vaughan Williams composition pupil who turned amateur musicologist and became secretary of the (Royal) Musical Association, and Sydney Shimmin, who taught at Cheltenham Ladies' College. Nevertheless, Howells must have been the first prominent composer roughly of his own generation with whom Finzi made friends; and prominent he certainly was, having been Stanford's golden boy at the RCM and with a reputation for technical virtuosity surrounding his rich harvest of youthful works. According to Howells himself (1974) the two saw a lot of each other during Finzi's Cotswold period, meeting about every third Sunday, when Howells went down to the country. The Howells family (Herbert, Dorothy and the three-year-old Ursula) stayed with the Finzis at Chosen Hill Farm for five weeks in the summer of 1925.

Their paths were to cross repeatedly and significantly, yet quite what they thought of each other, in the 1920s and later, takes a little unpicking. A photograph of 1925 or 1926 (see illus. 11) shows the two men, both short, side by side, Howells as dapper and photogenic as always, Finzi shy of face but casual of pipe and with pockets bulging with what could well be his *sedicesimo* sketchbooks. Both composers could take themselves too seriously and accuse the other of doing so. Howells fell out with Finzi over Finzi's intolerant treatment of his mother ('a wonderful woman') when he was composing (Howells 1974; Palmer 1992: 365). He himself could be vain and pompous when he was not being charming, and he probably patronised Finzi: he told Spearing that Finzi was his unofficial pupil in the Cotswold period – it is doubtful whether Gerald saw it like this – and a few years later when Finzi 'played him a Hardy song [he had written] . . . he said "a lovely poem" ' (19280714a). Finzi's retaliation, as related by Howells, was probably unconscious:

Every alternate Sunday morning, he [Finzi] would turn up at my house, and the other Sundays in between he would turn up either at Ralph Vaughan Williams' house, in Dorking in those days, or at R. O. Morris', in Chelsea; and he would pick our brains, quite legitimately; we'd discuss what he'd done, and sometimes we'd make suggestions, which ran counter to what he'd done perhaps. But we never any one of us knew that he ever took the slightest notice when we saw the finished work: we'd been put in our places! (ibid.: 364–5)

Plus ça change: that was Vaughan Williams's habit too.

Palmer explores Howells's complex character well, and probes the private sensuality underneath what Diana McVeagh lists as his three public facets, 'the professional, the pontifical, and the flirtatious' (ibid.: 199). His was very much an actor's persona, and Finzi was never the sort to warm to this; indeed, many of Howells's contemporaries thought he toadied to Stanford and to the establishment in general.

It may be, however, that any positive dislike of Howells came as much from Joy as from Gerald, and came later, after their editorial work on the Gurney songs in 1937. (Finzi did not send Howells a copy of *Dies natalis* when it was published in 1939. Most if not all of his other colleagues got one.) Joy painted an unflattering, 'sad' verbal portrait of him to the present author, probably because of what she saw as his neglect of Gurney, for apparently he was of no use at all in helping Finzi and Ferguson edit Gurney's music, unable to elucidate and hardly even seeming to understand the idiom (J. Finzi 1974). Nor does he appear to have contributed to the Gurney asylum fund. Certainly there was something amiss in the relationship between Howells and Gurney, fully weighed up by Palmer, though one might add that a note of mockery seems present in Gurney's letters to Howells, despite their apparent warmth. Joy Finzi, quoting a letter from Gerald to Robin Milford, bore stronger witness:

Who will ever know that so far from Gurney & Howells having been great friends – & any article by Marion Scott & even several loyal articles by Howells himself go to show this – that Gurney had the greatest contempt for Howells.

J. W. Haines, who knew them well in Glos says that Gurney used to say 'Oh, Howells will just get married, & that will be the end of him, and a Dr of music which is what he is best fitted for'. Both of these tragic prophecies seem to have come true . . . (J. Finzi 19400529)

Such comments are unfair if they ignore the fact that Howells had to earn a living, and chose to do so as a teacher and examiner and by writing for the vocal and church markets, whereas Finzi for most of his life did not. They probably also represent no more than the usual rivalries and jealousies between colleagues. Elsewhere Finzi acknowledged Howells's career constraints and viewed him in just the same way as most of his contemporaries must have done during the apparently fallow decades after the débâcle of his Second Piano Concerto in 1925, as 'the brilliant young composer with a great future behind him' (G. Finzi 1954: 181–3). During this time there was distance as well as tension between them – Finzi, writing to Howells in 1947, surmised that they had not met *en famille* for many years ('Christopher & Nigel are flourishing. I don't know whether you've ever seen them, but they are now 10 & 12' [19470215]). This was partly because the Finzis felt that to see such 'flourishing' sons would be unbearably painful to the Howellses after the death of their own, Michael, aged nine, in 1935; and Howells's inner emotional life was in any case so private that the Finzis' demonstrative liberalism at Ashmansworth would have grated against it.

Yet Finzi was fond of Howells's Elegy for viola, string quartet and string orchestra, which had entered the Newbury String Players' repertoire: 'We have done it a lot & never tire of it,' he told Howells (19470215). Eventually their paths converged again, more happily, when both had major choral works premièred at the 1950 Three Choirs Festival in Gloucester, Howells his masterpiece *Hymnus paradisi*, Finzi his *Intimations of Immortality*. Indeed, Finzi was instrumental in bringing *Hymnus paradisi* to the light eighteen years or more after its inception when in 1949 he confirmed Herbert Sumsion's high opinion of it and encouraged Howells to have it performed; this was before it was shown to Vaughan Williams. From here on relations were cordial, for they could afford to be now that each had achieved his recognition, though they both trod a wary critical path as Finzi was preparing his *Musical Times* article on Howells (G. Finzi 1954). Howells 'very sweetly included G in his new Clavichord book' (J. Finzi 19520909) – though he suppressed the fact that the piece he wrote the day after Finzi's death in 1956 was therefore a second version of 'Finzi's rest' (there are two in the RCM), which brings us up against something of the old theatricality. Joy admired Howells's speech for the Vaughan Williams eightieth birthday dinner at the ISM, though she found it 'affectedly spoken' (J. Finzi 19521006). Gerald praised the *Missa Sabrinensis*. Mutuality was by now their watchword, though there was little time left to cultivate it, and Finzi's last surviving exchange of letters, hardly more than a week before he died, was with Howells, about a lecture series Howells had invited him to give at London University the following year.

As artists, they were in many ways similar. Both adored Vaughan Williams and were particularly influenced by his pastoral modality following the First World War. Both learnt to engage with early English music in their own compositions, Howells with the virginalists, Finzi more with the baroque, both found original outlets for this in keyboard works of the later 1920s (Howells's was *Lambert's Clavichord*, Finzi's the Grand Fantasia), and both developed unique contrapuntal styles. Both aspired to the numinous, be it in *Dies natalis* or *Hymnus paradisi*. Both commanded prose as well as music and published articles, both were closely related to the Georgian poetic movement, and both 'adopted' a poet (de la Mare and Hardy respectively) and set him to music through some deep if ultimately inexplicable personal affinity. Both steered relatively clear of symphonic composition, to the detriment of a consolidated reputation – for instance, unlike their friends Bliss and Rubbra, neither achieved a chapter in Bacharach's *British Music of Our Time* (1946) – though both wrote cello concertos (Howells's remained incomplete). Both eventually rose to large-scale choral works with orchestra.

Yet the differences are as instructive, and they bring us back to what was going on in the early 1920s. We shall never really know what Howells thought of Finzi's music, though his praise for *Dies natalis* was generous and genuine. Finzi, for his part, had remained fairly unimpressed with Howells's Concerto for Strings – 'a charming Elgarian slow mvt, but I forget the rest' he told Howard Ferguson (19381227), apparently impervious to that movement's tragic poignancy – and in the 1954 article did not pull his punches about 'where note-spinning begins to replace invention' in Howells's music (:181). The point is that in 1922 they both had to find a way out of pastoral modality – though Howells was already much less bound by it than Finzi – and did so by different routes. Finzi kept his feet on the vernacular ground, gradually readmitting tune, tonality, harmonic function and *chiaroscuro*. Howells, with his more impressionistic, Franco–Russian sensibility (something Finzi never saluted), moved further into the world of existential modality with its flux of octatonics, winging rhythms and ecstatic lines. Finzi was seldom seduced by these broader, sometimes libidinous horizons, and like a spoilsport he resisted their enriching of the Piano Quartet in its 1936 revision and could hardly bring himself to welcome such a strong work as the Third Violin Sonata of 1923, with its unmistakable influence of the magnificent Second Violin Sonata of John Ireland (see G. Finzi 1954: 181). It is an important difference to grasp, for it helps mark off the potential territory of each composer for the later 1920s and thereafter. All in all there is plenty of common influence in their scores, be it of Elgar or Vaughan Williams, but of mutual influence one would be hard pressed to isolate examples.

So much for setting the compositional scene. Where the poets are concerned, one would similarly like to know when Finzi first met Haines – their correspondence begins only when Finzi moved to London in 1926. A friendly and congenial figure who was a Gloucester solicitor by day but a man of letters to the 'Dymock poets' by night – 'a stable point of reference to whom poets like Frost, Thomas, Gibson, Abercrombie, Kerr, Harvey and Gurney could refer' (Thornton 1991: xxi) – Haines may have been something of a role model for Finzi, who was a generation younger, if they were in touch as Finzi began to build up his own collection of poetry (if not yet of poets). He was a 'Forgotten genius . . . who scarcely / Wrote a line himself but knew the knack / Of making others write them' (Norman Nicholson, quoted in Ely 1995: 61), though strangely enough Finzi seems not to have possessed the one volume of poems that he did produce in 1921. Haines's 'extensive library' included a 'superb collection of . . . modern poets' that he put at his friends' disposal, though Finzi never shared his enthusiasm for first editions as such, being 'a vandal in that direction and . . . not in the least worried by the fact that one copy has precedence over another on account of a missing comma on the fly-leaf!!' (19370713).

His third artistic acquaintanceship of the Cotswold years requires a longer introduction, and it concerns the broad English movement that Jonathan Bate has termed 'romantic ecology' (Bate 1991). This was, crudely, the 'green' seam of thought that rejected industrial materialism and that Bate traces to Wordsworth and his prizing of community, geography and a sense of locality above historicism. The politics of such pastoral ideals, especially of contrasting images of town and country, past and present, folk and bourgeoisie, are complex and have been forever shifting in art and literature, as Raymond Williams (1973) has best demonstrated. Nevertheless, that a movement in opposition to the dominant ideology of progress and struggle gained shape and force towards the end of the nineteenth century in England is a significant fact of artistic and cultural history. How does Finzi fit into it?

John Ruskin and William Morris, in their varying spheres, were the two leading influences after Wordsworth, both preaching craftsmanship above mass production, vision above greed, quality above quantity, the vernacular past above the cosmopolitan present, mediaeval organicism above classical poise. By Finzi's time both were dead and their authority half a century old, though Morris's late, Utopian novel *News from Nowhere* (1890) and his guild socialism continued to affect the Edwardian generation. There was plenty of Morris in Finzi's library. Ruskin was less well represented and was considered too Victorian to remain current reading in the 1920s. Nevertheless, he was an influence and an important link between Wordsworth and Finzi's own environment, in two ways.

The first was a matter of general continuity in cast of mind that can be illustrated through specific continuity in turn of phrase. Bate quotes a passage from Wordsworth's best-selling book *A Guide to the Lakes* describing Lakeland cottages, which may be said rather 'to have grown than to have been erected; – to have risen, by an instinct of their own, out of the native rock' (:47) – and Ruskin, of course, retired to that same region of native rock. A century or more later, Joy Finzi described the ancient stone sexton's cottage on the top of Chosen Hill as 'looking like something that had come up through the ground' (Bennett 1991). In between, we have Ernest Gimson's Stoneywell Cottage in the Charn-wood Forest, an extraordinary stone building of 1899, as an early *locus classicus* of such organicist vision on the part of the Arts and Crafts architects. With enormously thick walls, it has, as Pevsner notes, a main chimney 'built into the rock' (1960: 258). Alastair Service puts it more forcefully: 'The composition is rooted in the great chimney which grows from the upper rock of the outcrop' (Service 1977: 26). Finzi's talk and writings, and still more those of his wife and her circle, were saturated with similar images of growth and organicism, of roots and branches and soil and husbandry.

The second link with Ruskin was more personal. The architect Detmar Blow was Gimson's foreman and builder for Stoneywell Cottage, and he had been handed Ruskin's torch directly when in 1888 Ruskin, 'then in his declining years and suffering from intermittent bouts of madness', had found him as a young man sketching in Abbe-ville Cathedral and took him under his wing as companion for a trip around Europe (Aslet 1982: 246). Blow was a direct and proud descendant of the composer John Blow and possessed one of the original portraits of him, but our concern with him here is because he was a crucial figure in the Arts and Crafts and conservation movements. So was Alfred Powell, another architect and artist with a vernacular mission. The National Trust, founded in 1895, harnessed the energies of both men, Powell restoring the Clergy House at Alfriston, the very first building acquired by the Trust, in 1896, Blow supervising the preservation of The Old Post Office at Tintagel eight years later, a project undertaken in collaboration with the Society for the Protection of Ancient Buildings, founded in 1877 in response to Ruskin and in outrage at the Victorian trend of over-restoration of which, paradoxically for Finzi, the young Thomas Hardy had himself been guilty when he was an architect. The same assumption of stewardship underlay this movement and the collecting and preservation of endangered music (folksongs), and they gave rise to similar facelifts and imitations; Aslet and Powers liken Stoneywell Cottage to 'folk-song arrangements ... such as Percy Grainger's "Country Gardens", slightly too good to be true' (1985: 63). Parallels abound. Vaughan Williams and his kinsman G. M. Trevelyan took it upon themselves to conserve folksongs and landscape respectively (Trevelyan became highly active in the National Trust). Blow 'edited' old buildings and built new ones on occasions to look old; Finzi did the same with music. Finzi even paralleled himself: 'indeed,' wrote Vaughan Williams, 'he was almost as keen on reviving forgotten varieties of apples as the works of forgotten English composers' (1956, R.1995). Bliss added stray cats to the list of things Finzi rescued from oblivion.

The more general revival of old music in Britain was part and parcel of the Arts and Crafts movement. Arnold Dolmetsch was a friend of William Morris, played the virginals to him as he was dying, and to all intents and purposes inaugurated the British early music revival with his lectures and concerts at the Century Guild in London in 1891. Casting the net a little wider soon takes in Detmar Blow, for Blow's group of close friends included, besides Finzi, Neville Lytton and Charlôt Geoffroy-Dechaume. Dolmetsch was a friend of the Geoffroy-Dechaume family from 1912 when he was working for Gaveau near Paris and a colleague of the artist and writer Neville Lytton, who around 1913 'was said to be the only person to play the eighteenth-century flute' (Campbell 1975: 198). Lytton was also the architect Edwin Lutyens's brother-in-law. Blow's musical connections did not stop with this or with his ancestry, or with the fact that he had designed houses for two patrons of music, Edward Speyer and the Hon. Mary Portman. 'In part musician and in part architect' himself, 'labourers and tenants were treated as equals; they came to him freely with their troubles and in the evenings he would play the old country dances to them on his fiddle' (anon 1939a and b; Blow 1986: 22).

In course of time, Finzi became closely acquainted with Alfred Powell as well as Detmar Blow. Powell, brother of one of the founders of

Bedales School, was drawn by Joy Finzi when he was eighty-seven, in 1952. By then his daughter Catharine was playing flute with the Newbury String Players; Gerald, meeting him at this time, found him 'an enchanting person' enjoying 'rather a glorious [old age]' (19520724, 19520711) and was instrumental, through Edmund Blunden, in getting his recollections of W. R. Lethaby's aphorisms printed in the *Times Literary Supplement* the following year. But it is Blow and his wife Winifred, daughter of the Hon. Hamilton Tollemache, who claim attention here, for they took Gerald under their wing in the 1920s to the extent of becoming virtually his surrogate family, just as the Geoffroy-Dechaumes, at exactly the same time, became to Elisabeth Lutyens 'my adopted family, closer to me than my own' (Lutyens 1972: 25). Exactly how and when they met we do not know, but it was hardly surprising that they saw a lot of each other once they were living two miles apart on opposite sides of Painswick, the Finzis at King's Mill House, the Blows at Hilles, spectacularly placed on the Cotswold ridge overlooking Gloucester. Hilles, built but not finished around 1914, recreated the seventeenth-century Cotswold vernacular – a sizeable manor house yet one with a thatched roof (until a fire in 1948) and many other homely features. It is a building of great character, though not a pioneer piece in the sense that the 'butterfly' house Happisburgh Manor in Norfolk, probably Blow's most important work, had been in 1900.

To grasp the essence of the Blow family's intercourse with Finzi and aspects of Finzi's lifestyle that remained with him to various extents for the remainder of his days, reinforced by his marriage to Joy, it is worth sketching how and why the Cotswolds became a nexus for Arts and Crafts. Far enough away from London to have remained economically backward 'before they were invaded by rich Midlands businessmen and aristocrats escaping from the Irish troubles after the First World War' (Davey 1980, R.1995: 162), the Cotswolds retained, in places such as Chipping Campden and Broadway, picturesque, apparently organic mediaeval townscapes and almost feudal communities in which local materials and traditional methods were still used in building and design. Morris had started the colonisation and inaugurated a Cotswold myth when, with Dante Gabriel Rossetti, he leased Kelmscott Manor in Oxfordshire in 1871. Kelmscott is on the Thames near its source, and Morris made much of symbolically tracing the river upstream from Hammersmith to the Cotswolds in *News from Nowhere*, as though the river of English life could be traced thither as well. His famous frontispiece for *News from Nowhere* is a woodcut-style drawing depicting Kelmscott Manor – an idea borrowed decades later by Blow in a card depicting Hilles (19400101b). After Morris, into the Cotswolds came 'a stream of disciples . . . forerunners of the multitude of weavers, potters, silversmiths, furniture-makers and painters now to be found sprinkled over the small towns and villages of England' (Finberg 1977: 188). The first was Gimson, who moved to Pinbury Park near Sapperton (the other side of the Stroudwater Hills from Painswick) in 1892 and set up workshops for the production of furniture and other artefacts together with Edward and Sidney Barnsley and, later, Norman Jewson. Decades later, Joy and Gerald Finzi often visited the workshops, and they loved hand-crafted furniture. The second nucleus of activity was five miles to the north, nearer still to Painswick, at Whiteway. This bleak spot, 800 feet up, became a Tolstoyan colony, founded in 1898 and still in existence. The idea was of communistic self-sufficiency – the deeds of the land were burnt once they had been acquired – but the odds were steep, and their most successful enterprise, the bakery, eventually went private. Their leather worker suffered vegetarian pangs of conscience, and the whole enterprise was all too close to self-parody:

. . . the colony attracted a reputation as a nest of eccentrics – as well it might when some of them wore Greek dress, struggled to learn Esperanto . . . and lived in direct opposition to the mores of the period. The early reputation of Whiteway as far as the sober citizens of Cheltenham were concerned was that of a place 'where they run about with nothing on and swap wives every night'. (Darley 1975: 174)

Shades of Rutland Boughton or even of Finzi's own grandfather! The third colony was the Guild of Handicraft, which C. R. Ashbee moved to Chipping Campden from the East End of London in 1901. This incorporated Morris's Kelmscott presses after his death and in addition to its core skills ran vacation courses for teachers and 'encouraged choral singing, provided new uniforms for the brass band and revived the Morris dancers and the Mummers Play' (Finberg 1977: 191), though only until the economic slump of 1905.

The list of artistic epiphanies in and around the Cotswolds at this time could be continued almost indefinitely. Architecture would dominate it, though music was also significant, and Ashbee concluded his Guild retrospect with a paean to 'its Song Book printed and published by the Essex House Press in 1905, and entirely ignored by the general public':

Up & down the gamut of human life and thought from childhood to old age they are grouped, these songs of the Guild singers, into ten sections – songs of praise, of comradeship, love and courtship, of loyalty & the land, songs of the sea, songs of the crafts, & many that were written for the singers themselves. Somehow this little book has brought them into touch with the sweetest & the kindliest, the most remote and the most modern, the greatest of the poets and the humblest makers of the folk song . . . and the subtle thread that ties it all together is melody, now in the form of plain song, now of chant, chorus, madrigal, now majestic, now burlesque, handled by the skilled musician, or hummed and whistled at the bench. (1908: 230–1)

In short, music was central to the 'merrie England' myth which was at its height in these years – years that were 'the last moment of the greenwood . . . [of] an England where it was still possible to get lost', as E. M. Forster put it in his 'Terminal note' to *Maurice* (1971: 240). The consolidated mythology of a greenwood musical past climaxed with the publication of Sharp's *English Folk-Song: some conclusions* in 1907.

All this was not just part of Finzi's background but his vital foreground. We have already encountered his vegetarianism, 'violent socialistic tendencies' and interest in folk culture. He wrote to Cecil Sharp with a folksong query in 1921. Erlebach was a folk-dance colleague. He attempted a setting – it looks early – of J. D. C. Pellow's 'After London', a ballad published in *Georgian Poetry 1920–1922* whose theme, rural reclamation of the capital, is that of *News From Nowhere*. Best of all, he and his mother bought an old Cotswold mill, complete with ghost.

King's Mill House is a wonderfully mellow, large, rambling, L-shaped old building of Cotswold stone and traditional design with a spectacular row of continuous mullioned 'weaver's windows' and an exquisite site in a valley, with stream and mill-race, on the southern outskirts of Painswick. It would be difficult to imagine a more idyllic spot. Little short of a mansion today, one wonders whether even in 1922 such a property could possibly have been afforded by the Finzis unless at the time only parts of it were domestic space, the rest still unconverted or derelict. One of a fine series of seventeenth-century cloth mills on the Painswick Stream, it goes back further in time, since a mill was already in existence on the site in 1495. In the nineteenth century, like the others, it became a pin mill, functioning in that capacity and using only water power until the early 1900s and reminding us that for all its Arcadian qualities this part of the Cotswolds was and still is industrial.

The problem with King's Mill was staffing and upkeep, and the Finzis must have been caught squarely in the massive economic shift of the middle classes after the First World War, when they could no longer find or afford many servants, and family units became more nuclear. But Painswick also brought the Finzis up against the particular social conundrums of the Arts and Crafts movement, whose Utopian naïvety was always easy to mock. The story of Ruskin's Oxford Museum pillar having to be rebuilt behind his back is well known, and Morris's 'earthly paradise' was dubbed 'the earthly paradox' because his craftsmanship was so labour-intensive. His maid had to stay up tending the fire till 2 a.m. while he and his friends sat around it discussing socialism; H. G. Wells found to his horror that the house Voysey was building for him was 'a house built by hands – and some I saw were bleeding hands – just as in the days of the pyramids' (Davey 1980, R.1995: 244). The Blows' social ideals were nothing if not thoroughgoing, and given the impression they made on Finzi as an intimate visitor to the household, Aslet's account of the regime at Hilles, and of the house itself, is worth quoting at length. Things would have been in full swing in the early 1920s, after Detmar returned to his as yet unfinished house following ambulance service in the war:

'The rooms are large and full of light,' wrote Detmar's friend the Hon. Neville Lytton. 'The hall is paved with stone, which does not fear the muddiest boots. The long drawing-room has a floor of raw elm, which also cannot be injured by large boots with nails in the soles . . . There is little furniture – one or two beautiful chests and chests of drawers; three or four tapestries and three or four pictures; a splendidly solid dining-table, a few good chairs; an old organ, and one beautiful frieze carved by the owner.' The Long Room served as a living hall, and a wide staircase, without banisters or any other ornament, gave off it. All the bedrooms faced south.

Blow ran his little kingdom on 'sovietic' lines. Contrary to usual practice, Mrs Blow did everything herself for the children. She breast-fed and washed them, and the nurse who was also employed was 'merely an understudy'. The children were not beaten when they were naughty, but corrected by means of persuasion, example and kindness – although even Lytton had to admit that the drawback to this system was 'a period of monstrous anarchy between the years of five and ten'. There was no nursery to keep the children out of the way of the rest of the family; and there were no proper servants' quarters. For a time, family and servants ate together in the kitchen, at separate tables but sharing the same food and some of the same conversation, but this proved so embarrassing to both parties that the experiment had to be abandoned.

Since the Blows were agnostics, daily prayers were abolished; folk culture, however, had a kind of sanctity in Arts and Crafts households, so each morning the children sang a hymn or a folksong in the hall before starting work. The two maids and the odd man as often as not joined in too. Generally there was country dancing after tea, with the servants helping to make up the sets. (1982: 247–9)

This curious yet characteristic mixture of self-sufficiency and seign-eurial patronage eventually drew a considered response from Finzi in a letter to Vera Strawson (as she had become). By then, like many another idealistic guildster sneaking back to the wicked city, he had given up Painswick and his own manor and settled, with a housekeeper, as a young professional composer in a small terraced house in London:

There was a time (alas, that I can already say 'in the days of my youth') when I believed that one shd do *all* work. That was when we did away with serv-ants! I suppose it had its good side. It certainly made mother work & so added 20 years to her life. I still believe it, but it did not become practical as work grew stronger than social ideals. (I still think it wrong to pay other people to do work so that one can be lazy & do nothing at all: I'm obviously referring to you.) So now I feel, more strongly & strongly, that it is the business of an artist to *get on with his job*. His interest shd be wide, but that does not mean distracting himself . . . It was one of the troubles of Kingsmill. If one is to have the distraction of a lovely garden & house one must be able to afford to pay other people to see to it. That we cd not do (192705).

This letter needs considering. Gerald, wanting to be independent of his mother, was, like countless latter-day offspring dealing with ageing parents, trying to get her settled with minimal costs, upkeep and inter-vention from him; she, equally typical, doubtless dreamed of an establishment that would entice him to it as often as possible. Things seem to have worked out to his satisfaction when she eventually moved to Suffolk and he stayed in London.

The point is that only after he had established his freedom could he once again look further than his 'job' in the metropolis to an oppor-tunity to expand beyond himself, to compose his own lifestyle in a form of husbandry of resources to be shared with others, much as one shares creative work by publication, performance or display. Once he had married Joy, whose financial means enabled them to build their own house, their joint 'performance' of those resources became a remarkable perpetuation of the yeomanly myth of manorial hospitality that he had found acted out at Hilles. The degree to which together they learnt and taught that performance will become evident as this study of Gerald Finzi unfolds, warranting admiration mixed with a little critical distance.

There were certain crucial ingredients, at Hilles and eventually at Ashmansworth: a spacious building; open house; life and conversation centred in the kitchen; a 'great man' in repose or at his workshop; collections of artefacts, such as Gerald's and Joy's books, antiquarian music, drawings and sculpture and Winifred's and Detmar's paintings, furniture and tapestries; music in performance; conservation, be it of country dances or apple trees; self-sufficiency; children; animals; a commanding vista; and above all, mechanisms for hosting sympathetic and articulate visitors not only susceptible to the ideology but with the creative potential eventually to enshrine it (with the implication of blocking out any negative aspects) in their turn. This meant, effectively, that friends had to be artists, a snobbery of sorts, and Anthony Scott testifies to how difficult Joy and Gerald found it to 'place' his wife Ruth, who was not one, until they discovered she had studied cordon bleu cookery.

Was it an exercise in real life or in artifice? Alan Bennett raised the question in *Forty Years On*, with his masterly set pieces about 'hear[ing] the nightingales down at Kimber', about 'those houses where we stayed . . . Grabbett, Lumber, Clout and Boot Lacy, their very names . . . a litany of a world we have lost', and about being 'a young man on a summer afternoon at Melton or Belvoir, sitting in the garden with my life before me and the whole vale dumb in the heat'. Since then we can never again hear such accounts as the following in complete innocence. The first is from an anonymous obituary writer describing Hilles:

. . . he was a link with so much that was rich and fruitful in the social and literary life of England before the War. The friend of Balfour and of George Wyndham, he was an intimate at Clouds, at Stanway, at Hewell . . . But if there is one house above all others that comes to the mind of his friends at such a moment it is Hilles House, Gloucestershire. No one who loves Hilles can liken it, I am sure, to any other house that they know. It has an extraordinary charm and an extraordinary personality, and like most houses that architects plan for themselves, it is left to this day unfinished in part so that there is always the possibility for growth in the future. Standing grandly out over and above the valley of the Severn, its gables dream down over dramatic and far-flung prospects. Here Winifred and Detmar Blow built up a background for their children and an ideal of hospitality for their home that will live in the minds of their friends for ever; for I cannot conceive anyone who has ever experienced it forgetting all their lives through the inspiration that was to be drawn from the lamplight and firelight of Hilles. (anon 1939a: 19)

Finzi's friend and fellow-intimate of Hilles, George (Jack) Villiers, knew how to play on this string to maximum effect, and his account, in a letter to Gerald, not of Hilles but of a visit to neighbouring Stanway whilst staying there is such a classic of the genre that it deserves to be quoted at length. It also shows the power of assimilation for the English – his 'envy malice & all uncharitableness' last only 'for a moment':

Yesterday was such a day as makes one wonder what more of beauty could be possible or desirable even in paradise. What good is it to postulate a mythical heaven on the other side of death, if one cannot enjoy the infinite heavens provided on this? Really, an early summer day in England is part of life everlasting, a thing that lives on for ever in one's consciousness & upon which one can draw, years afterwards, for strength & peace & power.

... we packed into the motor, Bimmy, Winnie, Detmar & myself, & drove, a heavenly drive, through the sleepy summer country to Stanway. Do you know Stanway? It's one of the heavenliest spots on earth. A gabled house the colour of summer-evening sunlight looking over hedges of clipped yew, with quiet lawns & a great old barn and – (but of course you know it backwards, so enough of this Vers Libres!) ... Well, we found old Lady Wemyss & the Oliver Bakers on the lawn. Baker we took for Bernard Shaw in the distance & so we advanced across the lawn brightening up our epigrams, so to speak ... Bimmy was reluctantly given over to a band of strange children, & Detmar & I & Winifred wandered off into the trees & looked & explored, till a gong summoned us to tea. The trees at the back are gigantic & ageless, & there is a grass avenue that crosses the lawn & leads down a vanishing perspective almost to Broadway. And there was that kind of peace & comfort about the place that you only get in places where generations of delightful people have lived sensible & delightful lives, making the place entirely their own, & handing it on to their sons & daughters, till even the very rabbits in the park have a family likeness, & grow proud & keen about the tradition. *How* I should have loved to inherit a place like Stanway. I should have loved fussing over it – standing for hours with my feet in the mud talking with keepers & woodcutters, & determining which trees should come down, & whether or not we should run a length of chest-nut fencing down a certain belt of trees – & all the infinitely important policies of the country-side. I think I might have done it rather well!

Anyhow yesterday Stanway was a great heart-ache to me & as we came down the hill to tea my heart was filled for a moment with envy malice & all uncharitableness that the fates had not seen fit to endow me with such a possession. Tea was the usual rather shy affair round a huge table in the hall . . .

After tea we wandered out again & soon were taken by Lady Wemyss onto the lawn where Lord Balfour – the great AJB – was resting in the shade. He is the sort of honoured guest & familiar of the house & has been for forty years. And now he is old & suffering temporary eclipse through a heart attack & must keep quiet & play no more tennis, & make no more political speeches. We found him stretched on a long chair in the shade, incomparably charming with nothing old but his body, & that lean & spare, & only temporarily out of action. He greeted us as if at last the moment of his day had arrived, & that our coming was the one thing he had been looking forward to for twenty-four hours. By his side was a garden table & upon it, besides a bottle of medicine, I was amused to see a book. We had seen him from various points on our rambles before tea reading, reading, reading, as if his very life depended upon it. And as I sat by him I glanced at the title of the book. 'On the Nature of Things' by Bragy [*recte* Bailey – his translation of Lucretius?]. So that questing spirit is still questing, still hair-splitting & wondering & searching for a clue. It was significant & delightful to catch him, like this, at his old tricks, still considering the difference between Appearance and Reality & wondering, wondering, wondering . . . Not that he talked at all in this vein. But rather of the watersheds of the district & which way the little streams ran & whether they debouched into Severn or Thames.

I shall always think of him there under the Stanway trees, with his dark velvety eyes & irresistible manner, waving his long thin hands in the air, & talking of trivialities, while beside him on the table lay the book, entitled, (so exactly what you'd expect) 'On the Nature of Things'.

We motored back latish through a mellow golden evening smelling of musk & the pollen of things, & I went to bed all lazy & sleepy with the sun & the memory of pleasant faces & quiet voices, & the consciousness of sharing yet another delightful day with people that I love. And what more of heaven is there than that. (19280528)

Finally we have Jeremy Dale Roberts describing the Finzis at Ashmansworth in the 1950s, all the more potent an essay in nostalgia for being self-aware, even down to the Traherne reference (hovering on Villiers's horizon too), which suggests that there is a *will* on his part, probably on everybody's, to make it all add up:

Difficult to recall Gerald Finzi without recalling the whole 'lost domain' of Ashmansworth in our youth; scenes from some gentle, bucolic – possibly Hardyesque – tale, often played out in the kitchen, with Jack and Olive much in evidence, and cats, and Scotts, and Shush, and Liddy; and as yet no tinge of sadness or tragedy. A large cast of family and friends and visitors, in which Gerald came and went unobtrusively: indeed, his presence most markedly signalled by his absence.

Everything made a profound impression. Quite as astonishing and 'formative' as meeting a real composer was my first encounter with yoghurt; all sorts of doors were unlocked. The place seemed paradise, and its natives – well, incredibly beautiful lively and free – (or am I reading the past with Traherne's eyes?). A wonderful blustery afternoon, high on Inkpen, flying kites ... Quietness in the car on the way back ... a space around the silent man sitting in the passenger seat in front, as we bumped our way back. Tea – Lapsang, served without milk and sugar, from a handsome faded Rockingham teapot, lustre on the cups: everything – like the Aran sweaters, the muesli (authentic), the obscene Bulgarian 'culture' on the windowsill – exotic to this very young novitiate. Later, as the light faded, lamps would be lit. Gerald would disappear to the book-room with Joy: always the sound of typing – like a kind of drone. Afterwards, much horseplay as we got ourselves ready for bed ... (Dale Roberts 1990)

The number of motifs and images these accounts share leaves one in no doubt that, however unconsciously on the part of the writer or indeed the participants, all of them are trading in enjoined ritual. 'Is it my fancy?' Bennett asks in *Forty Years On*, 'Did I ever take tea on those matchless lawns? Did apricots ripen against old walls and the great horn still sound at sunset?' Perhaps this is all summed up in Rupert Brooke's 'And is there honey still for tea?' because the tone of the rest of 'The Old Vicarage, Grantchester' (a source duly included in *Forty Years On*) makes it clear that he for one knew exactly what he was doing in creating a scene that was at the same time satirical and irresistible. Whether Finzi, at the head of his *Severn Rhapsody*, quoted Brooke's lines in this spirit is less certain.

There is a sad sequel to the happy influence of Blow. During the First World War, Blow became heavily involved in the affairs of the 2nd Duke of Westminster, 'the dreadful Bendor' as Aslet justifiably dubs him (1982: 250). He had designed houses for Bend'Or's Grosvenor Estate, covering most of Mayfair, before the war, but by the 1920s he was not only manager of the estate but Bend'Or's private secretary, living with the family and doing little if any architectural practice.

Bend'Or was personable and generous, but had a penchant for destroying his friends, and Blow, 'by nature an innocent' (ibid.), seems not to have seen it coming to him, despite Bend'Or's undoing of his own brother-in-law William Lygon, Lord Beauchamp, in 1931. Blow had been granted 'certain Mayfair leases ... [but] what precise use Detmar could make of the properties was never made quite clear' (Blow 1986: 22). In 1933 he was accused of embezzlement because he had sublet some of them. It was indeed Blow who had ensconced Finzi in 21 Caroline Street, Sloane Square, in 1926, presumably as a sublet, and at an especially low rent in the hope of encouraging a better class of tenant into the area, though this was probably not one of the disputed leases, being on the Eaton rather than the Grosvenor estate. Blow was dismissed in mid-1933 – at almost the same time that Finzi got married and left Caroline Street – and suffered a nervous breakdown from which he never fully recovered, retiring to Hilles for the remaining six years of his life and doing little further work. Had it not been for this, one wonders whether he might eventually have designed Finzi's own house for him. As it was, and despite encouraging the Finzis to build near Hilles, he died a month before they moved into Peter Harland's new house at Church Farm, Ashmansworth, in 1939.

In view of the wealth of affinities, associations and ideas that the Blows and the Cotswolds furnished for Finzi's artistic and (eventually) family life, the actual music he wrote during this period is disappointing in scope. Other than the songs already discussed, plus one or two more, it can be divided into two categories: a group of sacred choral pieces, aimed partly or wholly in Bairstow's direction (perhaps at his invitation), and two internalised, elegiac personal statements, A Severn Rhapsody and the Requiem da camera, which Finzi himself later in life wished to group together, revised, to form English Pastorals and Elegies, his Op. 3.

'Up to those bright and gladsome hills' Finzi went to live in June 1922, and to that text (a metrical version of Psalm 121 by Henry Vaughan), in that month, he set what was planned as the first of Six Anthems for Baritone Solo, Chorus & Orchestra. Judging by their disposition and seventeenth-century metaphysical texts, the other five probably included 'The recovery' (Traherne), published as the second of Two Motets ('Psalm 121' became the first), 'My God and King' (Vaughan) and 'The search' (Herbert), and possibly 'The brightness of this day' (Vaughan). Of these, only 'The search' and 'The brightness of this day' have a baritone soloist, and 'Psalm 121' does not use the double choir found in the others. 'My God and King' and 'The search' are grouped as Nos. 2 and 3 of Three Motets in the manuscripts; perhaps this was after 'Psalm 121' and 'The recovery' as well as 'The brightness of this day' had been separated off by their acceptance for publication by Stainer & Bell (all three pieces appeared, with organ accompaniment, in 1925, the Two Motets dedicated to Bairstow). The orchestration of the Two Motets, that of 'Psalm 121' incomplete in the manuscript, is not very satisfactory, though it is not incompetent. Bairstow was right: 'there is too much brass in them' (19250425). 'My God and King' and 'The search' seem not to have been scored up, and of the orchestral score and parts for 'The brightness of this day', originally lodged with Stainer & Bell, there is now no trace.

'The brightness of this day', subtitled 'Christmas hymn', is a setting of Vaughan's 'The true Christmas', omitting the first ten lines. It may not have belonged to the projected set of six anthems, but if it did, it was probably written second, sent to Bairstow in December 1922 and rejected by Curwen before being accepted by Stainer & Bell in November 1923. Bairstow may have given it its first church performance in 1923 ('We can only do it at the Minster at Xmas but with some of the choral societies next season'), or this could have been two years later, at Christmas 1925, when he said he would 'give [it] a trial' (19231118, 19251213). Nor is it clear whether he performed it, unseasonally, with orchestra (scored for strings and/or brass with organ) along with the Two Motets; it seems not. Since it was essentially a three-verse harmonisation of the folksong 'The truth sent from above' which Vaughan Williams had collected with Ella Leather from a Mr Jenkins in King's Pyon, Herefordshire, in 1909 (and had arranged himself in his Fantasia on Christmas Carols of 1912 and Eight Traditional English Carols of 1919), Finzi initiated his correspondence with his hero to ask permission for the tune to be used once he knew his composition would be published.

As with the Two Motets, Finzi later wanted 'The brightness of this day' withdrawn from publication and 'utterly destroyed' (1941, R.1951). In spite of this, Stainer & Bell have reissued it, for it is not that bad. True, the choral harmonisation lies too high, its instrumental clothing and interludes (in the form of subdominant statements of the folksong) are fussy, the last two lines of poetry have to be repeated to fit the final verse of the tune, and there is no real reason for the two choirs. But the form is original, fresh, and indicative: the first eight lines are given in modal recitative to the baritone solo (rather like the tune itself at the beginning of Vaughan Williams's Fantasia on Christmas Carols, similarly over a pedal), thus superimposing a psalm-like antiphonal structure on the poem – solo homily and choral response – in a way that, as we shall see, runs very deep with Finzi. Not only that, but the baritone's opening words suggest the presenter of some Christmas pageant acted out in a vernacular, homely, old-world setting with 'music, masque [and] show', 'gallant furniture' and gleaming 'plate' – at Hilles, perhaps, or one of Ashbee's community performances – and despite his negative protestations, and helped by the excision of the earlier text, they conjure a bright personal warmth as he sets the Christmas scene. Once again, as with 'Time was upon the wing', the plan of *In terra pax* is foreshadowed; indeed, something of its idea – Finzi's unique sense of place and of the numinous within domestic experience – is already felt.

The four 'motets' are more of a piece. Vaughan Williams's Five Mystical Songs (1911), also for baritone, chorus and orchestra and to metaphysical poems (by Herbert), are the obvious model, his Four Hymns, first performed and published in 1920, perhaps an additional stimulus. It is of Holst, however, that the music itself is most reminiscent. This was noted when the *Musical Times* covered the first performances of the Two Motets, given under Bairstow by the Leeds Philharmonic Chorus and Symphony Orchestra in Leeds on 18 March 1925 and (twice in the programme) by the York Musical Society in York the following day; the reviewer(s) nonetheless found them 'well written', showing 'distinct originality', but pointed out somewhat gratuitously that 'the Philharmonic Society is said to be in financial difficulties that threaten its existence' (lxvi [1925]: 453, 455).

'Psalm 121', the first of the Two Motets, is a particularly Holstian conception, structured on a ground bass of descending major scale in crotchets, which puts it into 7/4 metre. The pattern is sometimes broken, which is good, but it contends with some awkward stabs at originality, which are not – off-beat *a cappella* word-setting, a rapid-fire upbeat into stanza three, text in diminution at one point in the bass line, and, in the printed version only, a quotation of the opening of Byrd's 'Attollite portas' ('Lift up your gates') from the 1575 *Cantiones sacrae*. Still, the 4/2 broadening and inversion of the ostinato against a mixolydian point of imitation make for a satisfying ending, and the vocal part-writing is sound. 'The recovery', probably not composed until after Finzi had been sent Traherne's *Centuries of Meditations* in November 1923, begins with the kind of chordal clash patented by Holst in *The Hymn of Jesus* (ex. 3.1.a). Bairstow tightened up its voice-leading on its choral return, and said that he could not 'quite get to like' the folk-like trumpet 'victory' fanfare later on in the piece (19240812); the real problem, however, would seem to be the reconcilement, at the start and elsewhere, of the Holstian marching topic with Finzi's changing tempi (see ex. 3.1.a).

Bairstow understandably found the Two Motets too strenuous and uniform when placed side by side, but the incorporation of the other two (or three) surviving motets would have overcome this, and since they are the more interesting and inspired creative flights it is a shame Finzi did not persevere with them, though he did heavily revise 'My God and King'. Both 'My God and King' and 'The search' attempt relatively large structural spans and intense spiritual moods and succeed in conveying them despite problems along the way, mostly with contrapuntal tangles; the setting of 'The search', one of Herbert's poems that powerfully invest religious intimacy with erotic language, is particularly expansive, and Finzi omits only one of Herbert's fifteen stanzas.

The opening of 'My God and King' (ex. 3.1.b) is once again extremely Holstian, in its triadic austerity and sideslipping, its 'metaphysical agony' chord at x and its embrace (rather misplaced here) of differential

EX. 3.1.a (orchestra)

EX. 3.1.b (choir and orchestra)

barring; 'Butterworth thirds', however, are also present, and they form a motif binding this and 'The search' together. Both motets handle with real skill the return of opening material and its mapping onto the poem's argument: 'My God and King' after opening out into a broad march climax, 'The search' with a ritornello passage that comes three times, the last, as given in ex. 3.1.c, moving in its lyrical simplicity and beginning to give us more of Finzi than of Holst. The motif y in ex. 3.1.c has in the interim been developed into another march, making for a somewhat lopsided form but quite impressive as it carries choral

EX. 3.1.c (baritone, chorus and orchestra)

repetitions of 'Where is my God?' rather reminiscent of the finale of *A Sea Symphony*. All in all, these motets, particularly the unpublished ones, laid the foundations of Finzi's partnership with the metaphysical poets a good deal more than has been noticed, both in the highly self-conscious moments of penitential or pietistic address and in the striving towards ecstasy (compare the last words of 'The recovery' – 'Heal, feed, make me divine' – with the end of 'The rapture' in *Dies natalis*). One wonders how a young man barely in his twenties could have been drawn so firmly to such material (and with Traherne still only recently rediscovered at the time), for his identification with it is already more personal and specific than in Vaughan Williams, and Holst's 'The evening-watch' was still a year or two off. But what Traherne meant to him must await later discussion.

To turn to *A Severn Rhapsody*, written at Painswick in 1923, after these works is to re-enter the world of Finzi's early songs; indeed, the opening bar of 'Only the wanderer' (see ex. 2.11.b) is the opening motif of *A Severn Rhapsody* re-used down a tone. Even though Finzi eventually wanted to retitle the work simply 'Rhapsody', the motif therefore clearly signifies the meandering river and its plain in both cases – the view Finzi described on a later visit to the Blows at Hilles: 'I play with the children and look over twenty or thirty miles of country and see the shining Severn winding below' (19280409/10?). That is no excuse for the piece itself to wander, which is its main shortcoming compared with its obvious model, Butterworth's *A Shropshire Lad* rhapsody in which the larger orchestra, with its pairs and blocks of instruments, affords solidity, depth, harmonic precision and contrast where Finzi tends unproductively to equate single instruments with single lines and the multiplication of them with force, particularly when he is attempting a build-up. Both Butterworth's 'cherry tree' phrase from the song 'Loveliest of trees' (ex. 3.2.a) and the opening of his rhapsody (ex. 3.2.b), its thirds harmonically underpinned like Finzi's, demonstrate the connection, as does the sequel, which is another phrase from 'Loveliest of trees' in the Butterworth (ex. 3.2.c), a *Pastoral Symphony*-like pentatonic motif in the Finzi (ex. 3.2.d). Butterworth's strikingly Holstian pre-coda – a kind of 'aftermath' section really, surely indebted to that of Debussy's *Prélude à 'L'après-midi d'un faune'* – also finds a parallel in Finzi's 'With great peace' section with its oscillating chords, but again with less defined effect. Finzi's biggest problem is that he cannot develop the *character* of his material, unlike Butterworth

EX. 3.2.a

EX. 3.2.b

EX. 3.2.c

EX. 3.2.d

who puts it through considerable dramatic paces, *à la* Tchaikovsky and Wagner. Thus the climactic restatement of the opening motif at figure E works because it emerges from developing lines, whereas an even louder one seven bars later, a fourth lower, adds nothing and leads nowhere.

However, the *Rhapsody*'s elegiac feeling makes its mark despite all these problems, and one can see why it received one of the six or seven annual Carnegie publication awards in 1924, rated confidentially 'A–, well worth doing' by Vaughan Williams and officially as 'a picturesque and imaginative composition, written with a genuine sense of style' by him and the other two adjudicators, Hugh Allen and Dan Godfrey (Foreman 1996, Anderson 1928: [13]). Dedicated to Vera Somerfield, it was published at the end of the year, by which time its first performance had taken place at a Bournemouth Summer Symphony Concert conducted by Godfrey on 4 June. The following year, on 1 December, it was one of two Finzi pieces performed at a concert in London given by the Contemporary Music Centre section of the British Music Society, which was effectively the British branch of the International Society for Contemporary Music. Vaughan Williams was there, and told R. O. Morris that Finzi provided 'the best of what he heard that evening' (19251206) – though with the remainder of the programme made up of chamber works by Hindemith, van Dieren and H. E. Randerson that was hardly surprising. Ernest Newman, covering the event in the *Sunday Times* and mistakenly thinking it the *Severn Rhapsody*'s première, was highly complimentary:

Mr Gerald Finzi's 'Prelude from Requiem for Chamber Orchestra' and 'Severn Rhapsody for Chamber Orchestra' both created an excellent impression; from a young man who can write as well as this we shall expect good work as he develops. Mr Finzi does not, as a goodly number of his young contemporaries do, write for mere writing's sake: he does not pose, and he apparently has no desire to impress us with his cleverness. He sets down straightforwardly what he has felt about things, and as his imagination is poetic, and his idiom in perfect consonance with it, the results are very pleasing and decidedly promising. He has a sense of proportion, and he never strains, so that our interest in the music is never chilled; and even when he reduces his parts to two or three there is still vitality in them . . . There was an excellent body of string and wind players for all these works, under the enthusiastic leadership of Mr Anthony Bernard. (6 December 1925: 7)

Finzi had comparatively few bad reviews in his life; he was starting here as he meant to go on. 'Rather a shock to find . . . that EN . . . liked it – but you'll live that down in time,' R. O. Morris commented laconically (19251206).

The other Finzi work in the programme, the Prelude from his *Requiem da camera* dedicated to the memory of Farrar, really was a first performance, the only one that any part of the *Requiem* received in Finzi's lifetime, though this does not mean that he lost interest in the work. In January 1923 he had composed a setting for male voice and piano of Hardy's celebrated war poem 'Only a man harrowing clods' ('In time of "The breaking of nations" ') and clearly thought enough of it to elicit and act upon criticisms from both Bairstow and Vaughan Williams, the latter's indicating an early meeting of which there is no other record, probably before the rest of the *Requiem* was added and certainly before February 1925. In 1924 the song became the third

87

movement of the *Requiem*, which was scored for baritone solo, mixed chorus (or solo voices) and chamber orchestra. It was joined by an instrumental Prelude, with the same specification as *A Severn Rhapsody* except for the addition of a separate cor anglais player and a harp, and choral settings of stanzas from Masefield's 'August, 1914' and Gibson's 'Lament' from *Whin*, demonstrating once again Finzi's engagement with Georgian poetry, possibly direct from *Georgian Poetry 1916–1917* in the case of the Gibson poem. (See, however, Leach 1991: 23 – and :18 for the veritable Masefield phase Finzi went through around 1918–19. The 1918 edition of *Whin* was also in his library.)

After the 1925 performance of its Prelude, Finzi continued to think about the *Requiem* and tried to get it published. In November 1927 he was asking Howard Ferguson for information about horn signals (the 'Last post' is quoted twice) and the following month Ferguson made a piano duet version of the Prelude for a new fair-copy score. Finzi submitted the work to the Carnegie Trust for a publication award, but without success: 'They turned down my poor old cinderella-of-a-Requiem a second time. I shd really begin to think it a bad work and destroy it, if the recipients had not been Rootham and Stanley Wilson – neither of whom is worth twopence' (19280422). By then Finzi had decided to omit 'Only a man harrowing clods', probably because he was unsatisfied with the setting but possibly also because he was thinking of including it or a revision in his planned Hardy cycle of fifteen poems that would eventually become *A Young Man's Exhortation*; it certainly fits the theme. Eventually, perhaps in the early 1930s when the Hardy cycle was reduced to ten poems, he entirely rewrote 'Only a man harrowing clods', cast it in B♭ minor rather than D minor, and put it back into the *Requiem* (changing the last movement's 'III' to 'IV' on the manuscript in question), though he only made a rough draft of its orchestration, the missing details eventually being filled in and the whole work edited by Philip Thomas long after Finzi's death, in 1984. The *Requiem da camera* was first performed, in this edition, by Richard Hickox, Stephen Varcoe, the City of London Sinfonia and the BBC Northern Singers at the Spitalfields Festival in London on 7 June 1990, and was issued on disc the following year and in print in 1992.

Its weaknesses, outweighing its strengths, are very much those of the other early works so far discussed and hardly need explaining again, their (and its) effect well summed up by Thomas as 'one-paced, elegiac sweetness' (1990b: [15]). Finzi's later thought, on one of the manuscripts, of crossing out the work's title and substituting 'Elegies?' acknowledged but scarcely solved this. Yet Thomas adds, properly, that 'for all its stillness, this *Requiem* is a protest – a desperate cry for some certainty in a faithless world', which makes us wish once more that Finzi had had the technique to make the cry sink in, for by the time he had acquired it the cry was no longer so urgent. And for all this there are some very beautiful effects in the *Requiem*, making it unsatisfying but not disownable. The 'magical, unaccompanied start of the second movement' (Parker 1992) is among them, using only three-part harmony at this point, without tenors, distinctly Elgarian and affording an extraordinary transparency to the beautifully judged entry of poetic rhetoric following the Prelude. The return of the orchestra after Masefield's first two stanzas is equally magical, when a cadence note (the tenors' $B^{\natural}$) expected to be the root of a triad is underpinned as the minor third, a trick also used in the early song 'To a poet' at the words 'I was a poet, I was young' but even more effective here, where its *pianissimo* muted string chord and melodic response (ex. 3.3.a with imitation instead of parallel thirds) yet again recall the opening of Butterworth's *A Shropshire Lad* rhapsody. A comparably effective treatment occurs at the end of this movement, when Finzi cuts off the last eight stanzas of Masefield's thoughts about soldiers departing for the First World War never to return, closing instead with the lines 'and knew no more . . . the dear outline of the English shore', echoing their last visual impression of home by transmuting it into a verbal one with a memorable snatch of speech-melody repeated in the orchestra.

Unfortunately this approach to the moment cannot sustain the whole, and 'From "August, 1914" ', like the Prelude and the remaining, shorter movements, loses its formal way through the same general lack of contrast, clarity, relief and sturdiness of material that clouds Finzi's other early works. Yet he was not trying to write music without structural foundations, and given that the *Requiem da camera* was his only extended symphonic design prior to *Intimations of Immortality* and the two concertos of his last decade – that is, the only one, unlike the Violin Concerto, allowed to stand, if only because it never got as far as a complete performance – these need uncovering.

The work's binding motif is z in ex. 3.3.b, representing the plodding, stoical rhythm of continuing rural life as expounded in 'Only a man harrowing clods'. This 'stewardship of the landscape' as 'a metaphor for everything lasting' (Thomas 1990b: [15]) is a more ambivalent proposition than might at first appear, for in the farming civilisation referred to in the Hardy and Masefield poems individual people are taken away and die: only the place and the process remain, even if 'Dynasties pass' and, by implication, other people, even conquerors, are brought in to work the land – a deeply apolitical, proto-pacifist implication which the later Finzi would have thought through rather differently. Ex. 3.3.b, the clash at *w* flowering into a brief fanfare, unifies both versions of 'Only a man harrowing clods' and is also found in the Prelude, two bars into it, where it is shortly followed, rather inaudibly, by the melody of the poem's first line, ex. 3.3.c; it comes again later. The plodding is more thoroughly sustained by *y*, however, growing in ex. 3.3.d directly out of *z* as a Holstian 5/4 bass in counterpoint with a wan clarinet motif. Much prone to inversion, *y* develops

EX. 3.3

Second movement

EX. 3.3 cont.

into the seven-beat ostinato outlined in (e), underpinning the central reaches of the Prelude and, with its upward seventh, imitatively glossed with quavers into the pervasive melodic figure with upward stems in (e), Finzi's most exact quotation yet of Butterworth's 'cherry tree' motif. Such contrast as there is in the Prelude is afforded by *x*, the upward pentatonic collection (0257) heard at the outset in motif (a), which occasionally returns, and in (f) which might be thought of as a kind of unrecapitulated second subject, for there are dim ghosts of sonata form in the movement. A vague association with *x* informs the line spun at the end of the Prelude (and presaged earlier) that plays, not quite as expressively as it should, with the outline of the 'Last post', its tonic triads dissonantly flavoured by a flattened $\hat{6}$ in the bass – something of a cliché among British composers.

The second movement ('From "August, 1914" ') uses the loose head-motif technique later favoured by Finzi in strophic contexts. The first three lines of Masefield's first stanza are set to a melodic outline that recurs, down a tone and rescored with altos instead of sopranos, for the first three lines of the third stanza (before being paraphrased in the ostinato (g) in the strings) while for the lines and stanzas in between the music goes its own way. Like its converse, a refrain, and with a function of which Finzi was conscious (as we shall see from his dealings with Blunden), it provides just enough binding between the verbal and musical media for his purposes. Ex. 3.3.h then takes up the mood and the thread in the orchestra, but one is conscious of an all too loose succession of imitative points for the voices and the verse. These are sometimes reminiscent of one or another motif from ex. 3.3 but are not sufficiently offset by the ostinato (i), which is another manifestation of x, once again a way of dealing with the middle reaches of a movement and here the embodiment of the 'unknown generations of dead men' whose march down the ages spans the central stanzas of those which Finzi sets, a march climaxing in the revelation of 'Death, like a miser getting in his rent' with its further imagery of stewardship.

The imagery in 'Only a man harrowing clods' is lyrical and pictorial, and Finzi rightly felt that he could do it greater justice than in his earlier setting. Thus in the later one, (j) acts as a contrasting motif for the second stanza, representing the 'thin smoke without flame'. This sets up a ternary expectation, yet what happens is typical of Finzi's mature partnership with Hardy: instead of a 'closed' ABA resolution, the third stanza provides elements of an 'open' release from the first two by establishing the relative major with new 'aria' material, that is, music more melodically defined or simply more tuneful than in the early stanzas. The classics of this form are songs such as 'Proud songsters' and 'In years defaced' (though in none of these other cases does the relative major prevail in the postlude); here the transformation is for the lines about the 'maid and her wight', prefaced in the later version by the violin solo motif (k). Yet the later version of the song is not all gain, for the way this release is handled in the earlier one has a candour and attractiveness all of its own, as shown in ex. 3.3.n. This is not least because the metamorphosis of the 'Dynasties pass' phrase into x inverted and then x in the tonic major plus a delightful new melody and countermelody for the maid and her wight give the whole thematic process a focus and purpose not so pointedly argued anywhere else in the Requiem. Bairstow's criticism that the song 'is, as usual, rather high

EX. 3.3.n (voice and piano)

for baritones & low for tenors' was beside the point. One can see why his pronouncements *de haut* must have sickened Finzi, for they wither the very things that make his songs so distinctive and show how little he understood the emerging style of his pupil. 'When will you learn that people's voices are like their feet – of different sizes, and that only a very few have voices of abnormal compass,' he complained. 'The main difficulty wd be the *pp* F♯. E flat is quite high enough for *pp* with the average baritone' (192303). Finzi should not have offered the alternative lower vocal tessitura in the last two bars of ex. 3.3.n, for it ruins the very heart of the song, Hardy's whispered, intimate secret, something that a high baritone *can* communicate on that top F♯, and a foretaste of a yet more magical moment of revelation in a Hardy poem, 'In years defaced', at the title phrase of *Till Earth Outwears*, of which again the vocal alternative makes nonsense.

The *Requiem*'s fourth movement uses a short poem, so structure is less problematic. Various motifs – (d), (f), (e) – return or are echoed and combined with two new ones, (l) and (m), that vaguely emerge, the former equally vaguely reminiscent of the opening of Butterworth's first *English Idyll*. There is a brief, lonely soprano solo as at the end of the second movement; the 'Last post' passage and some of its surroundings recur in a postlude that is actually a seamless sewing together of three or four separate passages from the Prelude; *x* has the last word, perhaps of modified benediction, except for the final upward fifth on the flute that suggests, as well as a bugle call, the corresponding final gesture (Butterworth's self-quotation) in the *Shropshire Lad* rhapsody; other shadowy shapes and correspondences that may have been sensed all through the *Requiem* are no further defined. It is all rather touching in its way, but does not proclaim the making of a real composer. That needed quite different stimuli, to be found in London.

Finzi completed one further song in the Cotswolds: 'Days too short' (W. H. Davies), dated 1925 and yet again setting a poem found in one of the *Georgian Poetry* volumes. It sports much breezier two- and three-part pianistic counterpoint than found hitherto in Finzi's songs, and may well have been influenced by one or more of the comparable *jeux d'esprit* that were beginning to supplement the English 'sensibility' song in the output of other composers, if one thinks of Vaughan Williams's 'A piper' or perhaps 'The water mill', or Howells's 'Miss T.' from *Peacock Pie*, all published between 1923 and 1925. But like theirs, its rhythmic and contrapuntal manners make little impact and Finzi still lacks harmonic grounding (he appears to be using a lydian mode).

As for the events of his life at this period, from the few that can be chronicled it seems to have been extremely uneventful. He attended the 1922 and 1925 Three Choirs Festivals at Gloucester and the 1923 one at Worcester, where he got close enough to Elgar to report that he wore stays but probably never met him. He went on holiday with his mother to Dorset and again to Wiltshire in September 1923, delighted to be lodging in Dorset with a Mrs Hardy. He occasionally stayed with Bairstow in York, where he played table tennis with him, and revisited Harrogate; he also made visits to London, staying with Erlebach and his parents in Highgate at least once and going to concerts. He bought a car (a Jowett with a dicky-seat) in 1925 and had an accident when he swerved to avoid a duck – hardly surprising, if his habit of getting his mother to read out loud to him as he was driving along had anything to do with it, though perhaps this was his characteristically original way of dealing with a nervous passenger. He was never a good driver, as he himself admitted. He and his friend Villiers helped found the first Painswick Music Club (the present one must be the second), and from 1925 onwards reports of its impressive activities were periodically sent to the *Musical Times,* not surprisingly with a good deal of English music and some early music on the menu – Léon Goossens playing Bax, the Brosa Quartet playing McEwen and Eugene Goossens, Sybil Eaton playing Moeran, and Violet Gordon Woodhouse playing the harpsichord. Apparently *By Footpath and Stile* featured too (see Dressler 1997: 6). He also coached a local amateur string quartet, 'sometimes . . . in the tiny drawing-room of the odd little council house we then lived in' as a friend recalled after his death (19560928t).

But Finzi was also looking further afield, for the sense of freedom had turned to isolation and technical frustration. As early as February 1923 he asked Bairstow about R. O. Morris's counterpoint textbook, and in March 1925 he and Villiers went to see Adrian Boult in Birmingham where Boult was conductor of the CBO. Perhaps they were there to pick his brains about young artists they could engage at the music club; but according to Joy Finzi (1987b), Boult also advised Gerald at this meeting to go and study in London, though it is not quite clear whether he went as far as recommending his fellow-tutor at the RCM, R. O. Morris – Ferguson thinks he did. To Morris Finzi then went, for a private course on sixteenth-century counterpoint between April and the end of July, presumably at Morris's house. By this time he and his mother had sold up and were back at Chosen Hill Farm, but he lodged in London with a Mrs Marsh in St John's Wood when he needed to, on other occasions coming back on the milk train after going to the theatre or a concert.

The course was exactly what was wanted. 'It was . . . the greatest help when I came to a temporary stop,' he later told William Busch, 'to start again at harmony & cpt exercises' (19420409a). By the end of

1925 he had decided to move to London. Urgent in spirit and, in a certain manner, ambitious as he was, this was imperative; but for all his impatience with his mother and his meagre musician's circle it was a daunting change for an introspective, socially inexperienced young man. The Cotswolds offered one very particular benediction, which Ursula Vaughan Williams chronicled after his death:

We had a wonderful Sunday [at the Three Choirs Festival in 1956] when the Finzis drove us out to Chosen Hill and Gerald described how he had been there as a young man on Christmas Eve at a party in the tiny house where the sexton lived and how they had all come out into the frosty midnight and heard bells ringing across Gloucestershire from beside the Severn to the hill villages of the Cotswolds. (1964: 374)

We have encountered that tiny cottage before and shall meet it again. The experience formed the basis of *In terra pax* but also, much more immediately, of his Nocturne (*New Year Music*). He dated this work 1926, so the party could have taken place in any of the preceding four years. Most likely it was in 1925, when Finzi was staying not just in the region but on the slopes of the hill and was about to seek his fortune in the lonely city.

The associations of *New Year Music* encompassed both Christmas and New Year and literary works by Charles Lamb and Robert Bridges, as Finzi explained in his prefatory note to the published score and in letters to Robin Milford on consecutive seasonal occasions when he told him, 'I love New-Year's eve, though I think it's the saddest thing of the year' and '... for me, Christmas will always be a time of silence & quiet, like Bridges' "A Frosty Christmas Eve / When the stars were shining..."' (19400111, 19401215b). He would have identified all the more strongly with Lamb's – or rather Elia's – constitutional misgivings about change and a fresh start if his hilltop epiphany did take place on the eve of his move:

It is no more than what in sober sadness every one of us seems to be conscious of, in that awful leave-taking ... I am, naturally, beforehand, shy of novelties; new books; new faces, new years, – from some mental twist which makes it difficult in me to face the prospective ... If I know aught of myself, no one whose mind is introspective – and mine is painfully so – can have a less respect for his present identity, than I have for the man Elia ... God help thee, Elia, how art thou changed! Thou art sophisticated ... And you, my midnight darlings, my Folios! must I part with the intense delight of having you (huge armfuls) in my embraces? Must knowledge come to me, if it come at all, by some awkward experiment of intuition, and no longer by this familiar process of reading?

Shall I enjoy friendships there, wanting the smiling indications which point me to them here, – the recognisable face – the 'sweet assurance of a look' – ?

Nonetheless, like Elia, he put the past behind him with determination and looked for a place to live. Detmar Blow, as we have seen, found him the little two-bay house in Caroline Street (now Caroline Terrace), Belgravia – part of a neat post-Georgian terrace on the north side of the street, built in 1834 in an area still intimate and unspoilt today. He moved in early in the new year. When he interviewed a prospective resident housekeeper, all he asked her was 'Do you like cats?' (J. Finzi 1987b). Edith Pyke, whose husband Wilf was a policeman, evidently did, and the couple ensconced themselves in his basement.

CHAPTER 4

London

Michael Trend, in his survey of composers of the British musical renaissance, finds it 'impossible not to speculate on what Finzi – while probably losing something of his own particular freshness – would have gained from a proper musical training' (1985: 215). 'Proper musical training' Finzi's first years back in London may not have been, but they undoubtedly cemented professional associations, peer-group friendships and influences that lasted for the rest of his life. Despite earlier tutelage and the Arts and Crafts legacy of the Cotswolds, this was his formative period as a composer, though even then the best elements of his style had to wait until after 1930 for incorporation.

Reginald Owen Morris (1886–1948) was at the centre of this world. Directly, what Finzi gained from him was contact with a fastidious but undogmatic mind exercised on both compositional technique and historical musicology that enabled Finzi too, and his fellow-pupils Edmund Rubbra and Howard Ferguson, to become scholars as well as composers. Indirectly, Morris introduced Finzi to the circle and mindset that remained his milieu thereafter. Ferguson (b1908), whom he first met over tea at Morris's house, became his lifelong closest friend and most trusted colleague, while his exact contemporary Rubbra (1901–86), whom he got to know around the same time and who had in addition been a student of Holst, was of similar aesthetic cast and taste – 'we were both ardent vegetarians' (Rubbra 1981) – and would often find his equally un-English-sounding name bracketed with Finzi's when their generation of English composers was being discussed. (Where its pronunciation was concerned, at Finzi's indelicate suggestion he later 'took the bull by the horns & said RUB-Bra' [19460309].) The reciprocal influence between Finzi and these two composers extended to common stylistic fingerprints and even turns of phrase as well as shared creative plans and mutual reaction. Like Holst and Vaughan Williams, Finzi and Rubbra 'took our music to each other, and criticized it', as Rubbra testified. He went on: 'until his death we remained very close friends. He had a great influence on me' (Grover 1993: 13), also stating, in his obituary of Finzi, 'I cannot remember a single occasion when, in contact with him, I did not carry away something of vital importance' (Rubbra *et al* 1956, R.1995). Finzi and Ferguson enjoyed the same mutuality and were even closer, particularly during Finzi's London years. With Ferguson there was a temperamental kinship not matched by Rubbra, close friends though they and, in time, their wives became and remained. As for Rubbra's music, Finzi may have relished Arthur Bliss's description of one of the symphonies as 'like yards and yards and yards of brown linoleum' (Ferguson 1974–96), and he recognised that such a large output was bound to have weak spots, but when Ferguson wrote to him, about the first broadcast of Rubbra's Third Symphony, that 'I was very disappointed by [it] – as a work, I mean – at first hearing', Finzi fiercely defended the work by scribbling on the bottom of the letter: 'Well, he won't be on a few more hearings' (19410320). After the première of Rubbra's Sixth Symphony Finzi wrote to Bernard Herrmann: 'I have a great admiration for him and it is always a pleasure to see a thirty-year-old friend, in whom one has always believed, earning just recognition' (19541102). What he admired most about Rubbra was the strength of his individuality: 'from the word go everything he has ever written has been Rubbra,' he insisted in a letter to Thorpe Davie (19541124b).

Morris was actually absent from London for most of Finzi's first three years there, for he took up a teaching post at the Curtis Institute in Philadelphia in September 1926. Indirectly, however, this led to further lifelong friendships, for with him as his assistant went John (Herbert) Sumsion, a promising young organist. When they both returned two years later, Sumsion had acquired not only an American spouse, Alice, whose host family in Philadelphia the Morrises had met on the boat going over, but a job that catapulted him to eminence when he was called in 1928 to succeed Herbert Brewer as organist and choirmaster of Gloucester Cathedral. Thereafter he afforded Finzi one of his most trusted friends and colleagues; Alice Sumsion and Joy Finzi would also become very close friends.

Then there was the Vaughan Williams connection. Morris and

Vaughan Williams had married two sisters of the formidable Fisher family, Emmeline (known as Aunt Jane) and Adeline respectively, and the two couples shared their rented house at 13 Cheyne Walk, Chelsea. Finzi soon became an *habitué*, not least on account of the cats that dominated the Morrises' lives. Arthur Bliss (1891–1975), of Howells's slightly older generation, was another inmate. Not only did he play chess with Morris (thus the later dedication of *Checkmate* to him); he had actually composed there:

I did a lot of preliminary work on this [Colour] Symphony in the home of Vaughan Williams in Cheyne Walk ... There was a wonderful atmosphere of quiet sustained work in that house. Vaughan Williams lived on the top floor, then below came R. O. Morris' study, whilst I had the room on the ground floor. Morris, who was a quiet worker ... compiling his scholarly work, Contrapuntal Technique in the XVIth Century, acted as a sound-proof barrier between Vaughan Williams and myself ... I loved working there in so sympathetic and creative an atmosphere. (Bliss 1970: 74)

This was about four years before Finzi came on the scene, and in the meantime Bliss had spent two years in America (where he married Trudy, who herself became a Morris pupil back in England). But in due course Finzi and Bliss met, corresponded from 1927, and became lasting friends, employing the same architect when they built their own houses. As will be argued below, the influence of Bliss on Finzi, particularly at a crisis in his stylistic development around 1930, was crucial, but it has been underestimated or ignored by omission from standard accounts. To complete his colleagues' circle came Robin Milford (1903–59), yet another RCM pupil of Morris, as well as of Vaughan Williams who bracketed Finzi and Milford together in a major performance opportunity in London. Finzi had already contacted Milford in 1926, though the friendship probably did not become close – and demanding at times because of Milford's increasingly tortured spirit – until they were living relatively near each other on opposite sides of Newbury from the mid-1930s. (Copley [1984: 19–21] cannot be right in saying that Milford moved to Berkshire in 1932 'partly to be within closer proximity to Finzi', since Finzi was still in London at the time. Their letters only recommence in 1938.)

Other composers frequented Finzi's circle or vice versa until he left London in 1933, and to a lesser extent afterwards, though none as centrally as these. Elizabeth Maconchy (1907–94) and Gordon Jacob

(1895–1984) were of more or less the same generation, Benjamin Britten (1913–76) of a slightly younger one; their paths all crossed in various ways in the late 1920s or early 1930s, sometimes through a shared performance such as in the Macnaghten–Lemare concerts, and they viewed each other as young contemporaries, though not always charitably. Finzi employed Britten at least once as a copyist and later revelled in saying so. Like everyone else, Finzi took lessons in orchestration from Jacob, though this was an informal and, it would appear, on one occasion a reciprocal arrangement. There was contact with Grace Williams (1906–77), as there was of one kind or another with Elisabeth Lutyens (1906–83) and Lennox Berkeley (1903–89); and even Aaron Copland (1900–90) appeared briefly on Finzi's horizon when he was in England. Alan Rawsthorne (1905–71) did not settle in London until 1935, but the following year Finzi shared a première with him at one of Iris Lemare's concerts and was generous about his now forgotten Overture for chamber orchestra, calling it 'the most important thing in the concert' (19360207–12) in preference to his own Milton Sonnets; after the war he became a regular and respected colleague.

William Busch (1901–45), three weeks older than Finzi, was his closest contemporary. Preternaturally modest and now almost entirely forgotten, he was a composer of particular comparability because although his background was continental (his parents were German and his training cosmopolitan) his sensibility was by and large English pastoral. Eventually he became a rather special friend and correspondent, perhaps because of this, but it is not clear how much contact they had before the mid-1930s; nor does it appear that Finzi personally knew Busch's teacher and near-namesake Alan Bush (1900–95), who was in Berlin for part of Finzi's London period. E. J. Moeran (1894–1950) was older but a further friendly presence who perceived Finzi as part of this general group, for in January 1934 he wrote to the *Daily Telegraph* about the Queen's Hall's programming policy where new music was concerned, complaining: 'It was a pity an opportunity was not found to include something by Jacob, and I should have liked to hear something by Finzi, Rubbra and Elizabeth Maconchy, who seem to claim attention more than anyone else of that generation' (reprinted in Foreman 1987: 169).

One name missing from the list is that of Michael Tippett (*b*1905). He would in due course become the most distinguished Morris pupil of all, but it is unlikely that Finzi took any steps to cultivate him upon moving to London, for Tippett was too slow a developer at the RCM to be much noticed by his peers. By 1929 Tippett had moved to Oxted, and his period of study with Morris was not until 1930–32. One imagines that Finzi and Tippett might have had a lot in common had they been thrown together – a genteel Edwardian family background sharply fractured by the war; painful schooldays; intellectual breadth, stubbornness and self-reliance resulting both from circumstances and from character but untested by training; and that peculiarly innocent vernacular radicalism that marks out English privileged socialism of the period and that we have traced through Finzi's Cotswold years. Finzi's musical starting-point was not very different from Tippett's, and what both of them owed to a course of private study with Morris, after earlier teachers and a period of rural seclusion had failed to unlock it, was not so much their stylistic maturity as a technical common sense that would enable them to find this for themselves in due course. Most important of all, perhaps, they shared a tendency to cultivate interdisciplinary friendships rather than climb the professional ladder, surely because of a lack of executant skill. This limitation in practical musicianship was a highly significant shaping factor, and it made for slow and hard-won recognition in Tippett's case, a circumscribed output in Finzi's; indeed, according to Howard Ferguson both Morris and Harold Samuel had real doubts about Finzi's abilities, and Samuel thought his Piano Concerto showed amateur incompetence.

Though they were to find themselves on different tracks, there was warmth and respect, certainly on Finzi's part, when he and Tippett did later meet, an attitude contrasting sharply with his view of the early success of Britten, whom he and Ferguson both tended to dismiss – though not without extensive hearing – as a writer of 'piffle'. He was enthusiastic about Tippett's Double Concerto, though he found A Child of Our Time embarrassing ('like love letters read aloud', as his friend Tony Scott put it [19480311]). It should be added, looking ahead, that Finzi tried to do something for Tippett in June 1943 when he was sentenced to imprisonment for violating the terms of his registration as a conscientious objector (see p. 276), and that his measured assessment of Britten came, like everyone else's, after the Peter Grimes première in 1945. This can be savoured in a letter to Scott worth quoting at length because it shows something of how Britten eventually split the musical establishment right down the middle (it is nonetheless a good deal more charitable than Scott's fulmination about the *Sinfonia da requiem* which gave rise to it):

I'm 'allergic' to Britten's music! It's beyond me, the Britten boom. See Mrs Behrend's eyes light up at the very name! It's very difficult to say in public what one thinks about one's contemporaries, as it's so often mistaken for jealousy! I still go on getting his works as they come out, in the hope of finding a spark, but up till now, with the exception of 'Peter Grimes', they've struck me as being derelict & dead. Rubbra's description of them as having 'no central core' struck me as being good. My first impression of soap-bubble music still holds good. Wonderful iridescent colours & then, puff, & it all disappears into thin air. I think he has, technically, a most brilliant flair, a gift for placing notes & bringing things off, but as a rule what he brings off isn't worth a rat's dropping.

How odd it is to find quite a number of people who think Walton a mere nothing next to this most wonderful Benjamin 'the first English composer of international reputation' as they are now saying & as they said of Walton 10 years ago, Bliss 15 years ago, VW 20 years ago & Elgar 30 years ago!

However, there's always the chance that Britten may develop into something better & that he may grow out of his arid opportunism. And 'Peter Grimes' *was* a good opera, though I know that opera doesn't postulate good music (any more than it postulates good drama). Still, it succeeded in doing what it sets out to do, which is more than 95% of his other work does. (19451216a)

London in 1926 was a place of limitless opportunities, and here was a young man enjoying a bachelor existence, and with only a self-imposed occupation, near the heart of it in the little terraced house behind Sloane Square. With the jazz age at its height, he could have foxtrotted and Charlestoned to Ambrose or the Savoy Orpheans and Debroy Somers, no doubt with redoubled skill after the publication of Victor Sylvester's *Modern Ballroom Dancing* in 1928, bought their new electrical gramophone recordings or 'listened-in' to their live radio broadcasts, for the BBC was rapidly becoming a cultural force, about to receive its royal charter and soon to take over the Proms from Chappell's. The West End theatres were thriving, though increasingly with American musicals, and the silent cinema represented the biggest mass market ever. Dining out was becoming rapidly popular among those of Finzi's age, 'young enough to have avoided decimation in the First World War' (D. Scott 1995: 59).

He did little or none of all this, of course, this man of 'aloof and astringent style' not yet 'growing into comparative ease and geniality', as he himself later described Morris (1949a: 55), and much of it he would have dismissed as escapism. He did not spurn the wireless, but neither did he possess one (nor apparently a gramophone at this stage). He was certainly not a social dancer, and if he ate out it was at a vegetarian café. Though he frequently visited the theatre his world was exclusively on the dark side of the footlights. And even by 'serious' standards his musical world was carefully circumscribed, though not closed.

The Austro-German tradition had lost its hegemony since the war, except insofar as Schoenberg and Berg were seen as its heirs. Strauss was no longer 'the music of the future' – 'the Philharmonic was bloody . . . like a fool I stayed to hear Heldenlieber [*sic*] . . . I left in the middle,' wrote Ferguson to Finzi (19280506). They and their friends were not enamoured of the Second Viennese School, though they did listen. They were drawn to Mahler but had little opportunity to imbibe him. 'I heard the 4th Mahler Symphony at College on Friday: *most* interesting. It is very long indeed, but seems to have great beauty, of the kind of the Songs of the Wayfaring Man. It has a strange simplicity and very great sincerity,' Ferguson wrote in June 1928 (19280611). Finzi replied: 'It was interesting to hear about the Mahler. I wish I cd hear some of his big stuff or see some of the scores. Hearsay holds him in contempt, but I never feel like that as I know he went through Hell in his life time, and I've a sympathy for the metaphysicians' (19280615b).

Finzi was not alone in his distaste for the Franco–Russian aesthetic, for British music at the time was divided into cosmopolitans like Bridge, Bax, Ireland and Goossens who went with it and the folksong nationalists headed by Vaughan Williams and Holst who ostensibly did not. Rubbra, reminiscing late in life, summed up the situation with reference to his two teachers, Evlyn Howard-Jones (piano) and Holst (composition):

Howard-Jones . . . was a friend of John Ireland, Bax, Goossens, and that school of music, as well as Cyril Scott. On the other hand, Holst was a friend of Vaughan Williams, and the two schools of thought were much opposed to each other. Howard-Jones said rather nasty things about Vaughan Williams's school, and the other side said equally nasty things (although not quite so much) about the school that Howard-Jones championed. But Holst didn't know much about what was being produced by these other composers . . . It was odd that at that time there were these two schools of thought that never came together; they were entirely separate from each other. (Grover 1993: 14)

It was a somewhat false division, for the Holst of *The Planets* and the *Perfect Fool* ballet music could be as Franco-Russian as anybody, Vaughan Williams was on friendly terms with Ireland and Bax (up to a point), and they were influenced by him, and Bliss confined himself to neither camp; but a perception of 'two schools' it certainly was. Finzi, of course, was firmly on the nationalist side – witness his strong dislike of Bax, whose facility he distrusted ('G was interested to hear [Boult] say . . . "that he found it impossible to remember one Bax Sym. from the other",' Joy's journal later reported [J. Finzi 19410313]). Vaughan Williams, in a note introducing Finzi to Boughton, wrote 'He's one of us!' (Liley 1988: 69).

Nor did Finzi see the point of French neoclassicism, and Ferguson wrote a spoof piano piece for him called 'Cantilever' (1927), systematically bitonal and marked 'vif et gai'. Stravinsky was something of an unweighed quantity: 'See Stravinsky's "Noces" if you get a chance; I liked it – not as European art, but rather in the same way as we shd like some curious oriental or asiatic music,' Finzi wrote to Ferguson (19280714a), on another occasion praising *Oedipus Rex*.

It was not just a matter of musical style. Where British composers were concerned, it is evident that Finzi, for all his self-education, was an establishment man when it came to his choice of friends and colleagues. Nevertheless, like Vaughan Williams he had a natural respect for those with an ideology further to the left than his own, a sympathy applied to Tippett, as we have seen, and Alan Bush. He admired Bush's Piano Concerto, respected his 'astringent mind' (19560217), and deplored the BBC ban on his works in the war. But he steered clear of bohemians and patricians such as Lambert, Berners and Warlock, and Warlock's name scarcely appears in the Finzi annals. 'You've always slightly despised [him],' Robin Milford told him (19450408?), and he was impervious to *The Curlew*, describing it as 'mildly decadent' (A. Scott 1996). He liked the *Capriol Suite*, however – a later repertoire item of the Newbury String Players – when he heard it at the Proms in 1929, even though the composer, wearing Constant Lambert's trousers and John Ireland's tailcoat, 'made a pitiful exhibition of himself . . . rather drunk & completely unable to give a beat of any sort. The baton just trembled & shook!' (19290901–12). Finzi did have contact with van Dieren, their works thrown together in more than one concert, and his influence on the Milton Sonnets and one or two of Finzi's more intractable passages of the 1920s cannot be ruled out. Walton never became a friend, perhaps because he moved in rarefied circles, but he was soon admired by and influential on Finzi, Ferguson and even the idiosyncratic Rubbra. 'Did you hear "Belshazzar's Feast?" I thought it wonderful – it bowled me over: but R. O. [Morris] couldn't see anything in it! Who is right?' Rubbra asked Finzi after a broadcast (19311221). He must have sided with Rubbra, judging by this work's eventual impact on his style, as evident as the influence of the Violin Concerto's opening on that of his own Clarinet Concerto.

Walton filled a gap from the late 1920s, but until then other composers seemed equally central. Bloch was a particular enthusiasm of Finzi's:

I listened in to the Bloch [Violin Concerto] & liked it v. much. It's easy to imagine posterity finding a style of the age & giving VW & Bloch as examples, whereas you cd never find it say, between Bax & VW. Bloch's music always (no, not always) strikes me as being extraordinarily English! The slow mvt of the Concerto Grosso, the 4tet, the sacred service, this work, might almost be written by VW's brother. (musical brother, not blood!) & if one find, probably by suggestion, slight oriental turns, what cd be more oriental than 'Flos Campi'. Of course, biblical is the word, not oriental, but you'll know what I mean. (19390310b)

Ferguson pored over Jarnach, and Falla pleased them both. Ravel was still regarded as a man of the moment: '[he] knows perfectly well what he is about & is a brave little composer, courageous and looking forward, & in his way as many-sided as VW – only with the Devil's technique' (Finzi, 19281020). Bartók was admired rather than loved, though Finzi found the First Quartet 'a magnificent work' (19351105) and greatly enjoyed *Bluebeard's Castle* in 1937. Prokofiev, Szymanowski and Honegger appeared on the horizon from time to time but stayed there. If there was any affinity with the 'new simplicity' of Busoni it was probably more of a latent propensity than something conscious. In any case, once Sibelius was in the ascendant others were sidelined. Finzi made piano duet sketches of the beginnings of the Fourth and Seventh Symphonies of Sibelius – Constant Lambert's favourites – and was probably present at the British première of the Seventh Symphony in December 1927. Rubbra found the Violin Concerto 'magnificent' at the Philharmonic in 1931 (19310116), Ferguson was 'vastly struck' by *Tapiola* the following year (19320713). Then came Lambert's eulogy in *Music Ho!* (1934: 221–41), and by 1938 Finzi could write to William Busch:

I shd really feel suicidal if I didn't know that a song outlasts a dynasty & that, seen in perspective, Walton's Viola Concerto, VW's F Symphony, Howard's Octet, Sibelius No. 4, Gurney's songs, perhaps your new Piano Concerto, will make present day Germany look very small indeed, just as Napoleon & his ravages are now a dream, whilst Beethoven & obscure Schubert are the realities. (19381008)

Such were his contemporary co-ordinates, sufficient for the rest of his life, though they were by no means exclusive or even summary. True, by 1933 the general battle-lines of contemporary music had hardened. Unlike Walton and Lambert, neither Finzi nor friends such as Rubbra and Ferguson were on a fast enough career track to become denizens of the ISCM, and there appears to have been no contact until after the war with its president, Edward Dent. In 1946 Finzi told Anthony Scott: 'I've never sent anything in myself because I just feel that I'm not the ISCM cup of tea, interested as I am in new stuff' (19460329). Yet this was the point: Finzi remained constitutionally curious, alive to music he did not know and fully susceptible to enrichment and surprise in any artistic sphere, even after his own style had become more or less fixed and complete in the early 1930s. Roy Harris, for example, was a later enthusiasm. Receptivity is also the hallmark of the following extract from a 1938 letter to Ferguson:

Joy & I went to the Hindemith Ballet – *Nobilissima Visione* – & found it very moving. I've liked nothing better in the Ballet line since *Job*. There are bad patches in it, & it's not such completely 'realised' music as 'Job'; but for once, Hindemith's dry & wooden music takes on an almost ritualistic feeling. It's a symphonic type of work (if Hindemith's music can ever be called that) rather than a set of short mvts, & for once I think he has done a good thing. The choreography & decor was lovely, straight from the Italian Primitives, & now I know that the only sort of dancing that moves me is when something speaks through the dance, rather than when the dance speaks for itself, which is only another word for ritual, I suppose. Anyhow, 'Job', those Hindu dancers from Serakaila, this Hindemith Ballet, a morris jig like 'I'll go & enlist for a sailor' or the dance of the Kings of the Isle of Man (as danced by Billy Cain) – anything of this sort makes the flimsy-flamsy-on-the-toes, pas-de-deux-corps-de-Ballet stuff just too ridiculous for words. Do see *Nobilissima Visione* if you get a chance. (19380803)

During the London period Finzi enjoyed such a close bond with Ferguson that they set about their musical discoveries hand-in-hand, or rather hand-by-hand. Finzi's keyboard limitations prevented them from doing much of this in regular piano duet form, which is still one of the best ways of getting to know music from the inside and a standard item of self-education at that time. Rather, they had their own makeshift procedure, as Ferguson's account tells us. We pick it up after their first meeting, which must have been in or before early September 1926. Their second, 'both accidental and more significant', was outside the Royal Albert Hall on Tuesday 9 November:

Richard Strauss had been conducting one of the very early BBC Concerts, and during the noisiest climax of his *Alpensinfonie* the thunder-machine was seen to topple over slowly and crash unheard into the middle of the startled orchestra. As we were leaving the hall Gerald and I cannoned into one another, both of us helpless with laughter; and from that moment our friendship was sealed. For the next eight or nine years, until he moved permanently into the country after his marriage to Joy, he and I would meet about once a week, either at his home or mine. We went through each other's compositions, talked, and made music ceaselessly. Being the less fluent pianist, Gerald always stationed himself at the extreme upper end of the keyboard and there played whatever vocal or instrumental part came his way, several octaves too high, rather loudly, and with a distinctly capricious sense of time-values. So far as I can remember, we were pretty omnivorous; but I was then particularly fond of Beethoven, Brahms, Fauré, Debussy, Bartók and the up-and-coming young William Walton. (Ferguson 1989: 8–9)

(Finzi cannot have been too bad a pianist – see pp. 300 and 464; nevertheless, he 'always vowed he had an excellent sense of rhythm, but that his fingers, alas, wouldn't do what his brain told them' [Ferguson 1957a: 130].) Nor did they restrict themselves to music. Both were highly literate men (though uncertain spellers), wide readers, and eager to explore what the other arts had to offer. Finzi probably took the lead where poetry was concerned ('large as his music library was even then, there were many more books in the house than there was music' [ibid.: 130–1]), Ferguson for fine art – Flemish art and Blake exhibitions at the Royal Academy, Stanley Spencer, and other topics crop up in their early correspondence. They also went walking together, often getting out of London on a Sunday for a day in the country, best of all on the Berkshire Downs.

It was, perhaps, a surprising friendship, though clearly an extremely lively one ('So rare to get you & Fergie together. Such clash of wits,' Emmeline Morris observed in 1929 [192907–08?b]). Ferguson was seven years the younger of the two and not yet eighteen when they first met. Finzi was already a professional composer, and he taught Ferguson his quick, neat musical handwriting; yet with his isolated and unconventional upbringing he must have been gauche and immature for his age, while Ferguson was precocious, and much more of a practical musician, thereby and in other respects the more active and challenging partner, opening out and relaxing Finzi's attitudes and responses just as Finzi probably deepened and tempered some of Ferguson's. It was not a homoerotic, let alone a sexual relationship, for Ferguson, though gay – Finzi, of course, was not – was never in love with him. One has to recognise that a friendship can be intimate, perhaps even the most important partnership in a person's life (though not quite in this case), while it keeps certain areas of self off-limits for safety's sake. Finzi never told Ferguson that he was Jewish; Ferguson did turn a comparable stone, and paid for it, for he eventually came to believe that Finzi did not accept his practising homosexuality. This was why he was less close to him in later years and did not keep Finzi's letters after 1947, though he stresses that Joy was utterly accepting. (Finzi was homophobic, for he feared that the succession of talented youths with whom Ferguson tended to turn up at Ashmansworth in later years would have a corrupting influence on the children, and when Jeremy Dale Roberts showed him some Denton Welch poems he had set to music he described them as 'the product of a diseased mind'.)

Ferguson had been in London for just under four years when they met. He was a student at the RCM, which offered a genial foil to Finzi's autodidacticism, but all in all his upbringing had been just as unusual. Like Finzi, he was a fifth, last and unintended child, but unlike him enjoyed a close, warm, unproblematic and continued relationship with his mother and his father (who was Director of the Ulster Bank). The most important musical influence of his life appeared suddenly in the shape of the celebrated pianist Harold Samuel when he was thirteen. Samuel was adjudicating a Belfast competition, heard Ferguson play the piano, and promptly asked his parents to let the boy study with him in London. To Ferguson's lifelong amazement they immediately agreed and he went there, first as a pupil of Westminster School while he lodged with an American family, then, from Summer Term 1924, as a student at the RCM, where Morris taught him composition, harmony and counterpoint and Sargent conducting while he continued piano lessons privately with Samuel. By the time he met Finzi he had moved in with Samuel, with whom (along with his Irish nanny, later joined by her niece) he lived until Samuel's death in 1937. Samuel was a bachelor, and gay, and Ferguson, who stresses that their relationship was never sexual, recognises that this must have propelled the arrangement all along though he was unaware of it until he was about twenty. He was presented with extraordinary opportunities, including a five-month visit to America in the first half of 1927 (where he was able to continue lessons with Morris in Philadelphia and, of course, with Samuel), and reading his letters to Finzi from New York it is difficult to grasp that he was still only a lad of eighteen. Yet there appears to have been nothing oppressive about these unconventional circumstances, due perhaps to Ferguson's natural geniality, though they may help to explain the strength of the bond with Finzi, older yet not an elder.

Outwardly, Finzi's life in London was uneventful. After the 'short and sharp' counterpoint course (G. Finzi 1949a: 54) – about a dozen lessons in all – he continued to have consultations with Morris once he was settled in the city, and Morris, evidently following Vaughan Williams's example, set his pupil to work on his own scores in lieu of payment: Finzi made piano duet versions of his Symphony and *Concerto piccolo* in 1926–7. He visited the Morrises at their rented holiday houses in Surrey and elsewhere, continued to exercise his uncertain talents in photography on their cats, and humoured – and was probably humoured by – the 'distinctly peculiar' but lovable Aunt Jane (Ferguson 1985–96). There was a sense of dry fun in their dealings; Morris, 'this strange fantastic creature', as Finzi described him after his death (194812?), called him 'Burlington', after his lavatory, and it was Gordon Jacob who guessed Finzi's authorship of the following letter in the December 1928 issue of the *Musical Times:*

Sir, –

Your correspondent, Dr C. W. Pearce, has given some remarkable horoscopical coincidences. May I add, for the benefit of your readers, the following important cases:

A former housemaid of mine who was very musical, and always sang at her work, died on April 3, 1897, *the day on which the immortal Brahms died.*

My old friend Dr Thomas Smith, organist of Whelcaster Parish Church and composer of an excellent service, was presented with his third son on June 5, 1925, on which day the great Orlando Gibbons died, three hundred years before.

My mother, who was a pianist of no mean ability, died on March 2, 1909.

She was very fond of Chopin's pianoforte music, and it should be noted that he died exactly a hundred years and a day before.

Ludwig van Beethoven was born on December 16, 1770, and I was born on the same day in 1856.

I have composed but little myself, but am considered to be very musical by my friends, and have studied the rules of harmony and counterpoint.
– Yours, &c,

121, Caroline Street, sw1. R. Burlington

[The instances cited by Mr Burlington are indeed remarkable. Some in our own experience run them very close, however. For example, on April 1 – but we refrain. In fact, this correspondence is abruptly closed. – Editor.]

Once, during Morris's two-year absence in America, Finzi took his arrangement of the Symphony to Rubbra to try over with him, which seems to have been their practical way of beginning to get to know each other, though they had first met through Rubbra's piano teacher, according to Rubbra's somewhat imprecise memory:

... one day when I was having a piano lesson (which took place in Eaton Terrace, opposite Caroline Street), Howard-Jones told me of a young musician of about my age who wanted to meet me. He lived there and worked privately. I met him and we went upstairs and talked about music. (Grover 1993: 13)

At Caroline St. he had dinner guests, including Rubbra, and Winifred Blow and her children to tea. He went to stay with the Blows at Hilles from time to time and spent Christmas there in 1926 and 1927. Christmas 1928 was spent with his mother at Hundon, near Clare, Suffolk, where at the beginning of the year she had at last found a house in which to settle, 'The Limes'. It was large and gracious, with a tennis court, gardens, orchard and paddock, and over the next twenty years she became a well-loved local figure: very short, rotund, perennially smiling, deaf (with a repertoire of ear trumpets to match her neat, old-fashioned dresses), kindly to children and generous to the poor, still a good pianist, but increasingly dotty as she took to following spies down the village street and telling friends about her famous son coming home from overseas. Henceforth Gerald would frequently go to Hundon for quiet in which to work once London began to tell on his nerves. 'Cd I bang away at a piano without my next door neighbours banging away at the wall, as sometimes happens at 21 Caroline St (but what cd one expect of a couple named Hoare)?' he asked Vera Strawson when she was looking at a house in Hampstead for him with a view to purchase, near the Blisses who were in the process of moving there (1928 or 7?). (It proved far too expensive.)

Finzi wrote a fair amount of music during his first years in London, to be discussed in due course, though much of it is difficult to chronicle and assess because it remained largely unperformed and entirely unpublished at the time and later revision covered the original tracks. His chief creative endeavour, however, can be fairly well documented. This was the Violin Concerto, a work that failed but holds a key position in his development, since it was his biggest London première of the pre-war years (arguably of his whole career) and his only full, completed symphonic essay prior to the Clarinet Concerto.

It was written for and performed by Sybil Eaton, not least because Finzi was in love with her – unrequitedly, if she even noticed, for until Joy appeared on the scene 'he had [only] fallen in love from remote distances', Eaton the first of such infatuations and 'one of his idols' (J. Finzi 1950s?). The elegiac slow movement seems to have been written first, which is no surprise; Finzi dated it 'Churchdown 1925' when he later salvaged it for publication as the Introit. Sketches intended for the finale also date from 1925 (Sketchbook B: 4–5), but they went into the first movement instead, while the third matured into the Hornpipe Rondo rather later: work on it was held up by a bout of flu at New Year 1927. Meanwhile he had completed the first movement, its full score dated 1925–6, the piano reduction 'London 1926'. Eaton planned to perform the work on 17 March 1927, but as she was paying for the orchestra and could not afford it, it was postponed until 4 May. By this time Finzi had become dissatisfied with his first movement (the piano score of its 6/8 version – it was first written in 6/4 – is headed '*Damned* Concerto for small orchestra & violin solo'), and the performance took place without it. It was given by the British Women's Symphony Orchestra under their regular conductor, Malcolm Sargent, at Queen's Hall in a programme including Vaughan Williams's *The Lark Ascending*, the Franck Symphony and a couple of overtures. It was not well played, as Rubbra attested and Ferguson (who was on his way back from America) was told – according to Ferguson (1974–96) the BWSO was habitually 'pretty awful', and at this or the next performance Finzi, with characteristic candour, told Eaton that she had played out of tune in the slow movement. The *Times* was unenthusiastic, finding the slow movement 'too monotonous in mood and certainly too long' and preferring to reserve judgement on the whole until more than two-thirds of it could be heard (5 May 1927: 14).

At the end of May, Finzi went on holiday with his mother to the Ridgeway chalklands, staying at Woolstone near the Uffington White Horse, though neither this opportunity to retire and lick his wounds nor a session on 12 June with Morris, who was home for the summer from Philadelphia, seems to have produced any further rethinking of the concerto. Nothing more was heard of it until November, when Vaughan Williams, whom Finzi had consulted the day before its performance in May, asked to have a second look at it. This may well have been a Morris ploy to get Finzi to finish it. If so, it worked: Vaughan Williams announced his intention of putting it in the programme of his Bach Choir concert in February, along with his own *Sea Symphony* and Robin Milford's Double Fugue for orchestra, and Finzi quickly had to write a replacement first movement. This was done by Christmas, when Ferguson was working on the score in Ireland with a view to accompanying Eaton in rehearsal. Back at Queen's Hall, the work was heard again, this time complete, accompanied by the LSO and conducted by Vaughan Williams, on 1 February 1928. There were orchestral rehearsals that morning and the previous afternoon evidently attended by the Blisses for moral support, much needed when the orchestral players began to scoff – as they always will at new music – though Vaughan Williams knew exactly how to deal with them:

I don't know if I will have told you that VW made a speech to the orchestra saying that he very much wanted the work to go well, for although the composer from youth & inexperience had miscalculated his effects in places he liked the work, & believed that he (G.) wd do great things some day. Wasn't that nice? (Eaton to Finzi's mother, 19280206b)

Holst was probably at a rehearsal too, for according to Ferguson he sat up all night with Finzi helping him to make alterations.

Again the performance, while 'certainly a better one this time' (Rubbra, 19280206a), was imperfect. 'Bless his heart, but VW is not a born conductor!' Ferguson exclaimed (19280201a). And again the *Times* review (2 February 1928: 10) was not very helpful (see Chapter 1), describing the Hornpipe as 'of a frankly British type' and pronouncing the first movement 'rather dry'. Finzi himself was still unsatisfied with his first movement, and, frustrated at getting it wrong twice, must have gone around asking everybody at gunpoint what was the matter with it, for Jack Villiers, who had come up from Gloucestershire for the concert, wrote from his hotel, 'I think I know what's wrong with the first movement – but daren't say!' (19280202), Ferguson said, 'I see what you mean about altering the structure of the 1st movement, and I believe I agree with you' (19280201a), Bliss gave a general diagnosis, that 'the quick tempo you are not so at home with yet' (19280201c), Rubbra thought that 'the 1st movement didn't seem to have much shape . . . although perhaps the scoring made it rather seem on a dead level,' adding 'You looked very uncomfortable in your "backed shirt"!' (19280206a), and Milford feebly hazarded doubts about the middle section ('but whether it was in the scoring or in the music itself I could not make up my mind' [19280312]). Finzi's reply to Milford shows that he was still hostage to the misplaced earnestness of his early style – that he had not yet learnt the relaxation that comes with playing with sounds on instruments and events in time rather than with counterpoint:

I was v. anxious to hear any criticism you wd make about that concert, as I knew something was wrong, without being able to say exactly what it was. Perhaps the best thing to do will be to put the 1st movement aside & have a look at it later on. It's annoying, as that's the second first mvt I've done, and I have just the same difficulty that you mention about extended work – more particularly in quick mvts. Don't you think the cause is plain enough? It's much easier to build big structures if you can write a chord & hold it over fifty bars by means of tremolos, Alberti basses, arpeggios and the like. In that way a lot of people seem to find it quite easy to expand no ideas at all! But, with a close and concentrated texture it's a much more difficult job. (19280322)

This was still essentially what one might call a pre-classical or even pre-Raphaelite aesthetic after which he was tenaciously grasping, and it ties in with Ferguson's comment that in the early days when they were playing something through Finzi would say ' "This is just repeating itself, we can leave this out" and so seemed to fail to recognise the [architectural] importance of these passages' (Liley 1988: 7). Sibelius and Walton undoubtedly helped him see beyond this viewpoint in due course, as did Bliss and Ferguson himself.

The concerto's first movement was indeed put aside, and Finzi moved on. There were two later performances of the slow movement alone, as 'Introit', one given by Anne Macnaghten (violin) and conducted by Iris Lemare at the Ballet Club Theatre on 31 January 1933 (this was the concert at which Britten's Sinfonietta was premièred), the other under Dan Godfrey in Bournemouth, also in 1933, on 8 November, with Bertram Lewis as soloist; these sealed the fate of the rest of the work. A reworking of the (replacement) first movement was begun as the third movement of a Concertino for clarinet and strings, apparently in the 1940s, but it led to nothing – except, perhaps, to composition of the Clarinet Concerto proper. Meanwhile, the Introit was revised for publication with piano reduction in 1935, and again when the conductor Alec Sherman took it up with the violinist Henry Holst during the war, whereupon OUP issued a full score, copyrighted in 1943 but not appearing until 1944.

The strain of preparing the work had taken its toll of Finzi's health, and he was ill at the end of February; then, and again a month later, Ferguson expressed concern about his digestion and general overwork. An 'importunate lady' (Ferguson 1985–96) who was in love with him and to whom he had to write 'dispell[ing] the illusion' (19280307) may not have helped matters. He was alarmingly active on multiple fronts: still composing; thinking of writing a comic opera; going through *The Bartered Bride* and *Fennimore and Gerda* with Ferguson; attending concerts, plays (including van Druten's *Young Woodley*) and an early two-piano playthrough of Vaughan Williams's *Job* and portions of *Sir John in Love* at Morley College (the latter containing 'the worst music VW has ever written', the former 'quite another matter . . . the beginning and the end . . . as lovely as the loveliest parts of Flos Campi' [19280409/10?]); going for out-of-town walks; imbibing the recently deceased Thomas Hardy's *Winter Words* poems as they appeared one by one in the *Daily Telegraph*; and getting away, perhaps to Hundon, for recuperation.

Eventually a medical specialist was consulted, Finzi was told he had a mild attack of tuberculosis in one lung, pronounced 'of some years standing' (19280507a), and was ordered to spend four to six months in the King Edward VII Sanatorium near Midhurst in Sussex. The suddenness and potential seriousness of this diagnosis in the days before antibiotics (penicillin was discovered the very same year) shocked his friends, including Winifred Blow, Vera Strawson (who offered to lend him £100 to cover the expenses, since funds were low), the Blisses, and R. O. Morris when he heard about it in America. Finzi himself did not believe there was anything much the matter with him, and was proved right once in the sanatorium at the end of April where, after he had spent the first five days in bed with a temperature, the doctors could find little amiss, reducing his sentence first to two months, then adjusting it to two and a half while telling him he must not swim or run for two years. He came out on 7 July, and years later, when Howells was afflicted with something similar, summed up the experience as 'pleurisy, suspected TB in the left lung, the warning, enforced rest . . . & so on' (19400521).

Nevertheless, it was a worrying time for him. Beforehand he went to Hilles for a fortnight, to stay in the family warmth of the Blows 'till my time comes' (19280409/10?), playing with and photographing their children and meeting Ethel Smyth, a lunch guest, who had never heard of Walton, as it transpired when Finzi switched on the radio to listen to the *Sinfonia concertante*. 'Of course she walked all over the place, hat on one side, coffee-cup in hand, singing (?) the two interlinked French folk-songs!' he told Ferguson in a letter written 'between the intervals of painting three savage looking red-indians, and being killed (and eaten) by them as a bear' (19280422). He wrote a Grace for the Blows, but after that composition was out of the question. Entering the sanatorium and losing his freedom and status were just like being back at school – 'Shakespeare's whining schoolboy, in his first term, never had a greater sinking-feeling in his vitals than I' (ibid.) – and the parallel was so strong that he discouraged his older friends from too much contact: 'Tell Eric not to ask for particulars of my progress, as he said he wd. At least not for a long time: I don't want the feeling that I had at school, when my good mother used to write to the masters in a similar way!' he instructed Strawson (19280501). It was not exactly boring, for enforced routine filled most of the patients' waking hours. But it was tedious, and in addition to treatment at the hands of an incompetent dentist, his tribulations included highly uncongenial company – though even Strawson, long used to Finzi's fulminations, baulked at his attitude towards it:

They are such complete *fools* here. Ordinary intelligent people have resources of their own: if it rains, they can read, or think, or look at the trees (lovely lovely lovely) or write music, or play chess. But here, on a wet evening, they must organise whist-drives and the like. Thus, GF has the prospect of at last two free hours before going to bed, when some bloody little bank-clerk comes in to beg his card-table (which he has bought to write on, *when* time allows) for a whist drive! The surprising thing is that, in spite of my peculiar name & still more peculiar work (as it must be to a set of half-wits) I get on pretty well & normally with most of them: they don't regard me as an oddity. But it is a great trial to be cooped up with that deadly upper-lower & lower-middle class vacuity – a day or two wd be all right, but a month . . .! However, I can talk their talk – TB or cricket or bawdy, & thank God, they don't talk mine. One or two rougher Irishmen are worth knowing. (19280521)

This has the tang of Gurney's letters, though Finzi was probably not familiar with them at the time. And his faith in ordinary intelligent people writing music on wet evenings is touching.

Still, the building and the grounds were splendid. The former, dubbed 'the Caliphate' by Finzi (with letters addressed from 'Pinnacle of the Golden Dome'), was a major Arts and Crafts monument, designed by Charles Holden and with woodwork by Ashbee's Guild in the chapel. After a while Finzi was able to enjoy visits and long walks, and Ferguson, who was staying with Samuel in a summer cottage at Misbrooks Green near Godalming, cycled over to see him for a weekend ('it nearly killed me,' Ferguson recalls) and, rather less energetically, later managed a second one by a combination of bicycle and train. The Blisses visited on one occasion, Arthur Bliss and R. O. Morris on another when Finzi took them out to tea (this time Morris was home from Philadelphia for good). Meanwhile, as he described to Tony Scott years later, he found that 'your exasperation reaches a sort of boiling point – in fact, rather like a real boil, bursts' – whereupon he was left 'in a state of more or less dumb acceptance' (19400819a). At last it all came to an end, and after a busy few days in London he retreated to Hundon for most of the rest of the summer, busying himself with composition in an environment that was to prove fruitful at various times over the next eighteen months. He was back in London by mid-September and resumed his round of concerts, theatre, galleries, social meetings and weekend walks, marking the end of the year by preparing the Nocturne (*New Year Music*) for submission to a competition, probably the Patron's Fund (for performance at the RCM), in early January.

1929 was a good deal more settled and relaxed. He and his pocket sketchbooks enjoyed a marvellous lone walking holiday in May and June, heading for Bampton in Oxfordshire to see the Whitsun morris and then on to Somerset and North Devon and Cornwall, as far as Hardy's Beeny. This followed the pattern of extensive walking holidays in East Anglia in 1926 and 1927. Between London and Hundon for much of the summer of 1929, he returned permanently to Caroline

Street for a lot of 'Promming' from late August onwards, including the première of Walton's Viola Concerto on 3 October, followed by Beecham's Delius Festival ('I'll face five out of the 6 days, but can't swear to the "Mass of Life" again,' he told Ferguson [192908]). On the compositional front he was chiefly wrestling with a concerto for piano and strings (nicknamed 'David [and Goliath]' in letters to and from Ferguson), the Hardy song cycle that would eventually become *A Young Man's Exhortation*, and, probably towards the end of the year, a Chamber Symphony, of which we hear surprisingly little in his correspondence, though he took it to Bliss for comment. The Grand Fantasia, completed at Hundon in August 1928, was intended as the first movement of the Piano Concerto, despite Vaughan Williams disliking it and Morris saying 'it can't be in a piano concerto, but must be the fantasia for a fugue' (19280903). The second movement was finished by May 1929 (Rubbra 1929); the third gave him trouble and was never completed. He must have put the concerto on ice by the end of the year and returned to it later with various attempts at completion. This involved expanding the opening movement into a prelude and fugue or prelude with some other consequent, according to prescription, with the Grand Fantasia there to be quarried as needed. But he eventually gave up and re-used the Grand Fantasia in the 1950s, as will be discussed in Chapter 11. The original slow movement became the posthumous Eclogue.

Meanwhile, Oxford University Press seems to have rejected his Hardy songs and the Patron's Fund his *New Year Music* – 'I'm blocked whichever way I turn,' he complained (19290601). His friend the photographer Herbert Lambert then helped arrange for Maurice Jacobson to look at the songs for Curwen, but he was not keen on them either, at least not enough to persuade Curwen to put money into them, despite telling Lambert some of them were 'absolute masterpieces' (19300107). The *Farewell to Arms* 'Aria' and the last two movements of *Dies natalis* 'were turned down by every publisher under the sun' (19460926).

These setbacks were counterbalanced by two positive pieces of exposure during the year. The first was an article on Finzi's music, commissioned from Rubbra by Richard Capell, editor of the *Monthly Musical Record*, in his series 'The younger English composers'. Rubbra himself had been treated in the series earlier in the year, and Bliss, Warlock, Berkeley and Constant Lambert had also been featured.

Rubbra borrowed Finzi's scores, wrote them up critically and efficiently, and the result appeared in the July issue. In fact it was the only article to appear on Finzi for another seventeen years, with two marginal exceptions (Lee 1938 and Westrup 1940). The other piece of publicity was an hour's invitation recital at OUP's Amen House on the afternoon of Wednesday 20 November; it included the Hardy songs, the Chamber Symphony and the Grand Fantasia. Ferguson accompanied the singer John Armstrong in the songs and joined Kathleen Long (who played the solo part on another piano) in the Grand Fantasia. Ferguson can neither remember whether he and Long played the Chamber Symphony as a piano duet, nor whether Finzi himself paid for the concert.

Perhaps he had already decided to shelve the Piano Concerto as a cyclic work and let the Grand Fantasia stand on its own for the time being; but it must have been galling to realise that he was not getting anywhere with the Chamber Symphony either. This was a three-movement conceit intended to consist of slow Prelude, lively central movement and elegiac finale, an all too characteristic configuration despite what was a precedent of sorts in the Walton Viola Concerto. At some point, perhaps right from the start, it was entitled or subtitled *The Bud, the Blossom and the Berry* – that is, seen in terms of a triptych about growth, flowering and decay, rather like *A Young Man's Exhortation*. The title was a quotation with which he had been familiar at least since November 1922, when he wrote to Vera Somerfield, living in Australia:

Ma'am. I wonder whether you wd say such things about the English climate if you were to see the holly in the hedges & the hips & haws – berries as sweet as any flower?

Bud, blossom & berry,
Hey, down-a down derry.

After all, there is a lot in a sharp frost & a warm fire. (19221112a)

Yet again, however, he could not conjure up the requisite fast music and began to shy away from symphonic completion after the November concert (at which one presumes the two slow movements were played), a decision made in consultation with Bliss, from whom he was taking 'advice' (Rubbra 1929: 193) if not lessons at the RAM at this stage. Bliss told him to 'Let the [third] movement stand by itself / Elegiac Movement for Chamber Orchestra' (19291122). He did, eventually, and by 1934 it had become *The Fall of the Leaf*, borrowing its title (though no material) from Martin Peerson's tiny almain in *The Fitzwilliam Virginal Book*. Even on its own the movement had a difficult and protracted passage. The point is that at eleven or twelve minutes it was his longest single-movement span so far, by no means intended as another example of the rapt self-sustenance of the Introit and Eclogue but demanding dynamic direction, contrast and climax, which he could not yet manage. Not until 1942 did he feel sure, in a letter to William Busch, that it was 'at last finished (but not scored): I know now that it *is* complete & that the previous 5 versions (stretching over 12 years!) were only sketches in various degrees of compilation' (19420616). He never did finish scoring it, and the short first movement also saw the light of day only posthumously, as the Prelude for strings, though Finzi must have intended performing it himself with his orchestra since an autograph set of parts survives. Later in life he had alternatively planned for it, but not begun to execute, a subsequent contrasting movement and cyclic framing as a second-movement interlude.

This was a curious portfolio of four years' work: nothing to follow up the publications of the Cotswold years; three symphonic casualties despite a high-profile and not unappreciated performance of one of them; a number of striking but isolated, circumscribed and unheard or only privately performed individual movements; and a burgeoning number of solo vocal pieces beginning to draw attention to Finzi's 'wonderful sense for vocal writing & . . . gift for making real music of a contrapuntal texture (I could see this in your songs . . .),' as Herbert Lambert wrote to him on the very last day of the 1920s. Clearly something distinctive had been achieved with the help of a professional London environment. But what, and how was it still wanting?

CHAPTER 5

A problematic portfolio

Before beginning to assess the music of Finzi's first five years in London the problem of dating must be addressed. Because, as is well known, 'years might pass between the start and the completion of a work, even of a brief song' (McVeagh 1980b – see Ferguson 1957a: 131–2 for a more detailed account of this habit of work), it is too easy to assume that Finzi's style did not change over the years. This may be largely true after the early 1930s, but the main reason why so much music from the 1920s was left unpublished or incomplete is because there were certain essential things he did not yet know how to do. Once in London, he was undoubtedly aware of this and honest about it, which is what distinguishes the period from his Cotswold years; and the reason he was aware of it was because more experienced composers such as Bliss and Vaughan Williams told him so, in a friendly but realistic professional environment where his earlier arrogance had no place. (Indeed one wonders whether, had he met Howells at this stage rather than earlier – and without his mother constantly looking over his shoulder – they might have got off on an easier footing.) When he did eventually revise or complete an earlier work, in most cases he destroyed the original manuscript, so it is extremely difficult to know how much was changed or added to, and what proportion of the eventual whole really owed its essence to the earlier material. In Chapter 2 we have already seen, when the evidence does exist, how an early work might be deepened and transformed. Applying the test to works of the later 1920s, particularly the songs, is less easy.

Dies natalis is the crucial case. Finzi stated that 'Wonder' and 'The salutation (Aria)' were composed in 1926 but 'Wonder' was 'entirely rewritten' later (19460926, 19400521); in fact 'The salutation' probably began even earlier, for parts of it feature in a sketchbook dated 1925, much the same as eventually published. However, McVeagh (1980a: 596) also dates the first two movements of *Dies natalis* to 1926, probably on the evidence of Rubbra's 1929 reference to 'the *Intrata, Recitative, and Aria* "Dies Natalis" (1926) for soprano solo and strings, words by Thomas Traherne' (:194). The testimony of works such as the Violin Concerto, surviving complete in manuscript from the same period, belies this. While it is possible that the somewhat uningratiating first eighteen bars of the instrumental 'Intrada' were written that early – though even these have an easy-going harmonic rhythm that was probably acquired later – the next eighteen surely cannot have been, for they show a melodic breadth and rhetorical persuasiveness (to which the performance markings bear important witness) that only later experience released (ex. 5.1.a). And their harmonic depth, its cycle-of-fifths mobility indeed implied by the melody, was something he had not yet plumbed – it belongs to the same stylistic world as 'The phantom'. Similarly, while the first four bars of the following *sempre con moto* section exemplify, up to a point, Finzi's 'Bach' idiom, which had been acquired by 1926 (witness 'The salutation'), it is extremely unlikely that the next four, with their spacious texture, easy give-and-take between the upper parts, and 'strumming' series of $^6_3$ harmonies (ex. 5.1.b), pre-date the opening of Bliss's *Pastoral,* performed in 1929 (ex. 5.1.c – note too the opening low sonority, another later Finzi fingerprint), or the second movement

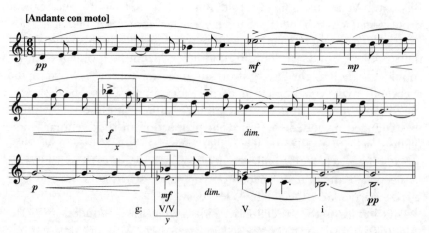

EX. 5.1.a (strings)

EX. 5.1.b

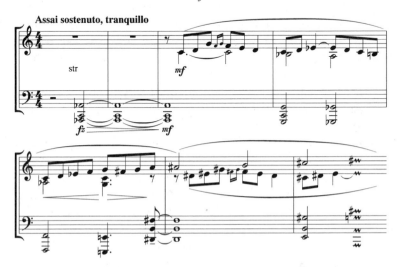

EX. 5.1.c

of his *Serenade* (performed 1930), with its similar strumming texture and a sprinkling of the relaxed $^6_3$s and $^6_4$s that were an eventual hallmark of both men's harmonic idiom.

It is much more likely that the 1926 'Intrata' was a different piece altogether and that Rubbra's 'Recitative' was 'Wonder' in its original guise. Rubbra makes no reference to the opening movement of *Dies natalis* being instrumental (that, perhaps, was another legacy of Bliss's *Serenade*) and sees nothing to comment on in the work beyond the 'Aria'. The obvious implication is that it was not the wonderful 'Intrada' as we know it but the eminently forgettable song of the same title but different music (setting the opening of Traherne's first *Century of Meditation* rather than, in 'Rhapsody', that of the third) that was published posthumously in *To a Poet*, presumably transposed down-

123

wards. This 'Intrada', while supple in its word-setting ('profitable wonders' is idiosyncratic), nevertheless suggests an early origin in several ways, notably in its 'classical' recitative touches, alien to the later Finzi's *arioso* fluency (see the Neapolitan-sixth imperfect cadence at 'but containeth nothing'), and lack of genuinely ruminant instrumental interludes (the piano links are nugatory). As for *Dies natalis*'s second movement, Finzi may equally well have retained and substituted or supplemented certain passages from the *Third Century* when he came to rewrite it, or set new ones entirely, given how easy it was for him to stitch together individual phrases of Traherne's prose from different paragraphs (which he does in both the *To a Poet* 'Intrada' and 'Rhapsody'). Indeed, in view of this very ease, one wonders exactly when he did create the statutory (and related) first and second movements, for they reflect a massive idiomatic breakthrough and it would be good to know whether Traherne's *arioso* prose helped entice him

EX. 5.1.d

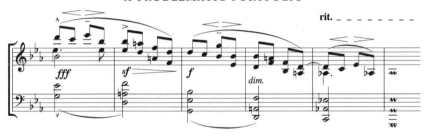

EX. 5.1.e

EX. 5.1.f (baritone and piano)

into affectionate harmonic warmth and sensuous textures. But if further parallels with Bliss are to be believed, that breakthrough must have already occurred elsewhere (compare ex. 5.1.d, e and f, the first from the second movement of Bliss's Clarinet Quintet, which Finzi first heard in 1933, the second from the comparable winding-down after the climax of *Dies natalis*'s 'Intrada', the third, surely a further echo of the Bliss, from Finzi's 'Channel firing'). Or perhaps 'Rhapsody' was taking gradual shape in the early 1930s. A query in September 1931 to a Harrogate antiquary friend, Walter Kaye, about the mid-seventeenth century pronunciation of 'dream'd' suggests that it was under way at this time.

Proper discussion of Finzi's mature style must await the next chapter, but these same questions have to be borne in mind with several works from the second half of the 1920s. The Romance for strings (dated 1928, performed in 1951 and published in 1952) is one of them. The main theme, with its harmonisation, relaxed and Elgarian enough in idiom, is present in Sketchbook L (:r2), probably from the 1920s, but one doubts whether the introductory bars, their train of thought unfolding with exquisite simplicity, can be this early; more likely they were conceived after Finzi began to explore his 'instrument', the Newbury String Players' orchestra. It is the same with 'I say I'll seek her', a Hardy song dated 1929: its piano sonorities, breadth of figuration, clear and economical textures and emotive harmonies, particularly in the first 11 bars, seem well in advance of anything in the other settings destined by this date for *A Young Man's Exhortation*

EX. 5.2.a

EX. 5.2.b

or about to be jettisoned therefrom. Indeed, Finzi was still revising the copyist's manuscript from bar 12 – utterly rewriting the passage, in fact – after gathering the song up in his last years, as though time ran out on him. This is exactly what happened with 'The temporary the all', another early Hardy setting. In this case the 1927 manuscript does survive, because although Finzi began a revised version of the song he never got to the end of it, so there exist both a complete early fair copy for tenor and an incomplete late one for baritone, each with its own annotations and further revisions. That revising could mean entirely rewriting is demonstrated by ex. 5.2.a and b (from the 1927 and late versions respectively). They prove the argument. So do the various piano-duet scores of *The Fall of the Leaf*, the first dated 1929 and presumably the one used for the OUP concert; five versions later, whole sections have been rejected, substituted, cut, transposed and added, and a sensitive listener to the posthumous end product can probably guess which material was written in the late 1920s and which in the early 1940s, though from the start it was more firmly characterised than most of what he had written hitherto, which was why he persevered with it. Nor can we be sure that rewriting was only done when the prospect of performance, publication or completion of a work was approaching. For no obvious reason other than a 'field day' at Ashmansworth the previous Christmas, we find Finzi writing to Ferguson in February 1940: 'I've rewritten the middle of that song – The market girl – as you suggested. It's a great improvement & I always knew it needed it' (19400205).

With all this in mind, we must concentrate on those passages, pieces and concerns that definitely do belong to the 1920s rather than later. Morris's influence is difficult to assess. If one looks at his Carnegie Trust publication, the Fantasy for String Quartet (published in 1922 but dedicated to Butterworth presumably while he was still alive), it shows, for all its original interpretation of the renaissance 'phantasy' brief, precisely the pallid and rather disembodied traits of the 'water colour school' Finzi needed to get away from, as Finzi himself (1949a: 56) later recognised. Nor can we be sure that his understanding of Morris's approach to sixteenth-century counterpoint stood him entirely in good stead at this juncture. There is a further sacred choral piece by Finzi dating probably from the Cotswold years and more likely attributable to the months of study under Morris than to Bairstow's continuing watch. This is his unaccompanied setting of the second section ('Beth') of Psalm 119 ('How shall a young man') in the metrical version taken from Byrd's *Psalms, Sonnets and Songs of Sadness and Piety* (1588). It gives rise to his own metrical experiment: although the word-setting is syllabic, it is done on the mixed principle of quantitative and accentual scansion that Holst felt had been a breakthrough for him when he tried a similar thing in 'My leman is so true' from his Four Songs for Voice and Violin and that Rubbra hailed as his 'discovery that most English poetry naturally falls into either a five- or a seven-beat bar' (Holst 1938: 106; Rubbra 1932, R.1974: 31). Finzi's setting is in 5/4, and this simply means in practice that the eight- and six-syllable ballad metre lines are spread out over two bars (ten beats) each by lengthening, on average, between one and three of the syllables as accentually appropriate. This gives a rhythmic flux not dissimilar to that of the original metrical psalm tunes themselves, and is fine for homophony – see ex. 5.3.a, which gives Finzi's second solo stanza (in a form that disposes the nine stanzas in choral groups of two or three broken up by two solo stanzas). The problems come with polyphony, and Finzi's, imitative from the start, is unconductable, possibly unperformable, and ruinous to the word-setting when nothing coincides with or even echoes anything else metrically. It is not really the sixteenth-century principle it seeks to rediscover, for it lacks the regular pulse of dissonance, though admittedly Byrd's own vocal polyphony at its densest and least Italianate approaches it; and when one senses a kindred experimentation in Tippett – via Morris in both cases? – it is in his instrumental works such as the string quartets. Although he did later build on this kind of writing to a certain extent in his Bridges partsongs, and had one successful further attempt at it in 'All this night' (see Chapter 11), Finzi came to a parallel realisation that in general such flexible vocal accentuation of the English language needs a regular framework if it is to be offset contrapuntally, as his 'aria' style of *Dies natalis* and elsewhere demonstrates, as Rubbra (1929) must have recognised, as (for what it is worth) American popular song composers such as Gershwin were discovering as they simultaneously developed their sophisticated uses of vocal syncopation and cross-rhythm based on selective syllabic lengthening, and as, to be fair, Morris would have been the first to point out (compare Morris 1922: 37, 69).

Nevertheless, Finzi did later plan to salvage 'How shall a young man' (which is not to be confused with the Anglican chant setting of Psalm 119 he made for Richard Latham and St Paul's, Knightsbridge, during

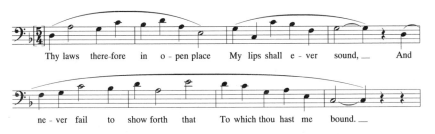

Thy laws there-fore in o-pen place My lips shall e-ver sound, __ And

ne-ver fail to show forth that To which thou hast me bound. __

EX. 5.3.a (basses)

the Second World War – Latham being a colleague of his at the Ministry of War Transport). The idea was to include it and 'Now Israel may say', both needing 'much revision' – indeed completion in the latter case, which he may have forgotten (G. Finzi 1941, R.1951) – in a group of Three Psalms to form Op. 4. 'Now Israel must say', dated to the 1940s by Howard Ferguson, is again a metrical psalm setting, an unaccompanied eight-part one of William Whittingham's version of Psalm 124. Finzi made meticulous notes on the three different versions of the text and their complex provenance (largely from psalters in his own collection), his hymnologist's impulse evidently here stronger than his composer's, since the music peters out half way through the second of four stanzas. The opening (ex. 5.3.b) echoes the metric principle of 'How shall a young man', but this time it is homophonic, already between sketchbook and draft proper the rhythm at bar 4 has become more conventionally accentual, and the succeeding lines are straightforwardly rhetorical.

Morris himself was moving with the times when he graduated from scholarship on sixteenth-century counterpoint, and the composition of music influenced by it, to the pedagogy of harmony and figured bass (see Morris 1925 and 1931) and the production of baroque-orientated works (such as his *Concerto piccolo* mentioned in the previous chapter) of more forthright harmony, melody and rhythm. Finzi began to do the same, very much in line with a general shift in the rediscovery of early music, not just in Britain – and indeed as part of a cultural trend not just in music. Although the neo-Tudor impulse that had given rise to Sir Richard Terry's liturgical performances, Vaughan Williams's Mass, the English Singers and a great deal else, such as the craft and guild activity discussed in Chapter 3, was sustained between the wars (for instance in semi-detached housing), it was joined by a rediscovery of

EX. 5.3.b (chorus (sketch))

the eighteenth century in the 1920s (see Haskell 1995: 521–5). Fashion this may have been, but it lent a much-needed layer of colour and substance to Finzi's music, and he perhaps benefited more from it than most of his fellow-composers when it led directly to the Grand Fantasia for piano and to puissant formulae generally remaining available within his settled style even if they still needed a further idiomatic dimension to offset them.

He was not greatly touched by the more chic or camp manifestations of the post-war pasticheurs, as Constant Lambert called them, who gave the neoclassical decade so much of its impetus, in the form of Stravinsky's reddening of noses and 'adding [of] moustaches and beards in thick black pencil' to Pergolesi (Lambert 1934: 51) and Margot Beste-Chetwynde's perpetration of something similar on King's Thursday in Waugh's novel *Decline and Fall* (1928). The 'amusing' world of gilded or periwigged frivolity of which even Walton partook on occasion (see Core 1984: 10) was certainly not his line, for all the charm of Claude Lovat Fraser's or Rex Whistler's art and designs or Nigel Playfair's ballad opera productions at the Lyric Theatre, Hammersmith, or Vivian Ellis's '18th century drag' in the 1929 musical *Mr Cinders*, though he did go to see Playfair's celebrated *Beggar's Opera* and enjoyed its stylisation and lightness.

The more sober musicians' world had its own version of neobaroque and neoclassical: it is all very well for Imogen Holst (1951: 73) to refer to 'the miscalled "back-to-Bach" movement' in connection with her father's Fugal Overture of 1922, but that is exactly what it was – not a first rediscovery of the baroque, of course (witness the 'Georgian survival' element in Elgar, Parry and others threading its way through the later nineteenth century), but a distinct phase of it. Holst's slightly later Fugal Concerto (1923), one of the three most likely models for Finzi's Violin Concerto (especially in its third-movement *quodlibet* introduction of a folk tune), is more straight-facedly Bachian than most new works of its time – not 'wittily opportunist' like Stravinsky (Evans 1995: 191) – and so is Bloch's Concerto Grosso No. 1 (1925), a piece Finzi must have heard at the time he was writing the Violin Concerto, for he sent Ferguson on a mission to bring back the newly published score from America in early 1927. The Bloch was a work that stayed with him, and it eventually entered the repertoire of the Newbury String Players. The third piece in this Bachian trilogy, and the nearest in certain details to both Bach and Finzi, is Vaughan Williams's *Concerto accademico*, also from 1925. This adopts baroque manners in having the solo violin play from the start, as does Finzi's original first movement (and compare Finzi's title: Concerto for Small Orchestra and Violin Solo), and it paraphrases the Bach A minor Violin Concerto's opening upbeat motif, just as the beginning of Finzi's third movement, in addition to another echo of this, refers to that of the first movement of Bach's Third Brandenburg Concerto – as well as to 'the Hornpipe immortalised by Sir Henry Wood' (Cooper 1985: 96) – see *x* in ex. 5.4.a.

Citation of such details may seem finicky, but they are part of a wider context. Elgar had orchestrated Bach's C minor organ Fantasia and Fugue in 1921–2. Vaughan Williams first conducted the *St Matthew Passion* with the Bach Choir in 1923. 'Bach flourished' at Henry Wood's 1924 Proms with the Fifth Brandenburg – and he would make the strings stand to play No. 3 – while his first pair of substantial Bach recordings, the first ever orchestral ones of that composer, dates from 1924–5 (Jacobs 1994: 200, 428; Hamm 1975: 258). Harold Samuel's

EX. 5.4.a (violin and orchestra)

EX. 5.4.a (violin and orchestra)

biennial Bach Weeks at the Wigmore or Aeolian Hall began in 1921. Dolmetsch's Haslemere Festivals offered amateur enthusiasts pioneer contact with the more intimate end of the eighteenth-century musical spectrum, and with its most refined stylistics; four of the twelve concerts in the first festival of 1925 were devoted to Bach. Finzi attended the third festival in August 1927, and it was probably there that he met Herbert Lambert, the photographer and early keyboard instrument maker who was to become a close friend. By November, John Morley was making him a clavichord at Lambert's suggestion. He attended the festival again in 1928. Himself something of an Ernest Pontifex, he also knew his Samuel Butler, Handelian *extraordinaire* who actually includes a musical example in *The Way of All Flesh* (ex. 5.4.d, from the last of Handel's *Six grandes fugues*), and this $\hat{5}$ $^\flat\hat{6}$ [$\hat{5}$] $\hat{4}$ $\hat{5}$ *petite phrase* seems to raise echoes not only in Finzi (for example in ex. 5.4.e, from the 1920s Prelude for strings; see also Sketchbook P: 5) but also in the last of Morris's *Canzoni ricertati*, a 'grave and lovely' work, evidently from the early 1920s, highly prized by Finzi, who thought it was Morris's 'one genuine masterpiece' (194812?; 1949a: 56). One even wonders whether there is a further connection with Samuel Barber's *Dover Beach*, where the phrase and cognate treatment of it may again be observed. Barber was a student at the Curtis Institute while Morris was teaching there, but Heyman (1992) does not mention Morris, and one must accept that turns of phrase like this were in the air and remained there: a work such as Rubbra's first set of Spenser Sonnets (1935) offers further concordances. So do Morris's own back-to-Bach violin concertos, a single and a double (the *Concerto piccolo*), written at about the same time as Finzi's and a possible further influence in either or both directions between teacher and pupil.

EX. 5.4.b

EX. 5.4.c

134

EX. 5.4.d

EX. 5.4.e

Stravinsky's example was not entirely shunned for this more loving handling of the past. The gentler reaches of his pandiatonicism, such as the enticing lines in ex. 5.4.b (from the *Pulcinella* suite, 1922), are close to Finzi's in the boxed *y* of ex. 5.4.a, whose every sonority is non-triadic, and still closer to those of the introductory theme of *The Fall of the Leaf* (ex. 5.4.c), with its tenor imitation on bassoon (the instrumentation Ferguson's decision: Finzi had substituted clarinet for bassoon in his sketches). On the whole, though, Finzi – as with Rubbra throughout his career – was more concerned than Stravinsky that such passages should spin respectful and sustained counterpoint, virile and satisfying enough as it is in the last twelve bars of the Violin Concerto's finale (ex. 5.4.a), especially where it posits a bass entry of the main theme against both its second sentence in the solo violin and a sequence in the upper orchestra. And there was already a specifically English strain of pandiatonicism that he could draw on. One thinks not just of the higher-diatonic dissonances favoured ever since Ward and Wilbye but of something a little more rugged, perhaps most indicatively seen (because for keyboard) in Vaughan Williams's *Three Preludes Founded on Welsh Hymn Tunes* of 1920, organ pieces, particularly 'Hyfrydol', in which 'the interaction of triadic harmony and strong-willed melodic lines [is] . . . raised to an exceptional power of diatonic dissonance, . . . the model . . . the "experimental" Bach of "Christe, du Lamm Gottes" from the *Orgelbüchlein*' (Banfield 1988). Parry had gone surprisingly far down this path in some of his late Chorale Preludes for organ (and compare the opening of his 'Martyrdom' with that of Part II of Elgar's

135

The Dream of Gerontius); eventually a circle of sorts would be closed when Finzi arranged a Parry Chorale Fantasia for strings, though the main point is how the tradition, which could probably be traced in parallel through English folksong accompaniments of the period, helped mould Finzi's piano writing in his songs of the later 1920s.

Finzi's 'Bach period' (Rubbra 1929: 194) began in 1925 with 'The salutation (Aria)' of *Dies natalis*: there are a number of sketches for it in Sketchbook B, which is dated 1925, and another one in Sketchbook A, probably from the same year or slightly later, all of them a tone lower than published. Sketchbook B also contains various other attempts at broad melodies ending with the $\hat{3}$ $\hat{4}$ $\hat{5}$ $\hat{1}$ $\hat{3}$ $\hat{2}$ $\hat{1}$ $\hat{7}$ $\hat{1}$ cadence found at bars 6 to 7 of 'The salutation', itself an echo of the *grave* cadence in Bach's 'St Anne' Prelude for organ. This cadence is also paraphrased in Finzi's other 'Aria', 'His golden locks', clone of 'The salutation' and written a little later: its opening section appears at the beginning of Sketchbook F, dated 1926, in the published key but beginning on the first beat of the bar and with altered and conflated details (the voice enters after two bars). It was composed once Finzi had settled in his Sloane Square neighbourhood, for he later told Iris Lemare that he associated it 'with old age in general (and Chelsea pensioners, who were in my mind when I wrote it – for I used to go to their garden most fine afternoons)' (19410127). This second 'Aria' was similarly destined – if not, in this case, originally intended – to stand as part of a solo cantata, though unlike the more substantial *Dies natalis* it was never so designated. Its title (*Farewell to Arms*) was fixed early on, by 1929 according to McVeagh (1979b), presumably triggered by that of Hemingway's novel published the same year.

There are obvious Bach models for Finzi's 'aria' style as found in these two movements, for instance the chorale prelude movement of Cantata 140 (*Wachet auf*) for its winning and ingenuous instrumental melody broadened by the voice into a three-part texture, 'Air on the G string' for its descending bass (in *Farewell to Arms*) and melodic opening on the mediant, and the 'Agnus Dei' of the B minor Mass for the downward melodic sevenths and a certain turn of phrase. More generally baroque is the reliance in both arias on a ritornello for continuity, repeated wholesale or in segments a number of times, and on *Fortspinnung*. *Farewell to Arms* finds these ingredients tonally sufficient, and as McVeagh (1980b) has pointed out, manages 'a song of some 60 bars without one accidental in it'. *Dies natalis*'s 'Aria' does signal relative-minor contrast (and it is there in the early sketches) but never articulates it beyond a slight imperfect cadence. This is a more severe restriction than the workings of a real baroque *Affekt* ever were. McVeagh finds such tonal innocence unconscious, but it seems more likely to have been 'an article of faith' at this stage, as with syllabic word-setting. That seems evident if one compares Finzi's harmonically uninflected melodic style in general at this period with that of Vaughan Williams in 'Linden Lea', where accidentals are still admitted to ease the cadences. Finzi savoured austere diatonicism's protected confines while he might, fully aware that it would prove an inhibiting limitation in larger contexts unless he could learn how to offset and broaden it. In any case, *Farewell to Arms* breaks its momentum and its late baroque manner with a short passage in compound time, country dance-like for the warrior's move 'from court to cottage' (compare the galliard section in *New Year Music*). This was astutely referred to by the *Times* reviewer of its first performance who called the song 'an essay in the style of Bach which lapsed into pure English in the end' (8 February 1936: 10), a description that might also be applied, in a different sense, to the Elgarian wistfulness that begins to overlay, rather more successfully, the white sonority of 'The salutation' with the advent of the second violins' downward-seventh countermelody (bars 16–19).

Finzi's 'aria' style stands him in good stead on several occasions in the Violin Concerto, notably in the main theme of the slow movement (the Introit), where its lyrical winding down from $\hat{6}$ to $\hat{1}$ is happy and variegated enough (see the top line of ex. 5.5.a for a reference to this later in the movement). This unravelled diatonicism is Finzi's denotation of timelessness and ecstasy – 'the 100s of carved angels . . . were static from very ecstasy,' he told Joy in 1939 of his perception of the double hammerbeam roof of March Church, Cambridgeshire (J. Finzi 19390202) – and it can remain serene and winged in faster contexts if kept texturally transparent, as in bars 6–13 of ex. 5.4.a. Its problems come with a more earnest distribution of counterpoint: in the preparation of the formal return in the Introit (ex. 5.5.a) the descending top line and first half of the main theme posited against it in the middle part salute the breadth and rhythmic flexibility of renaissance counterpoint, but the bass does nothing but plod (as it has throughout the movement), treading the same ground twice and ruining any sense of controlled flight. (Iain Cooper [1985: 16–17] traces the origins of Finzi's stepwise bass lines to left-footed organ technique. Finzi's invariable use

EX. 5.5.a

of downward stems for bass lines in his sketchbooks might seem to bear this out. See also Stunt 1996: 44–8 for the more metaphysical implications of these bass descents.) A comparable problem besets the concerto's replacement first movement when, avoiding dominants in his modal diatonicism, Finzi repeatedly finds his material plummeting flatwards, often into bitonality when the bass slips down a tone or a fifth – a bad habit probably picked up from Vaughan Williams and one Finzi never entirely got rid of. Ex. 5.5.b demonstrates it clearly enough; Finzi's invention-like *Fortspinnung* (which is all this movement consists of) desperately needs dominants, secondary and primary, such as those at x and y in ex. 5.1.a to restore its equilibrium, and without them, for all its rhythmic momentum and thematic unity, lacking in the first attempt at the movement, it is a disaster, quite incapable of climax and tangible shape.

There was one other thing Finzi could already do, and it shows in the Violin Concerto: he knew how to write a good folky tune, such as the

EX. 5.5.b

EX. 5.5.c

first episode in the Hornpipe Rondo (ex. 5.5.c). This may be termed his 'ditty' style, waiting to be harnessed to metrically intricate verse. The tune, beautifully taken up by the soloist, is reminiscent of such English folk 'standards' as 'O waly, waly' and, more particularly (and topically), 'The dark-eyed sailor' (see Cooper 1985: 97). Unfortunately, so is that of the second episode (visible in augmentation, without its dominant upbeat, in the bass at the beginning of ex. 5.4.a, and also present in the top line of the orchestra at this point), which is presented in very dense *stretto* counterpoint. The movement thereby lacks sufficient contrast, the hornpipe's traditional connotation of nautical clutter and bustle notwithstanding. Yet it probably deserves an airing for its élan, and even the two first movements have a breezy energy that one is loth to discard completely from Finzi's canon, for it is distinctive; they also contribute to motivic shapes and transformations that operate across the whole work. Curiously, though, it is to a minor composer such as Whitlock or Gordon Jacob that one turns for more satisfactory explorations of the tenets of both the outer movements, if one thinks of the Allegro Risoluto and 'Chanty' of the former's *Plymouth Suite* for organ (published in 1939). Perhaps Whitlock heard Finzi's concerto. More likely they were both simply speaking the *lingua franca* of their environment, similar in cause (they were about the same age) but to different effect.

Whatever the romantic impulse behind writing the Violin Concerto for Sybil Eaton, it did not show particularly in the music – unless 'Introit' indicated rapt worship. Two further works of the period, the Nocturne (*New Year Music*) and the Two Sonnets by John Milton, were more overtly personal, the one programmatically so, as we have already seen, the other in its choice of texts. Listening to a broadcast of *New Year Music* (by Charles Groves) on 2 January 1948, Adeline Vaughan Williams wrote to Joy Finzi: 'We could just hear those deep notes that are like the first steps in a dark wood – & later might Hardy have called it "a young man's aspirations"?' (19480104b). This opening section is gloomy indeed. Possibly Finzi had Lamb's melancholy poem 'The old familiar faces' in mind at the time of writing, as well as his 'New Year's Eve' essay and the Bridges work. If so, he was thinking not just of the passage of time and space but the separation of death, casting a last look back to his early mentors, met and unmet, for when he began setting 'The old familiar faces', in an archaic-looking compound-time metre comparable with that of the central section of *New Year Music*, it was on manuscript paper that 'came from either Ernest Bristow Farrar or Geo. Butterworth,' as Howard Ferguson explained on the fragmentary sketch itself.

Finzi himself, realising how much he had outgrown his adolescent morbidity, tended to refer to *New Year Music* in later life as a 'dismal' piece, though he also admitted 'I like something about it' (19501226, 19550603b, 19480126). He was an acute critic of his own early music: '[*New Year Music* is] 25 years old & I'm 25 years younger since then. It's that particular linear & somewhat constipated texture that is the real problem & I don't write that particular sort of texture nowadays. At least, I hope not' (195012?). Nevertheless, after its murky introduction it clears up and cheers up into a first section proper in G major rather than C♯ minor with a main theme on the cor anglais that has more immediate tenderness than any of the motifs in the *Requiem da camera* and elicits enough of the diatonics of his 'aria' and 'ditty' styles to help carry the section through to its consequent. This turns to compound time, and it helps to know that at its first performance the piece was entitled *New Year Music (Pavan)* (Lloyd 1996b), which also makes sense of a discarded title page 'PAVAN/for full orchestra/John Hodgson' – probably the work's pseudonymous guise for Patron's Fund submission. In other words, the central section is a galliard, in a traditional antecedent/consequent pairing that, rather as in 'The brightness of this day', lends an Arts and Crafts touch to the whole conception, especially when the galliard begins to gleam with golden, hymn-like radiance. Vernacular suggestiveness is well handled here: ex. 5.6 takes its hint from Delius (*On Hearing the First Cuckoo in Spring*), as does the overall scope of the orchestration, with its broad central tutti and short, intimate solos. (Delius's own similar melody has also been compared with the innocent cowboy tune in Copland's *Billy the Kid*.) Given the pavan/galliard element and Finzi's developing fondness for open, AB structures – which is indeed what Lamb's essay represents with its

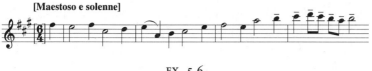

EX. 5.6

caesura at the attitude to death ('In the meantime I am alive') – it is perhaps surprising that he decides to round his form with a return to the A section, neatly handled though it is. As usual, we do not know how much he changed the work when he 'considerably revised' it (G. Finzi 1941, R.1951) in 1945 or 1946 prior to Groves's performance and its publication in 1950, but three pages of full score in his worst 1920s pastoral-modal style survive (Thomas n.d.) and make one thankful that he excised the passage and banished the idiom. Some touches in the finished product sound like mature rethinkings, such as the muted horns before letter K, foreshadowing those of *Intimations of Immortality*. Long before, he was already unsatisfied with it: 'Looking over the score again I find it to be a *dreadful* work, but I shall go through with it, if only to hear my trombones,' he wrote to Ferguson in anticipation of a BBC play-through on 20 January 1930 (19300107). It used a big orchestra from the start – or rather from the point at which he orchestrated it, late in 1928 – for a double bassoon is mentioned in a letter to Ferguson (192812?); and it may be that Finzi undertook the revision as a warm-up for handling identical forces, the biggest he ever used, in *Intimations of Immortality*. (*For St Cecilia* of 1947 uses them too.)

Finzi was also his own best critic of the Milton sonnet settings, when he sent a copy of them to Robin Milford:

Here are the Milton Sonnets. You'll find them rather gnarled & uncompromising. But they come off better in performance (with orchestra) than they look as if they would. So after the first performance – (&, so far, only one, an Iris Lemare concert) I published them myself. I was in a queer state when I wrote them, so you needn't say you like them if you don't!! (19380929)

Milford's reply may have been diplomatic: 'I shall look forward to getting to know them' (19381002). Rubbra, to whom Finzi dedicated the songs on publication, dated them 1928 in his *Monthly Musical Record* article (1929: 194) – and had the order the other way round, with Milton's 'VII: On his being arrived to the age of twenty-three' ('How soon hath Time') first and 'XIX: On his blindness' ('When I consider') second. However, the first line of 'How soon hath Time' is already present in Sketchbook F of 1926, down a third in D minor and without the right-hand accompaniment (but with the gratuitous, bitonal false relations), and there is also a fragmentary sketch of a different setting of the opening two lines of 'How soon hath Time', perhaps for a choral elegy and perhaps from Finzi's 'three and twenti'th year', if contemporaneous with his other early approaches to the metaphysical poets. The sonnets seem not to have been orchestrated until nearer the time of the first performance (given by the tenor Steuart Wilson at the Mercury Theatre, London, on 6 February 1936), since the title pages, instrument names and text in the full scores are written in the hand of Joy Finzi, presumably happier – or urged – not solely to 'stand and wait' in her service of the composer. (She habitually prepared the barlines of Finzi's score paper too – see Burn 1988: 5.) As for Finzi's 'queer state' as their immediate *raison d'être*, it was most likely a mixture of two things. Echoes of discouragement at the perceived failure of the Violin Concerto would have been raised by lines in 'How soon hath Time':

> My hasting days fly on with full career,
> But my late spring no bud or blossom show'th.

while in 'When I consider', Milton's description of

> how my light is spent
> Ere half my days, in this dark world and wide,
> And that one talent which is death to hide,
> Lodged with me useless,

matches the frustration Finzi felt, as we have seen, at the prospect of being cooped up in a sanatorium unable to compose for months. As Diana McVeagh asserts, these come across in the settings not as localised frustrations but as 'big emotions' (1979b); they suggest that, for all that he did not feel seriously ill in 1928, Finzi knew that it might turn out that he was. And having worked through such an identification in these sonnets, perhaps that helped him muster seemingly exceptional reserves of equanimity when he came face to face with mortality a second time twenty years later.

Sonnets, with their taut, linear argument, are seldom easy to set to music, as his reviewers wasted no time in telling him. Nevertheless, Milton's Petrarchan form, habitually emphasising an antecedent/consequent structure between octave and sestet – articulated as question and answer in the one, statement and reflection in the other – suits the *arioso*/aria AB preference already beginning to characterise Finzi's forms. He was right in his comment about the orchestration, for it does help to articulate this structure, plangent woodwind tones (especially the cor anglais in 'When I consider') tending to give way to richer, brighter string sonorities with horns and a flute edge in both songs, just as 'elaborate free polyphony . . . becomes gradually smoothed out into simpler figuration and finally into plain harmonic writing,' as Eric Blom pointed out in a review (*Music and Letters* xviii [1937]: 102–3). Motivic working is expressive, placed more firmly in harmonic and textural relief than in his earlier vocal works, and thereby effective as analogue to poetic thought: one senses the influence of Gurney's treatment of it, as in 'Even such is Time' and 'The folly of being comforted', in the Wagnerian chords, pauses and single lines preceding the first vocal entry in 'When I consider' and in the cathartic upward instrumental phrase at the end of its last line. Still lacking, however, are pace, tonal direction and clearly sustained and contrasted figurative material. Patience's reply in 'When I consider' does gather momentum and a certain exultation for depiction of the angelic hosts, but it leaves no clear image, while the processional resolution in 'How soon hath Time' is ushered in awkwardly, diffusing rather than focusing the structure – it simply needs more tuneful characterisation and bolder tonal grammar. Holst could have shown Finzi how to do it in his contemporaneous 'Envoi' from the Humbert Wolfe songs, where a kind of expanded sonnet (see Banfield 1985: II, 338–9), comparably philosophical, is pointed with limpid and modest but more memorable musical events, including refrain elements that are artfully sneaked in.

We do not know whether Finzi continued trying to set Hardy to music in the years immediately following *By Footpath and Stile*. Many fragmentary sketches for Hardy songs survive, apparently from all periods of his life from the 1920s onwards, but there is no evidence of anything moving towards completion until he was well settled in London. Ferguson must have seen some songs in the spring of 1927, for he refers to 'that one about the Comet, which you showed me when I saw you last' (19270607a). Rubbra's 1929 article describes what was shortly to become *A Young Man's Exhortation*:

In the years 1926–1928 a song-cycle for tenor and piano was completed. It consists of fifteen settings of poems by Thomas Hardy. It is divided into two parts, the first dealing with various moods of youth and love, and the second with philosophical retrospect, under the shadow of age. The cycle is not to be considered as a series of separate songs but as a unity; and unity has been achieved, in spite of the diverse character of the settings. (:194)

Finzi's manuscripts date most of the songs that must have comprised these fifteen. If we include those in the cycle as it eventuated, those published later (doubtless transposed where necessary to fit a lower vocal range) but dated by him presumably because they were early, and two strays (one never quite completed and the one excised from the Requiem), the overall list of contenders is as follows:

> A young man's exhortation
> Ditty (1928)
> Budmouth dears (1929)
> Her temple (1927)
> The comet at Yell'ham (1927)
> Shortening days (1928)
> The sigh (1928)
> Former beauties (1927)
> Transformations (1929)
> The dance continued
> Only a man harrowing clods (1923)
> The temporary the all (1927)
> The market-girl (1927)
> So I have fared (1928)
> Two lips (1928)
> Waiting both (1929)
> At a lunar eclipse (1929)
> I say I'll seek her (1929)

Of these, the first ten became the statutory cycle. McVeagh (1985) dates the song 'A young man's exhortation' '1926?', presumably because Rubbra said the cycle was begun that year and it is placed first in the score. However, the last song in the published cycle, 'The dance continued', is undated, the only one without its own title page in Finzi's manuscript, and subject to more revision on the manuscript itself than most of the others, which suggests that it was added later, without the leisure of a separate fair copy, and it may well be that 'A young man's exhortation', similarly undated, was added at the same time to replace others jettisoned, thus providing the whole cycle with its title (unmentioned by Rubbra). As stated earlier, there is stylistic doubt about 'I say I'll seek her', not because Finzi had not yet learnt to be so passionate, but because he had not yet begun to transfer the passion already found in the Grand Fantasia to his Hardy settings; with its agonised, involved emotion neither the poem nor the music quite fits the theme and its detached tone. 'The temporary the all', on the other hand, was undoubtedly intended for the set that became *A Young Man's Exhortation*. Its manuscript fair copy of 1927 was prepared in the same format and on the same type of paper as those of most of the other songs in the cycle, and it is not only very much a part of the subject and its motifs with its first-person dittyings and refrains ('So self-communed I') but with its clever fusing of past and future offers a kind of summary of it. It would have made, poetically, a logical preface (it is the very first poem in *Wessex Poems*, indeed in Hardy's *Collected Poems*), or an interlude or epilogue. That is not to say that it was musically tractable; it was not, hence its loss, and hence also, perhaps, its lack of a completed later revision.

Whether or not this is a correct guess at what the fifteen songs were, they had probably been reduced to the ten of the published cycle by the time of the Oxford University Press concert in November 1929. Ferguson's recollection is of playing the piano for *A Young Man's Exhortation*, and there would not have been time for as many as fifteen songs. Moreover, it was probably not long afterwards that Finzi sent his songs to Steuart Wilson (for when he commented on them to Finzi in April 1930 he said he had got down to studying them 'at last' [19300423]), and these were the statutory ten, it would seem from an annotation in Finzi's hand on the letter of reply.

It makes sense to consider all the listed songs here with the exception of 'I say I'll seek her' and 'Only a man harrowing clods' (see Chapter 3 for the latter), and to let them show us where Finzi's stylistic development had got to by the end of the 1920s, though the Grand Fantasia has temporarily to be left out of the reckoning for this purpose.

In general their strongest suit is Finzi's 'ditty' style, by which is meant the creation of overall flow and span through simple, vernacular-sounding melody with little or no tonal rhetoric. He never had any trouble thinking up a tuneful snatch of melody – the sketchbooks are full of them, from texted fragments to rounded instrumental tunes – and particularly where Hardy offered plenty of refrains, short and variegated lines and strong rhymes it is easy to see how, as Finzi himself later described the process of lyrical composition, inspiration flowed: 'He may read some lines. Instantly, with the reading, musical phrases will bind themselves to the words, almost like Pirandello's "Six Characters in search of an author" crying for birth; it may even be brought about by the actual sounds of the words, irrespective of the sense' (1955: II, 4). The setting of the words 'Tenements uncouth' in 'The temporary the all' points up one such inspiration, it and the triplet 'Wonder of . . .' being the only snatches of melodic (as opposed to rhythmic) identity retained between the early and late material in ex. 5.2, in the sense of lying on the same scale degrees. If we take 'dittying' to involve the setting to music not so much of something lyrically simple as of something contained or containable – capturable in tune, as it so often transpires with Finzi (see Banfield 1985: I, 282 for some examples) – the compositional issue becomes one of how such inspirations are welded together.

One of the things about Finzi's style that ought to strike us most – though it rarely does – is the curious formal contract between him and Hardy. Almost all of Hardy's thousand-odd poems consist of parallel stanzas. That is, and allowing for his liberal quantification of weak syllables within a poetic foot, they contain between two and, in the longest poems, thirty or forty stanzas with the same metre and rhyme scheme. Up to a point this is a normal condition of lyric poetry, but it is particularly striking in Hardy, and what is more, the schemes themselves are extraordinarily varied and inventive (see D. Taylor 1988: 71), even more so than with the experimental prosodist Robert Bridges. One rarely finds the same one twice, which places Hardy at almost the opposite extreme to Housman, three-quarters of whose *Shropshire Lad* poems are cast in four-line stanzas, the vast majority of them ballad metre. One could therefore distinguish most of Hardy's poems by their *form*, regardless of content. There are exceptions to the parallel-stanza construction, including his few sonnets (which he tends to tabulate as three or four separate stanzas), one or two poems with differentiated stanzas or two interspersed metric blueprints, and some single-stanza entities, but Finzi only sets three or four of these exceptions in all his Hardy corpus. More striking are the instances in which Hardy additionally binds his parallel constructions with refrain lines and particular rhymes persisting between stanzas. Finzi latches onto a number of these, as one might expect a musician to do, for a refrain offers identical structure between music and poem and rhyme can do something similar when allied to cadence. He avoids Hardy's poems of more than ten stanzas but otherwise seems to relish the poet's metric invention and intricacy.

Yet Finzi very rarely composes a song that is simply strophic – that is, one in which Hardy's parallel stanzas are matched with parallel melody – and 'Budmouth dears' is the only one in the group under observation, where it comes very much as a diversion from more serious business. This is despite his fluency at dealing with lyric lines of irregular length or number, a fluency amply demonstrated by ex. 5.5.c, which one could easily imagine as a five- or six-line strophe (10.8.10.8.5 or 10.8.10.4.4.5, in hymnbook shorthand). Instead, he demonstrates three main approaches to Hardy's periodicity, though doubtless they were instinctive rather than rationalised in this way. Sometimes he spreads a 'quadratic' melody – that is, one built up conventionally of two-, four- and eight-bar units – across more than one of Hardy's stanzas, normally across two. At other times he pairs and offsets a quadratic melody, or part of one, in one stanza with something quite different in an adjacent one; this tends to produce his *arioso*/aria AB structure, often on more than one level across more than two stanzas and sometimes in reverse. Thirdly he may parallel certain musical phrases between stanzas but not the whole tune: a kind of strophic variation but often chimingly intricate. This last approach in particular corresponds with his working method of crossing out lines of text on the written-out (or, after his marriage, typed-out) poem as he found music for them, often in short, isolated stretches; if it looked as though the same or similar melody could be used for another line in the same stanza or a parallel one, especially where Hardy's verse included a strong rhyme or refrain element, this would be crossed out too. In the longer songs two or more of the three approaches may be combined, and we need also to consider the structural effect of ritornelli in the accompaniment – the baroque influence once more – frequently supplementing or replacing these other devices.

'Two lips' is the simplest instance of a 'ditty' spread across two stanzas. As often with Finzi, one can posit a notional quadratic blueprint of folk-like modal melody from which he diverged rhetorically to create the song itself (see ex. 5.7.a). The point of this kind of melodic span is that it offers an articulated form but demands no structural tonality beyond an imperfect-cadence caesura between the stanzas. We find this 'caesura form' again and again in Finzi's music, within movements and between them (such as with *Farewell to Arms* in its eventual guise as 'Introduction and Aria'), when the idea is articulated about a central pivot, normally reflective or silent. Structurally, its origin is seventeenth-century, as in the recitative/aria pattern of the cantata, the pairing of dances, or the linking of prelude and fugue; psychologically, we shall examine its import in due course. In 'Two lips' we see how Finzi may accomplish the caesura not just with marks of separation (here a lengthening of the periodic structure by silence, and a *poco ritard.*) but through 'tropes' in the accompaniment – inserted melodic reflections, preparations or tangents between vocal periods. These become one of his most expressive devices in the later songs; the little motif marked *n* in ex. 5.7.a is a tiny, embryonic example, transposing and interverting the last three notes of the first stanza's melody. 'Waiting both' also spreads a melodic strophe over two stanzas, though with much less finite material; here the caesura is composed out using one of the two segments of the song's 'astronomical' ritornello, the other recurring after a ferocious instrumental trope inserted into the second stanza after the pregnant line 'Till my change come', which together add almost a

EX. 5.7.a

148

cadenza and thus a miniature concerto element to the song's overall form.

Melodic strategies serve Finzi well in *A Young Man's Exhortation*, and of the canonic ten songs it was the ones with the 'ditty' element most to the fore that Steuart Wilson liked best and sang at an Oxford Musical Club concert on 13 May 1930 – 'Ditty' itself, 'Budmouth dears' and 'The sigh'. Vaughan Williams shared this preference, responding at an unknown date to a performance of the whole cycle:

I like the obvious ones best – Ditty & When she sighed – though I like the apple man very much – though is he a bit too sinister?

I want to give a lecture one day on the English song – showing how you & Gurney & Robin & one or two others have at last found the musical equivalent of English poetry only that wd mean an intensive study of all your songs which my natural laziness boggles at. (19??1014)

He said much the same thing in response to a broadcast of two of Finzi's Hardy songs on 8 January 1939, Adeline concurring: 'though it's quite absurd for me to say a word I want to thank you for "The Sigh". I listened with the thought "can it go on being so perfect" & it did to the end' (19390109a). No wonder they were in sympathy, when Finzi quarried 'Linden Lea' so effectively for his melodies (see, for example, the first vocal phrase of 'The sigh', the opening of stanza four of 'Ditty', the last two bars of the piano ritornello of 'Her temple' and, outside this group, the piano introductory motif in 'Summer schemes' and 'Rollicum-rorum').

Yet the five-stanza 'Ditty' is quite complex melodically. Its piano ritornello introduces only the odd-numbered stanzas (and only half of it is used for stanza three); then it is a matter of each stanza including certain melodic phrases which occur in one of the others. For instance, the first four lines of stanza two are set to the same music as those of stanza four, while only the first two of stanza three recur at the start of stanza five; stanza two then continues with two lines of music that are re-used not in stanza four but in stanza five, and the next two of stanza five are also found in stanza four, but placed slightly earlier in the verse; lines four to six of the first stanza's melody recur not in the voice but in the piano as a kind of postlude to stanza five (but before the final refrain); and so on. Something comparable happens in 'The dance continued', except that with as many as ten parallel three-line stanzas the amount of melodic cross-reference has to be even more carefully distributed and restricted if strophic periodicity is to be avoided. The 101 scraps of music manuscript on Finzi's desk must have presented formidable puzzles as he put them together in these instances – and they cannot be easy songs to learn except insofar as the words carry the musical memory through, which of course is the point.

Chiming refrains are important, and that of the last line of each verse of 'Ditty' is the only point at which the melody runs parallel in all five stanzas. Conversely, in 'The sigh' the verbal refrain variants ('But she sighed', 'Why she sighed' etc) are joined – though not precisely paralleled – by melodic variants rather like the quarters of a clock (something we shall find elsewhere); the 'sigh' motif also informs the piano introduction, in an echo of Denis Browne's 'Epitaph on Salathiel Pavy', and appears inverted as the start of the vocal melody. But 'The sigh' combines these 'ditty' elements with an overall caesura form. The first four stanzas form an ABAB musical pattern, though without any pivoting caesura between the A and the B – each stanza is melodically self-contained. The fifth, though metrically parallel in Hardy, is treated as a consequent to the first four, the caesura at this point taking the form of a change of key, from G to E major. Tonally open, this bold gambit closes the poetic interpretation perfectly as the protagonist climbs out of the narrative frame to reflect on the picture ('It was in our May, remember / And . . . now I near November'). It creates a kind of bar form, with each AB unit as a *Stollen* and the fifth stanza as *Abgesang*. We see something similar in other Hardy songs, though rarely anything identical. For example, 'So I have fared' looks as if it is going to adopt the same approach as 'The sigh' but rings intricate melodic changes throughout the first four stanzas that would render a distributional analysis quite a challenge. Then comes the imperfect-cadence caesura – all the previous stanzas have ended with a full close – followed by what should be the *Abgesang* at stanza five ('So I have fared'), with its resolution into one of Finzi's processional arias on a completely new melodic groundplan. Yet this too turns out to be antecedent to a deathly coda, the pivot heavily articulated with a downward instrumental motif as trope (ex. 5.7.b) and the form tonally opened once more, since it ends in A minor. We shall eventually need to consider to what extent this kind of unrounded, antithetical structure represents a poetic philosophy shared between composer and versifier. It will not have escaped notice that where caesura form is at issue it offers a microcosm of the shape of the *Young Man's Exhortation* cycle as a whole, with its Psalm

EX. 5.7.b (baritone and piano)

epigraphs about the flourishing and withering grass (note the concordance with 'Only a man harrowing clods'), and that the pair of epigraphs neatly demonstrates the antiphonal verse form of psalmody itself, very much a part of Hardy's cultural heritage. In the overall cycle the caesura comes after the fifth song, though it would be unwise to read too much intentional tonal resolution between the end of 'The comet at Yell'ham' and the start of 'Shortening days', given Finzi's limited perceptions in this direction, as Ferguson has testified: 'You are quite right in saying that he had little tonal sense. Indeed, I'd go further and say that he had none, and simply wrote (in both small- and large-scale works) in whatever key he happened to find himself. He was, I think, oblivious of the structural aspect of tonality' (1985–96).

Where the 'ditty' melodic style is lacking or inappropriate, Finzi's reference to strophic form may take the looser guise of a head-motif, as noted in the second movement of the *Requiem da camera*. This happens in 'A young man's exhortation', whose first three stanzas begin with it, each in a different key, prior to intermittent further usage. The term and the treatment both suggest Tudor music, and this song's contrapuntal opening epitomises Finzi's habitual reaching back farther than Bach, to the English verse anthem with viols of Gibbons, Byrd and Morley, sensitively re-created in his four- and five-part imitative texture, walking pace, flexible rhythm and unforced, confidential verbal rhetoric, all done more stylishly than with most of his contemporaries (ex. 5.7.c). As Morris would have stressed in his course on renaissance counterpoint (if Bairstow had not already drummed it in), treatment of consonance and dissonance rather than harmony as such is the vertical

EX. 5.7.c (tenor and piano)

issue, false relations (as on the word 'crumpled') representing the limit
of the composer's emotional authority. If the head-motif signals strophic
variation in the first three stanzas of 'A young man's exhortation', the
last two are akin to those of 'So I have fared' in suggesting a diminishing
– or is it an augmenting? – perspective of musical and philosophical
consequents to the accumulated antecedent. Stanza four ('For what do
we know best?'), with its broader harmonic rhythm and country-dance
triplet figure, is like a new section in a renaissance viol fantasia (compare
Byrd's five-part one), but this soon gives way to one of Finzi's 'aria'
signals, in the form of a Holstian processional for the men dying 'Of
all scope dispossest', itself indicatively petering out into a heavily flagged
caesura (slowing harmony and tempo, a *diminuendo* to *pianissimo*,
fading texture, rests in all parts, an inconclusive $^6_3$ chord, a *fermata* and
a double bar), all of which leads to the least goal-directed ending
imaginable, a dreamy unbarred tune reminiscent of *The Immortal Hour*
(particularly at 'the passing preciousness of dreams') that does not even

cadence in the current tonic, which in any case is a tritone away from the key of A♭ in which the song began.

The head-motif of this title song (ex. 5.7.c, x) could be seen as having a modest binding significance in the overall cycle as published, if the tiny piano epilogue that rather touchingly concludes the last song ('The dance continued') and thereby the whole sequence is heard as thematically related to it. More to the point, perhaps, is that in this epilogue Finzi is still faintly echoing Butterworth's delicate pastoralism (see the end of the *Shropshire Lad* rhapsody). And the temptation to draw the first three notes of 'Shortening days' into the web – they were added on the manuscript, squeezed in – needs checking in the knowledge that they will have been as much a practical afterthought (to give the singer his note following a midway break) as a conceptual one. Otherwise rising and falling fourths and fifths will begin to appear under every bed. Nevertheless, there is at least one other hint of thematic cross-reference in the cycle, and it links in with some further motivic working within a song, namely in 'Transformations' where above all one would expect it. Alas, this is one of the clumsiest songs in the group, not least because of the gaucheness of the motif that opens and closes it and recurs elsewhere, unfitted for its lively tempo (which just produces frantic counterpoint), ungrounded harmonically, and unsuited to singing. This is all the more regrettable when we notice that the piano's reference to 'the fair girl long ago / Whom I often tried to know', and who is now being transformed into one of the growing plants that this song's own restless motif represents, calls up the opening phrase of 'Her temple' and transforms it back into this motif (ex. 5.7.d, y leading to z, all three showing a $\hat{1}$ $\hat{2}$ $\hat{3}$ rise followed by a disjunct further rise and fall). Finzi was right to attempt this kind of symbolic procedure, above all where Hardy and his women were concerned, but to give it transparency and poise he needed to go back to Wagner and Brahms. 'The phantom' was not yet on the horizon.

This is a relatively uncharacteristic example of a song pivoting on

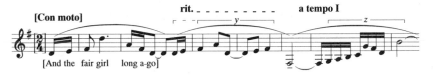

EX. 5.7.d (piano part)

continuity rather than on contrast most often articulated by silence. And when an AB form is articulated, beyond the songs already discussed it generally consists of an *arioso* resolving into an aria-style strophe. This happens in 'The comet at Yell'ham', 'Shortening days' and up to a point with the jig consequent in 'The dance continued' (though a recapitulatory coda follows). It is particularly striking in 'The market-girl', for here the consequent arrives in two layers, each at an imperfect-cadence caesura, the first in B♭ major at the words 'to take a bargain so choice away', the second in F major and with an element of reflexivity, since Hardy's words describe the musical release itself ('And so it began; and soon we knew what the end of it all must be'). Yet the reverse of the form is found too: in 'Her temple' the more periodic span comes first, followed by an *arioso* one, its verbal pace less lyrical because of Hardy's dialogue and added weak syllables, its metrical and tonal quadratics gradually disintegrating along with the community's memory of the bashful lover until the framing ritornello returns in F minor rather than E♭ major. Hardy loved to point up the tricks time plays on us, and this apparent reversibility of musical direction is a concomitant of what one reviewer of the cycle's first performance thought Finzi was doing with notions of prospect and retrospect when he or she pointed out, ingeniously if not entirely accurately, that 'the poems . . . fall into two divisions, in one of which a young man looks back, and in the other the young man grown old looks forward' (*The Times*, 8 December 1933: 12). The prefatory vector of 'The temporary the all' in *Wessex Poems* has been described by Michael Millgate in terms rather similar to this reviewer's, though he seems to say the opposite, that in offering the volume's structure in microcosm it moves 'from a hopeful past to a melancholy, backward-looking present' (1985: 393). The poem gave rise to a musical form that for once looked both ways, additive peaks of aria (for the damsel and the 'visioned hermitage') and processional (for the 'high handiwork') following an initial *arioso* and themselves sinking back into unperiodic obscurity.

With his penchant for processional consequents and codas and epilogues, his dispassionate notions of time and space, his folkloric melodies and compound-time dance sections, and his diatonic cleanliness, Finzi consolidated his monument to Holst and Vaughan Williams in *A Young Man's Exhortation*. He needed to get away from them both, and would soon do so, but the tributes are not all unwelcome. 'I wonder what Holst thought of the plagiarism from the "Grecian Urn"?' Rubbra asked after the Oxford University Press concert, which both had attended (19291120b). He was referring to the section 'Who are these coming to the sacrifice?' in the slow movement of Holst's Choral Symphony (1924) and Finzi's setting of Hardy's line 'Who is this coming with pondering pace' in 'Shortening days'. Finzi borrowed Holst's marching bass, his melody rising from the tonic through the scale, and his initial rhythm, reasonably enough in view of Hardy's Arcadian plagiarism from Keats, but Finzi's processional is the less sonorous, and he refuses to treat it to the harmonic kaleidoscope that keeps Holst's on the move, although the cider maker, when revealed, is one of his best inspirations in the cycle because he does have some human harmony – almost its graphic first appearance in his music beyond the sketchbooks. (And had he been listening to Henry Wood's first British performance of the Janáček Sinfonietta [10 February 1928] when he came to write the cider man's bass motif?)

Egdon Heath must have influenced 'At a lunar eclipse'. This is a sort of fugue (Hardy's poem is a sonnet), complete with four-part exposition, two episodes, two sets of *stretti,* and one final entry, and its subject has (although unbarred) the exact 7/4 rhythm of *Egdon Heath*'s brass theme at figure 2 together with something of that work's initial melodic austerity. This is one of three 'astronomical' songs in the group; in the other two, 'Waiting both' and 'The comet at Yell'ham', outer space is encoded in harsh chromatic counterpoint, falsely related or bitonal, a style also used to signal the withering effects of time at the opening of 'Former beauties'. Rubbra (1929: 194) was dismayed by the bitonality in Finzi's Violin Concerto, where ex. 5.5.c is suddenly subjected to canon at a semitone's distance, and unlike Holst – who in 'Betelgeuse' was contemporaneously exploring his own astronomical fancy through song, but with a far more integrated bitonal premise – Finzi would probably have been included in R. O. Morris's assertion that 'Any fool can write in X^n keys and make it sound like X^n keys' (Holst 1938: 143). That way his future did not lie, though there is some poetry in the correlation between this ungrounded dissonance and tessitura: the tonal gravity increases in both 'Waiting both' and 'The comet at Yell'ham' as the pitch comes down to earth (and lightens on going back up again in 'The comet').

Frank Howes was probably referring to *A Young Man's Exhortation* when in 1938 he said:

As a final item in a rough computation of what folk-song has given to English music over and above itself I would mention that the most considerable and best modern English songs, besides those of Vaughan Williams, are written by composers who have nourished themselves on English folk-song. The greatest achievement in this field during the past ten years, so far as I know, is Gerald Finzi's Hardy cycle. Finzi, like Hadley, is a lyrical writer. To both folk-song was like counterpoint, a part of their education. Finzi wrote to me once: 'Folk-song has been to me like food, grammar or counterpoint, it helped to build me up'. (:47)

But the folksong aesthetic notwithstanding, it is Finzi's intellectual tribute to Hardy and his ambitions therein for English song that make the greatest strides in *A Young Man's Exhortation*. No one could have failed to wish him encouragement in this, when he was beginning to discover an ability to show and share, through a singer, the full measure of Hardy's poetry in a song such as 'At a lunar eclipse'. The overall intractability of his austere and limited 1920s idiom remains – Christopher Stunt is not absolutely right to say (1996: 38) that 'there is not a single perfect cadence in the whole set', though the point is well made – but when linked with such verse it does offer an experience of greatness that is more than the sum of the parts of music, poem and performance, and there is something uniquely touching about the last song of the cycle in particular. The same 'added value' is found, to very different effect, in 'Waiting both', though here one suspects a quantity of 1930s rewriting. This is not thought of as one of Hardy's great poems, but it becomes one with the help of Finzi's questing tropes and laconic form and tiny, unforgettable vocal phrases.

As a symphonic *vade mecum* – or albatross around the composer's neck – throughout the following decade (see Chapter 4), *The Fall of the Leaf* requires later discussion, and little remains to be mentioned before turning the page on the 1920s. The Prelude for strings is very much a product of its half-decade: aria-like in its main melody; wholly devoid of accidentals until the cadence in the first section, in the middle one full of dubious false relations that betray insecurity in the handling of a minor key masquerading as archaism (see ex. 5.4.e); tonally gauche in its transition to the *grosso*-like *concertante* of the B section, abrupt in its final phrygian cadence; and with the expected baroque impulse overall, the initial throbbing pulse conveying something of an *actus tragicus*.

One work, however, does seem to present us with elements of a sudden stylistic breakthrough that, the lack of unrevised manuscript evidence notwithstanding, would appear to belong incontrovertibly to its date of inception, given its inherent audacity. This is the Grand Fantasia of 1928. Perhaps it was a joyful and spontaneous response to Finzi's release from the Midhurst sanatorium. Ferguson, however, recalls Finzi writing it while he was still there. It would be ironic but understandable if the adverse conditions of his confinement were precisely what liberated his creative thoughts – Bliss, as usual, would have been right: 'you will come out after an enforced slack with much fresher ideas. You can pity from your seclusion the numerous other Composers who are at liberty to write but simply can't do so' (19280430a).

The Fantasia's wild, improvisatory structure and strong emotional colouring, though founded closely and idiomatically enough on works such as Bach's Chromatic Fantasia and the G minor organ Fantasia, almost have the quality of automatic writing. Yet a simpler explanation for every phrase carrying not just a depth of feeling or a degree of tension but also a precise technical mass unprecedented in Finzi's earlier music – qualities soon to be transferred to his illustrative tasks, particularly where Hardy's more stormy conceptions would be concerned (as, indeed, in 'I say I'll seek her') – would be that for the first time he is writing piano music rather than abstract counterpoint. The right-hand thirds, the distance and functional differentiation between the hands, and the gestural role of the rests in ex. 5.8.a all give an embodiment and a weight to his music that had been crying out for release. They bring and henceforward keep him close to Brahms, perhaps not surprisingly with the professional chamber pianists Rubbra and Ferguson constantly at his side. ('I love Brahms through & through,' Finzi told Cedric Thorpe Davie in a heated exchange of letters about his formal procedures [19330713?].) Gone too at last is his flat modal landscape, for chordal rhetoric such as at x demands tonal commitment, and here Finzi suddenly seems to discover that he can write a powerful dominant and modulate to it, thereby acquiring a three-dimensional facility in the handling of his habitual short scraps of inspiration that brings him back to Elgar, whose idiom is sensed at the end of the example. With this comes for the first time the exploration of minor-key scale inflection, including false relation, for the painful joy of dynamic thrust, rather than the spinning of modal ambiguity for static introspection: every moment of sonority, direction and tension in ex. 5.8.b – a particularly fine and prescient passage (even though, being for the orchestra, one

(accidentals apply only to the notes they precede)

EX. 5.8.a

EX. 5.8.b (orchestra)

does wonder whether it was a 1953 addition) – is due to the colourings of the melodic and harmonic minor scale, and now he is not afraid of the emotional openness of the augmented second that such contexts

EX. 5.8.c

produce (see also the tensions between C♯ and B♭, F♯ and E♭ in ex. 5.8.c). This raises a huge and explosive question of hermeneutics: was Finzi in some sense beginning to explore and accept his Jewishness? He was certainly beginning to come to terms at last with his romantic musical heritage, most notably Wagner and Brahms, who hold as much of a key to his mature style as any other composers, as will be seen in the next chapter, and that this was linked in his mind with his family heritage is made explicit in a letter he wrote to Cedric Thorpe Davie a week before he died:

[Wagner] created an extraordinarily individual musical texture, and even if one dislikes the qualities of his mind which exude through every bar, one can't escape the greatness, the sheer intellectual force, combined with emotional force, of nearly all his later work. The fact that he used a large harmonic unit, rather as Sibelius does, doesn't lessen him in my eyes.... I have never been able to make up my mind about Liszt. My Mother was a good amateur pianist and my babyhood and childhood was rather brought up on things like Liebestraum! One can never afterwards view things detachedly. I can only say that, when in comparatively recent years I have heard big works of Liszt for the first time, I have been pretty horrified, and against that, when I got the Liszt Society publication of some of his very late keyboard works I found them very impressive and interesting. (19560920b)

Be that as it may, Rubbra and his wife were in no doubt about the advance the Grand Fantasia represented: 'We both thought the works grew much more interesting as they neared 1929, which is as it should be!' he told Finzi after the OUP concert. 'For me the Grand Fantasia seemed by far the best work (I have always thought highly of this), but that may be because it was performed on the instrument that it was composed for' (19291120b). Rubbra was returning a compliment, for Finzi had been greatly struck and no doubt directly influenced by his Introduction and Fugue, Op. 19c, for piano, in which the Introduction, while much smaller than Finzi's Grand Fantasia, is comparable (though paradoxically it was the Fugue that impressed him).

Clearly Finzi not only had the confidence and energy to forge ahead beyond the Grand Fantasia to the rest of the Piano Concerto after 1928, but also the self-knowledge to stop and search afresh for something more simple when he found he could not see it through. He knew there was a basic, common-practice fluency that had still not come to him and would need to be worked at because there was no substitute for it. 'I've just come back from Noel Coward's "Bittersweet",' he wrote to Ferguson in August 1929. 'Really I don't know whether his tongue is in his cheek or hanging out. It's the music that "everyone does", only perhaps a little more derivative. Yet how I wish I cd do these ordinary things that everyone else seems to be able to do' (19290802a). How was he to discover ordinariness? Arthur Bliss's prescription following the OUP concert (19291120a, 19291122) was forthright:

The weakness of the songs as a body was in the sameness of emotion in each. You are at present harping on one string, however deliciously. The last work played gave promise of something more, something different to the somewhat nostalgic country dreaming that permeates a good deal of the rest. I was honestly much impressed by passages that had promise of a very deep and original outlook.

What you want for the full consummation of it is not more writing, but more living. You must have your full nature exploited by fate – (and luckless man you will! –) before we shall get the real you. And I believe that is going to be very worth while waiting for.

Good luck anyhow.

In other words, he needed to fall in love. Bliss, who had once gone all the way to Switzerland in pursuit of a recalcitrant *inamorata*, knew what he was talking about. 'I take it you don't mean mistresses,' Finzi must have written in response. 'I *do* mean the mistresses!' Bliss replied.

CHAPTER 6

Marriage and maturity

Between the beginning of 1930 and the end of 1936 Finzi produced very few new compositions: seven partsongs, a handful of solo songs – mostly Hardy settings for baritone – and an Interlude for oboe and string quartet. Yet within the course of these seven years he finally found his voice, wrote three or four truly great songs, and paved the way for his becoming a Boosey & Hawkes 'house' composer. 'Wait until you see it as a miniature score & you will then feel yourself to be among "the Classical Masters",' Ferguson wrote of the Interlude in May 1936 (19360519), proud that it would stand alongside his own Octet, recently published, in the Hawkes Pocket Scores catalogue, a growing list already beginning to include such moderns as Elgar, Britten, Bush, Webern and Bloch and soon to encompass Shostakovich, Copland, Bartók and others of the most cosmopolitan flavour. During the course of the same period Finzi also got married, left London and produced two sons. In 1930 he might well have asked, along with W. H. Auden,

> Will it alter my life altogether?
> O tell me the truth about love.

By 1936, as 'a more complete & happier person married to my Joyce' (19330823), he could reply in the affirmative.

Was the one transformation the key to the other? Did Joy unlock his artistic maturity? The answer must in broad terms be yes, though neither the chronology nor the channels of cause and effect are quite as simple as romantic biography would have it. Many other factors played their part, and they all need consideration.

His discovery of personal happiness in the early 1930s took place against a background of growing frustration and depression at his slow career and with London in particular. 'They knew he was unhappy in London,' Ursula Vaughan Williams wrote of Ralph and Adeline, 'so, whenever they went away from Dorking, [Finzi] had the use of The White Gates where he stayed and worked' (1964: 196); he first visited them for Thursday overnight stays with tennis in the summer of 1930 and house-sat for them for a week or so at Whitsun in 1931 and again, twice, in 1932. 'You must forget all about 21 Caroline St, & I shan't be sorry to do so myself,' he told Ferguson when he finally left Belgravia before his marriage (19330817).

By 1930 he was spending as much time as possible out of London, particularly outside the main concert and theatre seasons. He often visited Hundon and worked there. He had always enjoyed walking in the countryside, and day excursions with Ferguson and others continued. But doubtless with his tubercular health still in mind, he also took every opportunity of going away by train and then on foot for several days or even weeks at a time. There was no shortage of casual accommodation, for hiking – the word from America, the idea from Germany – was rapidly becoming a major national pastime, part of the general cultural trend that gave rise to the Council for the Preservation of Rural England in 1926 on the one hand and the Youth Hostel Association in 1930 on the other. The real boom began in 1931, and by 1934 Constant Lambert was complaining of

the hideous *faux bonhomie* of the hiker, noisily wading his way through the petrol pumps of Metroland, singing obsolete sea chanties with the aid of the *Week-End Book*, imbibing chemically flavoured synthetic beer under the impression that he is tossing off a tankard of 'jolly good ale and old' in the best Chester–Belloc manner. (:125)

Finzi kept well clear of the herd, and we have already traced his lone footsteps across a large swathe of the West Country in 1929. But he did find a walking companion around this time, probably in 1930. Christopher Finzi recalls his father describing how he was sitting alone at a restaurant in Cornwall when he heard another solitary diner saying in a loud, pompous voice, 'I like my herrings soused'; they looked at each other, laughed, and once again a friendship was sealed in a moment of humour. This was Graham Hutton (1904–88), an economist and diplomat described in his *Times* obituary as 'pamphleteer extraordinary' (15 October 1988: 12) but apparently no relation of the 1990s popular economist Will Hutton. At the time, Hutton, married to a Swiss first wife absent on the continent some of the time – though she joined them for at least one weekend walk – was a research fellow and tutor at the London School of Economics, though he was called to the bar in 1932 before becoming assistant editor of *The Economist* in 1933. Later he worked as a consultant with a particular understanding of American economics, following service with the Foreign Office and Ministry of Information in Chicago during the war. He was an intellectual extrovert, and this mental availability together with his 'passionate dedication to the causes he espoused' (ibid.) immediately appealed to Finzi, whose deepening articulation of liberal thought must have owed something to those causes' 'common thread[:] . . . the defence of human freedom against the despotism of the State' (ibid.). Hutton also had a breadth not just of interests but of productivity that Finzi's was beginning to match. He was a poet as well as a pianist and Bach enthusiast, and in addition to his books on economic development he published a study of English surnames, an introduction to *The Adventures of Tom Sawyer*, and several books about the Americas. He became an expert on English parish churches, writing the excellent and encyclopaedic Thames & Hudson volume (Hutton and Smith 1952, R.1976) that is still in print, with a rare synthesis of architectural detail and human understanding in its historical portrait. Finzi was therefore not being entirely fair in representing him as 'the dead poet [who] lives in many a live stock-broker' – for it was undoubtedly Hutton he had in mind when he made this comment in his Crees Lectures (1955: II, 6), having long pondered their shared but divergent paths since their careers began to develop in the 1930s, as a letter to Robin Milford in 1938 shows:

old-age *can* retain freshness . . . But, of course, there's no doubt that something usually does disappear, round about the late twenties, & young men, who have published a slim volume of verse, or made a few songs, soon pass their moment of ecstasy, & once the adolescent urge is spent they settle down to be critics, doctors, economists, biologists, solicitors, politicians & so on. You wd be amazed at the number of middle aged people with an unsuspected & well hidden past of that sort! You may have seen that a series of lectures on the Balkans or central Europe, or something of that sort, are being given by Graham Hutton, in Newbury. Amongst my books I've got 'The Macmillan report & The International gold standard' by D. Graham Hutton 1931 – also 'Twilit corners' by D. Graham Hutton 1925.

Well, it's an old story. As Maurice Baring says, in his lovely book 'C' –

'Remember that verse is the blossom of many minds, the fruit of few', & Hardy in 'Desperate Remedies' talks about 'the age at which the clear spirit bids good-bye to the last infirmity of noble mind, and takes to house-hunting and investments'.

I suppose it's a matter of adjustment to life. The square peg won't fit in the round hole, & in its efforts it throws off chips & sparks, which are the works of art. Most people get adjusted – emotionally I mean – in early manhood, but the artist is someone whose make-up doesn't allow this. And I suppose this is what is meant by the saying that something of the child remains in every artist (though this shd not be confused with an unhealthy refusal to grow up & face responsibilities).

Anyhow, it's a simple enough theory, which may or may not work, but if it doesn't I'll leave you to find a better one! (19381109a)

On the other side, Hutton retained a deep affection for Finzi, though they did not keep up regular contact, and he contributed an obituary in which he recalled their Whitsun walk of 1930:

... [Gerald] was a great talker and arguer, and was both mentally and physically as lively as a grig. In our twenties he and I tramped weeks on end – in Cornwall and the Scillies, round Uriconium and 'on Wenlock Edge,' and once, unforgettable, barefooted for long – from Pewsey, off that early train on which one breakfasted, through Marlborough and Avebury across the Ridgeway to Radcot (where we read The Duchess of Malfi in a punt) to Oxford, all for a Whit weekend (Vaughan Williams *et al* 1956, R.1995).

It was on a trip to the Scillies, possibly just after they had first met but more likely a year later, in 1931, that they attested an unlikely truth, as Hutton wrote in an unidentified newspaper cutting found among Joy Finzi's effects:

SINGING TO THE SEALS

Sir, –
Disbelievingly, the late Gerald Finzi and I took a sailing boat round the outer (western) isles of Scilly in March, 1930 [*recte* 1931?]. Old Ernie Guy, the boatman, attesting its truth, we all sang for seals. They came. What's more, they crowded and stayed embarrassingly close. It must have been dear Gerald's musical charm. The bit near the Round Island lighthouse was best: and the seals preferred sea shanties. We lost our voices for a couple of days, as we sang for two hours.

Graham Hutton, Ernie Guy and the seals must have been among the few creatures ever to hear Gerald Finzi sing. A rather less dubious privilege was that Hutton was with Gerald in Sussex when he first met Joy; they were walking in and around the Ashdown Forest.

Finzi's walking holidays, following Holst's lead, were solitary or men-only affairs, much less frequent but not entirely abandoned after his marriage. John (Herbert) Sumsion joined him for five days in Wales, including the ascent of Snowdon, in May 1935. In April 1940, with the Ashmansworth house under siege from 'this damnable "spring cleaning" ' (19400320) and Joy away with the two children while the younger, Nigel, had his tonsils and adenoids removed, he escaped for what he described as an 'almost annual' pilgrimage to Hardy's Wessex – 'I was particularly anxious to see the Hardy room in the museum, which wasn't there when I was last in Dorchester,' he told Toty de Navarro (19400421). The itinerary on this occasion gives a good indi-cation of how energetic he must habitually have been, though he curiously fails to mention that he was in the company of John Sumsion:

The next morning I walked to Sturminster Newton where [Hardy] spent the two happiest years of his early married life. A much nicer little house, externally at any rate, than Max Gate, standing right above the river Stour (& all very much like 'Overlooking the river'). Then on to Shaftesbury & then a marvellous walk on the top of the downs from Shaftesbury to Salisbury & then on to Andover & home yesterday. It was a pleasant few days' walk . . . (ibid.)

A postcard to Milford further indicated that Milton Abbas was on the itinerary between Dorchester and Sturminster Newton. That would have made seventy-five or eighty miles altogether if he walked it all, even if much of it was an easy stride on ancient drove roads. He travelled light on such occasions, wearing only a mac, as Joy put it (she did not quite mean that), 'with a toothbrush in the pocket and carrying a pair of light pyjamas' (Highfield 1978: 4), and stayed in modest inns or private lodgings.

There were also mixed-company jaunts to Rhossili on the spectacular western tip of the Gower peninsular in South Wales, where Herbert Lambert, again very much in tune with the decade's healthy if sometimes stoical holiday pursuits, had established a permanent camp at Great Pitton Farm; Finzi joined Lambert's family and guests there for a week or so on two or three occasions in 1930 and 1931. Lambert and his wife Georgie were among his closest friends at this time, and he also stayed with them at their country home near Bath; to a certain extent they probably took over from the Blows the role of surrogate family, though Herbert, twenty years older than Finzi, had an impetuous personality and vociferous set of musical prejudices that cast him more in the role of old fogey than wise uncle and kept Finzi firmly on the side of the moderns, even unto Prokofiev, Schoenberg and Bartók. Finzi also went on a lengthy canoe trip down the Kennet and Avon Canal with their son John in July–August 1932, inspired by a *London Mercury* article by the waterways enthusiast William Bliss with whom he later corresponded. It must have been quite an expedition, for they paddled all the way from Salter's Wharf in Oxford – on the Thames at first, therefore – to Bath, and there would have been many portages. After his death Georgie Lambert provided a characteristic reminiscence of Gerald *en famille*:

Gerald was fond of long walks & so were we, & I remember day excursions such as to Bradford-on-Avon along the canal tow path to see the famous Tithe Barn & Saxon Church, to Stratton-on-the-Fosse & Downside along the Roman road, to Binegar & Maesbury Camp on the Mendips, to the Celtic tumulus at Wellow, Gerald always with a well thumbed & heavily pencilled book of verse in his pocket from which he & Herbert would read aloud during our picnic lunch & discuss the relative merit of this or that poem from the musician's point of view (19561207).

Herbert Lambert's involvement with Finzi had other facets. He photographed him in 1930, though with some difficulty, for Finzi invariably pursed his lips when he was having his picture taken, creating 'the "prunes & prism-y" expression' that Lambert lamented as 'quite unfamiliar to me probably because when we are together we are always talking & you don't get a chance to look "proper"!' (1930). Lambert's solution was to stick a pipe in his mouth (see McVeagh 1980a: 595 for the result). It was Lambert who helped Finzi amass a small collection of keyboard instruments through the early 1930s, including the Morley clavichord and a couple of square pianos that complemented the two or three modern pianos acquired and exchanged over the years and distributed between music and drawing-rooms at Aldbourne and Ashmansworth.

The Lamberts were also responsible for bringing several Finzi compositions into being. One was the oboe Interlude (see below), another a four-part *Short Fug(e) in praise of the G.C.C.* in C major for keyboard, formally annotated by the composer with deadly analytical seriousness. It is not a very good fugue, but fortunately it was not supposed to be.

He wrote it for Georgie, subsequent to a 'fantastic correspondence' with her (ibid.), after she had made him a Grand Composing Costume in November 1931, a white-knight invention 'rather like Churchill's Siren Suit' (Ferguson 1985–96) made of thick rug plaid and zipped up so that he could contemplate the stars outdoors in creative warmth. History does not record what he looked like in it.

Concert-, theatre- and festival-going carried on without much change of emphasis throughout the early 1930s, though Haslemere was given up. Finzi still went to many of the Philharmonic Society and BBC concerts, especially when new British music was on the programme (such as Bax's *Winter Legends* in February 1932). He attended many of the Three Choirs meetings, notably at Gloucester in 1931 with Holst's new Choral Fantasia, Milford's *A Prophet in the Land*, Morris's C major Sinfonia and Howells's *In Green Ways* on the programme, plus Elgar and Vaughan Williams works conducted by their composers. He saw operas, such as Smyth's *The Wreckers* at Covent Garden (September 1931), and plays, particularly the London Shakespeare productions of the day. Vaughan Williams performances remained vital occasions for him, above all the stage première of *Job* by the Camargo Society in June 1931, for which he was invited to share the composer's box. He was now also firmly on the list of invitees to the private, critical run-throughs of Vaughan Williams's latest 'tunes' on two pianos: he had already first heard *Job* in this fashion, and went to those of the Piano Concerto and – surely a red-letter day – the Fourth Symphony at St Paul's Girls' School in July 1931 and January 1932 respectively. Despite firm befriending and acceptance on both sides, Finzi was still slightly in awe of Vaughan Williams at this stage, and Adeline's natural formality may have been a barrier; only when Joy came on the scene did the two couples more fully relax as older and younger friends. Virtually to the end Vaughan Williams remained 'Uncle Ralph' to Finzi, an object of intimate affection but also 'one about whom most of us feel as Morley felt about Byrd, "never to be named without reverence" (or words to that effect),' as he wrote to Bliss (19421009b), though that did not prevent Rubbra, Howells and Finzi all agreeing that his Piano Concerto was a dreadful piece when they heard the first performance in 1933.

Once there was a Vaughan Williams enterprise of a rather different kind: his organisation of a concert of R. O. Morris's music at the Wigmore Hall on 14 November 1930. Finzi, along with many other friends and pupils, guaranteed £5 and may have been involved with more than just the financial responsibility, for Ferguson was writing to him the next day telling him to look after himself – perhaps Vaughan Williams was not the only one who was 'very anxious about the concert' and 'looked a wreck' afterwards despite its success (U. Vaughan Williams 1964: 185, quoting Adeline). Morris's diffidence about his own works made him a tricky customer, even if he had not yet reached the stage when 'even to mention them was ... the gravest of social indelicacies' (Colles and Ferguson 1980: 591, quoting Rubbra).

The one new item on Finzi's cultural calendar was a rather unlikely interest in brass bands, exacting annual attendance at the National Championships at the Crystal Palace. It probably began with the first performance of Elgar's *Severn Suite* in September 1930, and the following year Finzi got up a party to go and hear Hubert Bath's *Honour and Glory* played by ten bands first separately and then together. Ferguson, Lambert and the oboist Sylvia Spencer probably joined him; Howells wriggled out of it. It was the experimental period, dating back to 1928 and Holst's *A Moorside Suite*, in which highbrow composers were being commissioned to write test pieces and the leisured artistic classes were making 'a modest "discovery" of the movement' (Herbert 1991: 88). Howells, Bliss, Bantock and Ireland all wrote for the championships within the next few years, Bliss wrote about bands in *The Listener* and the *Musical Times* in 1935–6 (though Finzi seems to have been interested in them long before he was), and in 1938 Finzi was urging Robin Milford to think about contributing a suite, whilst demurring himself ('I'd have a shot ... if I wasn't so damned *slow*' [19381127]). The interest eventually waned, but not before he had found out 'what is supposed to be not found out – that of the Elgar, Ireland & Holst brass-band works only the last scored his own work' (193405), probably through speaking to Denis Wright, whom he knew. He was not impressed with Bliss's *Kenilworth* when it appeared in 1936; nor was the *Musical Times*, and the Crystal Palace responded by burning down a few weeks later. Finzi kept in touch with the Aldbourne Band when he lived in the village, however; it would wind up at his house for refreshments at 4.30 on Christmas morning – 'It's lovely to hear Christmas Carols, coming nearer & nearer, in the early hours, & it shd be especially lovely this snowy Christmas,' he wrote to Milford in 1938 (19381224). What is strange is that Graham Hutton said in his obituary that Finzi had composed for brass bands; there is no evidence of this, though the Aldbourne Band, which distinguished itself nationally after the war, did ask him to.

These activities bespeak continuing vitality; but where overall purpose, achievement and direction were concerned Finzi's life had to get worse before it got better. He inaugurated the 1930s with a new responsibility: teaching harmony and counterpoint one day a week to ' "second study" composition students' (Highfield 1978: 5) at the Royal Academy of Music. Bliss, who was already on the staff, probably got him the job and may have bequeathed some of his pupils to him (both of them taught on Tuesdays); Bliss realised that Finzi needed something to take him out of himself if his ambitions and abilities were not to disappear for ever in the receding mists of 1920s pastoral modality. He may also have needed the money, if his allowance was suffering in the Depression. Finzi faced his first pupils at the 'Royal Crematorium' on 14 January 1930, forced to instruct 'Molly Selby, Audrey Thomas, E. Talbot, Joan McTurk, Leila Goulden, G. Robbins & Mary Donnington in the theory of music, harmony, the first species & such things about which I know nothing & care less' (19300107). It was pure drudgery. For one thing, he was unprepared (see his later letter to Lambert (1930) about which textbook to use); and the students were doubtless of a low standard: they all seem to have sunk without trace. Yet he carried on until his marriage three and a half years later (when Rubbra wanted his job), for despite Lambert urging him to try to get real composition pupils – and he may have made an unsuccessful bid for them with the Principal, Sir John McEwen – he must have known that Lambert was right when he wrote, 'I feel that if you do not do something of this kind you will go through life only meeting the people you choose – which is all very pleasant and comfortable but has I feel some definite disadvantages' (1930), however much he might protest – which he did indignantly to himself and posterity on the letter itself:

I think not. The composer is within himself & externals are of no consequence. Life cd never be pleasant or comfortable or even worth while for this composer, but *for composition*, & since he does not exist outside his composition, which is his only real delight, why waste time in a grocery or haberdashery establishment, which is all that outworn theoretical teaching amounts to. Others can do it so much better. (ibid.)

And it is quite likely that being forced to think logically and functionally about harmony helped him achieve the simplifed and humanised style his own works began to adopt around this time, on the tried and trusted premise 'That if you become a teacher, / By your pupils you'll be taught.' If so, it proved the formal musical education he himself had never had, and Bliss probably knew that he was doing him this turn.

However, the RAM did sport a New Music Society; in fact Finzi was probably one of its co-founders, since Norman Demuth is known to have been another and likewise joined the teaching staff of the Academy in 1930. Demuth tried – managed? – to get a Finzi work, probably the Introit, into its December 1932 concert. Earlier in the year Finzi had himself organised a student concert, on 16 June, attended by his friends. The Bax Oboe Quintet was scheduled for performance by Sylvia Spencer and the Griller Quartet, but illness seems to have caused its postponement and the Kutcher Quartet played instead, in a programme including something by Delius, some Vaughan Williams songs, and Ireland's Cello Sonata accompanied by the composer. This last work occasioned the following comment from Lambert:

I liked the Cello Sonata especially the slow movement & the last one & I though John [Ireland] played better than he usually does – not so hard and harsh – though he found the piano stiff & uncomfortable –

If you could write him a word he is one of those men who appreciates that sort of thing. I know him better than most people & for all his grim & rocklike exterior he is an almost pathetically sensitive human being – a man of sorrow & acquainted with grief. When he writes like he does in that slow movement I can hardly bear the poignancy of it. I feel you don't agree & probably see little in such music but that is how it comes to me. (19320617)

Lambert was probably right about Finzi's reaction, if there is any truth in the legend that he once crawled under a buffet table at a cocktail party to avoid being introduced to Ireland by the hostess, even if he later stuck up for him in correspondence with Robin Milford and said that he thought 'he grows bigger with the passing years' (19450428).

Finzi's continuing determination to make his name as a composer and not get sucked into hackwork survived other blandishments and advice at this period. He declined Richard Capell's invitation (made via Rubbra) to write an article on R. O. Morris for the *Monthly Musical Record* in 1930, timed in accordance with the Wigmore Hall concert, even though it meant that no one else did so. Two years later he turned dispiritedly to Holst for support following publishers' rejections, but while he rose to the exhortation that he must simply keep trying and not anticipate failure (19320711a), he did not follow up Holst's other suggestion:

Have you ever thought of doing any newspaper criticism? I have often felt that you would do it very well, but I have no idea how one starts as I hardly ever see any critics. Do think it over, but not too much as I am talking about what I do not understand. (19321017b)

He did have ongoing exposure. John Armstrong and Howard Ferguson performed some of his songs at a music club concert, probably in London, on 15 January 1931, and six were heard at another OUP concert on 17 February 1932, the first in a series of three featuring the younger British composers (Pitfield 1995: 9). In June 1931 Finzi submitted the Drummond elegies and 'Nightingales' to Charles Kennedy Scott, and it may be that Scott's Oriana Madrigal Society performed one or more of these items at the ISCM festival held in Oxford and London that summer, the most likely explanation for Emmeline Morris's comment, 'I hear you were easily the outstanding success of the Oxford Fest. – apart from your ignominious flight when the Warden's wife inconveniently appeared' (19311212b), and her reference to his appearance in evening dress, 'an imposing figure . . . especially from a North-West aspect' (ibid.), as well as a later comment by Scott about having been 'glad to try to perform' 'Nightingales' (19341207). Dan Godfrey and the Bournemouth Municipal Orchestra premièred *New Year Music* at an afternoon concert in Bournemouth on 16 March 1932 – Godfrey kept his ear open for new British orchestral scores and had probably heard about it from the BBC run-through two years earlier, or from Patron's Fund readers. This must have been Finzi's radio début, for the performance was broadcast. But he was further than ever from completing a satisfactory instrumental work, and if he was now thinking of making *New Year Music* the first movement of something symphonic, as Holst's comments on its orchestration (19320711a) would seem to suggest, it was a desperate remedy indeed. He was probably still working at his Piano Concerto at this period – he drafted three and a half movements at some point or at various points – but Harold Samuel had evidently reacted negatively to it when he tried some of it over with Ferguson in July 1930; one almost suspects Finzi of retiring from Ferguson's company to lick his wounds for a while after this, since he kept silence for a couple of months, even where a trip to the continent was concerned. Ferguson, though still only in his mid-twenties, was beginning to forge ahead of him as a composer, and had certainly done so by October 1932 when his excellent First Violin Sonata was performed at the Wigmore Hall by Isolde Menges and Harold Samuel.

Another, very different cause for worry may already have risen above his horizon. Finzi was quite happy not to have left Britain since the age of thirteen – 'Chartres is one of the few places abroad to which I have always wanted to go, but doubt if I'll ever get there,' he told Ferguson in 1935. 'I feel so un-at-home out of England' (19350923). This attitude in an inquiring artistic spirit may astound us today, but in the days of Empire much of the English intelligentsia seems not to have had any desire for foreign travel, and Finzi was not especially domiciliary among composers: John Ireland, for instance, only once went further than the Channel Islands, for all his francophone music; nor did Robin Milford venture abroad until he was over fifty. British values, especially where spending and being able to afford relatively genteel seasonal time in the countryside were concerned, must have seemed far more self-sufficient and imbued with quality than they do now, and foreign cooking and manners far stranger. The formalities of dress and uncertainty of hygiene made southern heat much less of a pleasure than it has become. Upper-class travel or residence on the continent had in any case been undertaken very firmly buttressed with expatriate hotels, resorts, churches, shops and above all servants throughout the Victorian and Edwardian periods, and when this lifestyle collapsed with the First World War, together with the trauma of hostilities and the subsequent rise of fascism and communism it soured the European experience for a whole generation or more – or at least for some of its representatives (not for such as the Sitwells and many visual artists). So did the sad business of 'frontiers', as Adrian Boult entitled a laconic chapter of his autobiography, pointing out that before the First World War 'there were no passports in Western Europe' (1973: 87). Even Vaughan Williams travelled little on the continent between the wars. It was different where rising mass tourism on the one hand – cruises were becoming popular – and, on the other, trips to America and South Africa (still by sea, of course) were concerned, but neither of these appealed to Finzi, and he was not a performer, which kept Ferguson by contrast in far more cosmopolitan circles. It was also a matter of what he chose to spend his money on: all this time, in addition to the general purchase of books and music, he was building up his collection of English poetry as a steady priority. Finzi's diet, too, would either have restricted him or marked him out, for although no longer strictly vegetarian by the time of his marriage it was evidently based on what sounds like a rationalisation of kosher upbringing – he had complained to Vera Strawson of 'milk following meat, which is ruinous to teeth' when he was in the Midhurst sanatorium (19280501).

So when in late July or August 1930 he took a motor trip to France, Belgium and Germany with the Strawsons, it was quite an event, made all the more so when they had an accident courtesy of the *priorité à droite* system and he was injured. If despite this he enjoyed the trip, he was at no pains to write home about it; it is far more likely that he was at greater pains than ever to distance himself from things cosmopolitan because the spectre of his Jewishness was beginning once again to loom. By the end of 1935 at the latest, Finzi was well aware of Hitler's designs on the Jews, and by the time of the Munich crisis in 1938 he was desperate about it and the attendant 'essentialisation' as one of them (see Brett 1994) that this perforce meant for him, after all those years of putting it behind him; it is unlikely that this recognition came to him suddenly. He still had German relatives, reason enough to keep an eye on what was going on in their country. We know from Joy Finzi's journal that the 1938 Munich crisis caused him insomnia or nightmares; it is surely no accident that an earlier period in which he slept badly, at the end of January 1933, coincided exactly with Hitler's accession to the German Chancellorship. A still earlier bout of insomnia in October 1931 coincided with the attempted Pan-German customs *Anschluss* of Germany and Austria.

By the latter part of 1932 Finzi, for whatever combination of causes, was by his own reckoning on the point of a nervous breakdown. Georgie Lambert tried to get him to stay with them in Bath for a complete rest. Instead he embarked, literally, on the most curious episode in his life, one that caused his friends amusement and amazement: a six-week banana-boat voyage at Christmas to Egypt and back for £5 (did his father's old firm arrange the cheap passage?). In contrast with the sanatorium, this time he found the physical and social confinement pleasant. The crew were civilised and friendly and did not regard him as a freak, and when he got to Cairo he was soon enjoying himself immensely, 'seeing a good deal quite outside the usual tourist itinerary & . . . going round with cotton buyers into the most incredible villages, made of mud & dung – yes, and drinking coffee with Sheiks!'

(19321224). Alas that no sooner had he come home feeling very well than Hitler began to spoil everything.

Help was already at hand, however – no thanks to 'the charming Lady of the French letters' (19330101), an over-sexed French literature academic who was chasing him and in his absence tried to get Howard Ferguson into bed as the next best thing, but in the shape of Joyce Black (Joy, as she became more commonly known). As already stated, Gerald had first met her in the company of Graham Hutton; this was a year earlier, in December 1931, when they were staying at Bingles Cottage, Lye Green, near Withyham, which Joy and her sister Margaret (Mags) rented out while living nearby with their widowed mother. Joy first met Gerald when he called her in to the cottage with 'a list of complaints' (Burn 1984c) and because the fire smoked.

He had clearly come away from this encounter with magic as well as smoke in his eyes – Hutton noticed it, and Joy stated that 'we immediately became implicated' (J. Finzi 1950s) – and although we find no further references to Joy in his correspondence throughout 1932, they must have stayed in touch, for Howard Ferguson was kept abreast of developments enough to be told 'Mrs Black is dead, poor thing. But I'm glad she didn't suffer' in early December (19321204). After the trip to Egypt things began to move quickly. Perhaps Joy's mother's death brought them closer together emotionally. Equally likely is that Finzi had hitherto felt he could not afford to get married but Mrs Black's legacy to Joy now changed their prospects entirely. In February Gerald went back to Bingles Cottage on a visit of several weeks, coming up to London when he needed to but staying in Sussex off and on until the beginning of April. For some or all of this time he was cohabiting with Joy, but in exactly what sense Ferguson has been left to ponder:

G told me, or wrote me, that he was going to stay at Bingles for a week or a fortnight 'on approval' (those were his words) before they were actually engaged. I wondered at the time, and have wondered since, precisely what that meant; but alas have never been able to decide. I can only guess that theoretically his vaunted broad-mindedness would have approved of bed-before-marriage; but against that, his very real puritanical side . . . might have disallowed it (1985–96).

Lottie Dummett, Joy's old nanny, knew about their engagement in mid-April; Gerald's friends seem to have been told in May. For much of April Gerald was in deepest Cornwall, staying at Helford, possibly with Joy.

She and Mags then rushed off to the west coast of Ireland to be present at the final stages of shooting *Man of Aran*, the famous film by the American documentary pioneer Robert Flaherty released in 1934. Joy had a passion for the Aran Isles, immortalised as they had been in Synge's *Riders to the Sea* (of which Vaughan Williams had just completed his operatic adaptation). There she stayed with the film's principal character, Tiger King, and witnessed the harpooning of twenty-six-foot sharks, which provided a sequence 'regarded as the chief screen event of 1933 [*recte* 1934]' (Graves and Hodge 1940, R.1971: 232).

The great change in Finzi's life had occurred, and by now Ferguson was being asked to procure three tickets for shows or concerts they liked the look of – Ferguson had been invited to Bingles to meet Joy for a weekend in March and they immediately hit it off. Finzi even threw aesthetic caution to the winds and went to a variety bill at the London Palladium on 19 June:

I went to hear the Duke of Ellington last Monday. Worth it, if only for the attack & precision & to *see* how all these odd noises that one hears are made. Slightly aphrodisiacal, & all far too dazzling for my slow mind to be able to follow. Otherwise the whole show is pretty worthless; It, & the audience, made one feel that there's something to be said for a Hitler.

(There was one attempt at a joke – about 'some people liking chamber music, but personally I think it's all pose'.) (19330621)

He was still unsusceptible to some normal practicalities and priorities: when Joy cut her hair short before one of his visits to Bingles this summer he did not even notice at first. But new energy, self-esteem and confidence shout out from his letters, however much of an 'unsettling business' (19370309) he found the marriage preparations. He was at Bingles for his birthday, and took Joy to meet his mother in Hundon, the Vaughan Williamses several times with Mags in tow, the Morrises once in their summer residence at Peaslake, and Holst in his Ealing nursing home, as Joy herself described: 'Holst asked me to sit on his bed and tell me what I was going to make G do when I married him. I said that I thought it would be an advantage if he could be persuaded to sit down to eat his meals rather than walk around with a plate in his hand!' (J. Finzi 1984).

Gerald did one more walking trip in August, and then in September he went to reside officially in Dorking for a fortnight before his marriage, lodging in theory if not in fact with a Mrs Eveleigh. Determined at all costs to avoid a family wedding – Joy's mother's relatives would no doubt have been as daunting as his own – he kept the details secret even from Ferguson, and he and Joy were married on Saturday 16 September 1933 in the Dorking Registry Office, with Ralph and Adeline Vaughan Williams and Mags as the only witnesses. No one else was present: 'I'm afraid we were quite ruthless about hurting people's feelings over our nuptials,' he later told Thorpe Davie (19370309). Joy, for all her brightness and vivacity, had a pleasantly dotty side even then. When the Registrar asked who the bride was she looked around the room for some moments; when he gave her her marriage lines she 'said matter-of-factly that she would put it away with her dog licence' (U. Vaughan Williams 1964: 197). Gerald stood on the office steps in the photographs so as not to appear shorter than Joy.

Joy Finzi, an artist of distinction in her own right, outlived her husband by thirty-five years – half as long again as the time during which she knew him – and developed her own very distinguished circle of friends, including, in addition to a number of musicians, Sylvia Townsend Warner, Helen and Myfanwy Thomas, Laurence Whistler, Richard Shirley Smith, Jim Ede, John Schlesinger, Ursula Le Guin, Barbara Gomperts, Ann Hechle, Edward Storey, Richard Eurich and Reynolds Stone, most of whom Gerald met once or twice at the end of his life or not at all. With her gracious but indomitable personality (Simona Pakenham was terrified of her) she became something of a legend, and it is not easy to peel away the cultural layers of her later years – or even of his – to imagine what she was like when he first met her. Gerald himself was of no help: 'Repeatedly I asked what she was like,' Eaton reminisced, 'but he seemed to find her quite indescribable. Eventually he came out with "Well, she is *not* like Harriet Cohen!!" ' (1986: [13])

Joy was tall and slim, fairly dark-haired, with features that have been more frequently described as 'handsome' than beautiful, the chin and mouth particularly strong, the voice probably rather deep, for it became very cracked as she aged, accompanied by a throaty cough. In her younger days she seems to have been quite a fashionable dresser; later attire was very distinctive – 'little jackets with interesting buttons . . . longish skirts' (U. Vaughan Williams, in C. Finzi 1992: 38) and invariably a headscarf. She suffered badly from asthma, for which there was little medical relief during much of her lifetime. There was a pre-Raphaelite look about her, especially with her shortened and bunched hair – it was never grown long again. The rather masculine features were more accentuated in Mags, two years younger, who had Joy's vigour without her intellectual sharpness and was passionate about horses. Mags had a 'mannish' girlfriend known as Horace, though in due course she married a Newbury estate agent, Joseph Neate, thus remaining geographically close to Joy. Joy was devoted to her sister, and the only occasion on which Christopher Finzi ever saw his mother cry was when Mags died – in the spare room at Ashmansworth, where Joy spent her own last days nearly twenty years later. For Joy, phenomenally resourceful hostess, calm and indefatigable administrator, magical portraitist, and wonderfully warm friend to many as she was, was personally reserved and unemotional. 'Affectionate always, she remained undemonstrative: to greet her was like kissing a hollyhock,' as Laurence Whistler observed (ibid.: 47). She was lonely at heart, particularly after Gerald's death but not just because of that, for it was the fundamental loneliness of an artist. 'She hated anything that put a focus too close to her own deep well, and was much happier as the "eternal observer",' Christopher (Kiffer) observed, pointing out that Gerald, though in many ways a lonely artist himself, was temperamentally the opposite: 'He, who "could not disguise a passion, dread or doubt in weakest fashion, if he tried", provided the emotional fuel and volatility, whilst Joy gave the frame or combustion chamber that allowed it to fire so purposefully.' This made them 'a wonderful complement to each other,' their marriage 'much greater than the sum of their two individual halves' (ibid.: 7–8). In some ways they conformed to gender stereotypes, Gerald the intellectually restless masculine striver, Joy radiating feminine stability and intuition, even mysticism where her famous pendulum was concerned (which in her last years she repeatedly used to predict the date of her own death – always wrongly, with many an extended deadline).

She was born in Hampstead on 3 March 1907. Thus she was only twenty-four when Gerald first met her; he was thirty. Her father, Ernest Black, was, like Gerald's, a commercially prosperous north Londoner (and where Gerald's paternal grandfather was a dentist, Joy's was a doctor). Ernest married Joy's mother, Amy Whitehorn, at St John's Wood Presbyterian Church in 1889. Nothing more is known about the Blacks, and nothing at all about Joy's maternal grandmother, but Ernest's mother, Rosalinda Blow, belonged to an old Scots Presbyterian family with a Northern Irish branch that had distinguished itself in the printing trade in the eighteenth century. Both the Blows and the Whitehorns claimed a connection with their respective English composers, though it cannot have been direct descent in the latter case, since Thomas Whythorne had no children. There was Presbyterianism as well as music on both sides of the family, for Roy Whitehorn, Principal of Westminster College, Cambridge from the mid-1950s and well-known as a religious broadcaster, was Joy's first cousin; another relative is Katharine Whitehorn the newspaper columnist. The Whitehorns were a very fecund family. Joy also had an uncle Bertie Drummond, 'one time Moderator of the Scottish church' (19370118b).

Joy's birth certificate described her father's occupation as 'East India Merchant', and her parents lived at Cochin on the Malabar Coast. A son, Harold, was born in India a year after their marriage but died at eighteen months. Their second son, Geoffrey, born in West Hampstead in the care of Ernest Black's mother in 1892, died of blood poisoning at the age of twenty-one just before the First World War, so Joy would have had only childhood memories of him. She and Mags were very much a second brood, separated from the first by nearly twenty years, the most likely explanation being that Geoffrey's health was weak, both sons might therefore need replacing, and they had not wanted to bring up any more children in India. By the time Mags was born in Eastbourne in 1909, her parents must have retired there, and it is where Joy grew up. Her father died in 1926 when she was nineteen.

When Gerald first met her she played the violin, but otherwise her artistic talents were undeveloped. They were, however, both obvious – decades later a school friend remembered 'the awe with which she looked up to her as of one with brilliant gifts in everything!' (19510520a) – and assumed, insofar as her schooling at Moira House, Eastbourne, had been Dalcrozian. Gerald immediately encouraged them. Her initial view of him was set down, with characteristically idiosyncratic grammar, in the short account she wrote of it after his death for Diana McVeagh (1950s):

... Shyness and enormous vitality – a kind of zest which fed his inner urgency. This, I discovered later, never allowed him rest.

His shyness and ill at ease in a public situation, quickly melted with his unusual empathy for people and interest in them. He was not at ease with highly sophisticated superficial people, and had a liking for simple men. This prompted him to often sign himself anonymously when on his walking tours, to enable his contacts to feel at ease with him, one of themselves. He knew that he could share their problems, but they never his.

He experienced the isolation of the artist – the eternal onlooker. His lonely, hurt, incompatible early surroundings made his books his companions and his few deeply chosen friends. Aristocratic, acutely sensitive he built round himself an emphatic positive reaction to life and work. His urgency gave him an unswerving self-discipline – a dedication with which to wrestle with his utterance. Despite all this strong sense of direction his capacity for anguish was acute.

He was singularly inarticulate. Felt insignificant – plain to the point of ugliness. Inhibited and aware of it . . . I had never met anyone so sensitive and capable of hurt yet with such boundless vitality.

The insecurity of life had made a lasting impression on him. Even our meeting which was such an enormous impact, filled him with grave apprehension, and I think he discussed with Howard whether anyone needing such an isolated dedicated background should marry. He wondered whether it was right to expect me to happily share this with him. In our home he had seen people flow in and out, and he knew he needed specialised conditions in which to wrestle with his work, more especially as he was so ardently interested in all life and so easily distracted.

. . . He wished to show me everything that had been of significance to him, he was so starved of that warmth that makes for all flowering, and the need to communicate was so strong. That was why he laid such strong emphasis on environment as against heredity, and knew himself to be capable of drying up in inarticulation –

Like all who have known the shadows he had an immense capacity for enjoyment. A great appreciation of many things – and infinite delight & humour.

The sense of precariousness made delight an ecstasy.

Here Joy was scrupulously avoiding any reference to the transformed being he became with her support – how soon and how much he relaxed, multiplied his interests and outlets, and learnt easy sociability, hosting of friends and visitors, even the command of institutional rigmarole. Not that he lost his nervous hypersensitivity – he did not need to, for Joy, as her account makes clear, utterly accepted it as the artist's lot and therefore the artist's wife's burden. Today we are more likely to baulk at such protection from a spouse, but even in Finzi's day it required nerve – on his part, not hers – for it took his importance as a composer for granted. However diffident he might have been about marriage, once the step had been taken it required Joy's absolute belief in him – belief, that is, that he would spend the rest of his life and the whole of their combined material resources on his remaining a composer. And for her to have that belief, he had to have it himself, for there was as yet precious little to show for it – a handful of premature publications, no major work waiting in the wings, no institutional qualifications whatsoever, and no dazzling executive ability to vouch for his talent. Yet he was prepared to cast himself in the role of professional artist ministered to by devoted spouse, who would henceforward prepare his scores for him, type out his texts, and copy out passages from his letters for her journal before he sent them off. There were plenty of romantic precedents for this high-minded view of a struggling, missionary partnership, of course – not to mention parallels with a priestly 'calling' or at least a sense of ministry that may have drawn atavistic resonances from both their families – but one in particular was probably at the back of his mind. Finzi was the same age as Elgar when he married; both wives came from secure families in the Indian service, and both needed unlimited faith in a self-taught artist with as yet little reputation and no proof of attainment. If this was good enough for Elgar, it was good enough for Finzi. We are left realising that the sheer force of his personality must have carried it off. Both partners were taking an enormous risk. If Finzi, described as a 'composer of music' on his marriage certificate, failed to make a name for himself, there would be absolutely nothing to fall back on.

How much of a name for himself did he believe he would make? This is an intriguing, unanswerable question, and one which renders the task of biography stranger in Finzi's case than in many another, for although his output and influence were those of a minor composer, something about his profile, the way he went about his job, the breadth of his thought, the depths of his personality and its impact on others, in short his *individuality*, always suggested something greater. It was almost as though he could not stop himself from becoming one of Vaughan Williams's best friends, from saving his correspondence for posterity's use, from setting some of the greatest poems in the English language to music and thereby becoming, eventually, something more than an insignificant footnote to those poets themselves. There was something patrician in his assumptions that he was quite incapable of disguising or denying, for all his shrinking from conventional channels of competition and ambition and measurements of self-worth. We shall never know how much Joy understood of his hereditary background that must ultimately be seen as the source of this mixture; but she accepted the mixture, and helped him make the most of it.

In fact he was beginning to make more of it already, and it is time we returned to his music. Inevitably, as with Schumann's *Liederjahr*, it is bound up with Joy at this period, and he seems to have gone out of his way to set poems with references to 'Joy' in them. This has been rather downplayed by commentators, understandably enough while Joy Finzi was still alive. But it is difficult to deny the double meaning when it is so blatant, and it sticks in the mind, needing clarification (Milford, for instance, got the 'Joy' songs mixed up – see 19420214, 19420218). Two of the Bridges partsongs deflect any crassness in the self-referential idea away from the composer by locating it in the poems themselves. In 'My spirit sang all day' the poet explains his new-found eloquence, emotion, discovery of beauty and of music, all in terms of the female personification of joy:

> She also came and heard;
>   O my joy,
> What, said she, is this word?
>   What is thy joy?
>
> And I replied, O see,
>   O my joy,
> 'Tis thee, I cried, 'tis thee:
>   Thou art my joy.

'I praise the tender flower' is again self-referential, in the age-old paradoxical tradition of the lover's song as both intensely private and by definition public, insofar as it is at the same time a secret, unconfessing self-communion, not uttered directly to the beloved, and a performance, a serenade that sings the secret to the world, like the carving of initials within a heart on a tree (suggested perhaps by the word 'bind' in the last stanza):

> I praise the gentle maid
> Whose happy voice and smile
> To confidence betrayed
> My doleful heart awhile:
> And gave my spirit deploring
>   Fresh wings for soaring.

> The maid for very fear
> Of love I durst not tell:
> The rose could never hear,
> Though I bespake her well:
> So in my song I bind them
> For all to find them.

The other set of references to Joy is in poems by Edmund Blunden, where they refer quite straightforwardly to his infant daughter of that name who had died in 1919. The only one Finzi completed in the early 1930s was 'To Joy'. The poem had been published in the collection *To Nature* in 1923, but Finzi set the text as revised in Blunden's *Poems*, 1930, an omnibus volume whose appearance may well have sparked his particular interest in the poet. 'To Joy' was evidently composed during or immediately after Finzi's first meeting with Joyce Black, since he showed it to Ferguson who was impressed enough to write, on a postcard, 'I think "To Joy" is a most moving and beautiful song' (19320207). (The posthumous date of 1931 is not on the manuscript.) In the poem the child is 'motherless' because it has died, but all too soon, within the year, the sense would have uncannily and perhaps rather unfortunately adjusted itself to apply to Joyce Black, now bereft of her mother:

> Is not this enough for moan
> To see this babe all motherless
> A babe beloved thrust out alone
> . . .
> How shall you go, my little child,
> Alone on that most wintry wild?

Finzi did try to publish the song. This could imply that a whole Blunden set, planned around some of his other 'Joy' poems, was a later idea. Yet most of the other sketched Blunden settings seem to be contemporaneous. One of them, 'The time is gone', begins on the back of a title page for the Piano Concerto. Another, 'The child's grave', is very much in the musical vein of 'The phantom' of 1932 (see ex. 6.1.a). The third 'Joy' poem intended for the set was 'The shadow', its setting again probably sketched before Finzi's marriage, because the poem is written rather than typed out. One regrets that this set was never completed, for 'The child's grave' is enticing and was more than half finished in separate sections, most of 'The shadow' is there, and 'The time is gone'

EX. 6.1.a

has a striking (and complete) second half. It would have given his relationship with a living poet a kick start, and there are times when his ruminant method of composition seems infuriating because of its incomplete results. Finzi seems to have returned to the sketches towards the end of his life, adding (on the back of a Cello Concerto sketch) an introduction for 'The time is gone' on which he wrote *Joys of Memory*, possibly a title envisaged for the whole set, tidying up the end of 'The time is gone', and confidently beginning a fair copy of 'The child's grave'. Texts of 'The waggoner' and 'Water moment' were also typed out, and there is a fragmentary beginning for 'The long truce'. 'Water moment', about a predatory eel, would have been a challenge; it is one of Blunden's most characteristic poems, finer perhaps than 'The pike', comparable and better known. The opening of 'Harvest' was sketched on the title page of the fair copy of 'The child's grave' and turned out to be the only other one of the songs that he saw through, in mid-August 1956; according to Joy, writing at this point, it had been started 'some years ago' (J. Finzi 19560816).

One might argue, however, that a more powerful tribute to the transforming influence of Joy than all these is 'The phantom', about the joyful image of the young, horse-riding beloved, who 'sings to the swing of the tide', that accompanies the poet everywhere. It is one of the greatest of Hardy's remorseful poems about Emma that poured out of him after her death, and whether or not Finzi had Joy equally in mind when he made his setting, it is his deft conjuring up of a lilting *idée fixe* and his pacing and saturation of the song with it that makes it one of his first really superb achievements. Finzi has suddenly learnt how to give a song both instant character and lasting momentum through the use of a simple, flexible and vivid accompaniment motif – something which Schubert or any of the *Lied* composers could have taught him years earlier, and perhaps did now if he was having to teach them in his RAM work. The little cantering figure, used some thirty times, stands for the impregnated image and, unlike the skipping country-dance topic in 'Former beauties', does not attempt a melodic and textural continuum of its own but just weaves symphonically in and out of straightforward harmonic periods (see *x* in ex. 6.1.b), very much as Wagner or Strauss used triadic motifs in their operas (and in fact Finzi's 'ghost-girl-rider' has not a little of the Valkyrie about her). Now urgent,

EX. 6.1.b (baritone and piano)

now wry and pointed, as in the song's beautifully poised ending, it further demonstrates the virtue of letting point, mass and line keep out of each other's way in terms of hands on a keyboard, not lines of polyphony in a score (ex. 6.1.c), though at the same time it is still the accompaniment's *discourse* that guarantees the 'quasi-symphonic effect' (Hutchings 1974) upon which Finzi's strengths are henceforward built. Chromatic harmony has now been mastered too, as ex. 6.1.b demonstrates: perhaps Vaughan Williams's Fourth Symphony had already influenced the BACH contour of the chords in the first two bars, though the dissonances such as the dominant at *y* and on every main beat for the succeeding five and a half bars are becoming very much Finzi's own, traditionally but finely judged to lie under the hands and give maximum sonority or propulsion to the voice part or the motif. In addition to such general matters of technique, 'The phantom' is packed with one felicitous touch after another. They include the casual snatch of tune in the introduction, so well suited to the offhand reference to 'a man I know' (and a classic example of Finzi's spontaneous, piecemeal inspiration); the broadening of pace in the accompaniment for the 'moveless hands / And face and gaze', creating an effortless but magical paragraph of melodic rhetoric in three-bar phrases for one of Hardy's moments of reverie in which time and place suddenly enter another dimension; the thirds-related, hushed modulations that offer something of the same poetic corollary and that we have already noted in the *Requiem da camera* (before 'And what does he see' and after 'What his back years bring'); the trope in the piano, deliciously physical (because of its keyboard weight, phrasing and sonority), as the reader or listener takes up the poet's question about 'what does he see when he gazes so?' – a real operatic moment; the *x* motif's transformation into the left-hand syncopated figure that follows this, as the fragrant vision unfolds, in a relaxed rhythmic idiom unthinkable in the early Finzi but

EX. 6.1.c

an indispensable part of his stylistic armoury from now on (again one wonders about the influence of Schubert, for instance 'Die Taubenpost'); the workaday, antique chromaticism for the 'sweet soft scene / That once was in play'; the exploitation of what can only be described as musical insidiousness, with a dance-band air to it, as the phantom takes hold (ex. 6.1.d); and the mastery of minor-key inflection and false relation, already discovered in the Grand Fantasia, used to propel the vision and the song from this point on. Only at the climax, in the poem's last two lines, does Finzi spoil things by falling back on the creaky diatonic clatter that had hamstrung the first movement of his Violin Concerto. Above all, the song is passionately and urgently persuasive, in an intimate personal voice rarely achieved in the earlier tenor songs. This has a lot to do with the baritone tessitura, which can use depth for secrecy, height for earnestness rather than *cantabile* beauty. For Finzi the baritone range comes more and more to represent the authentic, vernacular voice of the poet's experience – Hardy's in particular – possibly because it is what the untrained male produces, even with bits of falsetto at the top end, when he sings privately to his own accompaniment, as indeed the pop revolution has more recently shown us. Was Finzi only now beginning to sing his songs to himself, or to Joy? He certainly accompanied himself in private with just such a voice in later years, as John Carol Case (1996) has testified.

Clearly this point about range and vocal relaxation cannot be taken too far. The mature Finzi commands a number of 'voices': but they do seem to have each their inevitable location. *Dies natalis* was written for soprano but is now almost always performed by a tenor. In 1956 Joy Finzi observed in her journal: 'G finished another song . . . "At middle field gate in February". Hoping it was going to be a tenor song it turned,

EX. 6.1.d

in the final making, into an inevitable baritone' (J. Finzi 19560221). The same thing had happened, in the period under review, to 'Proud songsters', composed for tenor in D minor and another great song sharing many of the idiomatic gains of 'The phantom'. It is the extended role for the piano, a whole landscape against which the voice is cast as observer or viewpoint, not as enactor or mimic, that makes this song in its baritone guise so remarkable and so moving. All the comparisons with Britten's setting, cast by contrast as a *performance* for a tenor and a piano who *represent* the birds, miss the point utterly if they fail to grasp this.

Finzi's harmonic and rhythmic relaxation deserves further consideration. It boils down to the discovery or acceptance of metric models that permit a strong harmonic rhythm, by which is meant a relatively slow-paced, regular grid of full-textured harmonic change in the interstices of which highly characterised rhythmic motifs and other gestural activity (including word-setting) can have free play. There is nothing in this that the later nineteenth century had not taken for granted, but Finzi and his contemporaries needed to turn the corner on the drynesses of the 1920s before they could re-accept it. (It brings Finzi much closer to Elgar in his later, mature music, though it would be difficult to say whether this was more a matter of discovery or rediscovery.) We have already noted this development, and Bliss's probable influence on it, in Chapter 5, and 'The phantom' shows it in its most common embodiment, an easily swinging or jogging compound time, perfect for the depiction of the 'diurnal round . . . / In peerless ease, without jolt or bound' that is its eschatological concomitant in 'In a churchyard'. The relaxed use of triplet division or ternary movement within a binary or ternary pulse was a favourite resource of Bliss – see, for example, the last movement of his *Pastoral* and the first of *Morning Heroes* – and such a swinging harmonic rhythm, whether or not in compound time, often sets up a strumming pulse in both him and Finzi, as in the pizzicato chords in the 'Intrada' of *Dies natalis* and the middle section of the oboe Interlude. The wide sonorities and reiterations of these chords, based on tenths, are not a million miles away from the blues, and they remind us that much the same 'topic' of harmonic rhythm, texture and 'swung' pulse – because the swing keeps a sense of lilt or momentum when the chords come slow – was being developed in big-band jazz and 'stride' piano at the same time. Indeed, stride is exactly the idiom of the piano part of Finzi's 'O mistress mine', undoubtedly if covertly influenced by Billy Mayerl or his contemporaries. We may also reflect that it was from this moment around 1930, at which the harmonic rhythm of jazz slowed down, that its emotional content could best serve 'classical' composers. The searing harmonic rhetoric of Walton at his finest owes a lot to such incorporation, above all in the first movement of the First Symphony, where intensely exhilarating 'swung' rhythmic activity sits effortlessly on correspondingly broad and magisterial harmonic rhetoric, making him 'The Rolls-Royce of music!' as Finzi astutely observed (19360814). Finzi knew that he could only hope to make a moiety of such virtuosity his own, but it was unquestionably a beacon for him, probably flaring first with Walton's Viola Concerto – that touchstone of modern emotional honesty that caused Guido Adler, of all people, to hail it as 'the real thing – at last' (Kennedy 1989: 289) – whose plangent opening and closing proposition Ferguson thought was 'the most beautiful music he has written' (19360817). Nor should the first movement of Elgar's Cello Concerto be forgotten, another potent rhythmic model with its *valse triste* properties. Both of these probably rubbed off on the opening of *Dies natalis*.

As we have already seen (p. 125), that opening's vocal sequel ('Rhapsody') may have already been under way in the latter part of 1931, around the same time as 'To Joy', which shares 'Intrada''s 6/8 metric blueprint (and its melodic beginning, complete with imitation). Their strongest common origin is in the second of Vaughan Williams's Four Hymns, more or less the first of his newly published works of which Finzi would have been aware as a young man; even the key (F minor) is the same as that of 'To Joy', and Blunden's opening lines ('Is not this enough for moan / To see this babe all motherless . . . thrust out alone / Upon death's wilderness?') seem to invite an echo of Isaac Watts's ('Who is this fair one in distress, / That travels from the wilderness'). 'To Joy' continues the parallel with 'Intrada' when it goes into a 'strummed' duple/quadruple-time middle section. This now proposes less of a march-like consequent than is the norm in *A Young Man's Exhortation*, more a dainty, slightly archaic and ghostly dance (see the motivic imitation at 'I would weep / My blood away'), though Finzi still finds it difficult to place this as a contrasting middle section within a rounded tonal form: the transition back to the compound-time opening, with its $F\flat/E\natural$ pivot at the word 'storm', sounds forced and hollow. Elsewhere in this song one senses that, now that he has found a harmonic framework for them, his style is rapidly settling into that armoury of idiomatic 'topics' – melodic phrases, rhythms, accompaniment patterns, harmonic and textural gestures – that makes it so distinctive. Compare, for instance, the setting of 'Upon death's wilderness?' with that of 'A ghost-girl-rider' in 'The phantom', or 'A babe beloved – thrust out alone' with ' . . . so many of worth, / Still in the flesh' from 'In a churchyard'.

The Bridges partsongs, composed over the same period as these solo songs, do not enable the mature style to flourish so colourfully. Their genesis may have been a further example of Herbert Lambert's influence, to judge from a letter he wrote Finzi at the end of 1929:

My dear Finzi,

My suggestion about 'part songs' evidently touched you on a sensitive point & your reply has done the same thing to me – I want to put my point of view – for years past I have spent a lot of time every year searching for part-songs for our MSMC and it has been a deadly business just because there is such an amount of stuff of the Cyril Jenkins Bantock type – Heaven forbid that you should think me capable of asking you to add to this land of journalistic plague.

My feeling was that with your wonderful sense for vocal writing & your gift for making real music of a contrapuntal texture (I could see this in your songs and don't agree with Jacobson on this point) you might find 'your proper work' to use your own phrase in making some music which might come upon us with the kind of refreshment and delight with which I remember finding such things as H[erbert] H[owells']s 'The Little Door' & 'The Spotless Rose' & even on a lower plane some of the exquisite part songs of Charles Wood – some of his simple 'children's music' is I think perfect of its kind & perfectly adapted to its purpose.

There are things of VW's and Percy Buck which to my mind can stand on the level of the finest music & at the Competition Festivals these things are done with the loving care and enthusiasm which music hardly ever gets on the concert platform with an audience before the singers' mental eye.

I have heard performances of music at our own Festival here, with possibly no one in the room but the competing choirs, so perfect in their musical spirit & understanding that I carry the memory of them about with me as a standard of what musical performance should & could be if only it is approached in the right spirit.

The great trouble is the lack of music sufficiently good for the purpose. Too many composers think of the Competitions as you do as lifeless routine music makings and write their partsongs for bribery as you suggest.

I have a theory that the present day refusal to believe that good music can be written for a purpose – that is, *for performance by some realisable combination of people & instruments on some particular occasion,* is a pernicious fallacy & if anyone is prepared to deny this I shall point out that it was exactly in this way that Bach wrote all his music, the most intimate choral preludes even being just part of his day's work while at the other end of the scale the sleepless Count Goldberg could be provided with equally great music for his occasion!

I hope you will now see my point of view when I made the suggestion that the writing of a partsong might be considered 'proper work'.

We must meet as soon as you get back from the country and talk this over. With all the best wishes to you for 1930.

Yours sincerely,

Herbert Lambert

Finzi had evidently been sniffy and characteristically bullish about the partsong genre, just as Bliss later imagined him reacting to a minor criticism of *Dies natalis* – 'I can see you snort immediately at this, though in my presence you would be too polite to make instantaneous objection, but would turn on your heel for one turn of the room, one hand on pipe, tother in the pocket, & *then* say No' (19401009). Lambert may have converted him up to a point, though we need to consider the possibility that, knowing well how to spur Finzi's professional dignity, he actually commissioned or (perhaps goad enough) offered to commission the Bridges partsongs, as he was shortly to do with the oboe Interlude. And it was only up to a point, if Finzi's later comments on the partsongs when he sent some of them to Navarro are to be trusted: 'Part-songs probably won't interest you & may even conjure up horrors of the local choral society. These at least have the merit of being too difficult to be sung except by expert choirs!' (19370721a).

Half a decade earlier, in 1926, still in his first 'metaphysical' phase, Finzi had composed the Three Short Elegies to poems by William Drummond of Hawthornden (1585–1649), revising them to an unknown extent prior to publication in 1936. The texts are uniformly lugubrious, and their effect takes us back even beyond the 'queer state' of the Milton Sonnets. Yet Drummond's particular sensibility stayed with Finzi. He quoted him more than once in later life, as in this letter to Edmund Blunden, with its proposition – the one that Rubbra (1929: 193) had noted – that 'Life is flux':

Well, I suppose it's much like the arts and letters and Drummond said all that is to be said about it in Flowers of Sion –

> All only constant is in constant change,
> What done is, is undone, and when undone,
> Into some other figure doth it range;

He said it in other words many times, and I really don't know whether a volume on the transmutation of matter could say more. (19550802)

One of Drummond's sonnets from the spiritual collection *Flowers of Sion*, 'No trust in time' ('Look how the flower'), ends with the couplet

> Thy sun posts westward, passèd is thy morn,
> And twice it is not given thee to be born.

and it is hardly surprising that the Finzi of the Milton Sonnets who felt himself being chased by 'Time's wingèd chariot' should have attempted a setting of this poem too, in their austere style and doubtless around the same time, as part of an envisaged cycle for tenor and string quintet to be called *The Posting Sun*; it is even possible that the two Milton settings would have been part of this cycle, its fifth movement another *Flowers of Sion* poem, 'Change should breed change' ('New doth the sun appear'). *The Posting Sun* as such never got any further, but after his marriage Finzi contemplated a *Flowers of Sion* cycle for baritone, chorus and orchestra, began a setting of the sonnet 'The court of true honour' ('Why, worldlings') as its second movement, worked further on 'No trust in time', incorporating new material in his updated style, and had Joy type out the texts of no fewer than eleven of the *Flowers of Sion* poems (nearly all sonnets). He also made sketches for an unac-companied SAATTB setting of 'The angels for the nativity of our Lord' ('Run, shepherds, run') (Thomas n.d.), but these are later still, some being written in ballpoint pen.

To return to the Elegies, their philosophy is summed up by the first line of the first, 'Life a right shadow is', and in all three poems it resolves into something funereal – 'So near our cradles to our coffins are' in the first song, 'Old age with stealing pace / Casts up his nets, and there we panting die' in the second ('This World a hunting is'), '[This life] . . . / As swell'd from nothing, doth dissolve in nought' in the third ('This life, which seems so fair', best known of the three texts). This occasions loose versions of Finzi's AB form with processional consequent in Nos. 2 and 3, old age's 'stealing pace' counterpoised by a modicum of motivic liveliness for the antecedent hunting in No. 2, where it is well placed at the centre of the group; and one cannot deny that such a formal approach is well in accordance with that of the renaissance madrigal – for instance, in the placing of the pavan rhythm of the imitative point at the line 'But in that pomp it doth not long appear', after a pivotal silence, in No. 3. (In fact Drummond entitled all three poems 'Madrigal' – though they were not set to music in his time – and took a particular interest in the genre.) However, none of this makes for much musical interest in its twentieth-century environment, and for all that the unaccompanied choral writing is competent and doubtless pleasurable to sing, because genuinely madrigalian with its balanced polyphony, judicious word-setting and the odd telling sonority, there is precious little melodic, harmonic or formal overview to engage the listener in any of the songs. Their angular, largely diatonic counterpoint is another instance of what Finzi left behind him with the 1920s or learnt to cradle in contrasting warmth.

This diagnosis does pinpoint some of the wider problems of the twentieth-century British partsong, however, and we can understand why Finzi was reluctant to get involved with them. He did not feel he had solved them in the Bridges settings, in which he took no great pride, as this letter to Milford shows:

Dear Robin

Firstly to thank you for the new Bridges part song. It makes me realise my own limitations in that sort of work. You do much bolder & braver things than I do, probably because I lack experience with choirs & am never certain how much they can really bring off. It makes my efforts seem positively old maidish. Though I did set myself certain limitations (– mine are, for instance, 3-part 4-part & 5-part *songs*, rather than part-songs that divide at any moment, – the difference is in the hyphen) – I realise how much further I cd have gone if I had been less finicky. (19460530)

Nevertheless, the Seven Poems of Robert Bridges are a serviceable and characteristic work, if not of the calibre of his finest Bridges setting, *In terra pax*.

Finzi was bound to have a special interest in Bridges, the Poet Laureate of his formative years (from 1916 until his death in 1930) who had brought Hopkins to the public, experimented, if somewhat ponderously, with metrics, became an expert on hymnody, and revived the baroque tradition of active collaboration with a composer (in the extended odes and other poems he wrote for Parry). Like Parry himself, to whom he was in Finzi's view 'something of a parallel in letters' (1949b: 4), Bridges could be stuffy and Victorian and seem irredeemably profuse. Finzi knew this, and there was never any question of the depth of personal response Hardy evoked; but he also knew the value of Bridges at his best and became 'enraged' when Cyril Connolly dismissed him 'as a ridiculous bore who got a few ideas at the end of his life' in a newspaper review (19530113). As Finzi's interest in Parry continued, towards the end of his own life, he made an attempt to get the Parry–Bridges correspondence published, gave him full consideration in his Crees Lectures (:II, 16–18), and three months before he died went to Yattendon to visit Bridges' niece, 'who had much to tell me about his musical activities,' as he wrote to Blunden:

Heavens! How he ran his choir, – and the parson, and the village! He seems to have been a terrific martinet. But, alas, his choir withered away when he left and was no longer there in person to enforce rigid musical standards. Now it is all forgotten in Yattendon. (19560707)

The seven Bridges partsongs comprising Op. 17 were completed and published separately over a fairly wide period in the 1930s, but a few more were envisaged and fragmentarily sketched, intended to make a total of ten, one of which would have been a five-part, mixed-voice setting of 'Thou didst delight my eyes', whose beginning survives along-side partsong sketches for another Bridges poem, 'The idle life I lead', possibly from 1930, the likely date of Sketchbook W in which one of them appears (:15; see also Thomas n.d.). A later setting of 'Thou didst delight my eyes' for unaccompanied male voices, made in 1951, was published on its own in 1952 and earmarked as the first of a second Bridges set, Op. 32, for male voices, though its companions never materialised. It could almost be added to the 1930s set in performance, since it is stylistically congruent with them despite having been composed twenty years later.

Finzi was already varying the vocal specification within the original collection. One of the unfinished ones was 'An anniversary', cast by Bridges as a dialogue between 'He' and 'She'; male-voice passages for 'He' were sketched in four parts, so presumably the female ones would have brought the total to seven or eight. In the order in which they were eventually brought together under one cover in 1939, the seven completed partsongs of Op. 17 begin with one for SATB ('I praise the tender flower') and then one for SAT ('I have loved flowers that fade') followed, rather like Parry in his *Songs of Farewell*, by a gradual increase, in this case to SSATB ('My spirit sang all day'; 'Clear and gentle stream'; 'Nightingales'; 'Haste on, my joys'), though the last song ('Wherefore to-night so full of care') reverts to four parts. The idea of increasing the number of parts is a legacy of English madrigal publications, and Finzi is strict about not subjecting the specified parts to any casual further division. ('It really shd be done with an intimate choir, just one or two voices to a line,' he wrote to Milford about 'Clear and gentle stream' [19390423/30?], though the total of eight singers used for the set's first performance struck Ferguson as 'typical of the BBC's genius for compromise . . . the worst choice possible' [19390104].) Other unfinished settings included 'Awake, my heart, to be loved' for SSATB, which got as far as the start of a fair copy, 'The birds that sing on autumn eves' (SAATTB), 'Say who is this with silvered hair' (SATB), 'I heard a linnet courting' (apparently for SAT), and two for TTBB, 'I made another song' and 'Pater filio'. This last may well be later, perhaps intended for Op. 32, its text of a darker poetic colouring than those of the others. Several of the fragments include page references to the complete edition of Bridges' works first published in 1936, but 'Say who is this with silvered hair' must be earlier than this, since parts of it were sketched on the back of workings for 'I praise the tender flower', published in 1934. As with 'Pater filio', its enigmatic poem makes it something of an odd-man-out; Holst had already set it to music in his own very different Seven Part-Songs to poems by Bridges (1925, with strings), and one imagines the two composers, when they met socially in the early 1930s, discussing their various Bridges settings – Holst's including the recent Choral Fantasia, dedicated to the memory of the poet, whom he knew. Finzi quoted what Holst had said about 'Say who is this?' in the Crees Lectures (G. Finzi 1955: II, 4).

Of the completed songs, 'Nightingales' may have come first, since, as we have seen, Finzi sent it to Kennedy Scott in manuscript in 1931 and his 'expert choir' seems to have performed it shortly afterwards. It was published by OUP in January 1934, when Finzi also sent it to Vaughan Williams and Holst. All three men liked it, but Scott had gently criticised Finzi's habit of beginning 'imitations or entries on a note which is being sung in another voice' and Vaughan Williams feared for 'the tenor lead at b.7. – which *may* sound a little dreary (you know what tenors *can* be when they try)' (19340122). 'I praise the tender flower', 'I have loved flowers that fade' and 'Clear and gentle stream' appeared a little later, probably in May, for Holst did not have time to thank Finzi for them before he died. Vaughan Williams now complimented Finzi on 'that real English–Bridges quality' and thought 'the most successful *as a whole* is the 3 part one – probably that's the one you don't like!'; he felt that 'Clear and gentle stream', lovely at the edges, 'falls to pieces a bit in the middle' (1934?). Kennedy Scott and the Oriana Society performed some more Finzi, probably these settings, at the Aeolian Hall on 9 June 1936. Publication of 'Wherefore to-night so full of care' followed in November 1936. 'Haste on, my joys' was probably composed next and was performed along with 'I have loved flowers that fade' and another new one, 'My spirit sang all day', on 29 January 1937, at a concert in Westminster School conducted by Iris Lemare and sung, rather gruesomely (*The Times*, 1 February 1937: 10), by the combined forces of the Carlyle Singers, the John Lewis Partnership Society and the St Stephen's Singers. Someone from Boosey & Hawkes must have heard them, for the firm then offered to publish the two latest ones, or possibly a whole set, which Finzi found infuriating because it was too late to rescue the others from OUP, who would (and did) nevertheless require a personal subvention from him to complete the series, which happened when 'Haste on, my joys' and 'My spirit sang all day' appeared in September 1937. Finzi had to dig into his own pocket again to see the seven songs brought out as a volume in September 1939, specifying that the volume's order (see above) be adhered to if the songs were sung as a group. Sadly, they were re-issued separately when Boosey's acquired the copyright in 1969 and did not appear again under one cover until 1995. The first performance of all seven partsongs was on the radio on 29 December 1938, given by Trevor Harvey and the BBC Singers.

Finzi realised that the choric persona of a partsong performance is a very different matter from the dramatic monologue of a solo song and offers no comparable platform for image, narrative, figure and ground, stance, reflection, viewpoint – all the things that lend accompanied solo song, particularly in Finzi's mature approach, its personal, often rather cinematic dimension. Even the past tense tends to lose its perspective, of someone *telling* someone else something, when the voice is choral and composite (contrast this with the intense voice of personal history in *Dies natalis*). However, in thinking this through he had also firmly decided that that was no reason to avoid the first person singular, and in fact the text of every one of his partsongs (though not those of the Drummond Elegies) speaks as 'I' rather than 'we' (though 'Say who is this with silvered hair' employs both); he must have already made this decision *vis-à-vis Intimations of Immortality* and saw it as no more of a problem than had Weelkes and Wilbye in their madrigals. Yet it has worried some people in *Intimations*, and it worried William Busch when he heard the partsongs in January 1937 – 'I still feel that that lovely Bridges poem (the first) is almost too personal to set for a choir, but I fully admire the way you did it,' he wrote to Finzi (19370202). Finzi must have responded with all guns blazing, citing a number of precedents including *The Dream of Gerontius* (which does avoid the choral 'I'), and Busch retreated cap in hand, admitting that he had 'not really given much serious thought to the question' (19370210?). It is a pity that this reply does not survive.

What the choral voice tends to do is elide subject and object, and the poems Finzi chose for his Bridges set reflect this well, given the self-referentiality already mentioned. Many of them are songs about songs or singing – about themselves, in other words. The very first words of the first song are 'I praise', describing the process of utterance itself: the language has a 'performative' function. This performative 'I praise' returns to seal the overall act at the end of the last song, and in between every song except 'Haste on, my joys' has song itself as explicit subject in the text, with the nightingale as its corollary at the core of the set, the five-voiced No. 5. Even in 'Haste on, my joys' (and in 'Wherefore to-night so full of care') the subject is kept rhetorically self-referential by apostrophising aspects of it ('my soul', 'my joys'), which minimises the unwanted risk of having someone in the choir *tell* something to someone else, even when the pronoun 'you' is used. Most of the sketched fragments would have maintained this reflexive world, most blatantly in 'I made another song', a kind of private serenade about a public one.

Kennedy Scott seems to have felt the power behind such reflexivity when he wrote of the songs to Finzi: 'When one gets a cue such as Bridges gives how different the value of music seems too' (19370914b); it was his view that 'the combination of Bridges & Finzi approaches perfection'. Finzi's choral mode is certainly very tightly unified by Bridges' poetic conceits, and the music itself lives by an equally strict code:

With odd exceptions (most notably the very first phrase of 'Wherefore to-night so full of care'), every voice enunciates the whole text, and does so to rhythms of 'just declamation'. No word or verbal phrase is ever repeated in an individual voice, there is not a single melisma, and feeling comes from the effect and underlining (with melodic contour, rhythmic stress or quantity, and harmonic depth) of the text on its syntactic axis, rather than from musical structures, ideas or images. (Banfield 1995: 436)

In some ways this puts expression and structure on an even shorter leash than Parry's, whose expansiveness and shapeliness even in a modest partsong such as 'O Love, they wrong thee much' are beyond Finzi's. That is not to say that Finzi does not contour his lyrics: the melodic peaks across all three stanzas of 'I praise the tender flower' do this well. But the absence of *Gestalt* is problematic. To give one example, Finzi, unlike Elgar in 'Serenade' (Op. 73 No. 2), never uses a group of voices to accompany or foil a single line with a figure or wash of sound. Nor is plain strophic form used, any more than in the earlier solo songs, and as with them head motifs and strophic variation signal formal correspondences rather slimly, though their point is to leave flexibility for imitation, which makes sense when the composer knows that he wants to maintain the madrigalian ideal (of equal and individual worth in every voice part most of the time) from the singers' point of view whilst not losing sight of the lyric simplicity, which is strophic, from the poet's. It is not always clear where this leaves the listener, however.

Nonetheless, there are rewards and subtleties. The very avoidance of exact musical repetition whilst maintaining, on the whole, a balance of phraseology and cadence, is something of a technical feat and must have been a highly conscious one. Repeating a snatch of something curiously out of phase instead of in simple strophic parallel occurs rather as we saw in *A Young Man's Exhortation* and is evident in 'I have loved flowers that fade'. Imitation is often deliberately inexact, though this can become irritating when it feels routine and unschematic (ex. 6.2). What Finzi would have seen as organic correspondences rather than mechanical ones occasionally strike home, and are in fact closely comparable with the structural techniques of the English madrigalists. Most of the songs' initial head motifs share a basic shape rising, with some scalic motion, to the upper dominant at its first peak; it is most obvious, almost as though illustratively, between 'My spirit sang all day' and the abandoned 'I made another song', but can really be sensed in all the completed songs except 'Nightingales' and 'Thou didst delight

EX. 6.2

my eyes'. In 'Clear and gentle stream', at the centre of the set of seven, it begins to be contoured downwards as well as up (again illustratively?), rather pointedly in the third stanza ('Many an afternoon') and then again at the beginning of 'Haste on, my joys', whose initial upward octave and its imitation also seem to be echoed in the later line 'O youth, O strength' with an element of augmented recapitulation, though it has to be said that the rather thrilling promise of a broader musical form in this song when 'Lo! I have seen the scented flower' comes in with the thematic contrast of a second subject is not fulfilled, for one longs for a recapitulatory reference to that too. Touches of harmonic colour in the set are rare but sufficiently well placed in 'Nightingales', as a succession rather than a continuum, that every one of the textual images imprints itself with their help (a technique to prove invaluable on a larger scale in *Intimations*) – the 'starry woods', 'barren . . . mountains and spent . . . streams', the 'voice of desire', 'throe of the heart', 'forbidden hopes profound' and 'dark nocturnal secret', all counteracted at a stroke by the 'innumerable choir of day'. Opposite this, as it were, is the succession of repetitions of 'joy' in 'My spirit sang all day': twelve of them altogether, each as a cadence chord, all but two simple triads, all except Nos. 1 and 3 differently approached and differently spaced, and all in a different key except for two in the middle in C♯ minor and the four G major tonic ones at the beginning and end. That must have taken some doing, and goes a long way towards vindicating Finzi's abhorrence of conventional formalism, as indeed it does again in 'To Lizbie Browne', written around the same time, with its eighteen chiming refrains, their differences and repetitions carefully planned out.

The other work seemingly set in motion by Herbert Lambert, the Interlude for oboe and string quartet, is very different. Lambert, who like Léon Goossens seems to have had a weakness for talented young female students, came up with the idea of commissioning Finzi to write an 'Oboe Concerto (or Suite)' for one of them, Goossens's oboe pupil Sylvia Spencer, following a party in July 1930. 'Of course I do not know the price of an Oboe Concerto (white mice I know are 3½ each),' he added, 'but I think I could afford the sum of £12 sterling – you to retain the copyright' (19300717?, 19300818). The proposal may have taken immediate root, if Sketchbook W belongs to that same year of his German holiday (it includes a German folksong) and ex. 6.3.a and a 6/8 fragment, both from the book (:4, 6), are early ideas for the Interlude (compare ex. 6.3.b). But if so, it was with typical slowness. Finzi went to hear the first performance of Imogen Holst's Oboe Quintet in December 1931, and in the spring and summer of 1932 Lambert, Ferguson and Holst were all badgering him to get his own finished, Holst and Ferguson suggesting that he should submit it to the *Daily Telegraph* chamber music competition by October. It was another year before he managed to complete anything, and only then, in the heady days just before his marriage, by dint of staying up all night at Bingles Cottage in August in order to meet a further submission deadline, probably to one of Iris Lemare's reading panels. It was a single movement, not at this stage envisaged as self-sufficient. 'There's some decent

EX. 6.3.a

EX. 6.3.b

music in it,' he told Ferguson, '& a certain amount of rant, which I had to stick in to fill things up when I got rather rushed towards the end. Later on I'll unscrew it & put it together again, & I rather fancy it really has the makings of a first mvt and not a middle mvt'. Ferguson, who had by now firmly overtaken him as a composer with the completion of his own Octet, wisely realised that this was just the sort of pressure, excitement and confidence he had needed all along and predicted that some of the padding would turn out to be 'the best music of all' (19330817, 19330819).

Finzi soon heard that Spencer and the Macnaghten Quartet did not intend to perform it. His reaction to this, to Ferguson in a letter written on his honeymoon, was less perturbed than might have been expected and suggests a quiet confidence in the new style of the work, whatever its problems:

Anne writes that they dont think it up to my level!!! I'll be very, very interested to hear what you feel about it. I'm *sure* the form is unsatisfactory at present, but feel that the stuff is not so bad. Executive artists are usually foul judges, but at least they've heard [it] & I haven't. So I've asked them if they wd mind just running through it, so that I can get an idea. (193309/10?)

In December it was another quartet, Jessie Snow's, and a male oboist called Butterworth who gave the piece a playthrough in Finzi's presence.

There are two things we do not know here. One is whether Goossens stepped in to prevent Spencer from playing the work: he was notorious for stealing pieces written for his pupils, and did eventually take its dedication and give the first performance himself. The other is (as usual) how much Finzi changed it before publication. Sections may well have been developed or added as the prospect of making it into a three- or four-movement work receded. (Finzi never gave up the hope of producing a full-scale oboe quintet and reserved Op. 22 for it in his catalogue of works; the Interlude is Op. 21.)

Whatever the case, it languished or grew until the end of 1935, when Bliss advised Finzi that the work's best chance of being broadcast by the BBC would be if front-rank players had already expressed willingness to perform it. It may be that the BBC had been sitting on it all this time – Finzi later told Milford about them 'keep[ing] the score for 2 years & then los[ing] it ... though I got it back after making dire threats' (19451124). He then sent parts to Ivor James, cellist of the Isolde Menges Quartet, possibly 'on spec'; and they and Goossens gave the

first performance at the Wigmore Hall in a Lemare concert on 24 March
1936. It was well received, though not widely reviewed, Goossens asked
for the dedication and was lined up for a broadcast, and Boosey &
Hawkes, who had sent along a Mr Ruch to listen, offered to publish
it, much to Finzi's surprise. Sadly, Herbert Lambert died rather suddenly
in March, two weeks before the concert.

The score appeared in August. Given that *Earth and Air and Rain*
had not yet been published (though some of its songs had already been
sung by Steuart Wilson and Keith Falkner), this was the first real
manifestation of Finzi's mature idiom. Vaughan Williams was somewhat
taken aback by it, finding it 'rather different perhaps from your style
as I know it – but all you all the same (including some "wrong notes"!)'
(19360816). Rubbra, however, was delighted with 'the greater harmonic
freedom' and said it was 'a work that I admire immensely' (19360926);
he reviewed it for both the *Monthly Musical Record* and *Music and
Letters*. Ferguson, already familiar with the work, was struck afresh
'by the ease and beauty of the writing for that awkward combination . . .
you seem to have the knack of writing for string quartet (never to
mention the oboe)' (19360817a).

These are all fair comments, and it is the sinuous baroque sensibility
of the chromaticism, as in ex. 6.3.b, that brings it close to Rubbra's
own flexible note-to-note procedures, as does the relaxed compound-
time rhythm. How anyone could continue to hear in this 'a compound of
Byrd, folk-song, and Vaughan Williams' (M. Scott 1936: 456) goes to
show how firmly Finzi's image was already fixed regardless of the actual
sounds he made. Texturally the new flexibility is a great advance, for
the main motif x, rather as in 'The phantom', is a simple enough
proposition (technically a *nota cambiata*) to fit virtually anywhere. In
a piece that lasts ten minutes or more, however, it is undoubtedly over-
used, and even near the beginning there is a sense of disappointment
when its apparent function as a lilting dominant preparation for something else on the tonic (ex. 6.3.c) leads to nothing new. However, there
is no lack of instrumental agility, even virtuosity, and ex. 6.3.d has the
sort of rich, splashy energy that Finzi may well have learnt from Bliss's
Oboe Quintet of 1927. It leads to a kind of *tutti* second subject for the
string quartet, and it is after that that the continuity, though fluent,
begins to feel unnecessary – x modulates developmentally but without
much direction, and the issue is perhaps shelved rather than solved by
the insertion of the duple-time central section. Finzi scrupulously avoids

EX. 6.3.c

EX. 6.3.d

almost all mechanical recapitulation: as the 'analysis' inserted into the pocket score tells us (did Finzi write it?), 'this is in no way a repetition of the first section, but a new presentation of the material which is given an added urgency and moves to a climax'. It is subtly thought out, for instance in holding back until this point any statement of *x* that continues directly with the crotchet/quaver rhythm (rather than landing on the dotted crotchet) – see ex. 6.3.e. The second subject and

EX. 6.3.e

its antecedent return a step higher, and the only other exact repetition is of ex. 6.3.c, now a tone lower. Perhaps all this effort at developing variation is slightly misplaced, however, for it seems to over-extend itself rather than make a compelling point. The coda recalls the rhythm but not the melody of the central section, though there are ghosts of earlier derivations (see ex. 6.3.f for these).

Publication of the Interlude was a particular stroke of luck, for if Boosey & Hawkes had held out for a full-length Oboe Quintet they might never have got anything at all. They were doubtless astute enough to realise that Finzi would need strong pressure put on him to complete cyclic works – they were shortly to take exactly that line with *Dies natalis* – and that this could best be applied once he was under their roof. What has to be recognised, however, is that songs and partsongs were at this time still seen as belonging to a quite different market from cantatas and chamber works – Boosey rather than Hawkes, indeed the Winthrop Rogers Edition (which Boosey had bought up) where Finzi's solo songs were concerned – and that they sold best individually rather

EX. 6.3.f

than in sets. It was still a sizeable market, but its clients, English recital singers of less than international status, not to mention students and amateurs, would not programme more than four or five modern English songs together, between which and *Winterreise* there was a huge gulf for all purposes other than a one-off composer's benefit concert. Nor would the BBC – 'I wonder whether [they] wd let him do 25 minutes of one composer!' Finzi asked Busch, whose friend the blind bass/ baritone Sinclair Logan was offering to give the first (broadcast) performance of *Earth and Air and Rain* (19361106). BBC programming was very much in 15-minute slots at this time, and back came the answer in the negative when Logan broadcast only half of the set (Nos. 1, 2, 3, 7 and 6) on 20 February 1937. Even Holst failed to get his twelve Humbert Wolfe songs published as a volume in 1930: 'I went to buy [them] today & find that they are all published separately at 2/- + 1/- making nearly £1 – isn't it disgusting?' Rubbra complained (19300305) – and this was after three publishers had rejected them altogether. As for the record companies, as late as the early days of LPs Finzi declined an offer from Decca or EMI of a recording of *Earth and Air and Rain* because they were limited to twenty minutes per side and wanted to cut out one or two of the songs.

By being determined that his songs should be published and performed in sets of ten Finzi was thus making history for his generation. With folksong arrangements, children's songs and the odd posthumous set as exceptions, no British composer seems to have published a volume of more than six or at the very most seven songs between Somervell's *Maud* and *A Shropshire Lad* at the turn of the century and Britten's *Les illuminations* (1940, followed by *The Holy Sonnets of John Donne* in 1946) – that is, unless they had charitable backing or financed it themselves.

This was the price Finzi had to pay too. Where *A Young Man's Exhortation* was concerned, it must have taken careful thought and some courage to proceed with a course open to accusations of vanity publishing, especially since in a book published the same year Hubert Foss described many of the works in the OUP catalogue as 'nothing but youthful indiscretions pressed upon the public so that the composer may get himself known' (1933: 90). Finzi took an informed and philosophical view, as a later letter to Milford shows:

... a good many composers are forced to make a contribution towards their publishing expenses. It's regrettable (& unfair on those who can't afford it & have no private means to help themselves) but even a Robert Bridges has had to do it; both VW's 'Pastoral' Sym, & early songs were done that way, & Ruskin spent thousands & thousands on his own publication. One cd go on *ad infinitum*. (19391023)

His aspirations as a song composer doubtless paralleled those of a lyric poet who would publish a volume of verse when there were enough individual poems ready to fill it. His aspirations for his profession in general may have been to aim towards the point at which his works would appear comprehensively grouped and consolidated by Boosey & Hawkes on the back cover of each publication, but the evidence and history suggest that this was not so high on his agenda, nor a piece of image-making grasped from the start, while he continued to seek the best deal from whichever publisher work by work. It was not, in any case, a point reached in his lifetime, for some of his earlier works remained with OUP until after his death. Nor was it a goal without commensurate risks, still rife today, if the publisher suddenly decided or was forced to abandon the 'house' composer. This is exactly what happened to Robin Milford in 1959 and precipitated his suicide.

It was clearly Joy who made self-subsidy possible, either directly by providing the money or indirectly in that two could live more cheaply than one and she could house the couple while more of Gerald's resources were available to promote his career. She probably also pushed him and began to act as an extra arbiter, for shortly before their marriage in 1933 he not only decided upon the final selection and order for *A Young Man's Exhortation* with Ferguson's help, delivering the songs to Hubert Foss at OUP on 8 June, but then, with 'all the Baritone ones to be gone through' (19330621), immediately fixed up another session with Ferguson in London on a day when Joy was with him. They became an editorial team of three, and we shall later see how they worked on the Gurney songs.

For whatever reason, the tenor John Coates rather than Steuart Wilson was lined up to sing *A Young Man's Exhortation* in a concert at the Grotrian Hall on 5 December, its inclusion presumably arranged (and sponsored?) by Finzi himself to coincide with the cycle's publication (Finzi was insistent that these songs formed a cycle, the later ones sets). Once again Finzi shared a concert with van Dieren, whose Fifth Quartet was also in the programme, along with a trio by one of Finzi's *bêtes noires*, Christian Darnton. Coates was an interesting choice for a work about youth and old age, for he had started his career as a baritone and was now sixty-eight, though still in good voice. He had sung in the original production of Gilbert and Sullivan's *Utopia Limited* and created the solo tenor parts in Elgar's *The Apostles* and *The Kingdom*. Finzi went to see him at his home in Northwood in August, where Coates's idea of making him feel at ease was to have some Italian music on display (McVeagh 1980c: 30). In the event heart trouble in November prevented him from seeing it through, and the young Frank Drew, who had sung in Finzi's RAM concert the previous year, took his place, learning the cycle at two or three weeks' notice, though still with Coates's pianist Augustus Lowe. Most if not all of the songs were now at least four years old and had already been heard in public by Finzi's friends, so it was not a great event, though the composer must have been gratified by an appreciative *Times* review three days later, which spoke of 'a contribution of value to that marriage of voice and verse which is English song' and found Drew and Lowe respectively 'admirable' and 'plastic' except when Drew 'failed to convey [the] imaginative quality' of the less forthright songs, wanting suitably 'veiled tone' (:12). Busch said he would have preferred 'a darker and richer tenor voice' and made it clear he only liked some of the songs (19331213). Plunket Greene missed the performance but was sent a copy of the score which made him 'wish I was a tenor (I don't really)' (19331208).

Well before this point, however, the main job was to get the set of Hardy songs for baritone completed. 'The phantom' and 'In a church-yard', both dated 1932 by Finzi on their manuscripts, were crying out for companions, as apparently was 'Amabel', though she would have to wait longer for hers. 'Proud songsters' had also been composed, was about to be sung by Steuart Wilson in its tenor guise (on 19 January 1934), and was thereafter due for downward transposition. Most likely, as we have seen, so were 'Waiting both' and 'So I have fared'. The remaining five songs ('Summer schemes', 'When I set out for Lyonnesse', 'To Lizbie Browne', 'Rollicum-rorum' and 'The clock of the years') were probably written after 1932 (since Finzi did not bother to backdate their fair copies), and all must have been finished by October 1935, when they were being copied prior to Ferguson and Keith Falkner trying them through as a set and when Finzi first approached Bliss about a BBC broadcast. 'To Lizbie Browne', Finzi's first composition to employ the characteristic marking 'Ravvivando al Tempo' (which he could have picked up from either Sibelius or R. O. Morris), was probably the 'work' whose completion made him neglect his correspondence in July and early August 1935, since he was consulting Ferguson about it then, though he was doubtless finalising the other songs too. A sketch headed 'After rereading [*sic*; the rest of the title, rubbed out, is illegible] . . .' (ex. 6.4), in Sketchbook O (:1) which may be as late as 1936 since it contains part of 'In years defaced', suggests that Finzi was either thinking of supplying an introduction to 'So I have fared' and transposing it into E♭ major or even, at a very late stage, contemplating a completely new setting of the poem.

After rereading . . .

EX. 6.4

By the new year the songs were sent to 'old Boosey' – who was not at all old, unless Finzi meant Leslie Boosey's father Arthur, head of the firm. Around the end of January Boosey offered to publish six of them. This was where Finzi's business sense came in, and where one begins to see that he was lucky to have caught the firm late in the day for Boosey, as it were, and early for Hawkes, the two partners doubtless more flexible than, respectively, they had been or would later be ('Marvellous to think that Leslie Boosey would look at anything less tawdry than Sanderson!' Bairstow wrote [19361114]):

Being away, I haven't done anything about the OUP or old Boosey, but it has occurred to me that the best plan wd be as follows. Wait until the oboe work has been done. If Hawkes takes it (and I don't think for one minute that he will, for he has already been bitten over one short oboe work, & Britten has a much bigger name than I have), then go into the question of old Boosey publishing six songs, as offered, and me doing the remaining four. Naturally, I don't want to do this, but it might be a way out of the difficulty. I shd have to aim for a bigger royalty – in proportion to the ⅓rd that I shd be forking out – &, published in one volume, there cd be no question of old B putting it on the shelf, (as he undoubtedly wd if it had cost him nothing, & he got nothing out of it) because he wd have been responsible for ⅔rds of it. How one wd manage over the separate issues I don't quite know. However, all this presupposes that Hawkes will do the oboe work. If, as I genuinely expect he won't, well then, I must just carry on with the OUP. (19360217)

We hear no more, so this was presumably the kind of agreement they came to.

Earth and Air and Rain appeared in November 1936, and 'To Lizbie Browne' and 'Rollicum-rorum' were also published separately – 'the two worst songs in the set,' Finzi observed (193609?). This time Busch was unreservedly enthusiastic: 'There is something wonderfully attractive about these songs . . . it is like meeting someone, a stranger, whom one knows instinctively is going to be a real friend . . . I think you are doing such admirable work, Gerald!' (19361104b, 19370202). Falkner had already sung some of the songs in public, as had Steuart Wilson 'When I set out for Lyonnesse' at the Iris Lemare concert that also saw the Milton Sonnets and the *Farewell to Arms* 'Aria' premièred in February 1936 (Finzi transposed it into G minor for him). At yet another Iris Lemare concert at the Mercury Theatre, on 11 January 1937, Falkner, with Ferguson, performed a group of five (Nos. 1, 3, 6, 8 and 10) 'magnificently' (19370116b). Some, possibly all, of the *Earth and Air and Rain* songs were murdered by locals in Newbury on 7 November 1938, but where a complete professional concert performance was concerned the set seems to have had to wait for Robert Irwin, Howard Ferguson and a National Gallery concert on 24 March 1943 (see Dressler 1997: 40), further evidence of how unusual the programming of such an extended sequence still was.

This lack of a timely first public performance, and the fact that the complete scores of two Hardy sets were published only three years apart while individual songs from both circulated in performance and in print ('Budmouth dears' and 'The sigh' were issued separately in 1935, 'Ditty' and 'Her temple' in 1938), rather obscured, and has continued to obscure, the extent to which *Earth and Air and Rain* seen as a whole marks an incalculable advance over *A Young Man's Exhortation*. In some ways it is Finzi's richest score. Characterisation now runs to vignette and *divertissement* in the two songs that, though it irked Finzi, were seen by Boosey to deserve particular popularity, 'Rollicum-rorum' and 'To Lizbie Browne'. The former is a straightforward strophic drinking song with a good tune, its text from *The Trumpet-Major*, its upper-octave ending suggested by Keith Falkner, and its accompaniment, while still betraying some of the mannerisms of the Guild folksong arranger, excellently weighted and driven home for all that, with some Waltonian touches. The chiming refrains of 'To Lizbie Browne' have already been mentioned, but not the scheme of their disposition, one at each end of nine stanzas on an ABACABAC¹A musical plan, nor the doubtless unconscious analogue between their change-ringing and the teasingly complex succession of similar four-note chimes that we hear every day from Big Ben. Up to a point a gift from Hardy, since each line of the poem has four syllables, this analogue nonetheless offers Finzi the perfect expression of time's differential passing ('So swift your life, / And mine so slow, / You were a wife / Ere I could show / Love') and makes the song doubly English, already strikingly and tenderly so in its soft, Elgarian diatonicism (it contains one accidental, a relative minor allowance as in 'The salutation'), perfected in the piano's trope of the word 'disappeared' (ex. 6.5.a). The third *divertissement* song is 'When I set out for Lyonnesse', which Finzi

EX. 6.5.a

209

scored up with small orchestra for the Mercury Theatre concert. It is a march and trio, with a ritornello at each juncture, as exquisitely phrased as anything by Sousa, its obvious model (of approaching and receding procession and tattoo) the song 'Ethiopia saluting the colours' by Charles Wood; no one but Finzi could get himself into such an apparent mess as a return of the A section that begins a semitone too flat, and then get himself out of it so triumphantly, cocking his favourite snook at formulaic recapitulation in the process.

Against these character pieces we have two songs with almost a cantata dimension and two others, the first and last, with something of a symphonic one. 'The clock of the years', its opening labelled 'Recit: Drammatico', uses its melodramatic poetic conceit as an excellent pretext for a tiny solo cantata in which one can count as many as three or four incipient arias interspersed with passages of *arioso* and discursive instrumental tropes. As with his earlier songs, the aria passages are signalled by caesura, head motif (an upbeat î 2̂ ♭3̂ 5̂ figure recurs) and the comfort of a lilting, settled accompaniment pattern, but now all far more poised and relaxed than previously. Again a ritornello

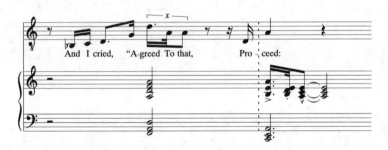

EX. 6.5.b

EX. 6.5.c

EX. 6.5.d

EX. 6.5.e

EX. 6.5.f

(the returning recitative) binds the structure, but so does a motif, as in 'The phantom': the splendidly romantic, Brahmsian gesture for the protagonist's bargain with the Spirit as he cries 'Agreed / To that' (ex. 6.5.b, *x*); of course it returns to haunt him (ex. 6.5.c, d and e). It is also transformed, between ex. 6.5.c and ex. 6.5.f, into a sobbing appoggiatura figure; *y* in ex. 6.5.f and then ex. 6.5.d shows it changing back again into the *x* motif. All these examples show that the secret of Finzi's word-setting, far from being simply a matter of 'natural' syllabic stress or quantity, lies in its motivic and hence dramatic force. Best of all in this song, however, is the way the tonal movement through the cycle of fifths reflects the time sequence: upwards (i.e. cadentially in reverse) all the way from D minor through A, E, B, F♯ and C♯ minor as the Spirit rewinds the clock, and then suddenly fracturing back into B minor with a *pianissimo* as the narrator realises 'it was as if / She had never been' (ex. 6.5.f). He briefly tries to recapture sharps (see ex. 6.5.d and the succeeding aria passage), but in vain, and the music quickly returns, with a broader fracture, to D minor and a present bereft of the perspective of memory. One never quite knows how deliberate such manipulation of tonal levels can have been with Finzi; but it works, as it also does in 'In a churchyard'. Here the point is not cyclic return but 'open-form' enlightenment: the poet leaves the churchyard a philosophically different person from the one who entered it (due, above all, to the linear passing of time 'as the day wore pale'). All the preceding music consequently resolves into the relaxed, rather Schubertian 'aria' or 'Lied' passage in D major (ex. 6.5.g). This passage's signification as song, while using the same melodic contours as the corpses' testimony (now transformed into a $\hat{5}$ $\hat{1}$ $\hat{2}$ $\hat{5}$ motif – clock chimes again), lies paradoxically in the acceptance of the 'strange tale' rather than the actual telling of it, which had been going further and further underground, both in tessitura and tonality (all the way from D minor to D♭ major) until this sudden emergence as enlightenment with a phrygian cadence. But enlightenment means acceptance, and this involves the opening D minor ritornello closing the song in B minor, retaining

EX. 6.5.g

the minor mode but lower in terms of actual pitch, philosophically right though not quite 'resolve melt[ing] into doubt' as Cline (1992: 12) claims.

'Summer schemes', appropriately enough for the first song in a musically and poetically broad scheme, builds more firmly on the sonata impulse beginning to be felt in 'Haste on, my joys'. Hardy has encouraged it, with his two quite lengthy parallel stanzas, each divided into thesis (the first seven lines) and antithesis (the last two) signalled but also unified by refrain motifs ('calls again' and 'We'll go' in stanza 1). Finzi uses the motif of a falling fourth for these refrains, augmented to provide a kind of second subject (at ' "We'll go," I sing') as well as inverted for the opening tune as first subject, though it is the movement towards the dominant (at the first 'We'll go') and the development of quite an abstract and continuous fast piano figuration in the middle reaches of the first stanza that really makes this song feel like a sonata allegro. The second stanza telescopes development and recapitulation, moving off from an exact return into development of the motif *x* from the opening tune (ex. 6.5.h, upper system) and reverting effectively to parallel material at the second subject.

The form of 'Proud songsters' is more intriguing. There is a whole miniature exposition in the piano prelude, with three pregnant, rather Sibelian motifs or subjects (ex. 6.5.i, j and k, one of them yet again like a four-note chime). Ex. 6.5.i's second appearance in this prelude (at bar 10) recalls Finzi's Bachian 'aria' style, and it is this that offers a rhythmic and textural continuum over which the voice eventually enters, melodically free, with only the slightest of references to ex. 6.5.k. Its effect, coming after the piano prelude, is more like the second (solo) exposition of a concerto than anything else, and it does lead to a *forte* recapitulation of the song's opening. But the poem's second stanza is then sung to new material, in one sense like a second subject on a properly broad scale, as though the piano prelude had been only a deceptive miniature,

EX. 6.5.h

Andante

EX. 6.5.i

EX. 6.5.j

EX. 6.5.k

in another functioning as a final consequent 'aria' for the whole set of songs, still undecided until the very last moment between an open-form D major ending to the song itself – though even here with a tiny hint at the opening tune of 'Summer schemes', and thus at a 'twelvemonths'' cycle, in the piano postlude (see ex. 6.5.h, lower system) – or a more obviously cyclic B minor one. Yet the song is tremendously moving, undoubtedly symphonic in scope – the lovely passage at the title words 'earth, and air and rain', reminiscent of the magical ending of the slow movement of Elgar's First Symphony, alone ensures that – and absolutely right in its inexplicable form. Finzi summed it up: 'when a work can't be fitted to preconceived ideas they call it "formless". Formality has about as much to do with form as bugs with buggery' (19330713?).

CHAPTER 7

Aldbourne and Ashmansworth

The Finzis travelled to both family enclaves for their honeymoon: East Anglia and Scotland. Sauntering first through Suffolk and Norfolk, presumably by car, Joy noted that Gerald's wish 'to show me everything that had been of significance to him' encompassed trying to find a 'blue-eyed love who had sold postcards in a shop in East Anglia'. They learnt, regretfully, 'that she had married a parson and had several children. G felt a Hardy sigh!' (J. Finzi 1950s). Catching the first night of a good production of *Romeo and Juliet* at the Maddermarket Theatre in Norwich, they proceeded to Edinburgh via Newcastle upon Tyne and got as far as Loch Lomond before returning home in October.

Home was not Caroline Street but 30 Downshire Hill, Hampstead. Gerald had continued his vain attempt to find a house in Hampstead he could afford to purchase, but now his prayers had been answered in another way. Downshire Hill, situated at the lower end of Hampstead on the edge of the Heath, is one of the pleasantest streets in the area. Variegated Regency houses line both sides of the road 'in a setting of generous foliage' (Pevsner 1952: 197), and a stuccoed Palladian parish church, St John's, stands on the acute angle of an even more delightful road leading off Downshire Hill: Keats Grove, named after the poet's dwelling on its south side, Wentworth Place, still there today in its sylvan grounds (though minus the nightingale). Aunt Lily, who was Ernest Black's sister and Joy's closest emotional tie after Gerald and Mags, lived at 24 Keats Grove. It had been very important that she approve of Gerald before they got married; luckily she did, and he in turn found her 'this most remarkable & lovely character' (G. Finzi 1939). They lunched with her on the day of the wedding, and she must either have owned the house in Downshire Hill or found it for them to rent. With three storeys plus basement, on the north side of the street, it is part of a pleasant terrace though not one of the area's showpieces. Gerald, who could not bear people hearing him work at the piano, had a first- or second-floor studio 'soundproofed at vast expense – with seaweed or something' (Ferguson 1974–96). Now the Blisses, as well as Howard Ferguson and Harold Samuel, were a few hundred yards away across the same corner of common that Keats would have traversed to visit Leigh Hunt. Hampstead, where Constable had painted, died and is buried, was after all still the best place for uninstitutionalised artists, if they could afford it, though the less well-off tended to live further out on the Northern Line at Golders Green and Finchley, like William Busch and Rubbra. The only problem with Hampstead was that the Heath remained the destination of the great unwashed every Bank Holiday, but Finzi was happy to report that his first one there passed without incident – 'no one used our front garden as a lavatory' (19340403/04).

Joy took up sculpture and went to study for a term, presumably in the new year, with John Skeaping at the Central School of Art and Design. He 'worked direct in his material' and she 'wanted to learn about tools and techniques that were necessary' whilst 'feeling shape beneath my hand' (J. Finzi 1987a). Her first work was a head of Horace, Mags's friend; her second, begun on 27 January 1934, one of Howard Ferguson that took about twelve sittings at Downshire Hill and was not completed in plaster until the following year. (It was then cast in cadmium in 1936.)

By April, Joy was six months into her first pregnancy and they retreated to the country while retaining occupancy of the Downshire Hill house. Once again Finzi was following Bliss's example, for Bliss was having a country house built on the Wiltshire–Somerset–Dorset border. The Finzis settled at the other end of Wiltshire, in Aldbourne, through which Gerald had rambled barely a week before his marriage – a large, attractive village, complete with green, pond and interesting mediaeval church, between Swindon and Hungerford. Aldbourne is in an exhilarating and idyllic position, for it nestles in a high, dry valley on the Marlborough Downs, rich in their prehistoric antiquities, and is quite isolated despite being on a main road. The Finzis bought a stylish and substantial early nineteenth-century house with large grounds, called Beech Knoll. This was an interim measure while they looked around for a permanent house or site – for Joy had persuaded Gerald to turn his back on the London rat race – and saved the bulk of their capital for it. Clearly they had not yet restricted their options to the area around Newbury and Hungerford, for Steuart Wilson interested them in a house at Knockholt on the North Downs at the highest point of Kent and, as we have seen, there was some question of moving back to the Cotswolds.

Finzi certainly wanted a high, open position, however, as Joy noted in her journal, quoting his conversation:

'I realised why hollows are never satisfactory. You must be in high country or in flat country to fully see the stars & the whole arc of the sky. Otherwise it's like being in a bucket.'

G has always had a touch of claustrophobia, which he thinks is very probably due to being shut up in a cupboard as a child – frequently – He doesn't know why. 'This may account for my love of East Anglia, the fen country – Wiltshire downs & the edge of the Cotswolds, & for my dislike of the inside of the Cotswold – & the high hedges & small hills of Devonshire. The lack of spaciousness'. (J. Finzi 19371002)

Altitude was also supposed to suit Joy's asthma, though late in life she denied Gerald's claim that this had been a factor in purchasing the Ashmansworth site – 'Oh, well, maybe GF pretended that was the reason,' Christopher Finzi commented (1990–96).

The Downs had been William Cobbett's ideal landscape, though when he took one of his 'rural rides' through Aldbourne in October 1826, finding it 'manifestly, once a large town' with a church 'as big *as three of that of Kensington*' but now somewhat depopulated, though still with a market, he admitted that its high and dry approaches were 'too naked' to please even him. He added, nevertheless: 'I love *the downs* so much, that, if I had *to choose*, I would live even here, and especially I would *farm* here, rather than ... in the vale of Gloucester, of Worcester, or of Evesham' (Woodcock 1967: 411).

Finzi, too, loved the chalk downlands above all other landscapes. They were Hardy's terrain, after all, as well as Cobbett's, and they extend right across Wessex – the long walk from Dorchester to Ashmansworth was nearly all on the chalk. With their ancient ridge-ways, thankfully unadopted as modern roads, and almost complete absence of settlement between the pretty and hospitable villages, they make for perfect, invigorating walking in creative solitude, undisturbed by people or obstacles: a plateau of broad spans, clean lines and measurable spaces. It is like striding across an empty sheet of paper. Finzi could maintain a brisk, purposeful pace in such countryside, which was rapidly becoming, above all in poster advertising, the symbol of a clean Englishness worth fighting for (see Howkins 1986). He thought nothing of covering eighteen miles in a day (19380217a), alone or with an intrepid visitor, and was thoroughly evangelical about it. 'I am incredibly proud of this and expect to be congratulated heartily,' Trudy Bliss told him when she first managed a similar distance (19290808?). In fact he could walk up to thirty.

Finzi must have been very happy spending the first years of his marriage at Aldbourne. He and Joy began to spread themselves and relax into the country lifestyle that would be theirs thenceforward, still going up to London for concerts, opera and professional purposes, but also having friends and parties of friends to stay for days, weekends or even weeks. That they now had means was evident, for they employed four or five domestics and seem to have maintained the Downshire Hill house as well as Beech Knoll, though only until mid-1935. (After this Gerald would stay with Ferguson when in London and Joy with Aunt Lily in Keats Grove, not necessarily at the same time, for they gave each other personal space – as we should say today – and retained independent interests, though they also did a lot of things together.) They shared a car (of sorts), and were on the telephone for the first time at Downshire Hill and at Aldbourne. They began to raise a family. Gerald developed a keen interest in gardening, particularly fruit-growing; and, as we shall see, he began editing Ivor Gurney's music, a task that kept him away from composition for a good deal of 1937, and spending increasing amounts of 'research' time on poetry and musicology, with the help of his rapidly growing library and in critical exchange with friends and colleagues, particularly the amateur poet Toty de Navarro. He was keen to encourage Joy's creativity, 'and drove her to do most of what she did'; he had to, for she was a reluctant genius ('I hate it,' she told Tony Scott). But Gerald's own impetuous artistic impulse was so deeply ingrained that Joy's inevitably took second place: Christopher Finzi recalls his father 'once locking her in the studio so as to make her get on with her carving, only to dash up half an hour later to ask her to type a letter for him' (1992: 8). She enjoyed ministering to his needs, and when he was in London for the première of Vaughan Williams's Fourth Symphony in April 1935 he returned home to find that Joy had spent two days arranging and cleaning all his books for him in the attic at Aldbourne, in spite of her asthma; but Howard Ferguson felt that she was over-protective and neglected her own career in the process.

He had found his personal style as a composer and could afford, intellectually and economically, to let it fertilise works at its own pace; yet he had compositional ambitions that would test his powers considerably further, and it is surely this aspect of his make-up that accounts above all for what can only be called his artistic demon. So many obstacles had beset him and would continue to do so: lack of family grounding in and support for an artistic career; lack of early technical aptitude as a musician and social aptitude as a student, and an overriding creative slowness resulting from them; the pressures of cultural assimilation in a disintegrating world order as the 1930s wore on; the massive and tragic disruption of World War II; and to cap them all, his truncated life expectancy in the 1950s. Yet beyond all these, and in a sense making them irrelevant, he was continually driven to accomplish more than he had yet learnt how to do, and to pursue interests and conserve knowledge in broader spheres and wider arcs than time and circumstances really permitted. Life simply offered too much: for him, accomplishment could never catch up with possibility, and he knew it. This was both his joy and his despair, and surely no further explanation is needed for both the great vitality and underlying pessimism, for it all followed once his character had first been set in motion. Ferguson describes how 'anyone who met Finzi personally will remember his bubbling sense of fun, his humour and his electric nervous energy. As I picture him in conversation he is always striding restlessly about the room, never seated at rest.' He adds, 'Fewer will know that beneath this incisive, buoyant exterior lay a deep and fundamental pessimism.' He astutely couches this in terms of Finzi's own bass-dominated music, 'his haunted sense . . . that there would never be sufficient time for the completion of what he had it in him to write,' a thought that 'ran constantly in his mind, like a ground-bass to his whole existence' (1957a: 134). Others are similarly constituted: he was an artistic type. But few showed or expressed the type so acutely.

This is the key to his beautiful, melancholy setting of 'Proud songsters' – as if the sudden great discovery of his own voice, a gift forged, like the song of the thrushes, finches and nightingales, out of nothing but 'particles of grain, / And earth, and air and rain', is both a marvel and a sadness, for as it has come so it will go, perfect only for the moment, which passes unnoticed, before driving with a sad, continual throb towards new possibilities and uncertainties. There will always be the next work, the dissolution of achievement even before its moments have been savoured – 'Where went by their pleasure, then?/I, alas, perceived not when.' It is the Faustian doom, if expressed in parochial, pastoral terms. The birds and their song are but part of Nature's cyclic process. So is creativity. It never settles, never rests, enjoys itself only in what it must do next. Even the delay in moving on, in finishing something, is because all that will happen then is that another vast door will open. No wonder Finzi enjoyed *Bluebeard's Castle*!

Perhaps even more potently than in 'Proud songsters', this all seems to be summed up in a Hardy setting composed in April 1936, just at the point of his first obvious success (with the publication of the oboe Interlude) but not published until after Finzi's death: 'In years defaced'. This gets us to the heart of him and may well be thought his greatest song. It is not so because he mirrors Hardy's structure and argument, for on the surface he does not, reversing Hardy's emotional perspective between the first two stanzas. Hardy, rather as in 'Where the picnic was', moves from light to dark, from the spark, the kindling of memory as emblem of past passion in the first stanza to the blown ash, as it were, of the cold present in the second: as another of his 'Emma' poems it commemorates the death of love in a diminishing perspective of two 'after' stanzas to one 'before' – itself highly congruent with Finzi's typical formal perspectives. The difference from 'Where the picnic was', however, resides in the opening of a deeper layer of emotional landscape, in which personal love is subsumed in Nature's continuity; and this is where Finzi gets the 'structure of feeling', as Raymond Williams (1973) would put it, exactly right. The poem has not quite that same structure as another of which it is inevitably reminiscent, 'In time of "The breaking of nations"', for after a central stanza in which it seems to be preparing for a comparable philosophy of cyclic natural process as triumph over human striving and desire, it actually says the opposite: that that one moment of love in that very precise place will never be equalled and will therefore always retain its identity through its uniqueness: somehow it will have changed the world for ever, though it can never be recaptured. Like all moments, it is something utterly lost before ever grasped (the couple were scared and hoping for the impossible rather than enjoying it), yet even the grass will never grow in quite the same way again because of their impression on the knoll.

Finzi's wonderful trope into the second stanza, transforming minor into relative major, the 'guilty', passionate, historical or goal-directed desire of 'human' chromatic tonality into the timeless innocence of Nature's modal diatonicism – one is tempted even to say from Finzi's Jewish past into his English future – catches perfectly this catharsis, the recognition of Nature's ability to receive, to transmute and assimilate human impressions and destinies, and the song sets its stamp on it when Nature herself sings, in the 'faery sound' of the unforgettable phrase (actually borrowed from Vaughan Williams's *Sea Symphony*) cunningly used by the composer's posthumous editors for the title of the whole set of songs of which it forms the core, *Till Earth Outwears*. Yet however one chooses to interpret Hardy's natural philosophy and Finzi's view of it, it is the musical technique that makes the song cohere, and that is perfect and unique: unique, because as with most of Finzi's songs it disregards formal orthodoxies and blueprints; perfect, because once again he develops an organism solely through transforming a motif with consummate skill and feeling. The motif is the two-quaver/crotchet one, initially on the scale degrees $\hat{2}$ $\hat{1}$ $\hat{5}$ at the words 'years defaced', and its progressive transformations, highly Brahmsian in their developing variation, carry it through all the coloured and variegated tissue of the song until by the end it has replicated itself some forty times. Especially notable ploys are how it points, weights and reifies the text, especially in the first stanza – at the words 'Two sat here', 'transport-tossed', 'wilted world', 'nothing of', 'momently' and 'could not be'; how it uses the long piano trope for converting itself into one of Finzi's clock chimes for the opening of the second stanza; and how it spins itself into a motoric, scalar continuum for the 'gust and gale' before changing back again, after another accompanimental trope, into a more discrete shape, but still a more flowing one for the suggestion of the 'faery sound' in the piano's countermelody to the 'lonely shepherd souls' – an afterthought, as a surviving sketch (Sketchbook O: r17) shows. These techniques make the intimacy of this song so acute that one cannot avoid seeing in it a memorial to his own life and its love, happiness and transience, if one knows about the composer's idyllic marriage, and about Aldbourne and its four prehistoric tumuli a mile away up a track onto the downs, to which Joy and Gerald would walk, sitting on the first, which they called their own, even if today the 'faery sound' of their passing has to compete with the hum of the M4, thrusting through the grandeur of the chalk barely a further mile away.

Another song that can be read as a memorial to the Aldbourne years is 'On parent knees', composed in 1935 shortly after Gerald had become a father. It is a tiny, sixteen-bar setting of an epigram translated from the Arabic (whether by the great eighteenth-century Orientalist William Jones or his younger contemporary the poet Samuel Rogers is the subject of a learned footnote by Finzi himself). The epigram's reversed terms around a central caesura – the baby crying while onlookers smile, the dying man smiling while onlookers weep – are nicely matched in the song's single strophe, its own caesura bringing coloured harmonic release as a counterpoise to plain diatonicism elsewhere, though the motif woven through the fabric rather as in 'In years defaced' does occasion a little additional harmonic shading in the reflective prelude and epilogue. Joy later stated (1982) that 'On parent knees' was composed for David and Rachel Willcocks when their first child was born, but that can only have applied to a postwar revision.

Both the Finzis' sons were born while they lived at Aldbourne, Christopher – who soon became known as Kiffer (spelt 'Cipher' by the organ-builder Tony Scott) – on 12 July 1934, Nigel on 9 August 1936, though Joy returned to Hampstead and Aunt Lily for both confinements, at a period when the husband would not have been let anywhere near the *accouchement*. With no further hazards than the usual whooping cough and measles, they grew into healthy, delightful and extrovert boys, if wild and undisciplined. 'I loved the little boys bringing themselves up,' Winifred Blow commented when she visited Ashmansworth after her husband's death [1940/411029?]). *Dies natalis* (the phrase signifies a saint's anniversary) may have been a thank-offering for the wonder of infancy embodied in Christopher, but he was no angel, and Ursula Vaughan Williams claims later to have been the only person ever to smack the boys, when they were fighting on a Cornish precipice. On another occasion Christopher petrified his mother by running around the edge of the parapet on the tower of Gloucester Cathedral. Both boys were musically groomed from an early age (Christopher on the cello, Nigel on the violin) and soon became the very symbol of Joy's and Gerald's environmental security and nurture: for how many other mid-twentieth-century English composers can one think of with sons (daughters still did not really count)? Admittedly there was always domestic help on hand (nanny, cook, gardener), at least until war economics took over, and Gerald dreaded family holidays and wriggled out of them whenever he could; but it was an enviable, thriving family until sundered by his death. Both sons gave eloquent and moving addresses at Joy Finzi's memorial concert in September 1991, Christopher's paying tribute to his parents' marriage as a heaven on earth, one which, though doubtless not without its share of tensions, only ever produced one major eruption that he could recall, when 'Dad had tried to paint the tops of some jars with silver paint while Joy was in Newbury. She came back to find far more paint on everything in the house other than the lids and was so angry that she picked up the garden shears, rushed out, and started chopping off the tops of his precious apple trees with furious vigour' (1992: 7). Happy indeed is the family that has weathered one or two such incidents and incorporates them into its lore.

Life during the five years at Aldbourne was relatively uneventful, though it was certainly not secluded, for Gerald, sometimes with Joy, continued his visits to London for concerts and operas, staying in town for a night or two, sometimes for nearly a week, increasingly for performances of his own works and especially, whilst lodging with him, for 'field days' with Ferguson about their compositions – they proofread each other's works for the rest of their lives, and Finzi always consulted Ferguson about creative and editorial details, occasionally also asking Vaughan Williams about some trick of the trade. Ferguson, always the more practical musician of the two, never quite ceased to have to prop up Finzi's 'acute uncertainty over matters of detail ... not only ... between ... slightly different versions of a phrase, but in all questions of articulation and dynamics':

With the latter he tended to solve the difficulty by leaving out such indications altogether, until it was pointed out to him that this did not make the life of the performer any easier. He would then agree, rather reluctantly, to a *piano* here and a *forte* there, and an occasional slur to show the beginning and end of a phrase, adding under his breath that the performer, if he were any sort of a musician, would instinctively do it like that anyway. (Ferguson 1957a: 132–3)

– though he acknowledges that such problems 'began to vanish miraculously' when Finzi started conducting his own orchestra in the 1940s.

Trips and holidays during the Aldbourne period included further festival visits, not just to the Three Choirs but to Glyndebourne, Boughton operas (*The Ever Young* and *The Lily Maid*) in Bath and London and Shaw's *The Simpleton of the Unexpected Isles* in Malvern, a seaside holiday at Tyneham in Dorset with the Sumsions and their children in 1938 (when John Sumsion junior disgraced himself on a visit to Hardy's birthplace by asking, 'Where's Laurel's birthplace?'), and precious time spent on their own as a couple. In view of late twentieth-century domestic norms it comes as something of a shock to realise that Gerald was first discovering Joy's culinary talents on a Cornish cottage holiday in February 1936 (she also discovered his, but put an embargo on them after his sardine dish repeated). The following year Gerald accompanied Joy back to the Aran Isles, which must have really taken him out of himself, judging from the description he wrote Ferguson:

In case you imagine that the 6 ft Islanders have slaughtered me, I thought I'd let you know that I'm quite safe: in fact, getting on very well & happily here. Of course, it's a great help that Joy is still remembered with admiration, & so, perhaps, I get a share of reflected glory! 'It's a fine woman you have' I'm told. And I can hardly disagree. They really are a remarkable lot – especially on Middle Island, where practically no English is spoken & life is really as primitive (& priest-ridden) as it might be in what the missionaries call 'darkest Africa'. Physically the men are mostly superb (except for teeth, which are deplorable) and some of the women are incredibly lovely. And it's all done on bread, potatoes, tea & occasional fish. There's no longer any opening for fishing & kelp and no living of any sort. In this way, I think the Film gave a pretty good idea of the hardness of the life (except for humbug of the whale-hunting) but what no-one wd realise from the film is the laughter, humour & dancing. It's rather wonderful to go into a cottage & find it quite a normal procedure for a melodeon or gramophone to start up & a young couple stand up in the middle of the room & dance a jig, reel or hornpipe. And marvellously they dance, too. As usual, the priest is the villain of the piece & a good many of them are very much under his thumb, though he hasn't yet succeeded in stamping out this wonderfully innocent pastime, as he's trying hard to. I say innocent, because their morals are really remarkable. Not a marriage for two years on the Islands, so great is the poverty & the impossibility of expansion, yet there haven't been more than 2 bastard children in 40 years (one of them was strangled at birth, I gather). One might imagine that they know too much, but according to Pa Mullen, drunk or sober you cd trust a man with a woman 'even if you put them in the same bed'.

Another great dancing sight is to see the crowd that gathers on a Sunday night at dusk (it is still dusk here at 11.0) when they dance on the 'slip' next to the quay. The nailed boots, a score of them, on the cement floor, make a wonderful 'swish' which puts the clip & the clop of 'Tarantella' in the shade.

I can't follow the movements of the sets, any more that I can follow a jig or a reel, but they dance with a great precision & rhythm. (19370530)

'Pa Mullen' was the father of the young Barbara Mullen, who became famous as a dancer and actress. Faber had just published her early book about growing up in America (without her father) and the Finzis found them a remarkable pair, even if when they subsequently stayed at Aldbourne over New Year Gerald told Ferguson that having to converse with the house guests over three meals every day made him feel 'murderous' (19380101a), though he liked them enormously.

Other friends visiting Aldbourne besides Ferguson himself included the Vaughan Williamses, William and Sheila Busch, the Rubbras, Rann Hokanson (a dashing young American pianist, protégé of Harold Samuel and friend of Ferguson), and Cedric Thorpe Davie, later with his first wife Bruno on their honeymoon, for which Finzi fixed them up in a hotel in the next village. Edmund and Antoinette Rubbra moved to the country in the same year as the Finzis, settling in a quiet Chiltern valley, Speen Bottom, too far away for frequent contact but equally idyllic and still more productive where the composer was concerned: there he began his astonishingly fluent succession of symphonies and, in parallel with the Finzis, acquired two sons, Francis and Benedict (the former adopted). Thorpe Davie soon graduated from being somewhat breezily treated as a student by Gerald – they had met in London through Ferguson – to becoming a close friend of the family, his racy sense of humour delighted in (and matched) by both Gerald and Joy. Gerald was not convinced by his creativity, however; 'I think what you feel about the "something bound up with his whole character" which will prevent him being a real composer,' he wrote to Ferguson, 'is that his nature lacks the upper & lower notes of the scale.' He felt that the urge would recede, 'its disappearance . . . made all the more easy & painless by his having a teaching routine' now that he was on the staff of the Scottish National Academy of Music (19370402?).

Another friend with whom Finzi could enjoy risqué exchanges, though in rather more of a male club atmosphere of unbridled wit, was José Maria de Navarro (1896–1979), known to everyone as Toty. Finzi met him through Ferguson. He was an archaeology don at Trinity College, Cambridge, and a closet poet (though Finzi did not know this initially), as fond of Hardy as Finzi and more than once the instigator of Finzi's later settings. The La Tène site in Switzerland and its Iron

Age Celts were his professional speciality, though he never completed his *magnum opus* on it for the British Academy, publishing only Volume I in 1972. He was also a highly cultivated amateur musician, and a bad enough pianist and singer that Finzi felt uninhibited about going through his own songs and playing duets with him – a relaxing and timely foil to the professional distance Ferguson could not but maintain. The family was wealthy, for Toty's grandfather built the 'El' in New York City, while his father, 'a cultivated New Yorker of Basque descent', had married 'the former Mary Anderson, an American actress of out-standing beauty who had retired from the stage at the early age of 28' (Ferguson and de Navarro 1980: 9) and who now, having banished Toty's father to Belgium, held court in some style at Court Farm, Broadway, in the Cotswolds, with 'occasional lapses into declamatory Tennyson' (J. Finzi 19370906) amid frequent soirées – or rather mati-nées – at which the best professional musicians performed and to which such as the Poet Laureate, Masefield, came. Ferguson had begun to get to know Navarro and his mother a decade or so before Finzi did, when he played at Broadway with Harold Samuel. The friendship really began for the Finzis when Toty invited them to join him for a long weekend's sailing and primitive living on Blakeney Point in Norfolk in July 1937 (duly retailed by Emmeline Morris as 'a *yachting cruise* with *Ivor Novello*! VW was bubbling over with it & wondering whether Joy had succumbed to his charms' [19370815]). Ferguson was there too, and so was Ann Bowes-Lyon, cousin of the (present) Queen Mother, who was just publishing her first and, as it turned out, only volume of poems with Faber. (Finzi's later opinion was that it was 'that pontifical, withering T. S. Eliot advice ... which stopped the flow' [19510530].) Toty was in love with her, but his mother and her family made difficul-ties, Ann had a severe breakdown, and he later married Dorothy Hoare, an English don at Newnham College, Cambridge. Gerald and Joy offered a fair bit of support as this emotional drama unfolded, and the participants were soon thoroughly integrated into their circle; Ann stayed at Ashmansworth, and Toty also got to know Hokanson and the Thorpe Davies, and while this was probably as much through Ferguson as through the Finzis, it was Gerald and Joy whose hospitality and solicitude tended to bring everyone together. Gerald's friendship meant a great deal to Toty, as did the Blakeney weekend that cemented it, after which he let him in on the 'secret' of his poetry. An inveterate reviser (and thus a bad influence on Finzi), he sents drafts and queries to Gerald and Joy, who typed, edited and commented on them, and Gerald began to respond by lodging copies of his music, especially the unpublished songs, with Navarro, who was a great fan and lost no opportunity of introducing his friends to it. Gerald's evangelical spirit would fain have reciprocated, but he felt that he was under a lifelong vow of silence concerning Toty's poetry and never managed to persuade him to try to publish it, his attempts probably causing Navarro to withdraw further into his shell.

Finzi had never lacked strong views and decisive reactions, but it is extraordinary nonetheless to see how quickly, with his marriage, his role changed in many respects from that of an individual needing reassurance and advice from others to that of one providing it. Robin Milford and Anthony Scott both swam permanently into his ken during the Aldbourne years, both lame ducks at the time, though in very different ways. Finzi had kept contact with Milford to the extent of going to a concert of his works in Epsom in 1931, but their correspondence only recommences, ten years on from their proximity at the Bach Choir concert, in May 1938. By this date Milford, yet another friend with whom he could share 'our Common faith' (19400910) – the love of Hardy – had been living for some years at Hermitage, north of Newbury, in a house he had built in the grounds of Downe House School, where he taught. Though two years younger than Finzi, he had on the face of it gone further as a composer, with an oratorio performed at the Three Choirs Festival in 1931, a Concerto Grosso conducted by Malcolm Sargent at Queen's Hall in 1937, appearances at the Leith Hill Festival and a fair corpus of works under his belt: he was very prolific. But he agonised over the charity from family, from friends, from the philanthropic Balfour Gardiner (who had earlier lived nearby at Ashampstead), even from himself, that this creative livelihood entailed. His problem is summed up by Diana McVeagh: 'He found life hard but composing easy' (1981b).

Milford's songs are closer to Warlock's idiom than to Finzi's, though they pale beside both, for he never really consolidated his style. Fluent, generally lightweight though with flashes of deep, even vehement feeling, and with many fresh if easy-going pastiche touches from the 1920s aesthetic of Holst and Vaughan Williams, one can appreciate the 'curious mixture of the innocent & sinister' that Finzi found in it (19401109; see, for instance, 'The pink frock') or bewail this as insipidity leavened with false modernity, the diversion or conscience of a lively critical intelligence rather than the determined integration of it. However, he did have a real gift for melody, and settings such as 'So sweet love seemed' and 'Cradle song' belong in the pantheon of English song. Finzi delighted in some of his compositions while realising that at bottom they were dispensable, which must have tempered the two men's common points – these including not just their settings of Hardy but of a number of other poets such as Bridges (both around 1933, Milford in a set of four solo songs), and Herbert ('The search' features in Milford's *A Prophet in the Land*).

Milford knew his limitations and let them depress still further his low self-esteem, exacerbated as it was by a family of high-flyers – his father was Sir Humphrey Milford, head of Oxford University Press, his cousin the poet Anne Ridler. His self-depreciatory tone and the spectre of family expectations are summed up in a letter to Finzi of June 1938, when he appears to have been recovering from one of his many breakdowns: 'As my mother said, very pertinently to me recently when I said I felt I was no good as a composer, "Well, you can't do anything else", & that is true' (19380620). He expanded on this in typical vein:

It is very nice of you to have rung up again & offered to come & see me. I think, however, I may go off to my parents for a couple of days, but don't know – I never can tell beforehand now what I shall do, or seldom.

I am better, in fact I've done a little composing again, but I don't think it's going to be much good. You see I have conceived a distaste for my previous music, & I think it has been a long time growing on me. Sometimes I like a thing of mine, & then I play through something like your 'Ditty', & I realise that that is the kind of music I should *like* to have written, or the VW 'Love bade me welcome'. All – yes, I think *all* my stuff sounds meretricious, not first-rate, artificial in some way or other, & often vulgar, or worse, common-place. Also often slightly mawkish.

I like music to be clean & fresh, as yours is (what I know of it) or Sibelius or the earlier VW, or Bach or Mozart. I have a spiritual affinity with Tschai-kovsky & I hate that.

Well, enough of this. The lesson to learn is SUBMIT, always, (as far as one is *personally* concerned) to everything. Only then can I achieve peace of mind, I believe; but then what is left? How can I teach, indeed what *can* I do? . . .

And then I become a washout for my family too, which is worst of all – However, I *am* better, & perhaps I shall achieve some sense of direction again by & by – though I am very, very confused at present.

Now, for heaven's sake don't answer this! I know you think well of my work, & it gives me pleasure to know this, though curiously enough it gives me little confidence if my *friends* like my work – I feel they are biased. This is terribly ungrateful, & I think a little warped; but there it is. Anyhow it will save you feeling you have or ought to write to me!

Of course Finzi did answer, as he always did, in an effort to instil a little more self-worth into Milford. But that could only be done with reference to his own certainties and securities, which probably made things worse. Neither of them could ever resist goading the other into replying, and the more Milford wallowed in his penitential Christianity, the more Finzi found himself asserting his agnostic rationalism. It was a psychological double-act that continued in their letters until Finzi's death. This is not to say that they were not genuinely good friends; but as friends can afford to, they did slightly despise each other, at root because of their opposite responses, over a whole lifetime, to how one asserts an identity in the face of family inheritance. Finzi's temperament could never see why Milford was beyond self-help; and Milford was sometimes scornful of Finzi's – indeed anybody's – bastioned self-importance: 'Gerald Finzi takes his L[ocal] D[efence] V[olunteers] terrifically seriously,' he wrote to Anne Ridler in 1940. 'He *hates* . . . anything that disturbs the peace of his excellently ordered composer's life . . . unassisted by teaching . . . nor even, so far as I can make out, any particular belief in God – though a terrific ideal of the Importance of the Artist' (Copley 1984: 58). Milford undoubtedly needed Finzi's friendship, but at his deepest level of mental torture it could not save him, and Finzi, for whom the only enemy to human achievement through effort was time, must have found this difficult to accept, though he also recognised when circumstances make even a close friend unreachable, as when the Milfords' five-year-old son Barnaby was killed in 1941. To the parents who had loved not wisely but too well by investing everything in him, Finzi could offer no philosophy, only pity, an impotence that must have shocked him:

Yes, it was a most terrible tragedy about little Barnaby Milford. Robin had been staying with us two nights before. We had done his lovely little Suite for Oboe & Strings at the Newbury Festival concert & he was in unusually good form, enjoying the concert & enjoying meeting some congenial musicians (a rare thing for him to enjoy). He returned home again with the intention of bicycling up at the weekend, to meet Tony Scott who, with Ruth & the children, was spending a rare weekend leave with us. Imagine the horror of hearing over the phone that they cdn't come 'as Barnaby has just been killed by a lorry'. Knowing what you feel about Nicholas, or what a good many parents feel about their children, it may sound strange when I say that we never knew any parents to whom a child meant more – in fact, absolutely everything. They were marvellously brave, but I think their anguish was everybody's anguish when, after the funeral, those two dear people left, indefinitely, for Oxford (with his father) without any plans for the future, without hope & with the whole focal point of their lives buried in a little remote country churchyard. There was *nothing* one wdn't have done to help, yet nothing that one cd do to comfort... the whole thing was, & is, terribly on our minds. (19410526, to Busch)

Milford's reference to Tchaikovsky's suicidal tendency in the letter quoted earlier was not flippant, any more than was his use of the word 'despair' in the well-known dedication of his song 'The colour', inscribed 'For Gerald Finzi, whose own settings of Hardy are at once my delight and my despair' when it was published in 1939. He attempted suicide more than once during his decades of correspondence with Finzi, though he outlived him for three years before succeeding in it.

Tony Scott, a friend of Milford as well as Finzi – he lived between Downe House and Thatcham – had difficulties of a different kind. Joy met him first, when she was playing his Fantasia for strings, among the violins of the Newbury Amateur Orchestral Union at a concert of works by local composers conducted by George Weldon, and took issue with the local disapproving music teacher as to its merits (see C. Finzi 1992: 13; J. Finzi 1984. Scott seems to have conflated two concerts in the former memoir). Scott turned out to be a cousin of Ann Bowes-Lyon, and soon he was having weekly private lessons with Gerald, who never charged for them and never found a way of forcing Scott to surmount his composer's block, despite setting him to work adding a third part to some of the Bach Two-Part Inventions, shutting him in the music room until he had written something, and generally exhorting him to 'buck up with the work' (193812–193902). The problem was that Scott was in awe of Gerald and preferred basking in his artistic company to producing something of his own, though at the same time he was not keen on Finzi's music (which scarcely featured in their discussions) and they argued about everything. It may also have been that Finzi was too generous with his ideas to be a really good teacher, though Scott, who was his only composition pupil, praised his 'catholic taste, essential for teaching,' that made him 'as happy analysing a song by Parry as a quartet by Bartók, and, in the work of his pupil . . . as much on the look-out for a little originality in some bars of two-part invention as in a gigantic symphony' (Bliss 1956–7: 6).

This friendship started early in 1938 when Scott was in his mid-twenties. Finzi probably found him dashing and certainly 'delightful', for he had 'arrived at music through a strange past of organ building & horse breeding!' (19380212a) and had married the daughter of his Harrow housemaster whose drainpipe he scaled for clandestine meetings with her while still at school. He had also studied with Howells at the RCM. Milford's view was that 'Ruth & Tony make me uneasy – she with her desperate anxiety not to lose her personal charms, & he with his obstinate determination to go his own way but uncertain of what that way is. But I like them, specially him' (19390420). Finzi's diagnosis, in response, was that Scott was 'really furious with himself the whole time' (19390423/30?). Ruth and Joy never quite got on (Joy's portrait of her shows this).

Neither Finzi nor Milford knew how to goad Tony Scott into productivity, and Milford mused further on 'poor old Tony & his beautiful music-room with vernal aspect, & ½ a fugue in ½ a year' (19390508b). Eventually, after surviving unscathed twenty-five RAF raids over Germany in the war as a navigator and bomb aimer, Scott did become more fluent, though he built little more than a local reputation, as organist of Lambourn Parish Church, despite some BBC exposure and a modest tally of publications. But it took him ten years to complete and publish his Prelude and Fugue in G minor for organ, dedicated to Finzi (who had written the subject and who performed a string version of the work with his orchestra in 1946) and even longer for a larger Introduction and Fugue for orchestra to see the light of day (see Burn 1984a: 31). Finzi did feel that the latter was worth waiting for, writing to Milford after a BBC try-out in 1947: 'It's full of Tony's twisted thwartings & repressions, but it does make magnificent music . . . There's an extra-ordinary power behind his music' (19480111).

Such collegiality between Finzi and his friends was the result of his having exchanged a metropolitan environment for a provincial one. Finzi had the choice of treating the Berkshire downs as a dormitory and remaining aloof; of not just accepting the convivial pleasures of a local artistic community but submitting to its standards, limitations and jeal-ousies; or of imposing his own will and vision on his surroundings, as

Britten would do at Aldeburgh with both dazzling results and breath-taking ruthlessness. In time, Finzi chose something of a middle way when he founded the Newbury String Players, largely amateur in their personnel and economics, yet professional in their approach to stan-dards and in their repertoire, stiffening and soloists. It was a highly successful solution. Meanwhile, now that he had found his own voice and the makings of a national reputation as a composer, and was settling into his preferred personal lifestyle, the friendships of such as Milford, Navarro and Scott suited him and Joy well enough as a corollary. They did not make demands he could not now resourcefully meet.

Interpersonal demands of a very different kind were taxing him sorely at this period, however: the totalitarian states' threat to civilisation and in particular the Nazis' persecution of the Jews. Finzi's fear and insecurity as a Jew was a largely or entirely unrecognised *cantus firmus*, to be discussed in the next chapter, but around it in 1938 he was constructing two lively counterpoints that can be dealt with now. One of them was his house, the other his musical output, which needed and was given a definite sense of direction after the publication of *Earth and Air and Rain* and the Interlude. 'No more songs,' Finzi wrote when he sent a score of the former to Vaughan Williams, who wondered 'what *is* it going to be[?]' and told him to 'remember what was said about Madame d'Arblay[:] that she must see that the works of art kept pace with the works of nature' (19361123). He had every intention of seeing that the works of art kept pace with the works of nature, for he was turning from songs and partsongs, in which he had honed his techniques of solo and choral vocal writing, to two compositions that would draw on those techniques to underpin musical transcendentalism on the broadest scale. This project entailed not only the completion of the Traherne cantata *Dies natalis* but the launch of his long-considered setting of Wordsworth's great 'Immortality' Ode; both works were to be for high voice and orchestra, with strings in the former and chorus and full orchestra in the latter. For the moment neither had a dead-line, and the size and scope of *Intimations* in particular meant that he left few markers as to its progress. Joy Finzi (1974) said that it had taken twenty-three years to write, which would date its beginnings to 1927, shortly after the early work on *Dies natalis*, though Finzi's own comment in a letter to Ian Davie was that it had 'simmered for about sixteen years' (19551014b). Joy also remembered Gerald suddenly singing 'And the Children are culling / On every side', in the car, around the time of their marriage. And it is worth noting that as early as September 1931, at Hundon, *Dies natalis* and *Intimations of Immortality* were being considered or sketched in tandem: at the same time as asking Kaye about Traherne's pronunciation (see Chapter 5, p. 125), he consulted Haines about Wordsworth's stress in the phrase 'shout round me'. One wonders whether at this stage he was considering a single *Bildungskantate* juxtaposing portions of both poets' texts, for which there was an exemplar in Walford Davies's Twenty-One Songs, published in 1931 and including a portion of the 'Immortality' Ode and various settings of other poets from his earlier cycle *The Long Journey*. (Nor should the Walford Davies precedent be forgotten in consideration of Finzi's determination to group songs into large sets.) Be that as it may, *Intimations* was well under way by the end of 1936, so that it is perhaps no accident if it occasionally sounds like Constant Lambert's *Summer's Last Will and Testament*, one of the few metropolitan English choral works of the 1930s by a member of Finzi's own generation; he had attended its première on 29 January, though he was not over-impressed. To this period belongs the famous 'bilge & bunkum' letter written to Ferguson after he had been taken bumptiously to task by Arthur Hutchings in the *Musical Times* (lxxvii [1936]: 1091) for setting Milton's sonnets:

. . . what a slating the two Milton Sonnets get! I don't mind the adverse criticism at all – it's quite impersonal & without animosity – but I do hate the bilge & bunkum about composers trying to 'add' to a poem: that a fine poem is complete in itself, & to set it is only to gild the lily, & so on. It's a sort of cliché which goes on being repeated (rather like the phrase 'but art is above national boundaries'). I rather expected it & expect it still more when the 'Intimations' is finished. But alas, composers can't rush into print, particularly where their own works are concerned – (though I do sometimes have a sneaking wish that editors wd ask for one's opinion!) Obviously a poem may be unsatisfactory in itself for setting, but that is a purely musical consideration – that it has no architectural possibilities; no broad vowels where climaxes shd be, & so on. But the first & last thing is that a composer is (presumably) moved by a poem & wishes to identify himself with it & to share it. Whether he is moved by a good or a bad poem is beside the question. John [Sumsion] hit the nail on the head the other day when we were going through a dreadful biblical cantata, which Armstrong Gibbs had sent him – Kapellmeister music of the worst sort, only brought up to date. John said 'He chose his text, it didn't choose him'. I dont think everyone realizes the difference between choosing a text & being chosen by one. (They shd see Pirandello's 'Six characters in search of an author'.) But what, to my mind, settles the whole argument is the fact that people will listen to songs sung in a foreign language, of which they don't understand a single word. Sing the Milton Sonnets to a foreigner & he has to judge them as music. This may be good, bad or indifferent, but it can't change its value according to the country in which its sung. (19361219)

He was saying the same thing to Busch over a year later, when he wrote to tell him 'I'm half way through my choral work (Ten. chorus & orchestra) & I think, & hope, it's going to be "not too bad". There are also odd movements here & there, two mvts towards the cantata for sop. & strings etc.' (19380214b). Then we hear of no more progress on *Intimations* until the late 1940s, while *Dies natalis* proceeded relatively smoothly to its completion, as we shall see.

Further evidence that Finzi felt he was settling down to his 'real' output after the oboe Interlude and *Earth and Air and Rain* can be found in his dedications, which, beyond the one Goossens had asked for, were more or less systematic. The only reason for composing the Prelude and Fugue for string trio, dedicated to R. O. Morris, in July 1938 seems to have been that it was the first in an intended series of appropriate tributes to his mentors and colleagues. A letter to Tony Scott in 1942 suggests that *Intimations of Immortality* was to have been his seventieth birthday offering to Vaughan Williams, for he was anticipating that, with *Let Us Garlands Bring* as its substitute, it would be 'A melancholy occasion for me as the work really intended for that event lies on the stocks, ½ finished & must so remain till the end of things' (19420414); this – with its delightfully broad variants of 'two thirds finished' and 'more than a 3rd done before the war' in other letters to friends (19420411, 19450915) – cannot refer to anything else, 'things' being the war, of course. In other words, the elderly Vaughan Williams and Morris needed their dedications first, while there was yet time. Bairstow presumably did not deserve one, and younger friends could wait. Having missed the boat, the *Intimations* dedication was then deflected to Adeline Vaughan Williams when it appeared in 1950 (she died the following year). Ferguson in due course received *For St Cecilia*, John Sumsion *In terra pax*, and John Russell the Romance for strings. Early works lay outside this scheme, as did the earlier song sets (including *Dies natalis* except insofar as it was associated with his son Christopher) and commissions, so it is not easy to see why Rubbra was given the dedication of the Milton Sonnets when they were published in 1936, unless it was as an acknowledgement of his comparable Spenser Sonnets of the previous year or in memory of the 1929 article. Nor is the absence of a dedication to Bliss explicable, unless he would have been the recipient of the symphony Finzi was planning at the time of his death. Joy seems to have been intimately associated with the Cello Concerto and this probably did not need public acknowledgement. One could speculate further, where Finzi's workshop of the late 1930s and early 1940s (up to the time of his call-up) is concerned: a string Serenade was on the stocks – that might have been for Bliss, originally – as was a Violin Sonata (with the Elegy as its second movement), probably for Sybil Eaton, who reappeared at Ashmansworth around the time of its gestation.

As for the house, the Ashmansworth site was found early in 1937. They had been looking for somewhere since 1935, and the idea of building their own house with Peter Harland as architect probably stemmed directly from their first visit to the Blisses at Pen Pits in May 1934. At that time, and while they stayed in a cottage *in situ* or even camped out, Harland, a close friend of the Blisses, was building them a 'suntrap' country house, modernist and ship-shape, on a thirty-acre woodland site that they had purchased, complete with mysterious ancient craters; there is a painting of the house by Bliss's friend Edward Wadsworth, done in 1936, and another of the pits themselves by Paul Nash in the Victoria and Albert Museum (see Bliss 1970: 102–4; Powers 1985). Harland (1900–73), whose wife Lisa became a director of the Ballet Rambert, had graduated from and taught at the Architectural Association and was predominantly neo-Georgian in sensibility (hospitals were his speciality), though he was fully conversant with modernism and handled it enthusiastically enough at Pen Pits. Like all architects he was also firm with and ambitious for his clients, and the Finzis would find themselves having to cut back drastically on his plans, just as the Blisses had to abandon their swimming pool, and Harland's idea of giving the house the plan of a grand piano, because of expense.

Harland visited the Finzis at Aldbourne in June 1935, though it is unclear where the housing question stood at that time. It appears that he first built a cottage for the Finzis' gardener William Sampson and his wife Doris, their cook, in the grounds of Beech Knoll. Ferguson, who was present at Harland's first visit, also remembers them pursuing a site in the Lambourn valley. Nothing further happened for some while, however, perhaps because they were having to save more money than they had anticipated, and in November 1936 Finzi told Ferguson that they did not expect to purchase a house or a site for another year or so.

Two or three months later, however, he and Joy went to view a sixteen-acre farm that was for sale on high ground in North Hampshire, 700 feet above sea level on the chalk and with a view all the way to the south coast. This was Church Farm, Ashmansworth, seven miles south of Newbury on the old road to Andover that had long before been by-passed. Ashmansworth village is more elevated still, and lies at nearly 800 feet on a ridge leading up to the highest point of the British chalk, Walbury Hill near Combe Gibbet. If the chalk is England's torso, this is its very bosom (though a northerner would say something similar about the Pennines). Cobbett knew the area well, and after the treacherous descent of a chalk hanger elsewhere in Hampshire he 'bid my man, when he should go back to Uphusband, tell the people there, that *Ashmansworth Lane* is not the worst piece of road in the world' (Woodcock 1967: 84), notwithstanding that he loved the place. He must even have known Church Farm with its Regency farmhouse, for he referred to 'the astonishing depth that they have to go for the water. At Ashmansworth, they go to a depth of more than *three hundred feet*' (ibid.: 210), and there is indeed a well of that depth in the Finzis' garden, the only one in the neighbourhood.

'The first time we came to Ashmansworth, up the narrow climbing lane from a warm green valley,' Joy Finzi wrote in her journal, 'Blue shadows lay with an intensity on snow, that I have only seen in Switzerland. The ash trees made strong pattern against dark sunny sky. George Bissill with berry [*sic*] on head, gumboots & a sketch block, tramping about' (J. Finzi 19371002). Bissill lived next door to the gardener's cottage that went with the site, and they stopped to ask him the way to Church Farm. He had been a coal miner, and they found that he was an unexpectedly good artist when shortly afterwards they went to see an exhibition of his at the Léger Galleries in London. Although purchase of the site proved complicated, it was theirs by July and they took possession in September. Harland had visited it and they decided not to try to save the ruinous farmhouse. By October they were 'in great trepidation' about the size and risks of the commission and struggling with Harland as to what they wanted and could afford. 'He [being] a personal friend partly creates this difficulty,' Joy acknowledged (ibid.). Her poetic approach as opposed to his technical one ('it will be a quiet place, with a wide sky, to think in. Quietness sounds there, & the earth has hospitality'), sounding like nothing so much as the Lake Isle of Innisfree, may not have helped matters, though they differed over details too, holding out for a steep pitched roof – a flat one would have been disastrous in the exposed position – and no horizontal glazing bars and thus severing two of the most obvious links with modernism that the house might have had.

Harold Samuel had died, following a heart attack, in January 1937, only months after he and Ferguson had moved into their Willoughby Road house in Hampstead. Ferguson had no desire to stay there after Samuel's death, and by 1938 had sold up and needed a place to live while he considered his options. Not surprisingly, the Finzis tried to persuade him to follow their lead and buy a site at Ashmansworth, and he did pursue one for some months while they let him live in their gardener's cottage, which by April had been rebuilt. He stayed there until November, by which time he had decided to move back to London, managing to buy a fine house in Hampstead when the market plummeted after the Munich crisis. Thus Ferguson and Finzi never lived at Ashmansworth at the same time.

Meanwhile, demolition of Church Farm and renovation of one thatched barn and some of the other outbuildings began in January 1938, and soon Gerald was finding his almost daily visits from Aldbourne, eighteen miles away along tiny country lanes, 'a great distraction. Of course it's going to be well worth while & we're really enjoying it all tremendously,' he wrote to Busch, 'But I must admit that this perpetual poring over plans & rushing up to the site to see about demolishing some ruined barn, or seeing whether a wall shld be 6 inches higher or not, is not easy to combine with composition!' (19380214b). Gerald photographed every stage of the operation. Cost was still a major headache, and Harland's plans had to be cut back again and again. They were not agreed until early May, when there was a three-month respite before construction began on 8 August. The Finzis and their friends toured local brickyards and eventually chose 'warm multi-coloured bricks with some traditional "flared" blues from Pine Wood Kilns, Hermitage' for the house (Powers 1985: 563), while they salvaged flints from the demolished buildings for a new perimeter wall – which upset the locals, who speculated that the strange couple must be nudists.

Harland was ill while the house was being built, and the Finzis had to do a great deal of the works supervision themselves. They secretly reorientated the pegging-out one evening so that it would not face due south, as Harland had insisted, and form an acute angle with the outbuildings. Harland never noticed the change, and 'it was a matter of enduring pride that there is only one crooked wall' (Popplewell 1995) – an endearing anecdote at this distance, but a risky thing to have done and a snub that would have enraged Gerald had his own profession been its target, given his 'feeling of sickness' when dilettantes, especially literary ones, trespassed on it (19410331).

Planting trees and then digging the foundations unearthed a wealth of ancient potsherds, and Gerald spent happy hours piecing some of them together into a large but incomplete vessel. Some Belgic (Romano–British) fragments were found, but one of Navarro's colleagues pronounced the pot 'late Bilge Period (Mediaeval)' (19380617), a verdict confirmed by Harold Peake of the Newbury Museum, a well-known scholar who was rather less excited about it than Gerald and spurned his offer of it, or rather its conditions of further reconstruction and permanent exhibition, since they were short of space and already had a 'still larger and quite perfect specimen' (19400413). Nevertheless, the finds fuelled Gerald's ideas about racial identity and assimilation: 'When this pot was made, 2 or 3000 years ago, there was not a single person in the whole of the country, who could consider any present day inhabitant other than an alien,' Joy quoted in her journal – 'We should not have one word in common and hardly any so called racial characteristics' (J. Finzi 19390202). He and Joy reciprocated by burying a small collection of artefacts, as was the fashion at the time, under the porch, as Gerald explained to Navarro:

I did my duty to future holders of your Cambridge office by digging a hole beneath the foundations & putting in a large sealed glass bottle, well bricked around, & in it a few coins in current use. I shd have liked to have given a few things representative of our times (for I'll never consider pins, hairpins, beads, representative of any times!) but when one came to think about it, it became so impossible that all I did was to copy out on the toughest paper I cd find, a few poems by Hardy, Housman, Blunden, Bridges & others, which is very nice for the bottle, even if the future never finds them! (19380830)

By 30 August the building had reached the damp course; when Chamberlain was in Munich trying to construct an edifice of European peace it had reached the roof-line; the exterior was more or less complete by November, when Harland first visited it, and in good time for a very snowy Christmas; the removal started in earnest in mid-February with the arrival of Mags and her horse box; and they moved in on Wednesday, 8 March 1939, in fine weather, to the address that would last 'for the rest of our lives, I hope' (19390305a) and to which a telegram from Howard and a letter of good wishes from Harland were sent. It was chaos at first –

we're still in a really bloody muddle, un-curtained, without rugs, or half the furniture we need . . . So at the moment we're cluttered up with papers that have no place for them. The problems are 'where shall this inkpot go?' 'Oh, put it on the floor until the desk comes next month'. 'Here's a box of drawing pins & a 60 watt bulb; where do they go?' 'Oh, put the drawing pins on the window sill until - - - - - and the bulb must wait until the wall-plug has been moved to its right position' etc etc . . . What will be the garden looks like a devastated Flanders village. (19390403b)

– but they never regretted it for a moment, even with the debt still hanging over them, and Gerald told Navarro that 'The mistakes have been few & easily rectifiable – if not now, then in the future when & if we can afford it' (ibid.).

'This is what I have always longed for & now that it is ours we must work hard to justify it,' he said to Joy (J. Finzi 19390316). Gerald and Joy were supremely happy in their house, and Church Farm, like Blow's Hilles before it, has rightly become a byword for artistic hospitality and the open hearth of English yeomanly mythology (and they never locked the door). 'You can do, say, or think anything you like in that house,' Jean Stewart told Ruth Dyson. Not that Gerald was always at the centre of things: when Joy organised country dancing on the lawn, even with the Enborne morris dancers, he would remain firmly in his music room. The Ashmansworth tradition has continued posthumously, with frequent Finzi Trust Friends meetings there and, for an apogee, Christopher and Hilary Finzi's munificence at the posthumous Joy Finzi celebration in September 1991, when a *Times* announcement of the event, with its buffet lunch in a marquee on the lawn, simply read 'all welcome'. But it cannot honestly be said that the house itself lives up to its role stylistically, however kind Powers is to it, and however 'light, white, very new and modern, with . . . summer sun streaming through a vast expanse of window' it felt in its initial surroundings, as a Downe House schoolgirl reminisced, probably in the early 1940s (anon n.d.).

The entrance side, on the north, with its horizontal row of landing windows, actually holds the greater visual interest; the garden front, now in any case obscured behind a conservatory, is bland and looks all too much like that of an extended council house, despite the ghost of a Cotswolds reference in the proportions and mullions of the windows. The Arts and Crafts latched front door, now enclosed in a porch, accords ill with both its heavy neo-Georgian surround (which Joy disliked because she thought it made the house look like a bank) and the basic language of brick walls and metal windows elsewhere. There seems to be a poverty of detail without modernism's dynamic lines and masses to compensate. Perhaps Harland was the wrong architect for these firm customers and compromise neutralised their conflicting ideas.

Nevertheless, it was and still is a very comfortable and, with its views, exciting house to live in, even though the original central heating proved too expensive to run and had to be taken out, the soundproofing was not entirely successful and the original insulation was slight (and wartime austerities must have made it very cold at times). As Powers points out (op. cit.: 562), Gerald and Joy went for modern fittings and started afresh with new, albeit vernacular, furniture, commissioned from 'one of Ernest Gimson's successors, Harry Daroll' after they had had a sale at Beech Knoll. One of the most attractive features is the hall and dining-room flooring, in blue-black tiles that were Joy's discovery. The house has been added to and altered over the years, but not violated. It looks larger than it is, for it is only one room deep, essentially on the traditional 'E' plan but with porch and main staircase as part of an east-wing service mass and with the west wing projecting on the garden rather than the courtyard side. Without this west wing the main layout would be similar to that of Pen Pits. Gerald's ever more impressive English poetry collection was housed in the spacious room on the ground floor of the west wing which in 1974 was more or less recreated, with its contents, as the Finzi Book Room in Reading University Library. Above it was his music room, and the two are isolated from the rest of the house by double doors and interconnected by their own staircase under which, indicatively, he had a secret hiding cupboard built for himself. The living room and main bedroom over it form the centre of the house, with transverse hall and landing alongside. The guest bedroom, over the dining room and an open sun porch (later closed in) at the south-east corner, commands the best views, and at the north-east extremity, as far away as possible from the shrine of Art, were placed the lesser altars of cooking and child-rearing in the form of kitchen below and nursery above, though this end of the house was eventually enlarged by Christopher (who literally built it himself) into a separate dwelling for his daughter Clare and her family. A third bedroom, plus service and utility quarters downstairs, allowed for one or two live-in domestics, whose role immediately merged with that of refugees and evacuees – Rubbra was probably not the only one to discover that refugees solved the servant problem – until the end of the war, which put a permanent stop to both. Joy's studio was among the outbuildings, in a loft above the garages.

The great sadness and frustration for both Gerald and Joy as they settled into Church Farm was that the gathering war clouds made a productive compositional routine psychologically impossible. But somehow or other *Dies natalis* was completed there under this threat, and it is time to retrace Finzi's output leading up to it.

'No more songs' could not be taken literally when Finzi was still as susceptible as ever to Hardy and had now conquered so much of his expressive and structural territory. He was excited by William Rutland's biography when it appeared in 1938, and in May of the same year looked in on the auction of Hardy's library in London, depressed that it would all go to dealers but putting a £3 reserve on Hardy's walking stick and having to pay an extravagant £9 for it. By August 1937 he had composed 'I look into my glass', and Rann Hokanson and Toty de Navarro went through it while they were staying at Aldbourne. One of his very finest Hardy songs, 'He abjures love', followed early in the new year, and four other Hardy settings for baritone appear to have been composed prior to that date: 'Amabel', 'Overlooking the river', 'Let me enjoy the earth' and 'I need not go'. McVeagh (1985) dates the last two 'before 1936' and 'Amabel' to 1932. Stylistic evidence would put them all in the early or mid-1930s, with their plain but relaxed diatonicism, roughly comparable with the constraints of the Bridges partsongs, though the vestigial touch of false relation at the end of 'Let me enjoy the earth' was initially built more firmly into the song, at the opening phrases of its first and last stanzas, which may take its gestation back as far as 1927, the date on Sketchbook G in which these two fragments appear (:r2). Whichever ones had been written by 1935 may well have been considered for inclusion in *Earth and Air and Rain* before it was reduced from twelve songs to ten (see p. 58).

Three of the songs are in E♭ major ('Let me enjoy the earth', its initial sketches in D major, was composed for baritone in E♭ but was later transposed by Finzi up a minor third for tenor). This is a key which Finzi seems to associate with a particular mellowness of sonority and figuration or with romance and memory, if one compares 'Amabel' with 'To Lizbie Browne', the Romance for strings with 'Romance' from the Five Bagatelles, and all these compositions with Vaughan Williams's 'Silent noon', whose opening chord and mood seem echoed particularly in the clarinet 'Romance' and whose kingcup fields reappear in 'Overlooking the river', taking both songs into triple time. Another anchor for style and sensibility in 'Overlooking the river' is the intimate, sustained keyboard polyphony of its opening, like that of a Bach allemande, especially in the second bar (ex. 7.1.a); this is Parry's chorale prelude idiom as utilised by Gurney in his song accompaniments, and it offers further evidence of Finzi relaxing into his romantic heritage in a way which he would not have allowed himself in the 1920s, and which pays further dividends, delightfully, in the *Fortspinnung* of the trope after stanza two of 'I need not go' (ex. 7.1.b).

EX. 7.1.a

EX. 7.1.b

The poem's structure in 'Overlooking the river' occasions a musical form for each of the first three stanzas in which the first two lines, firmly tonicised despite a lovely flat seventh in the first stanza, are repeated to the same music at the end, the middle two lines offering a midway pivot on the mediant. It is intriguing to see something of the same structure operating macrocosmically in 'Let me enjoy the earth', where the two middle stanzas have parallel music, again with a mediant half-close as pivot (in this case between them), and so do the outer two. In this latter case equivalence is signalled, as so often in Finzi, by little more than a head motif, and that is also the process by which those three stanzas in 'Overlooking the river' share not just the same form but the same music, though it is not the refrain lines but the middle ones where the parallel melody is pursued most exactly. It all contributes to the flux of form, in which melodic refrain and melodic discourse have to be kept in balance; but in both 'Overlooking the river' and 'I need not go' that balance is finally tipped, as in so many of Finzi's earlier Hardy settings, by the poet's open-ended consequent, involving a final stanza in which he distances himself from the framed vision by interrogating it or, in 'Overlooking the river', literally turning his back on it. The poem 'Overlooking the River Stour' has usually been taken to refer to Hardy's failing to notice his happiness with Emma while it was at its height in their two years at Sturminster Newton (Finzi was aware of this, as we have seen on p. 165); but Millgate's point (1985: 191–2) about Hardy's maid's unnoticed romantic melodrama at the end of that 'wet June' adds considerable punch to the *mise-en-scène* by ironically deflating its pastoralism. Finzi was not to know this, but he does reflect the nagging worry about 'the more behind my back' by harping so much on the mediant, the chord of G minor, not just in the three pivots within stanzas but with two larger ones, first as one of his accompanimental 'tropes' between stanzas two and three, then as a colon into the final, musically free-standing stanza, where it forms a kind of composed-out phrygian cadence in dropping by step to F, on which (minor) chord the song ends. Unlike 'Overlooking the river', 'I need not go' resolves its doubts after raising them more dramatically in a quasi-*recit.* opening to the final stanza, and he neatly tucks his opening tune in to the last half of the stanza, all the more effectively because Hardy at this point is still in rhetorical recitative mode with his 'me' repetitions. Finzi also makes the most of the three upward steps that form the song's binding motif by effortlessly fitting them to his last notes and the poem's last words (ex. 7.1.c); the paradoxical expression of passive acceptance ('suffer it so') through assertive upward scale degrees onto the dominant offers the perfect analogue to the fact that in the poem the lovers' fidelity is frictionless because the girl is in her grave!

'Amabel', although like 'Overlooking the River Stour' a poem of very specific personal reference (it is about Mrs Martin, the 'older woman' of Hardy's childhood), is more of a ballad portrait than an idyll, and so is Finzi's setting. Folky in its simple tune, it is very much in the Cecil Sharp/Stanford tradition in its accompaniment, whose expressive, contrapuntal and descriptive touches are probably the best offering Finzi ever made at that shrine – witness Amabel's 'knell', her 'step's mechanic ways', her chromatically sweet laugh, the beautifully broad, warm, sung 'strain' recalled by the poet (a touch of John Ireland here), the piano that 'weeps' sympathetically while the voice part creeps into its attic, and so on. Yet these illuminations are relaxed and personal, not doctrinaire, and in a review of a folksong publication perhaps written around the same time as 'Amabel', Finzi recognised that 'the attitude towards accompaniments has travelled a great way since the days when any note in the setting that was not in the tune was looked upon as a dangerous intruder' (1935). He knew all about variants in folk tunes, too, and sets about them as schematically as ever in his vocal melody. Each pair of the poem's eight parallel stanzas forms a musical strophe (encouraged by Hardy's *enjambement* of a thought and then a speech in the second half of the poem), its caesura accounting for four of the 'Amabel' refrains, all on the dominant note over a dominant or mediant chord. The other four refrains, like those in 'To

EX. 7.1.C

244

Lizbie Browne' and 'My spirit sang all day', ring the changes on other scale degrees and shape the song's overall harmonic argument: submediant, over a supertonic chord; mediant, *on* the mediant; supertonic, on the dominant; and finally dominant, prior to tonic closure. The first half of each strophe (i.e. for the odd-numbered stanzas) has the same melody each time, varied only by the rhythm of declamation; the second half is always different – it has to be, to arrive at the various refrain notes – though formal closure is suggested when stanza eight echoes stanza two.

The first three lines of strophic ballad melody in 'Amabel' are found again in the first four-line stanza of 'I look into my glass', but the point here is to dislocate the ballad framework. This happens in two ways. Firstly, after a mediant caesura has been reached at the end of the first stanza (as so often, pointed up by staccato quavers in the piano), the second half of the quadratic melody, for stanza two, is presented a step lower than expected. This has the effect of concluding it not in the relative minor (E minor) but in D minor, which in an odd sort of way accords with the song's introduction and its presentation of the opening melody as mixolydian D rather than on the dominant of G major. Yet this apparent consequent, in the second gesture of dislocation, proves to be in itself the antecedent of the real one, the poem's third and final stanza. Here the throbbing D becomes a dominant once more, so that the song ends in G minor. The song as a whole, therefore, operates ambiguously between unified and 'progressive' tonality – a composed-out drop of a fifth – and between different modal interpretations of a basic d to d^1 melodic ambit, a multiple perspective that accords well with Hardy's poetic one, in this, the last and one of the finest of his *Wessex Poems*, of the apparent closure of old age being opened out again by the 'throbbings of noontide' in the 'fragile frame at eve'. It is quite likely that Finzi arrived perforce at this unorthodox whole by stitching together disparate sketches, but that would not invalidate the result.

'I look into my glass' is not only formally shrewd but expressively rewarding, its chromatically passionate harmonies at the one end foiled by the vainly dispassionate ones at the other, in neoclassical equipoise (for the image of the mirror) and with something of the sixth-, second- and seventh-based sonorities of Britten or Tippett (ex. 7.1.d). But for even greater emotional richness in song and Finzi's finest encapsulation of Hardy's double time frame, of the tension between feeling that one has moved on irrevocably to something else and sensing that one may

EX. 7.1.d

later still be proved to be only circling, or rather spiralling, back to an anterior position on a larger radius, we must turn to 'He abjures love'. Here the ambiguity is built into the diction itself: is the poem's fourth word in the present or the past tense? If the former, then the first four stanzas are all antecedent, a review of the poet's life before and during love prior to the single melodramatic moment of love's banishment at the beginning of stanza five. If the latter, then he has *twice* attempted to put off love, once in the first stanza with its effect of 'hav[ing] no care' in stanza three, and again, after a second ensnarement in the second half of stanza three, in the last two stanzas of the poem. Hardy probably intended the former, but the latter interpretation adds a level of epic enrichment and is encouraged by half-hidden parallelisms and ambiguities in the prosody: the third and sixth stanzas begin similarly ('I was' / 'I speak') and both place 'But . . .' at the beginning of their fifth line, while it is the second and sixth stanzas that share a variant rhyme scheme (abbcaddc instead of abcdabcd).

Finzi picks up on all this. On one level, he casts his song as a very broad recitative/aria structure, the aria beginning with the marching bass at the start of stanza four. This, if you like, is the more 'innocent' interpretation of the younger man, who believes that he can turn his back on the past once and for all. But the irony of Hardy's sneaking parallels, the sense that one cannot escape the cycles of history, that you make your mistakes repeatedly – that, to borrow Finzi's own despairing quotation from his 1938 correspondence with Busch, 'what you were you are, what you are you shall always be': this demands his most powerful structural response yet, not just to Hardy but to any formal proposition; and it comes in the shape of sonata form, as a triumphant fulfilment of the possibilities first grasped in 'Summer schemes'. The first subject of his exposition, as rich and momentous in its succession of expressive ideas as Hardy's first two stanzas are in their single-sentence sweep, wings its way to the (double) dominant, C# minor, in a tonal flight that for him is unprecedented, its consequent the haunting, Brahmsian second subject of a loveless fate (ex. 7.1.e), itself with a mid-way caesura before Hardy's 'But . . .'. Stanza four constitutes both development of the first part of the first subject and a substitute for its recapitulation, which then proceeds, without the voice and greatly truncated, to a new transition to the second subject. At this point the 'aria' is simply inserted as an interlude before the second subject is recapitulated, as exactly as the situation allows, in the tonic. This double musical form is powerful, unique, deeply symbolic, and perhaps Finzi's first wholly puissant musical structure. It is a tribute to the strength and security of his creative instincts that he discovered it not through a musical exemplar but through a poet and his philosophy.

A few months later he had composed his one work whose whole point is musical exemplars: the Prelude and Fugue for string trio, undertaken while he was trying to help Anthony Scott struggle through his own fugue. As a tribute to Morris it attempts to be both technically immaculate and 'grave and lovely' like Morris's *Canzoni ricertati*, and more or less succeeds in both these aims. Though it offers little to care deeply about, it does demonstrate how far Finzi has travelled since the days of his unnegotiable false relations and diatonic dissonances. Now the dissonances function within traditional norms of consonance, the very first sound in the piece, an 'English' simultaneous flat and sharp seventh, is not only resolved smoothly but fully integrated into a tonal world of harmonic sonorities at a later appearance (ex. 7.2.a), and he even avoids consecutive fifths (Vaughan Williams would have moved

EX. 7.1.e

EX. 7.2.a

EX. 7.2.b

the viola part in parallel with the outer ones in ex. 7.2.b). The short Prelude alternates, in a surprisingly classical manner for Finzi, two contrasting periods, those of ex. 7.2.a and b. The first two bars of the fugue subject are based on ex. 7.2.b, while its third bar contains a ♭7̂ ♭6̂ 5̂ 4̂ ♭3̂ descent that has previously been outlined by the top part of ex. 7.2.a and its antecedents, though this is not 'explained' by the music until the final bars of the piece, when it then does so almost like one of Hans Keller's Functional Analyses by presenting a unison statement of the fugue subject, pointing repeatedly to its high G, and then substituting the opening of the prelude for the scalic descent, thereby bringing the work to a close with admirable promptness. Finzi's own analysis, published with the miniature score in 1942, marks out the unexceptionable course of the fugue – exposition with regular countersubject, three middle entries separated by motivic working, two *stretti*, a dominant pedal, and tonal and thematic development to the climax of the final tonic entry. The middle entries sink far flatwards on the cycle of fifths, but rise again through the *stretti* and compensate not just with sharpwards movement but with tonal shifts by thirds (compare those in the Prelude) when the dominant pedal in A minor rises to another in C♯ minor. The work, well written for strings, was taken up by various groups after its first, wartime appearance in Birmingham at an Appleby

Matthews lunchtime concert at Queen's College Chambers on 13 May 1941, the very day another Queen's concert chamber, in London – where Finzi's début had taken place – was bombed and burnt out. David Martin's string trio played it at a National Gallery concert later that year, and in 1942–3 it was broadcast by the Philharmonic and Grinke Trios.

The Prelude and Fugue's autograph manuscript was originally headed 'II / Preludio e Fuga Accademico'. It is not possible to tell whether the idea of making it part of a multi-movement work, or indeed that of the dedication to Morris, was present from the start; but by 1941 Finzi must have decided to channel further sketches into a separate String Trio, for which he reserved a different opus number in his catalogue of works. A few jottings for its first movement exist, but nothing continuous. Perhaps earlier than the Prelude and Fugue of 1938, he seems to have been undecided as to whether he should write a string trio or a string quartet: a passage clearly presaging the opening of the Prelude appears in Sketchbook J (ex. 7.2.c) alongside another marked 'String 4tet', the heading also given to a further cognate fragment in Sketchbook E (ex. 7.2.d).

Dies natalis was the last work Finzi completed before the Second World War. To summarise the argument presented in Chapter 5, 'The salutation' had been composed as early as 1925 and will have needed

EX. 7.2.c

EX. 7.2.d (string quartet)

EX. 7.3.a (Elgar)

little alteration when Finzi returned to the cantata. 'Wonder' is also early (though probably not that early), but was 'entirely rewritten', presumably in 1938, the date of the first two movements as we know them. 'The rapture' was composed at the eleventh hour, during the first half of 1939 in the midst of the move to Ashmansworth; Finzi always needed forcing to produce enough fast movements in his works, and he always did them last.

A deeply personal statement *Dies natalis* may be. But one cannot help wondering whether its completion was triggered not only by the presence and wonder of his own growing children but also by the fact that Ferguson, who had never previously been to a Three Choirs Festival, had a performance at Gloucester (of his Two Ballads) in 1934 while Finzi, a loyal *habitué*, had not yet achieved a commission or a hearing in any of the three cathedral cities. Hereford, where Traherne had been born and with his parish of Credenhill nearby, was the obvious place for *Dies natalis,* and the approach of a festival there in 1939 may have meant that Finzi broke off sustained work on *Intimations* to rewrite or complete his cantata instead, though against this argument is the fact that he seems to have been unusually diffident about submitting the work.

Another speculation bound to modify our inherited view of *Dies natalis* as an act of creative candour to match Traherne's concerns the first two movements. It is easiest to assume that the essence of their inspiration lies in 'Rhapsody', in which Traherne's prose sets the tone of discourse, and that the material of 'Intrada' was extrapolated from it, like that of an opera overture. The truth is almost certainly the other way round. Moreover, 'Intrada' shows all the hallmarks of having been the first movement of a string serenade, if its opening is compared with that of the Elgar Serenade (ex. 7.3.a and b), its *Sempre con moto* section

EX. 7.3.b (Finzi)

is seen for the debonair strumming it is and considered further in the light of Bliss's *Serenade* and general persona, and its final chord substituted for the *attacca* which has been its inevitable yoke ever since it became a standard work. With a little effort one can still imagine many another movement following it. To view the material of 'Rhapsody' in this light is to realise that, skilful and highly affecting though it is as vocal expression, virtually none of its text-setting is thematic. There are only two exceptions. One is the very first phrase, where the rhythm of the initial four notes fits the text well enough to fix the illusion that the musical curtain is going up on the first scene proper; the way Finzi ensures this is as knowing a stroke as Traherne's 'roll up!' showman's language ('Will you see . . .?') at this point. The other exception is a couple of phrases in the E♭ major section, though even here the 'Intrada' melody is stretched and realigned rhythmically (compare figure 5 of 'Intrada' with 'O what [venerable] creatures did the aged seem! / Immortal che[rubims]', and figure 7 with 'I knew not [that] they [were] born [or] should die', the syllables in square brackets being thematically extraneous). In this latter instance the instrumental thread (from figure 5) is spun out a bit further while the vocal recitative rides it, and figure 7 is then transformed and extended. Elsewhere the movement, which is quite a lengthy one, is held together in two ways: by simple recitative (its longest span beginning at 'The corn was orient and immortal wheat'), and by Finzi's 'trope' technique, in which memorable but tiny melodic fragments are separately conjured up as word-setting and then pondered in the orchestra: see 'innumerable joys', 'I was entertain'd', 'splendour and glory', 'melody to Adam than to me', and so on. The best and most extended of these troped phrases, strategically placed, are, first, 'strange and wonderful things', which is instrumentally transformed into the E♭ march section with its 'image procession' of strange and wonderful things indeed – the aged, the young men, the maids – and then, at the end of the movement, the climactic 'all in the peace of Eden', which paves the way for the coda. It is a method of composition that works for Traherne's prose (of which Finzi selected odd, separate phrases from the first three of his third 'century' of meditations, chopping them up and changing their order), but it is essentially synthetic, a far cry from his melodic grasp of Hardy's refrains, metres and structures, and a matter of sustained working technique, not piecemeal or sudden inspiration. Milford hit the nail on the head when he rambled on, a few years later, about the 'Introduction' being added to the 'Aria' in *Farewell to Arms* in a similar manner:

I was thinking how well . . . you've managed to bridge the 20 years' gap . . . between the Recit. & the Air. I suppose the thing is that one *ought* (now & again anyhow) to be able to turn out a simple & beautiful tune-movement (excuse the phrase!) at *any* time of one's career, oughtn't one? (surely, if one has retained any of one's youth at all, which I suppose in a way is the only thing worth retaining) . . . [whereas] perhaps almost the only point of the rather disgusting business of getting old is to improve one's technique, don't you think? – I mean, you *couldn't* have written the Recit 20 years ago; you *could*, as I say, repeat an equivalent of the Air; & I think the fact that the two in this case go so well together proves it. (19450215)

None of this is to decry the beauty of *Dies natalis* but to suggest that its centrality in Finzi's output belongs more to its reception than to its composition. 'Intrada' may well have been initially intended for 'that foul serenade' (19370101) that Finzi was working on at the beginning of 1937 and still envisaged completing when he got another of its prospective movements, presumably the Romance, into shape four years later. In early 1938, as we have seen, he told Busch he had completed two movements of the cantata, probably meaning that 'Intrada' had by now been incorporated and 'Rhapsody' composed. Any touching-up necessary in 'The salutation' and the rewriting of 'Wonder' were most likely accomplished over the next few months, for by mid-August he had shown *Dies natalis* to Milford, recognised that he still had to write a fast movement, and agreed with Milford's suggestion that he submit the work to Percy Hull, organist of Hereford Cathedral and musical director of the following year's Festival. He did so the following month and was doubtless surprised at its acceptance by Christmas, with Elsie

Suddaby as soloist and Sumsion (at Hull's invitation) as conductor, provided he could write the fast movement, still unborn through the unsettling months of Munich and appeasement.

'Wonder' is the cantata's weakest movement; Ferguson did not like it and he, Finzi and Sumsion all had the greatest difficulty in wresting its phrasing and dynamics into shape after it had been rewritten, though Finzi stuck by its intimate, lyrical flow. To Ferguson's criticism that 'it belongs to the period when you relied, as I see it, too much on emotional rise & fall as a means of giving shape to a work, and not enough on a synthesis between emotional rise & fall and purely musical shapes, such as you have now so successfully achieved' (19390104), he replied: 'I wdn't write it nowadays, yet still I like it!' (19390116b). Doubtless the rewriting had involved some entirely new passages, and one guesses that bars 16–18, 23–5 (possibly 23–32) and 38 or 41 onwards were among them, redeeming the whole.

Three other Traherne poems were typed out by Joy: 'News', five stanzas of 'The world', and three of 'The preparative'. All were probably considered for *Dies natalis*'s central movement. No music survives for 'News' and not much for 'The preparative', but Finzi did have a shot at an easy-going 'Air', marked 'III', for 'The world' – the title beginning to suggest his interest in the English eighteenth century – before steeling himself for the more Dionysian effort of 'The rapture'. He kidded himself that it would only be an additional 'short section' (19381103b), but truth will out, and it had to form the cornucopian centrepiece of the cantata. He hated working under pressure but could do it when he must, and Joy was pleased to record in her journal that, while 'Booseys won't definitely agree to publishing until they see whether it provides sufficient contrast to the other three slow mvts,' and despite all distractions, it was going well – 'an angelic roundabout!' (19390202). Gerald had been thinking again about the March Church angels (see p. 137) and those of Botticelli, doing their round dance in his *Mystic Nativity*, but the ecstatic had by now found an utterly new mode of expression in his music, his highly secular 'stride' style, 'novelty' syncopation and all (ex. 7.3.c). The 'angelic roundabout' is, appropriately enough, cast as a rondo, though like Finzi's later instrumental ones it rather creaks as its sections revolve, despite firm thematic linkage into and out of the main motif (ex. 7.3.d) and its episode themes. The 'all aboard' trilling call to the carousel (ex. 7.3.e) is reminiscent of the opening of 'Der Trunkene im Frühling' from *Das Lied von der Erde* but is equally likely

[Allegro vivace e giojoso]

EX. 7.3.c (piano reduction)

EX. 7.3.d

EX. 7.3.e

to have been influenced by that of Mahler's Fourth Symphony when it comes back in the vocal finale, his soprano singing of the childlike joys of heaven where Finzi's praises the heavenly joys of childhood. 'I hope Elsie Suddaby will get the . . . real feeling of youthful rapture in Dies Natalis,' Joy commented (ibid.). She did, though the work had been assembled with Sophie Wyss rather than Suddaby in mind. (It is not clear whether Wyss ever sang it. She wanted to give the 1939 first performance.)

Dies natalis may have been knitted together 'from far, from eve and morning', but something beyond Traherne's limpid, irresistible voice and Finzi's elective affinity with it binds the work firmly. It is Finzi's string writing that does this above all, so naturally and refulgently that one has to be reminded that the work was completed before he began to study and interpret the repertoire with his own orchestra, up to which point his experience in the medium remained very limited (though he had made an arrangement of his oboe Interlude with string orchestra at the end of 1937). The English string tradition seems to come to a nodal point in the late 1930s. Tippett finished his Double Concerto within days of Finzi completing *Dies natalis*; Howells's Concerto had received its world première at the end of 1938, Bliss's Music for Strings its British one at the end of 1935 (Finzi went to both, and loved the Bliss). Britten's Bridge Variations date from 1937. Finzi's contribution was to unite Elgarian warmth and lucidity with something of Warlock's and Delius's nostalgia for villanelle and roundelay, and if on top of this there is less of Vaughan Williams and his Tallis Fantasia's mysticism than might be expected in *Dies natalis*, there is more of Bliss (see ex. 7.3.f for a typical Bliss sonority): if for Bliss in the Music for Strings 'the sympathies of an English pastoralist . . . give a persuasive ardour . . . without stifling textural invention of an incisive kind' (Evans 1995: 206), so they do also for Finzi in 'The rapture' when he weighs anchor from decorum and sails on an expanded technique.

On the spiritual side, Milford, for all his shortcomings as a composer, was probably best placed of all Finzi's close friends to sympathise with the transcendental innocence that *Dies natalis* aims to express, all too soon to be associated with his own dead son, and to appreciate how closely the composer's voice accorded with the poet's. It would be wrong to measure this accord against Finzi's fidelity to Hardy, for in *Dies natalis* he was at bottom quarrying an author and his thought for a representative cantata rather than responding repeatedly and separately to individual poems each of which needed its (for him) one musical solution; indeed, in 'The salutation' and 'Wonder', the first two of Traherne's 'Dobell' poems, Finzi omitted half the stanzas. But it was equally right that Milford should have been the one to prod him into getting *Dies natalis* floated, and it was Milford's cousin Anne Ridler who prepared one of the standard editions of Traherne after both composers' deaths. Even then, in 1966, one of Traherne's manuscripts had only just been discovered and was yet to be published; yet more

EX. 7.3.f

astonishingly, another unknown manuscript work by him was plucked from a burning rubbish heap in Lancashire the following year. Never was one of Finzi's works surrounded by more fragility or his urge to clutch at permanence through art more sharply focused. By the time *Dies natalis* had been finished, accepted by Boosey, its vocal score set up on the presses and proofed in time for its first performance scheduled on 8 September 1939, its scoring and part-copying completed in urgent haste by Finzi, as was its bowing with the Rubbras' help at Ashmansworth, and its first two orchestral rehearsals held, in the composer's presence, in London at the end of August, Hitler had signed his non-aggression pact with the Russians. The British government banned gatherings and decided to start putting its evacuation plans into action, which restricted transport and meant the abandonment of the Three Choirs Festival on 31 August. The following day a pile of evacuees and another of newly published scores of *Dies natalis* arrived at Church Farm, Ashmansworth, and Hitler invaded Poland. War was declared on 3 September, and *Dies natalis* remained unperformed.

CHAPTER 8

Finzi's war

'I can't possibly tell you what a difference you make to his life,' Kirstie Milford wrote to Finzi about her husband Robin, probably in January 1939; 'I only hope you feel strong enough to shoulder the burden of being Chief Prop to both him & Tony. How have you achieved your own strength & serenity? (A rhetorical question, obviously.)'

It may have been a rhetorical question, but it needs answering. Finzi had achieved his strength and serenity at a price that few knew and that was becoming higher and higher as the war with Hitler approached, in that he had invested everything in identification by self rather than by others. He had forged his complete, watertight identity as the English freelance composer, model of professional artistic integrity in his standards and aspirations, at the same time as seeing himself as heir to the great tradition of the inspired gentleman amateur (as exemplified by Traherne and other seventeenth-century divines) in his intellectual freedom as a provincial man of letters with its resistance to institutionalisation. He had been wholly assimilated, and had 'married out' with the effect that his children would no longer be Jewish (Jewishness is traditionally transmitted through the mother). Yet Hitler's voice was telling him more and more hysterically that he himself was still a Jew. It is hardly surprising, therefore, that no one recognised the need to fight Nazism earlier or more forcefully than Finzi.

There could be no personal question of pacifism, no limit to the effort he would make to retain his achieved Englishness. True, and as his correspondence quoted below will show, he recognised a disinterested need to uphold the liberal values one believed in, indeed civilisation itself, by force when necessary rather than take them for granted and lose them. But alas, that however much he was prepared to fight for the Jews to be saved, he was, underneath it all, fighting for himself *not* to be one of them!

Finzi's story, perhaps like that of many another assimilationist who had travelled equally far down his road, takes on a deeply ironic dimension at this point, for just as Nazi ideology would have completely discounted all aspects of his identity other than his Jewishness in dealings with him, so did Finzi insist on essentialising himself as entirely English to the complete discountenance of his Jewishness. Was it also potentially tragic, in that he wanted one thing at the expense of everything else? If so, he was never called upon to act out the tragedy in his lifetime, to stand up and be counted too late as 100% English *and* 100% Jewish, but a posthumous critical jury must surely ask itself whether he showed or lacked moral courage; whether he acted for the best or courted hypocrisy in never 'coming out' and therefore appearing to be above the battle, patronising the victims of oppression rather than identifying with them; and whether in making such a wilful, summary break with his family history he was simply asserting his own identity, as we all have to, or in fact succumbing to as totalitarian a mindset as the Nazis themselves.

It has to be remembered, however, that many of his friends were as blind to Hitler's intentions or as complacent about fascism and ethnic cleansing as the British populace at large, and could not have been counted upon to grasp anything much about the forces at work. Hokanson was contemplating a trip to Germany in January 1937, whereupon Finzi wrote to Ferguson: 'I hope he doesn't swallow the Nazi bull-shit, as X – seems to have done! If things appear all rosy there let him tell his first German acquaintance that he is a liberal – no need to go as far as Communist! – or that his grandfather was a Jew!' (19370104b). And though manifest anti-Semitism would have had little place in his liberal circle, we need look no further than the following unthinking passage in a letter from Milford to be reminded of the general level of ignorance, prejudice and stereotyped attitudes. Milford is referring to the refugees who have descended on Downe House, and are in and out of his own dwelling, in May 1939: 'This house fairly swarms with Jews & Jewesses now – just like a ghetto, or is it called a pogrom? – they seem to swarm like the locusts in the bible' (19390508b) – though it is fair to point out that he was well enough disposed towards them:

Kirstie is *really* kindly, & I retire to my room & Barnaby loves Heidi; so we don't do badly! – & the Ebels are *charming* – we don't mind how often we see them. What a lot of talent these people have – they gave us (the Frankels) a marionette show last night, entirely home-made, out of bits of wood etc, & all done in that little hut where they live, sleep, eat, & everything – & the scenery beautifully painted – really extraordinarily talented, I thought, & a *marvellous* triumph of spirit over circumstance. (ibid.)

The totalitarian menace must have been constantly in Finzi's thoughts from the mid-1930s onwards. In October 1937 he was musing on what it took to make a Hitler: 'to be civilized you have to be tolerant – to be tolerant you have to be cynical. In the obvious way, those who move mountains are always little people. Could a person who saw both sides of things – with a sense of humour, be a dictator?' (J. Finzi 19371001). Reflection gave way to deep anxiety when Hitler marched into Austria on 12 March 1938: 'G has had bad sleepless nights,' Joy noted in her journal two days later, 'and has been too disturbed by political events in Austria to do much work. "More persecution for the individuals who do not fit into a regime of physical force." ' Appeasement, which he called 'peace without honour' on 30 September when Neville Chamberlain returned from Munich, seemed a mockery; 'no feeling of relief or satisfaction anywhere with us. Everyone [else] rejoicing,' Joy wrote. After Chamberlain's first meeting with Hitler, a fortnight earlier, they had paid a lightning visit to Gerald's mother at Hundon – to find that she had painted her conservatory brown and sold all her white chickens so that the Germans would not spot the aerodrome nearby. We laugh at her precautionary logic, but how do we react to Gerald spending his three days there destroying 'her accumulation of papers' (J. Finzi 19380919)? Joy probably never saw them, for she was running a temperature during their stay. Gerald must have asked Joy never to mention his Jewishness to anyone (Ferguson was not told about it, whether despite or because of his great intimacy with Harold Samuel and Myra Hess, and never guessed). Under what restrictions did he place his mother?

By now many others were equally worried about the future. Ferguson returned from a holiday in Austria at the end of September and told Gerald how shops were daubed with the word JUDE and had their windows broken. He, like Gerald, was 'unable to work during this waiting – and suspense,' as Joy recorded. 'Brought him home for the night and we talked of war & our abilities in relation to it. Air-raid precautions begin & London starts evacuating' (J. Finzi 19380926). Newbury was a 'reception area', and they thought they might put up twenty evacuee schoolchildren! Yet still the view of Chamberlain's appeasement as a triumph for peace and, even worse, of Nazism as right for Germany had to be countered and challenged. Finzi, once again sleeping very badly (J. Finzi 19381005), joined impassioned debate over this with Busch, who had Nazi relatives, and since these letters are among the most eloquent he ever wrote and represent not just the central crisis of his life but his whole philosophy of history, they exact generous quotation. At the same time, two things should be borne in mind. First, they are not a unique outpouring, for he did conduct various other epistolary debates, reminiscent of the early Somerfield ones, particularly in the early years of the war and particularly with Milford and (again) Busch, though never with such urgency or at quite such length. (Overall, judging by what survives, 1938 and 1940 were the two most voluminous years in Finzi's correspondence.) Second, Busch's woolly thinking was a soft target. Finzi rather bullied him, and trod the same ground more mildly where a professional intellect, that of the academic Navarro, was concerned (compare 19381107a).

Busch set the ball rolling on 7 October when he proposed self-congratulation that 'Having weathered this dreadful crisis we can now look forward to the establishment of a firm basis for general peace, provided we all support our truly great Premier.' Finzi responded the following day:

I agree with you about Chamberlain, but only in the sense that the crucifixion was greater than the crucifiers. That Hitler wd have been prepared to force Europe into war is quite enough to convince me that a firm basis for peace has by no means been established. – Nor do I see how it can be, with a paranoid of that type. I'm sorry, my dear William, but I feel more than ever that the Nazi octopus is one of the most evil & retrograde things in the world – quite as bad as the communism it pretends to counter. I entirely see the right of the Sudeten cause (even though Hitler's, & his henchmen's, foul-mouthed abuse doesn't exactly appeal to my reason!) but knowing how German minorities suffer – far more than any Sudeten minorities suffered – my thoughts are with the new batch of civilised people, social democrats, Jews, liberals, pacifists etc receding before the Nazi tide. You will not, I know, take this for an attack on the fundamentally fine Teuton, but I can't understand how a very civilised person like yourself can stomach a party, which, to suit an ignorant ideology, has scattered everything that a civilised person values, from religious tolerance to scholarship, reduced a one-time tradition of culture to a farce, denigrated & exiled some of its finest minds, & set new values on truth which, at their mildest, can only be called lies. I think something pretty low has been reached when a Niemöller has to suffer as he is now doing; when a Dr Schuschnigg – (who, I think you will admit was a patriot, even if not exactly the particular patriot that Hitler wd have wished him to be) – is played with cat & mouse fashion, till his nerve & spirit are broken & is then faced with a trial, which if it comes off, will be about as preposterous as our own trial of Sir Walter Raleigh some 300 years ago ... when 'The Lorelei' has to become 'anonymous', & Mendelssohn's memory is obliterated from the conservatorium which he founded; when every profession is closed to the Jews, & even their names are removed from the war memorials (can you beat this for caddishness & pettiness); when – – – but this cd go on indefinitely & you know it all as well as I do; only I rather feel that your gentle spirit is trying to forget or overlook it, in the hope that 'it will all be much better when things have settled down in Germany'. Well, I hope so too, but whilst things are as they are at present I can't feel that humanity exactly benefits by the absorption of the Sudetens & probably the eventual disappearance of Czecho-Slovakia.

Busch's reply does not survive, but we can guess its tenor from Finzi's next letter:

Your long letter was much appreciated ... But I can't let you run away with the idea that I have the least animosity towards Germans. Naturally I wrote to you regarding you as nothing but an Englishman – (knowing quite well that one's parentage means very little compared with one's environment) – but I have great admiration for the German character, always excepting the unbearable arrogance of a certain class which, fortunately, has no parallel in England ... No, I can't dislike Germans on account of a regime, otherwise one wd soon have nobody in the world to like, if one thinks of Mussolini in Italy, the St Bartholomew massacres in France, the persecution of the Puritans in England & so on, back as far as history goes.

I'm not at all certain that your 'psychological' explanation of the Nazi revolution is *entirely* right, because these movements exist elsewhere (& have existed in the past) without any such possible explanations. It's as likely as not that they are symptomatic of something much larger – in fact, a genuine receding tide. The world has seen dark ages before & is certainly seeing them now! But that's beside the point. What we must remember is that two wrongs don't make a right & that if we blame the Nazi revolution on to England & France's post-war attitude, we can blame the war on Bismarck & 1870, & that again can be blamed on to Napoleon & he can be explained by the French revolution & so on to the beginning of time. All events have antecedents to explain them & one can only take each event on its own merits or demerits.

No one can object to a 'captain steering his people to the open sea' (a good simile of yours). What one objects to is when the captain runs down every frail craft of decency that may be in his way. I only mentioned Schuschnigg & Niemöller as being representative of so many thousands of these frail craft. Incidentally, I have not met a single exile 'shrieking calumnies & denunciations'. The few I have met, ranging from Pastors (we have had a self-exiled one staying here) to unfortunate Jews, have, without exception, been examples of dignity & restraint. One can't wonder if there is a certain amount of embitterment & I wonder if you & I wd really retain our equanimity under the strain of losing everything in the world (including a usually beloved country) & being left with nothing but our lives, for no *real* reason at all. The 'shrieking calumnies' come from Hitler & Co.

What you say about the decadent Jewish element in post war Germany is probably true (though if it had come from Nazi sources I shd doubt it, knowing how unscrupulously they cook their figures, an example being their notoriously falsified statistics about Jews who fought in the war) but one must remember that there was a general post-war laxity & decadence all over Europe – by no means the prerogative of the Jews. (Is Der Stürmer, by the way, an example of 'Aryan' morality?) I think a great deal is due to the fact that one *notices* if Gluckstein has been had up for keeping a disorderly house, but one doesn't notice it if John Smith is had up for the same reason. (Mosley's gang makes great capital out of this sort of thing, reading out the foreign names involved in Fascist clashes & omitting English ones!) One sees quite a lot of it even in England, where an anti-Jewish movement has been deliberately & artificially stimulated. You hear quite reasonable people say that the Jews have taken all the cottages in the country to escape air-raids & that there's nothing left for the others. It then turns out that there is indeed a Jew in a cottage, but nobody remarks on the 40 others who are not Jews! Howard, for instance, has had to give up the idea of his site at Ashmansworth, for the reason that the farmer tried to get an excessive amount of compensation. His name was Heath & I suppose that is what is called business. If his name had been Levi it wd have been called something different! I myself was 'blackmailed' (by a judge, too!) into paying £200 for a piece of land worth £30 because he knew that I *had* to buy it, as it was a wedge running into our site. His name was not Stein. This is one of the reasons why I'm always rather suspicious when one hears that the Jews occupy all the key positions, and surely the Jews in Germany weren't so numerous as to prevent anyone else getting a job? I doubt whether your nephews cd have got into the cocoa & chocolate trade in England, since it is in the hands of the Rowntrees, Cadburys, Terrys & Frys, but I see no reason why the Quakers shd be persecuted on that account. When I see that 5000 doctors in Germany are to have their degrees revoked, not because they are bad doctors, but because they are Jews or half Jews, I feel that something has been done that not a hundred years can put right. It stands to reason that the 5000 who will take their place must be lesser doctors, in so far as they are shackled to ignorant ideologies, and cannot be taught 'pure medicine'. Meanwhile, the 5000 doctors, the best of whom are true servants of both humanity & Germany, are obliged to cease practising (& think what that implies) on account of a racial theory which no responsible ethnologist apparently recognises. I wish I cd feel that this Jewish problem was purely a matter of Germany's own internal life, but she spreads these ideas with nothing short of malevolence wherever she can get a foothold. It's wonderful to read now that Duff-Cooper, Churchill & Eden are a war party backed by the Jews!!

I knew of the afflictions of the Sudeten Germans & told you that I saw the rightness of the Sudeten case, even though they suffered considerably less than the minorities in Germany; & now I'm waiting to see whether Hitler will negotiate with Mussolini for the return of the Tyrolese Austrians, who shd never have been handed over to Italy, or whether he has sold them for 50 pieces of silver (by way of the axis).

How horrible it all is that a fundamentally good humanity can be so played upon & played with. (19381012)

The judge's name may not have been Stein, but the purchaser's was Finzi, and one begins to boggle at his so clarifying the one side of the equation while so obscuring the other.

Later that month, at a run-through of Busch's Piano Concerto, the Finzis met his Nazi cousin from Germany: 'I longed to tell her that if only she, or people of her kind, cd be in the place of rat-like creatures such as Goebbels, there might be some hope for the world! Joy & I thought her most delightful & "sympathetic",' he wrote to Busch (19381101b). But Busch's reply started them off all over again. 'It may perhaps comfort you a little to know that people of her type are coming more to the fore in Germany,' he wrote on 2 November:

She is a convinced Nazi (though formerly not), and in her district, that of the large island of Usedom on the Baltic Coast (which is really part of the mainland) on which her town, Swinemünde, is situated, she says that the high officials are now of a very fine type and much loved by the people. She says there are 60 Jews in her town, that the landlord to whom she pays rent for her flat is a Jew, and that they are well-treated, except for the ban on social intercourse. I am afraid that she firmly believes that Jewish and non-Jewish races do not mix satisfactorily, but she also declares that the whole question has been pursued too rigorously, and much more time should have been allowed for a solution of the problem. She dislikes Goebbels, but says that his sort of propaganda has been thought necessary to give ordinary non-political-thinking people a sense of unity and pride in their newly-won greatness. His words are, she says, not taken seriously by anyone else. She has implicit faith in Hitler and is absolutely certain that his aims are peaceful and not imperialistic.

She disapproves of bans on Jewish musicians etc, and says that sort of thing will pass. – These are all *her* views, so please do not feel you must answer them and spend your valuable time in so doing. She has promised me, however, to reply to any criticisms or queries I might make respecting actions by Germany, as she numbers amongst her patients and friends people whose views are pretty official. While over here she avidly read the papers and was very distressed at the almost entirely negative aspects of Nazi Germany which are printed here, and also claimed that, as far her own & one or two other large districts go (of which she has personal knowledge) these negative aspects are largely untrue.

Of course Finzi had to answer these views, which he did the following day:

I certainly rejoice to think that people of your cousin's type are coming to the fore in Germany – (if it is so) – but how can one fail to be appalled thinking of the 60 Jews in her town being 'well-treated, except for the ban on social intercourse'. Just *think* what that means. Once a caste system is started it is practically inescapable. Children born into such an environment can never hold up their heads, or feel, or be, self respecting citizens, nor can they function intellectually, morally, or physically as they wd otherwise do. That is why no Mendelssohn, Heine or Einstein were born into the ghetto. Nor will they be into the new ghetto.

Take the case of the Eurasians. I used to believe that they were wretched people with all the vices, & none of the virtues, of White & Black! It took some time to grasp that if they were barred by the whites on account of their black blood & by the blacks on account of their white blood, they must of necessity, *though not for any inherent reasons*, become outcasts. The caste system, such as in India, produces the same results. If you are born an 'untouchable' you remain an 'untouchable', & nothing in the world will raise you to a higher caste. But you know as well as I do that if it were possible to bring up an 'untouchable' as a Prince's son, he'd as likely as not take on all the attributes of a Prince's son! Though it's difficult to pass opinions on other people's religious beliefs, we naturally disbelieve in the Hindu ideas of Karma that make the caste system so inviolable, and it shd always be remembered that Nazi theories about race, amounting almost to a religion with some people, were not formulated by authorities on the subject, but by ignoramuses to whom any authorities have had to toe the line. If your cousin really believes in such Nazi theories as that Jewish & non-Jewish races do not mix, she ought to smuggle back a few books by world authorities on the subject, people like Huxley,

Haldane & Carr-Saunders & see what *they* have to say on the matter. After all, their opinions are worth more than Rosenberg's, & incidentally they have no axes to grind.

Of course the Jewish question is complicated enough by the religious question. One must admit that nonconformist minorities in any community are always a difficulty, even though one respects them for their integrity, whilst holding that their beliefs are tarradiddle & nonsense! But when people desire to belong to the community at large & feel themselves a part of the whole, rather than of the minority, & are prevented by a bogus racial theory, one's sense of justice is naturally roused. I absolutely agree that in times of emergency it is necessary to remove disintegrating elements, whether Jewish or non-Jewish, (though even here there are difficulties; to distinguish between opposition that is constructive & opposition that is destructive – Shelley & Beethoven wd never have survived an English or German Fascist revolution) but now that German unity has been achieved I sincerely hope that you are right in thinking that the worse side of things will recede. Personally, I do not think that Jewish artists will be able to practise in Germany, *for* Germany, for generations & perhaps centuries. Meanwhile the Japanese are accepted as 'Aryans' & theoretically there are no objections to Japanese artists exhibiting, creating & performing in Germany!!

Busch's reply, on the seventh, widened the discussion of segregation while firmly upholding his belief in appeasement:

When I read your remarks I really feel that I absolutely agree with you. Fundamentally, I feel that we are all (all humanity) of the same 'mind substance'. I feel that the true nature of this is positive good, and not good and evil. It is difficult in a few words to describe my faith, but I feel about evil that it is a tremendous lie about good, that when we get right down to the bottom of things, through all the distortions, beliefs, suppositions and what-not, we find good. Perhaps this sense is what underlies my feeling that there is a certain amount of good in everything, if one looks for it, and that wholly to condemn a person, a movement or a nation for the wrong things it does or exposes, is to shut out – as far as oneself is concerned – the possibility of helping that person, movement or nation towards the enlargement of that good. Of course, by 'good' I mean something very much more active and all-embracing than the word usually signifies. It would take too long fully to explain my meaning. However, I feel that though the *real* and sometimes practically dormant part of each individual (the acorn of the oaktree, a poor simile) is concrete good, yet I know that the individual, the nation or race, humanity, is in many a different state of evolution or unfoldment (a word which I prefer), and that we cannot simply go out and say 'let us all mix together, we are all of the same substance anyway'. We cannot do this *yet*, because each race is so to speak a symposium of its own thoughts and culture and seems but to evolve along its own lines. I am thinking of race in a very broad sense of course, such as you mention, white & black & yellow.

It is really a difficult question, when it comes to particularising about races. I feel personally that although I am ready to grant absolutely equal status (speaking impersonally of course) to a member of a different race I would still be very much against wishing to incorporate him as a member of my family, *not* out of any feeling of superiority but because I feel we as races are unfolding along entirely different planes of thought and culture. Possibly in centuries to come, with wider dissemination and greater unfoldment of the culture of different races, their mental and physical characteristics will tend to become less different, and harmonious merging will be more possible. – The Nazi conception of the Jew as being of Oriental race and therefore of a totally different culture is undoubtedly exaggerated, although strangely enough, the orthodox Jew will be as stern about mixing his race with the non-Jew as the most fanatical Nazi. I think there is no question, however, that the Jew has a different culture, and racial attributes entirely of his own, although he is very adept at the adoption of extra-racial characteristics when this adaptability is needed. The ban on social intercourse in Germany is, I feel certain, only a temporary one, although this 'temporary' may be for our generation (I hope not). I deplore it as much as you do, but I do feel that to allow our indignation over this & other things to blind us to the good in many other directions, which anyone with an open eye who takes the trouble to go and see for himself, *will* see, is, as I said before, to shut out our chance of helping towards the enlargement of this good and the eventual transformation of the bad.

Finzi was prevented from replying to this until the fourteenth, but had by no means cooled off in the interim:

A visit to London interrupted this & there was lots I wanted to say about the rest of your exceptionally interesting letter. Not that there's anything one wd wish to dispute about your ideas of good & evil, though I rather feel that they're both like knowledge & non-knowledge – two sides of the same coin. Black is white & white is black, not only when it comes to, say, manslaughter as conceived by English law & as conceived by Australian aborigines, but also all around us. Moral & Ethical ideas are in such a perpetual state of flux that it is impossible to draw a fixed line between the two ('To thine own self be true' is about the nearest approach to such a thing) or even to know the difference between the two. Custom & morality are so inseparable as to be almost husband & wife! To be a pacifist in England in 1914–1918 meant humiliation & suffering, but to day it is almost a hall-mark. It gave one a halo in Germany after the war, but now it leads to the concentration camp, or even to the axe. However, it's clear to everybody that the virtues of one age are the vices of another, & I realise quite well that the 'fundamental goodness' about which you write is a much wider concept than the comparatively superficial view of right & wrong amongst human beings.

Still, if the small boy is cruel to the cat you can't overlook the cruelty on the grounds that the small boy is fundamentally good. His beastliness may have been brought about by the people around him, & we may know that one day he will grow out of his cruelty. He may have a delightful side to his character in other ways, but what about the cat, & all the future cats that get into his hands? The parallel may appear simple, but it's near the mark.

I think you're quite right when you say that humanity is in varying states of 'unfoldment' & that the idea of all mixing together may be an ideal, but it certainly isn't practicable. I'm un-idealistic enough to hope that neither Nigel nor Christopher will marry the above-mentioned Australian aborigines! I'm also un-idealistic enough to feel that art is by no means 'above national boundaries' (as this aggravating cliché goes) & in this way I shd have said that I was far more of a Nazi than you! However, one must recognise that occasional composers do arise who are not to be placed in categories – Delius for example – & that in the past a universal style seems to have been workable. But as a rule the cosmopolitan style in art leads to nothing but disintegration, & a national concept does make for boundaries & limitations, which is all to the good. But nationality is *not* a matter of race & blood. It is a matter of culture, custom & environment. Assimilation, so far from being a prerogative of the Jews, is about the most important & universal fact of existence. And how does race apply to a country like England, which has assimilated Latins, Saxons, Celts, Danes & dozens of other groups of people? Even the American now forms a definite type, after only a couple of centuries of the melting pot. If anything, the trouble with the Jews seems that they are less assimilative & adaptable than many other people – probably owing to the strength of their culture & environment, as well as to outside pressure preventing assimilation.

I admit the difficulty of the orthodox Jew, who, you say, wd be as 'stern about mixing his race with the non-Jew as the most fanatical Nazis'. The crime in Germany, it seems to me, is in *preventing* assimilation of those more enlightened Jews who have risen out of all that medieval nonsense & who were/are quite as much part of Germany as are most of the Nazi gang – & have possibly actually been settled in Germany for as long – (for it wd not be tactful to trace back the ancestry of Hitler, Goebbels or Goering too far. No Jewish blood might be found, but sub-man certainly wd! Yet the Nazi concept of race is 'what you were you are, what you are you shall always be'.)

I think it wd be about as intelligent, & equally foul, if we made scapegoats of all the thousands of Huguenot descendants, who have become completely assimilated into English life, traced them back to their refugee ancestors, & then forced them into a separate unit, outside national life. Or shall we send

Vaughan Williams back to Wales, where some century or other, an ancestor must have come from? Or Elgar to Denmark, or Grieg to Scotland. Holst's grandfather was a political refugee. Sibelius has hardly any Finnish blood in him. Wd you not say that all these, if not in themselves, then at some point in their ancestry, showed that they were 'adept at the adoption of extra-racial characteristics where this adaptability is needed'? The charge might be levelled at nearly everyone – at Van Dieren's son, at you, at Rubbra etc etc. Meanwhile, what is the typical Jew, & has he any existence outside prejudice & imagination? Is it that loathsome Whitechapel type, or is it the abstruse Saint-like philosopher like Professor Alexander? Is it the proverbial miser or that most generous of men, Harold Samuel? Is it the slick, superficial artist or the Myra Hess type? Is it the music-hall vulgarian or Sarah Bernhardt? Karl Marx or Joachim? (Both had beards.) Is it the stock exchange parasite or is it Einstein? Is it the man of feeling like Mahler, or the man of intellect like Schoenberg? And so on *ad infinitum*.

(No wonder the Nazis blame the Jew for being both International warmonger & pacifist; capitalist & communist!) Surely the answer is that all these types exist amongst all civilised people. There is no Jewish race & no Jewish type, except where environment has made it.

But Heavens, this is more like a pamphlet than a letter! Since our discussions started, further events have taken place in Naziland which must make even you feel less tolerant. I *know* that the worst side doesn't prevail forever, but Ghengis Khan was a reality for enough number of years to devastate a good portion of the world. His followers were no doubt healthy & happy, if that was sufficient justification.

Finzi's 'further events', which caused Busch to write that he was 'horrified and very upset over latest developments in Germany', and assure Finzi that 'my family are all very depressed about it' (19381114), were the dreadful pogrom of 9–10 November, when Jewish shops and synagogues were looted and burnt in a night of violence throughout Germany and Austria in revenge for the murder of the diplomat vom Rath in Paris by Herschel Grynspan (Tippett's 'child of our time'). The position of the Jews in Hitler's Reich was summed up by Lord Rothschild (one of Toty de Navarro's colleagues at Trinity College, Cambridge) in *The Times* two days later: 'Almost the only thing left for them is death; for many that would be a welcome and blessed relief' (12 November 1938: 13). But it was not so much this unambiguous outrage that put a stop to the debate, which otherwise could have gone on indefinitely, as the fact that Busch's Piano Concerto had just been announced for a BBC performance in January. An excessively nervous pianist ('Hadn't we better subscribe to buy him a pair of waterproof pants?' Ferguson asked [19390104]), he now had to practise hard and had no further time for correspondence. He probably never guessed that when Finzi wrote 'etc etc' in the last letter quoted, he really meant 'me' but dared not say it.

Preparations for the move and for *Dies natalis*'s début at the Three Choirs Festival may have taken Finzi's mind off the Nazi threat temporarily, but not for long, for the family had scarcely been at Ashmansworth a week before Hitler marched into Czechoslovakia, demolishing what was left of the state. Again Gerald became insomniac, and a short recuperative holiday, mostly at Hundon, in April was accompanied by a further rapid worsening of the international situation as Hitler turned his sights on Lithuania and Mussolini invaded Albania. Britain was having to re-arm ever more rapidly and all too late, while Finzi's attention, which had already had plenty of psychological gunnery practice with Busch, was drawn to Hardy's poem 'Channel firing' by Toty de Navarro for a possible setting. He began one enthusiastically but got stuck where God says 'Ha, ha' (Toty suggested he cut one of the 'ha's). There was just time for a final bucolic holiday, with the Scotts and both families' children, in Norfolk at Burnham Overy windmill (owned by the architect Hugh Hughes, a cousin of Ruth Scott), and for as many of their army of friends who could – Ferguson, Navarro, the Thorpe Davies, the Rubbras, Jack Haines, Ann Bowes-Lyon, fellow-fruitgrowers Justin and Edith Brooke and possibly the Busches, Milfords, Harlands and Vaughan Williamses – to visit the new house at Ashmansworth, before war broke out. By that time, and with the interior decoration of Church Farm still unfinished, 'black-outs were needed instead of curtains,' as Alan Powers puts it (1985: 559).

Finzi put up the shutters on composition as well as on Harland's new plate-glass windows and wondered when he would be called up. Milford, who had retreated to Guernsey as Downe House was given over to refugees, volunteered immediately for active service, pronouncing lugubriously that 'my chief object, if I get in, will (I hope) be to get killed before killing or wounding' (19391013) – which was hardly the spirit – while Finzi, who knew Milford would not last a week without a breakdown (nor did he), was rather more circumspect. 'There *is* a danger, with all of us, of a sort of withering up from over-refinement – rather like a plant which hasn't enough soil for its roots to get down,' he admitted in reply. 'In that sense tough company is a good antidote to the drawing room.' But on the whole he thought it was 'better to wait till one's wanted ... I'm afraid neither of us will make good soldiers. Like me, I suppose pop-guns & bows & arrows were your last firearms' (19391018).

In the meantime, London was dark and deathly quiet with the 'phoney war' while domestic life at Ashmansworth resembled a battleground with its swarms of evacuees. Joy, who knew no one and would therefore be fair, was put in charge of billeting for the whole village. East End children may soon have drifted back to London, but friends were more tenacious. Frank and Vera Strawson, their vehicle piled high with furniture, descended on Church Farm from St John's Wood and stayed there for most of the war, arriving before their postal forewarning and proving a terrible trial to Gerald in his less sociable moods: Vera's ineffectuality drove him mad. In time, she was put in charge of the chickens while Frank looked after the vegetable garden. He was no trouble though equally inactive: a lazy man at heart, he had made a fortune smuggling jewels in India and invested it in stocks and shares which he spread out on the floor every morning. He was of German Jewish stock, had changed his name from Strauss, and was one of the chief shareholders and a director of Gollancz's publishing house. They brought with them his cousin Lydia Riesenecker, a delightful, unobtrusive Czech who had known Richard Strauss, been wooed by Ysaÿe and forced to leave behind her husband Kurt (she returned after the war to discover that he had married an Aryan). Peggy Bendle, Christopher and Nigel's nanny since Aldbourne days, was also in residence until 1941 (when she left to marry Wilf, the man who built the flint wall), and another Jewish refugee, Gisa Dietz (now Cartwright), who had been employed by an uncongenial German family in London until Joy improved her lot, lived in as cook, in the room next to the kitchen, from 1940 to 1942. As if they were not enough, an unidentified woman secretly known as 'the black slug' joined the household for a while in the autumn of 1939, as did Iris Lemare, sleeping in the open porch with her dog (whose effect on the Finzis' many cats is not recorded). Later, in 1941, three Walthamstow children arrived temporarily after their mother had been strained to breaking point by circumstances and means; 'we infinitely prefer having children to having Vera!' Gerald told Navarro. 'The boy in particular, aged 13, with the manners of a king and whose gentleness and sensitiveness strike Joy as being quite exceptional' (19410728). This was Ronnie Coombes, who became a chauffeur, remained in touch with Joy and testified to how much the experience had meant to him, as did others who stayed at Ashmansworth (see C. Finzi 1992: 17, 20–21). Life at Church Farm was communal, with Joy doing most of the cooking. Her war must have been even more exhausting than Gerald's, and it was the crucible of her reputation for unlimited resourcefulness, though this took its toll in her many and severe asthma attacks, from at least one of which she thought she would die. She looked after her charges all too well; Lydia tried decamping to Mrs Straker's across the road for a week but soon returned after her new hostess phoned up to ask how much to charge her for a cup of tea.

It all sounds homely enough, even glamorous, in retrospect, but no one was enjoying such conditions at the time, and Iris Lemare recalled her Ashmansworth stay as a most unhappy period for her; Gerald's attitude was overbearing until she managed to find some farm work. (His patronage was surely not unmixed with guilt at having himself so far escaped the uprooting suffered by most Jews.) Finding a personal role in the war effort was urgent for most but not easy at first while the phoney war dragged on, especially for freelance musicians whose teaching and playing had immediately dried up. There was no general rush or encouragement to volunteer for military service, as in the First World War, for this time the government picked its men and women slowly and more carefully. Tired of arguments with pacifist friends, Rubbra took part-time work on a poultry farm. Ferguson was lucky, catapulted straight to the heart of things when asked by his friend Myra Hess to help run the National Gallery lunch-time concerts that within six weeks of the start of the war were filling the great cultural chasm that had opened up when all artistic events and entertainment summarily ceased. Finzi, now nearly forty, could do nothing much except revise one or two old compositions, go to a few concerts and plays in London once the initial siege mentality had receded, and, with Joy, ponder like latter-day Thoreaus the terrible ice storm that hit Ashmansworth in January 1940, destroying a hundred years' growth of trees:

> Twig weighed with ice, 28 oz
>   "   " without " 1 "

A new friend, Alfred Chenhalls, came to stay several times. He was accountant to a number of musicians and more than anyone else sharpened Gerald's responses with his 'cowpat' view of most English music, a doctrine beginning to become a terminal bugbear to the Vaughan Williams school as figures such as Lutyens and Edward Clark to whom the continental avant-garde was no longer the great enemy came quickly to the forefront of cultural respect, not least because they stood side-by-side with so many refugee artists. Finzi and Chenhalls manoeuvred each other into faintly ridiculous positions:

We loved having Chenny, & all biked over to show him the Stanley Spencer chapel on Sunday morning. Stopped for beer, gin & ginger wine before tackling the hill home. Chenny puffing & out of condition. We were all tired & happy when we got home. A late evening by the fire – talking & sipping wine & playing music – C. thinks all music should start with a bang – his dislikes include VW, Elgar, Delius, Holst – & English music generally for its lack of presentation & meandering introductions. His musical appreciation & judgement run parallel with his attitude to life. A muddled genius, with a rare generosity, & love for music & painting. Inside the bon vivant & city man & raconteur a sensitive, unhappy spirit. 'He is like a guelder rose – sterile.' (J. Finzi 19400227)

Chenny for the weekend. He brought the manuscript of the new little Walton pieces. Duets for children – quite delightful, but without any special individuality . . . Mags came on Sunday night to meet Chenny & we all played duets for 8 hands. Smetana & Haydn, which sounded mostly like Hindemith. (J. Finzi 19400526)

Chenny, the man of the world as ever, managed to bring wine even in the middle of this war, & much appreciated by G. Many arguments. 'It makes one feel so hopeless, when one finds one's whole point of view is so misunderstood, that one doesn't speak the same language at all. I feel it would really be better not to know a person like Chenny, who tries to demolish arguments by setting up false & entirely unrecognisable premises. Our values are so different & our approaches so dissimilar, that he makes of me – of us – of our way of life a gross caricature.' A revealing argument at table. Chenny's contempt for the larger figures of our age – VW etc & indeed, he sees no permanent values in Sibelius or even his dear Willie – rather nettled G. At some mention of Borodin & Moussorgsky, Chenny said: If those are important figures, I can understand you thinking VW is important. G asked, 'Who do you consider a great man?' Chenny replied 'Hitler.' This explains a lot & one can understand how Hitler's 'success' appeals to Chenny. To G Hitler is a powerful person, a dangerous person and a disease, but a completely unimportant person, who will leave nothing behind except a chapter in the history books. His whole world pales into insignificance next to the at present unknown work of some obscure poet, sculptor or composer. (J. Finzi 19401011)

This belief in the artist as the only true representative of a civilisation, and of artistic value transcending time, place, obscurity, politics, science, technology and social history, may have been hyperbolically expressed but it underpinned Finzi's entire life and work, a philosophically based creed but one no less passionate and dogmatic than those he despised in others. It was at this period that he gave it its most concrete expression, in his *Absalom's Place* essay and the revised setting of 'To a poet a thousand years hence'. As for Chenny, his salute to Hitler was ironically and tragically repaid. He looked like Churchill and was mistaken for him later in the war by a German spy, who spotted him boarding a plane at Lisbon along with the film star Leslie Howard. They were shot down and killed.

The phoney war came to a swift end in May 1940 when Hitler attacked the Low Countries. Churchill replaced Chamberlain as Prime Minister, and by the end of the month all British troops were evacuating the European mainland at Dunkirk as France fell to Hitler. On 10 June, Italy declared war on the Allies, but by the fourteenth the Germans were in Paris and on the twenty-second France signed an armistice; there were now no Allies left, only Britain, alone against the Axis powers and desperately short of weapons and personnel. 'G never slept that night,' Joy wrote after the French surrender. 'Rose at 3 & took Bromide [and] though it quietened him, he couldn't sleep. Even next day, unable to sleep after lunch' (J. Finzi 19400622). The Channel Islands were occupied shortly after the Milfords (and John Ireland) had escaped on one of the last boats back to England.

By this time Finzi had joined Dad's Army, the Local Defence Volunteers inaugurated by Anthony Eden in May and later called the Home Guard. It reminded him of the Wessex militia – 'just like a Hardy scene of England during the Napoleonic Wars' (19400529) – and was something of a community joke from the start, what with an initial dearth of rifles and as motley a crew of volunteers as TV would later have us believe. Frank Strawson joined up with Gerald, and when an officer giving a talk about the Bren gun invited questions he asked, 'Can anyone tell me what to do about my broad beans?' Friends' visions of Gerald chasing enemy parachutists along Doiley Bottom proved irresistible, and he so hated loud noises that he secretly stuffed his ears before rifle practice (once they had actually got some guns). Nevertheless, he was as proud as a schoolboy when he proved rather a good shot, and wished he could show Ferguson his 'battle dress, forage cap &

three stripes (awarded by virtue of possessing a telephone)' (19400830). The redomiciled Milford was amused to see how seriously he took it all (as indeed he did everything he undertook), describing it in a letter to Anne Ridler:

in the corner of his music-room, cheek by jowl with a table of music MS, stands a gun, and various notices also lie about the room as to 'How to behave in air-raids', etc; and he talks steadily about the war lasting 10 years, and how bitterly disappointing it must have been for all the people who died between 1803 and 1815 (wasn't it?), and so never saw or heard of Waterloo!! (Copley 1984: 58)

It was easy to scoff, but war takes place in the countryside, as Fussell observed (1975: 231), and soon enough, as Britain came within an inch of its life in the battle of the air at the end of August, there were dogfights overhead, a nearby village was strafed, and with the area's strategic altitude huge searchlights appeared in fields and a small wireless training station in the village, the Finzis avoiding further billeting of personnel at two hours' notice because Gisa Dietz counted as a dangerous alien. Gerald's weekly all-night Home Guard watch – he also did three evenings a week – was supplemented by a mysterious general stand-to in the middle of the night on 7 September: it was the first major nocturnal bombing of London, and the East End was devastated. By Christmas Southampton was a red glow on the horizon every night.

It was an extraordinarily tense time, as 'day after day the sun shone warm and the news grew worse' (McVeagh 1981b), and there were plans to ship the children off to America to join John Sumsion's family should the Germans invade. Yet until that moment Finzi would be an indistinguishable part of the British nation, protected and accepted by it and with something to fight for not alone but alongside every other citizen. At least he was no longer the freakish, lonely composer but, for the first time in his life, a cog in the great turning wheel, awaiting his call-up along with every other male of his age and trusting in Churchill's 'great & imaginative strokes' (19400920). Pre-war political uncertainty had been agonising and enervating, whereas he could bear, almost revel in the stress and apprehension that came with hostilities. Yes, he was afraid, like every other British resident; but he was also stimulated, and creativity returned. As he later stated in a letter to Milford, 'so long as we retain the capacity to feel I don't think much is lost. I certainly think that the loss of awareness & a peculiar clarity of mind & the power to

1 Birthplace of Gerald Finzi (53 – now 93 – Hamilton Terrace, London)
2 Jack Finzi, *c.* 1886
3 Kate, Felix, Douglas, Edgar and Gerald Finzi, April 1904

4 Jack Finzi with Douglas and Edgar, August 1907
5 Lizzie Finzi with Gerald, c. 1917, Harrogate

6 Ernest Farrar   7 Edward Bairstow
8 Detmar Blow   9 Winifred Blow

10 R. O. Morris   11 Herbert Howells and Gerald Finzi, *c.* 1926
12 Joyce Black at Bingles Cottage, *c.* 1933   13 Portrait of Gerald Finzi,
probably 1930

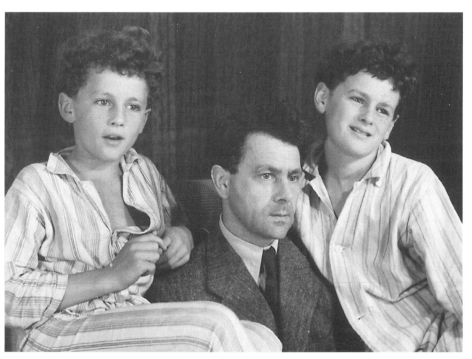

14 Joy Finzi, Howard Ferguson, Norah Nichols, Arthur Bliss and
Gerald Finzi, Pen Pits, 1937
15 Gerald with Christopher and Nigel, Church Farm, 1947

16 Church Farm, Ashmansworth
17 Portrait of Robin Milford by Joy Finzi, 1945
18 Portrait of Edmund Blunden by Joy Finzi, 1952

19 Left to right: Eric Greene, Sir Gilmour Jenkins, Jean Stewart, Gerald Finzi, Herbert Sumsion and Benjamin Frankel picnicking between rehearsals for *Intimations of Immortality*, Hyde Park, London, August 1950

20 Gerald Finzi, Ralph Vaughan Williams and Howard Ferguson's arm, Three Choirs Festival, Gloucester Cathedral, September 1953

21 Gerald Finzi with Edmund Rubbra, Cheltenham Festival, July 1956

22 Autograph sketches for the 1956 song, 'It never looks like summer', in Finzi's hand. The sheet was torn in half, discarded, and rescued from the wastepaper basket after his death.

bear tenseness & excitement is the loss of everything that matters' (19450303). He never lost that power, except perhaps in the utterly draining later years of the war, and in 1940–41 it was probably at its most acute.

There was accordingly a minor rush of compositions in the spring and summer of 1940. 'It was a lover and his lass' was drafted by 20 March and finished by mid-April, the more topical but equally seasonal F. L. Lucas setting 'June on Castle Hill', which 'came very quickly' (J. Finzi 19400703), by early July. The Elegy for violin and piano was also composed in June, and 'Channel firing', Finzi's longest song, was finished by mid-September. 'June on Castle Hill' and 'Channel firing' constitute an immediate and complementary pair of responses to the moment – the closest a composer of Finzi's cast, through making settings, could get to being a 'war poet' – and in some ways it is a pity that they were split up for publication. Another spurt of activity followed in the spring and early summer of 1941: 'To a poet a thousand years hence' was rewritten in April, the Romance for strings (as the second movement of his Serenade) and two of the clarinet Bagatelles, probably 'Carol' and 'Romance', in June. A third Bagatelle ('Forlana'?) followed in July, when Finzi also prepared his catalogue of works, *Absalom's Place*, with its message to posterity, and revised *The Fall of the Leaf* for the last time ('it really *is* finished now' [19410729]).

By now the relatively easy flow of the pen had become ironic, because once again time's axe was about to fall and put a stop to it. 'This next call up will include men of Gerald's age,' Joy had written in March 1941; 'to him it is now only a few weeks until "the billows go over my head." ' Milton's talent 'lodg'd with me useless' again sprang to mind, and he cried out in frustration, 'There is so much music I want to write and I can't with the sword hanging over my head' (J. Finzi 19410316 and 19410322). Perhaps for the first time ever, he was feeling conventionally competitive, as was everyone who was not a pacifist, for it was imperative to find a role for oneself in the nation's superhuman effort. He believed passionately that his proper duty was to remain a composer, tending the flame of civilisation's one unchanging asset in the midst of such upheaving conditions, all the more so because he had at last found how to write fluently: 'The passing of time at such a vital moment in his life when he was just achieving an easier technique is a constant remorse,' Joy wrote later in the war, acknowledging his 'fear of never re-capturing it again' (J. Finzi 19430601). Yet the government would not recognise uncommissioned composers as pursuing a reserved occupation, and he knew that this cause was hopeless when he fulminated to Howells that 'the creative artist shd be recognised as contributing to the national effort. As it is, any blue nosed comedian is reserved for entertainment purpose, whilst men like Rawsthorne, Rubbra & Tibbett [*sic*] have no status at all' (19430712). Nor did his 'rather useful' Home Guard work count: 'I'm only the platoon sergeant. If I were the platoon commander I shd possibly be left alone. I think I told you that if I were a mole-catcher I shd also be in a reserved occupation!' he explained to Ferguson a month or two before he had to register for active service (19410224). This state of affairs was rendered all the more painful by the fact that he was neither a conscientious objector nor, unlike Ferguson and Rubbra, a performer. The former might be left in peace (as was William Busch after his tribunal, though evidently on health grounds), the latter could in many cases continue playing or singing for the nation's entertainment or edification through CEMA or the forces and indeed might enjoy for the first time the luxury of a ready-made engagement diary. This seemed positively ironic in the case of an executant conscientious objector like Britten, who could continue to be a professional musician, with more exposure and recognition than ever, even if performing took up more time than he would wish. 'It makes me wild to think of you, whose contribution to music is of vital worth, "stewing" in a Government office, while Britten, because he decides to conscientiously object, is left scot-free. It's a curious piece of "justice",' wrote Rubbra (19420921). This was after Finzi had found his substitute 'reserved occupation', which did not prevent him from trying to continue to make the point. He saw Tippett, a similarly non-'reserved' musician because he was not a professional performer, as being in the same boat (though at Morley College he was doing what Vaughan Williams testified was teaching work of national importance). Tippett refused to work on the land after his tribunal in 1942 and was given a prison sentence the following year, at which point Finzi attempted to drum up signatures from colleagues for a letter to the press about it. Most of them, however, including Ferguson, Hess and Howells, felt that his argument confused the issue of conscientious objection with that of the role of the musician in wartime and declined to sign.

Rubbra had been in a similar situation to Finzi, though once he was called up he quite enjoyed his anti-aircraft postings from within the ranks (where his shorthand ability kept him in an office) and he had not only the temperament and a sufficiently established technique to be able to carry on composing on the side but also the specific abilities first to give music appreciation lectures and start an amateur orchestra in camp and then, eventually, to be commissioned into a piano trio playing for the troops. Ferguson's executant skills had been called upon much earlier, because he was younger, and he joined the RAF musical establishment at Uxbridge in August 1940 as pianist in a quintet with the Griller Quartet, though in 1942 he was released in order to continue his National Gallery work full-time.

Finzi was left high and dry by all this, though his founding of the Newbury String Players at Christmas 1940 was doubtless in part a competitive response to the various outlets his colleagues had been offered or were creating. He would have been wrong to claim that there was no war work for cultivated composers, since writing for the Ministry of Information films was an example to the contrary, and a tantalising reference to film music (19400306) suggests that Finzi may have applied, or have considered applying, to do this. If so, nothing came of it. Then, once again, it was Bliss who helped him forward. Bliss had been stranded with his family on an extended visit to the USA when war broke out and at first took an academic job at the University of California at Berkeley. It seemed advisable for Trudy, who was American, and the children to remain on that side of the Atlantic, but Arthur, like Benjamin Britten, felt an overwhelming need for active solidarity with the British people. He had already offered his services to the BBC and the British Council, and came back in June 1941 after he had been invited, presumably at Boult's behest, to become Director – or was it Assistant Director? – of Overseas Music. Ten days after disembarking he was writing to Trudy: 'to-morrow I have Gerald Finzi for lunch & hope to get him into the BBC somehow' (Bliss 1970: 142). There was little time to lose, for Finzi had registered for military duty at the end of May and was expecting to be called up in August following a medical.

What happened next was explained by Finzi in a letter to Busch:

A short time ago I had a tentative offer of a BBC job. It was the usual sort of thing, where one wd have been involved with a little music & much muck, office work, concert agency & all the BBC schimozzle! I turned it down, as I wd really prefer to be in the army than do that sort of thing, though it was exceedingly kind of anyone to think of me with regard to it. About the same time I was asked by an acquaintance if my name cd be considered for an appointment in the Ministry of War Transport, where a particular type of person was needed. I went up before the board, thinking what a fool I was to waste their & my time, & noticing that all the other applicants had got the right suits on (whereas mine was my one & only, bought off the peg at a Harrods sale in 1924 or 1925!) & presuming that they had all the correct & orthodox educational records; matric, school certificate & all that standardised drivel, whereas I had never taken an exam in my life & shd probably never have passed one, as I can only do things *my* own way. Yet a day or two later I had a letter offering me the appointment & I've accepted it. I take up duty at the end of this month or first week in August. It's going to be a hard job, with responsibilities, & means (horror of horrors) working in Berkeley Square daily from 9.0 am till 6.30 pm, with only Sundays off to get down to Joy & the children, & to look into my own affairs. I have been lucky in getting rooms in Frognal Lane, which is not too far out, thanks to some friends who have evacuated to the country, but left their furnished house in charge of an old housekeeper who won't budge. It remains to be seen whether I shall have enough energy left in my evenings for music, especially when the blitzes start again. However, the war won't last forever & I wd rather be doing something totally unrelated to music than that sort of half & half BBC job. And I ought to be very grateful to have a chance of using brains instead of brawn, for I shall at least be of more use than doing sentry work on Dartmoor.

Clothes are my chief difficulty, as I really *will* have to get a suit, & Joy, presuming that I wd be called up, used all my coupons on underwear (for myself)! (19410718a)

This needs glossing slightly. Joy Finzi (1987b) states that the BBC opening was 'the job that Arthur had just left', and it seems likely that Bliss had initially been appointed as assistant to Kenneth Wright, who ran the department, but that immediately on Bliss's arrival Wright moved on and Bliss moved up. The two first interviews were on the same day, and before the second BBC one Finzi was already telling Bliss that he had been more impressed with the Ministry of War Transport and thought they would offer him the job. He gave him a further reason for being uncertain about the BBC post: 'Also I'm suspicious of you! To work with you is invigorating, but I suspect that you'll be flown in 6 months!' (19410712). He was right, though it was within the Corporation that Bliss became airborne: he was appointed Director of Music at the BBC in the following year.

The Ministry of Transport and the Ministry of Shipping had been merged to form the Ministry of War Transport in May 1941, which nonetheless must have had to take on extra staff rapidly as the war intensified and especially, where its Foreign Shipping Relations Division was concerned, as co-operation with the United States broadened until they became an Ally. Under the new Ministry's Director-General there were three Deputy Directors-General, two for Shipping and one for Inland Transport. One of the Shipping ones was Gilmour Jenkins (knighted during Gerald's time at the Ministry), and he interviewed Gerald and clearly rooted for him. He was the archetypal civil servant with immaculate taste who sings in or runs a choir or excels in some other branch of the arts, and he later became a friend of the poet Ursula Wood, whose first husband died in 1942 (her second of course being Vaughan Williams); Gerald, who together with Joy knew her through the Vaughan Williamses (having first met her at the 1942 birthday concert), introduced them. Although there was a divisional chief, the Assistant Secretary W. C. Weston, between the two men, Jenkins struck up an affectionate friendship with Finzi, later remarking on 'a real bond of sympathy from our very first meeting at my round table' (19440609). He was deeply grateful to Gerald for getting him 'out of the official rut & . . . interested once more in real things & meeting people with real interests outside Government & transport circles,' added that Wednesdays (probably the evening meetings of Ursula Wood's madrigal group, in which both men sang) had been a great tonic, and thanked 'the good God who guided you here for an interview so many years ago,' but for which 'I should never have known you or Joy or the two children. It doesn't bear thinking about' (19450703a). This was doubtless all true, but it did not stop Gerald getting Vaughan Williams to write a letter to his boss to try to have him released when he could bear being away from his freedom no longer.

Gerald was appointed Temporary Principal or Assistant Principal in the Foreign Shipping Relations Division and put in charge of South American Shipping, presumably a steady job given the countries' neutrality but a responsible and hard one in a world war involving so much submarine and convoy activity and requisitioning of transport, though Ursula Vaughan Williams states, somewhat mischievously, that they called him 'Frenzy' at the Ministry and that his sole task was to get some ship into South America and then get it out again. It was a wonderful irony, though one he chose not to dwell on, that he had to all intents and purposes come full circle to his father's occupation of shipbroker.

He started work on 30 July, quizzical yet immensely pleased with himself: never before except in the odd composition award had he achieved something on other people's terms. 'To think that I, who wrote Proud Songsters – Dies Natalis – Farewell to Arms – am to become a Principal in the Foreign Shipping Relations Depart[ment] of the Ministry of War Transport. How fantastic – how unbelievably fantastic' he exclaimed to Joy (J. Finzi 19410729), echoing Chamberlain's 1938 speech about Czechoslovakia ('How horrible, fantastic, incredible it is that we should be digging trenches and trying on gas-masks here because of a quarrel in a far-away country between people of whom we know nothing!' [Graves and Hodge 1940, R.1971: 447]). Joy went up to 14 Frognal Lane with him, 'lay[ing] London shirts in a strange drawer & manuscripts on the work table' (J. Finzi 19410730) while he reported for duty 'like the smallest boy going to the largest college for the first time' (and, she might have added, with the most desolate parent, or in this case spouse, having to return home alone). The big red-brick house at the bottom of Frognal Lane belonged to David Watson of University College, London, a palaeontologist who had become a neighbour at Ashmansworth for the duration of the war while his department migrated to Bangor, and it included a fine piano as well as the indomitable housekeeper. Finzi does not seem to have had any close shaves with bombs, though he did return from work one day to find that the house had been ransacked by burglars. He had to move out of it into spartan accommodation provided by Richard Latham's church towards the end of his four years at the Ministry when Professor Watson returned to London.

Gerald's job stood him in good stead in a number of ways. It gave him a full-time salary – over £600 a year – for the first time in his life, while Joy got a married person's allowance, and he probably began collecting antiquarian music in earnest during his London lunch-times, when prices were low and shops surrounded him (but see Chapter 10). It greatly enhanced his general confidence and his interpersonal skills (as we should call them), prepared him for useful committee and panel work after the war, including the responsibilities of the chair, and made him much more used to working decisively and to frantic deadlines. As a result, he wrote twice as much music, and for much larger forces, in the ten years after 1945 than in the fifteen preceding ones, despite his burgeoning postwar responsibilities, interests and activities in other fields. In many respects it was the making of him – Milford recognised this when he wrote 'the "drain-pipe existence" has made you greater' (19420503) – though it did not fundamentally alter his creative persona.

This is not to say that the job did not become a weary, grinding drudgery: it was bound to, especially in wartime, and within three weeks of starting he was writing to Milford:

My present job goes on – & on. Off early each morning & then papers & papers & telegrams & files; an hour off for lunch & then more papers & telegrams & files till I get home at 8.0 or 9.0. It's extraordinarily tiring, if only by sheer weight of material one has to master. It's all very absurd, when you think of the transitoriness of it all. Anything that is more than a month old is quite definitely old history ... Thank Heaven in real life my job deals with more permanent values. (19410815)

Nevertheless, and despite the fact that as a composing mortal 'you can live other people's lives, but they can never share yours' (19411005), he was not in uncongenial or desultory company, as he described to Rubbra:

I am lucky in liking most of my colleagues at the Ministry, and in being treated like an adult. The fact that one does not have to 'clock in', and is allowed to do one's work in one's own time, means that everybody works much harder as a result of the trust that is put in them.

I have certainly had to change any views I had about civil servants. The higher grades are a first rate lot of people. I often wondered how one could 'place' R. O. Morris, and now I realise that he is very typical of that type, with his all round brain, peculiar humour, and many other qualities.

As an organisation, the civil service is really rather like the technique side of the creative mind. Anyone of average intelligence can be taught to 'compose' in a routine academic way, just as anyone can master normal civil service routine. Both are really the wheels on which the creative mind moves. A Churchill must have the civil service organisation for him to function, just as a composer must have a good technique to run on. I find the analogy crops up very frequently as one sees diplomacy based on the foundations of our work!

However I can't begin to give you any idea of what we do, and when it is all over, I hope I shall forget it in quicker time than I have learnt it! (ibid.)

Gerald found that he was too tired when he got home each evening to do much except read poetry and write the odd letter, and even concerts and theatre were no longer regular diversions. Although he did manage the occasional evening with Howard Ferguson or a friend passing through London, composition was of necessity shelved, and the completion of a handful of single pieces took the utmost effort, with no spirit of delight to reward it. For him and for everyone else during these deepest war years there was little in Britain, still less in London, to lift the spirit: drab and insufficient food and a general, acute shortage of goods; blackouts everywhere; and air raids most nights, especially at the beginning and (with the advent of flying bombs and V2 rockets) the end of his Civil Service period. Once, in June 1943, he was sent home on a month's sick leave, fearing a recurrence of his tuberculosis but simply in a state of collapse from complete exhaustion. Joy, who was also working harder than ever, must have been in constant worry, not just about his spiritual and physical health but for his physical safety too.

Who can say whether the Newbury String Players were a lifeline or an additional drain on his energies? He got home three weekends out of four (he was a duty officer for the fourth), but not until Saturday afternoon; often he would go straight from the train to the weekly rehearsal in Newbury (which had been moved from Sundays to Saturdays at some point), returning to London early Monday morning.

At a time when there was still relatively little music-making because of the war, though its level had crept back up since 1939, Gerald had offered to conduct an amateur string orchestra if Joy fixed the players. She herself was one of the second violinists, and in due course their two sons would become good enough string players to join in when they were home from boarding school. The orchestra made its début in the tiny, ancient parish church of St James, across the lane from the house at Ashmansworth, on the afternoon of 28 December 1940, doubtless a relief for all concerned from the convivial rigours of the season, and the first of their annual, candlelit Christmas concerts. For the next thirty-nine years, the orchestra rehearsed weekly except for a summer break and a short Christmas one and gave a total of 379 concerts, a dozen or more a year in the first few seasons. It played in churches large and small, parish and town halls, colleges and schools and corn exchanges, throughout Hampshire, Berkshire, Wiltshire and Oxfordshire, bringing the classical string repertoire to obscure venues (such as Ashmansworth Church) that had certainly never heard it before but also helping to revitalise many a local festival's and school's music-making after wartime dispersals of teachers, choirs, parents, pupils and classes had depressed their community or competitive gatherings. The Newbury String Players performed primarily in their own concerts, with vocal and instrumental guest soloists, but were also joined by a choir from time to time or provided part of a festival concert programme, their appearance every spring at the Newbury Festival chief among these.

The players were initially recruited from the Newbury Amateur Orchestral Union and were, predictably, mostly female. Finzi referred to them as his twenty-five 'old ladies' until rebuked by Vaughan Williams, who protested that 'your excellent orchestra ... includes several young & lovely women (including your own wife)' when he first heard and saw them at the Newbury Festival in 1945 (19450803b). The first leader was Rosie Roth, a local refugee, and she played the Bach E major Violin Concerto at the début concert, which also included Holst's *St Paul's Suite*, Boyce's Symphony No. 4, and the Pastorale from Corelli's 'Christmas' Concerto. She was not unproblematic ('what *must* the Budapest conservatoire have been like,' Finzi exclaimed [19410101b]), and later they opted for a paid leader, May Hope coming up from Oxford in the earlier years, John Kirby succeeding her for the remainder of the orchestra's life. As an amateur orchestra they were bound to have personnel difficulties of one kind or another – of finding a double bass player, of house-training local organists and continuo players when needed, of maintaining attendance at rehearsals. Wartime conditions can hardly have helped Joy's immense burden of administration. Petrol rationing, for instance, threatened to stifle the NSP's very existence in 1942, and although Vaughan Williams may have pulled some strings on their behalf and they got a small allowance, it must have remained a difficulty (and generally restricted the Finzis' mobility) until it was relaxed several years after the end of the war. As for finances, at first the aim was to raise money for the bombed-out residents of Southampton, and they had collected £100 by the time Gerald started his MWT job, after their first seven months. This will partly have explained the intensity of their schedule, especially since it was not at all clear whether the orchestra would be able to keep going thenceforth until Gerald knew that he could get home most weekends. Later, when the players' commitment entailed continuing sacrifices of scarce commodities, financial assistance was sought from CEMA, and after the war they received an Arts Council grant for taking music to the region.

The first NSP concert at Ashmansworth was something of a turning-point in Finzi's life. With one stroke it consecrated the *genius loci* of his new, chosen home and hallowed his secular yet transcendent vision of music in the community, though it trod on toes in a way scarcely imaginable today, so completely secularised has British life become since the war. Concerts given by the NSP in churches could not be so described but were dubbed 'An hour of music'. Even so, and without applause (never permitted in church until two or three decades ago), Milford expressed regret at the programming of non-sacred pieces on this first occasion, which elicited one of Finzi's epistolary star turns:

Here we are, once again, at the roots of this *intolerance*, which all beliefs (as opposed to 'ideas & feelings') seem to beget. Thus Mrs S— of our village, was horrified that Mrs W— a confessed unbeliever, shd come into the church to hear the music & went as far as to say that she shd not have been allowed in. Mrs W—, on the other hand, was appalled at the Vicar's prayers, which she thought quite out of place. Mr A— the churchwarden thought the collection of £11.1.6 very remarkable.

Oh, how much *bigger* music is than all this & why shd it be tied down to earth by a Communist rope, or a Fascist rope, or a Church rope or a Chapel rope or a pagan rope or any bloody rope. It *is* sufficient in itself. Incidentally, if it has to be the handmaid of religion, *which* religion? And why was the Bach E major concerto any more religious that the Holst, & was that lovely Sinfonia necessarily suitable for a church just because it prefaces a church cantata: it happens to be also used as the slow mvt of a secular concerto & so on. I shd have been just as happy doing that music in a village hall as in the church, but I admit that the setting was marvellous & that in itself was part of the art. I didn't rejoice that only 4 people go to Church on a Sunday & 100 came to hear music on a weekday. It doesn't matter to me whether 4 or 40 go to Church, as I have never yet found anyone better or worse for going or not going. But I did rejoice to think that, perhaps for the first time in history, most of the Chapel attended the church, & that agnostics, RC's, Anglo C's, Jews, chapel & C of E were all gathered together, seeing a beautiful sight, listening to decent music & with all their ridiculous differences dropped for at least an hour. (19401230)

'Thank you so much for your letter, but oh dear! oh dear! oh dear! oh dear, oh dear, oh *dear*!! – I disagree with almost every word of it,' Milford replied (19410101a), and off they went on one of their extended arguments. Without wishing to join in posthumously, one might point out that the problem with Finzi's liberal viewpoint, which implies that culture is good in itself and that people therefore *are* to be found 'better or worse' for imbibing or shunning art, came to a head after the war in George Steiner's 'after Auschwitz' theory, which says ' "We know that some of the men who devised and administered Auschwitz had been trained to read Shakespeare and Goethe, and continued to do so." For Steiner, this revelation puts into question the "primary concept of a literary, humanistic culture" ' (Doyle 1989: 116, quoting Steiner *et al* 1964: 23). This would have been the debate of a lifetime for Finzi had he lived to take part in it.

The NSP début additionally marks the start of Finzi's active career as an eighteenth-century scholar, to be examined more fully in Chapter 10, for before long he was having to scour the repertoire for, and eventually began to make performing editions of, baroque works for his players; he also made string arrangements of later music such as Gurney songs. It goes without saying that the orchestra also consolidated his position in provincial musical life, for though various other, separate involvements with Newbury and with Hampshire and Berkshire music were inevitable in due course, he never attempted to dominate or appropriate these. In this Finzi's preference – and limitations – contrasted sharply with Britten's. Britten actually turned up to a Newbury String Players engagement at Bradfield College in May 1942 (as, by an extraordinary coincidence, did George Dyson, who was passing through and heard Bach being rehearsed) – he was staying for the weekend with the concert's soloist, Sophie Wyss, and her husband Arnold Gyde. He was not impressed by the orchestra – 'amateur (and how)' – or by Finzi's enthusiasm, which he described as the ' "I prefer this to those horrible professionals" sort of thing – ugh!' But there were enough pretty schoolboys around to console him (Mitchell 1991: II, 1055–6).

The orchestra must have sounded scratchy and uncertain enough at first, but Milford assured Finzi that as early as May 1942 they had 'improved out of recognition (honestly, if I'd been behind a curtain I don't think I'd have known it was the same band as when I first heard them in Ashmansworth Church)' (19420503). They undoubtedly went from strength to strength, continuing to flourish after Finzi's death, when the cellist Jennifer Ward Clarke wrote to Joy: 'that orchestra was a wonderful thing . . . I have heard from many sources that it has the reputation for being the best amateur string orchestra in the country' (19561004b). At one time the double bass player – was it Lawrence Ashmore? – drove over from Kent every week because he enjoyed it so much. A list of the orchestra's soloists, many of them promising young college students or professionals Finzi had heard about, would be impressive, including within his lifetime Isobel Baillie, Joy Boughton, Julian Bream, Bernard Brown, Wilfred Brown, John Carol Case, John Constable, Colin Davis, Ruth Dyson, Sybil Eaton, Howard Ferguson, Léon Goossens, Eric Greene, Frederick Grinke, Henry Holst, Philip Jones, Richard Latham, Kathleen Long, Denis Matthews, Marion Milford, Yfrah Neaman, William Pleeth, Bernard Rose (baritone!), Antoinette and Edmund Rubbra, John Russell, Mollie Sands, Anna Shuttleworth, Julian Smith, Jean Stewart, Herbert Sumsion, Norman Tattersall, David Willcocks, Sophie Wyss, and the well-known Dutch flautist and musicologist Johannes Feltkamp, who greatly enjoyed performing with 'people who arrange, organise and play just for love of art and the fun of playing . . . even if not everything was done with the technical perfection a professional orchestra may command' (19501220). Even the rank-and-file players included some eminent names, such as Albi Rosenthal and Professor Stephen Smith of St Thomas's Medical School, then an Oxford undergraduate. Up to a point, the orchestra also offered a platform for young composers, pre-eminently Kenneth Leighton but also Stephen Dodgson and one or two others. In this it was far from the expected provincial model and in effect formed its own reading panel on occasions. For instance, in May 1951 Finzi reported to Milford that they had had 'a flute afternoon' with Catherine Powell, reading through 'a set of Variations by a Dutch composer, Andriessen, dull, negative stuff, & a Suite by Stephen Dodgson, interesting but rather ungrateful writing, which no-one except the composer, a nice chap, enjoyed! The Interlude [by Milford] was the only work we felt we wanted to do' (19510522). The surroundings were extraordinarily unpressurised for such meetings of performers and composers, amateurs and professionals, though Finzi was not as firm with his players in rehearsals as he should have been. The adjournment to the Bandar-Log Tea Rooms in Newbury at seven o'clock on a Saturday evening after the three-hour rehearsal became legendary.

'Well, I shall never make much of a conductor,' Finzi admitted to Ferguson after his first concert (19410101b). It was not the very first time he had tried to conduct, and indeed he had gained 'his first very valuable . . . experience' with another local body run by Joy, a choir in Sussex, before their marriage (Highfield 1978: 5–6). But apart from this, the previous occasions were attempts at his own works and had been 'a nightmare & a dismal failure' (19410117), one of them in July 1935 when he was let loose on a BBC broadcast of his *New Year Music*, a performance he kept singularly quiet about. Now, however, 'I shd never have any qualms about conducting my own stuff in the future . . . a weekly rehearsal with a few picked amateurs in Newbury has made me feel much more at home with a baton,' he told Busch (ibid.). Sure enough, five years later he did make a satisfactory professional début, conducting *Dies natalis* at the Three Choirs Festival in Hereford – in Tony Scott's morning suit, his doctor Tom Scott's dress shirt and collar, and John Sumsion's tie ('together with John and 4 assistants to help me put the things on in the right order' [19460916a]). He coped well enough, though Rubbra pointed out 'one mannerism [that] worried me & I felt myself doing the same in my seat! – that is your habit of *leaning to the right always*, whatever you are doing' (19460917b), and Anna Shuttleworth (1995: [10]) writes that 'he waved his arms in an imaginative style and we all did our best to follow him' in the Newbury String Players. Carol Case's verdict is that 'he wasn't as bad as VW' (1996). He had only two disasters in his first five years with the NSP, when a movement broke down because of a mistake he had made, but was very upset on both occasions. He was not a good loser.

With a war on, a demanding full-time job as a weekly commuter, and an orchestra to rehearse and conduct, Finzi had more than enough to keep him busy. Most of the NSP's fifty or sixty wartime concerts were at weekends, but not all of them, and the others took up the bulk of his Ministry leave. So a small tally of compositions at this period is hardly surprising. More so is its high quality, which he tended to belittle, perhaps because he had willed rather than enjoyed the effort.

Finzi's fingerprints, found on all his scores, are at the same time rather more period-specific than is generally recognised. Thus the introductory 'vamp' of 'It was a lover and his lass' reappears to herald in the tonic major section of 'June on Castle Hill' two months later, and is again re-used in the 'Forlana' of the Five Bagatelles. Lucas's 'Not a tower now, / Not a stone:' in 'June on Castle Hill' inevitably recalls another of Finzi's Shakespeare songs, from the same period, 'Come away, come away, death', with its 'Not a flower, not a flower sweet' at the start of the second stanza, though strangely enough it is Quilter's setting of these lines, not Finzi's, that the melody set to Lucas's words resembles. And the opening motif of 'June on Castle Hill' is reminiscent of that of 'The market-girl', in the same key, which he had revised earlier the same year. 'June on Castle Hill' has an odd and disturbing structure, reflecting that of the poem, for the 'release' of the first stanza's site of ancient battle into the grassy, springtime peace of the present day in the second stanza brings only a temporary and deceptive lightening with the music's tonic major: what really happens overall is that the music's structural fall to tonic closure at the end of the first stanza ($\hat{5}$ $\hat{4}$ $\flat\hat{3}$ $\hat{2}$ $\hat{1}$ in the melody) is eventually continued on downwards through another half-octave ($\hat{8}$ $\sharp\hat{7}$ $\sharp\hat{6}$ $\hat{5}$) to the low D on which the melody terminates, while the accompaniment remorselessly sinks to a tessitura an octave below its initial one. Like the descent of an everlasting staircase in a dream, this is much more disconcerting than one might expect, and gives one Finzi's 'fundamental pessimism' in a flash. Shades of the same 'Fallings from us, vanishings; / Blank misgivings' are intimated not so much in the setting of these words in Finzi's Wordsworth Ode as in his instrumental prelude to it, where between figure 2 and the entry of the voice at figure 4 the throbbing harmony keeps sinking until the bottom would fall out of its world, though in this case (not in the Lucas setting) the music suddenly pulls out of its reverie with the *fp* chord (ex. 8.1.a). Is there something of the manic depressive in this recurrent persona?

The even more murky C minor opening of 'Channel firing' is like the tonic to the G minor modal dominant of 'June on Castle Hill'. 'Channel firing' is Finzi's most ambitious song, though it misses the structural integration of 'He abjures love' and does not quite compensate by hinting at a demonic four-in-one symphony in miniature, almost like a tiny Liszt B minor Sonata (the octaves at 'So down we lay again' and the Mephistophelian skeletons with their momentary scherzo, as well as the overall Teutonic cast of textural weightiness, prompt the comparison). In one respect its centrepiece is God's anti-war sermon – a deeply ironic set number in view of Parson Thirdly's scepticism about

EX. 8.1.a

preaching – covering four stanzas, of which the middle two themselves form a central stormy Allegro following a slow introduction. But in another sense this Allegro is merely a lyrical strophe with central caesura on a half-close – or a toccata, even, leading to some unspecified and unfulfilled consequent. This is the whole point: that the consequent never comes. Even in the strophe of the sermon there is a false musical perspective, the half-close itself giving way to a bigger one at the word 'threatening' (whose only consequent is a laugh, while the music continues flatwards through the cycle of fifths). We may look for it in an Allegro recapitulation. There are hints of this in the rhythmic motif setting the words 'I blow the trumpet', echoing the phrase 'The world is as it used to be' which had inaugurated the Allegro, though Finzi, in a rare and fatal misunderstanding, spoils this reference when he misses Hardy's point about God's Armageddon as opposed to man's by failing to provide the proper accentuation for the line 'It will be warmer when *I* blow the trumpet'. Or, if instead of rising at the last trump, the corpses are to sleep on undisturbed for ever, then the consequent should be the slow throbbing march in B♭ minor that raises expectations of an aria after 'So down we lay again'; but this too is shrugged off by the skeletons' cynical scherzo. The only real recapitulation or fulfilment of existence is not God's but man's, who structures time not with an achieving symphony but with his wretched rondo of war, 'Again the guns disturb[ing] the hour' as the song's opening ritornello returns, providing the only formal certainty and, if you like, defensive security in the whole song.

Finzi plays with form in 'Channel firing' as Hardy plays with time and eschatology, his teasingly incomplete, layered musical sections and their interrelationships matching Hardy's blasphemous theology, in which a mouse can partake of the remains of the Host, gunnery practice can smash stained glass, and corpses can imagine the Judgement-day in the *past* and subsume it into the eternal perspective not of any last day but of an infinity of earlier days implied by the eighteenth-century, Arthurian and prehistoric points on the line of history in the poem's last two lines. He also plays with musical space in terms of a highly unbalanced tonal centre of gravity, its dominant (therefore goal-orientated) rise in the central 'strophe' hardly compensating for the obsessively flatward descent everywhere else, resolved only in terms of a large-scale phrygian cadence for the song as a whole. One cannot quite accept 'Channel firing' as the masterpiece it needs to be, and to bring it off completely would make formidable demands on the greatest baritone, for Finzi does not really grasp the narrative voices with the dramatic characterisation of colour, pace and tessitura that they demand. Hardy, utilising something of the mummers' conventions (as when God says 'for Christés sake', and in his general demeanour towards humanity – compare *Noye's Fludde*), is for once not fully served. One hates to say it, but Britten would have done it better, though there is in any case something Brittenesque about the sonority of Finzi's opening 'gunnery' motif, with its abstraction into an *étude* of thirds in wide hand spans, and the doggedness of the later battering accompaniment. What is decidedly not Brittenesque is the Elgarian sympathy evinced betweentimes, not least for the cow.

'To a poet a thousand years hence' is another meditation upon the past and the future, and it was one of the poems Finzi placed in his time capsule in 1938. It illustrates perfectly his belief in the 'telegraph wires' of communication across the ages through art (see p. 11). Accordingly, his setting comes closest of all his songs to a definitive personal testimony. At least, this is true in terms of sensibility of thought: the music itself is somewhat uneven and seems to betray its early origin, particularly in the fourth stanza, where the fabric for the 'wind that falls at eve' is polytonally creased in the Vaughan Williams manner he had long left behind and needs tucking in. Such an extensive central span of A and E major, in a C minor song, also stretches unity too far, not just in tonal but in registral terms, old Maeonides (and who was he?) suddenly conjuring up a tenor rather than a baritone (all the more so before the song was transposed down a tone for posthumous publication). To judge from 'The temporary the all', this was a join of separate material never fully soldered, and a tiny sketch, probably from around 1925, of a different setting of the words 'How shall we conquer?' (ex. 8.1.b, from Sketchbook A: r6), affirms a higher tessitura. Nevertheless, 'To a poet a thousand years hence' is an achingly beautiful song, not least because it speaks directly in the second person singular, from the first person and the present tense – a rare voice even in as lyrical an art as Finzi's, its intimacy scarcely matched in 'Her temple' and 'To Lizbie Browne', in which the 'I' and the 'you' are also employed. It is an ardent love letter written to span the ages, to Flecker from his imaginary poet, from the poet, and all poets, to the composer, from Finzi to any who 'will understand' when they listen. A presumptuous transference, yes, if his 'sweet archaic song' is itself to last a thousand

EX. 8.1.b

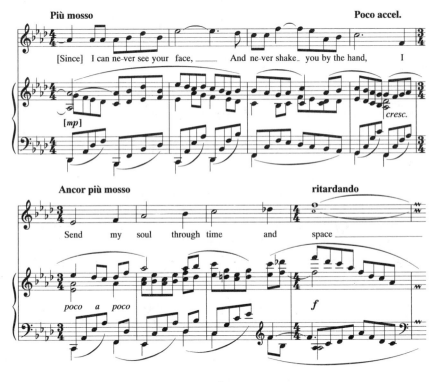

EX. 8.1.c

years, but an idea to which his material is equal, from the magical mixolydian touch for the 'sweet English tongue' and its student (a lovely irony to use this for the future rather than the past) to the passionate embrace of the sonata- or rondo-like tune that shows a new fluency and with its broader melodic partner in the voice part achieves a real climax as the ravishment of time that is art is consummated (ex. 8.1.c).

Finzi's poetic statement in 'To a poet a thousand years hence' was soon joined by a prose one when he compiled a catalogue of his works and wrote a preface for it, entitled *Absalom's Place*, immediately before joining the Ministry in July 1941. It summarises his humanistic belief in the value of the minor artist – and, almost equally important, of scholarship as the handmaid or even the bridegroom of art, if there is always to be a 'student' or two motivated to read the work, whatever tricks posterity plays with the artist's reputation, and if the stewardship of a circumscribed or incomplete output is not to fail (as he himself had not failed Gurney). It is short enough to be quoted in full.

Absalom's place

It was Thomas Hardy who wrote

'Why do I go on doing these things?'

and, indeed, if appreciation were a measure of merit and cause for self-esteem, it wd long ago have been time for me to shut up shop, class myself as a failure, and turn to something of what the world is pleased to call a more 'useful' nature.

Yet some curious force compels us to preserve and project into the future the essence of our individuality, and, in doing so, to project something of our age and civilisation. The artist is like the coral insect, building his reef out of the transitory world around him and making a solid structure to last long after his own fragile and uncertain life. It is one of the many proud points of his occupation that, great or small, there is, ultimately, little else but his work through which his country and civilisation may be known & judged by posterity.

(As to stature, it is of no matter. The coral reef, like the mountain peaks, has its ups & downs. 'If he cannot bring a Ceder, let him bring a shrubbe.')

It was, then, in no mood of vanity that Henry Vaughan wrote

'*Ad Posteros*'
Diminuat ne sera dies praesentis honorem,
Quis, qualisque: fui, percipe Posteritas.

(Englished by Blunden thus:

To After Ages
Time soon forgets; and yet I would not have
The present wholly mouldering in the grave.
Hear then, posterity:)

Nor was Absalom guilty of mere self-aggrandisement when we read in the second book of Samuel:

> Now Absalom in his lifetime had taken and reared up for himself a pillar, which is in the Kings' dale: For he said, I have no son to keep my name in remembrance: And he called the pillar after his own name, and it is called unto this day, Absalom's place.

And what of the main-spring of this curious force, this strange necessity?
There is no need here to go into the labyrinths of aesthetics & to discuss whether art is based on the need for communication or the need for organised expression. For me, at any rate, the essence of art is order, completion & fulfilment. Something is created out of nothing, order out of chaos; and as we succeed in shaping our intractable material into coherence and form, a relief comes to the mind (akin to the relief experienced at the remembrance of some forgotten thing) as a new accretion is added to that projection of oneself which, in metaphor, has been called 'Absalom's place' or a coral reef or a 'ceder or shrubbe'.

It must be clear, particularly in the case of a slow worker, that only a long life can see the rounding-off and completion of this projection. Consequently, those few works of mine fit for publication can only be regarded as fragments of a building. The foundations have (perhaps) been laid, odd bricks are lying about, though comparatively little of the end which is envisaged is to be seen. Long may Absalom's pillar grow, but in the event of my death I am anxious for as much as is finished & fit for publication to be issued, preferably in as uniform an edition as possible. It would be unwise to issue definite instructions; likely as not, with constantly changing conditions, they would soon be out of date or unpractical. I should like the whole question of revised publications, new publications & withdrawals to be dealt with systematically & I suggest that the advice of Howard Ferguson should be asked. Not only does he know my systematised marks of expression etc but his practical advice has always been of the greatest help. That, together with my dear wife's judgment, shd be sufficient.

Gerald Finzi
July 1941

Finzi's lifelong combination of urgent pronouncement with modest career and output is bound to strike us with a touch of sententiousness, and as it happened he and all his manuscripts survived the war unscathed. But almost exactly ten years after consecrating *Absalom's Place* he would have further portentous occasion to revisit it, one less easily gainsaid.

The particles that Finzi did manage to add to his coral reef during the later war years by no means reflect their grim times and are actually more blithe and relaxed than anything he had yet written. The Shakespeare songs appeared first, published and performed as *Let Us Garlands Bring*, Finzi's contribution to Vaughan Williams's seventieth birthday celebrations. 'Fear no more the heat o' the sun' had been composed in 1929 and probably did not require much revision. The others were more recent and more mature (though 'Fear no more the heat o' the sun' is powerful in its early austerity): 'Come away, come away, death' was written in July 1938, 'It was a lover and his lass' in the spring of 1940, as already mentioned and by now with the specific object of a set of Shakespeare songs in mind, and 'Who is Silvia?' some time before January 1941. As usual, it was counsel, conscience or inertia that caused the composer to add a fifth, fast number to the work only after he had persuaded himself that it was complete without it. 'O mistress mine' accordingly followed in May 1942, 'a pleasant light, troubadourish setting', though it had taken Finzi 'more than 3 months to do its four pages' while feeling 'baulked, thwarted, fretted, tired, good for nothing & utterly wasting my time' in his Berkeley Square prison, where no nightingale sang (19420515).

Boosey for once made no difficulties over publication, though the set's florid title (admittedly Finzi's idea) pleased him more than it did Finzi's friends. *Let Us Garlands Bring* was issued in time for the first performance, given by Robert Irwin and Howard Ferguson at a National Gallery lunch-time concert on Vaughan Williams's seventieth birthday, 12 October 1942 (though his age was omitted from the score's title page at Adeline's request). Irwin, a fine musician and one extremely sensitive to words and poetic sense, was something of a find and became Finzi's foremost baritone exponent for some years afterwards, though later, following a terrible road accident, he lost his concert nerve (Ferguson 1974–96). He and Ferguson gave a fine performance, despite Ferguson's lumbago, which Finzi assured him did not affect his playing, even if 'you cd not conceal that something was wrong somewhere by your attempts to walk across the platform. Probably most people thought you wanted to go to the lavatory!' (19421012b). The press was laudatory, and after the concert, which also included Vaughan Williams's Double String Trio and Fantasy String Quintet, Joy and Gerald threw a lunch party attended by the Vaughan Williamses, Denis Matthews and Mira Howe, Ferguson and a friend, Ursula Wood and Toty de Navarro. There was another concert of brief musical tributes from various composers (and of various shades of quality, according to Finzi) later the same day, broadcast from one of the BBC London studios and apparently compèred by Hubert Foss, who against expectation 'appeared to be absolutely sober' (ibid.). Six days later Finzi's tribute had its own broadcast, in an arrangement of the songs with strings made by him and performed by Irwin with the BBC Symphony Orchestra conducted by Clarence Raybould.

'I wd rather listen to a deft, delightful, light, movement by Ed German, or Fauré or J Strauss or Elgar than all the ponderous integrity of Bruckner or the constipated integrity of Schoenberg!' wrote Finzi just after he had finished 'O mistress mine' (19420616). It is the cycle's vernacular lightness that distinguishes *Let Us Garlands Bring* so radiantly and earns Finzi what was after all his privileged position of being the one composer of all Vaughan Williams's friends and juniors to share the platform with him at the focal birthday event. In this homage as much to Shakespeare as to Vaughan Williams, he was filling a gap that had opened up between the often forced jollity of the folksong ideal, by now decidedly outmoded in relation to mass taste (if folksong settings had ever appealed to it in the first place), and the much more slick and sophisticated cheerfulness of the new urban light music for radio, resort and theatre, as practised by Eric Coates, Haydn Wood and many others. Walton was already bridging the gap, and Malcolm Arnold about to, in instrumental music, especially for films, but it lacked a vocal mediator between the dying drawing-room tradition and the rising Hollywood and Broadway one, someone who could set the English language to music with both integrity and the broadest possible appeal. True, Warlock had earlier achieved something germane, but Finzi is at pains to avoid both archaism and alcohol, respectively twee and rumbustious, as refuges (rather than merely allusions), and settles instead in 'O mistress mine' and, pre-eminently, 'It was a lover and his lass' for a relaxed and stylishly idiomatic wardrobe of modern enough yet casual and comfortable clothes. They have worn extremely well, and Touchstone will continue to make a better showing, as he struts down Piccadilly or the main street of Henley-in-Arden, in Finzi's costume than in most if not all of the other 350 he has been asked to wear over the centuries (see Gooch and Thatcher 1991: I, 134–58) while he listens to the two pages singing 'It was a lover and his lass'. Finzi came as close to the universal appeal of an English vernacular in the music of this song as Shakespeare ever did in his characters and

EX. 8.2.a

aphorisms; perhaps it is because it all sounds so natural that he hardly seems to have noticed the achievement, though it is one that should have pleased him more than anything else in the world. It was a noble piece of war work. Nor did it remain unnoticed at the time, at least by Robin Hull, who praised Finzi's 'wellnigh inconceivable' freshness in a first proper treatment of the composer within the covers of a single book (1946: 222–3).

Deftness of technique and characterisation are the hallmarks of three of the songs in the cycle. For instance, Finzi is (at last!) getting quite adept at tonic return and therefore structural balance – witness the third stanza of 'It was a lover and his lass', which begins in the double subdominant (D major) but pulls itself back up without effort but with two splendid touches, the F natural whole-tone dissolve and the rising major seventh (rather than fourth or fifth as in previous stanzas) that realigns the melody (ex. 8.2.a, x and y). 'O mistress mine' capitalises on the idiom invented for 'The rapture', with its novelty vamping yet

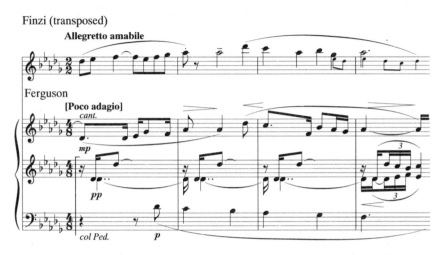

EX. 8.2.b

not without Italianate trio sonata touches in the interplay of the top lines. 'It is a curious phenomenon in you – some atavistic trait coming to the surface?' Tony Scott asked (19430426). What also comes to the surface in this song is a strong echo of the slow movement of Ferguson's Piano Sonata of 1938–40 (ex. 8.2.b). 'Come away, come away, death' on the other hand is reminiscent of William Denis Browne's 'Epitaph on Salathiel Pavy' (Ben Jonson) – another Elizabethan lament – with its descending ritornello bass and rising î 2̂ ♭3̂ motif above it. It also contains Finzi's most famous melisma, on the word 'weep', too obviously Bachian to require further comment, but effective because its indulgent chromaticism and syncopation are so well prepared in previous voice-leading and rhythmic interplay (ex. 8.2.c), themselves set up by a serenade-like strumming that keeps the whole song sensibly within a generic context. 'Fear no more the heat o' the sun', felt by Ursula Vaughan Williams (1964: 250) to be 'one of the most perfect songs ever written', certainly offers the best possible match for the gravity of Finzi's early diatonic style, which allows the vocal line to soar, unconstrained by any accompanimental persona, in wide, emotional arcs perfect for the weight and range of a baritone voice. The veiled *envoi* enters another world, one that brings the tune back in D♭ major, but a *tierce de Picardie* offers the right tonal return and emotional closure. 'Who is Silvia?' has never commanded the affection

EX. 8.2.C

lavished on the other songs, and Vaughan Williams himself was not sure what he thought about it (19421013). The detail, including some Elizabethan touches but also those of an English baroque 'air' (the Newbury String Players' repertoire perhaps already beginning to rub off on Finzi's own idiom), is too fussy for such a common-property poem, though Finzi's 'aria' style is neatly incorporated into the second stanza. The cycle's title phrase, thus centrally placed, occasions a ceremonial curtsey as though in some *branle*-like dance and signals the more dramatic engagement with Shakespeare to come four years later.

Ferguson heard the string orchestral version of the songs' accompaniment on the radio on 18 October. He was not impressed:

With the exception of 'O mistress mine' which takes kindly to such treatment, it seems to me that they are all too literally transcribed from the piano version. One longs for a real string lay-out, instead of the close writing which the limitations of one pair of hands imposes. This type of writing would be all right for part of the time, but there is too much of it. Apart altogether from the monotony of sound – and it is a curiously enervating monotony, for the fiddles play so much in their dullest register – it seems such a waste of the resources and opportunities of a string orchestra. The low tessitura of the accompaniment in the first three songs is a bit risky even in the piano version when they are sung in order; in the string version it is fatal . . . I feel you ought to consider very carefully either (a) re-thinking them as a whole for the new medium, or (b) withdrawing the string version altogether. Honestly I am not sure that the latter would not be the better plan, for they do seem to me real piano songs – apart, that is, from 'Fear no more', which would in any case require a fairly large orchestra to do it justice. I say this because I feel very strongly that performances of this version would do no service to the songs or to you yourself. (19421018b)

How Finzi responded to this blunt admonition is not known. Its effect may or may not have been mitigated by Busch, a far less astute critic, saying exactly the opposite – 'They are fine, Gerald, and certainly it needs the strings to help them do full justice, and you seem to have laid them out perfectly' (19421019b) – but he probably knew that despite some promising touches (the opening mixture of *pizzicato* and *arco* in 'Come away, come away, death', for instance) Ferguson was on the whole right, for, as he had told Navarro, 'all my scoring has to be done round about midnight which isn't the best of times' (19421013a). 'Who is Silvia?' would have stood to gain most from a more three-dimensional string version, especially at the dominant preparation before the final stanza, where one longs for a real Elgarian athleticism of texture. The second stanza of 'Who is Silvia?' may nonetheless have had bona fide string origins or associations, for a version of its opening, a sixth higher in B minor, appears alongside the melody of the middle section of the Romance for strings (see below, ex. 8.5.b) in one of Finzi's Serenade sketches, in such close juxtaposition as to suggest a connection. But a restricted tessitura does indeed affect all the songs, and except occasionally in 'O mistress mine' and at the very end of the cycle, the violins never dip more than a toe in the invigorating waters of the third octave above middle C.

If Finzi took the criticism to heart, it shows in the last of the Five Bagatelles, where he fully explores the clarinet's range (there is a leap of nearly three octaves at one point). This, the only one written after *Let Us Garlands Bring*, was forced agonisedly out of him in the summer of 1943, after the other four had already received their first performance, given at the National Gallery earlier that year, on 15 January, by Pauline Juler and Howard Ferguson. (He had found time to compose what must have been No. 1 whilst taking his annual leave at Ashmansworth at New Year in 1942. 'It has turned out to be rather larger in scale, & more difficult, than the others & I only hope that it's not outside the "Bagatelle" radius,' he told Ferguson [19420114a].) Leslie Boosey, cautious to the last, wanted to publish the pieces but not as a volume, though by now Finzi was beginning to know his value: 'I'm not accepting unless they agree to do them together,' he told Busch after Juler and he (!) – Ferguson was unavailable – had been to play them through to him. Boosey gave way, perhaps after Finzi had agreed to add a quick finale, though still reluctant to face its necessity even after the first performance when 'several people' said it needed it (19430122). Neither party can have regretted capitulating, for the entire edition of the Five Bagatelles, issued in July 1945, sold out within a year of publication. From that day to this they have probably appeared on the examination platform as frequently as any staple of the solo wind repertoire – a success rather resisted by Finzi, who always claimed that 'they *are* only trifles' (19430117a) and took no pride in the 'Fughetta''s facility. 'I'm sure that Gordon Jacob cd have done it just as well, in a fraction of the time,' he told Milford (19430812). One reviewer, N. G. L[ong], also resisted such popularity and facility, finding the whole set 'a perfect summary of the commonplace', and the Fughetta 'banal to the last degree' (*Music Review* vii [1946]: 55).

But the Bagatelles are top-drawer Finzi, whether he and N. G. L. liked it or not. Howard Ferguson indirectly brought them into being. He was friendly with Juler, a young clarinettist whose later career is a blank simply because she stopped playing after her marriage to Bernard Richards, the cellist, in 1948. Not long before adapting his own Four Short Pieces for clarinet and piano from early piano pieces, Ferguson had tried his hand at learning the clarinet himself – with Frederick Thurston, not Juler – perhaps following Vaughan Williams's example (though with more success). In public he restricted his prowess to their piano part, however, with Juler as clarinettist, first at one of the Navarros' concerts at Broadway, then at the Wigmore Hall. They are shorter and more epigrammatic than Finzi's pieces, and were paradoxically reduced from five to four for publication in 1937. Something of their white-note modality (see Matthews 1989: 36) may nonetheless have influenced Finzi's most substantial Bagatelle, the 'Prelude', which to the approval of the *Times* reviewer of the first performance 'shows that a diatonic scale may still be used as the basis of a vigorous theme' (16 January 1943: 7) – even if between Ferguson's 'Pastoral' and Finzi's 'Fear no more the heat o' the sun' the influence would seem to run strongly in the opposite direction. To make the connections still more complicated, Ferguson wrote his own set of Five Bagatelles in 1944, though for piano solo, and they were published in the same year as Finzi's.

A more unexpected but even more likely influence on Finzi's 'Prelude' was Koechlin, the first movement of whose Second Sonata for clarinet and piano (1923) sounds uncannily similar. Finzi certainly thought Koechlin was an underrated composer, for he told Robin Milford so in pinpointing his 'elusive quality' (19451022), and it needs recognising that the further towards abstract or sonata logic Finzi ventured the less he relied upon his erstwhile English models, though there may also be something of the genially neoclassical opening of John Ireland's Piano Sonata about that of the first Bagatelle. The 'Prelude' sets the agenda well for the rest of the collection, its festively pealing diatonicism (ex. 8.3.a) presaging the seasonal imagery of 'Carol', as do the triplet quavers of its gentler middle section those of 'Romance' and its occasional oom-pahs and the rougher spirits of its dominant preparation (after figure 6) the robustness of 'Fughetta'.

The dominant preparation is a false one, leading to a recapitulation in B♭ rather than C, and this too is matched in the later pieces: all four of the ternary ones recapitulate the A section in the wrong key, always flatwards, though they end in the right one. Essentially this is the opposite of conventional sonata relations, for except in the 'Fughetta', Finzi, like most tonal composers of his and the preceding generation or two, avoids dominant goals in his first sections, which in these ternary rather than sonata movements in any case achieve or posit tonic closure. The movement to the dominant therefore comes, instead, in the repeat of the A section. Sometimes it works well, as at four bars after figure 6 in 'Romance' and in the 'Forlana' (in which the opening eight-bar period of the first section is simply omitted at the return, picking it up where it had first modulated to the subdominant). At other times

EX. 8.3.a (clarinet and piano)

301

the tonal unity sounds forced, particularly in the 'Prelude', where the regaining of C major disconcerts with its straightforward cycle-of-fifths spectrum (one looks for a further mediant or submediant twist). It is difficult to know whether Finzi planned these excursions, perhaps with Schubert in mind, or simply recapitulated in whichever key he had rambled too, preferring to face the problem of the return journey once fortified with the refreshing delights of earlier enharmonic fancies. Certainly there is no inherent reason why he should not be allowed his varieties of textural complexion – because at different tonal altitudes – in the initial material of a movement rather than, more conventionally, in its later periods, and though those with perfect pitch no doubt find it the more psychologically unsettling, he was vehement in his refusal to bow to tonal convention. 'I don't care a damn what the key is (always supposing that it's satisfactorily done & provides the contrast),' he had told Thorpe Davie, adding 'Nor do you, really' (19330714–16?). Later he cited Vaughan Williams's heretical views on tonal unity to Busch, who replied: 'It is delightful to hear of VW's remark about not being able to tell whether a movement ended in the same key. That is really encouraging!' (19401015).

The return of the opening of 'Romance' a fourth higher, with new details and new countermelody in the piano, enhances the ethereal magic of this poetic piece which seems to refer to both Vaughan Williams's and Ernest Farrar's settings of 'Silent noon' in its outer sections – Vaughan Williams particularly in the key and initial gesture (perhaps this was why he was not too keen on the piece), Farrar in the gently impressionistic detail that follows (ex. 8.3.b and c). Unlike Vaughan Williams, however, he is not out to develop erotic intensity, which he gives all too wide a berth in the middle section, steering instead into the blameless purlieus of the organ voluntary. 'Carol' is one of Finzi's best early inspirations in his 'ditty' style, an innocent conception yet full of character; one is surprised that it has not been converted into a real vocal carol with words until one sees how subtly interwoven are its periodicity, countermelodies and interludes and therefore how difficult that would be to do. The striking of the Christmas-morning clock at the end – is it 6.00 or 7.00 a.m.? – is a touch of genius, enhanced by the ghost of a waits' horn-call. Here was a theatrical imagination waiting to be released, as it could be, Howells tells us, by the very young:

EX. 8.3.b (Farrar)

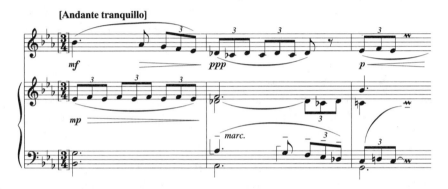

EX. 8.3.c (Finzi)

... he was delightful with children, he used to come often when both my children were young; and there's a lovely tune, published as a clarinet piece, which he first wrote as a carol for my two children, when they were very young. I used to play this tune to them. And when he published it years later he must have forgotten what he'd originally written it for (quoted in Palmer 1992: 365).

'Forlana' may well date from the same period as 'The phantom', for it shares some of its turns of phrase, if not its intensity, being serviceable rather than inspired, its countermelody fifths in the clarinet part dutifully inverted for the rustic middle section. Finzi's greatest worry about it seems to have been what to call a cross between a forlane and a berceuse (Rubbra, not one to share his agonising indecision, rather unhelpfully suggested 'What about Berlane or Forceuse?' [19430107]). 'Fughetta' is better than Finzi thought, and one relishes its relaxed prodigality of detail, not one phrase of which is routine – something of

303

an achievement in a fugue. One feels for the composer, wrestling with it against his inclination to write the piece at all. There are a number of sketches for it in his pocket sketchbooks, at a time when he had no freedom for country walks. Did he take them to work? Use them on the train?

Tonal relations did concern Finzi, after his own fashion, at this period, and his Elegy for violin and piano shows this, for he revised it in order to bring the initial theme back in the tonic (F major) towards the end of the A section (two bars before figure 3 in the printed score) rather than in D major. This section's tonality wanders around quite enough as it is on its ternary restatement, which sounds for a moment as though it is going to be simply a shortened version of the first A section, cutting swiftly to the dominant statement of the theme, but turns out to be more a mixture of development and coda. Such continuous invention is admirable in a way, and part of Finzi's deliberate resistance to block repetition, but when the first section already has the monothematicism and textural continuity of a baroque *da capo* aria's A section (which in the revised version it resembles tonally, making a ramble rather than a drama out of the dominant), it leaves him once again with his inveterate problem of a slow movement of beautiful *Affekt* but excessive rhapsodic length. The Elegy is the best of his three central slow movements salvaged from uncompleted or discarded symphonic cycles, and its Bachian intimacy of rhythmic invention within a rich harmonic continuum (much like that of Gurney and, still, of Vaughan Williams) is often delightful. But its B section, based on x in ex. 8.4.c, is insufficiently contrasted, and the attempt, as the corner is turned into the recapitulation, to prove that its subsidiary rising scale motif is really both y (ex. 8.4.c) in inversion and capable of transformation back into x does not quite convince, given the homogeneity of all the material in the first place. One cannot take Finzi's obsession with this type of movement entirely seriously when it is so difficult to tell his three examples of it apart – see ex. 8.4.a, b and c, the opening themes respectively of the Introit (from the discarded Violin Concerto), the Eclogue (from the incomplete Piano Concerto) and the Elegy (all that was written of the Violin Sonata). They are so stereotyped as to threaten to make even the Cello Concerto's slow movement (ex. 8.4.d) into a caricature of itself. All four movements are too long, and the nine-bar cut made in the Introit in 1943 for the publication of its full score solves one problem while creating another, for it excises all clear treatment of a

EX. 8.4.a (Introit)

EX. 8.4.b (Eclogue)

EX. 8.4.c (Elegy)

EX. 8.4.d (Cello Concerto)

subsidiary motif which is thus left unexplained on its reappearance at figure H (the cut was three bars before figure E).

The Romance for strings, already mentioned in Chapter 5, avoids these problems and, perhaps together with *Dies natalis* (if that contains Serenade material), demonstrates that Finzi's continuing difficulties were not with slow movements *per se* but with 'sonata' rather than 'serenade' or 'bagatelle' thought. The Romance is a much more straightforwardly balanced structure than these other slow movements, and one is tempted to say that it is simply a better piece than any of them because it is contrapuntally unpretentious, texturally varied, and melodically fresh, with conventional goals and contrasts: a dominant mid-way cadence in the A section (though turned aside for the mediant); a central section with a new tune, new instrumentation (solo violin), new speed, some subsidiary motivic wit (ex. 8.5.a), a broad, relaxed climax and, most important of all, a ternary structure itself; and a shortened A section return, the whole enveloped in the introductory material with a neat but emotionally telling brevity rare in Finzi's instrumental works. As already indicated, the main section's melody would seem to be from 1928, the middle section's (ex. 8.5.b) from 1940, but overall in the Romance one can only hazard the conviction that 1940–41 speaks more loudly than 1928 and 1951 perhaps most audibly of all in the transparent buoyancy of the string writing, even if the fact that Finzi simply described the work as 'very ancient (1928)' when he sent a copy to Thorpe Davie (19521014c) rather goes against it. One senses the influence of Moeran in its climax, but the sharing of a peculiarly potent, Elgarian phrase between his Violin Concerto (1942) and the melody of the central section (ex. 8.5.b, *x*) must be coincidence.

Finzi's Serenade sketches, mentioned earlier, deserve further comment.

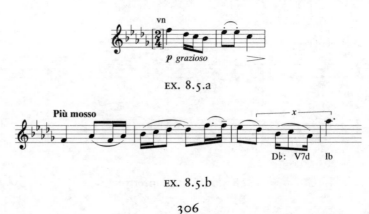

EX. 8.5.a

EX. 8.5.b

Two of them are unusually sustained: neat and fluent (though not very good) ink continuity drafts for fast movements, an opening one with introduction in D major, 4/4 time, and a third or fourth one in A minor/major, 6/8 time (starting very much like ex. 6.1.d and perhaps contemporary with it). Both drafts break off, the former at some point prior to a middle section, the latter, after as many as 150 bars, before a return, and both are supplemented by a good many shorter workings, including some labelled alternatives for recapitulation purposes as well as for preferential choice, mostly in pencil. It is difficult to tell whether the continuity drafts were initial, determined attempts to embark on an idea and simply keep going or whether they represent collations of other fragmentary or pencil workings that have been destroyed. In either case, in terms of quality they would unfortunately not make satisfactory end products even if the return could be completed in the 6/8 movement (one of whose pencil workings does get to the end). The first movement sketches are probably from a later period than these 6/8 ones, for they use a cueing system not considered by Finzi until 1947 (see below, p. 451). There is also quite a lot of promising material for a 2/4 intermezzo, possibly the movement from which the Romance's middle section was eventually derived (a variant of ex. 8.5.a is present), the opening of a slow movement or alternative intermezzo labelled 'II', and the introduction to an E♭ Allegro of unspecified 2/4 content labelled 'III'. At one point, probably (to judge from the handwriting) when the Serenade was first mooted in the late 1920s or early 1930s, even the original first movement of the Violin Concerto was pressed into service – for a few bars, at least – as the third movement. One cannot say that by any date the Serenade was categorically doomed, for *The Fall of the Leaf* proves that Finzi's tenacious hold over an early piece might eventually produce results after four or five widely separated attempts at resurrecting it, but it does seem as though he finally gave up on it in the late 1940s, refashioning a passage from the first movement (ex. 8.5.c) into the Clarinet Concerto's finale theme before rescuing the Romance.

As for *The Fall of the Leaf*, Uncle Tom Cobley and all seem to have had a hand in it. Bliss had advised its rescue from the debris of the Chamber Symphony in 1929. Ferguson was pressed into critical and practical (piano-duet) service on its behalf in January 1940 and in a long letter tried his best to persuade Finzi it was not up to scratch,

EX. 8.5.c

feeling that it 'shows signs of its chequered genesis' and 'like Mr Dolmetsch's famous harpsichord ... buckles in the middle when you play
on it,' adding, 'I do not think that tinkering about with details is going
to put the matter right' (19400204). He and Finzi played it through to
Ernest Chapman at Boosey & Hawkes, in the presence of Basil
Cameron, who happened to be there and who suggested, instead of 'the
long rhapsodic diminuendo', an 'alternative climax' – 'a real improvement & G has reworked it,' Joy commented in her journal (J. Finzi
19400227). 'Chenny' also made 'some very helpful suggestions' about
the end of the piece when he stayed at Ashmansworth for a weekend
(ibid.). But even after Finzi had knocked it into its final shape in 1941
(or had he? – see 194402?) he could not fire himself to complete the
orchestration, working on it spasmodically during his time at
the Ministry but getting it little more than half done. There is no
evidence that he ever took it out of the drawer again, and it was left
to Ferguson to finish scoring it after the composer's death (see Ferguson
1957c: 10–11, reprinted as 'Editor's note' on the full score; also
McBurney 1989: 51–2 for a detailed if idiosyncratic critique of the
task).

It betrays its early origin in every bar in which that is not too
obviously concealed. The initial strands of material are fragmentary
and contrasting enough to have symphonic potential, but they lack
vibrancy in their vestigial, pastoral cast. (Ex. 8.6.a and ex. 5.4.c show
the introductory motifs, ex. 8.6.b and c those of the 'poco allegro'.)
Ex. 8.6.b runs in an 'aria'-like groove that is far too short-winded for

EX. 8.6.a

EX. 8.6.b

EX. 8.6.c

the context, for ex. 8.6.c in the dominant follows it a mere four bars later yet is the only thing Finzi has to offer for his main climax, where he states it – twice – without development or reinterpretation (it nonetheless has a definite 'meaning', that of 'abid[ing] / Till my appointed change', if its concordance in 'The sigh' is to be considered). Well before this, ex. 8.6.b has itself returned in a tonic 'a tempo' which, coming after a winding-down based on ex. 8.6.a, sounds like the A section returning within a tiny ternary form; the only other thing it could be would be an exposition repeat, though it has left nothing pregnant behind in the meantime. As for the climax, it is all over well before the half-way point, and all the epilogue fragments that are piled on in the second half of the piece can do nothing to conceal the fact that the stable door has been locked after the horse has bolted; nor can Cameron's 'alternative climax', if such is the *fff* at figure 19. A miniature somehow eludes capture in the first half of *The Fall of the Leaf*, for which its second half becomes a melodramatic and impotent complaint.

Farewell to Arms dealt rather more successfully with an early remnant when Finzi added an 'Introduction' to his eighteen-year-old 'Aria' around 1944. 'I was lucky to come across *c*.1670 Ralph Knevet's doggerel (in Norman Ault's "Treasury of Unfamiliar Lyrics") which makes an excellent foil for the aria – a setting of Peele's "His golden locks",' he explained to Navarro (19450113), the point being that both poems contain the image of a warrior's helmet being made into a beehive, couched in almost identical iambic pentameters. Such serendipity must have made Finzi thankful that Boosey had refused to publish 'Aria' on its own when he submitted it in 1941; in 1945, though still anticipating peace, its sentiments were more timely. Finzi scored up *Farewell to Arms* for small orchestra, though he offered strings alone as an alternative, perhaps with one eye on the Newbury String Players (who did very occasionally perform his music, though he was anxious not to make a habit of it), and it really does not need the wind. As with *Dies natalis*, his idiom of 1926 in the 'Aria' contrasts rather than conflicts with the greater harmonic *chiaroscuro* of the 'Introduction'. Unlike *Dies natalis*, *Farewell to Arms* uses a head motif to bind the two pieces, the first three notes of the 'Aria' appearing parenthetically as a mordent in the 'Introduction'. The 'Aria' ritornello is also more directly anticipated at one point. The *arioso* technique of the 'Introduction', while generally similar to that of 'Rhapsody' in *Dies natalis*, is rather less discursive but actually more mature harmonically, building a broad paragraph towards the dominant half-close that acts as a caesura into the 'Aria' and thus achieves a fair structural span.

The BBC honoured Finzi by broadcasting *Farewell to Arms* from Manchester on Easter Sunday, 1 April 1945, performed by the tenor Eric Greene and the BBC Northern Orchestra under Charles Groves two days after they had premièred the work in a Manchester concert. Joy and Gerald travelled to Manchester for the event. Two or three weeks earlier Gerald had 'just sent a copy to my chief saying that it's an unusual, but perhaps more interesting way of giving notice!' (19450311), though he saw 'little hope of getting home much before the end of the European War,' as he explained to Thorpe Davie. By this time the Ministry was frustrating him keenly, and he continued:

But then I have been promised very early priority. How I agree with you about the duty value of these things having gone. 'Unbelievable nuisance' is putting it too mildly. I particularly resent it because most of my work has reorientated itself to a post war direction & I feel very strongly that my own post-war work is more necessary than putting the shipping lines on the map again or feathering the nests of wealthy shipowners. On matters like that I don't feel able to cooperate. Colleagues of mine have already been called back to their peace time jobs, but that's because there's something to call them back, a museum or that sort of thing. But a free-lance composer, unattached to an institution, has no such backing. (ibid.)

Towards the close of 1944, with the liberation of Europe well under way, Gerald had hoped to be released early in the new year, but first the Germans' counter-offensive on the Western Front and the continuing war in the Pacific kept him in the Berkeley Square office and then this awkward transition to demobilisation did. He was not officially to leave the Ministry until the end of June 1945, though he walked out on the first. The composition of *Intimations of Immortality* might be no further ahead than six years earlier, but in the meantime he had become a very different musician, and he returned home to find that *Dies natalis* had transformed his status.

CHAPTER 9

The Three Choirs composer

Finzi was glad to turn his back on London at the end of the war, and he did not even go to the performance of *Earth and Air and Rain* given by Irwin and Gerald Moore at the National Gallery on 2 July. He returned to the routines, pleasures and seclusion of Ashmansworth, and henceforth, for the remaining decade of his life, nothing much would disrupt these. It would be rare for him to spend more than three or four days at a time away from home, and apart from a three-year external examinership at St Andrews University (1952–4), an excursion to Iona and Scotland's west coast in connection with it, and a week's visit to some long-lost cousins of Joy's in deepest Ireland in October 1953 (when they both flew for the first time, thrilled by the experience), there were no enterprising trips, few holidays even.

The house and grounds were in good order, for Gerald had planted assiduously, fruit trees and bushes in particular, during the war, and the garden and its terraces had been levelled and paved by German prisoners of war. Joy kept bees – Gerald remained firmly indoors when they swarmed – and there were still chickens and geese, plus the innumerable cats. The shelves of the book room and music room were steadily filling up, for, as Gerald explained to Thorpe Davie, 'Books remain my only vice' (19470202b), and the walls of the house were being hung with Joy's art, for she had turned from sculpture to pencil drawing, inaugurating the magnificent series of portraits of which a comprehensive selection was eventually published in 1987 as *In That Place*. Perhaps encouraged by Howard Ferguson's friend Nigel Barnicott, another portrait artist (though anthropologist by profession), she began in 1940 with studies of Gerald and Professor Watson, the former, finished by December, 'a bit too heroic' by her own reckoning (19401008) but still a triumph – 'I've seldom known her so pleased' Gerald told Ferguson (19401202).

The refugees had all finally dispersed, but so had the family, for both children were now at boarding school. Not without agonising over sending them away for their education at the formative age of nine, and one hopes not without also remembering his own unhappiness at school, Gerald had agreed with Joy that they should go to a 'comparatively cranky school' (19430628), Bedales, near Petersfield. They wanted a co-educational one, and they were perhaps influenced by Justin and Edith Brooke, whose children were already there, though the Arts and Crafts philosophy of Bedales, based on William Morris's teachings, made it a natural choice in any case. Edward Thomas had lived nearby while his wife Helen taught at Bedales in its early years (and quite by chance Joy found herself buying their grandson's sports jacket for Christopher to wear while he was there); Alfred Powell had supervised the building of the school's hall and splendid timber-roofed library, designed, along with its furniture, by Ernest Gimson; Powell's brothers Malcolm and Oswald had taught there. By 1945 Christopher had been at Dunhurst, the junior school of Bedales, for a couple of years; Nigel left home to join him just as his father returned from London. Short of educating the boys at home, there was probably little alternative, for their earlier schooling, in Newbury, had entailed twenty-eight miles of driving every day until petrol rationing forced one parent to stay in town all morning or share transport.

In an empty house, and (probably for the first time in his and Joy's life) with little or no paid domestic help, Gerald at first settled down quietly to picking up the threads of his Wordsworth Ode. He may have made considerable further progress on it over the following year, for no other music flowed from his pen except for the revision of *New Year Music*. But the range of his interests and the level of his energies were such that he could never hope to concentrate exclusively on one activity unless terrorised by a deadline. Even then he and Joy lived life with an extraordinary intensity. One example, from the summer of 1952, may be taken as indicative. On 27 June he went to Oxford for a medical consultation; he was already under sentence of terminal illness, and knew it. The following day he conducted a Newbury String Players concert in High Wycombe, with Wilfred Brown and Rubbra as soloists, and he and Joy stayed the night with the Rubbras. On the 29th, after Rubbra had played through his new Viola Concerto to them, they picked up the Blunden family at Reading on their way home and arrived back at Ashmansworth for a late supper to find John Sumsion, also coming to stay for a couple of days, already there. Sumsion discussed Three Choirs programme planning with Gerald; Blunden, who stayed for a week, discussed poetry and all manner of eighteenth-century matters, not to mention the business of Alfred Powell and W. R. Lethaby, that then continued in correspondence. During Blunden's stay Siegfried Sassoon also came over for a day – and all this at a time when Gerald was frantically preparing and scoring his *Love's Labour's Lost* suite for its first performance at the Cheltenham Festival two weeks later, to be followed by the even more rushed composition of the Magnificat within the next six weeks.

One cause after another continued to claim his enthusiasm and conviction, his zeal uninhibitable, 'his dark face . . . always fulminating with rage at some injustice, a sort of walking *Manchester Guardian*,' as John Amis has described it (1985: 84), and overall, in addition to his accelerating number of initiatives on behalf of other living artists, he must have spent as much time on scholarship and conservation as on composition between the end of the war and his death 11 years later. First he set out to rescue rare and endangered English apple varieties; then Parry, and more Gurney; then – beginning alongside all of this – the English eighteenth century in music. His powers of advocacy also made him sought after as a lecturer, writer and broadcaster, and he even took part in some kind of Brains Trust event in 1953. He claimed to dislike such assignments, but often he did not refuse them. Similarly, his fair but passionate judgement saw him occasionally adjudicating a composition award or festival day. Such responsibilities catch up sooner or later with almost any career that has kept to the track, but it is a measure of the respect in which Finzi was held after the war, as well as of the country's general need for a new, confident musical establishment made up of the men (but not many women) of his generation, that he could undoubtedly have chosen his path through them to the highest levels. He preferred not to, unlike his friends Rubbra and Thorpe Davie who became respectively Lecturer in Music at Oxford University and master of music (later Professor) at St Andrews, both in 1947. In the same year Finzi was asked by Stanley Marchant to return to the Royal Academy of Music as composition professor 'to the cream of our Composition students' (including John Joubert) and 'at the top rate of payment' following the death of Theodore Holland (19471030), but he declined the offer and the job passed to Ferguson.

Some of his jobs must have been undertaken for financial reasons, for he and Joy were perennially hard up once they were paying school fees for both boys; Gerald even gave up pipe smoking in order to save money. Editions as well as compositions brought in royalties, and he always attempted to drive a firm bargain on them with publishers, relations sometimes bordering on the acrimonious. Similarly, talks and articles as well as commissioned compositions brought in fees, however small. Overall, it is difficult to judge whether the balance of Finzi's postwar activities would have been any different had he not had to think about money, for against his ideal of the rural artist composing full-time out of inner necessity there is the fact that relatively few compositional projects were planned out by choice once he had returned from the Ministry, and old creative stock once fulfilled or deflected was not fully replaced with new. The completion of *Intimations* was the great imperative. The Serenade withered on the branch, though something of its strain re-emerged in the Clarinet Concerto. The Piano Concerto was a revived project of the late 1940s and early 1950s, but it too eventually lost its impetus. Most of Finzi's remaining output was urgent because made to order rather than a personal compulsion. The Cello Concerto, *In terra pax* and a handful of songs were the exceptions to this. Not that the question particularly matters one way or the other: compositions prompted by whatever combination of urge and request would undoubtedly have continued to flow and bring both their artistic and modest financial rewards.

If anything, undertakings as a matter of pure idea or unconditional commitment were at their most striking outside the sphere of Finzi's own compositions, once *Intimations of Immortality* had been completed: there was no second *Dies natalis*. Finzi did not think this cause for lament, for he saw that the nature of the personal impulse changes as one matures: it was another manifestation of what he described as 'the danger of naming particular external associations with works of art, & the reason why the Romantic young mind tends to become more extrovert with the years as it realises the futility of external dependence' (J. Finzi 19521126). Perhaps most internally driven of all were his continuing devotion to the Newbury String Players and his support and promotion of younger composers of compatible cast, above all Anthony Scott. Be it selflessness, or the need for self-projection into the future, the quest for 'that chimerical immortality to which nearly all men aspire', as Couperin put it (1730, R.1970: ix), this portfolio made heavy demands on him and his inheritors. The Newbury String Players meant that he had almost no free weekends or potential rest periods, and by 1952 the orchestra could be reviewed as an encumbrance as well as a privilege:

A performance of this sort [one of their best, in Stockcross Church, 8 March 1952] pushes the ever recurring problem of continuance into the background. What a problem it is! An organisation started at the very beginning of the dark war years 1940 to keep spiritual activities alive locally has continued ever since right through each year with weekly rehearsals or concerts & has reached as high a standard as is possible for mainly amateur players – but it means that every weekend, except for a short break at Christmas & six weeks August–Sept is tied. G takes this responsibility seriously & it doesn't matter if odd players miss rehearsal now & then – but it is essential for him never to do so. After a 150 concerts (15 last year) & 12 years of constant work one sometimes longs for someone to share the work & take over entirely – for it's too valuable to drop & there is no money for salaried conductor & it seems impossible to find someone willing to do it voluntarily, at the same time able to deal with a crowd of 25 or so self centred amateurs, who for all their keenness & loyalty, have to put their musical interests 2nd to personal ones. Then it needs a musician not only interested in the standard repertory but always adding works new & old to keep alive both conductors', players' & audiences' interest. When one thinks of the first performances of works by young composers (G excludes his own works except on rare occasions) & the 1st opportunities that have been given to young soloists & instrumentalists one realises the importance of such an organisation is much wider than a purely local one. Yet no likely successor seems to be on the horizon – in the case of G suddenly having to give up. (J. Finzi 19520308)

This was written just as Christopher was about to leave school. He rather surprised his parents by wanting to take up music professionally – though Ferguson thinks the boys had really been reared for it all along, despite parental protestations to the contrary – and in the autumn of 1952 became a cello student at the RAM. He suddenly started joining in with his father's activities – lecture trips, editing tasks, operas in London, and a three-day examining visit to St Andrews ('Enjoyed having Kiffer with him now that he has left school & can share musical life with him,' Joy commented [J. Finzi 19520830]). Coming so soon after the diagnosis of Hodgkin's Disease, this must have shown an urgent need on Gerald's part to pass on his life and thought to his elder son while there was still time. As for the orchestra, Christopher swiftly and without fuss took it over from his father a month or two after his death, having directed it in rehearsal earlier in the year. Gerald conducted the first 164 concerts, Christopher the remaining 215. It was as simple as that, excepting the odd, augmented appearance under a festival conductor: the 'Finzi & Son' family business, just like any High Street grocer's or solicitor's. This is meant as a tribute to provincial life and its foundations, for such it should be. It is also a further reminder that blood is thicker than water, Gerald's perennial discountenance of the idea notwithstanding.

But Christopher was not a composer, and in this respect Anthony Scott continued to play the role of Gerald's musical godson. It was an emotional and sometimes tense relationship. On the eve of Scott's call-up into the RAF in 1940 Gerald had opened 'our last bottle of superb port, which G has had for 20 years & Tony's usually stolid face was holding tears when G toasted him. We played G's new violin mvt [the Elegy] to him & Ruth said afterwards – she had never seen him more moved' (J. Finzi 19400723). Later in the war Scott was stationed a mile or two from Gerald's mother and was encouraged to use her music room for composing, as one of the few people whom Gerald let anywhere near her (she left him in peace, interrupting only to tell him of suitable places to bomb in Germany). For most of 1945, after the Watsons had returned to London, Ruth Scott and the children lived in their house at Ashmansworth, though Tony was still away in the RAF and spent little time there. The Finzis hoped they would buy it and settle in the village, but the proximity would have been stifling, and Ruth explained their reasons for moving further away, to Horton, near Datchet, in a letter to Joy:

I think Joyce you know that as far as Tony's & Gerald's friendship goes, it is best for Tony not to be in the same village, he is a moody creature and also has a very great hero worship feeling for Gerald and this in Tony makes him rebel, as if Gerald took the place of Tony's father, it is a strange psychological thing in Tony and he seems to get obstinate and difficult with those who get a power of him. He is so fond of Gerald that it's best not to risk it, and when Gerald airs his theories and strong views it automatically makes Tony resist them and go against him. I hope we may eventually come near Newbury but not to Ashmansworth. (19460306b)

This was written after a visit to Horton during which Scott was beside himself with some kind of frustration. There may even have been an unrecognised homoerotic ingredient in the attraction between him and Gerald and an element of jealousy on Ruth's part. At any rate, the distancing clearly worked, and Scott became far more productive. Gerald continued to advise him, however, and his promotion of Scott's music culminated when in 1951 he hired the Kalmar Orchestra in London to play through his string Sinfonietta (the Newbury String Players also demonstrated Leighton's *Veris gratia* and Milford's *Elegiac Meditation*). This was for the benefit of, and probably paid for by, Vaughan Williams, who then financed a Boyd Neel Orchestra concert of all three works, whether because he believed in them himself or simply wished to put his money where Gerald's mouth was. Gerald loved the 'inward fury' of the Sinfonietta (J. Finzi 195202[18]), and it is indeed a most powerful work.

Despite this and his undoubted instrumentality in getting Scott's Chorale Variations performed at the 1953 Three Choirs Festival, he never managed to make Scott's reputation. By 1946, however, his own had largely been made for him by the reception of *Dies natalis*, which steadily gathered momentum towards the end of the war and fixed his identity with the public. Elsie Suddaby had given its delayed first performance in a lunchtime concert at the Wigmore Hall on 26 January 1940, during what Frank Howes called 'Finzi's week' (because his Interlude had been performed at the National Gallery four days earlier [J. Finzi 19400126]). She was accompanied by Maurice Miles's New London String Ensemble, in its début, and sang 'divinely', though Gerald did have reservations. She was too free with the rhythm, and without the Traherne texts in the programme and despite her adequate diction Gerald feared that the audience could not get the real gist of the work – and he was probably right, given that its spiritual apotheosis seems not to have begun quite yet, for all its positive reception from public, press and friends (who as usual turned up in force – the Navarros, the Scotts, Ferguson, Vaughan Williams and Rubbra were all there, as well as Basil Cameron). When Finzi sent Bliss, in America, a copy of the score later in the year, he described it as 'not a very enterprising work' (19401104). He thought of doing it with the Newbury String Players in 1941, but it was in America that its progress began to make it seem rather more enterprising after all, despite a partial further Wigmore Hall performance (three movements only) by

Suddaby under Boult in January 1942. Bernard Herrmann, of all people (who was later to compose the film scores for *Citizen Kane*, *Psycho* and *Taxi Driver*), conducted what must have been its first performance with a tenor, William Ventura, in a CBS broadcast that was recorded, its acetates making their rather expensive way across the Atlantic to Ashmansworth in due course. Finzi has always found sympathetic ears in the United States, perhaps because his emotional candour and idealism have fewer barriers of taste to penetrate there than in Britain, and it is good to think that one of the first pairs should have belonged to such a prominent and influential member of America's musical and commercial establishment. Herrmann, who in any case was a great Anglophile, became one of Finzi's strongest fans, and he visited him at Ashmansworth after the war (though without making much headway with the proposal that Finzi should reciprocate).

Finzi sent the score of *Dies natalis* to Henry Wood in the spring of 1943, but Wood told him that his Prom programmes for that year were already fixed. What was probably its next performance was the first conducted by Finzi himself, at Morley College on 19 December under Tippett's auspices – 'Tippett was apparently not very happy about it – & it certainly is very remote from his music,' Finzi told Busch, 'so young Antony Hopkins or John Amis... asked me to conduct it' (19431231a). Two days later it received its first broadcast, a fine studio performance, sung by Eric Greene and played by the Boyd Neel Orchestra. 'I'm sure this wld never have happened but for the U.S. performance,' Finzi maintained (19431129?). Vaughan Williams, who 'listened-in', still preferred a soprano to a tenor, but it was Greene and Boyd Neel who began to fix *Dies natalis*'s image and send it on its journey, though Neel sometimes performed it with a soprano. Greene, the foremost British Evangelist of his generation in the Bach Passions, made the work his own and promoted it avidly, writing to Finzi in September 1945:

We were fortunate enough to get another Broadcast of 'Dies' & a most splendid BBC recording. Also I have persuaded Sydney Watson to give it in Winchester Cathedral on Nov 8th . . . Most exciting of all I am tackling the British Council for a recording with Boyd Neel and a tour of Sth Africa with him making your work & the Four Hymns (VW) our features (19450913).

It is not certain that the South African tour took place, but Neel did successfully take *Dies natalis* to the Antipodes in 1947.

Meanwhile, Ernest Newman had focused on *Dies natalis* in no fewer than three consecutive *Sunday Times* features in July, just as the war was coming to a close (see Newman 1945), and praised it highly. On 15 July he compared it with Britten's *Les illuminations*. The following week, in a somewhat muddled argument, he acclaimed Finzi's word-setting as a historical break-through, an example of how, in a composer 'with the requisite blend in himself of musical imagination and poetic sensitivity, a vast amount of our finest poetry that has hitherto evaded musical treatment becomes susceptible to it'. This of course was the exact opposite of Hutchings's 1936 view and must have helped neutralise any misgivings Finzi felt about returning to his Wordsworth project. Newman continued his eulogy in the third feature, concentrating on Finzi's way with Traherne's prose, and although by this stage in Newman's career his terms of reference sound decidedly passé one suspects that his accolade did more than anything else to bestow authority on Finzi's melopoetics and invest *Dies natalis* with classic status. The 'sensibility' period of English 'music and letters', and Finzi's pre-eminence within it, became fixed by such pronouncements, at such a moment, though in the light of post-war aesthetics it was very much the moment of its passing, as we shall see.

By the following January Milford could write to Finzi: 'I am really glad to hear, from a number of sources, of the proper appreciation your *Dies Natalis* seems to be obtaining' (19460118). Finzi conducted it, at Vaughan Williams's invitation, with Bradbridge White at the Leith Hill Festival in April, and again at the Three Choirs in Hereford in September, with Suddaby – its first performance postponed for seven years, in effect. Dyneley Hussey gave it a further critical boost and probably helped get the British Council recording off the ground around this time, but Greene was bitterly disappointed when the recording, with Boyd Neel, went to Joan Cross rather than him (this was nothing to do with Finzi). It was ill-fated: Cross was not the person for it, a train strike in January 1947 left Neel stranded in Edinburgh for one of the recording sessions and Finzi conducting two of the movements himself (it has never been known which), and an electrical fault meant that they were at a slightly different pitch – the more's the pity, since it was the only commercial recording of any composition by Finzi during his lifetime other than that of 'White-flowering days' on the *Garland for the Queen* disc. A study score of *Dies natalis* was issued in 1946, without any mention of Traherne ('the words ... are presumably by the composer,' *Musical Opinion* guessed [lxx/834 (1947): 187]). Then, in April 1948, a Cambridge student, John Reeves, told Finzi that he and one of his contemporaries, Wilfred Brown, were performing the cantata in a Cambridge University Musical Club concert; 'his control is perfect, and his musicianship impeccable,' Reeves wrote (19480426). Brown, a Quaker, decided to become a schoolteacher, and coincidence shortly put both Nigel and Christopher Finzi in his form at Bedales. But the musical profession soon claimed him, and his orbit approached Gerald's ever more closely, for he had studied before the war with Kennedy Scott and now went to Eric Greene for lessons. In June 1952, at the memorable Newbury String Players concert at High Wycombe, he sang *Dies natalis* under Gerald's direction, but not until eight years after the composer's death, and with his former pupil, Christopher, conducting, did he make the second, definitive recording of the work. He died even younger than Gerald, of a brain tumour in 1971 at the age of forty-nine.

It was Brown's great musical intelligence and spirituality that capped *Dies natalis*'s reputation. The qualities he brought to the work are evident from an article he wrote for *The Friend* in 1958, drawing on his Cambridge training in modern languages:

It is . . . my duty to stand in all weathers at the crossroads of human experience, assimilating all that I observe, so that the quintessence of any given emotion may irradiate my voice as I sing of it and my listeners thrill to this as being the articulation of something within themselves. I cannot believe that this urge for articulation, be it direct in the interpreter or vicarious in the listener, is implanted in us for the vapid purposes of entertainment. Both urge and gift are God inspired, and I for one would not have given up my material security for anything else.

But to what purpose?

In one of his sonnets Rilke contemplates an ancient statue of Apollo so mutilated that only the trunk remains. He muses on its present, and what he intuitively knows to have been its past glories, and we share the exultation of spirit which this torso, despite the ravages of time, produces in him. Then comes his astounding conclusion: there is no part of this figure which does not see you: 'Du musst dein Leben andern.' (You must live differently.)

This work of art, imperfect as even the fairest of our human creations must be, has seen us as we are and shamed us into a sense of our own imperfection.

Many singers have doubtless sensed this power and obligation, but who else could have articulated it so forcefully? Janet Baker, perhaps, among

British ones; few others. Long before, however, Finzi's wartime audiences had begun to respond to *Dies natalis*'s own 'astounding conclusion' about innocence and unattainable perfection as the lost birthright of humankind and – what needed saying – the continuing birthright of art. Howells was one of the first to express this. 'I want to tell you how moved I was, on Tuesday night, by "Dies Natalis",' he wrote to Finzi after the 1943 broadcast. ' – It was strangely comforting: and (it seemed to me) it all gives one back a standard of beauty that virtuosity has so nearly wrecked in so much contemporary work' (19431224). Tony Scott put his finger on something similar when he told Gerald: 'I know of few works since the time of Bach, at any rate since Romanticism set in, which have just that quality of serenity and also intense emotion quite devoid of self pity. Very different from the arid sterility of the neo-classic phase of Stravinsky and his followers' (19460705). Non-musicians frequently felt compelled to more general testimony, and Finzi's first fan letters from unknown admirers were about *Dies natalis*. His own doctor, Tom Scott, wrote after its NSP performance at Enborne in 1948:

[*Dies natalis*] seems to me to be something which, like the words you have chosen, is ageless and dateless, and will live and be played and loved long after you are gone. You have managed in your music to express your own emotional outlook on childhood and life with which I feel in such sympathy; there is a feeling of contentment and happiness mixed with joy, enthusiasm and (as you say) rapture, which is a rare change from so much art that has come from twisted, frustrated and unhappy minds during the last 30 years. Moreover you have made the music express and emphasise the meaning of the words, not only in the general mood but also in the particular phrasing so that the words could be heard and the meaning comprehended which is such a rare thing. I think the Intrada is really beautiful and I found it awoke in me that rare feeling of contentment that I get from walking through beech woods in early summer or looking at a Cathedral roof, and that lovely melody haunted me halfway through the night. The Rapture gave me the impression of a huge spring bubbling up through the ground which someone kept trying to stop. Each time it was quiet for a few seconds & then burst out on the other side. It also reminded me of the children playing and it pleased me to think that the children of your mind and of your body were equally attractive. I felt that the whole thing had its roots deep in the past and its well balanced branches yet young with vigour. At any rate I love it and hope to hear it many times more, quite apart from the shadow of the real thing that I play on the gramophone. (19481212)

More power to Tom Scott's elbow for having the layman's courage to come clean about his mental imagery, which may be flowery but is notably specific, its emphasis on height and aspiration not unconnected with Finzi's epiphany on looking at March Church roof.

All three letters quoted above make the point that *Dies natalis* was in opposition to the prevailing artistic climate. It was this perception that made it somewhat distortedly into a representation of the whole of Finzi, rather than a side of him that he had no intention of re-exhibiting, even in the Wordsworth Ode. It became a weapon in the fight against the new technocratic cultural efficiency that swept almost everything before it in postwar reconstruction and was embodied in British music above all in the figure of Britten, his professionalism, ambition, cosmopolitan circle, *Angst* and all. Just as Holst and Vaughan Williams had been appointed – indeed, anointed – Britain's senior composers at a stroke when the end of the First World War rendered the positions psychologically vacant, Britten was similarly appointed, as is well known, at the end of the Second, with the production of *Peter Grimes*.

But those who felt that the war had shown art music on the whole, certainly from its younger exponents, failing an entire population in need of spiritual comfort (popular music was another matter, stepping very firmly into the breach), would have none of it and rejected Britten vehemently. The feeling grew among those of Finzi's cast that Britten had been deposited on an international fast track where few if any would be permitted to follow, and that, almost like the international money markets and, later, the multinational corporations, the whole thing was a 'racket' (19481107). Later, Finzi's bewilderment and antagonism – Rubbra's were even stronger – towards what he saw as a shallow art widened into anger at the wholesale arrogance of the dominant critical establishment of the postwar era, literary as well as musical, above all because of its élitism, its Leavisite habit of excluding all but a favoured minority of works, artists and approaches. What he and his contemporaries were witnessing was the wholesale professionalisation of musical taste and opinion-making in Britain to the point at which it seemed as sole a domain of the academy and corporations such as the Arts Council and the BBC as was scientific research, and to whose tune the quality press delightedly danced.

This needs further consideration in Chapter 11; the point to stress here is that although, as already suggested, there was plenty of room on the band-wagon for Finzi, he rapidly opted for vernacular cultural opposition insofar as he became prime representative of an art routed from London and defending its camp in the west in the cathedral cities of Gloucester, Worcester and Hereford. Every year from 1946 until his death, he, Joy and the children went to the Three Choirs, staying for the week, meeting their friends, together with Alice Sumsion organising an entire house party, and generally enjoying themselves and spending money in a holiday atmosphere unlike anything else in their annual calendar. Joy might precede the festival with a proper holiday with the children – they went on to Hereford after a fortnight at Coverack in Cornwall in 1946, for instance – but Gerald invariably stayed at home with urgent work to finish, not least because most years he had written or newly scored a piece for the festival. (One wonders whether in the end he did not regret not having devoted more 'quality time', as we might now call it, to his family away from home. There was another excursion with the Scotts to the Burnham Overy windmill in 1952, but Gerald spent it working hard, and the only holiday the four of them ever had together and on their own was a week in a caravan at St Davids after the Hereford Festival in 1955.)

The annual pattern established itself for the Finzis in 1946, when the Rubbras, the le Flemings and Eric Greene and his wife all stayed with them at Hereford and, as well as Finzi's first professional conducting engagement other than a studio broadcast, namely his performance of *Dies natalis*, witnessed a fine *Pastoral Symphony* conducted by Dyson and an appalling B Minor Mass conducted by Sir Ivor ('Saliva') Atkins. The following year at Gloucester Finzi conducted *Dies natalis* again in addition to the first performance with orchestra of 'Lo, the full, final sacrifice'; this time the latter was his first attempt at handling a choir in a professional context, and they went flat. His four orchestrated Gurney songs (the *Five Elizabethan Songs* minus 'Tears', arranged for the Newbury String Players and Sophie Wyss in 1943) were also performed. Again Joy convened a house party, and they met up with the Scotts, the Milfords and Jack Haines in addition to their cohabitants of the year before. In 1948 at Worcester 'Lo, the full, final sacrifice' was performed again (Finzi wisely left it to Sumsion on this occasion), and the 1949 Hereford Festival saw the first performance of the Clarinet Concerto. The 1950 festival marked the biggest occasion of Finzi's life: the première of *Intimations of Immortality*, at Gloucester. Most of the festival concerts were broadcast, and most radio broadcasting was still live, so the infirm Adeline Vaughan Williams, the work's dedicatee, was able to listen to it while her husband was present in person. Accompanied by Ursula from 1948 onwards, he was almost as regular an attender as the Finzis until 1956 (which was his last festival too), often conducting one of his own major works there and becoming the pride of the Finzi social circle for the last six or seven visits.

Finzi's string arrangement of Parry's Chorale Fantasia on an Old English Tune for organ, another piece he had scored up for the Newbury String Players (in 1948), was also performed at Gloucester in 1950. In 1951 it was *Intimations* again, this time at Worcester, in the cathedral, plus *Farewell to Arms* in the Odeon Theatre. The 1952 Hereford meeting and the 1954 Worcester one were the only two of the postwar decade without any Finzi in them, but the family still attended. 1953 saw the third festival performance of *Intimations*, back at Gloucester and this time under David Willcocks, plus the second of the Clarinet Concerto, played by Gervase de Peyer under the composer. In 1955 *Dies natalis* was revived at Hereford, and at Gloucester in 1956 *In terra pax* received its first performance with full orchestra, conducted by Finzi who by now knew how to handle the choir. This year's festival was not only Joy and Gerald's last but in many ways their best, 'one of the happiest . . . we have ever had', as Joy noted in a journal (19560902–08) still being written up in spare moments between those spent supervising a bigger and better house party than ever. At the same time it was an uncanny *envoi* to their presence and spirit in that it also included the first performance of Ferguson's *Amore langueo*, dedicated to them and performed by their old friends Sumsion and Greene, plus an exhibition of Joy's portrait drawings, her equally personal gift to her subjects – in more than one sense of the word – many of whom were present. It must have seemed incredible yet almost the fulfilment of a benediction when less than three weeks later Gerald's death after a short illness was announced.

The Three Choirs Festival has always been subject to ridicule, perhaps most famously by George Bernard Shaw, but it had to suffer a particularly cruel bout of denigration after the war as the new international festivals and summer schools threw its provincialism into ever stronger relief. A cold war of the critics' own broke out, the younger ones on the side of Edinburgh and Aldeburgh, Dartington and Darmstadt, the older ones 'mostly tired of music and . . . trying to keep Britain free of the moderns, free for Elgar . . . England and St George' (Amis 1985:

156). The Edinburgh Festival actually coincided with the Three Choirs, which lost out on press coverage and the best soloists. And Britten never visited the Three Choirs in Finzi's lifetime, or indeed in Vaughan Williams's, arriving at Hereford a fortnight after the latter's death to conduct *St Nicholas* and, in what must have seemed a grimly ironic valediction, the *Sinfonia da requiem* (see Boden 1992: 204).

In short, *Dies natalis* and its composer assumed more and more the mantle of Vaughan Williams. True, the early influence and hero-worship had in any case been paramount, while in later years the friendship became on Vaughan Williams's part the closest of all his associations after the death of Holst. But rather than take stylistic congruence for granted it may be suggested that at least where *Dies natalis* is concerned it was an identity not so much inherent in the work as one that overtook it. *Dies natalis*, in its lean, clean, Apollonian moments, and as a *Bildungskantate* that makes something of a break with the English song tradition at the same time as continuing it (see Banfield 1985: II, 393–5; 1995: 478), has as much in common with Tippett's contemporaneous *Boyhood's End* as with anything Vaughan Williams wrote. Finzi was content enough to enjoy not just Vaughan Williams's friendship but also to take over his role of dissenting lobbyist and spokesperson, but that does not mean that his mature music echoes the master's. His personality and techniques are quite different, even if they do produce similarities on certain occasions, such as in *In terra pax*.

Finzi's first postwar composition, 'Lo, the full, final sacrifice', makes the point, for no one notices that its last six lines of text were also used by Vaughan Williams as the third of his Four Hymns thirty years earlier, so differently conceived are their settings. Where a similarity does sound through is at the point in Finzi's anthem at which the liturgical stage suddenly clears for a solo treble voice proclaiming the 'Bread of loves': compare 'Music! Hark!' in Vaughan Williams's *Serenade to Music*. But in general 'Lo, the full, final sacrifice' breathes an intense, almost necromantic atmosphere, laden with incense, that is as far from the clear air of Vaughan Williams's metaphysical settings as it is from the artlessness and transparency of *Dies natalis*.

'That remarkable parson' Rev Walter Hussey, vicar of St Matthew's, Phippsville, Northampton, commissioned 'Lo, the full, final sacrifice' for his church's patronal festival day, 21 September, in 1946. Hussey, whose father had been the first vicar of St Matthew's (see Foster 1993), developed a lifelong mission 'to help re-forge the ancient link between the Church and the Arts' (19460606, 19460707). He went on to become Dean of Chichester, where his commissions included Bernstein's *Chichester Psalms*, but his efforts had borne their first fruits at St Matthew's in 1943, when Britten's *Rejoice in the Lamb*, Tippett's Festival Fanfare and Henry Moore's 'Madonna and child' sculpture were brought into being for its golden jubilee. Annual anthems for St Matthew's were squeezed out of British composers for many more years, and Arnold, Poston, Leighton, McCabe, Bennett, Howells, Christopher Headington and James Butt all wrote for Hussey. It was Rawsthorne's turn in 1944, and Rubbra – a local lad – stepped in with 'The revival' when his composition failed to materialise. Berkeley wrote his Festival Anthem for St Matthew's in 1945, and it was only when Rawsthorne let Hussey down a second time that he turned to Finzi, at rather short notice, on 6 June 1946.

Hussey, like many a cultured Anglican, liked his metaphysical poets, and suggested to Finzi: 'We have not so far had anything on the theme of the Eucharist . . . The sort of texts that pass through my mind are verses from Vaughan's The Feast, or his The Holy Communion, or Herbert's Holy Communion, and many others of similar and other sorts' (ibid.). Both Rubbra and Berkeley had already set Vaughan for the occasion, though Berkeley's anthem, much influenced by *Rejoice in the Lamb* (see Dickinson 1988: 102–8), was not at all to the taste of Finzi, who put a fence round his own creative patch by describing it to Scott as 'rather like a still-born turd' (19460707). Finzi's initial reaction to his first ever rushed commission must have been panic, for Hussey answered his reply to the invitation with 'Yes, I think the Vaughan "Up to those bright and gladsome hills" would be included within the limits' (19460612): in other words, the composer was thinking of returning to old work – very old work – at least to get him going. Hussey sowed further seeds of suggestion in this letter by mentioning 'devotional intensity' and stating: 'Some of the old latin hymns are lovely and very suitable . . . But other things being equal, I am inclined to think that an English text is to be preferred.'

Finzi delivered magnificently on all these counts when he set a partial amalgamation of Richard Crashaw's English versions of the St Thomas Aquinas hymns *Adoro te* and *Lauda Sion*. (Berkeley had comparably combined Latin sequence and metaphysical poet, though in juxtaposition.) 'Mine's only a little thing, organ & SATB,' he told Scott (ibid.), but the little thing frantically grew into by far the longest single span of music he had yet written, bar whatever already existed of *Intimations*, lasting between fourteen and seventeen minutes in performance. He was careful to ease its structure by shaping the text as strongly as possible, and he chopped up and interspersed Crashaw's stanzas a good deal in the process, also leaving out odd lines of dubious sensibility such as those about the 'vital gust' produced by the 'Rich, royal food', which would have been taking the shock tactics of the metaphysicals' imagery a little far, though he happily kept in the reference to the 'soft self-wounding pelican', surely the most alarming and memorable line in any English anthem. The opening stanza of *Lauda Sion* ('Rise, Royal Sion!') was placed in the centre, as the keystone of a musical arch, whereas the initial, title lines, repeated as a musical refrain before the final 'Amen', are actually taken from near the end of that poem.

Finzi's strategy is roughly to enact the liturgical drama of the Eucharist in narrative. The observer's gaze is initially directed towards the distant ritual with the opening (and recurrent) word 'Lo' and the reference to a 'Sacrifice / On which all figures fix't their eyes', and the first organ interlude (before figure 2), drawing marvellously on Anglican conventions of improvisation, suggests activity in the chancel, followed perhaps by the swinging of incense (see ex. 9.1.c) and movement towards the altar with one of Finzi's Holstian march signifiers (ex. 9.1.d to f, all loosely within a motivic first group). The sequence of the sharing of bread (Christ's body) followed by wine (Christ's blood) is then honoured, to an obvious exposition and recapitulation of lyrical 'second-subject' material – see the second (central) vertical column of motivic material in ex. 9.1 – though a second stanza referring to the bread, placed after the central climax presumably in order to sustain its vehicle of 'Triumphant Text', threatens to obscure this plan. The climax of the anthem comes after a third group of motifs, of fanfare character (see the right-hand column in ex. 9.1), has heralded both development and the 'Rise, Royal Sion!' episode (not shown in ex. 9.1 but coming between j and k); this circles back rhythmically to far-reaching transformations of the initial material. If one were to pursue the sonata analogy, the passage between figures 8 and 9 would be an elision of development and first-subject recapitulation, though the overall formal impression of the piece is more that of an arch (with 'Amen' coda), because of the literal first-line refrain near the end.

The progressive variation of motivic cells is instinctively loose yet subtle: ex. 9.1.c–f, for example, shows cumulative transformation by

EX. 9.1

changing first the rhythm, then the pitch contour, then a modicum of both. Most of the other connections in ex. 9.1 speak for themselves when thus tabulated, but what makes the form of 'Lo, the full, final sacrifice' work, exactly as in 'In years defaced', is that *words* verify moments of motivic significance. The outstanding, though utterly unselfconscious, example of this is when the motivically levelled figure for the trisyllable 'Legacy' is enharmonically replicated three bars later for the word 'Pelican' (x in ex. 9.1), another dactylic trisyllable with 'l', 'e' 'i' and 'a' sounds. Finzi makes it sound like the simplest of gifts from the poet, but one salutes the composer's technique that enabled it to take its place so perfectly. He knew exactly what he was doing in this mysterious and ungraspable musical structure, in which verbal phrases – 'Rich, Royal Food!', 'Lo the Bread of Life', 'the great twelve', and the 'dear Memorial', not to mention the pelican – jump out of the text motivically in flashes of transcendence, while the breathtaking flight of angels seems to materialise and intensify in the central reaches with their gathering harmonic movement. An extraordinarily bold and risky extent of anticipation precedes this climax, and in the aftermath, once again rather as in Debussy's *Prélude à 'L'après-midi d'un faune'*, one is left wondering whether it ever occurred at all – did one really see the vision? – in the impressionistic, almost post-coital lassitude of the 'come away' section. All in all, 'Lo, the full, final sacrifice' is a magnificent incarnation of the metaphysical experience, and in this author's opinion its opening page is the best thing Finzi ever wrote. Despite his dislike for the instrument, his understanding of organ sonorities is acute: it must have been more deeply imbibed under Bairstow than he realised, and here forms a fitting memorial to the man who died two months before the anthem was written. The power and the mystery of 'Lo, the full, final sacrifice' are lost with orchestral accompaniment, despite some thrilling colours, particularly on low flutes and muted trombones in the opening ritornello. Nor is the anthem's tonal structure as chaotic as the changing key signatures and Finzi's habits might suggest. The circumferential phrygian E, lovingly fulfilled in the final cadence with its D and F naturals, makes the most of its tonal penumbra at the outset, when on the first page the initial motif explores A, D and E polarities with Elgarian restlessness; marches duly sharpwards as the 'exposition' progresses; interprets lyrical contrast as needing an acute submediant, D♭; and places the central revelation in the relative major, G, moving to the tonic major (E) for 'heightened' return.

One of the bonuses of writing choral music in the days before photo-copying was the instant gratification of seeing one's work in print before the first performance: the choir would learn the piece from newly published scores. (This also explains why within such a culture orches-tration was regarded as a supplementary art, for the short score had to be definitive before a note of it had been heard, whereas the orchestral one could be adjusted after rehearsal and performance.) It was also a nightmare, demanding the strictest of deadlines from publishers, but it enabled a choral piece to be well and truly launched by the time of its first performance. 'Lo, the full, final sacrifice' was well received on St Matthew's Day, sung again by the church choir in November for the unveiling of Graham Sutherland's *Crucifixion*, and accepted for the 1947 Gloucester Festival. 'I have a feeling that Walter Hussey was dis-appointed with the work when I had a very rough run through at the piano,' Finzi told Milford (19460912a). 'It *isn't* like Britten, for whom Hussey has a great, great admiration!' Yet the 'remarkable parson' was pleased enough to ask Finzi to write him an unaccompanied Mass the following year. Finzi thought about it but did no more, and already his next composition after 'Lo, the full, final sacrifice', another rushed commission, had shown that he could explore his instinct for dramatic ritual in quite a different context. At a time when many of his closest friends would doubtless have been delighted to appropriate him as a religious composer – for Milford had turned Anglo-Catholic in 1940, Toty de Navarro had always been a member of the Roman Catholic church and Rubbra was received into it 'in 1947 or thereabouts' (Rubbra, quoted in Grover 1993: 20) – he turned to commercial secular-ity and wrote incidental music for Shakespeare's *Love's Labour's Lost*.

He was given three weeks in which to produce a score for sixteen instrumentalists accompanying a Home Service radio production to be broadcast on 16 December 1946. This was a live relay, as most still were, though there was talk also of a later transmission, presumably recorded on acetates or on tape, which was now beginning to affect patterns of broadcasting. Finzi's original instrumentation is not known, for his score is missing, but short-score drafts suggest that it consisted of nine strings and one each of flute/piccolo, oboe, clarinet, bassoon, horn, trumpet and side drum. If so, later amplification was a matter of adding second horn and second clarinet. The producer was Noel Iliff, the cast included Paul Scofield (as Berowne), Thea Holme, Ernest Milton, David Spenser as Moth (a real discovery, though he went on to be a producer, not an actor), and Pauline Letts; the conductor was Clifton Helliwell.

Iliff's wife, the actress Simona Pakenham, arranged the play for the broadcast, greatly cutting it for the standard Monday evening ninety-minute production slot. She had asked Finzi, whom she did not know, to compose the music on the strength of *Let Us Garlands Bring* and *Dies natalis*, having heard the latter at a National Gallery concert. (Though not a trained musician, she was already writing her book on Vaughan Williams and had completed about half of it. Finzi was not told this, and when in the course of their conversation he said 'Of course the opinions of amateurs on music are of no importance whatsoever' she went home and destroyed the manuscript. 'That's so typical of Gerald,' Vaughan Williams commented when he heard the story years later.)

In true theatre fashion, with BBC copyist at the ready, Finzi finished his scoring at 4 a.m. on the day before the broadcast, and despite complaining 'I am not made like that,' he was pleased with the assignment. 'I rather wanted to do it, just to show myself that I *cd* do it,' he told Milford, while to Scott he acknowledged: 'I thoroughly enjoyed the experience and liked the crowd I was working with, and they also seemed to like the music' (19461222a, 19461221). Pakenham thinks he had not known the play before; few people did.

At first he was doubtful of any future for the musical snippets, but in July 1947 Mollie Sands and Ruth Dyson performed the four songs in a Wigmore Hall concert and by the time of their publication the following year Finzi also had in mind an orchestral suite. His setting of one of the songs, Moth's 'If she be made of white or red' was not required for the radio production and he had written it afterwards to round out his contribution. He submitted the suite, 'part-made', to the BBC for consideration in a Midland Region programme of light music for the Cheltenham Festival of 1952, and they thought it 'so much better than all the other scores' that 'Finzi should be invited to complete the Suite, – the more so,' they added, with delightful geographical vagueness, 'since he is a West Country composer' (19520403). Perhaps he thought he had completed it when it was performed on this occasion (by the BBC Midland Light Orchestra under Gilbert Vinter), with the songs and six assembled instrumental movements (see Appendix on p. 498), but Ferguson was not happy with the sequence: he wanted more fast music and advised splitting up the Soliloquies, omitting one of them, and leaving out the songs (19520721). Finzi's solution was to leave the three Soliloquies in and keep them together but add two lively movements, a 'Quodlibet' based largely on the low characters' material and a 'Hunt' scherzo, together with a 'Nocturne'. These last two items were composed for Michael Greenwood's Coronation production of the play with the Southend Shakespeare Society in the open air at Leigh-on-Sea in June 1953, as were the Princess's entry flourish and fanfares for the three lords as they sign their oaths in the first scene (though the latter had to be omitted because of an inadequate trumpeter). The ten-movement Suite achieved its final form in 1955, when John Russell broadcast it with the LSO, and the Three Soliloquies were also made available separately. Altogether his originally commissioned twelve minutes of music (plus the songs) grew to nearly half an hour's-worth of Suite and an even longer 'quarry' of music 'from which to dig' for future productions (G. Finzi ?1955), one of which was a second BBC radio broadcast of the play using Finzi's music at some time in the 1970s.

Love's Labour's Lost is one of Finzi's least-known works, yet it is also one of his most vivid, delightful, and important in that it afforded a focus for his Englishness and scope for his maturing imagination as authentic and intrinsic as anything he ever engaged with, but for once (as far as we know) entirely unencumbered by residual material from earlier periods. The score surely offers better evidence of potential development beyond his fleeting final decade than any of his other compositions, even the Cello Concerto.

Why, then, had it taken a genuinely theatrical flair so long to manifest itself? The answer must lie largely with Finzi's self-education and its causes. Most composers would have been presented with opportunities to join the rough-and-tumble of musical society and its workshops by composing for their peers and neighbours in theatrical productions and other events whilst at college and even at school, or, like Tippett, would have made their own opportunities in almost any village or regional community even if they were not themselves accomplished performers, so long as they could adapt their aims sufficiently to gain immediate and ongoing practical experience. Finzi paid a heavy price for ploughing his own furrow so straight before the war and keeping his long-term objectives so entirely detached from short-term surroundings and expediency.

In fact, this was where time ran out on him most obviously, for it was not as if he had no interest in dramatic or theatrical music, rather that until he was fully established in other fields it never occurred to him that he might one day be in a position to exploit it. 'To me, the sound of *"live"* music in the theatre is one of the joys of life!' he wrote to Milford in 1951. 'And now that Stratford has live music again ... it adds an enormous lot to the performances' (19510831). Nor did opera cease to constitute the biggest of all musical events for him (together with the first performances of Vaughan Williams's symphonies), and after the war he and Joy went to the Britten premières, Bliss's *The Olympians*, Walton's *Troilus and Cressida* and Menotti's *The Medium* and *The Consul* (these three much admired, with some personal contact with Menotti), Wellesz's *Incognita*, Berg's *Wozzeck* and Berkeley's *Nelson*. He missed Tippett's *The Midsummer Marriage* because he was in hospital; it is intriguing to speculate on what he would have made of it. Earlier he had done all he could to see or otherwise imbibe Boughton, all the Vaughan Williams operas (and *Job*), plus those of Holst, Benjamin, Goossens, George Lloyd and Delius, as well as such continental repertoire as Weinberger's *Schwanda the Bagpiper*. He had always been a theatre-goer, in London both while he lived there and after he moved to the country, and latterly at Stratford and Oxford. Indeed, no English musical renaissance composer could afford not to be, for as the agenda for cultural Englishness gained force from the late nineteenth century onwards, with the Elizabethen golden age in particular as beacon, it was vital that music, omnipresent in Shakespeare's plays, find its proper role in the theatre and help reclaim the stage 'for England and St George', rescuing it from the Scylla of Italian and German opera and the Charybdis of increasingly vulgar and Americanised musical comedies. To Finzi's colleagues one of the most galling things about Britten's success was that in *Peter Grimes* he showed with one bound how two or three generations had missed their chance: it was all over for them and their dream of a classic, vernacular England, merrie or otherwise, on the musical stage, Vaughan Williams's *Pilgrim's Progress* included. Elgar's unfinished Ben Jonson opera *The Spanish Lady* symbolised the wreckage, as Sullivan's *Ivanhoe* and Stanford's *Much Ado About Nothing* had done earlier.

In the late 1920s Finzi, together with Ferguson, had devoted considerable time and thought to the problem. Holst's *At the Boar's Head* and Vaughan Williams's *Sir John in Love* were particular challenges, with all the right ingredients – Shakespearian comedy, a specific indigenous setting, folksong – but somehow still not quite the real thing. Finzi wanted to set Masefield's play *The Tragedy of Nan* to music in 1927.

In the spring of 1928 *Master Peter's Puppet Show* by Falla reinforced in both composers the urge to write a comic opera, whereupon their attention turned to pre-Shakespearian drama, Nicholas Udall's *Ralph Roister Doister* being considered for treatment later in the year. They seem to have had a pact to attempt scenarios or libretti for each other until they realised the extent of the difficulties. Ferguson did later begin an opera on *Ralph Roister Doister*, while Finzi excitedly planned one on Ashley Dukes's *The Dumb Wife of Cheapside*, a 'silent woman' play he heard on the radio in 1929. None of these projects came to anything, and the two friends were soon overtaken by their third, Cedric Thorpe Davie, who managed to complete a comic opera on *Gammer Gurton's Needle* (another source Ferguson had been considering) in 1936, scarcely out of college. Their response to early English comedy never diminished, however, and Finzi was as receptive as ever when he saw Dekker's *The Shoemaker's Holiday* in 1948, the year Ferguson composed a ballet on the 'Chauntecleer' fable found in Chaucer. Nor did Vaughan Williams ever abandon the challenge of the vernacular lyric stage: he and Ursula were working on a *Thomas the Rhymer* opera when he died.

No one has yet succeeded in the quest. Where Englishness in music had long found a comfortable dramatic niche for itself, however, was in incidental provision. Henry Irving had taken a good deal of trouble over the incidental music to his epoch-making Lyceum Shakespeare productions, keen to get the right composer and the right period flavour. Arthur Sullivan's and Edward German's Shakespeare scores are classics heading a tradition of British light music, though it was one that gradually moved away from the theatre and winter garden and into the broadcasting and film studio as it approached Eric Coates and then Finzi's contemporaries and juniors such as Arthur Benjamin and Malcolm Arnold. This was partly because the economics of 'straight' theatre gradually ruled out the slick sound of a Broadway or Broadcasting House march, and partly because Shakespearian taste tended to get too big for its boots, prey to hi-jacking by the all too mummery concerns of the Arts and Crafts movement when it encouraged Stratford to team up with the folk revival. At this point period flavour became historical recovery, entertainment became cultural concept, and wit, always the biggest stumbling-block for British opera, went out of the window. (See Kennedy 1964, R.1980: 64, 103–4 and 1982: 30–31, 78–80; Grogan 1993; Boyes 1993: 83–4, 107–8; and Greensted 1993:

84–6 for cameos of Vaughan Williams, Elgar, Cecil Sharp and others working within this frame, though the whole picture has yet to be painted. The revival of the masque is somewhere in the middle of it.) Up to a point, with the support of Henry Irving's namesake Ernest, British light music regained classic status in the cinema, above all in Walton's *Henry V* score of 1945 (see also Bax's *Oliver Twist* of 1948 and the other films listed in Kershaw 1995: 130–31, 133–5). Here at least, thanks to the rigid discipline of the studio, the comic spirit in the broadest sense, without which no composer can hope to stand up to Shakespeare or Dickens and with which, it has to be said, Britten was never wholly at ease, could find its expression.

Finzi's *Love's Labour's Lost* music stands at a crossroads surrounded by all this traffic. It is easy to see where some of the traffic is coming from – Quilter, Vaughan Williams, Walton, Rawsthorne, Fauré, even a current popular song all pass by, as do one or two earlier Shakespearians in music. The D major stateliness of the King and his court's music in Finzi's Introduction (ex. 9.2.a) is very much that of the opening of Vaughan Williams's *Serenade to Music* (another Shakespeare setting), with perhaps a touch of 'Rosamund' from Quilter's music to *Where the Rainbow Ends*, which Grainger had described as 'so kingly' (1947). Another double echo of Quilter and Vaughan Williams comes with the folky tune and busybodying G major strings of the Finale's C section, not unlike the latter's overture to *The Wasps* while carrying a suggestion of 'Over the hills and far away' from the former's *Children's Overture* (perhaps the King's 'Away, away!' before this entr'acte triggered this reminiscence, though it was cut in the production). A French lightness of touch pervades the atmosphere, in general with the Princess's music and its 'feminine' rhythms pattering on beyond the barline or downbeat (see especially *xy* in ex. 9.2.b) and in particular when the III/IV entr'acte (No 6C in the Suite; see ex. 9.2.d) takes its cue from Fauré's *Dolly* Suite (compare 'Tendresse', ex. 9.2.j) and 'The hunt' – a *jeu d'esprit* completely unprecedented in Finzi – its hint from Berlioz's 'Queen Mab' Scherzo. The smiling graciousness of the ladies of the French court comes straight from Walton's *Henry V* – the parallels between the two plays have not gone unremarked – but other nearby sounds are grasped more unexpectedly. In the introduction to the 'Songs of Hiems and Ver' (ex. 9.2.k) Finzi seems to be broadening his harmonic vocabulary in the direction of Rawsthorne (compare ex. 9.2.l, the opening of Raws-

EX. 9.2.a–i

EX. 9.2.j (piano duet)

EX. 9.2.k

EX. 9.2.l

thorne's overture *Street Corner* of 1944). And at various points in the Nocturne and Dance, Mel Tormé's 1946 hit 'Chestnuts roasting on an open fire' enters one's head, not altogether happily, through a recurrent motivic phrase (ex. 9.2.e); perhaps 'When roasted crabs hiss in the bowl' made it too strong an association to resist, especially when Finzi was writing his score in the run-up to Christmas.

As Finzi pointed out (?1955), Shakespeare's play 'calls for no extended music and requires no change of scene' (see Gooch and Thatcher 1991: I, 653 for the modest tally of musical stage directions). Nevertheless, its affectionate tone and pace, and its contrasted, concerted groups of characters and the modulations between them are invitation enough to any composer, and Finzi must have been pleased not just to be asked to provide a number of entr'actes (in addition to exit and entrance music) for the original radio production but to have the opportunity of extending and multiplying his cues for the more leisurely and primitive open-air conditions of Greenwood's production in 1953, where music had to abet the lighting (see McVeagh 1987). Altogether he provided enough music for joining every scene, should the producer desire it, and something each for most of the characters. Furthermore, the play culminates in a masque of sorts, though with only one extended dance (No. 5 in the Suite), followed by Shakespeare's 'rather miraculous end' (19461221), namely the two songs 'When daisies pied' and 'When icicles hang by the wall'.

Stringing most of this into a suite – all the entr'actes and signature tunes except for a few fanfares were eventually found a home – was a matter of rediscovering what the eighteenth century had first proved, namely that a medley can achieve respectability simply by being made into a ternary form or rondo, and this is what the first, second, sixth and tenth movements of the Suite are, while No. 5 was also extended into a rondo from an endlessly repeating functional ternary form. In McVeagh's inimitable phrase (1987), this enjoyment of self-contained, highly characterised strains 'loosened Finzi's sinews'. Perhaps it did so too much, when it came to stringing sections together in the fast movements of his two concertos. What cannot be gainsaid, however, is the new range of colour and texture that Shakespeare's characters drew forth. It is often the same story with British music: when it ceases to be serious or too self-sufficient it becomes so much more imaginative. Parry's music for the Greek plays; Ireland's for *Julius Caesar*; Stanford's in the operas, even his *Ode to Discord* – all these make one regret that illustrative work, above all in the theatre, is not standard training for the British composer. One suspects Finzi came to regret it too, though he did not live long enough to do much more about it. And where *Love's Labour's Lost* is concerned it was largely a question of taking care of the producer's needs and trusting the Englishness to take care of itself.

It did, along with the Frenchness, just as in Shakespeare's play Navarre effortlessly establishes itself as the world of home, no more exotic or Iberian than a clown called Costard, a flat-footed policeman and pedantic schoolmaster. Ex. 9.2.a–i (its layout conceptual rather than consecutive) shows Shakespeare's three character groups plus the fourth that foils them. The left-hand column is that of the King and his courtiers, their stolid, somewhat contrapuntal diatonicism taken as much for granted as the indigenous spiritual landscape as their park is for the physical one. The central column represents those foreign, or at least visiting, objects of desire, the Princess and her court, in ex. 9.2.b, plus the base caricature of their graceful qualities and concerted social identity that is the fantastics' oddball, antagonistic assortment. Costard heads the latter, his theme, which goes tonally awry after the bar quoted in ex. 9.2.c and is played on the piccolo and side drum (which should surely be unsnared, even though Finzi did not specify it, for his accoutrement is pipe and tabor), a distortion of the Princess's. The motley band he leads take their cues from his throwaway $\hat{5}$ $\hat{3}$ $\hat{1}$ fanfare tag that reappears in the masque when Nathaniel the feeble curate enters as Alexander (and with a joke on 'Some talk of Alexander' Finzi turns it into 'The British Grenadiers'), having also served for 'Dull's hey' at the end of Act V scene i, the constable's inevitable plodding exit on bassoon (ex. 9.2.g). Given that part of the point of such a play is to show how characters unwittingly reflect or caricature each other's foibles or aspirations, it is fitting that motifs should be susceptible to mutual transformation. Thus the Princess's arpeggio tag divides into the scale x that is ubiquitous in the Nocturne entr'acte and the Dance, to the point at which it seems to accompany the entire comedy of manners, while the gentle courtly wit of $y1$ is mirrored in the coarse buffoonery of $y2$. Somewhat outside all this, adding a more mysterious element of whimsicality and melancholy, is the third group of material, for the 'fantastical Spaniard' Armado and his foil, the page Moth. Obsessive and vulnerable, their fixed humours are embodied in oscillating motifs (ex. 9.2. h and i), in other words with fixed and obsessive shapes, within melodies that mark time harmonically: neither character seems to find a home in this world of courtiers and clowns, and Finzi's music for these two outsiders is among his most striking. Perhaps the sad echoes of the distant Mediterranean from the one and of the ancient greenwood from the other (in the viola rendition of the folk-like tune of 'False Concolinel') carry something of Finzi's own pondered, shifting legacy of heredity and environment with them. There is an exquisite melancholy, too, in Dance (No. 5), its plangent opening harmonies very much in the vein of 'Proud songsters', nicely gauged for presaging Marcade's announcement of the Princess's father's death, when the play of the play takes a sudden darker turn. There are further plangencies elsewhere, though not as many as the Nimbus recording would have us believe, containing as it does two howlers from Finzi's uncorrected full score (at 2′11″ and 2′34″ in the Nocturne, on clarinet and horn respectively).

Even the spread of this material does not give a full idea of how Shakespeare expanded and liberated Finzi's range. One also admires his orchestral resourcefulness – 'I... think the sound of brass by itself is marvellous,' he told Thorpe Davie (19360209), and one would never guess from listening to the Princess's entry music that opens the Suite that half the fanfaring instruments are woodwind. One wishes he had bitten the bullet of a rapid scherzo decades earlier in his career: he manages it perfectly well in 'Hunt', and it offers as much scope for his beloved Neapolitan relationships as any of his ruminative song structures and includes a galloping metric modulation from 6/8 to 3/4 that is a brilliant touch, like a fox suddenly throwing the chase off the scent. And one recognises above all that a single bold, economic stroke could be worth a great deal of prudent husbandry: an unaccompanied clarinet line here, a piece of instrumental mimicry there, a simple cantilena as background to a spoken sonnet – melodrama, in other words – somewhere else. The melodramas (the Three Soliloquies) are especially effective when one realises that the first and the third fit the number of poetic lines precisely and thus can supplement character portrayal as far as tone of voice and rhythm of speech, to the extent the actor desires. The King's love sonnet emerges as the most delicate and poetic, Dumaine's infatuation as a little more facile, and Longaville's 'stubborn lines' betray a brooding passion the eloquence of whose embodiment in clarinet arabesque looks forward to the Concerto while its smouldering harmony recalls the flashes of apprehension in 'Lo, the full, final sacrifice'. The means are simple and the emotional end no different from that of many a film composer; but the idea works, and throws both character and composer into relief.

Finzi's next composition, *For St Cecilia*, called for the further development of several of his aesthetic faculties at once. As a Ceremonial Ode, commissioned by the St Cecilia's Festival Committee for performance in the Royal Albert Hall on 22 November 1947, it was even more in the public sphere than incidental music. As an unbroken span of choral music (with solo tenor) lasting about seventeen minutes, it was a little longer than 'Lo, the full, final sacrifice' while a good deal larger in scale, since it was scored for full orchestra. Unlike the anthem, however, it presented Finzi with the challenge of setting, without cuts, a single poem, one moreover that he had not chosen himself. He could nevertheless help shape the text's final form, for it was commissioned, apparently at Frank Howes's instigation, from a poet whom he had long admired and with whom he could now therefore develop a working relationship: Edmund Blunden.

The close personal friendship that eventuated was a major new departure for Finzi, one which he prized highly and which became one of his greatest sources of satisfaction and fulfilment thereafter. His creative 'telegraph wires', at least where the partnership of setting poetry to music or editing another's work was concerned, had hitherto (if one excepts Harland) been connected solely to artists whom he had never met, even when they were still alive: Hardy, Gurney, Parry, Bridges and poets such as the Georgians had all been friends on the page, not in the flesh, so that it was in each case a one-way conversation. Reciprocal literary exchanges were honed on minor, behind-the-scenes practitioners such as Toty de Navarro and Jack Haines. Now, perhaps when he was ready for it, he could have his very own Georgian poet for colleague and friend – which would more than match Howells's name-dropping of the Georgians, if nothing else.

Not only had Finzi already made several Blunden settings, as we have seen, but he was familiar with his prose as well as his poetry. Blunden, discovered young, was one of the most enduring of the Georgians, partly because his academic career, prose and scholarship took him well beyond their orbit even if his poetic language never did. His modest, retiring nature – that of a 'harmless young shepherd in a soldier's coat' (Marsack 1982: 13) – would never have projected the claim, but it was fairly made by his biographer, that 'he spent more time in the trenches than any other recognised war writer' (Webb 1990: 50–51). He was in the firing-line for two years, and wrote about it in *Undertones of War* (1928), a minor classic re-issued as one of the early Penguins, though the book did not fully exorcise his experiences, for they returned to haunt him in his final years. Whether or not he and Finzi ever talked about the First World War, the presence in Finzi's later life of one so central to its literary mythology must have gone a long way towards filling the personal lacuna the war had represented to the composer too young to have experienced it as anything but arbitrary loss. Furthermore, Blunden had published a book on Thomas Hardy. He also knew Gurney, another source of allure to Finzi and the subject of their initial dealings, when Finzi persuaded Blunden to write a memoir of Gurney the poet for the *Music and Letters* tributes of 1938. Finzi, greatly struck by Blunden's beautiful handwriting, did not meet him at this point, but returning to his Gurney crusade after the Second World War went to see Blunden in his *Times Literary Supplement* office in London in October 1945 to discuss the problem of Gurney's unpublished poems. with him. They evidently hit it off, and soon found that they had many scholarly and antiquarian interests, particularly eighteenth-century ones, in common, furnishing plenty of material for ongoing correspondence for the rest of Finzi's life – which was just as well, since Blunden was not musical. Indeed, Blunden's rehabilitation of a minor 'vernacular' poet, John Clare, in his edition of 1921, must have strengthened Finzi's confidence in his own eighteenth-century protégés, above all John Stanley.

It was an ideal friendship, but it was not, practically speaking, a vital one – that is, beyond the success of Finzi's Blunden settings and of his efforts to get more of Gurney's poems published with Blunden as editor. Finzi's urgent temperament and freelance power base were very different from the more centripetal, and hence self-contained, springs of Blunden's creativity, which operated quietly between his desk at home and his office or university room. Finzi was a passionate correspondent, eager to share thoughts or stimulate arguments about anything and everything; Blunden, the hard-pressed institutional employee who had to conserve every possible ounce of creativity and critical perception, was a courteous one, tending to give back what he had received, in whimsical and elegant exchanges that Finzi occasionally found himself emulating. In any case, they remained on second-name terms, in an efficient professional relationship, until long after the composition of *For St Cecilia*. Blunden, *en route* to Japan for two years as Cultural Liaison Officer with the British Mission – he had to earn a living – missed the first performance, and it was only after he and his family had returned and spent a weekend at Ashmansworth in May 1951 that the two households proceeded to first-name intimacy, even though Finzi had in the meantime dedicated *Before and After Summer* to him, which smacks ever so slightly of lionising. (Later printings of the volume unaccountably omit the dedication.) All too soon the Blundens were off again, to the University of Hong Kong in 1953, which greatly exercised Finzi, who felt it a national scandal that Blunden had to earn his living abroad and spent a good deal of unfruitful effort trying to get his friends to agree with him and help him find a way of doing something about it.

'The poet has accepted the traditional manner, invoking the "Delightful Goddess ... resourceful Legend" in true seventeenth-century style,' wrote Frank Howes in his review of *For St Cecilia*'s first performance (*The Times*, 24 November 1947: 7). There was in any case a strongly Augustan side to Blunden, particularly in his language of 'arcadian resources' (see Marsack: 13–14). 'Dont pass the poem over as a piece of 18th century artifice,' Finzi accordingly warned Thorpe Davie. 'The more I got to know it the more I grew to love it, though I was very dubious at a first reading' (19481003). But the question is not so much whether he (and indeed Finzi) successfully combined the artifice with twentieth-century imperatives, as whether Blunden's verse structure lent itself to musical setting. Compared with Pope's and Dryden's St Cecilia texts, settings of two of which, by Handel and Purcell (1692, re-orchestrated by Rawsthorne), were performed in the same concert, Blunden's may appear too polysyllabic and intricately continuous in its syntax, with a dearth of short, exclamatory phrases, close rhymes and assonances and refrain motifs such as would enable the composer to build with small, variegated textual blocks rather than have to break down larger, homogeneous ones. This cannot have helped Finzi's habitual struggle with musical structure, though he probably did not see it quite like that. The only phrase that is turned directly into musical coinage is the very opening apostrophe, quoted by Howes, which becomes a kind of ritornello theme (ex. 9.3.a), with a dangerous weight to have to carry over such a long span. These misgivings would have been no surprise to Blunden, who was quite prepared for Finzi to 'revert to one of the old poems on the Saint', an option the composer dismissed notwithstanding his possession of 'a pleasant volume published by Bell & Dalby in 1857, which I have, and this gives a large collection, ranging from Fishburn, Oldham, Tate to Christopher Smart (though oddly enough omitting Collins' Ode) & including a great many enti-ties & nonentities, both in letters & music' (19470617). The poet was

[Maestoso, ma poco Animato]

De-light - ful God - dess,

EX. 9.3.a

344

well aware of the 'virtue in a variousness of allusions & "materials" for musical setting' (19470925), but if his ode was short on this Finzi saw its broad, sustained form as a converse virtue.

The poem alternates three eight-line sections or stanzas with three twelve-line ones (except that the first of these is missing a line). In the former Blunden rhymes alternate lines, interspersing tetrameters (and one final-line Alexandrine) with iambic pentameters and couching their rhetoric largely in vocative exclamation and question. The latter, consisting solely of heroic couplets, take a more distant, panoramic stance, and include the lists of saints and English composers respectively in sections two and four. The final section fuses second-person direct address (now to the audience) with the cooler perspective of historical narrative, though it originally also included a third catalogue, this time of musical instruments, and what Finzi saw as a fusion of the two verse forms by way of 'compromise between the Strophe & Antistrophe idea', which he felt 'defeats its purpose – again, from the musical angle' in its use of poetic antithesis: 'The last verse *must* build up' (19470617).

This clearly involved a substantial change to the poem. Finzi also asked for some minor ones, for reasons of singability, form, mood or simply improvement (at which he had had long experience with Navarro's poetry), sometimes suggesting the new wording himself. Blunden was quite happy to make or approve them. Thus 'Speak' was changed to 'Sing' at the start of the last line of the first stanza, a reference to 'modern Britain' in stanza two – suggesting to Finzi 'publishers' series, railway hoardings & technical magazines' (19470617) – was excised, and *Cecily* became 'melodious' rather than 'charming' in stanza two and her 'race' 'grace' in stanza four. A curious usage of 'ascends' in stanza five was changed to 'transcends', though not until seven years later, after 'a county music organizer' had written to Boosey & Hawkes pointing out that that made more sense (19540611a).

The last four lines were rewritten several times, Finzi adjudicating between and further refining alternatives supplied by Blunden, suggesting the open-vowel final rhyme of 'along' and 'song', and generally making sure that a final rhetorical crescendo was sustained. Stanza four's catalogue of composers caused Finzi misgivings, not so much of ranking and inclusion – though Arne and Wesley went while Gibbons (later replaced by Dowland) and Purcell came and Handel ceased to be 'chief' – as of treatment. 'Old Handel' was originally described jocularly, which suited poetic wit but fractured the musical continuum with a jarring couplet, 'stuck as it was, in the middle of rapt contemplation' (19470925). It was tempting on the one hand to make too much of the composers by referring to their styles or by quoting Dowland's 'song – so apt it is – "Time stands still with gazing on her face" after your line "Their looks turned listening to that faultless face" ' (19470918b), or on the other to omit the catalogue altogether. In the end Finzi went for what would best 'keep the rapt state, so that those four lines can be sung on the same level – really like a monotone' (ibid.), and consciously declined to illustrate Handel's 'choral zest'. He had, after all, already had his 'image procession' for the saints in stanza two, a delicate and for him unprecedented piece of orchestral sleight-of-hand, like a miniature version of the one in *Belshazzar's Feast*; yet it is regrettable nonetheless that the passage in Blunden's poem closest to music itself should be the one least embodied in Finzi's setting, a lacuna at the heart of things.

Finzi keeps roughly to Blunden's sixfold sectional division in his music, but for all that he felt he could draw musical shape and formal strength directly from it, the real question is whether he manages to do so from his own devices. Whatever the overall verdict, there are problems. They can be illustrated by a comparison with Parry, which was in Finzi's own mind when he wrote to ask Blunden

whether there is any reason why the original Handel couplet (or for that matter any other excisions or changes which you may regret) shd not go back into the Ode when you eventually publish it. One is bound to recognise that there may be poetical delights which are not necessarily suitable for musical use & I can see no reason why a poem shd not have its 'poetical' form as distinct from its 'musical' form – that is, if the latter does not do violence to the ideas of the poet ... This suggestion is perhaps rather an impertinence on my part, yet I have in mind Robert Bridges' Ode which he wrote for Hubert Parry, 'Invocation to Music'. The version which Bridges published differs from that which Parry set, & Bridges mentions this point in the preface to the original issue of it. (19470924)

To expect to echo Parry's working relationship with Bridges was indeed presumption – Blunden never did publish his ode – but to echo Parry's music made sense. Whether or not Finzi had seen the score of Parry's own *Ode on St Cecilia's Day* (1889) – a fine work, though little known – he was familiar enough with *Blest Pair of Sirens*, and he takes frequent cues from it in *For St Cecilia*. Both works start with resplendent, ceremonial orchestral prelude and stolid choral entry in E♭ major (though Finzi's oblique A♭ major starting-point creates difficulties). Finzi's consequent to this is virtually a quotation of Parry's (ex. 9.3.b and c), and both composers further contrast their opening pair of motivic propositions, which are rhythmically propulsive or persuasively positioned on the downbeat (and in Finzi's case, that is in ex.

EX. 9.3.b (Parry)

EX. 9.3.c (Finzi)

9.3.a and c, constitute the main thematic fount of the composition), with the more spreading, conjunctive poise of a three-note upbeat figure starting with 'And' (ex. 9.3.d and e respectively). Finzi's, though presaged earlier, comes farther on in the piece than Parry's, and articulates his (and Blunden's) second half, with its concerns of the 'host of mortals' whose terrestrial pilgrimage is evoked in the suitably Holstian terms of persevering march, redolent of quiet comfort rather than austerity – a national preference – and, unlike the cider-maker's, harmonically fluent enough to shift itself down a tone as we reach England. A further concordance between *Blest Pair of Sirens* and *For St Cecilia* occurs at the thematic turn-around before the peroration (ex. 9.3.f and g), though Finzi's relatively brief dominant pedal here is token rather than structural, again confusing A♭ with the real tonic, E♭ and no match for Parry's eight-part contrapuntal *tour de force* of real harmonic tension that follows ex. 9.3.f.

But Parry's phrase structure is what secures his motivic contrasts, and it still operates on a quadratic and tonal basis: ex. 9.3.b comes after

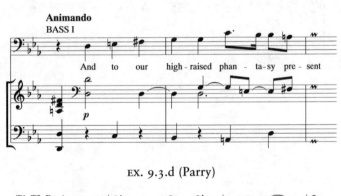

EX. 9.3.d (Parry)

EX. 9.3.e (Finzi)

EX. 9.3.f (Parry)

EX. 9.3.g (Finzi)

eight bars and a half-close on the dominant. Finzi's ex. 9.3.c, by contrast, appears in order to rescue a periodicity and tonality that have
foundered. The miscalculation is twofold. The 'Delightful Goddess'
figure (ex. 9.3.a) is treated in the first choral entry (between figures 1
and 3) as though it were a head motif rather than a ritornello, on both
of its appearances lapsing into madrigalian small-talk with shifting time
signatures and no tonal thrust. The exciting tessitura of the A♭ opening,
meanwhile, has been lost in the shift to E♭. The tonal expectation is, as
with Parry, that an initial move to the dominant signals a half-close,
the return from which will fulfil structural line and contour; but in
Finzi's ode we never regain those vivid above-the-stave ensigns of tonic
and dominant that make his instrumental opening so exciting – at least,
not until the words 'On this returning day', by which time momentum

has been lost and the choral entries have fallen flat. His tonal apostasy has, alas, come home to roost, while his choral contract with part-song has cut little ice with the demands of symphony.

There are some astute placings and continuities of material later on in *For St Cecilia*. Ex. 9.3.a returns more successfully as an instrumental ritornello between the first and second and third and fourth stanzas and duly re-appears to round off the whole piece (and while one again misses the altitude of A♭ major in the brass, the trumpets can end on a high E♭ triad by way of compensation). It also heads a transformed, conflated reminiscence of the first two choral paragraphs at the ode's half-way point (figure 14, marking the beginning of the fourth stanza), a paraphrase technique taking us right back to the second movement of the *Requiem da camera*, but appropriate enough here as Cecilia is transformed from heavenly goddess to terrestrial 'inventress' of music. One could argue that the head motif is also transformed from its $\hat{5}\ \hat{5}\ \hat{5}\ \hat{1}\ \hat{3}$ shape into $\hat{5}\ ^\flat\hat{6}\ \hat{5}\ \hat{1}\ \hat{5}$ for the first of the two tenor 'arias' ('How came you, lady of fierce martyrdom') and further into $\hat{5}\ ^\sharp\hat{6}\ \hat{5}\ \hat{4}\ \hat{3}\ \hat{4}$ for the obviously complementary second one ('How smilingly the saint among her friends / Sits'), thereby linking the second and fifth stanzas as Blunden had done with the first word of each, even if the one introduces a question, the other an exclamation. This second aria is delightfully sustained, with trio sonata counterpoint (plus occasional further proliferation from the tenor) and a fresh version of Finzi's 'stride' idiom in the accompaniment. Howes, in his *Times* review, thought this 'an air which might be set beside the fourth and fifth songs of *Dies natalis*, as one of the loveliest things in contemporary music', and there is a particularly felicitous touch when, at the modulation from G to E major, ex. 9.3.e's upbeat figure is also incorporated. It is something of a relief to hear one of Finzi's aria sections within a larger form properly rounded off for once, which he does before the final stanza. The penalty paid, however, is that the subsequent trumpet fanfares are embarrassingly lame and sound as though they have strayed in from *Love's Labour's Lost*. (Were they played by the Kneller Hall trumpeters, engaged for the St Cecilia concert?) They lead to choral entries ('Wherefore we bid you') that are no less pedestrian, and only a recapitulation of the 'devotion' motif (ex. 9.3.c) with added lustre (ex. 9.3.h, which could almost be from a film score by John Williams) saves the day for the peroration. Ex. 9.3.c had itself been earlier transformed into the funeral-march 'topic' opening stanza two at 'Changed is the age'.

Such musical topics are still handled incidentally by Finzi to signal structural consequents or to provide highly characterised objects in relief – a kind of macrocosm of the harmonic strategy observed much earlier in 'Nightingales'. There are plenty of them in *For St Cecilia*, more relaxed and congenial than ever – which is just what the poem and its occasion called for. The catalogue of saints and their attributes, especially St Swithin's rain, demonstrates and demands from the performers new-found scherzando virtuosity in details that fly by all too quickly; 'melodious Cecily' emerging from the company of 'many another saint' is painted with uncommon tenderness and invoked by the female chorus as though she were Pan in Bliss's pastoral landscape; her opening of the palace of music at the end of stanza three begins to suggest the ecstatic passages of *Intimations of Immortality*; and even more fleeting inspirations occur for individual phrases, such as 'Song's later-comers' (is this supposed to suggest anyone in particular?) and ex. 9.3.h already quoted.

Finzi's melodic gift was certainly not losing its freshness, and whether

EX. 9.3.h

or not one regards *For St Cecilia* as successful overall depends on whether one prizes these moments and their succession more than the structural engineering, which fails ultimately to show which of them dominates the others, in other words to produce a culmination point or climax. Ferguson, perhaps surprisingly, did think it a fine piece, and it was his admiration for Finzi's new public manner, probably coupled with relief that such a 'normal' composer's persona had appeared at last, that earned him the work's dedication. 'The work is a real beauty,' he wrote the day after the first performance (at which Vaughan Williams and Tony Scott were also present, while the Rubbras and the Blisses 'listened-in'). He continued:

not only that, it seems to open out (which is almost more important) such endless possibilities. You yourself may perhaps be too close to notice that anything has happened; but to me it seems so much larger in musical scope & intention than anything you have yet written. Your lungs have expanded & your muscles have loosened, & god alone knows what you may not do now. Beauty & sensitiveness were always there, & to spare; but now you've added real size to them without, moreover, spoiling the one or the other. It's a very great achievement.

I do feel so proud that my name should be at the head of it. (19471123b)

His own part in it had been far from negligible, for Finzi, not for the last time, needed last-minute help with the orchestration, having had to rush the work's composition, which occupied him throughout the late summer while Joy took the children on holiday to his sister's house in Essex. Ferguson put in about ten days at Ashmansworth in response to an SOS. As Finzi described to Thorpe Davie (who had also been asked whether he could come and help for a week or so): 'He has been down here twice; a wonderful help. I take such a long time in deciding about this or that point in scoring and Howard's presence in an armchair, reading or writing, is a great relief to be able to turn to' (19471102). Even then the scoring was not completed until November. As for Blunden, he first heard the work on his return from Japan when it was repeated at the Albert Hall on St Cecilia's Day 1950, performed by the Royal Choral Society and conducted by Leslie Woodgate. He was astounded not to be able to make out a word of his text. If, *pace* Finzi's collaborative enthusiasm, he had privately adopted the attitude that a poet's work relinquishes its identity entirely when set to music, it was probably just as well.

For St Cecilia gave Finzi an institutional foothold in London, and for several years thereafter he accepted invitations to the St Cecilia's Day lunch – 'one of the few annual functions he likes to attend,' Joy noted (J. Finzi 19521124) – which was part of the festival that had been revived in 1946. He was able to sit next to Isobel Baillie on one occasion, take Blunden as his guest on another, listen to speeches by Gerald Kelly and Cecil Day Lewis, and enjoy a further commission, 'God is gone up', in 1951. On the other hand, ' "Delightful Goddess" alone prevents St Cecilia being done [at the Three Choirs Festival]!' he complained to Tony Scott (19490215). It was not the only time the saint had faced exclusion, and Finzi's next work after his Ceremonial Ode was a song for the BBC for which he chose to set George Barker's poem 'Ode against St Cecilia's Day' from the six new, commissioned ones anonymously sent to him and five other composers by the Corporation, ironically while he was in the middle of his Blunden setting (McVeagh 1981b). It was a harebrained fit of zeal on the BBC's part, complete with questionnaire for the composers about melopoetic matters and choices. Finzi declined to answer this (ibid.), and one can see why in the light of his contemporary comments to Thorpe Davie about word-setting:

Personally, I have no theories about the matter. It comes just 'natural-like' and I can't see why a melodic line should not be just as beautiful with a decent accentuation as without. If it were a question of sacrificing the music to verbal accentuation I shouldn't hesitate to be on the side of the music, but I have never in my life found it necessary and I think these songs show that you haven't either. (19481003)

The BBC project foundered when none of the other composers completed their settings, partly on account of the poems – 'They were all appalling from the musical point of view and mostly bad from the poetic point of view,' Finzi told Jack Haines (19490104a; see also G. Finzi 1955: II, 1). Rubbra, who had also been singled out, wrote to Finzi: 'I'm almost inhibited when I even *think* about it: God knows what the result will be. In my desperation I've even thought of making a collage from bits of all the poems' (19480422) – but he cheered up when he discovered a few weeks later that Lennox Berkeley was another victim and was having an equally unproductive time of it. Finzi, not to be beaten at this stage in his career when he was beginning to find that he could handle material to order, had finished his lone setting by

December. He was probably rather proud of having conquered a text of the modernist generation: 'The [poem] I eventually chose,' he admitted to Haines, 'which had a sort of fury and magnificence such as one expects from Dylan Thomas, turned out to be by George Barker, and that has made me see his work in a better light' (19490104a). The BBC were obliged to programme the setting in a regular song recital broadcast, which they did on 15 March 1949 in a programme sung by the baritone Bruce Boyce, although Finzi had suggested that Robert Irwin would be the most sensitive exponent.

Barker's 'fury and magnificence' saturate his poem with words and images used at the temperature of expressionism, and his idea of silence being preferable to music in a 'black time' might have found apt yet very different interpretation at this date from an English Schoenbergian or Webernite. Finzi at least tries to be modern, and opens his song with gesture and texture nodding towards recent Britten and Tippett (the opening of the Donne Sonnets or 'To rise . . .' in *Boyhood's End*, for instance). This rather tails off, though he has no difficulty in matching the weight and texture of Barker's rich succession of poetic objects with his musical objects: vivid patches of sonorous chord and line sewn together out of the materials of fanfare, chorale, march, arpeggio, drumbeat, melisma, ruminative trope and so on, all in his dark romantic manner. He calls his song an 'arioso', and although its quilt is loosely stitched, the succession of fabrics is by no means random. St Cecilia has her own motif (the Elgarian one with the upward fifth at the line 'where once Cecilia shook her veils'), duly expounded between the tonic-and-dominant footsteps of her funeral march to which its fifth therefore relates. Once again a verbal correspondence is what seals the figure, when it is found also to fit the phrase 'long abandoned grandeur', a moment which unlocks the figure's proliferation into the fierce arpeggio at 'O stop the calling killer in the skull' (reminiscent of Holst's 'Come back, Persephone'), later balanced and reversed in the piano's angry hammerings before the final imprecation. Earlier, Barker's 'thunderbolt' has triggered a comparable feat of musical continuity and flux, as its reverberations subside into the central march. Further formal assistance comes from the opening idea of stepwise expansion from a single note, used several times later in the song.

It may well be that the commissioned Barker setting reminded or encouraged Finzi that he might without too much agony complete his second set of Hardy songs for baritone, though another reason for

finishing *Before and After Summer* at this stage was that he was beginning to find that it was a good idea to keep his hand in with the
composition of smaller pieces while he was wrestling with a larger one.
In this case it was the Clarinet Concerto, his largest and most naked
commission so far – in the sense that it entailed nothing on which he
could fall back, not even a text – from which he took time off to write
and rewrite a number of Hardy songs, completing them in the spring
of 1949. Robert Irwin was lined up to give the first performance, which
took place as a BBC broadcast on 17 October 1949 with Frederick
Stone as pianist. By this date, with the recent advent of the Third
Programme, there was no difficulty over programming a relatively
lengthy set of songs, though the Corporation rejected Finzi's suggestion
that the poems should be read between their settings (see 19490812).
It appears that the performance was pre-recorded, its relay delayed
since June and then repeated on 23 October. Complete publication was
also less of a fight than it had been, though, as Finzi described to
Navarro (19490607), Boosey remained as laconic as ever:

Howard, Robert & I went to see Boosey & ran through the songs. There can
be no one else in the world quite like Boosey. At the end of the performance
he pronounced the songs to be 'very charming'* & then added that his problem
was to know how much to charge for the volume.

*That includes 'Channel Firing'

'Overlooking the river', 'Channel firing', 'Amabel' and 'He abjures
love' were already in existence before 1949. So were three other songs
eventually excised from the total of thirteen mentioned by Finzi in a
letter to Milford (19490528). These included, no doubt, 'I need not go'
and 'Let me enjoy the earth', and the third would have been whichever
of his hitherto unplaced Hardy settings was in low-voice guise at the
time. Possibly it was 'Only a man harrowing clods'. 'The self-unseeing'
and 'The too short time' were quite new, composed in 1949, though
the latter poem, Hardy's original title for 'The best she could', had first
entered his consciousness in 1941 when Navarro sent it to him on a
postcard with the challenge 'What about it?' (Finzi replied thinking that
the poem was an attempt by Navarro at aping Hardy; it immediately
'roused musical ideas' in him [19410922?], and he was both pleased
and chagrined when he found out the truth.) 'Childhood among the
ferns' had got as far as Finzi's worrying about its last word

('perambulate') in June 1947, when he told Blunden it made a setting 'impossible' (19470629), so it must have been some time later that he solved the difficulty and decided to preface *Before and After Summer* with this song. The title song probably dates from 1946–7, to judge from its opening fanfare's congruence with those of *For St Cecilia* and *Love's Labour's Lost*. 'In the mind's eye' and 'Epeisodia' enjoy lean but jaunty counterpoint, relaxed pacing and supple melodic lines that surely indicate contemporaneity with the Clarinet Concerto.

In fact 'Epeisodia' is like a sixth Bagatelle, and all the new songs are marked by a kinetic clarity, a continuity and simplicity of textural character that contrasts with the brooding and weighty reflections, the flashes or shades of feeling, of the older ones. They have become more objective and extrovert, indicating that Finzi would never again be quite the same composer after having discovered, in the Bagatelles, how to make a musical point in a short piece and contrast it with its neighbours, with melody but without words. One senses that he can therefore set several intractable passages or even whole poems in *Before and After Summer* because technique is more flowingly at his command. Whether inspiration has waned in the process is a moot point.

The first three stanzas of 'Childhood among the ferns' demonstrate the change. The voice has perfectly good, memorable melodic phrases, but their succession is in a sense more formless than ever, because the limpid, toccata-like figuration of the piano part can support them indefinitely (appropriately enough, as the ferns' protection supports the child's innocence). No longer is the response of what comes next the burning issue, though admittedly it is the brilliance of the opening five bars that sets up the subsequent continuum, with all the old warmth and humanity in the initial 'sun' motif and the full weight of his gnomic imagination in the *chiaro* chiming figure that follows. Idiom apart, Finzi has something of the knack of Stravinsky in the authoritative placing of such pregnant musical objects. The second song, 'Before and after summer', illustrates the same point in its first stanza, which must press forward if it is to reflect the poet's mood of anticipation, though here one does begin to feel that the melody, while never actually violating Hardy's sound and sense, is becoming the arbitrary commentary to a pianistic study in sixths that provides the tonal analogue to the February weather (the opening fanfare inscribing a sixth modally interlocked with the one held in the left hand, somewhat *à la* Bartók). Neither of these songs is primarily concerned with motivic argument, or at least not with the resolution of musical substance, for although 'Before and after summer' does appear to transform its $\hat{1}$ $\hat{2}$ $\hat{1}$ $\hat{5}$ $\hat{1}$ antecedent fanfare into the $\hat{5}$ $\hat{6}$ $\hat{5}$ $\hat{1}$ melodic shape that begins the second stanza's march consequent, and continues to brood on the shape at the end of the song, to *achieve* anything substantial would work against Hardy's conceit of the unexperienced summer. If, accordingly, both songs have span (say, that of a sonata forelimb) rather than scope, it serves to calibrate rather than usurp the drama to come in 'Channel firing' and 'He abjures love'. For the same reason, both 'Childhood among the ferns' and 'Before and after summer' blatantly demonstrate Finzi's favourite antecedent/consequent structure which in this case is built into the very title of the work – and the collapse of the first song into unresolving recitative, with techniques reminiscent of the second movement of *Dies natalis*, is Finzi's boldest use of reversed form – while any temptation to organise the whole set of songs along the same lines macrocosmically is firmly resisted.

Over *Before and After Summer* as a whole, the change in the composer may not be noticed. But the beloved's ghost in 'In the mind's eye' is a flighty, whimsical creature, not at all the radiant, corporeal horse-riding phantom in the song of that name, even if the use of chromatically oblique triads to indicate her abiding presence amid shifting landscapes in both songs is what prompts the comparison (see ex. 6.1.b and ex. 9.4.a). The difference is indicative of Finzi's distancing himself from his earlier conception – or compositional method – of constructing songs such as 'The phantom' as conflated dramatic monologues or cantatas. Instead, more conventional song forms are now accepted. At least on the surface, 'In the mind's eye' treats its four tiny parallel stanzas strophically, each one except the last introduced by the piano's will-o'-

EX. 9.4.a

357

the-wisp bass figure of four quavers and trilled minim (straightened out and broadened for the vocal opening of the last stanza itself), though the shuffled distribution and paraphrasing of melodic material in different stanzas recalls Finzi's earlier way with 'ditty' elements: the fount of four basic features, each marking a line of the first stanza – namely upward quintachord, G–F upward seventh, triplets with downward stepwise motion, and downward fourth or fifth onto B♭ (later onto A) – is kept in balanced circulation but never allowed to parallel itself. This restlessness in 'In the mind's eye', further expressed harmonically and tonally (set in G minor, it begins and ends aslant in C minor and D minor respectively), makes the song too fussy. 'Epeisodia', on the other hand, handles its three exquisite stanzas with consummate grace. Hardy's scheme is a triptych of landscape scenes, upland, city and coast, but Finzi achieves ABA musical closure by contrasting the oppressive middle stanza, with its 'city walls' and 'foggy dun light', with the country air of the two outer ones. For his dark B section he contrives not just a new walking accompaniment motif and a different vocal melody strikingly lower in tessitura, but an upbeat placing of several of Hardy's lines that cleverly belies the parallel prosody of the three stanzas, and even a miniature character motif, inferred from two sets of syllables, 'footstep' and 'pit-pat', that makes Hardy's 'city' stanza sound as though intended all along as a march trio. Best of all in 'Epeisodia' is the instrumental link between the second and third stanzas, a vastly elongated 'trope' in origin but something quite different in spirit, showing this interpreter of Hardy now dancing rather than reflecting his way through life's shifting circumstances.

The obvious complement to the conceptual dance in 'Epeisodia' is the material one referred to in 'The self-unseeing', which gathers momentum as the poet's memory re-enacts the scene (and as his alliteration develops – see Renouf 1986: 167, glossing Christopher Walbank). Again Finzi treats the song to an ABA form, this time with the dance as the inner section rather than the outer ones, though, happy and conventional in its relative major, and even moving to the dominant as it blossoms, it spills over into the bulk of Hardy's final stanza, ternary closure being suggested only by the last line. The opening section entails mysterious chromatic chord sequences which Milford greatly enjoyed – 'I find all the old mastery, & an extraordinary sense of atmosphere – for instance, the opening of "The Self-unseeing" has an extraordinary feeling of the "ancient floor" & the "dead feet" (one can almost *smell* the mustiness of that floor!), quite unlike anything else in music,' he wrote to Finzi (19500204) – though in fact the sequence, which is repeated a tone higher when the voice enters, and the harmonic language are actually quite like Rawsthorne's in the slow movement of his First Piano Concerto. And if Finzi's utterance in his last few bars seems more oracular than ever (ex. 9.4.b), it matches Hardy's inscrutable irony in this minute detailing of his childhood home, for the 'unseeing' of the self in the poet's curious and characteristic gerund involves not only somehow undoing the vision of who one is and what one has become but recognising that, though the past can never be regained, its emotional meaning was not experienced at the time and is only felt years later, when the subject is looking at the scene and its structure from outside rather than failing to observe it because actually within it. Even in 'The too short time', which strikes one primarily as an *arioso*/aria pairing, there is formal symmetry. The introduction and first six lines of the first stanza are indeed a throwback to Finzi's much earlier unbarred and bitonal astronomical analogues, though here we are dealing with nothing more stratospheric than leaves on a tree, falling illustratively like angular, modernist versions of Butterworth's cherry blossom (we hear, if I have counted correctly, six leaves in about forty-eight seconds, which is exactly right for Hardy's 'nine leaves a minute'). But a slight refrain element binds the two stanzas with parallel music at and after the line 'Alas, not much!', though the equivalence, leading into F major the first time, D major the second, is downplayed, and one rather regrets that Finzi did not see fit to illustrate more graphically Hardy's parallel images of the motley leaves as a seaside Pierrot show

EX. 9.4.b

in the first stanza, autumn days as overdressed, ageing promenade gossips in the second.

As for the Clarinet Concerto, it followed indirectly from the Five Bagatelles, in that Finzi had 'half promised' Pauline Juler a concerto after her performances of them (19480904). When the Three Choirs Festival committee asked Finzi, in September 1948, for a new work for Hereford the following year (originally envisaged by them as a string piece *without* soloist), Juler was about to get married and Ferguson, who was consulted, wrote to Finzi: 'I have always thought that she was very keen to have children; so . . . a simple sum in arithmetic will tell that she might, perhaps be somewhat occupied in about a year's time.' He advised him 'to keep an eye on Paul's waist-line' (ibid.). Matrimony had indeed won the day, and the concerto was written for Frederick Thurston, though Finzi first tried its difficulties out on Stephen Trier, a local lad. Thurston gave the first performance with the strings of the LSO, Finzi conducting, on the morning of 9 September 1949, the last day of the festival, in a concert whose first half had included Part I of Haydn's *Creation* and which was rounded off with Myra Hess playing Beethoven's Fourth Piano Concerto.

We have seen how the replacement first movement of Finzi's Violin Concerto underwent fleeting resuscitation as the third of a clarinet Concertino with strings, probably some time after the founding of the Newbury String Players, if the rather more sustained attempts to complete the Piano Concerto with strings in the 1940s are indicative of the increasing influence of this medium on Finzi's thought from then on. We have also noted the connection between the abandoned Serenade and the Clarinet Concerto's last movement (see ex. 8.5.c, its bass thirds perhaps eventually transferred to those of the Rondo's first episode, before figure 4), and there are further incarnations of this theme and that episode among the fragmentary attempts at a full-scale Oboe Quintet and String Trio referred to in earlier chapters, as well as among the Concertino sketches. But little is heard of the Clarinet Concerto between the date of its commission and Finzi's announcements, respectively in May and July 1949, that he had done two-thirds of it and finished the third movement but not yet the first, and essentially it was a new work, uniformly conceived and quite speedily written.

This makes it the most smoothly-argued and best proportioned of Finzi's full-scale compositions, and it has become very popular. Like the Dag Wirén string Serenade, which the NSP played and which may well have influenced it, it represents a prime point of contact with the general consumer of classical music – as opposed to the more specialised constituencies of (in Finzi's case) church musicians, singers, clarinettists and assorted Anglophiles – and is a work now fully accepted into the canon. ('The clarinet is doing well these days with a new concerto from Malcolm Arnold in one week and another from Gerald Finzi in the next,' wrote the *Times* reviewer, probably Howes, of the first perform- ance [10 September 1949: 8; Thurston also premièred the Arnold].) It is not without its limitations, however, and they are characteristic: a first-movement orchestral exposition that promises struggle and vigour that never materialise once the soloist has deflected the discourse into more platitudinous conversation; an endlessly rapt slow movement; and a Rondo whose themes are delightful if inconsequential (the main one prompting outrageous vistas of Russ Conway and Dr Finlay) but placed in too pedestrian and arbitrary a succession. Some of these issues, and the forms that occasion them, we have met before; all will recur in the Cello Concerto. The Clarinet Concerto has generally had a good press in Britain, but it irritated 'R. S.', the *Musical America* reviewer of its first transatlantic performance, who found that 'one becomes fearfully restless before it has ambled through the three traditional movements . . . the composer indulges continually in sentimental "asides" until the whole work sounds like one long digression' (15 December 1955: 20). Nor was he or she impressed with the solo writing, finding it 'rather ungrateful' where *The Times* more diplomatically suggested that 'the writing for the strings was more conspicuously felicitous than the solo part'. The first-movement cadenza was inserted at Vaughan Williams's suggestion after the first performance, though it does not add a great deal to the soloist's technical portfolio, and the clarinet's propensity to soothe or rhapsodise while the strings appro- priate the weight of sonority and hence the real rhetorical power inherent in the material remains a general problem. There are almost no places where the clarinet actually drives the structure. Its peculiar lyricism, on the other hand, melancholy, fervently entreating, and with homespun cheerfulness by turns, does make for a double act with the strings of very strong character, one that if one listens with unprejudiced ear may be felt to exhibit in its overall discourse one Hebraic plangency for every Albionic rumination.

Nevertheless, those 'sentimental "asides" ' are the nub of Finzi's Elgarian mode, revealed as fully here as anywhere in his mature output, and the stricture might equally have been applied to Elgar's Violin Concerto, it being in both cases, as sometimes in Schumann, a matter of one small-scale harmonic gratification – a single progression with suspension or appoggiatura – leading to another with little to choose between sharp or flat triads of resolution and therefore with a propensity to meander in and out of dominant-related keys to no obvious purpose beyond intimate effect. Perhaps both Finzi and Elgar were more affected by their youthful hours in the organ loft than they would have wished, and in Finzi's case his eighteenth-century researches may have been a further dubious influence, for the baroque technique of a chain of $^6_3$ chords which suspends tonal direction, with or without 7–6 suspensions, is what lies behind the first two bars of ex. 9.5.a, whose third bar brings the inconsequential modulation to the subdominant that prepares the next piece of musical pillow talk. The restriction is apparent from the eighth complete bar of the first movement's orchestral exposition: this is all too early for it to be settling so comfortably into the $^6_3$ chain that follows, highly Elgarian in its three-part texture and in no clear rhetorical relation to the more athletic opening, whose muscles, flexed, it would seem, in distant response to the opening of Vaughan Williams's Fourth Symphony (sharing its key, two-part writing, stepping figures and semitonal clashes), are already in danger of atrophying. The peremptory, Waltonian dominant octave unisons before the clarinet enters seem aware of the need for sterner exhortation but, given the nature of the material surrounding them, come perilously close to meaning nothing at all, even though Finzi himself was at pains to stress that the idea of an octave leap was one 'from which much of the later material develops' (programme note, Bodl. MS Mus.c.394).

These are more than quibbles, but not sufficient to undermine a

EX. 9.5.a

EX. 9.5.b

generally satisfying first movement. The two main motifs, both with dominant crotchet upbeat, are the opening orchestral proposition – its placatory version seen at *x* in ex. 9.5.a – and ex. 9.5.b with its contrastingly chordal sonority. Finzi rehearses these twice in the orchestra before the clarinet enters, the initial statement tonally oblique (in the subdominant) in a manner which for once proves unproblematic, since the first bar of ex. 9.5.b also scans forcefully as a Neapolitan. The second motif, like the first, undergoes soothing dilution, minus its upbeat, at the hands of the soloist before transitional reassertion into a figure (ex. 9.5.c) that provides the accompaniment to the second subject, an unassuming phrase rather than period, reminiscent of Elgar's tone of voice in the Introduction and Allegro (ex. 9.5.d). Joined by ghosts of the 'meaningless' *martellato* dominants, it very soon reaches the exposition's peroration, where Finzi's string writing is at its best,

EX. 9.5.c

EX. 9.5.d

EX. 9.5.e

though he cannot keep up this kind of energy for long (ex. 9.5.e).
Indeed, it subsides so soon that the development, based on the oscillating background shape of the semiquaver figure with the upward octave
of *x* now accompanying, is in danger of being perceived as merely
part of that process and over before one is aware of it, so that what
one hopes will be an impressionistic episode over unfolding harmonies
(at figure 3) turns out to be the recapitulation; this is not quite right
psychologically, though a firm interpretation of the tempi and shading
of tone in performance can redress it. In the recapitulation there is a
carefully considered mixture of exact correspondence of material (in
a different key), shortening, inserted trope and rearrangement, the
reminder of ex. 9.5.b now coming between the second subject and
peroration, but as if to make up for the section's prematurity Finzi
appends a good deal of coda, indeed almost a second recapitulation,
which after a mediant pedal in E♭ minor goes over much of the earlier
ground again before eventually heaving itself onto a C minor dominant
pedal where, unfortunately, the strings scrub themselves painfully raw
in a misjudged build-up leading to their *martellato* figure and the
cadenza. The augmentation of the initial octave upbeat into the memorable clarinet trills and of the early Neapolitan into the triadic hammer
and swirl that end the movement is a fine touch, recapturing something
of *Dies natalis*'s 'Rapture'.

The opening of the second movement digests the first's Neapolitans by attaching a flat second to the octave shape, as well as to fifths and fourths, before exchanging semitone for tone in the movement's main theme (ex. 9.5.f). Or, to look at it another way, its first two bars taken together presage the return of first-movement shapes to come in the middle section. The attenuated atmospherics of this link between the movements are highly effective, and it is a pity that, as with the link into the Cello Concerto's finale, they have nothing to do, timbrally, with what follows, which is an ever-flatward process of repeat and paraphrase of the main theme as support for burgeoning clarinet rhapsody, some of which, across the registers, is very similar to figures in the oboe Interlude (compare ex. 9.5.g with ex. 6.3.d). No real contrast of material or perspective appears, for what, as with the first movement, at first promises impressionistic dissolution of motion and phraseology

EX. 9.5.f

EX. 9.5.g

Un poco più affettuoso

EX. 9.5.h

EX. 9.5.i

in a new section (the three-bar phrase at figure 3, its modal accent – a dorian touch – perhaps distantly remembering Howells's Clarinet Quintet) soon reverts to two-bar limbs of the opening theme in catechismic repetition, vaguely suggesting a first-section ternary form within the overall one. The real central section appears in triple time with the development of ex. 9.5.f, mentioned above, that reintroduces the first movement's melodic and rhythmic preoccupations (in the two downbeat quavers and contour of ex. 9.5.h). This accumulates considerable breadth and a *fff* climax, perhaps trying to justify them in retrospect when it issues in the false-relation confessions heard earlier in the movement (ex. 9.5.i), but these are too much a part of the general fabric, not just of the movement but of the whole concerto, to be genuinely dramatic, and one somehow feels that no real point has been made as they turn into partial recapitulation, which includes the modal passage now tonally (if too shyly) transformed and comes to rest with a Neapolitan release from Finzi's seemingly inescapable flatwards pull when a G♭ chord within F minor sinks straight to the tonic F major.

The finale's introduction breezily (and somewhat Brittenesquely) blows away the Neapolitan semitones by exchanging them for leading-note ones, a rising thrust also embodied in their sharp keys, F♯ and C♯ minor, which although soon subsiding into plain C major for the rondo theme are not entirely irrelevant, for that theme has a habit of coming back in A major, a welcome counterbalance to all the earlier flats, however awkward for the B♭ clarinettist. The symmetry of the semitone appoggiaturas attached above and below the tonics and dominants they emphasise is explained late in the movement, before figure 9, at the point of cyclic summary which is in a sense the climax of the concerto (again with a *fff* dynamic). Here the Rondo introduction is juxtaposed with passages from the first movement rather more subtly chosen than one realises (though one might have expected this after the *Requiem da camera*'s finale): a trope from the recapitulation, the $^6_3$-chain from near the beginning of the orchestral exposition, and the mediant pedal from the coda – all helping to justify their isolated existence in retrospect – followed by enough of the clarinet's first-subject exposition to round things off before the rondo theme is reinstated. In between, the course of the movement is unremarkable, and it rests unashamedly on the catchy main tune – its downward fifth from ex. 9.5.b – which, however, is never closed off like a classical rondo theme. If the first episode sounds somewhat irresponsible in its light-handedness, the second too much like an alternative piece of music (a Bagatelle), and both too long, Finzi is still aware of his structural obligations, for the first arises out of an inversion of the stepping figure in the concerto's opening bars (one hears the connection in the transitions) and later incorporates the *martellato* figure. Both are themselves in a kind of ternary form, the first with a delightful second tune, the second with central scherzando contrast, and both share their substantial lead back in to the rondo theme (which doubles as the returning A section in the first episode), ingeniously cast in triple time in the one case, quadruple in the other. The cyclic retrospect acts as a third episode.

The concerto soon made its way in the world, and Finzi conducted it a second time, with Thurston and the Boyd Neel Orchestra, in the Oxford Subscription Concerts on 24 November. Arnold Barter programmed it in Bristol Cathedral the following February, and what must have been its London première, given by Thurston, took place in a summer season of Serenade Concerts at Hampton Court on 1 July 1950. It was broadcast by Cyril Chapman at the end of this year, and Gervase de Peyer, a young player with whom Finzi was tremendously impressed, then took it on tour to Switzerland. Boosey postponed its publication until after *Intimations*, for reasons of cost, issuing the short score in 1951, the full score not until 1953. Presumably at the proofing stage of the former, Finzi was wondering whether to make adjustments to the opening, and consulted Ferguson, who seemed surprised and replied:

I don't know what to say about the opening of the Clarinet Concerto. The only time I heard it in the flesh – at Oxford – the opening in particular struck me as being tremendously exciting and impressive. It would therefore never have occurred to me that anything wanted doing to it. The trills in the vls and turns in the vlcs & dbs might certainly make it more exciting; but I don't really feel I know enough about string orchestral writing to say this with any certainty. Why not try them at the next performance and see whether it sounds more to your liking that way? (19510104)

This can only have referred to the treble C and bass D♭ in the first complete bar. Finzi decided to leave them unadorned.

Since the end of the war each new work had been bigger than the last in one sense or another, and except for the George Barker setting, between 1945 and 1951 Finzi produced only two short pieces in the interstices of his longer ones. One was an anthem, 'My lovely one', written for Mags's wedding on 2 September 1946 in Newbury and published by Boosey in 1948 (after Oxford had rejected it). The other was a unison song, 'Muses and Graces', with words by Ursula Wood, text and music 'written and composed,' a note on the score tells us, 'at the instance of Cedric Glover, Chairman of the Charlotte Mason Schools Company, and presented by him to Overstone School in commemoration of the twenty-first anniversary of its foundation, September 1950'. The first performance of 'Muses and Graces' was earlier, on 10 June 1950 at the girls' school in Northamptonshire, whose headmistress, Miss Plumptre, gives every impression of having stepped straight out of an Ealing Comedy, name and all:

Dear Mr Finzi,

There was great excitement this morning when your large envelope arrived for Miss Lasker, just a few hours before she said good bye to us for the holidays. She was thrilled with your composition and I expect will write to you about it herself. She was able to play it to the whole School before leaving. Our one hope is that we may be able to give a worthy rendering on June 10th . . .

I know that you and Mrs Wood between you have given the School something that they will praise for many years and which should be an inspiration to generations of girls. (19500329)

It is an uninspired piece, though dance topics charm the second stanza, and Ursula Vaughan Williams says it was done as a joke. Be that as it may, the reappearance of Finzi's hobnail-booted diatonic style at this stage of his development feels gratuitous and routinely applied so as not to divert inspiration from *Intimations*, on which he was frantically working at the same time – here the principle of the small complementing the large evidently not paying off. The tune, entirely strophic for once except for small rhythmic variants, is not very catchy, in fact rather fussy and lacking in the breadth that one expects (and gets from, say, Howells in his hymn tunes). Ursula Wood's 11-line stanzas with shapely distribution of rhymes and feet are tricky but surely not to blame. The song was published with piano in 1951, and Finzi also made a string arrangement of the accompaniment.

'My lovely one' is an equally slight work, but if its outer sections in 6/8 sound like material left over from the oboe Interlude and the central one begins with alarming similarity to the *St Cecilia* head motif in its stanza four guise, the overall effect is exquisite. The post-metaphysical verse of Edward Taylor (?1646–1729) repays its discovery, which was even more recent than Traherne's when Finzi approached it, his *Poetical Works* having been first published in 1939, two years after his manuscripts were found in Yale University Library. (Taylor, born in England, was a Harvard graduate who spent the rest of his life as a clergyman in deepest Massachusetts – see Beechey 1977.) Here the constantly rotating 'sentimental asides' of chromatic minor tonality, together with Taylor's preciously intimate protestations, suit the shy but overt tokens of passion a church wedding purveys, though Vaughan Williams thought otherwise: 'I don't care for the El Greco like sentimental affectation of the words,' he told Finzi, adding '(By the way poor blushing bride – no it will not do for weddings!)' (19481211b).

The completion of *Intimations of Immortality* was the overriding and overwhelming task after the launch of the Clarinet Concerto. By mid-October 1949 Milford had heard a rumour that it was scheduled for the 1950 Gloucester meeting, and one wonders whether Finzi's determination to get it finished at last was influenced by sight of Howells's *Hymnus paradisi*, for it was immediately after the 1949 Hereford Festival, when he was as usual recuperating at Ashmansworth, that Sumsion showed the score to Finzi. The ode's later stages of genesis are no more easy to trace than the earlier ones, and one would dearly love to know how and when its course was planned and its details written. Joy probably knew little more than posterity when she mischievously said, '*Intimations* was certainly with us all our married days and it is something of a mystery to me that although it was conceived some 25 years before, the house was full of copyists making parts for the orchestra on the last evening before the first performance! A rather acute piece of timing' (J. Finzi 1982). By the end of December 1949 the Gloucester festival committee had agreed to programme the score without seeing it, though Finzi had shown a completed extract to Ivor Atkins, about to retire from Worcester, who supposed that it represented perhaps a fifth of the whole. How much of Finzi's previous work on the piece this represented, how much a fresh draft, we can guess no more than whether at this or any stage he intended to set the entire poem. (In the event he omitted two of Wordsworth's eleven stanzas, VII and VIII. Is it mere fancy that hears a more expedient join at figure 25 than elsewhere, indicating a late, emergency cut?)

He finished the vocal score on 19 May 1950, and two weeks later a delighted David Willcocks answered the postman's knock before spending an extra hour in bed reading it through with a view to a second performance at Worcester in 1951. By the end of June, Finzi was having 'a terrifying time', getting up at six every day and keeping 'at it morning, afternoon, evening, and night' to orchestrate the work, and again he enlisted help: this time Thorpe Davie was down from Scotland, and spent a 'gruelling' weekend at Ashmansworth in mid-July helping to score 'the tuba & trumpet trills in "our" fanfare', amongst other things (19500624+, 19500707b, 19500724?, 19500831a). There were '56 more bars to go' on 16 August, and on the twentieth Finzi went to one of the choral rehearsals in Gloucester. Orchestral rehearsals followed in London on 29 and 30 August, at which not only the composer but also Joy, Howard Ferguson, Tony Scott and evidently a host of others were present (see illustration 19); Finzi was pleased with the scoring, including ' "our" fanfare', which, as he described to its conspirator, was 'a hell of a noise, but rather a wonderful noise all told!' and he only had to make one noteworthy alteration: 'Wherever I've let an oboe double the solo voice (only once or twice in the whole work) I'll have to cut it out. It's a bad sound' (19500831a). One of the final rehearsals was enlivened when Eric Greene, having discovered the footer 'Intimations of Immorality' on two pages of the vocal score, broke down in giggles, followed by the choir; subsequently 'some of the publishers' minions obviously had to sit up all night pasting corrections into the copies for sale' (Highfield 1978: 12).

The performance was on 5 September. Rubbra, the Milfords, Ursula Wood and doubtless the Scotts were present, as were Ferguson, with a friend who was permitted 'to bounce in & out' of the Finzis' house party as he wished (1950091oa), and Vaughan Williams, who conducted his own Sixth Symphony as the final item in a lengthy programme that had started with Haydn's *Creation* (*Intimations* came after the lunch interval). Finzi was on the whole happy:

Needless to say Boosey & Hawkes were bright [enough] to send down 24 copies to the music shop in Gloucester before the performance and then, after great pressure from various people, another 50 followed after the performance!

For an audience of 3000 this was hardly good business and much of my spare time had to be spent answering 'where can I get a copy'. Novellos with wiser organisation sent down 200 of the Howells work (a fine work, by the way). Anyhow that sort of thing doesn't matter much in the long run. The main thing is that I had a very fine first performance. Sumsion, Eric Greene, chorus and orchestra, were all at their best. The whole performance was fused. So I shall have no more worries for next year's performance.

Hardly anything to alter in the score, though there will have to be a few minor alterations in the chorus part which must be left to a second reprint. I did my usual book hunting in Gloucester and got one or two things I have been wanting including a full score of the Messiah which looks like a fairly contemporary piracy of Arnold, but seems to be pretty complete . . . I got it for 7/6! (1950091ob, to Thorpe Davie)

He wrote a letter of thanks to George Stratton, leader of the LSO, who was at pains to reply:

May I say how impressed I was with your work, and that a great number of compliments were paid about it by the orchestra, which as you know is a fair test of its great worth. On the other hand my wife, who is not a musician said how very much she enjoyed it even though she was sitting behind the orchestra. (19500915)

Stratton was himself a composer, however – he had an Oboe Concerto premièred at the Three Choirs two years later.

Intimations of Immortality tested Finzi's stature as nothing else had done or could do. His friends were as eager to see the whole of him between two covers and hear it in a single span as the critics were quick to put a fence around one of Wordsworth's, and therefore the nation's, greatest poems and tell him to keep out. Both reactions are worth savouring prior to a more relaxed critical assessment at nearly half a century's distance.

Howes at *The Times* (6 September 1950: 6) was dependable, though even he could not find the same enthusiasm for *Intimations* as for *Hymnus paradisi*, which he reviewed two days later. He put his finger on the musical problems Wordsworth's argument poses, not just in its theme but in its discursive syntax:

To set Wordsworth is ambitious and not easy because of the double thought in the text which veers from the fading glories of Heaven to the beauties of the Earth. Is the musician to depict praise and ignore the negative in

'Not for these I raise
The song of thanks and praise,'

and is he to give thanks loudly or softly for 'those obstinate questionings'? Finzi has steered round such difficulties by instrumental interludes that depict the general sense and allow some amount of word-painting in the vocal sections.

Other critics, less charitable, were 'inclined to echo that famous reviewer of Wordsworth himself and say, "This will never do" ' (Banfield 1992: [3]). Martin Cooper, in possession of a particularly strong line of attack, nonetheless conveniently ignored the many acknowledgements of the continental romantic heritage, not to mention the *lingua franca* of Walton, in the score, and began to hear what he wanted to hear when he complained that 'a great deal of the music seemed somehow irrelevant in 1950' because 'to use, as Finzi does, an idiom compiled not from those of the great masters of the past but from a selection of our own native (and confessedly lesser) composers of the last half century, is to incur the charge of being the epigone of an already epigonic generation.' Punching relentlessly, he continued: 'This harmless and derivative music, not very happily orchestrated, was wedded to Wordsworth's finest poetry. Such words would beggar even the greatest music and they showed the inadequacy of Finzi's painfully clearly' (*Musical Times* xci [1950]: 398). This last sentence was, of course, exactly the 'parrot cry of each decade' about unsettable poetry (19541105b) that Finzi had predicted as early as 1936.

Naturally the more detailed and considered responses came later. Wilfrid Mellers's review of the score in *Music Survey* (iii [1951]: 184) drew a distinction between the solo tenor confidences and the less interesting ' "noble" bits' in the chorus and concluded, 'What Finzi has to say he seems to have said once and for all in the Hardy songs', while Hans Redlich's in *Music Review* (xiii [1952]: 242–3) hit squarely below the belt: here was an Austro-German immigrant – the man who coined the phrase 'Second Viennese School' – criticising Finzi for his accentuation of English poetry!

Wordsworth's famous poem, inspired by 'recollections of early childhood' and delighting in the intimate imagery of pastoral romanticism, seems a singularly bad choice as text for a Cantata. The simple rhyming scheme of its 'poetical prose' seems unduly stretched by the rigours of a 6–8 part chorus, singing in elaborate madrigalian imitations. The scansion of the text is totally misleading in a principal subject such as the following, obviously emphasizing the unimportant word 'seem' alone for the sake of a formalistic imitation in the orchestra (cf. motif x) and at the risk of obscuring the actual poetical meaning: [here he quotes the opening words and solo tenor line as far as the word 'light'; his x motif is the instrumental 'trope' at the word 'seem']. The whole composition is curiously old-fashioned in technique and musical subject matter. The initial horn melody, strongly reminiscent of Brahms, but even more the stereotyped treatment of emotional words like 'joy', 'tears' and the like conjure up the atmosphere of Victorian Romanticism, probably released in the composer's subconscious mind by the fact that his score was being written for the Three Choirs Festival in Gloucester . . .

Redlich was right to mention Brahms, however inappositely to Gloucester ears (the echo is of the opening of the Second Piano Concerto), and, *pace* Cooper, courted further political incorrectness but nonetheless potentially fertile comparison when he drew a parallel with Pfitzner's *Von deutscher Seele* (1921) on Eichendorff poems (and he returned to the Pfitzner comparison in his *MGG* article on Finzi three years later – see Redlich 1955). 'It is, of course,' he continued,

quite possible that Finzi knows next to nothing of Pfitzner's retrospective tendencies and that he has arrived at a similar old-fashioned, slightly morose style of anachronistic romanticism quite on his own. Some of his principal melodies are beautiful in a faded, out-dated way, his pastoral scenes having the quaint flavour of engravings from the middle 19th-century, while the choral writing, especially in its more chordally treated sections, contains many truly poetic moments. I cannot help feeling that to write in 1950 a work so obsolescent is a singular quixotism for a composer still on the right side of fifty.

But, as we have seen from the 'bilge & bunkum' letter, he must have got Finzi's goat by referring to his 'choice' of text. The composer's friends knew better than to pursue this aesthetic line and would no more have attempted to deny him his poetic partnership than his 'choice' of wife on grounds of unsuitability.

Instead, they tended to accept the score's invitation to share his solicitous connoisseurship of lines, images, feelings, creative personality and ideas much as they would in the book room at Ashmansworth, by treating it as a kind of personal treasure trove. Bernard Herrmann, writing from North Hollywood and uninhibited by English reserve, let his response to the 'telegraph wires' of Finzi and his poet be warmly known after he had received the score:

My own personal favorite spots, and the ones that remained ringing in my head for days were as follows.

The Prelude and opening chorus. – the harmonies of the Allegro giojoso at [figure] 10; the interlude that follows 'the tabor's sound' [he quotes the rhythm of the passage before figure 12]; the beauty of the setting of 'the Rainbow comes and goes' and most of all the little turn in the tenor on 'love-ly is the rose'; the tenor solo from [figure] 38 and all of the joyful ecstatic choral moments. In other words I simply loved the work and find it hard indeed to signal out my favorite bits. It is certainly a masterwork – I am certain of that and above all personal and original – and full of beauty – a quality not in fashion to-day – and its great melodic lines will certainly be admired long after most of the music of the mid century has been forgotten.

Bravo – Bravo. I am as always a Finzi fan. (19520722)

Ferguson's appreciation, after the first performance, was more by way of general testimonial:

'Intimations' was a tremendously moving experience. It is a most lovely work & seems to me far & away the biggest thing you've done: not in size only, of course, but in conception, breadth of vision & sheer accomplishment. And so much of it has an ecstatic lyric beauty that brings one near to tears, besides & within the larger framework. It's a magnificent achievement, & (for me at least) it knocked the other new works into the middle of next week. Many, many congratulations on it. (19500910a)

But Bliss, like Herrmann, felt moved to single out particular passages:

Dear Gerald,

I came back here last night, and the first thing I noticed was the copy of your new score, and this morning I have been delighting myself by playing it through. It is indeed a beautiful and moving work, and when I got to the last page, even without the magic of the actual sound, I felt I had had a deep musical experience.

It seems to me to be done with real mastery – You always could set English supremely well, but the design of this long work is so satisfying that I believe it to be a great advance on anything you have achieved before.

As soon as I had entered the first choral section on page 4, I knew I was in for a good thing. I think your use of the tenor's first phrase as a sort of silver thread to knit the work together among others is very skilful.

I like immensely also the variety of feeling and texture p. 24–34 – the setting of the difficult words for the solo p. 64–66 – the deliciously timed reprise on p. 72 and the punctuality of your ending. But I have only chosen particular things almost at random in the work. It is a real achievement as a whole, and I am sick that I wasn't at the first performance, score in hand. I am sure you can be proud for creating so big a thing, and *apparently* with such ease, & I write at once to congratulate you. (19500920)

while Benjamin Frankel, as he had already done with *Before and After Summer* (19500219), loved the whole but took rather eccentric issue with Finzi's sense of closure, writing to him after a later performance:

I find it all the more satisfying that, in finding the music so lovely, it should be written in a manner poles apart from anything that I myself would attempt. Let me say, in fear and trembling, that I shall never agree with your final chord in the work. I don't think that all the lofty and timeless things that you are saying in the last pages need to be, or indeed can be brought to a conclusion in this (to me) rather tame way. Your 'too deep for tears' is so meltingly lovely and the sudden return of the opening horn theme so mystical that your oh-so-final chord tends to bring us back to earth with a bump. But there it is; why don't people take my advice I wonder? (19540712)

Nevertheless, he considered it 'his masterpiece' (19560930a).

How do we mediate these views, critics' denunciations and friends' eulogies, based as they are on such different premises? What sort of a piece is *Intimations*?

It is a continuous musical movement lasting between forty and forty-five minutes. That is about the length of a Puccini operatic act, and very roughly speaking Finzi's post-romantic musical techniques for holding it together are comparable, though Wordsworth's text is so much more wordy than a libretto, its every phrase and image demanding its 'setting' in the sense of critical exegesis and emotional weight, that finding the opportunity for a straight line of musical thought, a span of song or symphony, must have been the greatest problem. It was one that Wagner, his libretti often equally discursive, tended to solve by embroidering the voice as countermelody on an orchestral fabric of motivic quilting, but the candour of Wordsworth's 'I', the often innocently blithe metrical patterns of his 'false Pindaric' ode, and perhaps the presence of the chorus seem to have turned Finzi away from this approach, even though it is evident elsewhere in his output, for instance in 'The rapture' from *Dies natalis*, and was after all a part of his early 'aria' technique.

Nevertheless, symphonic *Intimations* is, and leaving aside the question of the poem's emotional curve, Finzi builds his structure more firmly and probably more self-consciously than one might have expected, and he does so around what is essentially a sonata concept, very much a macrocosmic version of the miniature symphonies and concertos inherent in 'Summer schemes', 'He abjures love', 'Proud songsters' and 'Channel firing'. But as anyone even distantly acquainted with Wordsworth's ode could guess, he also reflects its pivoted 'before/after' structure musically, again like a gigantic sequel to his Hardy songs and other works in which the antecedent/consequent articulation is uppermost. It is the use of these two principles on such a large scale, and above all the reconciling of them, that proves difficult.

Wordsworth's two poetic voices are also a challenge. His first two stanzas each pose the question the poem is trying to answer, the second by way of one of his 'ditty' passages, metrically part and parcel of the ode genre. This calls forth a 'ditty'-like *a cappella* interlude from Finzi –

> The Rainbow comes and goes,
> And lovely is the Rose,
> [etc]

– which is fine, and there are comparable metrical topics, with comparable treatment, later in the piece. But the partsong sensibility only really returns to reassert itself and balance this passage in Wordsworth's very last four lines (marked 'Epilogue' in fig. 1): the 'rainbow' unit can afford to stand out and create episodic tension because it is still within a multiple introduction. The introduction otherwise consists of the instrumental prelude plus the opening two tenor solos and two polyphonic choral debates, the second solo passage followed by the orchestral transition that links the first two stanzas (Finzi places an instrumental commentary between the limbs of every pair of Wordsworth's stanzas, though the one at the end of stanza V is very short). Again, its unconstrained pace can accompany Wordsworth's other poetic voice – the

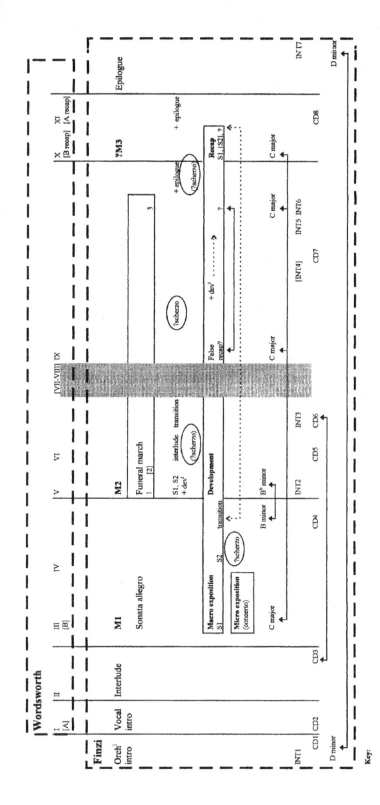

FIG. 1. *Intimations of Immortality*: formal structure

one that makes a single rambling sentence out of the ode's first five lines – because the main formal business has not yet begun. Later in the piece such a leisurely pace, with its reflection of the poet's 'variety of lyric modules' (Banfield 1989: 3), is less feasible, and it is worth noting that for Finzi, half-time (by the clock) occurs at the pivot between stanzas IV and V, whereas two-thirds of those parts of Wordsworth's text which he sets to music are still to come at this point.

In standard romantic fashion, Finzi uses a motto theme as binding. In fact he uses two, Bliss's 'silver thread' (ex. 9.6.a, first two systems) and the evocative horn call that opens and closes the work (ex. 9.6.b, final system). The horn call is mysterious and ethereal and represents the idea of pre-existence, the 'intimations of immortality' themselves; it is always presented with some kind of orchestral allure, be it the muting of brass, shimmering of strings or harp, or pointing of timpani, and with a touch of harmonic resonance – a chromaticism, a frozen dominant, a prick of dissonance, or whatever. The other motif is plain and earth-bound, rhythmically matter-of-fact, texturally stolid and unappetisingly modal (aeolian). It feels like a textbook first subject and sounds like that of the first movement of Ravel's String Quartet without its insouciance. Its word-setting is not endearing at first (why did Finzi allow the initial vocal crotchet at 'There was a time'? – a quaver following a quaver rest would have made such a difference) and one can see why

EX. 9.6.a

378

'Intimations' motif

EX. 9.6.b

Redlich complained about it. It may well be a prop left over from Finzi's initial work on the ode, for it perpetuates, at least to begin with, his early, heavy diatonicism, though like that style it conveys a certain stoic nobility coupled with regretfulness. All of this is in a way appropriate, for the theme represents the mundanity of adult existence, the existential problem of 'common day' that Wordsworth is trying to come to terms with, and indeed does take on a warm, compensatory glow at various points later in the piece as the poet stresses the consoling features of 'the years that bring the philosophic mind'. Both themes, like Tchaikovsky's 'fate' motifs, tend to be used at transitions and at sectional joins (see fig. 1), one of which recurs *verbatim* or rather *notatim* (see the connection between CD3 and CD6 in fig. 1). The 'intimations' motif is referred to six or seven times (depending on whether or not one hears a ghost of its initial upward 4th and tritonal signal in the horn calls for the 'guilty Thing surprised'), not always orchestrally and once as a vague recapitulation of the central funeral march topic (INT6 in fig. 1). The 'common day' melody appears on eight occasions – though that verbal phrase slips by more or less unmarked in Finzi's setting – its various guises including one by way of considerable head-motif paraphrase (at 'Earth fills her lap with pleasures of her own'), another, the last, more or less subliminal as Wordsworth himself recapitulates his 'meadow, grove, and stream' as 'Fountains, Meadows, Hills, and Groves'. The connection between the two themes

is explained aurally, in Sibelian manner, at the ode's central pivot: ex.
9.6.b shows the inscribed downward fourth of the first bar of the
'common day' melody repeated, extended and then inverted to form
the dominant/tonic upbeat prompt for the central funeral march based
on the 'intimations' motto, while Wordsworth's 'sinking feeling' conveniently justifies a chromatic gloss on the intervallic space. The
disjunction between the themes and the ineffable question posed by it
is pinpointed as early as bar 7, when we blink painfully at the pricked,
pizzicato unison that destroys the 'immortality' vision and brings us
down to earth. The Gloucester audience heard that effect, stereotypical
but still the right one, twice during festival week in 1950, for Howells
also uses it for a comparably filmic cut in the Sanctus of *Hymnus
paradisi*.

The other thematic transformation in the ode is less neat but more
pervasive. The positive rising contour of the figure that Redlich damned
for 'formalistic imitation' (ex. 9.6.a, second system) is turned into the
chorus's first entry in the symphonic allegro ('Now, while the birds
thus sing a joyous song') via the superb orchestral transition with its
syncopations and dotted-note fanfares. Every bit of material on
pp. 17–18 of the vocal score, ragtime xylophone and all, is about this,
and the third system of ex. 9.6.a offers just one link in the chain.
Subsequently, Wordsworth's third stanza, which propels the Allegro,
makes the distinction between universal joyfulness and the poet's
momentary but indicative grief, and as ex. 9.6.a shows, Finzi simply
inverts what has by now become the rising scale x and its cadence to
serve this polarity, initially for the setting of 'To me alone' (though the
motif has already been pervasively expounded in the orchestral prelude).
The two shapes can be traced, both literally and in vague correspondence, throughout this whole section up until the appearance of the 'to
me alone' figure appended to the 'common day' melody in the transition
shown in ex. 9.6.b.

The Allegro is the great glory of Finzi's *Intimations*, and the way in
which it sustains kinetic energy and orchestral force and pacing is quite
unlike anything else he accomplished. As the linchpin of a Lisztian
composite sonata operating across the entire work, there are various
ways of looking at it, and fig. 1 shows these. On the smallest level, the
Allegro simply encompasses stanza III, its first and second subjects
signalled by the x and xI motifs, and reaches its *fff* climax (the only
one at that dynamic level for the chorus, at the words 'Shout round

me') and subsequent orchestral peroration in one breathless, jubilant span; the peroration, containing some extremely fine writing, has the hallmark of a ritornello closing a concerto exposition – a choral concerto, perhaps. But the corybantic fervour of Wordsworth's verse continues right through most of stanza IV as well, and there is no respite in the music, which climaxes successively, after the initial high dominant G of the Allegro, on A, A#/B♭ (at 'Shout round me'), and B ('with joy I hear!'). On the larger level, this is all exposition, perhaps with the delightful piece of dittying in stanza IV, at the lines

> And the Children are culling
>   On every side,
> In a thousand valleys far and wide,
> Fresh flowers; while the sun shines warm,
> And the Babe leaps up on his Mother's arm: –

as second subject, prefaced by what must be one of the most sly pieces of mickey-mousing outside of Hollywood.

In the Lisztian three-in-one or four-in-one form, exposition stands for the whole, and the double perspective on what follows is accordingly that of both slow movement and development. This is the structural pivot of the poet's thought and the composer's form, as mentioned earlier, and to depict birth as a funeral march (starting in 5/4) is a brilliantly apt way of articulating it. The tonality slips a semitone from B minor (in the transition) to B♭ minor as the light goes out of things, and this too is highly effective. The difficulty, however, is that whereas in Finzi's music the preceding Allegro has quite properly been the work's core substance, material that will need balancing and fulfilling, Wordsworth's first four stanzas are still asking the question, posing the problem (which they do three times, at the end of stanzas I, II and IV), which he gets down to the serious business of attempting to answer in stanza V (and which came to him after a two years' break in the ode's composition). The only way to accept this discrepancy is as a counterpoint between the poetic and musical structures, but unfortunately the counterpoint or corollary to Wordsworth's structural argument is, in musical terms, a 'double decrescendo':

It projects . . . an interlocking double perspective on existence: as the intense yet shadowy joy of early childhood is to the glory of supposed pre-existence, so the dullness of adulthood is to the impulsiveness of youth. The effect is of a double decrescendo, a constant journey 'daily farther from the east', and

Wordsworth makes no attempt to reverse it by anticipating the afterlife, which is scarcely referred to at all in the poem. (Banfield 1989: 3)

Thus the music never has a chance to regain its momentum and concentration, and despite the many beautiful and memorable things in the second half of *Intimations*, and its growth in stature as the work achieves better performances and becomes more familiar as a repertoire piece, this will always remain a problem. Nor is it really possible to sustain the funeral march, for the poet's reflective discourse continues with too many fleeting shades of feeling and turns of syntax and imagery, all of which Finzi matches musically, inevitably on a more or less individual basis. The funeral march runs underground for a long way but rarely has a chance to surface (see the box and its numbered statements in fig. 1). Even when it does, the head-motif paraphrase referred to earlier (INT6) has to do symbolic duty, in immemorial Finzi fashion, for a whole section. The interim throbbing plaint (figure '[2]' on the diagram) is a variant of what might be seen as the slow movement's second subject (ex. 9.6.c). It is also the most obvious of three probable echoes of the finale of Vaughan Williams's *A London Symphony* in *Intimations* (compare the opening of the Vaughan Williams movement), the other two being the 'mighty waters' figuration, redolent of the symphony's 'London passing' Epilogue with its evocation of a journey down the Thames, and the 'common day' theme itself, shadowing a figure in the midst of Vaughan Williams's exposition (two bars after letter D).

At this point it is worth seeing how Arthur Somervell approached the problem of the poetic form in his setting of the Immortality Ode. Somervell, like Finzi, had a strong affinity with Wordsworth, more geographically grounded in that he came from the Lake District; he also made a setting of Wordsworth's *[On] The Power of Sound*. Finzi probably did not know Somervell's *Ode on the Intimations of Immortality* – Joy never heard him refer to it (J. Finzi 1974) – and may not

[Hea - ven lies _ a-bout us _ in our in - fan - cy! _]

EX. 9.6.c

have been aware of its existence, though a vocal score was published and Vaughan Williams ought to have remembered it, since its first and probably only performance shared the platform with that of his own transcendentalist choral essay, *Toward the Unknown Region*, at the Leeds Festival in 1907. (Somervell was let down on that occasion by an ailing, ineffectual soloist, but the work evidently meant a lot to him, for he revised it not long before his death. He also deliberately quoted from it in another composition – see Banfield 1975: 529.)

There are striking similarities between the two settings:

both composers wrote for one solo voice [bass in the Somervell], chorus and orchestra; both placed considerable weight on a lengthy orchestral introduction of a sort which presents a summary of the main themes, though Somervell considerably shortened his in the revised score; both cut stanzas 7–8, Somervell also omitting 6; and both wrote a one-movement structure of about 720 bars, Somervell's lasting approximately 30 minutes and Finzi's 40. (ibid.: 528)

Where Somervell scores over Finzi is in his simple, overt formal planning with its broad-brush musical paragraphs. This enables him to restrict stanzas I, II and IV to the bass soloist, while stanza III is given to the female chorus (SSA trio), not at all fey in its effect because he builds up a genuinely celebratory 9/8 scherzo, tonally immaculate, across its entire span, and also interweaves its rhythmic motif with the soloist's observing commentary in stanza IV. In other words, he holds back the full chorus's first entry until the nub of the poem, stanza V, is reached. (Like Finzi, he casts it as a funeral march reminiscent of Brahms's in his *Deutsches Requiem*.) But his musical arches carry Wordsworth's more orotund passages, negatives and all, only by descending, as he habitually does, to conventional, banal melody, sequences and all. Ex. 9.6.d, with its rippling triplet accompaniment, is too high a price to pay for the syntactical flow. If Finzi is scarcely more comfortable, certainly not at his relaxed, confiding best, in this difficult passage, at least his chugging bass semiquavers keep a kind of neutral motion going to tide him over it and foreground Wordsworth's diction (ex. 9.6.e).

Those semiquavers, started a little earlier and carried through to convey 'Delight and liberty, the simple creed / Of childhood, whether busy or at rest', offer a kind of intermezzo topic, here rather Schumannesque, and very much needed from time to time as a smooth musical ride between more cogitative, strenuous or argumentative reaches. Such passages have been labelled '?scherzo' in fig. 1, defining the term very

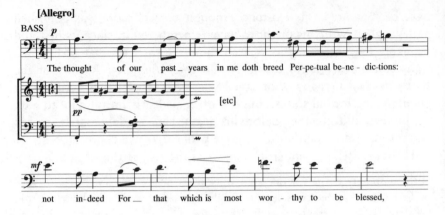

EX. 9.6.d

EX. 9.6.e

loosely to suggest the motoric flight of a deft musical texture, and it is one of the formal problems of the ode that its sonata analogue offers no opportunity for them to be joined or extended into a scherzo section proper. Somervell managed one, but only where Finzi opts for his Allegro; the other candidate for such treatment might have been stanza V, at the depiction of the 'growing Boy''s journey, but given its gloomy destination at the end of the stanza, Finzi's funeral march seems right.

The other severe formal limitation is Wordsworth's admission that 'nothing can bring back the hour / Of splendour in the grass, of glory in the flower': in other words, a full Allegro recapitulation or sequel by way of finale is out of the question. Finzi's truncated, telescoped return, taking its cue from Wordsworth's verbal one at the start of stanza X, includes a suggestion of second subject at the lines 'We in thought will join your throng, / Ye that pipe and ye that play' insofar as this corresponds to the ditty of the flower-picking children (balancing rather than recalling it, though the month of May is mentioned in both). The stanza X recapitulation comes as a release from the frustrated anticipation inherent in one or two earlier such 'recovery' passages that had proved unsustainable, at the beginning of stanza IX and perhaps also at the line 'Hence in a season of calm weather', between them affording a measure of C major unity to the inner core of the sonata concept, though it should be stressed that tonal structure is no more a touchstone of Finzi's thought here than elsewhere in his output, and the work's opening and closing in D minor is a token rather than an essence.

The effect of all this is that Wordsworth's consolatory epilogues are rather piled on to a musical structure that has not really been through a culmination or crisis point to any kind of resolution and has not therefore earned them. As if in recognition of this, twice on the home straight Finzi resorts to incidental blues throbbings rather than symphonic references (see 'the faith that looks through death' and 'The Clouds that gather round the setting sun'). This ultimate shortcoming is not helped when he seemingly misinterprets the syntax of Wordsworth's final four lines, making their 'Thanks . . .' sound for all the world like a freestanding grace or doxology ('Let us give thanks . . .') with his re-introduction of the partsong topic, rather than a projectile subordinate clause with the sense of 'Because of the blessings of the human heart . . .' (There is one other occasion on which he fails to realise Wordsworth's meaning: the implied emphasis when the poet says that 'We in *thought* . . . will join . . . Ye that . . . *Feel* . . .' is missing, and an opportunity to underline the whole point of the ode is lost.)

But the sheer persuasiveness and beauty of Finzi's setting taken as a series of discrete moments ensure that, unlike Somervell's when he exhausts his thematic material, it never sinks completely, and the panoply of romantic topics in his music sounds fresher rather than staler as the years pass, much to what would have been Redlich's and Cooper's surprise. Without wishing to compete with the lists of favourite passages drawn up by his friends, one must salute his mastery of sensibility in, and imprinting of musical memorability on, such lines as 'It is not now as it hath been of yore', 'Heaven lies about us in our infancy!', '... we come / From God, who is our home', 'that imperial palace whence he came', 'Did tremble like a guilty Thing surprised', 'moments in the being / Of the eternal Silence', 'Nor all that is at enmity with joy', '... the faith that looks through death', 'I love the Brooks which down their channels fret' and, best of all, 'Another race hath been' (where Finzi even overshoots the meaning of Wordsworth's 'race' in his entreaty). When we rally to the flag of unity we forget how difficult and creatively exhausting it is to maintain coalescent musical variety over such a long stretch, and this Finzi triumphantly achieves in rarely letting a single phrase of Wordsworth's slip through a vigilant mind and loving hand. By virtue of these and other moments, explored with something approaching Elgar's rare genius for particularisation (and often in Elgar's *Dream of Gerontius* style), he succeeded in making his Immortality Ode *the* setting of Wordsworth, not to be superseded in the forseeable future and an achievement that, however incrementally, adjusts and enhances our view of the poem and the poet for ever, just as every atom of scholarly and critical accretion does.

It was a curious way for a minor composer to court greatness, and like everything else Finzi did it was sidestepping the usual imperatives, if he could bring his courage, or arrogance, to bear on the determination to prove equal to Wordsworth. For this he did, surviving critics, the general impossibility of the task, and the weaknesses of his musical form alike, to arrive at the point – which he had to take on trust, indeed had not expected to occur, in his lifetime – to which the following testimony of a Finzi Trust Friend, John Savage, bears representative witness:

... hearing Finzi's setting of *Intimations* in 1950 was a revelation to me of the truth of Wordsworth's poetry (and poetry in general), and of his vision of the world 'apparelled in celestial light'. This led me to read English at Cambridge and to spend my life teaching. It has been a life-long love affair with literature and music... I count myself very fortunate. (*Finzi Trust Friends Newsletter* xiii/2: [2])

With this in mind, there is little need to labour Finzi's personal and individual affinity with the poet, his ode and its perceptions. True, he had studied Wordsworth thoroughly (see Banfield 1992: [4–5]). True, the expression of primal, god-like innocence and its broader background of belief in humanistic, liberal transcendence was a particular preoccupation with particular, highly congruent manifestations in his Traherne and Wordsworth settings. True also, Finzi's own childhood, with its specifiable 'shades of the prison-house' and subsequent determination to forge an adult life that both acknowledged and overcame them, was a potent fixed point which moved his creative vision. Other magnetic fields of precise attraction might be sought and mapped. Finzi was researching John Stanley at the time he completed his ode, and one wonders whether he pondered Stanley's childhood experience by analogy with Wordsworth's, for Stanley had been blinded at the age of two and would have had the most shadowy, dim, tantalising and peculiarly literal memory of 'things which I have seen [and] now can see no more'. And what about Finzi's own genealogical particularity? Did this, perhaps without him realising it, trigger his response to the exploration of pre-existence in the first place? It may be crass to suggest that, in contradistinction to the workaday, 'assimilated' modal resignation of the 'common day' motif, the exotic, shimmering allure of his 'intimations' theme somehow represents a Jew's lost home and heritage, forever beckoning, never again attainable because locked in the irreversible past. It may also be necessary to do so.

But the main point should be a more general one about the way the western cultural heritage has interacted with creativity in the twentieth century. Just as critical studies, biographies, collected and popular editions, academic respectability and common understanding eventually overtake great artists and their work, along with the other tricks posterity can play on them, so do musical settings, when the time is ripe. The time is ripe when the tools are available and the market is attuned. Where the tools were concerned, Somervell's setting was premature, in that Wordsworth's intimations, vistas and phraseology would only properly respond, musically, to a later distillation of romantic and postromantic signals, pacing and articulation of discourse, palette of tonal and orchestral colours, and patchwork of harmonic insights of the right emotional weight and accessibility. As for the market, a certain universality of musical understanding has to be in the cultural air, which will keep the setting depressed somewhere below the level of classic or artistically pure status while endeavouring to keep it above that of popular ephemerality or kitsch. Exactly the same could be said of settings of Dickens, which is why no Dickensian operas appeared in his own time but he has been well served with films and musicals in the twentieth century. Consciously or not, Finzi was the vessel through which this particular moment in the trajectory of Wordsworth and his ideas passed. Those ideas are as central to the English cultural identity as Goethe to the German, though on another level they partake of the international aristocracy of art, just one manifestation, a magnificent one, of the 'Beatrician vision' of first and second love that Dorothy L. Sayers (1958) traced back through Dante and other poets. On still another plane they are virtually folk property, which is why phrases such as 'trailing clouds of glory' and 'shades of the prison-house' can enjoy a proverbial afterlife and Finzi's orchestral and harmonic effects, stereotypical as they may be, could have made him a very fine film composer. (No wonder Herrmann loved *Intimations*!)

It was a rich moment, but it exhausted him. 'I'm not surprised the *"Intimations"* took it out of you; it's a bigger work than I cd. conceive,' wrote Milford the following April (19510414a). Who knows by what combinations of chance, cause and pattern the body's destiny is forged? Another shock to Finzi's physiological system came in February 1951, when he and Joy were driving to Gloucester and their Ford 8 baker's van, which had replaced their ancient, canvas-topped leaky Morris 8 as a kind of 'people mover', skidded into an iron fence at Cricklade. Joy chipped her front teeth, but they were otherwise uninjured, though without a vehicle for several months. And one can only speculate, as did Martyn Wade with poetic if not factual impunity in his play *Before and After Summer* (1995), on what Finzi's earlier experience – his lifestyle, illnesses, general health and heredity – had been storing up for him, for little is known about the origins of leukaemia. But at some point in the first half of 1951 he was suffering from a persistent cough and neck swellings. He told his doctor, Tom Scott, who was one of those general practitioners who can instinctively tell when a symptom is dangerous. Finzi immediately saw the worry in his eyes as he arranged for them to be treated.

CHAPTER 10

Scholarship and conservation

The rehabilitation of old music, started in earnest in the nineteenth century, has been a major fact of cultural life throughout the twentieth, especially in Britain, and we have already seen how Finzi was at least indirectly associated with it through his early contacts with Detmar Blow. Later, he was by no means alone among British composers of his generation in finding ways of rubbing shoulders with earlier ones: Britten arranged *The Beggar's Opera* and a good deal of Purcell; Tippett, Rubbra and Bliss (the last in consultation with Finzi) built works on seventeenth- and eighteenth-century themes by way of variation, arrangement and fantasia; Lambert edited Boyce, Warlock did the same for Purcell and the Elizabethans; Walton arranged Bach, Vaughan Williams conducted him; Howells pastiched the virginalists; Ferguson eventually turned full-time professional editor; and so on.

But with Finzi there were special factors. He was, first of all, in the organisation of his time and surroundings more of a man of leisure and man of letters than the others, and accordingly a significant collector: in addition to the 4,000-odd volumes of English literature, mostly poetry, and criticism now in the Finzi Book Room, and his extremely large general library of music and books on music, he sported by the time of his death an eighteenth-century antiquarian music collection, largely English, 'considered the finest of its period assembled privately in England at that time' (McVeagh 1980a: 595) and now in St Andrews University Library. Secondly, his interests included, almost uniquely for his period, the later nineteenth century (Stanford, Ernest Walker and Edward German as well as Parry) and even his own seniors (especially Gurney). Thirdly, with his own, admittedly amateur, string orchestra at hand he was in a stronger position than most to perform the music he was resuscitating – an unusual triple alliance with composer and editor. And finally, he did not confine his scholarly and conservationist labours to music: poetry and apples came into it too, and one is half surprised that he did not begin breeding rare varieties of cat.

Finzi's work in all these fields was of distinction – he never did anything half-heartedly – but also of distinguishable kinds. His pomology, while of practical usefulness insofar as he helped to propagate rare stock, was essentially a hobby, an enthusiasm shared with friends rather than with the world through publication. So were his textual interests in literature, whether he was making editorial suggestions to Hutton and Navarro on their unpublished verse or sharing notes, queries and opinions with Blunden – though with Navarro he (and Joy) came close to the role of professional editor. Other tasks were those of an enabler, often behind the scenes: the sorting and securing of homes for Parry's manuscripts, the publishing of Gurney's poems, and lobbying for republication of this and that and for performance of the other (from Vaughan Williams to Anthony Scott) were the actions of a good citizen and *littérateur* that have been described as modest, selfless devotion to others. True enough, though it has to be remembered that as a man who did not need or intend to earn his living Finzi was free to spend his time being a composer, conductor, archivist or impresario just as he saw fit. One could say the same about his third type of activity, professional editing for publication, though here financial reward probably did tip the balance of time spent on it when, in his later years, he was feeling the pinch and needed to get editions into print so that he could reap royalties. Whether they earned him enough to make much of a difference is doubtful, however. The fourth string to his scholar's bow was a matter of what one might call intellectual authority, or simply criticism: his overview of Howells, of Parry, of Vaughan Williams, of R. O. Morris, of 'music and words' and of one or two other general subjects achieved publication or delivery because he felt specially equipped or responsible for the task. One must add to all this activity the innumerable occasions on which he was consulted by friends and others because he not only had such sizeable and wide-ranging interests and collections but an extraordinarily active command of them. Christopher Finzi testifies to his father having been 'a voracious and extremely rapid reader' (Stunt 1996: 11), which, added to his apparent ability to pinpoint a quotation, a stylistic echo, or a concordance (see Walker's testimony [1959: 10] to his memory of the Berg

Piano Sonata), must have made a visit to Ashmansworth a byword for intellectual benison where many a senior or junior fellow-artist was concerned.

Perhaps because he took all his labours so seriously, Finzi's friends were apt to tease him about them. Ferguson felt that some of the old English apples would have merited their extinction. Vaughan Williams, as we saw in Chapter 3, noted the same enthusiasm applied to the apples and the English eighteenth-century composers whom Finzi revived, and refused to worship at the altar – a side altar, admittedly – of one of the latter when he sent Finzi the following:

Lines found in a wastepaper Basket shared by RVW & Crispin, authorship therefore uncertain.

> I fear I'm no judge:
> but the work of Rev: Mudge
> seems nothing but fudge,
> and you won't make me budge,
> in spite of his Herald
> to wit, our friend, Gerald (195412?).

Crispin was the cat. It was all very well for Vaughan Williams, who had been able to exercise his nationalistic instincts on folksong collecting early in the century; Finzi, coming later, had missed that opportunity, for which in any case his shyness would probably have disqualified him, though he did notate a mixolydian lavender seller's tune in London on his twenty-fifth birthday – it is found in one of his sketchbooks.

Finzi's scholarly bent must have been evident to Marion Scott as early as 1925, when she asked him to help her with the editing of the string parts of Gurney's song cycle *The Western Playland* for its Carnegie Trust publication. (Did he also get involved with the preparation of *Lights Out* the following year?) Side by side with Gurney on his musicological agenda, virtually from the start of his adult life, stood early music. There was plenty of it in the first issues of *Music and Letters*, inaugurated in 1920, to which he subscribed and whose influence on his intellectual development probably cannot be overestimated. As already mentioned, he went to several of the early Haslemere Festivals, met Herbert Lambert and was enticed, or enticed further, by him not only into the world of period keyboard instruments but of the presentation of old scores or tunes when he arranged, for piano and string quartet in November 1927, a Purcell sarabande and the dance tune 'Heartsease' for a play Lambert was involved with. This was a business in which he chose not to remain, however: his output includes remarkably few arrangements and transcriptions (as opposed to scholarly editions), partly no doubt because of his textual fastidiousness and bibliophilia, but perhaps also because he preferred to distil the essences of old styles into certain compositional topics of his own rather than deal aesthetically with *données*, being rather the opposite of Grainger in this respect. (His single folksong arrangement, 'A lullaby' for unaccompanied mixed chorus [1942, unpublished], is not very successful, largely because Calvocoressi's awkward translation of the original Greek words went against Finzi's melopoetic grain. It was in any case written by request, not volition – 'Calvocoressi asked several composers to make arrangements of certain Greek Folk songs for a Greek chorus which was to be formed by the Greek National Committee for Broadcasting during the war,' as Finzi's note on the manuscript, dated 2 January 1943, explained.)

Again in 1927, Finzi and Ferguson were planning to play through Rameau and Scarlatti operas, though this was thwarted when they were not allowed to borrow the scores they had discovered in the Parry Room at the RCM. (Emily Daymond, who appears to have been quite a character, must have been an influence here, at least on Ferguson, who pays tribute [1974–96] to how she helped him over scores and scholarly editions even before he was a student at the College, where she supervised the collections in the Parry Room. She had been one of Grove's earliest pupils at the RCM, a kind of secretary to Parry, the first female Oxford Mus.D. in Britain, and founder of the Music Department at Royal Holloway College [see Young 1980: 197].) Then in 1928, while Finzi was in the sanatorium, he and Ferguson first flexed their muscles on textual scholarship when Ferguson, still only twenty, went to the British Museum to copy out from the complete edition the Schütz *sinfonia sacra* 'Fili mi, Absalon', with which he and Gerald had been highly impressed when Keith Falkner sang it at a Gerald Cooper concert. Ferguson sent his score to Finzi and they discussed matters of proportional tempi (Finzi citing Morris 1922), *ficta*, instrumentation, performance practice and continuo realisation in some detail, only to discover that Daymond had already made an unpublished performing edition of the piece. The seeds of their later, separate endeavours had clearly been sown, and though Finzi's baroque and Georgian interests did not develop in earnest for the best part of two more decades, it is worth noting that in August 1929, still very much preoccupied with his own Piano Concerto, he had ordered scores of all the Field concertos, and that the following month he heard Angus Morrison play 'Arne's little Pf con.' at the Proms, doubtless under Constant Lambert's guidance, and found it 'well worth reviving: it can hold its head up in good company' (19290901–12).

Ivor Gurney's sustained claim on his editing skills and general devotion was based on his first hearing of the song 'Sleep' in York, sung by Elsie Suddaby in one of Bairstow's voice lessons, a revelation carrying the conviction that it was 'not being wise after the event to say that one can feel an incandescence in his songs that tells of something burning too brightly to last, such as you see in the filament of an electric bulb before it burns out' (G. Finzi 1955: II, 7). After the 1925 'prod' (see Chapter 3, p. 62) and a renewal of the attack on Marion Scott as custodian of Gurney's *Nachlass* around 1933, Finzi's vision of a Gurney memorial in print first became a practicality with the publication of Plunket Greene's book on Stanford early in 1935. A. H. Fox Strangways referred to Gurney in his *Observer* review of it, and Finzi felt that 'a better time for drawing attention to his work wd not be found' (19350414). He had already asked Vaughan Williams to consider writing an article on him, but Fox Strangways was willing to go further and commission two or more for a multiple tribute in the October issue of *Music and Letters*. Walter de la Mare was lined up to comment on the poetry, Marion Scott on the man, and for the music Finzi initially thought of Plunket Greene (to whom Gurney had sent some of his very best manuscript songs). This would have been in addition to Vaughan Williams, but one thing led to another when Vaughan Williams, rather than write more than a paragraph, encouraged Finzi to take authority unto himself: 'You are obviously the man,' he wrote (19350417). Finzi instead must have asked Howells to do the main musical survey, while Plunket Greene's short statement ended up supplementing Marion Scott's; but it was not until July 1937 that he wrote to Blunden for a second contribution to the poetic assessment alongside de la Mare's (Masefield had also been approached and Jack Haines thought of, but in the event Blunden and J. C. Squire supplemented de la Mare). The change of editorship of the journal early in 1937 from Fox Strangways to Eric Blom may have slowed things down, but the main delaying factors were Marion Scott's constitutional dilatoriness and, most of all, the death of Howells's young son.

This devastating event must also have been responsible for the fact that Finzi never met Gurney. Vaughan Williams went to visit Gurney in the City of London Mental Hospital at Dartford in the summer of 1935, whereupon Adeline asked Scott, his friend and custodian, whether they might get him into the country for a couple of weeks. She approached Gurney's doctors, who considered him too suicidal even for a car outing with two male nurses in attendance. She added, however:

It is very kind of Gerald Finzi to be willing to go and visit Ivor. I think there is a possibility it might be a success if he could pay his first visit in company with Herbert Howells. The arrival of the two composers together would seem very natural and it would start Ivor on the right lines with Gerald Finzi. (19350819, in 19350822)

Alas, she wrote this only a few days before Michael Howells was struck down with meningitis. Astoundingly, Gurney appears to have heard of Finzi notwithstanding, and long before: 'How surprising that he shd know anything about me as a composer – even only the name, especially as I had hardly started by the time he was already ill,' Finzi wrote to Scott. (19370208)

It must have been around 1936 that the additional plan (again Finzi's, we must assume) of getting two volumes of Gurney's many manuscript songs into print took root to the extent that Finzi began to acquaint himself with Marion Scott's holdings. Most of the best songs were still unpublished, some still uncollected, and gathering and sifting them must have been an exciting task. Grading was done, carefully, over a matter of weeks early in 1937 in conjunction with Howard Ferguson, who played the accompaniments on the piano while Gerald tackled the voice part an octave higher and Joy sat by to take notes (Ferguson 1974–96). It was not just a question of choosing the best songs but the best version of each, given Gurney's habit of producing a slightly or radically different one with each new manuscript copy. As with Finzi's own songs, a shortlist of twelve per envisaged volume of ten was drawn up, and then, in March, they went to play them to Vaughan Williams, who made the final selection. Next stop was Howells, whom Ferguson and Finzi visited in May, primarily with a view to his helping to unravel 'a few obscure points in the musical text' (M. M. Scott 1938) – a dampened hope, as mentioned in Chapter 3. By this time Finzi had himself

made the fair copies needed for submission and was evidently spear-
heading another attempt to get the composer moved from the asylum,
since Moeran wrote to him certain that nothing could be done; 'I doubt
whether he would remember me; it is years since we met', he added
(19370404). Gurney was by this time physically very ill, and it became
clear that he would not live much longer. But it was also clear that
Marion Scott was not the best person to speed his best songs on their
way to a publisher, and in July Vaughan Williams forwarded them to
Foss at OUP himself. Foss took twenty of them in August ('Ploughman
singing' was one of the jettisoned ones), hoping to issue them in time
to coincide with the *Music and Letters* tributes.

Finzi now recognised the eventual scope of the task he had taken on.
First there was the textual challenge, as he described to Scott:

The sorting has been even more difficult than I expected, chiefly because there
is comparatively little that one can be really sure is bad. Even the late 1925
asylum songs, though they get more and more involved (and at the same time
more disintegrated, if you know what I mean) have a curious coherence about
them somewhere, which makes it difficult to know when they really are over
the border. I think the eventual difficulty of 'editing' the later Gurney may be
great: a neat mind could smooth away the queerness – like Rimsky-Korsakov
with Mussorgsky – yet time and familiarity will probably show something not
so mistaken, after all, about the queer and odd things. However, there are some
obviously incoherent things and a good many others of which one can say that
it would be better for them not to be published. (19370130)

On the actual methodology of editing, Finzi took his cue from Ferguson
at this stage: 'Ferguson thinks an "Urtext" is what is needed, with
editorial markings in brackets,' he reported to Scott (ibid.).

Equally daunting was the challenge of Marion Scott herself. By May
1937 he had discovered something of the extent of Gurney's unpublished poetic legacy she had squirreled away in addition to the songs,
but even that was not all. He reported to Ferguson in no uncertain
terms on the three days' visit he and Joy paid her at the beginning of
August in order to get the whole collection catalogued:

It's terrible to think that all this might have been done a dozen years ago, if
his work had not been left in the hands of that possessive, incompetent, mulish,
old maid Marion Scott. You know the inside of it all & how impossible she
has been, but that was nothing to the 3 days Joy & I spent in London doing
the final cataloguing. This had been agreed on about a month before. The first

thing we found was that she had mislaid part of the List 1 music. This turned up the next day. Then she had not even managed to get copies of the published work to put with the complete works. She put every obstacle in the way of our 'phoning up to the publishers, but we managed to get our way & the copies arrived on the last day. Then, in the afternoon of the last day, I suggested looking into that large wooden packing case in her room, which she always assured me had nothing of importance in. I bundled everthing out on to the floor & found about 30 complete songs of G's best period, dozens of notebooks, some with complete songs in, and a few thousand papers of various MSS including 'lost' vln sonata mvts & so on. Joy & I worked till about 9.30 that night – the temperature of Maid Marion's room was 90° – & begged that we shd be treated like the piano tuner & left alone, whilst the Scott family dined in state. It is rather incredible when you realize that everything was supposed to be ready for the cataloguing, sorted & in order, two months ago. But what can you expect from someone who hasn't 'had time' to copy out those two little Vln & Pf pieces you asked for nine months ago! I'm so polite to this fragile fool that I've not had the heart to remind her that I *made* the time to copy out 24 of his songs in a month. However, the cataloguing seems to be done. 17 portfolios of coherent work & a chestful of asylum stuff, and it's taken me about four years' incessant prodding to make the woman move. Now, she says, all the music must go back into her bank! I'm reminded of the little beetle in the Insect Play, guarding his pile. I think Howells & VW are quite right in feeling that she has an unconscious resentment against anything being done for Gurney unless it's done by herself, but beyond 'guarding his pile' she is incapable of doing anything. Now there'll be all the bother over again if the poems are ever to see the light. (19370815)

Perhaps inevitably, this outburst had modulated into an entirely different key by the time he came to present a posthumous tribute to her (G. Finzi 1954b) describing the 'iron will equal to a great heart' that underlay her exterior of 'slightness and fragility' (:3). In any case, the extra finds cast only a minor spanner in the works, for Volumes III and IV were already gleams in Finzi's eye. He had hopes of OUP committing themselves to a collected Gurney after another meeting in London at the end of August, and at one point even proposed a volume of ten Edward Thomas settings to Scott, by silent analogy with his own Hardy sets.

Gurney died on 26 December 1937 – two days before Ravel. Finzi helped with the funeral expenses. 'It's splendid, though rather pitiful,' he wrote to Jack Haines, 'to see the attention which the papers are giving Gurney. They gave him precious little when he was alive...'

(19371229). The following day Joy filled Navarro in with further details:

I expect you will have seen the obituary notices of Gurney's death, & perhaps previously, the warming articles on the publication of Music & Letters. He lived long enough to realise recognition had come [to] him and said to Marion Scott 'You will understand that this is difficult for me to understand.' He died of TB of the lungs caused by after effects of gas during the war & 15 years sedentary asylum life. The last fortnight he was lying unable to move with weakness. Gerald is so very glad the articles came out in time for him to hold them & to know. G always felt he wouldn't live so very much longer. He is to be buried in the little cemetery at Twigworth near Gloucester – We shall be there. (19371230?)

They were there, and it was 'a sad little affair . . . H[erbert] H[owells] played "Sleep" & "Severn Meadows" on a wheezy little organ,' Finzi told Ferguson, 'whilst his [Gurney's] brother Ronald stood by, looking exactly as though he had won a medal, so pleased, complacent & high-collared! Poor Marion Scott, in tears at the end, but remarkably brave & calm considering how much it must have meant to her' (19380101a). Ronald Gurney, epitome of the British shopkeeper mentality (he was an outfitter) which is not only the opposite side of the cultural coin to the lyrical waywardness of such as his brother but – as Finzi would discover – frequently more than a match for it, had already been proving difficult. In later years he would make Gerald, and Joy after Gerald's death, earn every ounce of their pride in having got 'something, however much in the background . . . done, since his own "friends" hadn't the spirit to do it' (ibid.).

Meanwhile Gerald dealt with the songs' proofs, saw the volumes in print in the spring of 1938, and went to a Gurney recital to mark the occasion at Amen House on 13 April, though he had little to do with the BBC Gurney broadcasts that summer and deplored their choice of *Ludlow and Teme* for the first one, which did not prevent him from enjoying Sinclair Logan's performances elsewhere in the series.

Henceforward Finzi must have felt his responsibility towards Gurney hanging over him all through the war years, when little further could be done, though he continued to badger Scott in no uncertain terms about the poems. New songs were also continuing to turn up, including, in May 1941, fifteen from the publisher Felix Goodwin who had had them for an equal number of years. One of these, 'The happy tree', was subsequently included in Volume III, which appeared in 1952, this time bowing to current orthodoxy (under pressure from Finzi?) by including an additional note on performance practice by Marion Scott (M. M. Scott 1952).

He returned to Gurney's uncollected poems immediately he was released from the Ministry in the summer of 1945, having wrested their texts from Marion Scott during the war or in stages thereafter, with the collusion of Vaughan Williams and Ursula Wood as typist. First he and the Navarros graded a selection of the unpublished ones. The visit to Blunden followed in October, and Blunden started working on them for a selected edition with Finzi's support (and initial longlist), but the project was inevitably held up by his sailing for Japan in 1948 and only reached fruition on his return when Finzi managed to incarcerate him in his book room for the best part of a week in May 1951 while the rest of the Blunden family enjoyed the Ashmansworth air. This was none too soon, for by now postgraduate overtures from California were being made about Gurney in the person of Don Ray (and were being regarded somewhat snobbishly by Gerald). Blunden emerged from Finzi's study having made his selection of seventy-eight poems (excluding those in Gurney's early published collections *Severn and Somme* and *War's Embers* but including a number that Finzi had helped retrieve from published obscurity in the pages of the *London Mercury*, the *Gloucester Journal* and other sources), tackled the complicated textual problems, taken on board Gurney's 'asylum' verse (which continued to flow after composition had disintegrated) and written a splendid introductory memoir as preface. According to Webb (1990: 289), he was later 'to regret the speed of the volume's compilation and the selection of too few "Asylum Verses" ', though Kavanagh (1982: 20–2) rather implies the opposite of Blunden's 'eccentric' selection – that there was too much wildness in it. Nor did Blunden avoid serious misreadings (ibid.). Finzi, however, while keen to acknowledge that 'the selection was ... not intended as a definitive one' (19520630b), was relieved that he had at least found a way of getting the poet Gurney into print for the postwar era: after a number of rejections, the book was published by Hutchinson in 1954, by which time Blunden was in the Far East again.

Marion Scott lived long enough to comment on the typescript but died at Christmas 1953 after a few months' illness. 'One had always tended to ignore her complaints, but this time it was the real thing,'

Finzi observed in a letter to Haines (19540101). What he had not anticipated was that in a sense his Gurney problems were only just beginning with her demise. She had possessed Letters of Administration over Gurney's effects by virtue of being owed money by him which otherwise his family would have had to pay at his death, and this was seen as a clever way of keeping the intestate composer's posthumous affairs out of their hands. She passed the debt on to Finzi on the same pretext, but Ronald Gurney took issue with the legal ruse and insisted on administering his brother's estate directly. Fearing that he was paranoid and might destroy the manuscripts altogether, the Finzis repeatedly visited him in Gloucester and once again had to enlist Vaughan Williams's muscle. Even the publication of the poems in 1954 was held up while the tailor of Gloucester decided whether or not they were worthwhile, and it was only after Gerald's death that the fourth volume of songs achieved publication (in 1959) and Ronald finally allowed the manuscripts to go to the Gloucester Library on permanent loan. Joy Finzi, ultimate heroine of the Gurney saga, had exercised her 'magic' on him, as Howells put it (19600130), and took them there from his house in a wheelbarrow. The whole affair, which with hindsight all parties might have seen brewing once Gurney's work was beginning to accrue royalties, was an exhausting and classic tragicomedy of incomprehension, suspicion and tactlessness between the classes, between artists and traders, and between the rival claims of kinship and akinship, as Finzi would have put it. The dignity of art won the day, not least because its representatives were able to maintain a united front where family feeling was ultimately factious. The Finzis did an enormous amount for Gurney, but it would be unfair to let Gerald's fulmination against Marion Scott reverberate without antiphony. She had, after all, arranged for periodical publication of a number of Gurney's poems, had prepared a selection of them (as, apparently, had Jack Haines – see Kavanagh 1982: 18–19), and had faithfully and regularly visited him in his mental hospital for 15 years.

'My feeling about getting the manuscripts safely housed has been intensified ten fold by recent experiences with the Ivor Gurney manuscripts,' Finzi wrote to Dorothea Ponsonby, Parry's elder daughter, about her father's *Nachlass* in the midst of his troubles with Ronald Gurney (19540729). Luckily he had a good working friendship with Lady Ponsonby and no comparable problems arose. Even so, taking on Parry as well as Gurney was a daunting task, because of the size of his output, at which Finzi, with his much smaller one, not to mention freedom from institutional obligations, must have marvelled.

Finzi's interaction with Parry was on four planes, though none of them possessed the intense scope of his Gurney project. First there was Parry's influence on his music and his philosophy. Then there was what he gave back in his centenary talk and article and in public comments elsewhere. Thirdly, he helped Lady Ponsonby identify, catalogue and clear out her father's music and manuscripts and distribute the *Nachlass* to permanent homes in libraries. Finally, he endeavoured to bring certain works back to public attention through transcription, publication or re-issue.

He was not blind to Parry's failings as a composer, and would probably not have gone as far as Douglas Fox's endorsement, in a letter, of Ernest Walker's prediction 'many years ago that he would eventually outlive Elgar' (19470419). But Parry's strengths, achievements and suitability as a role model seemed so obvious to Finzi that they alone would have been sufficient to buttress his extraordinarily firm and prescient belief, a belief simply held through all the upheavals of modern times that he and his generation witnessed, that 'the opinion of today is not necessarily the opinion of tomorrow' (19560509), and that Parry's time would return. This belief, which Finzi had planned to expound at least in general terms in his London University lectures of 1957, was present in the first few sentences of R. O. Morris's *Music and Letters* article on Parry (Morris 1920), and one wonders whether this was specifically where his interest in the founder of the English musical renaissance began, or whether it was more widely inculcated through his early training under Farrar and Bairstow.

Whether Parry's radical liberalism was also a specific force in the formative days of his own is another unknown, but it probably cannot have rubbed off in too specific a sense until, years later, he had the opportunity to read *Instinct and Character* (*did* he read it?) and enjoy sharing in Lady Ponsonby's taste for left-wing visionary politics and civil disobedience (her husband had been a radical Liberal MP of some renown), which bolstered Finzi's pride in his son Christopher's conscientious objection (see 19541105) and gently but satisfyingly helped close a historical circle when Lady Ponsonby was staying at Ashmansworth in 1956. 'Her mind still big and vigorous and cantankerous,' Joy wrote on that occasion. 'Took her to ... the first Newbury Peace Meeting – A pathetic little gathering – Excellent speaker – who quoted from Lord

Ponsonby & was glad to meet Lady P' (J. Finzi 19560306). One rather wishes they had all been around a generation later to take sides over Greenham Common and the Newbury Bypass.

As his centenary radio talk of 1948 makes clear (it was published as G. Finzi 1949b), Finzi knew his Parry exceptionally well, especially the choral works, the familiar brown covers of whose vocal scores he must have sought out in second-hand shops over the years. And what his critical assessment of Parry shows above all, in addition to a shrewd, balanced, fully informed and sympathetic judgement of the music, is a parallel between Parry and himself of which he can hardly have been unaware. He describes 'two streams' in Parry, 'the Puritan and the man of feeling', the 'romantic . . . fighting Wagner's battles in England' and the Apollonian musician 'look[ing] back to Bach in nineteenth-century terms, in the same way that certain neo-classical works of recent years look back to Bach in twentieth-century terms'. He accepts that the later uniting of the two streams into 'an integrated personality' was not all gain, in that often 'the music suffers from a certain jog-trot quality: in avoiding extremes of emotion it settles down to . . . equability' (G. Finzi 1949b: 5). The parallel is not precise, of course: Finzi's equability was if anything more marked in his early music; his Grand Fantasia, unlike Parry's *Grosses Duo*, placed Bach's image firmly on the romantic end of the mantlepiece; and his *rapprochement* with continental romanticism was the opposite of a youthful indiscretion. Nevertheless, the example Finzi gives of 'that sense of serene well-being which Parry's music can convey' (ibid.: 6) is the ritornello to the chorus 'For everything there is a season' from *Beyond These Voices There Is Peace* of 1908 (ex. 10.1.a and b), and he must have realised that with it many of his readers would immediately smell a rat. 'I know that passage well and remember hearing the rehearsal of what, I believe was the first performance,' Vaughan Williams told him in a letter, further recalling Harford Lloyd on that occasion 'talk in admiration of it to Bantock. He (Bantock) said, rather tentatively it seemed to him to be an imitation of Bach's "Wachet Auf"!' (19500628). Exactly the same model, if not the exclamation mark, has often been proposed in relation to the fifth movement of *Dies natalis* and the 'Aria' of *Farewell to Arms*, but Finzi kept his scholar's and composer's functions separate and never divulged whether he had known the Parry as early as 1925 or was marking a powerful coincidence.

Finzi's voluminous correspondence with Lady Ponsonby gives the

Andante tranquillo espressivo

EX. 10.1.a

EX. 10.1.b

impression that, where attempting to keep Parry before the public was concerned, rather a lot of effort produced relatively little result. 'For everything there is a season' is a case in point, for Finzi attempted unsuccessfully to persuade Novello's to publish it, with an adjusted ending which he supplied himself, as a separate extract for choral use. He and Lady Ponsonby tried various two-pronged attacks, with the odd additional thrust from Vaughan Williams, on Harold Brooke at Novello's, for instance on the question of full scores, reprints and hire material of the choral works, but in the main they had to console themselves with Brooke's philistinism where Parry was concerned. There were long-running but bootless efforts to publish parts for the String Quintet (which Finzi's NSP leader John Kirby performed with colleagues at Exeter College, Oxford in 1955), and Finzi was keen first to locate and then resuscitate the Suite from *The Birds*, realising, with his *Love's Labour's Lost* hat on, the value of its 'charm' and 'good humour' in a genre 'not so much light music as happy and buoyant music' (G. Finzi 1949b: 5), qualities prized also in *The Pied Piper of Hamelin*, which he rightly placed 'among the *very* best' Parry (19550215).

Novello did publish Finzi's string arrangement of Parry's F minor Chorale Fantasia on 'When I survey the wondrous cross', an affecting

Adagio very much in the vein of Bach's chorale prelude 'O Mensch, bewein' dein' Sünde gross' and other essays in contemplative penitence. Finzi was extremely fond of this piece, which has the edge over Parry's other chorale workings in its intensity. Nevertheless, it would be difficult to argue that it possesses any particular string propensities (and his transcription is fairly literal), and one is apt to agree with Vaughan Williams, who 'got bothered' when he heard it because he 'thought it was going to turn into "Rockingham" all the time and it never did!' (19511128b). Overturning associations of words with tunes is a dangerous business, as every organist knows, especially when the composer has also written a lovely meditation on the hymn's standard tune.

As for the Parry manuscripts, Finzi's main labour of love seems to have been to sort a number of them and clear the family house in Kensington Square of autographs and printed scores that had been languishing there for thirty years, whilst taking soundings on how the RCM was dealing with its Parry holdings and becoming familiar with those at Lady Ponsonby's home, Shulbrede Priory. Always on hand to help and advise her, this was a task he and Joy undertook piecemeal over the best part of his final decade, relieved when it looked as though the Bodleian would happily take anything offered it, sketches and all. He was rightly concerned to keep track of particular manuscript works, especially since he feared that in her later years Emily Daymond (who died in 1949) had given bits and pieces to all and sundry – though his safe custody of the autograph of the Third String Quartet ironically led to its being lost for decades after his own death among a pile of his sketches in Joy Finzi's attic (see Dibble 1992: xv–xvi). Such devotion does not make for exciting biography, alas, but deserves recognition. And like those on Gurney's behalf, Finzi's Parry efforts had to continue after his death: to his son Christopher and to Eve Barsham fell the task of collating his prolific and chaotic sketches, following on from work done by Gerald on the music for the Greek plays 'and a number of shorter compositions' (see Crum 1968: 101; Barsham 1960).

Cedric Thorpe Davie's account, the primary one, of how Finzi began to research English eighteenth-century music must be somewhat romanticised:

He rehearsed [the Newbury String Players] weekly throughout the war and beyond, and for him it was work that was kept green by continually finding and playing fresh music. In searching for works that were within their technical capacity he discovered the eighteenth century; gradually the personalities of the composers emerged, and he responded to those whose music he felt to be significant. Opportunity and chance enabled him to build up his collection, and led to the publication of works by Boyce, Stanley, Mudge and Capel Bond. For him, music was a live thing that had to be played, and so he spent all his lunch hours when he worked in the Ministry of War Transport in London, searching in second-hand bookshops and endlessly keeping music alive during the war years when so much that was unfamiliar remained unheard; to him it was a life-line. (1982: iii)

This makes it sound as though the practical exploration of forgotten English composers began during the war. The NSP printed programmes for this period do not survive, but references to the concerts suggest that, inventive though his repertoire had to be from the start (and there was a Boyce symphony in their very first concert), it was until 1946 largely if not entirely a matter of performing what was available in standard format (Bach and Mozart concertos with strings at one end of the chronological spectrum, for instance, the Barber Adagio and Bloch's First Concerto Grosso at the other) and supplementing it with works for which he could obtain a 'modern' score but needed to write out parts or have a colleague such as Busch or Scott do so – string works or movements such as the Nocturne from Fauré's *Shylock* and single numbers from Handel oratorios or Bach cantatas. Nor is there evidence that Finzi even began collecting his Georgian minor masters until after 1945, and though the lunchtime searches in London may well have triggered such antiquarianism, it was obscure eighteenth-century literature, not music, and the poetical works of Isaac Watts that were on his mind in March 1944, when he was wondering whether Milford's father, Sir Humphrey, head of OUP, might consider republishing them.

Or perhaps he had already gathered together a number of volumes but was not quite sure what to do with them, given their inevitable missing parts, problems of realisation, and so on. Real musicology required a leap of confidence that he would not take alone.

He seems to have been on the springboard in March 1946, when he claimed the first modern performance of Purcell's Trumpet Sonata, presumably prepared from the York Minster Library manuscript but almost certainly by the soloist, Bernard Brown, or some third party rather than Finzi. Then, over the course of the next twelve months, it was two other soloists with the orchestra, Ruth Dyson and Mollie

Sands, who helped set him on his scholarly course. In November 1946 a Dyson engagement happened to coincide with a chance comment in a letter from Thorpe Davie, now embarked on his academic career at St Andrews and already having his brain picked by Finzi in more familiar areas of bibliography and scholarship. The manner in which this suddenly opened the floodgates of enthusiasm to release a tide of enterprise is best judged from Finzi's own words. Clearly Davie had said he was making an edition of the Arne concertos but thought that Finzi, with his antiquarian bent, might know something about missing parts. Finzi's response is that of a man joyfully coming out:

Dear Ceddy,

It's really most extraordinary how a number of people get on to the same thing at the same time, unknown to each other. I'm very glad you wrote about the Arne Concertos and will give you a bit of the past history, as far as I am concerned. I have always been on the look out for works for solo instruments and strings. As you know, one gets dreadfully fed up with the inevitable half-dozen concertos which one has to trot out season after season and year after year. A year or two ago I was re-reading Hubert Langley's book on Arne and, finding that we had some mutual friends, I got into touch with him to find out more about the six concertos which he mentions in the bibliography at the end of his book. About the same time I had a professional notice from Ruth Dyson, a young pianist whom I had met at one of VW's concerts at Dorking. The list of works which she submitted was very enterprising and included Arne Concerto No. 5. This I found was not published but existed on hire in an edition done by Julian Herbage. It is scored for strings and two oboes. I liked it so much, when I saw it, that I fixed up a number of performances with her, to the first of which Hubert Langley came. She, meanwhile, at my suggestion, had got in touch with Langley and had borrowed his set of the concertos and was busy re-constituting them – or one or two of them – from the piano score. Langley had no instrumental parts, nor are there any in the British Museum. (I also advertised for a set and managed to get the same piano score that you have, but no parts.) I found out that parts were definitely published, and have been in correspondence with the Bodleian about getting photostats, and I advised Ruth Dyson to hold her hand in her reconstructions till I could get the parts for her . . .

Now, on the very day that Ruth Dyson was staying with us for a performance of No. 5 at a school, your letter arrived. She was very sporting about it and said that she was delighted – the great thing being to get [the] concertos printed and available. I am also glad, more than I can say, because although I intended co-operating with Ruth Dyson and Langley in any way I could, I'm so pressed with other jobs at the moment that I doubt whether I could have got down to the job. In any case I think you would do it better than she or I. (Langley is, of course, an enthusiast but not a musician.) Incidentally I have written off to him to tell him the news so that he can stop anybody else wasting their time on the re-constructions. I do so hope that the OUP will really do the whole set of them and that they will let you do not only an edition, which is a practical performing one, but also one that is, at the same time, correct. In this respect I think their edition of the Boyce Symphonies, which Lambert edited, one of the most valuable contributions in the whole of their catalogue. Not all of them are, perhaps, first rate, but there can hardly be a string orchestra in England that does not make use of them and at least 4 of them are extremely good. In the last few years I have rather changed my mind about a lot of 18th Century stuff – Boyce and Arne in particular – and feel that we have been rather viewing the scene from the wrong hillock, if you know what I mean. So, although I dont think they are *great* works – (and are the bogus cello Haydn & Boccherini great works?) – once one gets back to their idiom and background I think they are extremely delightful works, in the same way that the Haydn D Major piano concerto is *delightful*.

I feel pretty certain that if the OUP publish them there will be the same demand for them (or even more) that there has been for the Boyce Symphonies, even though one or two may not be quite up to the rest. Our own little string orchestra would want scores and parts of the whole lot and they would be an absolute God-send to us, as indeed No. 5 has been, so that we could ring the changes on the [Bach] F minor, D Minor, the Haydn and the Mozart E flat KK449.

I hope the OUP won't omit No. 5, a really delicious work, which players and audience seem to love, just because Goodwin & Tabb circulate the Herbage edition. Not having yet seen a set of parts I don't really know if it is the genuine thing. Oddly enough only the other day I came across a Suite of Boyce pieces which Parry had edited, and I found it hard to get myself into the shoes of such a great man and understand why he should have been so completely insensitive to the period, and I am quite certain that the only sort of edition that is worth having is what Arne wrote; no more and no less, beyond a few dynamics and a few bowing marks. Then the edition is good for ever, and one does not make a fool of oneself as Parry did (in that case).

By the way, one interesting point cropped up, and that was whether cadenzas are wanted in the concertos. Though I am now pretty certain that they are not, when I tried to find out exactly when the virtuoso cadenza entered into the concerto I found it almost impossible. Have you any idea? They were not in JSB (one can't include a measured cadenza such as in Brandenburg No. 5) but they were right there by the time you come to Haydn. Now Haydn was born about the same time as one of Bach's later sons. His earlier son was contemporary with Boyce & Arne, 1710, and I could find no evidences of cadenzas in the 1710 group. Of course we all know about Handel and his cadenzas in the organ concertos, and Howard suggested that we should find our instrumental cadenzas coming from vocal cadenzas which probably first appeared in Italian opera. He thinks I am wrong when I say that it must have made its entrance between JSB and JCB. JSB was essentially north German and untouched by Italian opera and would have been therefore outside the influence of that particular innovation, whereas 'JCB was virtually an Italian composer to whom opera would have been vieux jeux'. Howard suggests that it arose contemporaneously with, or before, JSB. But in Italy since the set up of opera of that time was Italian Handel would have imported [it] into his organ concertos through his own Italian opera. It would therefore have nothing to do with the Mannheim school.

All this, however, is rather beside the point. Personally I am quite satisfied that Arne did not expect cadenzas in these particular concertos. What do you think?

Two other points – if I can't get photostats from the Bodleian – I am not yet certain whether they have the instrumental parts – could I get one made from the St Andrews set? and at the usual library charges? This is in case the OUP don't issue the whole set, as I should certainly want the complete set for myself. Secondly, do you think it would be a nice idea to let Ruth Dyson have the first performance of one of them which she is particularly keen on? . . .

You mention parts for *strings*. Oboes are mentioned in at least one of the concertos (in the short score) though I don't know whether they exist in No. 5 as Herbage's edition implies. (1946111b)

The spirit of the age could hardly be conveyed more clearly. Coming at the point of inauguration of the BBC Third Programme and its first music organiser Anthony Lewis, with an agenda of high seriousness and musical knowledge for its own sake, and when, 'once again, the aftermath of war engendered a renewed commitment to preserving Britain's musical heritage' (Haskell 1995: 525–6), here is the whole musicological bag of tricks and its postwar ethos of positivism that sustained the new British university music departments and their degrees, then just beginning, for forty years thereafter and eventually changed the face of the classical music profession and market: the excitement of 'scientific' collaboration between colleagues; the apparatus of library research, complete with its technological aids and far-flung geographical communication; the sense of a mountain of undiscovered historical knowledge waiting to be quarried; baroque repertoire enhancement as musical wealth creation; proprietorship of first modern performance as personal credit; and the notion of artistic truth in editorial faithfulness to the score and to the performing practice of the composer's own day.

Finzi was well ahead of Thorpe Davie in editorial wisdom, and as usual knew his own mind, awaiting only the opportunity to engage it. 'In 30 years' time you will be held up as a monster of unreliability. The eighteenth century knew perfectly well what it was doing,' he wrote a week later (19461119) after hearing of Thorpe Davie's proposed interventions, a comment repeated in his first published editorial preface; and he continued to advise him on his Arne edition over the next few months.

Meanwhile, the soprano Mollie Sands appeared on his horizon, probably introduced to Finzi by Dyson, her friend and recital partner. She sang groups of songs with the Newbury String Players at a concert in February 1947 and another in May, and since she had written a book on the Ranelagh pleasure gardens (Sands 1946) she was no stranger to the eighteenth-century English repertoire, indeed was already a widely published authority on aspects of it (see Johnstone and Fiske 1990: 511–12). Mutual support and furtherance of research ensued. She sang Lully and Rameau in her first concert, but it was Finzi who suggested that individual songs by Arne and Greene, lacking modern editions, should be included in her second. He outlined the current extent of his knowledge of Boyce:

I'm a great admirer . . . He was a real person with a most distinct individuality. We do most of the Symphonies which Lambert edited & I know the 12 Sonatas for 2 vlns, cello & continuo, which are first rate. The only songs of his I know, apart from the things like 'a song of Momus to Mars' are the 4 books of Lyra Britannica, which I have. (19470222)

He also asked her to consider writing a book comparable with Grattan Flood's on the early Tudor composers – 'short biographical studies which brought entirely new material to light. Why not think of something on similar lines about 18th century chaps, Boyce, Stanley, Avison, Roseingrave (a remarkable fellow) & others?' he suggested (19470504?), throwing out some of the names he would later uphold as 'definite personalities' and not 'mere imitators of Handel' when he started publishing editions (G. Finzi 1949c). On the other hand, it was she who went to the British Museum to check a host of textual details in the Arne and Greene songs against the original sources. Finzi had not yet learnt to darken its doors, it seems.

Had he already a special interest in John Stanley, or did this rub off from Sands? Her knowledge was surely his exemplar, and he was asking her about some of Stanley's manuscript works in May 1947. A year later, however, he could assure her that Stanley's oratorio *Zimri* was published, 'as I have it (Stanley's own copy)' (19480524). The following month he was asking her all kinds of questions about him (see 19480601a), presumably because he had finally bitten the musicological bullet and was preparing for publication a performing edition of the third of Stanley's 'Six Concerto's in Seven Parts' of 1742, a work which by now was in the NSP repertoire, 'scored from an early set of published parts [and] singularly refreshing' (ibid.). It was published by Boosey & Hawkes in 1949, competently edited with an introduction by Finzi fully accordant with up-to-date attitudes towards performance practice, though he still expected 'the pianoforte' to have to tackle the continuo part (G. Finzi 1949c) and put the original dynamics rather than his editorial ones in brackets. Curiously, for one who had always kept his efforts on behalf of others, however integrated into his own intellectual portfolio, as free as possible from any taint of self-publicity, Boosey veered to the opposite extreme and issued this and his later editions in a format uniform with that of his compositions, listing it as one of them. Perhaps no one can escape a touch of vanity sooner or later. His publisher even went as far as taking a revised version of Finzi's Royal Musical Association paper on Stanley, presented in May 1951 with Frank Howes in the chair, as an article in *Tempo* ('a quarterly review of modern music'!) in 1953 (see G. Finzi 1950–1 and 1953).

The RMA opportunity, graced with generous live musical examples, must have been a welcome outlet for its author, though Finzi baulked at exhibiting too many of his own antiquarian treasures on that occasion through the 'fear that this would make it into something like a parson talking about the Zenana mission, with pictures of groups of natives, mission houses in Africa etc' (19510421). The paper itself is a fine piece of work, lucid of prose and argument and, like his Parry assessment, extremely well informed and judiciously balanced. As with his later Crees Lectures, he puts his listeners and readers singularly at ease in a witty and allusive preamble – a touch of Tovey, perhaps, or testimony to many hours spent imbibing the eighteenth-century essay tradition. He highlights the Op. 2 concertos, particularly their fine fugues and formal originality (Stanley was fond of movements that alternated allegro and adagio sections), but is also fully alive to Stanley's vocal music. And he has this to say in general about the eighteenth-century solo cantata: that it 'carried within it the seeds of perfection,' being 'equally suitable for lyrical or dramatic expression' with its 'unity of subject-matter . . . conveyed in diversity of vocal treatment, the recitative, either stromentato or secco, and the aria' (G. Finzi 1950–1: 69). He might be describing his own *Farewell to Arms* or one of the Hardy songs.

The Stanley concertos were a joy forever to Finzi. He came to possess eighteenth-century copies of all three of their versions – for strings, keyboard and strings, and flute and harpsichord – and in time edited the whole set for Boosey, completing the series in 1955. The NSP played them, and after his death Christopher Finzi conducted the orchestra in a private recording of Nos. 1–4, with John Russell on organ continuo and strong solo violin and cello playing from Nigel Finzi and Anna Shuttleworth. (The first concertino violin part far outshines the second in Stanley's conception, and while the cello also has some prominent solo work, particularly in No. 2, it has been suggested that he was really writing organ concertos – see Holman 1989.) The performance style is typical of an informed approach of its time, and of, say, Boyd Neel's sound though with amateur allowances: clean but fruity, it employs plenty of middle, lively but stolid tempi (with massive cadential *ritardandi*), rather uncherished upper-note trills, little rhythmic assimilation and no unwritten ornamentation. The continuo realisations are simple, which is how Finzi liked them – so that he could write them in the car.

Finzi's other eighteenth-century godchildren were Boyce, Capel Bond (1730–90), John Garth (*c.*1722–*c.*1810), Richard Mudge (1718–63) and, somewhat later in date than these, Charles Wesley (1757–1834), brother of Samuel and nephew of John. Bond, Mudge and Garth were all obscure provincials, which no doubt constituted part of their appeal to Finzi, and they published one set of six concertos each in mid-century (in Mudge's case, virtually his only known work). All six of Garth's concertos are for cello, unusual at that time, while Mudge and Bond varied their solo instrumentation, each including a trumpet concerto of which Finzi published an edition. Garth was a friend of Avison, with whom he developed an indigenous form of trio sonata (see Sadie 1990: 346–8), and lived in County Durham. Bond was born in Gloucester but worked as organist to the city churches of Coventry and as a general musical force in the Midlands, conducting the first Birmingham Festival in 1768, which included a performance (by Mr Adcock, of Vauxhall Gardens) of his Trumpet Concerto in what is now Birmingham Cathedral (see Handford 1992: 27). He must surely have known Mudge, a cleric at nearby Great Packington and Bedworth and son of a friend of Samuel Johnson, and Peter Holman (1992: 5) points out the influence of the one trumpet concerto upon the other.

They do have individual personalities, and Bond is as delightful when he is attempting to be *galant* in the Bassoon Concerto (No. 6), while betraying at the same time a curiously rustic touch of country dance in his second movement (ex. 10.2.a), as Mudge, always earnestly high baroque, is impressive when he is showing his 'serious and philosophical mind' (G. Finzi 1954c). Bond and Mudge both command suave contrapuntal energy and Handelian continuity, which makes them good at fugues, the second movement of Mudge's Concerto No. 4 being a particularly fine example, resourcefully using a three-note stepwise motif in retrograde and diminution amongst other treatments (ex. 10.2.b) as well as for a brisk and imaginative ending. Mudge's Organ Concerto (No. 6) also packs a formal punch when its opening F major toccata leads with an almost Hardyesque darkening of the mental landscape straight into an F minor Largo; at the end of this work, 'quite

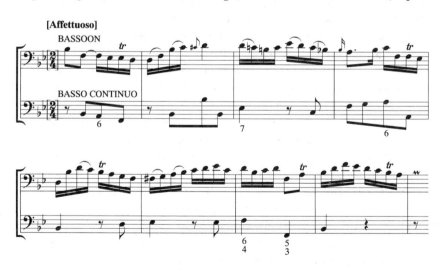

EX. 10.2.a

411

EX. 10.2.b

exceptionally, three voices join in with the canon "Non nobis Domine" formerly attributed to Byrd' (McGuinness and Johnstone 1990: 61), though Finzi's edition does not treat it as part of the concerto and omits it. Garth has turned the corner into classical ease and balance in his concerto form, and writes a surprisingly extended finale in the B♭ concerto (No. 2).

Wesley, as member of a formidably eminent family, was a rather different case from the others, but he fitted perfectly Finzi's theory of the value of early lyricism: 'genius faded into mediocrity' was his simple diagnosis (1953c). A pupil of Boyce publishing an opus dedicated to his master at the age of twenty-one was bound to earn Finzi's affection, especially when it was in a naïve idiom (part *galant*, part 'obstinate[ly] Handelian' as Samuel Wesley put it) and suitable for amateurs, '[string quartet] players who are making their way towards Haydn and Mozart' (ibid.). Finzi and Hinrichsen between them got as far as issuing Quartets Nos. 2, 5, and 1. Of these tiny works, each ending with a slightly earnest minuet suggesting that the young man had yet to test his charms in the ballroom, No. 2 with its fugue and wealth of suspensions shows the quaint persistence of 'Georgian survival' most obviously, and like everything the Wesleys did this seems peculiarly English, with a kind of innocent perversity in what it takes or leaves from continental fashion and revolution. The one concerto Finzi edited, No. 4 in C major from Wesley's Op. 2 published in 1781, is more completely *galant* or classical in its style, though not in the form of its first movement, which keeps harking back to baroque ritornello structures. It is a cheerful piece that makes one wish for the rest of the set.

It is clear from Joy's journal entries that publishing and performing these pieces gave Gerald enormous gratification in his final years and probably meant as much to him as his own compositions. They brought new friends with them, too. Scholars such as Thurston Dart, Stanley Sadie and Charles Cudworth came to Ashmansworth to use his eighteenth-century library (which included some scores Parry had owned), and he picked their brains. Prominent performers were enlisted for the concertante works. 'Concertos for solo bassoon and strings are rare enough at all times,' he wrote in his posthumous Preface to Bond's No. 6, 'and it would be hard to say where, in the whole repertory, a more charming example can be found, or how bassoonists could have lost sight of it for some century and a half' (G. Finzi 1957a). This one earned him the acquaintance of William Waterhouse, who gave its first modern performance with the NSP on 27 February 1955. A few hours later, that same evening, the Finzis tuned in to the Third Programme to hear from the studio not only the first performance of *In terra pax* but 'Stanley No. 1, Boyce "Now shall soft charity repair" & the magnificent Mudge No. 4: all G's discoveries,' as Joy proudly wrote (J. Finzi 19550227). Sadly he did not live to edit and publish all six times six concertos and quartets of his protégés, but he would have been pleased to know how satisfactorily a complete set can now sit on a compact disc, though not many of them currently do.

Finzi published two other Stanley editions, both modest though discriminating choices: the fifth of his *Six Solo's for a German flute*, Op. 4 (Rudall, Carte, 1954), actually a lively three-movement suite from a highly distinguished set (see Johnstone 1990: 182–3), and 'Welcome Death' (Hinrichsen, 1953) from the unperformed opera *Teraminta*, a bass aria which was in the repertoire of John Carol Case and the NSP and Finzi thought of as 'a sort of eighteenth century "When I am laid in earth" ' (1950–1: 72), a comparison that flatters it somewhat. (In his RMA paper, Finzi was the first to discuss the question of whether or not *Teraminta* is by Stanley; see also Sands 1952, Williams 1979 and Gillespie 1983.) Both must have afforded pleasant relaxation, as must his unpublished practical editions of individual Stanley arias extracted from longer works.

Editing Boyce's *Overtures* for *Musica Britannica*, however, was another matter. Boyce's claim on Finzi's attention had been growing since about 1950, principally on account of two important portions of his instrumental output. The twelve published violin trio sonatas of 1747, 'in freshness and vitality ... unsurpassed in British chamber music of the period', had been 'far and away the most successful English musical publication of the [eighteenth] century' (Johnstone 1990:

179–80) but lacked a modern edition (Finzi possessed a copy of the original one). On the orchestral front, twice as many overtures (or symphonies) again as Boyce himself had extracted from vocal works for publication as his *Eight Symphonies* (1760) and *Twelve Overtures* (1770) lay unexhumed as autograph manuscripts in the Bodleian, coming principally from the Birthday and New Year Odes he was obliged to compose as Master of the King's Band of Musicians from 1755 until his death in 1779 and had begun to quarry for the *Twelve Overtures*. Finzi discovered these, and probably had his first proper brush with antiquarian manuscript sources in libraries, after a lengthy and unsuccessful library quest for the second trumpet part of the *Twelve Overtures* had led him first to Leslie Bridgewater. (Bridgewater was musical director of the Shakespeare Memorial Theatre at Stratford and purveyor of huge amounts of light and theatre music, but Finzi discovered to his astonishment that he not only possessed an [incomplete] set of the published overtures but was a closet serialist: 'In private,' Joy wrote, 'he practices studies in twelve-tone scale music & showed G exercise books full of notes & some good specimens of this school – as well as analyses of works such as the Schoenberg piano concerto, bar by bar, which showed that he really understood the idiom. Rather a revelation...' [J. Finzi 19520124].) Finzi then visited the Bodleian, ordered up a shelf number, and found himself 'faced with a complete truck, with 50 manuscript volumes of Odes 50 ditto of original parts and 50 ditto of vocal parts' (19520123). Here, then, were the originals of the *Twelve Overtures*, missing parts and all, and so much else besides that Finzi felt 'despair at the amount of [Boyce's] music which lies unpublished' (J. Finzi 19520213) and began frantically working on it, to the point of reviving several of the overtures with the NSP over the coming year or two. He realised, as Boyce had, that there was little or no future in the vocal portions of the Odes – 'for all the words are rubbish' – but felt a great responsibility towards the composer's reputation as a whole: 'it is a dreadful thing that such a figure regarded in his lifetime as second only to Handel & thro' whose work a great personality exudes, shd remain unpublished & well nigh unrecognised except for a piece here & there' (ibid.).

Meanwhile he had pointed Herbert Murrill, a fellow eighteenth-century enthusiast, encouragingly and instructively in the direction of appropriate realisations of the Arne and Boyce trio sonatas, and having despatched the Arne ones, placing them with Hinrichsen as and when the publisher was able to take them (most of the seven had appeared by 1960), Murrill had begun to tackle Boyce's on the same basis. So when Anthony Lewis asked Finzi in February 1954 if he would edit the complete Boyce trio sonatas for *Musica Britannica* he explained that he could not very well do so in competition with Hinrichsen, for although Murrill had since died, leaving only one so far in print, Hinrichsen was still intending to issue the remainder. 'So Mus Brit idea is to give Hinrichsen a year or two to see if he continues as he says he wants to,' Joy noted, '& then if no more are issued to issue them in Mus Brit . . . meanwhile the proposal is that G shd do a volume of the Boyce MSS overtures in the Bodleian. G knows these Overt[ures] pretty well' (J. Finzi 19540218). No more of the trio sonatas did appear in Murrill's edition, and Finzi's own death prevented his having anything further to do with them. Stanley Sadie eventually took over the Hinrichsen sequence, but they are still not all in print.

The volume of overtures was not officially signed up until December 1954. Finzi was proud to be part of the *Musica Britannica* venture – 'The Concert Hall & "*Musica Britannica*" will be about the best long-term things to come out of the whole affair,' he had told Lady Ponsonby about the Festival of Britain (19510517a) – but daunted by the amount of work involved, even though it was textually a straightforward job, with immaculate autograph scores and parts to work from and little in the way of further manuscript or published sources to collate. He relied heavily on Christopher, who did all the copying (from photostats) and was pressed ruthlessly over it, but the checking and editorial commentaries (G. Finzi 1957b) were Gerald's sole responsibility, the Preface a challenge that 'meant revision & revision,' for 'as with all G's writing . . . the shape grows slowly with continual re-working' (J. Finzi 19560130). All in all 'the continuo parts & constant research & the following-up of every clue, checking of various copies, comparing original parts with the score & . . . much correspondence' kept him away from composition for six months, and although Lewis had wanted copy by the autumn of 1955 it was February 1956 before Joy could record: 'We celebrated the finish of the . . . Volume . . . (Kiffer had brought home the last of the 20 overtures he had copied) & drank to Boyce . . . A good job done & a good deed done for a great man characteristically neglected for nearly 200 years' (J. Finzi 19560211, 19560130). After this it was a relief to return to creative work – to his late Hardy songs, if not to the orchestration of the Magnificat – but even then he did not deliver all the finished material to Lewis until April, for the Preface needed further rewriting and the volume was too long. Two overtures, including that belonging to the Ode to Charity, had to be omitted.

It was a fine achievement, and one can take pride in the fact that Finzi was the first but not the only British composer versatile and altruistic enough to salute his heritage professionally within the series – Geoffrey Bush is another. No one but he could have spotted, in a footnote, a reference that links Boyce and Hardy. Sadly, however, he never lived to see the volume in print, and because until recently *Musica Britannica* did not publish parts, these overtures have continued to lag badly behind Boyce's others in diffusion and popularity, despite being in no sense bottom-drawer material (see G. Finzi 1957b: xv–xvi).

It may seem odd to have left consideration of Finzi's lectures about words and music (G. Finzi 1955), mostly on English song, almost until last in this chapter, but the fact is that given his already-quoted belief that a good classical composer's word-setting just comes 'natural-like' they are of less importance than might be expected in illuminating his own compositional choices and neither theoretical enough to have made a contribution to any particular scholarly discipline – aesthetics, history of style, melopoetics, musical analysis – nor sufficiently self-centred to be the key confessions of a composer. Finzi was perfectly well aware of this, and in any case had the good sense to know that no overall pronouncements upon the subject have ever done much good, quoting Robert Bridges' 'if it has not been given to me to assist in solving [the question] practically, I cannot venture to meddle with it further' (:II, 18). His talks' advertising flyer similarly assured the reader that the aspects of the subject to be treated would 'leave the birds still singing and Pilate's question unanswered', and he disconnected a further potential circuit of electricity on the very first page of the first lecture when he said that 'the little one knows of one's own methods of work are too personal to be any guide to the processes of others', though he did rather coyly refer to himself in the third lecture when he stated that 'some composers have never written a song or a choral work without at least a line being instantaneously matched with a musical equivalent on the very first reading of the words' (:6).

Those – presumably most – in his audience who already knew his music but not necessarily the man could live with this, and must have marvelled not just at the characteristically fair-minded coverage and common sense Finzi evinces, but at the breadth and, in a connoisseur's sense, profundity of his learning, in which respect the lectures are a superb tribute to his library irrespective of their further value. But it is not entirely clear on whose behalf he is otherwise communicating, and one misses the tenacious development of an argument or real programme of research that would have made him more than an occasional speaker except on his beloved eighteenth century. Many of his points we have already encountered in this book, in his correspondence or in Joy's journal, and there is a danger that they would have gone from being salient perceptions to hobbyhorses had he exercised them many more times. Already in the Crees Lectures his lifeline arguments about not confusing idiom with quality and about the change wrought on reputations by fashion are on the verge of speciousness, and they were due for a further airing two years later (see Chapter 11).

Nevertheless, as a characteristic *aide-mémoire* of Finzi's various concerns and influences, with more than a touch of his putative *Desert Island Discs* in the references and illustrations (performed by Norman Tattersall, Kenneth Byles, Gaynor Lewis, Valda Plucknett and Roy Teed), the lectures are stylish, engaging and highly civilised. His first one outlined the various problems and perspectives that the subject arouses; the second was a refutation of V. C. Clinton-Baddeley's *Words for Music* (1941) with its preference for the lyric as melopoetic craft over the poem as subject matter for the composer's discourse, and thus an expansion of his 'bilge & bunkum' complaint; the third looked at composers' stylistic traditions and their aesthetic implications but also, to his credit, at 'music for words' – the adding of words to pre-existent music, including translations (with a live example of *Blest Pair of Sirens* in German or Italian).

Parry, and Stanford perhaps even more, come out of it all very well; Elgar is shunned, not for musical style but for poetic susceptibility. The sixteenth-century musical renaissance is a fixed point but rather underplayed, the eighteenth century kept in conscious restraint though frequently referred to (and Finzi manages to get in a bit of research on Felton). The nineteenth century is surprisingly prominent, often in derogation but from an impressive vantage-point of knowledge, not excluding Italy on the one hand and Victorian divines on the other (a highly sublimated consciousness of family, possibly). Gurney is treated at greater length than any other figure, in the section on the 'divine madness' of artistic lyricism 'usually associated with the earlier years of life' (:II, 6); this is understandable, since it was Finzi's only real chance to write about him. Hardy is avoided altogether, a rather regrettable instance of decorum but one practically unavoidable without bringing in his own music. Modern English song is summarised without reference to Finzi. Yeats and music, Housman and music, and Bridges and music are all well represented, and one feels a research article coming on where Bridges is concerned. Schubert hovers in the background, perhaps a more significant lodestar for Finzi than has hitherto been accounted for; Ravel and French song's syllabic traditions are respected, perhaps even loved, whereas Italian *bel canto* is paid lip-service only, and Edward Sackville-West's 'long, sinuous, rhetorical Italian line' twice becomes Finzi's bugbear, explicitly because in English music it represents 'an un-natural graft on to a language which is primarily consonantal' (:I, 8; :III, 2) but implicitly because it stands for Britten, who is accorded a few polite words but, pointedly, no musical example, whereas Tippett is represented without prejudice in an example from *The Midsummer Marriage* (only three months old at the time) and Stravinsky not too uncharitably with part of *The Rake's Progress*.

One cannot imagine anyone else having done the lectures better, and even forty years on it would probably take a university course to find a match for Finzi's bibliographic adroitness. Opera is an obvious blind spot, though not sufficiently acknowledged as such, and these days the whole argument would have to be opened out with full consideration of popular, mediaeval and vernacular music – one rather feels he views Clinton-Baddeley from the wrong hillock, to coin his own phrase – though to give Finzi his due, he recognises the popular muse to the extent of dealing briefly with the accentual cross-rhythms of Tin Pan Alley, even if folksong is despatched (as a nineteenth-century vernacular phenomenon) with surprising cursoriness. Just once, however, Finzi seems to lower his scholar's guard and historian's equanimity and in a rather sad allusion near the end of the third lecture refers to Henry Vaughan's 'picture of those living with the idiom of their early days and finding discordancy in all new things around them', doubtless thinking of Boyce but also perhaps opening a brief window on that 'fundamental pessimism' that Ferguson identified in Finzi and showing us that the courage to be himself occasionally failed him and gave way to simple sadness at being out of step with the times. In his Boyce preface (1957b: xv) he was soon to quote Hawkins's comment, that 'having thus experienced the vitiated taste of the public, Dr Boyce abandoned the thoughts of giving to the world any more of his works'. What were his thoughts as he struggled not only with this last lecture but with the last movement of his last major work, the Cello Concerto?

Apart from the Howells article in the *Musical Times*, referred to in Chapter 3, and an eightieth birthday one on Vaughan Williams written for a more general readership (1954a and 1952), Finzi's remaining writings do not amount to much. There are one or two reviews and letters to newspapers, and a slight treatment of his favourite theme of the importance of environment (1950a). The *Oxford Guardian* guest editorial (1950b) was a dummy run for the Crees Lectures. The 'Critic on the air' script (1948) offers a rare view of Finzi reacting to a week's general broadcasting of classical music regardless of his own agenda. He hated doing this, but took it seriously (despite the date) and did it very well. The Vaughan Williams article is authoritative and keen to strike a balance between obvious fact and timely perception, as also between national pride and universality, though the fact that no discussion of Vaughan Williams has yet managed to avoid these terms of reference, however carefully it adjusts them, is itself something of a stumbling-block, perhaps one never to be overcome. Finzi does not quite avoid the author's trap of wanting to have his subject neatly tied up when he refers to 'the three later symphonies' (:65), as though he rather resented Vaughan Williams going on to write yet more. Indeed, his private comments and Joy's often give the strong impression that they felt he should have retired at 80 and were primly suspicious or disapproving of his new lease of life with Ursula as though it bordered on the irresponsible. However much the two couples enjoyed each other's company, there was a certain tension between Gerald and Ursula which probably reflects this. Gerald never accepted the *Antartica* as a symphony, was not unduly enthusiastic about No. 8 and never lived to hear No. 9, though much of it was written in his own music room after his death.

And the apples? The point about the crusade is that, rather as with folksongs, many of the 6,000 indigenous varieties had been squeezed out by international commercial pressures from the late nineteenth century onwards: as the Dominions increased their specialised export crops to Britain, British growers' only way of competing was to 'concentrate their efforts on a handful of good commercial varieties' as small, market-garden producers and the country-house culture that had produced the heyday of the English apple in Victorian times declined

(Morgan and Richards 1993: 96). The rescuers that this trend eventually threw up – the Baring-Gould, Lucy Broadwood and Cecil Sharp of pomology, if you like – were 'the nurseryman and connoisseur Edward Bunyard; his protégé J. M. S. Potter, the Royal Horticultural Society's Fruit Officer; and the scholar and linguist Morton Shand' (ibid.). Bunyard died in 1939, but Finzi must have known Potter and certainly had dealings with Shand, a remarkable if not very personable man in Finzi's own multidisciplinary image: scholar, linguist, and published expert on French wines and modern architecture.

Morgan and Richards (1993: 100–1) suggest that it was Shand's BBC radio broadcast in 1944 that turned the tide of conservation with lightning-flashes of recognition, conscience and fervour from Finzi and one or two others, including Leslie Martin, architect of the Royal Festival Hall. One can see why when they quote his stirring rhetoric, coming at a time when the whole of English culture was still fighting for its survival in the war and English cuisine and home-grown food were perforce at a premium:

What would the future be without the sort of apples that are part of the very stuff of the English countryside and its cherished local traditions? The apples men of Norfolk and Devon used to swear by, or that were honoured names to generations of Herefordshire, Somerset, Kent and Sussex yeomen farmers.

But if Finzi was so inspired by the broadcast as to write and 'offer his help immediately' (ibid.), he had nonetheless already been flexing a connoisseur's muscles on the old varieties for several years, as letters to his landed friends, particularly Toty de Navarro, make clear:

My pomological queries are rather urgent, so do please ask your curator! I had hoped that somewhere round about you might be an obscure fruit nursery where all these odd sort of non-commercial trees cd be obtained. I get as much pleasure from apple tasting, with these infinite varieties, as you do from gentian fatherhood! It's disastrous the way old slow bearing varieties are gradually being shoved out of existence by the inevitable C O pippins & Laxtons Superb. Both are wonderful apples, but a single D'arcy Spies, Court Pendu Plat, Orleans Reinette, Margil; Wyken Pippin, Claygate permain, Adams Permain, Sturmer, Ribston etc etc shd be in every orchard, if they only give a few pounds in a year, just for the joy of variety. (19421013a)

This was written the day after he had given Vaughan Williams 'the very largest apple ever seen' (U. Vaughan Williams 1964: 250), presumably from a tree in their garden, for his seventieth birthday. Navarro, who in the course of time graduated from a gentian enthusiast to one of the chief daffodil-growers in the country, was clearly his partner in crime where this kind of hobby was concerned, but the crucial impetus had probably stemmed from Justin Brooke during the Aldbourne years. Brooke, a highly valued older friend – 'more like Cobbett than ever,' Joy wrote in 1940 (J. Finzi 19400404) – and yet another country gentleman of multifarious scholarly leisure, had originated the Marlowe Society with Rupert Brooke and Francis Cornford and lived at Clopton Hall in Suffolk, near Gerald's mother, who perhaps facilitated the initial contact. He named a new apple variety, Clopton Red, after his house in 1946, and soon after the Finzis had moved to Ashmansworth in 1939 Gerald had sent his gardener William Sampson to Brooke to study his fruit-growing methods.

Finzi's collection eventually ran to about 300–400 trees, including some pears and quinces, planted around the house, against considerable expanses of boundary and kitchen-garden wall (the latter enclosing a nursery area), and in the two orchards, Church and New Pond, that adjoined the grounds. Gerald's plans survive, together with a typed, annotated index to his varieties that lists nearly 300 different ones, most of them sporting only one tree. He would have lived to see most of them fruit but not reach full size; indeed, many of them never did reach full size, for he – or his gardener Jack Theyer, who replaced Sampson in 1949 – tended to plant them too close together, and exposed at 700 feet on chalk capped with heavy clay and flint the site was a hopeless one for apple orchards. Nevertheless, he was able to help the Royal Horticultural Society and commercial nurseries such as John Scott of Merriott, Somerset, further their stock with his repropagation of some of the endangered rare varieties, which was the point of the exercise. He also scoured his friends' – and strangers' – gardens and orchards for venerable old trees and had them send him specimens of fruit so that he could get them officially identified, or let him take scions for propagation. Whether he ever found a 'missing' variety in this manner is not clear.

But almost all of Finzi's trees have now gone, which adds a final note of melancholy to an otherwise positivistic story of research and achievement. Perhaps that is as it should be; 'life is flux', and too many memorials are not a good thing.

CHAPTER 11

Time's wingèd chariot

In November 1951 Joy Finzi recommenced her journal, which she had kept sporadically between 1936 and 1945. Her first new entry was '*Nov. 15th* Finished slow movement of cello concerto', but the heading above it explains why she would maintain regular entries from now on: 'After the verdict & 1st course of X-ray treatment'. Time was running out for Gerald and for their marriage.

Earlier in the year Finzi had revised *Absalom's Place* and added a postscript, this time quoting Chideock Tychborne's lines written on the eve of his execution:

Since the preceding pages were written, ten years ago, a good deal more work has been written. Performances, publication & some kindly or generous notice, have all taken place, which I hope my development has justified.

But a serious, & possibly fatal, illness has now been confirmed by the Doctors. At 49 I feel I have hardly begun my work

> My thread is cut, and yet it is not spun;
> And now I live, and now my life is done.

As usually happens, it is likely that new ideas, new fashions & the pressing forward of new generations, will soon obliterate my small contribution. Yet I like to think that in each generation may be found a few responsive minds, and for them I shd still like the work to be available. To shake hands with a good friend over the centuries is a pleasant thing, and the affection which an individual may retain after his departure is perhaps the only thing which guarantees an ultimate life to his work.

Gerald Finzi
June 1951

He was suffering from Hodgkin's Disease (lymphadenoma), technically registered on his death certificate as lymphoid-follicular reticulosis and variously described as lymphoma (cancer of the lymph nodes) and leukaemia (a condition of the blood caused by the lymphoma). Then, as now, radiotherapy was the treatment, and then, as now, the patient's future was uncertain, though it has become less so. Not unlike AIDS, Hodgkin's Disease suppresses the immune system and offers the body less or no resistance to opportunistic infections (such as chicken pox). Possibly after the first course of radiation treatment had failed to destroy the lymphatic growths, Finzi was given at the most ten years to live.

Joy and Gerald bravely decided to tell no one outside the immediate family (which meant Christopher, Nigel and Lizzie), though Ferguson points out that a surprisingly large number of people did come to know about Finzi's illness, and that he himself heard the news from Tony Scott. Occasionally the mask slipped or a hint was dropped, as when Ben Frankel found out about the lymphoma by chance when discussing a similar case with Gerald. John Carol Case was told 'I'm afraid there won't be time' when he asked Finzi to write him a *Dies natalis* for baritone. Mags's niece, a nurse, spotted the radiation marks and knew. Olive Theyer, the home help, was confidentially told by Joy. In January 1956, sympathising with Bruno Thorpe Davie's radiotherapy and its after-effects (she had cancer), Gerald wrote to Cedric:

one must be very patient with anyone who has had intimations, even if not real ones, of death, and who from being a 'well' person finds themselves on the other side of the curtain amongst the ill and sick. It's a horrible experience which the 'well' find difficult to understand. (19560111a)

He could, of course, have been referring to his suspected TB of 1928.

Though it was not the first time Gerald had kept hidden something fairly momentous, the secrecy must have added an appalling strain to circumstances requiring the utmost courage, and we can only guess at the measure of both that were his and Joy's portion. Nor can we know what structures of feeling the mind invented to encompass the situation. Did Gerald accept the Hardyesque irony of the slow developer's shortage of time, by which he had always felt pursued, suddenly becoming so brutal a reality just at the point when he felt he was beginning to catch up with himself? After his early losses, TB scare and wartime pressures, was he already half expecting it? Was he able to maintain his agnostic rationalism, or did he begin to feel *punished* for his happy life and watertight identity, for his secluded, self-regulated pattern and pace of work, or for the prodigality of his multifarious interests and activities? Were his comforts and luxuries now demanding their price?

All that we can be sure of is that outwardly Gerald and Joy steered an extraordinarily positive, controlled course through their last five years together. Whether his intense productivity – not so much in composition alone but in its combination with scholarship, performance, social intercourse, lecturing and examining – was because he had by now reached a plateau of technique and energy that would coast along at this rate in any case, or because he dared not stop to think about his fate, is again unanswerable. One marvels at the energy all the more since he was being driven by Joy to the Radcliffe Infirmary in Oxford for weekly radiotherapy during a great deal of this final period. He dreaded these visits, and they not only took up time but caused subsequent lassitude and discomfort, sometimes to the point of vomiting; but perhaps they provided a routine of passivity, not to mention hope, to which he willingly submitted. He began to combine them with trips to the Bodleian to edit Boyce, which also gave him an alibi when friends were around.

Quiet acceptance undoubtedly masked quiet desperation, and when his blood count precluded further treatment in October 1953 and he was told he would later have to have his spleen removed, Joy even persuaded Gerald to undergo radiesthesia, a mysterious alternative treatment administered weekly (again in Oxford, but apparently also at a distance) by the appropriately named Mrs Ray, at least until mid-1954. No one can say whether it made any difference to his health, but it must have made a difference to their bank balance, not being available under the National Health Service. So must the private hospital bed they booked when Gerald had to have his spleen removed in January 1955. Their finances cannot have been eased much in the early 1950s, and in May 1952 Ferguson asked the BBC on his behalf why his PRS broadcasting returns had fallen to a quarter of their level of a year or two earlier (19520524). Gerald's dealings with his publishers also became decidedly prickly later in the year over royalty arrangements and the pricing of his editions.

They probably received good, reliable care overall at the Radcliffe from their consultant, Professor Leslie Witts, and Frank Ellis, the radiotherapist. Both newcomers, both were also remarkable, dedicated and distinguished men (see Burroughs 1978: 77–81, 152–3). Moreover,

Neville Finzi was on hand for an authoritative second opinion. In January 1953, for instance, Joy wrote in her journal: 'On Neville's advice & somewhat against Ellis's, but because of his admiration for Neville, they are going to treat glands inside the rib cage which show abnormal size.' It was also notwithstanding a Health Authority blunder of latter-day proportions when they returned from a holiday at Abbotsbury in October 1954 to find 'a highly embarrassing letter addressed to Professor Witts by Dr Ellis at our address,' as Joy explained:

as there were about 40 letters in a pile we did not notice the name & that it was wrongly addressed. This gave Ellis's confidential opinion about G – 'going downhill very rapidly'. G consulted Tom Scott as to whether to forward the letter or whether it wd embarrass them too much or get the sec into trouble & Tom, as a doctor, advised us to destroy the letter & say nothing about it. (J. Finzi 19541025–29)

She does not record what their feelings were.

The general pattern was of periods of radiotherapy on the spleen and on the enlarged glands in his neck, groin and stomach, under his arms, and inside the rib cage, followed by longer periods during which his blood count recovered and they waited to see whether swelling would return. The first course of treatment was in mid-1951, but by December the news was not good:

To Oxford for another examination. It was disappointing to find the glands again active. One had hoped that the quick reaction to the first course of X-ray & the ensuing fitness [meant] that by some miracle they were laid low for some time. Had two treatments on the spleen. Went to tea with Percy Scholes. A man with a dry sense of humour & a wonderful musical library indexed & cross-referenced in a wonderful method. (J. Finzi 19511212)

Further treatment followed, and Joy noted: 'G sleeping badly: the menacing awareness of the possible shortness of time left.' 'Dark days' followed, though by mid-January Witts was 'very pleased with G's reaction to the ray treatment', explained that they were 'working on this process as they feel it may be an intermediary condition to cancer', and ordered a respite of three months, barring fresh symptoms. The three months turned to six and longer as the glands remained dormant – 'How wonderful if one had got the better of them' – though optimism was tempered: 'this does happen in some cases & after a dormant period it re-appears. Nevertheless it's a breather ... every month is a precious asset in time' (J. Finzi 19511227, 19520103, 19520114, 19520407, 19520721).

Sudden swellings in the groin, however, in September 1952, soon put an end to this period of hope, and spirits sank as new areas of concern became apparent:

[At the Radcliffe] G mentioned Neville Finzi's use of oblique X-ray in invest-igating interior of rib cage. This Ellis had never done, on second thoughts he took G over to X-ray department to have this done... The X ray showed shadow on left side which has not yet been sufficiently clearly defined to determine treatment. Why had not this been done as routine & only as a result of chance remark! Tom says there is a seat of glands in rib cage which shows sign of enlargement – and we suppose this is the shadow. How long have they been enlarged? Ellis is away next fortnight in Denmark – on his return he will deal with this condition.

G tired & down. 'That I of all people should have to die so soon, when I have the seeds of growth in me'. (J. Finzi 19520905, 19520911)

They showed the X-rays to Neville Finzi over lunch in October. It was apparently the first time Joy had met him, and probably Gerald's first adult reunion, and they found him 'most interesting'. But while 'some doubt had arisen over interpretation' of these photographs it was soon time to combat the neck swellings again, at Christmas 1952. This time Gerald's physical response was less robust, with 'sickness & mouldiness' (J. Finzi 19521011, 195210, 19521222). Rib cage treatment began the following month, and a clue to Gerald's understandably fatalistic cast of mind, unable as he was to forget that he had been under sentence of death once before with tuberculosis, is afforded by Joy's journal entry for 22 January: 'G dreaded this, fearing that it might stir up all his old trouble. His cough ... has made him sleep badly.' One wonders whether the cough was therefore psychosomatic. 'Indigestion & heart-burn' followed further rib cage treatment, but a consultation with Witts in March showed 'knowledge of the illness ... still where it was, G just about stationary'. 'It's always re-assuring to see Witts on matters of guidance & experience,' Joy added, 'but there is really nothing he can do' (J. Finzi 19530216, 19530302).

The next bout of treatment, between August and October 1953, led to the splenectomy prospect – 'a great shock to G who did not realise he had got to that stage' (J. Finzi 19531015) – but much of 1954 passed before it became necessary, to Gerald's relief whenever he went for a consultation. However, radiotherapy had to begin again in September: 'Things not satisfactory & the glands all up.' He was 'very mouldy as a result' and after two more sessions was 'unable to do anything during the week' (J. Finzi 19540923, 19541007). He was now failing to respond and in November the doctors took him into hospital to try drugs and observe his overall condition instead, as Joy explained:

Sunday Nov 28th G to Radcliffe Hospital . . . very depressed inspite of the beautiful sister in charge. The intention was to give him a drug known as TEM which has the same effect as X-rays, but over the whole lymphatic glandular system at once. It is therefore rather dangerous & lowers the blood count in the same way as X-rays. G was to stay a week, but after various blood tests, a sternum puncture a barium meal & X-rays they let him go after 3 days without giving the drug. The verdict was that although the spleen was very enlarged & the arm glands up the general blood condition was better than when Ellis had decided to stop X-rays on account of the bad blood conditions.

The doctors decided that TEM might do more harm than good & that G could go on for the time being without any treatment, tho' the threat of the spleen being removed if it became an actual nuisance, was again raised. G very impressed by the organisation of the hospital & the care & attention given by the doctors. The nurses were charming but overwhelmed with curiosity at seeing G working in bed at music. He scored In Terra Pax for ten hours on the first day – a lovely chance of work without interruption.

By January 1955 the spleen was sufficiently enlarged to be causing pressure on the bladder, and Witts now advised its immediate removal. This was probably the point at which the full physical nature of his condition really sank in for Gerald, who reacted with instinctive resistance to surgery while he and Joy grasped at straws: 'One always has the feeling that after the spleen is removed the cure may be found by other means. The solving of the problem is just round the corner, and a spleen can never be put back.' Although 'aware of the enlarged spleen', he was 'fit in other ways & above all able to work & is terribly apprehensive of the ultimate effect of the operation – "that this should have come to me at the prime of my mental powers, with all my work before me",' he wailed, begging Witts to postpone the operation for six months (J. Finzi 19550110). But his own doctor, Tom Scott, advised compliance – 'we are all so ignorant' – and Neville had no alternative strategy, so on 24 January Joy 'took G to Radcliffe to have his spleen removed':

After discussions with all the authorities it seems inevitable & G felt it better got over now. Dark days – full of apprehension – but the decision to have it done will end it. 'I feel as if I'm going to be guillotined'; 'this worst crisis in my life'. I felt as when taking G to M[inistry] of W[ar] T[ransport] in 1941. (J. Finzi 19550124)

The following day Joy recorded: 'Operation satisfactorily over. 4½ lb. spleen removed instead of 4 oz.' Gerald, in hospital for a fortnight, made a quick recovery. The following day he 'sat up and dictated to [Joy] for several hours in perfect possession of himself & his faculties' (Harman 1994: 263–4), and when the Vaughan Williamses, who like other friends had been told that it was appendicitis, visited they found him cheerfully working 'under an enormous pile of scoring paper, which seemed to take up all the room on his bed' (U. Vaughan Williams 1964: 359).

This was not a cure, but it 'reduced the battleground' and permitted a new bout of treatment, that of the stomach glands, as Joy explained:

During these last months . . . G has been over to Oxford for regular weekly X-ray treatment on the tummy glands which have never been able to have proper treatment. Then arm-pits & groin & so far his blood-count seems to be standing up to this, the longest bout of X-ray treatment, & despite the continuous & intensive work G has been better than for these last years. (J. Finzi 19550622)

Despite this regime, which continued for much of 1955 though with an intermission in the autumn, by the end of the year she could refer to 'the years [recte year?] of grace with G looking so much better that people continually comment on it' (J. Finzi 19550207, 19560102).

Apart from the Cello Concerto, he was writing no music on quite the scale of the late 1940s projects during this time, but he was still composing prolifically by his own standards, and doing more editing, lobbying, committee and panel work, writing of articles and lecturing than ever before. As well as the Cello Concerto's slow movement, three small-scale pieces occupied him during his first period of medical treatment in the latter part of 1951: 'God is gone up', 'All this night' and 'Let us now praise famous men'.

To take the last, and smallest, first, 'Let us now praise famous men' was a two-part choral song with piano (plus optional strings) intended primarily for male voices, finished by December and issued early the following year, that set an Apocryphal text from *Ecclesiasticus*. It is not known what occasioned it, nor when it was first performed, and it is more or less futile to speculate on any personal identification with the words or even look too closely at their meaning, for it was hardly Finzi's style to praise 'our fathers that begat us', there was no particular occasion to laud Vaughan Williams (undoubtedly Finzi's favourite among famous men to be praised, and one who had made his own setting of the lines), one hopes he was not beginning to envisage himself as among those 'perished as though they had never been', and in any case it is difficult to see how the name of these can live for evermore if they have left no memorial – a semantic non-sequitur for which he had only himself to blame when he left out nine lines of text, understandably enough given that they dealt with the honouring of forefathers and with children remaining within the covenant and inheriting prosperity.

'Let us now praise famous men' is more tuneful than 'Muses and Graces' and its accompaniment benefits, like that of 'God is gone up', from its bright march character, though the swooping melodic contours and crisply constrained rhythms (for instance, for the 'musical tunes') can be slightly awkward in performance. The form, to a continuous prose text, suggests three-verse strophic variation or a bar form (AAB) with the last unit as *envoi* or epilogue and a tiny interpolated *arioso* for the 'Leaders of the people'; the opening downbeat quaver rhythm (to the initial exhortation, 'Let us now') holds the whole thing, rhetorical idea and musical structure, together.

Finzi had visited Shulbrede Priory, the home of Parry's daughter Dorothea Ponsonby, in the course of his researches, and one wonders whether the lovely poem 'All this night' by William Austin (1587–1634) about 'chanticler' proclaiming Christ's birth all night long reminded him of the entrancing sixteenth-century wall painting there, which shows the animals in the stable conversing onomatopoeically about the Nativity (the cockerel crows 'Christus natus est', the duck quacks 'Quando, quando?', the jackdaw croaks 'In hac nocte', the bull bellows 'Ubi, ubi?' and the lamb bleats 'In Bethlehem!') – or indeed whether also in his mind was Parry's setting of Dunbar's *Ode on the Nativity*, which like Finzi's Christmas motet has to muster unalloyed and unremitting joy, if on a much larger scale. 'All this night', originally described as a 'carol-motet' (later 'unaccompanied motet'), is a short piece but one of substance. For once there is hardly a flat in it and virtually all the movement is sharpwards, appropriately enough for the cockerel's reverse glossolalia, and a kind of analogue for that childlike reluctance to get any sleep on Christmas night that Finzi knew and loved in his own sons, perhaps remembered from his childhood, and had certainly experienced in the variant pertaining to the Aldbourne Band. Finzi was good with Christmas cheer; at the annual Christmas Eve party at Church Farm he would go up into the attic and shout mumblingly down the chimney as Father Christmas, whereupon all the children would rush outside to see if they could see him on the roof. And something of the old-fashioned Christmas family warmth of 'The brightness of this day' runs like a thread through his output's fabric and shows here in the galliard- or branle-like metric modulation in the second stanza. It also underlies his overall capacity to keep the emotional light blazing by suppressing routine thematicism and periodic balance as much as he dare (they are represented, as so often, by a head motif affecting only the first two lines of each stanza), so that the whole piece is like an extended fanfare – sounding 'very well and trumpet like' at its first performance in St Paul's Cathedral on 6 December 1951, as Joy noted (J. Finzi 19511206).

'All this night' is not without shades of colour, however; indeed, as an essay in plastic choral sound it is expert and triumphant. Finzi's use of *divisi* contracts and expands the texture just as his shifting rhythms keep the rhetoric ever fluent, like a radiance that hovers and changes shape continually (something similarly experienced in *In terra pax*). His placing of high notes and close-harmony thirds, particularly in the altos, is a skilful optimisation of vocal character, as is his gradual and sparing exploration of bass depths. One also notices that his imitative 5/4 section in the third stanza manages to maintain utter clarity of text and texture – mature technique's solution to exactly the problem he failed to solve decades earlier in 'How shall a young man' – and that each of his two flatward gestures encapsulates a world in a moment, the one a matter of mediant minor-triad relations, the other phrygian, both modal and both an undermining of tonal confidence, but not to be countenanced further because it is Christmas.

Charles Thornton Lofthouse had commissioned 'All this night' for his University of London Musical Society chorus, a group of 400 young voices which nonetheless 'sounded quite small in the vast building – but a lovely sound in the dome' (ibid.). St Paul's was full to capacity because Princess Margaret was there, though it is difficult to square this kind of choral zest and sense of occasion with John Amis's description of Lofthouse as a 'dear old thing' of a continuo player who 'fussed, hesitated and pernicketed, changing his mind constantly' in the record shop where Amis worked as a young man (1985: 59). Be that as it may, and illness notwithstanding, the Finzis were enjoying their social life at this period. They dined with the Lofthouses after the concert, not arriving home till 1.30 a.m.; the following evening was even more of a late night; and they then went on to score a hat trick:

To Oxford for the 1st performance of Wellesz's opera Incognito. Met VW & Ursula for dinner before. Dent was there also. Long opera over 11.30 – home by 12.30. Ovaltine & bread & cheese in the kitchen warmth & then sat over the wood fire talking. Cats perched on VW – at 3.30 he said 'I hope I am not keeping you young people up'. He was first up next morning & walking out to see the day while I made breakfast. Went home after lunch.

We to rehearsal & then on to Michael Rothenstein's lecture on Abstract Art. Brought him home for the night – after very good lecture. We enjoyed his stay. (J. Finzi 19511207)

Only two weeks earlier Gerald had had another sacred choral work premièred in London on a society occasion, something to which his style was becoming more and more equal. 'God is gone up' was first performed on 22 November at the St Cecilia's Day morning Festival Service – as opposed to the evening concert – at St Sepulchre's, Holborn Viaduct by John Dykes Bower, conducting choristers from the Chapels Royal, St Paul's Cathedral, Westminster Abbey and Canterbury Cathedral, with William McKie or C. H. Trevor at the organ. This time the Lord Mayor of London was in attendance, the Dean of St Paul's preached, and someone, probably Frank Howes, present as chairman of the Musicians' Benevolent Fund, even graced the service with a *Times* review, describing the new anthem as combining 'jubilation with a not too emollient euphony' (23 November 1951: 6). Blunden and Ferguson came and listened, and the combined choristers made a thrilling sound, though Ferguson complained about church musicians' sense of rhythm and Joy about the fact that the organ was too small – 'too weak for size of choir (church damaged during war & new organ installed)' (J. Finzi 19511120–21). And if this was a good send-off for a good piece, an even better one followed on 20 May, when it was repeated in London, with strings in addition to organ and again conducted by Dykes Bower, at the 298th Festival of the Corporation of the Sons of the Clergy in St Paul's. The Archbishop of Canterbury, Geoffrey Fisher, was present, clinching another hat trick for Finzi: music for the ears of powers royal, municipal and ecclesiastical, for the apogee (almost) of court, city and church – which did not prevent Joy from catching a flea amongst the evidently unwashed masses. 'Considering the dire echo & conditions,' she recorded, 'it was a successful performance. The strings gave point & clarity to the sound. Fine choir & masses of bishops' (J. Finzi 19520520). It was understandable enough that Finzi should enjoy basking in the company of 'masses of bishops' at this juncture: 1951 had, after all, been Festival of Britain year, and the whole Finzi family went up to the South Bank to visit it and attend a concert in the new Royal Festival Hall in September (at which they heard and met John Carol Case for the first time: he was singing *Let Us Garlands Bring*). But what relation do these performances of 'All this night' and 'God is gone up' bear to the Arts Council Music Panel's resolution, on 5 November 1948, that 'a Festival Psalm, to be staged in a thanksgiving service at St Paul's Cathedral, should be commissioned from Rubbra or Finzi' (Kildea 1996: 154)?

If 'All this night', for all its attraction, is still too loosely madrigalian to be really memorable – its principle, at the risk of repeating earlier observations, being the one Finzi had grown up with as his staff in the fight against formal orthodoxy, namely that of a varied succession of homophonic and imitative 'points' rather than the symmetrical unity of sectional repetition – 'God is gone up' at last capitulates more or less to structural conventions, being in plain ABA form and none the weaker for that, as Finzi might finally have admitted. A thoroughly successful anthem, rich and fresh in detail from the point of view of the cathedral repertoire while 100% *echt* in terms of Finzi's style, it has become one of the twentieth-century classics of the genre, and satisfies these two perspectives like none of his other sacred pieces. It also demonstrates how even the Deity – at least as conceived by the Church of England – has been permitted to partake of the British Empire's blithe swansong of ceremonial metropolitan marches, for the A section, even when in 3/4, has the trappings of Waltonian or Coates-like pageantry in its organ triplets, jaunty staccato quavers and semiquaver flourish (ex. 11.1.a), while the B section retains just enough offbeat step to serve as a trio (ex. 11.1.b) and trades in Arcadian nonchalance for all the world like a change of scene in a Shakespearean comedy or a down-home item in a newsreel. Perhaps this is the twentieth century's equivalent of the seventeenth's innocence of 'dissociation of sensibility', for having returned to Edward Taylor's poetry (two stanzas of his

EX. 11.1.a (choir and organ)

Sacramental Meditation No. 20) for his text, Finzi makes it sound sufficiently impersonal not to be intrusive on the one hand while metaphysical enough, with its courtiers flying downwards 'in flakes of Glory' and its 'Heart-cramping notes of Melody', on the other. The same could be said of his form, for though basically standard, the return of the A section, exact for much of its length, does curtail the 'Sing Praises' passage and strengthen the plane of A♭ major in its parenthetical function, in that initially this key had been approached via C minor and E

433

EX. 11.1.b

major and thus felt rather too grounded as it arrived by drop of a fifth. Yet Finzi still does not bat an eyelid at rounding off his A section with a fanfare ritornello a semitone higher than the tonic (F major as *tierce de Picardie* of F minor), nor at a premature tonic return after the B section (at 'More to enravish'), even while he takes pride in a clever tonal rounding-off at the very end, when the A♭ key, its tonic as climactic top note, pivots enharmonically back into E major, in other words down a major third where it had gone down a minor third (into F) at the equivalent point before the B section. As for 'the unexpected chord at the end' (technically an augmented sixth), Milford said it 'seems to me a stroke of genius!' (19520913), though not necessarily because as a dominant seventh it could be heard to echo the G major start of the middle section. This was hardly Finzi's characteristic logic, yet he could be as intellectual as Brahms when it came to progressive variation between motifs: see the transformation of part of the opening fanfare into the B section arabesque as tabulated in ex. 11.1.c. Not the least of the virtues of 'God is gone up' is its excellent accompaniment, full of life and character by analogy with orchestral identities on the one hand (brass, strings and woodwind are all suggested) and the piano figuration of one or two of his later Hardy songs on the other, yet always done in terms of the organ itself. Again one marvels that Finzi could write so well for an instrument he strongly disliked, and again realises (as he probably never did) how much he had to thank Bairstow for.

He was by now so engrossed in his editing and performances of

(may also
be aligned)

EX. 11.1.C

eighteenth- and early nineteenth-century British music, his scholarly work on John Stanley, and his external examining at St Andrews University that composition was in danger of being squeezed out altogether. True, he was composing, compiling and scoring his *Love's Labour's Lost* Suite for Cheltenham during the first half of 1952, and orchestrating 'God is gone up', but nothing else got written in these six months, and the Magnificat, which came next, was a rushed job. This time he sailed too close to the wind, as Joy's journal makes clear:

July 25th G hard at Magnificat for Smith College – time running out. Jack Henderson naturally angry & we hope Dee Hiatt will not mind it coming a month overdue. G, having had so many years of Church music background & the innumerable dreary automatic magnificats finds it hard to throw any new light on the words – the orange is sucked dry.

Henderson, at Boosey & Hawkes, was waiting to get copies printed and sent across the Atlantic for rehearsal, or possibly taken back by Iva Dee Hiatt.

Hiatt was Director of Music at Smith College, Northampton, Massachusetts and evidently (apart from Herrmann) the first of the many intrepid and determined Americans who have since beaten a path to the front door of Church Farm. She had brought a choir to Europe in the summer of 1951, on which occasion she turned up at Ashmansworth in August and was found 'very delightful' (19510820). Finzi agreed to write a non-liturgical Magnificat for her candlelit Christmas Vespers service, doubtless flattered to have an overseas commission at last, though Vassar College, it will be recalled, had sung another Nativity piece of his nearly thirty years earlier. She visited again with her singers in 1952, and somehow or other the Magnificat got written by 7 September, the eve of her sailing, when it was demonstrated to her at Ashmansworth. Two days earlier Joy noted: 'Finished the Magnificat: last Amen followed the zero hour post. Rather forced upon G and the product of the craftsman rather than any particular feeling. It may be better than he thinks' (J. Finzi 19520905). This was probably the Amen Christopher Finzi remembered his father writing in the car, and as if out of publisher's spite, it appears rather ignominiously on the back page of the published score. (There is, moreover, no Gloria.) Hiatt seemed satisfied with the piece, and duly gave it an idiosyncratic first performance (which survives on tape) with the All Smith Choir and her colleague Robert Beckwith's Amherst Glee Club on 12 December 1952. The British première followed at the Wigmore Hall on 29 May 1953, given by Audrey Langford (who had been married to the viola player Frederick Riddle) and the Orpington and Bromley Choir with Hammond organ; despite this expedient – did Finzi ever hear a 'proper' performance with organ? – they made a good showing, and he orchestrated the work in 1956 for their concert on 12 May, this time on home territory and with a professional orchestra. Joy noted that Gerald had intended orchestrating the Magnificat all along, and that the choir 'of about 130' (in number, not age) sounded good (J. Finzi 19560223, 19560512).

The Magnificat is better than Finzi thought. At the same time it shows why much of his best vocal music had to be written as the slow, ruminative response to an impulse, for without either the impulse or the rumination nothing stands out quite as freshly as it might. Nevertheless, it is much firmer structurally than his partsongs, 'Lo, the full, final sacrifice' and For St Cecilia (though at roughly ten minutes in length somewhat shorter than these last two), and this pays off, as a comparison of its opening with that of For St Cecilia demonstrates, for here the modulation to the dominant before the first chorus entry is properly counteracted at the second one, which kinetically reinstates the strategic C naturals (over a dominant pedal) omitted from its pentatonic predecessor. This kind of balancing period, basically classical, once again shows Finzi capitulating, sensibly it has to be said, to traditional norms, and the amount of repeated (as opposed to imitated) text, like the first phrase used here, in his Magnificat is a fair indication of changed priorities. In fact he immediately repeats the lines a third time before moving straight into a kind of second subject for the next portion of text. The motif used for these 'magnification' words themselves is a kind of eight-note diatonic series (ex. 11.2.a), rather Brittenesque not so much in its pitch collection as in the way it is immediately worked on intellectually, regardless of its *Affekt,* first in triplet diminution and then piecemeal to build steps leading to the first choral entry. The second subject (ex. 11.2.b) signifies lowliness or humility and is recapitulated for 'his mercy', while a third or concluding motif, speaking expositionally, is the figure marching through 'all generations' to the choral reiteration of 'blessed, blessed...' ('for ever, for ever...' in the recapitulation) (ex. 11.2.c).

Something of the telescopic sonata carries over into the Magnificat from *Intimations of Immortality,* for these recapitulations are broken up by suggestions of other movements operating within the Magnificat's continuous span – perhaps no different from many another composer's setting, liturgical or no, but indicative nonetheless. (Most of the sonata indications are clarified and proved by instrumental association in the orchestral version – brass for battling scherzo and concluding march, woodwind solos for second subject, and so on – a treatment which suits this extrovert piece a good deal better than it suited the mysticism

EX. 11.2.a

EX. 11.2.b

EX. 11.2.c

437

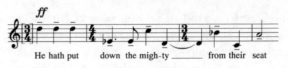

He hath put   down the migh-ty _____ from their seat

EX. 11.2.d

of 'Lo, the full, final sacrifice'.) First comes a hint of development, in
text as well as music, when 'My soul doth magnify the Lord' is repeated
once more prior to the line 'For he that is mighty hath magnified *me*'
(my italics), tightening up the Virgin's train of thought and transforming
the dotted rhythm of 'magnify'. After the second subject repeat, scherzo
topics join battle, in both triple time and triplets, for showing strength
and scattering the proud and, still combatively, fugue follows scherzo
when the 'scattering' motif is augmented rhythmically and intervallically
for putting down the mighty (ex. 11.2.d) – not a real fugue, but a
succession of entries, monophonic at first, rising by fifths and with
a countersubject added for exalting the humble and meek. This subsides
into a slight but subtle reminiscence of the work's opening – in D major,
which usurps the tonic – when the hungry are filled and the rich sent
empty away, for over this new section of text, which is repeated, not
only are the opening line and motif echoed once more, but, at the
second statement of 'He hath filled the hungry with good things', there
is a reference to the organ introduction with its melodic steps and
slightly Rawsthorne-like harmonies. The final section of text, spun out
over a flowing quaver accompaniment, has something of the function
of slow movement or intermezzo, leading via repetitions of the word
'Abraham' into the recapitulation of ex. 11.2.c. These repetitions are
puzzlingly emphatic from the exegetical point of view, though as so
often with Finzi the melopoetic reason for them is that they unify verbal
and musical rhythms and intonations, in this case those of 'Abraham'
and 'magnify'. One notes that the Amen's final cadence, at least in the
organ part, echoes the introduction of the Romance for strings – another
argument in favour of the latter's dating from 1951, perhaps.

Finzi's next two pieces, continuing a succession of choral commissions
whereby he was now in danger of becoming typecast, reverse the tight-
ness of musical formula evident in the Magnificat, and this is not to
their benefit, for both 'White-flowering days' and 'Welcome sweet and
sacred feast' sound rather loose, unmemorable and retrogressive by
comparison with the preceding essays. The former was commissioned

by the Arts Council in connection with the 1953 Coronation as a contribution to *A Garland for the Queen*, the latter by the BBC's Religious Broadcasting Department.

Undeterred by or ignorant of the BBC's burnt fingers in 1948, the Arts Council invited twelve British composers and poets (the latter via the former, with a suggested list) to contribute to the *Garland* and help celebrate a new Elizabethan age. The following guidelines were offered:

The poets and composers are invited to approach their problem by choosing some aspect of contemporary Britain which they feel moved to treat in a spirit of acceptance, praise, loyalty, or love. Humour need not be excluded, but it is advisable to keep in mind the bearing of the individual part upon the whole . . . an item of brittle, sardonic, or satirical wit will be out of place and damaging to the general effect.

So much for the manner. For the matter, the term 'contemporary Britain' should be understood in the widest sense, as including, for example, celebration of the countryside or city; the courage, skill or character of the people; the nobility or charm of their traditions and customs in public or private life; their jealously guarded and ancient liberties; their religious faith or tolerance. A search for modern parallels with the age of the first 'Oriana' may prove fruitful: the continuing spirit of discovery; the renascence of music or of the arts as a whole, loyalty to the monarchy, and compliment to the first lady of the land. (Undated Arts Council Music Panel memo, quoted Kildea 1996: 160)

As Kildea notes, 'In between the above draft and the formal commission, the *a cappella* pieces had become madrigals, and the collection "An Oriana Garland" or "A Garland for the Queen". It was a regressive view . . .' He also explains that Britten and Walton declined the commission, Britten because he was too busy with *Gloriana*, Walton because of the embargo on satire and sardonic wit – 'all my best sides', as he pointed out (:161).

Finzi, not surprisingly, used the opportunity to renew his partnership with Blunden. They had not collaborated further, except in the editing of Gurney, since *For St Cecilia*, though Blunden had sent Finzi a poem, 'March', in the summer of 1951 to which Finzi's response makes it sound as though either or both men now viewed such a gesture as half way towards a musical challenge, Finzi writing back:

I wish I cld enlist Claire on to my side in finding 'casuistry' a bit jarring. Perhaps it's only my composer's mind, seeking a musical equivalent & failing to find it. One can sing, say, 'argument' but 'casuistry' is impossible. (Try it!)

But of course I realise that under this test half the finest poems in the world
wld fail to pass, though all purely lyrical ones might succeed. (19510724)

He put the *Garland* proposal to Blunden when he was at Ashmansworth
in November 1952 for a portrait session with Joy, who noted that
'E B, who now regards himself as more or less a literary hack through
force of circumstances, seemed glad to do it but rather hilariously
chanted "as I stood at the corner of Piccadilly plying my trade"'
(J. Finzi 19521106). The following month Blunden, who got £15 from
the Arts Council for his pains (as presumably did Finzi), sent him two
poems from which to choose one, 'Spirit abiding' and 'Now the white-
flowering days'. Finzi was in his critical element, confident enough by
now in his friendship with Blunden to reject the former with forthright
comments – 'quite apart from the awkwardness (from the musical angle,
of course) of such a line as "genius ancestral", the sentiment of the last
verse is too like Wm Watson. It might even land you with a knighthood, & that wd never do!' (19521226) – and ask for substantial
changes to the latter.

His approach to Blunden's draft of 'White-flowering days' provides
exact verification of his partsong methods, dependent as they had
always been on head motif and refrain as the only overt unifying agents
other than the poem itself. At first he thought a refrain would be the
answer:

I like music to grow out of the actual words & not be fitted to them, and as
the verses are not strophic they will all need separate treatment. This is all
to the good, but it does mean a possible lack of some cohesive musical idea. If
necessary, cd some short couplet be devised (the same for all three verses)?
Not quite T[homas] H[ardy]'s

> Fill full your cups; feel no distress
> That thoughts so great shd now be less!

but that idea. What I shd really like is the chance of using the couplet or not,
according to how the piece shapes. It might even be something bearing on the
season-crowning idea, but I ain't no poet. Over to you. (ibid.)

This would have resulted in a musical archetype with some kind of
triple span. But he had second thoughts, reverting to his more frequent
notion of a pair of musical strophes, each covering two stanzas, the
strophes starting similarly, with a head motif, then diverging as they
approached the even-numbered stanzas:

I can see daylight now & what I shld dearly like is an extra verse, a penultimate one, if possible in the exact rhythm of the 1st verse. This will enable me to give it some musical unity, perhaps more satisfactory than the 'refrain' idea. You see, the particular rhythm of the first verse

Now the white flowering days

can't be applied to any other lines in the poem & therefore, *ipso facto*, that particular musical phrase can't be used elsewhere. The 'exactitude' need only apply to, say, the first three lines

> Now the white-flowering days,
> The long days of blue and golden light,
> Wake nature's music round the land; – (19530113)

Blunden obligingly came up with the extra (third) stanza, matching the syntax of the first in all five lines – 'Now' as first word of both, repeated as penultimate syllable of the third line; 'long days' paralleled by 'wild brooks', 'round the land' by 'take their stand', 'swift and bright' by 'far and near'; a semi-colon after 'sweetness' matched with one after 'songless'; and so on. He also grasped the necessity for congruence of idea sufficiently for the composer to be able to use the fanfare-like imitative point at the waking of nature's music for the 'Tall trembling blue-bells' as well – that is, once Blunden had assured him that bluebells were all right for early June (Joy had queried this). And although Finzi does not maintain Blunden's parallels right to the end of the two stanzas, he does repeat the text of the last clause of each, both times in imitation.

This is a madrigalian trait – repeating the text of some lines and not others – and it is worth noting how closely Finzi follows the practice of the English madrigal in other respects. Imitation in pairs of voices, in single parts or with one against three, interspersed with passages of special focus set in homophony; points alternately in triple and pavan-like quadruple time (the triple time encompassing 5/4 metre, not just cross-rhythm, in the modern context), alternately upbeat and downbeat (where the poem permits), and alternately in conjunct and disjunct motion; augmentations and variants of one or two basic shapes (here, the three upward steps followed by upward leap of ex. 11.3) in balance with contrasting ones – all this contributes to the flux of musical material that is so dissimilar to the periodic norms of later classical models, and 'Now the white-flowering days' is accordingly, and appro-

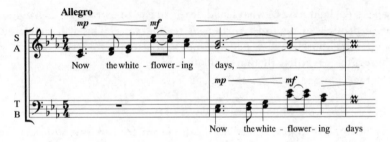

EX. 11.3

priately enough, the most Elizabethan of all Finzi's partsongs. At the same time the parallel with Farrar's turn-of-the-century partsong 'Margaritae sorori', suggested in Chapter 1, seems beyond chance, especially as Finzi was enquiring of Farrar's widow about his *Nachlass* in the very month of composition of 'White-flowering days' (see 19530123?, and compare ex. 1.1 with ex. 11.3). However, neither of the two blueprints, Victorian partsong or renaissance madrigal, has ever sufficed for the twentieth-century *a cappella* brief with its more libertarian harmonic environment, and although the general effect of 'White-flowering days' is virile enough, its details lack the pull of gravity that an instrumental grounding always ensures in the mature Finzi. Most disarmingly, the difference, following the head motif, between the flatward regions of the first two stanzas and the sharpward ones of the third and fourth seems offhand, an arbitrary shift upwards of an extra semitone at the words 'now none / Is bloomless'.

'White-flowering days' was not the only contribution to *A Garland for the Queen* to fall short of musical conviction (see Banfield 1995: 437). The other offerings were by Vaughan Williams, Tippett, Rawsthorne, Bax, Berkeley, Ireland, Rubbra, Bliss and Howells, and almost all of them failed to stand out in sufficient relief from their texts, their fellows and their predecessors, a number of which (including five of the *Triumphs of Oriana* madrigals) were also in the Coronation eve Festival Hall programme on 1 June. The *Times* reviewer, probably Howes, sensed this:

A sequence of 10 madrigals, to use a generic term out of its historical context, by living composers raises all sorts of questions about the relations of words and music, each of which was driven from the attention by the next, which pressed hard upon it. Is occasional verse good enough for music? If it is not occasional what is the point of putting its setting into this garland? Do modern composers in their search for something not said before overload their texture, or borrow dissonances from string writing that will sound dull instead of bright on voices?

Such questions will not be answered here . . . Whatever the individual merits of the several contributions, the sequence held together as such, though it had not a set refrain, like 'Long live fair Oriana' of its famous exemplar.

It . . . [was] sung by the Cambridge University Madrigal Society under Mr Boris Ord with an assurance and polish that concealed the cruel difficulties of modern choral writing. (*The Times*, 3 June 1953: 4)

Joy found 'things of interest' in all the partsongs except Bax's and Berkeley's, and 'After the concert set out for home – for one day of rest whilst the whole of central London was matted with 1000s upon 1000s of people in cold, showery weather trying to settle down for the night in the streets, for the sights of next day's coronation' (J. Finzi 19530601). Later 'White-flowering days' joined *Dies natalis* as the only other one of Finzi's works to be commercially recorded in his lifetime – again courtesy of the British Council, who issued the whole *Garland* with Ord and his choir.

Finzi received the invitation to compose an anthem for the BBC while he was writing 'White-flowering days'. Both sides made difficulties. He was not impressed with the fee offered, and tried to get it raised (it is not clear whether he succeeded). Then Cyril Taylor at the BBC pronounced the unspecified Donne poem that he had chosen to set unsuitable, being too intimate and not overtly Christian. 'Welcome sweet and sacred feast' did get written, however, when Finzi settled on a second choice of text. This was by Henry Vaughan, to whom he was returning for the first time since the 1920s, when two partsong settings, 'They are all gone' and the impressive 'Death (Dialogue between the Body and Soul)' had been begun in addition to the motets discussed in Chapter 3, though it will be recalled that Vaughan had also featured in his first thoughts about the anthem for St Matthew's, Northampton. And like 'Lo, the full, final sacrifice', what he now composed was a long – though not so long – meditation on the Eucharist, to a text as intense and far-seeing as Crashaw in its gaze but without the structural rhythm and drama Finzi had managed to realise in him and Aquinas. His best response to Vaughan's remarkable sparks of thought and feeling, which fuse the language of pastoral and Passion and range over the whole of nature, comes right at the end, when they are resolved into the acceptance of devotion to a Christ who is 'both food, and

443

Shepherd to thy sheep', both red rose and white lily. Finzi's turns of melody and harmony here, from his final *Tempo I* to the end, are as relaxed and open as he ever got (see Russell 1956: 630 for their genesis), and are given refrain status through their appearance in the anthem's introduction, all this making for a last page as achingly lovely in its way as the first of 'Lo, the full, final sacrifice', though one is additionally reminded both of Percy Buck's hymn tune 'Gonfalon Royal' at the *Tempo I* and of D. J. Enright's stricture on Crashaw's religious verse, that it is 'lovingly handled, but sometimes too lovingly fondled' (quoted in Ousby 1988: 237). Certainly the flat sevenths and sixth at the end verge on the sentimental in that they presuppose a resolution of tension, a claim to keepsake, that has never quite been earned by the composer.

The problem is that he cannot match the trajectory of heightened thought and feeling in Vaughan's first stanza (from which in any case he omits twelve lines), though he is quite right to attempt it in one span, for Vaughan perceives 'The way to thee' through the whole of time and space, from the turning leaf to the rending veil of the Temple, as if in a blinding flash. There is indeed a *fortissimo* climax at the breaking of the veil, but Vaughan's verse respires as well as gasps, and it is this ebb and flow that Finzi reflects the more and which stymies the first, and much longer, section of his anthem. The musical material, loosely interweaving ideas of downward fifths and upward steps (both initially for the word 'welcome', the latter echoing the 'come away' section of 'Lo, the full, final sacrifice' rather inopportunely so early in the proceedings), is simply not compelling enough, and one gets little sense of direction or agenda from it, fluent though it is. Vaughan's two marvelling questions that arise from his epiphany are set as an aria consequent, again rather unmemorably and therefore without the thrill of the pivot of his apprehension, though the modulation from B♭ minor to D minor for the aria does its best (if not helped by two missing G♭ accidentals in the score). The beginning of the aria also has an element of second-subject recapitulation about it, its prototype the metrically congruent line 'They, by thy Word, their beauty had, and date' and its music.

Finzi's friends were an honest bunch. 'We heard your anthem last night, and it left us a little puzzled. But perhaps it was the very dull performance,' Rubbra hazarded (19531012a) the day after the first performance of 'Welcome sweet and sacred feast' at a broadcast BBC evensong from St Martin-in-the-Fields on 11 October 1953, and though he liked it better on publication, Ferguson and Milford (who both spotted the misprints) registered disappointment when they received the published score in 1954. Colleagues and family noted wrily that by now he was coming suspiciously close to churning out compositions to order, something that would have been anathema to him two or three decades earlier, and they were not above teasing him about it, warning him that fame was going to his head when a young, ambitious pianist and conductor, John Russell, suddenly appeared virtually at his beck and call.

Russell lived in Reading and first met Finzi there as a fan in November 1947 when he (Russell) was preparing a performance of *Dies natalis* with his string orchestra. By 1951 he was coming over from Reading weekly to conduct the Newbury Choral Society, and the two men probably saw a fair amount of each other from then on; Russell certainly joined the group of intimates – Milford, Sumsion, Rubbra, Ferguson, Scott – who were played Finzi's new and progressing works in the privacy of his study. He performed *For St Cecilia* with the Newbury choir in March 1951 and later the same year, in Reading on 11 November, gave the première of the Romance for strings. He began to show himself Finzi's right-hand man from this point on. In 1952 he wrote an article on Ferguson's new Piano Concerto for the Boosey & Hawkes house journal *Tempo* after Finzi, who had been asked to do it and as an old friend could not refuse despite finding it a weak and disappointing work, had failed to provide enough copy; two years later he published an article on Finzi himself in *Tempo* (Russell 1954). He also began to influence the course of Finzi's composition when he showed an interest in the uncompleted Piano Concerto. 'John Russell came over to try through the slow movement of G's piano concerto, which he is scoring, with a view to running through it with the [Reading?] strings. This stimulated his interest in it & he is keen to finish it,' Joy noted in January 1952 (J. Finzi 19520112). Later that month he did finish rewriting the movement, which, it will be recalled, dated originally from 1929 or earlier, though it was only performed and published posthumously, with the editorial title Eclogue.

The concerto had never been entirely abandoned, and was apparently revived with a will after the war, for both Arnold van Wyk, who was a close friend of Ferguson's, and Robin Milford knew about it and probably heard the sketches: van Wyk proposed to stay at Ashmansworth in July 1946 and help Finzi with it (in his capacity as a pianist rather than composer), and the following year Milford was writing: 'Are you *never* going to produce your piano concerto?' to which Finzi replied, 'Alas, I wish I knew when I was going to . . . I suppose when the stuff I'm waiting for knocks at the door. I can't get the right music after that weighty introduction' (19470315, 19470321). This suggests that the D major sketches following the D minor introduction Finzi refers to may predate 1947, although there is also evidence, admittedly very slight, that an opening for a fourth movement – if that is what it was – drafted around 1930 resurfaced, transformed, as the 'John Williams' theme (ex. 9.3.h) in *For St Cecilia* later in 1947 (see Sketch-book X: r16, r17). Finzi had held on to a classic antecedent/consequent pairing as the envisioned shape of his first movement, though again other evidence alters and confuses the picture, for a British Library manuscript (Deposit 9365) places the Grand Fantasia as the first half of the *third* movement of the Concerto, its consequent followed by 'attacca IV' (no material for 'IV' being present). Whatever was being moved around on either side, the Eclogue remained second, Joy recording at the end of January 1952 that 'the piano concerto was written before our marriage & the slow movement twice reshaped since until he was satisfied with its eventual form ABA leading to climax & middle section leading back to A & B played together followed by Coda' (J. Finzi 19520130). She meant by this a ternary form of which the opening section is itself ternary, and added, 'Original movements on either side have been scrapped but some of the material may be used again' (ibid.). The following month, again according to Joy's journal, Finzi was working at the finale, but that is the last we hear of it, and although Milford made further enquiries in May, the concerto was scrapped once and for all when Finzi decided to salvage the idea of the composite first movement, and some of its material, for the Grand Fantasia and Toccata that eventuated in November the following year (1953) at Russell's considerable urging and in great haste. The urgency was because Russell had persuaded Finzi to let him have the première, playing the solo piano part under Finzi's baton, at a Newbury Choral Society concert in the town on 9 December at which he was also conducting *Intimations* (with the tenor Richard Lewis) and *For St Cecilia*. Joy tells the full story:

This was a bold & enthusiastic local step on the part of John Russell. Several months before G had mentioned a very early Grand Fantasia which he thought of revising & adding a Toccata to. On the strength of this John, who had always wanted to do Intimations with the choral society & without saying a word to G went to the committee & proposed a Finzi concert to which, with a few dissentions they agreed.

G never really took it very seriously or thought much more about G F & T until he found that the whole thing was a fait accompli & that the finished work was really expected from him. So between return from Ireland [on 24 October] & Dec 9th this was written & scored & with the help of Tony Scott & the usual last minute all night sessions it was done just in time. John did his best with a pretty bad choir & the orchestra was only made possible by a professional stiffening on a big scale. Consequently the Fan & Toc were the most successful performances, & G pleased with the work. (19531209)

What is not entirely clear in all this is the relation between the Grand Fantasia and 'that weighty introduction'. The latter, perhaps a postwar creation, is shorter and tighter, and though in very much the same stylistic vein as the wild, improvisatory Fantasia, is more of a stately French overture, based on a unifying motif (ex. 11.4.a). The implication of Joy's account is that Finzi had told Russell about the Grand Fantasia as something still separate from the Piano Concerto rather than an early study for its opening. On the other hand, that he kept the two simultaneously in mind is clear from the lifting of two passages from the 'weighty introduction' for the final version of the Grand Fantasia, duly crossed out in the Bodleian manuscript fair copy (in piano duet form) of the Introduction. And certainly the sketches for the Introduction's consequent – the 'right music' Finzi was struggling to bring to birth – were the starting-point for the Toccata, as a comparison of the opening of each (ex. 11.4.b and c) and their subsidiary, contrasting motifs, perhaps for a second subject in the Concerto (ex. 11.4.d and e), clearly demonstrates. Other material strengthens the resemblances.

The inherent passion and tension of the Grand Fantasia's piano writing are raised to an extraordinary, Beethovenian power by the orchestra's largely silent witness throughout most of it; this was quite likely a ploy of 1953 rather than 1928, since Finzi described the work as having been 'considerably revised, re-written and scored' at the later

[Largo maestoso]

EX. 11.4.a

EX. 11.4.b (Concerto)

EX. 11.4.c (Toccata)

EX. 11.4.d (Concerto) (strings and piano)

EX. 11.4.e (Toccata)

date when he annotated his own catalogue of works (G. Finzi 1941, R. 1951). The opening *tutti* flourish returns at the climax of the Fantasia, now as a dominant rather than a tonic, a semitone higher, and in a highly overwrought context, but the real destiny of confrontation and interchange comes at the end of the Toccata when it returns again, now on A♭ (whose tritonal route to the eventual tonic D is strongly mapped through a virtually entire duodecalogue of falling fifths), and the orchestra goes on rather shockingly to play the piano's free, opening music from the Fantasia, now notated in measured double augmentation and suggestive of an almost totalitarian programme of usurpation of the individual's property. There is something violent and heartless about this piece, and there is certainly nothing like it in the repertoire. It is not the only British *concertante* piano work to sit aslant the conventions of etiquette and sensibility – one thinks also of the piano concertos of Bliss, Britten and Vaughan Williams – and one is tempted to wonder what this might tell us about the national psyche where appropriation of the power of the rebellious individual is concerned. Perhaps it is not surprising, therefore, that *The Times* rejected the Fantasia's brief at its first professional performance – 'the Grand Fantasia left the orchestra unemployed for too long' (10 July 1954: 3). Ferguson, meanwhile, had by now lost patience (which he would nonetheless have heroically to muster again as Finzi's posthumous editor) with the whole idea of gathering up early material:

As to 'early & late work'. I quite agree that the limitations of the former are often part of its strength; & I can see no harm in using up self-contained slabs of old stuff, provided they are not mixed up with stuff of a much later vintage. When there *is* such a mixture, difficulties start crowding in. The chief of these in your case, it seems to me, being the amount of time you have to spend on tinkering at the old stuff in an attempt (unavailing) to make it fit with the new: time which, to my way of thinking, would be infinitely better employed on something wholly new – even if that were to mean jettisoning some of the old altogether. However, this is a very personal matter, and I don't think argument about it is of much avail: one either sees & agrees, or one disagrees. Having made the point, which has been weighing on me for some time, I shall forever hold my peace about it. (19540102a)

The real problem is that the Toccata is shallower than the Fantasia, dilute Walton (early, *Portsmouth Point* Walton at that) or, to look forward, breezy proto-Arnold, with a good deal of synthetic 1950s confidence but not much weight or substance – it sits well with the splayed legs and tubular frames of the Festival Hall furniture that witnessed its professional première. The obvious link with the Fantasia is in the opening two-semiquaver/quaver motif, now reduced to repeated notes and as such the cue for a good deal of the piano writing, the two hands hammering away xylophonically or in broken octaves and cognate figures. The formal plan is not straightforward, for while the general thrust, after the orchestral exposition, is that of sonata form, involving two statements of the material, in practice the ideas are disposed more like those of a baroque concerto, some passages coming again note-for-note over a fair number of bars, but not joined in the original order or with something new inserted mid-way, others not repeating at all, and the main theme jauntily sampling a number of keys and treatments. This undermines any sense of development towards tonic return, and one hopes Finzi did not think of figure 11 as the latter. (However he viewed it, it is an extremely weak moment.) The motoric, baroque frame of reference would have been unproblematic enough on a *concertino* scale, but fierceness and melodrama keep threatening. They need the opening movement of the Cello Concerto for their proper arena. Another way of looking at the difficulty is Iain Cooper's, when he likens the Toccata's main theme to 'a fugue subject heard in one voice only', recalling Morris's 'great perception when he suggested that Finzi follow his *Fantasia* with a fugue' (1985: 111).

The Eclogue requires little separate consideration from its siblings discussed in Chapters 5 and 8 (see especially ex. 8.4.a–d), for the issues are comparable. However, its opening ritornello, probably Finzi's last Bachian 'aria' to be put to bed, is one of his best, wise and humane of melodic gesture and rich in inner voice-leading. Joy Finzi's description of the movement's form is slightly disingenuous, since A has to be altered to fit B prior to their combination at the return, which therefore tends to sound like a varied ritornello – though in any case, A's *Fortspinnung* has been variegated all along, its head motif prefacing a number of rambles starting from the same spot. What Joy called the coda is a more exact recapitulation of the motif (and in the tonic), though it immediately darkens into an ominous tonic minor passage vaguely recalling lines from the movement's 12/8, Ab major middle section (with its echoes of *Dies natalis*). All in all this gives a distinctive emotional curve to the work, one that proposes the pursuit of serenity for as long as possible, since it proves elusive and clouded on recapture. Or is it a case of formal default? One is not entirely convinced.

The concerto's finale has been reconstructed by Jonathan Cook (see Cook 1994) and proves a long, rambling continuity draft – rather like those for the Serenade – of a lightweight rondo with strings, full of delightful potential but in need of a great many injections, surgical excisions and transplants to make it stand up, though it has a very good ending that includes a retrospect of the Eclogue's head motif. Finzi probably wrote the movement before mid-1947 and then reworked it in February 1952, for the earlier version of his draft includes rehearsal letters every ten bars, a cueing system he referred to as 'a mistake' in a letter to Milford of May 1947 – 'players prefer it at significant points, changes of harmony etc' (19470504b) – and subsequently abandoned. There seems to be no hope of reconstructing the concerto entire, however, for the sketches for the first movement's consequent part, though plenteous, are probably beyond use.

After Russell's December concert Finzi was without a commission virtually for the first time since 1946 apart from the respite after *Intimations*. It would hardly be true to say that the pressure was off him, for he still had a part-finished cello concerto on his hands and plenty of work other than composition to keep him occupied. The first half of 1954 serves as a good window through which to observe how much of that other work he was undertaking. In January he was working on his article on Howells for the *Musical Times*. On 3 February he struggled along icebound roads to conduct a Newbury String Players concert in Andover Guildhall with John Carol Case and Yfrah Neaman as soloists, and two days later was in London replying 'for music' to speeches given by the heads of the two senior conservatories (Ernest Bullock and Reginald Thatcher) and the Dean of St Paul's at the London University Musical Society's twenty-first anniversary dinner. Joy commented:

G feels how surprising it is when one looks back at his inarticulate past that he has developed such comparative ease at this sort of thing. 20 years ago – he couldn't have said ten words in public – but probably the experience of regularly rehearsing the orchestra & giving concerts to schools & talking to them has helped to make public speaking less of a bugbear. He certainly never *enjoys* it but can do it adequately without being nervous. (J. Finzi 19540205)

Two weeks later he was back in London for lunch with Anthony Lewis, when they agreed that he should edit the Boyce Overtures for *Musica Britannica*. The following day, 19 February, he conducted another NSP concert, this time in Newbury and with Ruth Dyson, who stayed two nights at Ashmansworth, playing Milford's harpsichord Concertino. Milford also visited Ashmansworth and played Gerald a new overture. The Howells article was finished in early March, after which he and Joy stayed with the Vaughan Williamses in London and went to hear him conduct the *St John Passion* in Dorking (with Christopher Finzi in the orchestra); in London Gerald chaired a Composers' Concourse discussion on a Bartók lecture by Colin Mason, which included Darnton, Lutyens, Edward Clark, Bernard Stevens, Alan Bush and Seiber ('Several people who like talking for the sake of talking had to be manoeuvred' – J. Finzi 19540310). He went to London once again a week later to hand over to Boosey & Hawkes the Grand Fantasia and Toccata (the latter revised in the light of comments by Vaughan Williams) and one of the Stanley concertos he had been editing, and yet another London visit the following week, with Joy, was for a wedding, sherry with the Day Lewises and an exhibition by the young artist Richard Shirley Smith, friend of Kiffer, at Harrow. A visit to Gloucester in early April mixed business with pleasure, the pleasure being a breakfast meeting with the ecologist Frank Fraser Darling and his wife the poet Avril Morley, the business a fraught attempt to wrest Gurney's manuscripts from his brother Ronald. They dropped in on Gerald's mother too, now in a nursing home near Painswick. Herbert Sumsion reciprocated the geographical exodus the following week when he stayed at Ashmansworth while adjudicating the Newbury Festival. Two more NSP concerts followed later in the month; one of them was attended by Vaughan Williams and Frank Howes and included a Wesley organ concerto Gerald had resuscitated plus a new work by Adrian Cruft. They visited Ronald Gurney again in May, and at the end of the month spent a week in St Andrews while Gerald examined there followed by a week touring western Scotland with the Thorpe Davies. Gerald returned to a pile of correspondence and proofs – of Stanley and Mudge concertos and 'Welcome sweet and sacred feast' – that occupied the rest of June, as did further work on his *Love's Labour's Lost* music, which was given a run-through at the RCM in the presence of Ferguson and Vaughan Williams by James Lockhart, then a student conductor, on the eighteenth. On the twenty-fifth he gave a talk on Marion Scott to the Society of Women Musicians in London, and three days later went to Marlborough where Joy and the NSP were helping out in a local performance of *Dies natalis*. Throughout all this time he was still visiting the mysterious Mrs Ray weekly, having occasional hospital check-ups, and keeping up his voluminous correspondence.

His own music returned to the forefront of things with a vengeance on 8 July, for John Russell, offered a conducting date with the LSO, had booked the Festival Hall, the BBC Choral Society, Richard Lewis and the pianist Peter Katin for an all-Finzi concert containing *For St Cecilia*, *Dies natalis*, *Intimations* and the first professional performance of the Grand Fantasia and Toccata; Russell's Newbury concert had been a dry run for this. Gerald, Joy noted, was initially 'much against the idea, as he felt that it wd bring a nearly empty hall and a devastating loss for John. But upon John asking the advice of VW he was enthusiastically backed up' (J. Finzi 19540707). Things turned out well, with good performances, a hall 80% full ('in some measure due to all the trouble to which John went'), friends in plenteous attendance, including Vaughan Williams, Ferguson, Frankel, Howells, Bliss and Rubbra among the composers, and 'an extraordinarily warm & enthusiastic audience' if a 'rather patronising' press apart from (predictably) *The Times* (J. Finzi 19540708). The poet and HM Inspector of Schools Leonard Clark, he and his wife both amateur singers, was also present. Finzi had heard of him years earlier from Jack Haines, and they now began a rewarding correspondence that, together with ongoing Blunden exchanges, kept Finzi's literary faculties on their toes during his last two years. (Clark also edited a further selection of Gurney's poems after Finzi's death, in 1973.)

Given the personal nature of the Festival Hall concert, it can hardly be considered the peak of Finzi's career. But it was an important juncture, and Frankel's subsequent letter of congratulation, part of which was quoted in Chapter 9, is worth sampling further:

I do want to say one or two things which you may find flatulent but which are not the less sincerely felt for all that disadvantage. One of them is that I have the deepest conviction that when all the noise and pother of our self-conscious prophets of 'the new' have died down, your vocal works will be there to remind them that music went on being created that could go to the heart of the human matter. Another is, that your work is a living proof that when one has something deep to say, the manner of the saying always becomes noble no matter what means are chosen. The last, and perhaps the most self-conscious (for which please forgive me), is that it has become intensely necessary to find out from each other not what style or technique we are working in but what we are saying to each other. With you I know and love it and would not therefore for a moment attempt to put it into terms other than your own. (19540712)

Of course, what lies behind this and the patronising press of the Festival Hall concert (see Mitchell 1954, though he is a good deal more generous than one might expect), is that since the war a greater and greater chasm had been opening up between the 'soft' or 'fuzzy' humanism of Finzi's functionally tonal – increasingly tonal – idiom and the 'hard science' of modernist technique, aesthetics and professionalism in music. Finzi was well aware of this, had stopped peddling the liberal 'representative of civilisation' line, and was bastioning not just himself but a number of young composers who turned to him with the manner/matter distinction made by Frankel. We shall need to consider this further in the light of the Cello Concerto, its reception and its position in his output.

Frankel's words may well have encouraged him to be himself in his next composition, written during July and August, one which, after the somewhat unmanageable side revealed in the Grand Fantasia and Toccata, is quintessential from beginning to end and idiomatically franker than ever. If ever a musical work justified the celebration of the minor masterpiece from the limited pen, that work is *In terra pax*. Perfect in its fusion of idea and shape (if you like, of manner and matter), it takes Robert Bridges' poem 'Noel: Christmas Eve, 1913', subtitled '*Pax hominibus bonae voluntatis*', and creates what Finzi, in his own subtitle, called a 'Christmas scene' by omitting Bridges' third stanza and substituting St Luke's account of the angels' visitation to the Bethlehem shepherds.

In terra pax is full of resonances, as is Bridges' own poem – the poet's *pax* devastatingly ungranted when World War I broke out eight months later – and it is difficult to separate the work from Finzi's life. It was his second attempt at capturing the magic of his Chosen Hill experience on New Year's Eve and led directly to his final one. The third hammer-blow of fate struck when he revisited the hill two years later after conducting the full orchestral version of *In terra pax*, his last première and public appearance and virtually his last creative assignment. With its message of universal reassurance and blessing – the 'Angels' song' of 'fear not', '[as] comforting as the comfort of Christ / When he spake tenderly to his sorrowful flock' – amid the great, agnostic gulf of 'th'eternal silence', it seems to bespeak an acceptance of life and the unknown and to communicate something that is every composer's ultimate wish within the specific terms of reference crowding in on Finzi at the end of 1954: the leaked knowledge that he was 'going downhill very rapidly', the first real acceptance of mortality as he faced his splenectomy, even the possibility that he thought he might not pull through the operation and that the Christmas of 1954, and its Ashmansworth Church NSP concert, would be his last. Yet the facts, while scarcely denying the spirit of this interpretation, do not warrant its letter. Finzi was planning *In terra pax* as early as April 1951, before ever he got ill, the echo of the Biblical text at the end being Ferguson's suggestion at this point. (It sounds as though Finzi had previously been wondering whether to retain all four of Bridges' stanzas, with the third, homing in on the rustic bellringers, as his heterophonous climax – rather as in Vaughan Williams's 'Bredon Hill' – followed by the Biblical passage and finally a repetition of the poem's last stanza; Ferguson advised strongly against this. See 19510414b.) He composed it before anyone was aware of his latest deterioration in health. And the speed of publication of its vocal score, issued in time to become his 1954 Christmas card to the orchestra and other friends, was a surprise when he handed it in at Boosey & Hawkes at the end of September and heard of their intention: the gesture was a bonus, therefore, rather than premeditated purpose (the work being in any case dedicated to Sumsion), though one does wonder whether Boosey's knew or guessed anything about his prospects when they executed their 'special act' of producing seventy-five copies in an edition without the price on it for the occasion (J. Finzi 19541219). One cannot even rule out the possibility that Finzi composed the piece as a commercial proposition, something that would bring in seasonal earnings (as indeed it still does). As he wrote in *Absalom's Place*, 'the real intention of the work was for 1955 and onwards', meaning Christmas; 'after all,' as Milford wrote, 'there is really very little to fill the gap between carols & "the Christmas Oratorio", isn't there?, so I do hope it may become an established favourite for future Christmas-tides' (19541228).

In the same letter Milford commended Finzi on 'the constant suggestion of "the first Noel" & "that first Christmas of all" which runs through the work', and it is this together with the other thematic images that sets the seal on *In terra pax* as the perfect analogue of his susceptibility towards the season's atmosphere and celebrations, musical and other, and epitome of his childlike serenity of style. The means and the mood would not have been so vernacular, populist or effective in the younger man, and when his use of the phrase from the refrain of 'The first Nowell' (ex. 11.5.a) comes into final focus with the Hardyesque suggestion of straining west gallery tenors on the refrain's descant, a few bars before the end of the piece, one wonders whether this closing cameo was an unconscious response to the use of it by others – Elgar in *The Starlight Express*, Conrad Salinger and Roger Edens in *Meet Me in St Louis*. But the resolution of a children's or family scene into a snatch of Christmas carol is an old dramatic topic. The other obvious representation of Bridges' 'distant music' (ex. 11.5.b) is at first more like a clock chime wafting across the stillness of the valley than a peal of bells, but when the company of angels bursts on the scene with their words 'Glory to God in the highest' its canonic splendour is campanological enough, perhaps first thought of as the depiction of Bridges' 'rattling ropes that race / Into the dark above / and the mad romping din' at this point in his omitted third stanza. A third suggestion of diegetic, 'real-life' music picks up on Bridges' opening cue, 'A frosty Christmas Eve' (ex. 11.5.c), redolent in both poet and composer of waits and their nocturnal announcements, and lends it too the magic of distance and clear, cold air in its initial scoring on the harp. These three motifs, particularly the first two, are all-pervasive, skilfully and effortlessly woven – in a piece that for once has no structural weaknesses or awkward joins – into all manner of harmonic and melodic shades

EX. 11.5.a

EX. 11.5.b

EX. 11.5.c

EX. 11.5.d

EX. 11.5.e

of phrase and period as the narrative progresses. See, for instance, the detail, or rather hear the mood, of the downward scale fragments at the lines 'And from many a village in the water'd valley / Distant music reach'd me'. This passage also utilises upward steps as ex. 11.5.a's inversion, more of a structural issue at the first entry of the chorus (ex. 11.5.d), and the angel's sudden appearance similarly takes place to a kind of inversion of the clock chime (ex. 11.5.e), while in between the rising and falling steps are combined to form the figure for the shepherds keeping watch – or rather falling fast asleep until rudely awakened by the angel, a touch of humour as nice as is the magic touch of Vaughan Williams and his own oriental pastoralism at this point, with its modal dissolutions of consciousness between A minor, G minor and E minor (ex. 11.5.f). And the initial third of ex. 11.5.c expands manifestly to become the fifth for the angel's 'Fear not'.

But the point of *In terra pax* is not how it unifies thematic material but how it unites all its feelings and images and familiar events into one simple, shapely musical narrative that anyone can grasp. How

457

EX. 11.5.f

many classical works – vocal ones – are so direct and universal in their communication? In its miniature way it partakes of some portion of the greatness of Bach and Handel in Christmas music, for it has an extraordinary quality of openness and empathy. This was something Vaughan Williams had always shared, and there is an echo of 'The infinite shining heavens' from his *Songs of Travel* with its astral subject matter at the words 'The constellated sounds ran sprinkling on earth's floor'. Mahler is another influence, obvious once one removes Albion-tinted spectacles – not for nothing the initial tempo 'Adagietto' and the translucent scoring for harp and strings (plus cymbal), to refer to a piece Finzi had conducted with the Newbury String Players. The tools of Finzi's idiomatic workshop, more eclectic than reputation would have them, fit the task perfectly at every turn, whether they be set to fashion dancing angels, bright stars shining, didactic messengers' arias, the march of speeding thoughts, or a Bachian rocking manger. And if these figures are a matter of naïve candour, what could be more appropriate to Christmas? – or to Hollywood, come to that, delightfully close at hand in the shepherds' fear heart-pounding on the lower strings and the great light in the sky glowing chordally with many a hairpin dynamic in the chorus (compare *Jaws* and *E.T.* respectively): not for the first time we observe Bernard Herrmann, John Williams and their compatriots as kindred pictorial spirits. For all this, however, *In terra pax* is a work of poetic courage when it resolves all its acceptance of feeling, community, reverence, naïvety, setting and tradition in the telling of the old tale – so similar to Hardy's bundle of values in 'The oxen' – into one 'eternal silence' as its personal correlative, the narrator 'heark'ning' for a sound, looking for a sign, any modern sign to match the comforting yet illusory old ones, the musician positing one bare note, a cavernous F♯ of ambiguous and ungrounded meaning, cold and alone whether phrygian tonic in F♯ minor, dominant in B minor or, as it turns out, mediant in D major. Bridges counterpoints this subjective agnosticism with the continuity of rustic faith, even the suggestion of a different, proletarian narrator, in his third stanza; by omitting this Finzi foregrounds the soul-searching subjectivism.

In terra pax is suffixed 'XXXIX', and Finzi reached only one further opus number, XL, for the Cello Concerto. His unconstrained creative agenda had not lasted for long, for no sooner had he finished *In terra pax*, the only work of his final years written entirely of his own volition (even the late songs were commanded by circumstances) than Sir John Barbirolli wrote, in September 1954, to ask for a major first performance for his tenth Cheltenham Festival the following summer. This meant finishing the Cello Concerto, but first *In terra pax* had to be orchestrated, and one can see why Gerald fought confinement and the splenectomy on practical, let alone psychological, grounds. He did much of the scoring in hospital, as related earlier, in time for the first performance, a BBC studio one, on 27 February 1955. He and Joy heard this over the air, having been present in London at the rehearsal the day before, given by John Russell and the Goldsbrough Orchestra with Myra Verney and Hervey Alan as soloists. Joy noted that Verney, Harriet Cohen's sister, was 'the wrong angel' and that the harpist was 'not quite up to it' but that the performance as a whole was good (J. Finzi 19550226, 19550227). Vaughan Williams, Ferguson and Nigel Finzi (now a violin scholar under Rostal at the Guildhall) were at the rehearsal, Ferguson writing after the broadcast to say that he agreed that 'Miss Verney ought to be put away (painlessly); apart from her, there was nothing to complain of,' and though he found 'the Angel's music a little too full of *human* emotion,' it was otherwise 'a lovely work & a brilliantly successful idea' (19550304a).

There was now no time to lose if the Cello Concerto was to be ready for its first performance with Barbirolli and the Hallé in Cheltenham Town Hall on 19 July. The slow movement, as has already been noted, was complete as early as 1951 and tried over and bowed by Anna Shuttleworth in January 1952 when she was staying at Ashmansworth for an NSP concert. Quite when Finzi found time to put in the bulk of his work on the lengthy first movement is not clear, though it was probably not a great deal in advance of 1955, if at all, since Milford was only played the slow movement when he visited Ashmansworth in the summer of 1953. It may have come in a rush upon his quick recovery from the splenectomy; in any case, it was finished 'all but the [last?] few bars' by mid-March, when Christopher Bunting paid the first of several visits to Ashmansworth to work on it. Ten days later, there was a further session on the concerto with him at the Vaughan Williamses' in London, where the Finzis were staying. Vaughan Williams was enthusiastic about it – the two extant movements, that is – but prompted the cadenza or its extension, effected the following month in another session with Bunting and authored, like some of the other solo passagework, partly by composer, partly by soloist. In April Finzi was wrestling with the finale, but one is astonished to realise that at this time he was also having to write his three Crees Lectures on words and music for the RCM (they were delivered in May and, much to his surprise, treated as a major public event, to the extent of *Observer* and *Times* reviews by Blom and Howes), his elder son was off to prison for three months – reduced in the event to nine weeks – as a conscientious objector to national service (the tribunal appeal having been rejected the previous December, possibly through refusal to confect the standard religious grounds), and he even produced another composition, albeit a single instrumental variation. This last was his contribution to *Diabelleries*, variations on 'Where's my little basket gone', a theme attributed to Alfred Scott-Gatty, by Vaughan Williams (who mischievously suggested the source), Ferguson, Alan Bush, Rawsthorne, Lutyens, Maconchy, Grace Williams and Jacob as well as Finzi. *Diabelleries* was a present to Anne Macnaghten and her new music group, presumably for old times' sake where her pioneering pre-war concerts were concerned, and was performed in London on 16 May. As we have seen, during all this time he was having weekly radiation treatment once more in Oxford, but his renewed vigour after the operation allowed him, probably simultaneously and in record time, to get through the composition of the finale and the scoring of the whole (the latter once more with the help of Ferguson, who put in two long weekends at Ashmansworth), though there is no doubt that the last movement was rushed and Finzi's mode of discourse simplified in the concerto's outer movements, with a more continuous, accompanied rather than conversational train of thought from the soloist than was his wont. He finished the concerto on 22 June, not having been helped by the 'seedy old man' Boosey's produced when he begged for a copyist (J. Finzi 19550622). Still changing things at the last minute, he handed everything to Boosey's, score and parts, only on 1 July, which to

Bunting's alarm was less than three weeks before the première, and on the tenth took the train to Manchester for Barbirolli's first rehearsal with the orchestra.

Barbirolli gave it his best, for he had been an admirer of Finzi since 1947 when he wrote to him appreciatively of *Dies natalis*, after performing it with Isobel Baillie. He was a cellist himself and must have been all the more delighted when he heard what Gerald had on the stocks for his commission. Finding the right soloist, however, proved more problematic. Zara Nelsova was spoken of, and then André Navarra, rejected because he asked for a fee of £130. Christopher Bunting was nonetheless an exciting eventual choice, a young player of 'fabulous technique' (J. Finzi 19550227) who occasioned Finzi's most virtuoso solo role by far, even if all the difficulties are of a traditional kind. On his first visit to Ashmansworth, Bunting, a Casals pupil, impressed the Finzis as 'a very remarkable person, a powerful mind & great sensitivity & bringing the grand manner to his playing in a way that is rare even among the best English cellists' (J. Finzi 19550312). He could play the notes with ease and great feeling but had difficulties with projection, and complaints of inaudibility in passagework were made of his performances of the concerto, a problem not solved during Finzi's lifetime (no one else seems to have played it for a very long time) although Barbirolli thought he could help Bunting with it. Cello concertos are always on the edge of practicability in this respect, so it was no severe reflection on the player, whose readings were warmly appreciated by most of Finzi's correspondents and much of the press, and certainly not on the work, which is well thought out in this regard.

Barbirolli loved the concerto, took it to the Festival Hall for its London première the following March, and wrote afterwards to Finzi, 'I felt tears in my eyes in the slow movement. There are only a few moments in music which do that to me & without going into details, I can assure you, you are in good company!!' (19560321b). He also programmed it for the Henry Wood Promenade Concerts at the Royal Albert Hall the following August. Extraordinary as it may seem, this was Finzi's one Prom performance of major significance during his lifetime, and only the third hearing of anything at all by him in the series. (The 1954 season had included *A Garland for the Queen* and *Let Us Garlands Bring* – the programme planners clearly had garlands on their mind – but Finzi missed them both.) Knowledge that Barbirolli had to go into hospital for the removal of a non-malignant growth and would miss this performance caused Joy and Gerald unease, for they were no fan of his deputy, George Weldon; and Gerald, backed up by Bunting, offered to conduct the work himself. But they were touched when Barbirolli wrote to them the day before his operation – asking Gerald for a new work for the Hallé's centenary the following season – and Weldon took reasonably good care of the performance, though the studio broadcast transmitted the following month was in the hands of Georges Tzipine.

Finzi had never before been taken up by a front-rank conductor like this, and it is sad that he only lived to see a year of such promotion. 'You know that I have the greatest faith in it and I am happy to be able to demonstrate this to you in the most practical way possible – that is, by giving performances of it,' Barbirolli wrote when the short score of the Cello Concerto was published in June 1956, adding, 'I do hope that B. and H. are sending out copies of the Concerto to all the leading European Cellists for I have talked about it quite a lot during my travels this year' (19560703). Evidently Boosey's did this, and when, a month later, Finzi received a letter in French from Casals in Prades, saying how much he liked the work, it was 'almost like getting one from Paganini or Sarasate' (19560811). Did Casals ever play the work? Apparently not.

The Cello Concerto dominated Finzi's final year – its first broadcast was the night before he died – though it had dominated his thoughts for a good deal longer. As mentioned in Chapter 7, it was possibly some kind of a tribute to Joy, its solo instrument's range perhaps analogous to that of her personality or even her voice; she herself referred to it as 'written since our marriage' as opposed to the Piano Concerto, belonging to the period before it (J. Finzi 19520130), as though each in some sense symbolised the separate individuals or the one represented the struggling single artist, the other the fulfilled man. Be that as it may, there seem to be more fragments in Finzi's sketchbooks for a cello work, or for gruff or stormy gestures seemingly connected with the Cello Concerto's opening, than for anything else, and some of these undoubtedly date back to the early 1930s. Sketchbook C, for example, containing a draft of 'When I set out for Lyonnesse' and therefore earlier than 1935 or thereabouts, includes both a distant foreshadowing of the concerto's slow movement theme (ex. 11.6.a) on page 10 and the real thing, in the right key, a few pages later, with other cello-orientated material in between. The sketch of the theme as

EX. 11.6.a

EX. 11.6.b

we know it may well have been added later, but the connection with earlier material is what proves the point. The central theme of the slow movement's episode is sketched, complete with its chromaticism (ex. 11.6.b), not only in a book datable to 1930 or 1931 but also in the middle of the Bristol Channel on an Ordnance Survey map used for walking tours in the same two years! This was even before he had met Joy. As for the gruff and stormy openings, they seem to have betokened a lifetime's determined symphonic proposition, and a sample is given in ex. 11.6.c–f, one of them, in A minor, actually labelled 'Sym[phony]'.

What is not present in these sketches is the unmistakably Celtic cast of the Cello Concerto's opening melody, with its Scotch snap and dorian sharpened sixth. This, and the movement's overall brooding, passionate lilt, could have been influenced by the equally fine first movement of Moeran's Cello Concerto of 1945 (as well as by Elgar's); they could also be something to do with Joy's Scottish and Northern Irish descent, or with the couple's holiday in western Scotland in May 1954, when they visited Fingal's Cave, for the motif is a kind of retrograde of Mendelssohn's opening one on the cellos (see ex. 11.6.g). Whatever the source of the urge, urge it is, giving this first movement a surging breadth that 'sings to the swing of the tide'. It lasts over fifteen minutes, the whole piece thirty-five to forty. The models Finzi must have drawn on, consciously or otherwise, for a romantic concerto of this size include any or all of the Brahms concertos, the Dvořák Cello Concerto, Rachmaninov's piano concertos and, closer to home, Elgar's Violin Concerto.

EX. 11.6.c

EX. 11.6.d

EX. 11.6.e

EX. 11.6.f

He follows them to the extent that all three of his movements are in standard, recognisable forms and utilise conventional rhetoric, though they are assembled in idiosyncratic ways. It is also worth noting that he played through the Tovey concerto and Parry sonata with Bunting.

The first movement has a full – and splendid – orchestral exposition of which the features earmarked for most use later on are the ubiquitous motif x (ex. 11.6.h), a rather Bliss-like lull in the waves to a sequence of $^6_3$ chords, and the figure y (ex. 11.6.i). One of the reasons why this movement has little by way of a clear development section is because, very much as with Elgar's sequential workings and 'asides' in his later

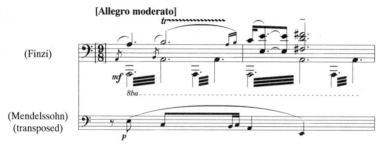

EX. 11.6.g

EX. 11.6.h

EX. 11.6.i

EX. 11.6.j

symphonic works, so much close development is inherent in the thematic material itself that it cannot be prised apart harmonically (see, for example, ex. 11.6.j). To keep the movement dynamic, fresh and consistent over its entire length when there is so much of this intimate interchange going on must have been no mean feat; conversely, one feels the change of texture, key (F major) and metre at the second

465

subject as rather a jolt, switching as it does to an 'aria' topic from a fully symphonic one rather than from some kind of *arioso* – possibly the first time Finzi had ever had to do this, except perhaps in *Intimations*. The exposition ends in the tonic – no matter – with a palpable codetta, but no sooner have we heard a development gesture of interest, a beautifully pensive three-bar figure repeated up a minor third, very much with the feeling of both Elgar and Vaughan Williams, than it becomes clear that we are not going to hear another, further development being merged with recapitulation from figure 11. This juncture is disguised because it lacks the start of the orchestral ritornello, is now in the subdominant, and, rather as in the Toccata for piano and orchestra, leads on from here towards blocks of exposition material revisited in a different order and with substitutions and a good deal of omission. The second subject returns in the relative major, with a further appearance in G but this time assimilated to 12/8. The new passage before the enormous cadenza is pure Bliss and with its semiquaver triplets begins to hint at the Hispanic finale. But what one carries away from this movement above all are the Fafner-like heavings that close it, the opening giant of a three-chord trick now turned into a monster whose writhings of major triads (and then minor) with a semitonal dissonance added to each in the bass threaten the cello's very life as it struggles with them for mastery. Romantic heroism enters Finzi's creative realm with a vengeance while, imagery apart, the chords and their counterpoint pursue a relentless logic that one does not associate with him.

The movement ends with a stroke of genius when the unison tonic dies away at such length that one eventually doubts its finality and injects suspense into it, which of course begins to make it into a dominant preparatory to the slow movement, whose serene opening is quoted in ex. 8.4.d. Again there is a Celtic element, in this case the repeated tonic, and again a little figure, the dotted-note appoggiatura at figure 1, will prove ubiquitous. This movement, for all its family resemblance to Finzi's other idylls, is uniquely beautiful, its opening cantilena all the more blessed for coming after the restlessnes of the first movement. But it is far too long, not in rapt stasis like Finzi's early slow movements but with a succession of climaxes in no clear relation to one another within an overall form that approximates to ABAXA, where X is development. Ferguson's diagnosis and remedy were clear, blunt, and right:

About the ... slow movement: I think the music is heart-breakingly beautiful, but that formally and emotionally it overbalances the rest of the work. That is to say, as the middle of a big work it is about a third too long. I have an idea that you are very unlikely to do anything about this point, or that you will agree with it, for I get the impression that the movement means something special to you; however, I feel I must mention it, since it struck me so *very* strongly. If it were my baby I would let the return of the opening music after the *first* climax be the real recapitulation, followed only by that very lovely quiet coda. This would cut out the second climax altogether, which seems to me altogether disproportionate for the material of the movement and the position of the movement in the work as whole, and it would cut out a largish wad of music which I also felt was redundant. However, it's *not* my baby ... (19550721)

There is another way of looking at this problem, and it seems that what Finzi was groping towards, though without reaching it, in Ferguson's 'largish wad of music' was a fantasy scherzo section within the slow movement. Rather as in *Intimations*, scherzo topics begin to be found as the composer delves deeper and deeper into his reflective material: they emerge with the 'pressando', 'più movimento' and 'accel.' markings following the recapitulation at figure 9, and especially with the bucolic clarinet duet with pizzicato dance chords shown in ex. 11.6.k, the *alfresco* impressionistic reinterpretation of the main theme at figure 10 that follows it (again with a pizzicato bass), and the sextuplet cello figuration that then virtuosically takes over. The obvious subconscious model for all this is the slow movement form of Rachmaninov's Second Piano Concerto (with some similarities in that of the Third), though the generic archetype goes right back to the Chopin nocturne with the flights of uncontrolled, often disturbing fancy that it frequently generates. But what in Rachmaninov becomes a breathtaking leap of imagination,

EX. 11.6.k

leading to a crisis at which it is broken off, never quite gets off the ground with Finzi, who seems not to have had the courage of his convictions about it and climaxes with yet another plodding march apotheosis of his main idea with its stepwise bass at figure 12, though his winding-down includes enough of a serenade topic (particularly in the pizzicati of the 6/8 bars) to make one see where his imagination might have taken him had technique been pushed a little farther.

In this last climax, in the thwarted scherzo, and above all in the inner recesses of the B section, we revisit, as McVeagh (1986) rightly points out, 'the melancholy grandeur that informs . . . *Intimations of Immortality*', and though the absence of words makes all the difference to how such grandeur can be articulated and sustained, the B section taken as a unit (which it should surely be, though the point is arguable) seems to want to reveal more of Finzi's emotional core than anything else he wrote. It is the way he *signals* inner depths rather than the material itself that conveys this message, for at figure 6, with the last of his magical 'Butterworth' modulations, he uses a trombone chord, with all the instruments' old sacral associations, to turn the key twice in a door leading into another, secret, perhaps lost world with the haunting phrase *z* in ex. 11.6.l. Some wonderfully tender and evocative wind solos inform this inner sanctum of the Concerto before its door is locked once more, even more poignantly when the sixth note of *z* is reinterpreted as the semitonal tonic against a Neapolitan accompanying chord.

Once again there is a subtle psychological link between movements, when the rhythm of the cello's exquisite final musings in the Andante is augmented (visually) to presage the Rondo, in an atmospheric introduction full of diegetic sounds like a city (Vaughan Williams's London?)

EX. 11.6.l

or landscape awakening. (This does not quite come off, and paradoxically needs to be longer.) The scene, when the sun rises on it, turns out to be overseas, and one can leave aside the question of whether or not the rondo theme digs up Finzi's Italian and Hispanic roots (whilst being at the same time a polonaise!) with the more functional suggestion that it further reveals the light music composer *manqué*. Ferguson disliked it, and it does give rise to some tawdry moments, the worst of them the shabby developmental link *X* in the overall formal plan ABCAXDCABYAZ. In this scheme C includes fugato references to ex. 11.6.g, *Y* is the obligatory (since Elgar) mournful retrospect, here rather uninspired and unnecessary, the final A a C major apotheosis of the rondo theme on brass, and *Z* a very short, skittish coda which furthers one's wish that Finzi's forty minutes had found proper place for the scherzo impulse, perhaps in a separate movement. The first return of the rondo theme, with an extended oboe countermelody added to the cello solo, raises another wishful thought: that Finzi had been granted time for someone to suggest that he return to this solo instrument in a subsequent work – perhaps for Lady Barbirolli.

In the 1920s and to a certain extent in the 1930s Finzi's austere early style, alongside works by such as van Dieren and Rawsthorne, went some way towards answering the aural challenge and penance of contemporary music, though even then he was not thought of as one of the 'moderns' (Lemare 1996). Now the challenge had irrevocably moved on and his style had in many respects moved backwards. The press at the Cheltenham Festival of British Contemporary Music found this hard to take. 'Is it possible to call "contemporary" a work so dominated by the figure of Elgar and one whose harmonic language and thematic character give no hint of what has been happening in music during the last 40 years?' Martin Cooper asked in the *Daily Telegraph* the following day (:10), while Desmond Shawe-Taylor in the *New Statesman* on 30 July (:132–3) was even more doubtful, maintaining that 'his Cello Concerto is conceived and executed so much under the shadow of Elgar that only by courtesy can it be called a new work at all'. He called its finale 'modified *Nell Gwynn*'. *The Times*, possibly in the person of Howes (though it does not sound quite like him), rather feebly put the opposite point of view when it summed up the festival's first ten years, concluding: 'it is one of our besetting temptations to overpraise the new because it is new, and another is to underestimate what is traditionally expressed merely because its language is not new' (29 July 1955: 6).

Finzi had had to learn to live with this debate more or less since the rise of Britten after the Second World War, and knew how to defend himself. But doing so might easily have exhausted him or made him dig himself too far in – which one can certainly argue is beginning to happen in the Cello Concerto – had he lived to run the gauntlet of an ever-hardening critical climate too many more times. What would the work for the Hallé centenary have been like? Or the Viola Concerto he had wanted to write ever since Bernard Shore wrote asking him for one in 1946? One wonders all the more because he put himself on display as a champion for younger composers who felt thwarted or victimised by the cold science of postwar modernism, even – and this is the sad thing – when their idiom was adventurous, if sometimes this was at the expense of their true inclinations. Leighton, Cannon, Anthony Milner especially, had reason to view him as a beacon of integrity. The Milner correspondence from 1956 puts Finzi's point of view very eloquently, and he was honest enough to let Milner know that he was using it to hone his arguments for the London University lectures the following year.

In March he had congratulated Milner on a *Musical Times* article, 'The vocal element in melody', and added: 'The real worry to me is not that of a new language – after all, it has been familiar for 30 years and I can understand it more or less, without wishing to speak it, – but the danger of a great art being narrowed down to a very few people and the consequent withering of its roots' (19560327). This would have been one of his themes in the lecture series to be entitled *Aspects of the Past, Present and Future* – 'the importance of the amateur in the life of a country's musical structure' (19560523). Four months later, after hearing a broadcast of one of Milner's works, he expatiated on another topic:

And now I suppose people like Colin Mason will start telling you (or rather the public) as he did in the case of Kenneth Leighton's new 'Cello Concerto, that your 'romantic idiom is very conservative', that you have 'a rather artificial fluency of melody', that you have 'shirked the real problem of all young composers today and made things too easy for himself by writing in a language which is as dead for the music of his generation, as Mozart's . . . etc' and that you have written a 'complete emotional fake' etc. etc.

I quote this from a cutting in front of me, as it's typical of the sort of pressure which is put on younger people to try and make them conform to a minority style, whether *or not it is right for their particular quality of mind and feeling.* Meanwhile the Colin Masons and Peter Heyworths go on writing straightforward English, in spite of the fact that English has been revolutionised by Gertrude Stein and James Joyce! (I've not yet heard the answer to this one!)

I feel so particularly angry about Kenneth Leighton because I feel that he has a natural and spontaneous lyrical quality which, whether it last or not, is too valuable to be sacrificed to Colin Mason's ideas of the right language for a composer to use. In any case there is no reason why the use of one language shd preclude the understanding of another. (19560805)

Here, then, was his second theme for the lectures, 'our faulty aesthetics which continually confuse idiom with quality' (19560523). It was pursued further in his final exchange with Milner:

I take it to be one of the glories of the world that it can hold a Byrd at one end and a Berg at the other: that we can appreciate a Bartók (which I was doing before Mason was born) and a Parry. Surely conservatism and liberalism are states of mind, not languages.

These little pip-squeaks try to *reduce* experience and appreciation, to narrow down understanding to what they alone think is worth understanding. Their pedantry and narrowness makes the Victorian pedagogues seem comparatively liberal. And when they describe the language which 97% of the musical world understands, as a dead one they are, by their tactics, alienating music from the very people who shd be encouraged to understand it.

I have worked so much amongst amateurs that I'm quite convinced that these little people wd be serving music much better if they tried to train a village choir or managed to teach a small boy the elements of string playing. But cd they? Not on your life! All they can do is to put a magnifying glass over two or three bars and try to prove that because three notes go up and three notes go down Walton, VW, Elgar, Brahms – all, all are past redemption! Ebenezer Prout isn't in it. (19560812)

Note also a foretaste of his third theme, 'change & fashion' (19560523), for one imagines this would have included a plea for rehabilitation of the Victorians, and not only Parry, since he had written to Herrmann a couple of years earlier: 'Poor old Stanford wrote about seven operas, and some of them make one wonder why they don't get revived today. But the time is against them' (19541102).

Whether or not Finzi's antipathy towards Colin Mason had been fuelled by the Bartók lecture he had chaired, it is only fair to point out that Mason himself was not antipathetic towards Finzi, and assumed the composer's own viewpoint in his review of the Cello Concerto's Manchester première:

Finzi's work is certainly conservative, but it is not to be dismissed with most of what falls under that label. Conservatism itself is no fault. The trouble is that in the arts it often accompanies, or is a manifestation of, an inferior sensibility. This was not true of Finzi, as this concerto proclaims, perhaps more strongly than anything else he ever wrote. His music had always shown, in spite of its relatively conventional language, a distinction of personality and thought, a fastidiousness of expression, and a fineness of taste that rejected all the banalities – lyrical, rhetorical, or jovial – characteristic of most conservative music, even by composers of real talent. In this work he showed himself for the first time capable also, without any sacrifice of this natural refinement of style (comparable in its more conservative idiom with Lennox Berkeley's), of a symphonic work of the same large proportions and high romantic ardour (still in its more conservative idiom, of course) as those of any concerto by Fricker. It is an outstanding success in a very difficult medium, with abundant and varied thematic material, some of it very beautiful, and all treated with invention and imagination, not least in the form, which is designed to leave the orchestra playing alone at the biggest dynamic climaxes in all three movements, so that we are never straining to hear the relatively weak solo instrument at these moments. To have managed this without any effect of contrivance, as Finzi has done, is a brilliant feat. (*Guardian*, 1 November 1956: 7)

Rehearsing his distinctions so carefully, as he does, makes one wonder whether he was here paying posthumous homage to an impressive debating position that had reached and convinced him.

On 18 March 1955, right in the middle of the composition of the Cello Concerto, Joy wrote that Gerald had completed a Hardy song, 'Life laughs onward', 'the first song he has written for some time'. She thought it was 'a good sign & one which so often happens when he is wrestling with urgent other work' (J. Finzi 19550317). It was not merely relaxation from a larger creative effort, for having made his will the previous month after the spleen operation Finzi was consciously beginning to put his affairs in order, and aware that there were a number of good songs to poems by Hardy and others that had not yet been placed in sets, he now attempted to finish, revise and add a number of others in the hope that there would be time to complete the four or five coherent volumes he envisaged. Some of the revisions that probably dated from the last eighteen months of his life have already been discussed; a brief survey of his remaining programme of song composition is now in order.

Five more Hardy songs were added to his total, all except one for low voice though with the hope that there would be another high-voice and another low-voice set. In addition, as indicated in Chapter 5, 'I say I'll seek her', which is a high-voice one, was probably re-written. Most of the others were also completions of extant material, and they can all be dated except 'For Life I had never cared greatly'. Joy's reference in July 1956 to 'the new five Hardy songs' (J. Finzi 19560714) suggests that, like the others, it belongs to the first half of that year. The first of the dated songs is 'In five-score summers (Meditation)', of which 'one verse had been written some time ago' when Finzi took it out again in mid-January 1956. Joy's journal comment, that 'G feels it alright as an extract from a diary but the words make it unsuitable for public performance', and its subtitle (which is Finzi's) suggest that he may have been concerned about its being too personal, even self-pitying in its correspondence with his morbid depression at this time as his final course of radiotherapy began; but the real problem is that the poem is Hardy at his Gothick worst, a mode calculated to show Finzi's sententious minor-key inflections, sonorities and chromaticisms in a cloying, melodramatic light, almost as self-parody. Once again one sees (and hears) the parallel with Mahler.

The other high-voice song, 'It never looks like summer', was another reworking, as Joy's journal entry for 23 February 1956 recounts:

whilst I went to Newbury G opened his Hardy poems & on reading 'It never looks like summer here' instantly set it. A little one but beautiful. This is a tenor song. Later this evening 'It's extraordinary how the mind works, quite extraordinary' – on looking thro' old musical notes he came on a page with sketches for the first line of 'It never looks like summer here'. When this first line sprang instantaneously to music on reading it this afternoon, it was quite unknown to him that he had previously worked at it over 25 years ago. The line written today had the same shape and fall as the previous germ & was obviously the completed idea after twenty odd years. 'If one doesn't live long enough one can't complete the hundreds of musical lines waiting final shape.' 'What makes one suddenly write a song?'

Two days earlier he had completed 'At Middle-Field Gate in February', 'an old draft with one verse written' (J. Finzi 19560221). This song presented him with the problem of Hardy's grammatical slip on revision, resulting in a rhymed verb that does not agree with its subject. He set Hardy's original as an *ossia* so that the performer can decide on the lesser of two evils; but before settling on his course of action he consulted Blunden, Navarro and the Hardy expert Howard Bliss about it.

Bliss, Arthur's brother, was a wealthy recluse whom Finzi hardly knew but who nevertheless responded by giving him the autograph manuscript of Hardy's poem 'We field-women'.

The February song foray was by way of playing truant from the orchestration of the Magnificat. 'I said to Love', his last Hardy song, was similarly composed in the interstices of a scoring job, that of *In terra pax* for full orchestra, and he drafted it in July, polishing it in early August. It was added to his corpus with the deliberate intention of filling out and balancing a volume, for, as Joy noted, it was 'more violent . . . than some of the recent ones – & therefore a help by way of contrast' (J. Finzi 19560805).

None of these last Hardy songs has the profundity and scope of his greatest earlier ones, though 'I said to Love' is highly impressive and something of a companion to 'He abjures love' and 'The clock of the years' with its transcendental melodrama in both text and music. This makes it more of a sport than a *credo* – an essay by poet and composer in seeing how far an idea can be taken, though the idea itself (that of 'nescience', the loss of humankind's will to self-perpetuate) was an obsession with Hardy. Its vision of a self-destroying humanity is rather like condensing Wagner's *Ring* into four minutes, and the music does something of this too. The sheer noise of its barnstorming chords and punctuating unisons is Wagnerian, and with their clangorous sonorities and with no fewer than seven markings of *fortissimo* and above they would orchestrate magnificently, though no voice could hope to ride the result. Wagnerian too is the suggestion of Wotan and his spear in the descending line at 'We fear not such a threat from thee', and of a stage fight to the death with the dragon Love in the extraordinary piano cadenza, followed by last-breath imprecations in the best operatic tradition. Or one can see these features as another legacy of the Liszt four-in-one symphony, the B minor Piano Sonata again hovering in the background, as with 'Channel firing'. Structurally Hardy's poem is another gift to a composer, like 'To Lizbie Browne', because of its four-syllable refrain lines (eight of them, at the beginnings and ends of four stanzas); and as in his settings of 'To Lizbie Browne' and 'My spirit sang all day', Finzi does something slightly different for each one, though here the emphasis is less on this than on formal simplicity – two pairs of stanzas with a dominant pivot between them, the first pair with an aria consequent leading to this, the second with development (and a nice episodic touch of Finzi's 'blues' style for Hardy's brilliant image of 'iron daggers of distress') which reverts to arioso after the cadenza, all within the tonal plan of a C major that closes as C minor.

'For Life I had never cared greatly' is, by happy contrast, a last Finzi bagatelle, one of his best tunes, cast in a continuously circling ABABA[1] format for Hardy's five stanzas – circling, in that until the end the tune only ever reaches the tonic harmonically as it begins again. It all sounds so natural, such an obvious corollary to Hardy's country-dancing lines, that one feels that anyone could have done it. Not so: and witness to the effort involved survives in the many Hardy poems Finzi began to set comparably but never completed, such as 'Weathers' and 'Afterwards' (see Banfield 1985: I, 289).

The idiom of the first two stanzas of 'At Middle-Field Gate in February' sounds like early Finzi, and one imagines that one or the other of them was what had already been written, its partly whole-tone ostinato then shifted up or down a tone for its new companion. This is the last of Finzi's 'aerial' Hardy impressions, it being this time a drop of water that falls through the foggy air, splashing down the gate bars, where in other songs leaves, or a comet, or the moon, or a star were suspended. The ostinato suggests Holst ('Saturn') or Debussy, the falling droplet perhaps Butterworth's cherry blossom once again, for there is a last echo of his phrase, or rather of its use in Finzi's other early works, between the second and third stanzas, before its descending tenor line is transformed into the 'late' baritone style and cadence of the final verse.

'It never looks like summer' is, like 'I look into my glass', a *trompe l'oeil* of keys and modes, though interlocking over two rather than three stanzas. That is, the end of the second is depressed far flatwards, into B♭ minor. As an analogue for Hardy's perception of life's pattern slipping disastrously beyond one's control or even one's notice, it excuses a Finzi mannerism. But the art, even the sad philosophical rightness of it in both men, is in the fact that one could have seen it coming and that its end is, in a twisted sense, its beginning: for the B♭ minor had been foreshadowed at the word 'drear' in the first stanza – an enharmonic perspective on the C♯ leading note of the pivotal dominant – and in any case leads ironically back into the regions of one flat when the song ends on its dominant, a chord of F, the irony all the stronger in that this sounds like the relative *major* of the original tonic. Hardy would have liked this view of things, and indeed it is almost as if Finzi is creating his own post-Emma retrospect in these last songs as he revisits so much early work from the standpoint of late experience and understanding. Yet there is still room for 'Life laughs onward', the perfect antidote to it all, as poet and composer revisit their old haunts to find them freshly inhabited as 'Old succumb[s] to Young'. Finzi's revisited haunts, rather as in 'I say I'll seek her', are a handful of his best idiomatic fabrics – bits of ditty, aria, wistful trope, melodramatic piano figuration, 'stride' for the loud gambolling children, syncopated sonata subject for the life force, and shy pastoral pastel for the missing self or beloved. Miraculously he manages to cram all these into a short song held together by the last of his clock chimes – joyful and rising – and the tiniest scrap of 'aria' head motif signified by a staccato quaver bass, with perfect word-setting and without a whiff of staleness.

His last songs to verse other than Hardy's amounted to rather less. Over the years he had begun settings of a great many poets, sometimes quite a number of the same poet – Housman, for instance – without them becoming sustainable projects. (See Banfield 1985: II, 444–7 for a complete list of fragments.) One or two longer-term goals appeared, however. *Three Dramatic Ballads* was mentioned in Chapter 2, *Flowers of Sion* and *The Posting Sun* in Chapter 6; another was an intended *Bestiary* cycle, to poems (and one piece of prose) about various animals from de la Mare's anthology *Come Hither*, though only one of these got as far as having any music added. *Dance Now and Sing* was a planned Campion partsong set, with some sketched fragments. A few Shakespeare settings were begun and abandoned, whether or not in connection with *Let Us Garlands Bring*. And the 1950s saw a new departure when an Oxford poet, Ian Davie, actually wrote an extended religious poem, *Piers Prodigal*, after he had heard a performance of *Dies natalis* and in the hope that Finzi would set it to music. This disarmed Finzi at first when Davie sent it to him, but also flattered and interested him enough that he began to work on it, for he thought well of the poem. (He also met Davie quite by chance at an NSP concert in Oxford. Davie published his poem after Finzi's death, in 1961.) The foremost intentions that remained, however, were, as mentioned earlier, a de la Mare and a Blunden volume, and to these he now added a song each, 'The birthnight' and 'Harvest' respectively. ('The birthnight' was written some time prior to mid-June 1956; see Chapter 6 for the background to 'Harvest'.)

It comes as something of a shock to realise that Finzi had by now been wedded almost exclusively to Hardy in his completed solo song settings for over twenty years. Shakespeare and his single George Barker song were the only exceptions, unless one includes *Dies natalis*. There is accordingly the concomitant shock of a slightly new musical voice in both 'The birthnight' and 'Harvest' as fresh poets' accents are explored. It is more noticeable in the de la Mare setting, with its strong touch of Gurney (who also set de la Mare with great feeling) in the highly intimate D♭ major key, caressing slow syncopations and memorably rapt melodic openings (for the line 'A sighing wind' as well as the first one). It does not quite match Gurney's intensity, and though the return to the initial melody is aimed in that direction, it is immediately counteracted by a typical Finzi gesture in the opposite one: the *envoi* away from the tonic (in this case the subdominant, sounding curiously bright), which wilfully opens out the whole structure. It expresses the outcome of intimacy and wonder in the innocence and surprise of new birth – the converse of the repose and consecration of death at the end of 'Fear no more the heat o' the sun'. 'Harvest' offers a more familiar personality, but one tempered and made somewhat austere by Blunden's kind of introspection, compounded of curiosity and diffidence and with no capacity for Hardy's emotional melodrama and indulgence. The music on occasions seems to weigh out its notes and define its textures as economically as Blunden his words in his letters to Finzi (see ex. 11.7.a, reminiscent of the 'fugue' in the Magnificat), with an emphasis here and elsewhere on bare seconds. But this only throws the 'aria' resolution of the song's and the poem's problem into all the more delicious relief when it comes with a Purcellian refulgence that even Blunden the nonmusician must have appreciated (ex. 11.7.b). Finzi never used this device

EX. 11.7.a

477

But hush – Earth's __ val-leys sweet in lei-sure lie; __

pp molto sostenuto

EX. 11.7.b

more beautifully, and the image of the composer accepting his unfulfilled personal fate and descending the hill to enjoy nature's cornfields in harvest is not just a touching but an uncannily prescient one, given the role that both hill and cornfields were to play in Gerald's life the following month – his last.

Equally uncanny is 'Since we loved', to a tiny poem by Robert Bridges. Finzi cannot have known or guessed that this would be his last composition, for when the end came it was swift and without warning. Yet nor could he have written a more beautiful and perfect final love letter to Joy, to his art, and to life itself (even if the line 'All my songs have happy been' is glaringly untrue!), and the last music he ever wrote has an almost unbearably simple poignancy (ex. 11.7.c). He composed or rather finished the song on 28 August, not at all at reflective leisure, for he was between flying visits to London to take *In terra pax* rehearsals and attend Cello Concerto ones, with his last meeting with Blunden, on Blunden's last day in England on an equally flying visit from Hong Kong, sandwiched in the day before and the Prom performance three days after. The day after the Prom the whole family decamped for Gloucester and their annual house party.

ritard.

mp

EX. 11.7.c

The only possible way to end this account of Gerald Finzi's life is with Joy's courageous account of his death. We pick it up at her description of their last Three Choirs Festival, in which everything seemed to come together: the first performance of Ferguson's searing *Amore langueo*, dedicated to Joy and Gerald and as much a tribute to the white heat of their love as to his own experiences; Joy's first portrait exhibition; and the chance, at some point during the week, to take the Vaughan Williamses up Chosen Hill to show them the spot that had inspired *In terra pax* and *New Year Music* thirty years earlier, the sexton's cottage still sitting in the churchyard 'looking like something that had come up through the ground' and offering a welcoming cup of tea or whatever from the occupant whose children were in bed with chicken pox.

2nd–8th [September 1956] This has been one of the happiest Three Choirs we have ever had, with some of the best performances too. The house party which consisted of the VW's, Meredith Davies, David Willcocks, Howard Ferguson, Peter & Sheila Godfrey, Richard Shirley Smith, Harold Brown & one or two others was very gay & with others constantly looking in. The hospitality was, as usual, endless, & though one met more or less the same people in the constant round of lunches, teas, receptions & sherry parties, it was good to see something of Herbert Howells (who conducted a superlative performance of his Hymnus Paradisi) [and] the Le Flemings whose youngest boy Anthony, aged 15 but more like 19 has the makings of a rare musician. VW to everything. His Symphony 8 got a fine performance under Meredith Davies. He can hear very little of the quiet stuff, tho' he seemed to like In Terra Pax, which he said was 'flawless.' G got a very good performance of this [on 6 September] & tho' it came at the end of a heavy week the choir remained fresh to the end. It really got an atmosphere & quiet playing & the Angel at the top of the organ loft sounded miraculous. Bruce Boyce sang well. Nigel overheard some of the choir saying how much they liked singing under G & that he got what he wanted out of them, which pleased but surprised G. Rubbra, John Russell & others came & were very generous. The orchestral version is certainly more exciting under those conditions & the angels' wings & shepherds' fear were thrilling. Howard Ferguson's Amore Langueo which is dedicated to G & JF had a magnificent first performance under Sumsion. It has a fine shape with the climaxes marvellously placed. The general texture is continually moving & restless as perhaps befits such an erotic poem, but it is a beautiful & successful work. J's portrait exhibition in the rest room was visited by about a 1000 people – it looked surprisingly well, though hung very closely. We did not stay for the Messiah on the last day & visited a Mrs Neilson at Upleadon who had a large collection of Paul Nash paintings & some very exciting books & one of the best Ivon Hitchens. Nash was a great friend. Mrs N's book collecting has been varied & intelligent, ranging from the Wise forgeries to 2nd 3rd & 4th Shakespeare folios – altogether a civilized & delightful house. We took Shush [Richard Shirley Smith] with us who was very interested. A civilized house. We also visited the Price's & Davies & G looked at orchards. We saw the VWs off by the 8.15 AM train – he was tired after the exertion of conducting The Lark & general festivities. We feel he shdnt conduct anymore, even though he enjoys it. Everyone rose in the Cathedral as he came on – which was impressive & fitting but there was an agonising start to the performance when he found he had started conducting with the piano score. Fred Grinke continued his opening cadenza while he scrabbled for the full score – even then the strings were not quite certain about his beat & made a bad entry – but despite everything it was a moving occasion. His cousin R. L. Wedgwood & great friend to whom the early Sea Symphony was dedicated suddenly died – he saw the notice on the last day & it was rather a shock for him. They were the same age & had been to Cambridge together. We look back to the week with great pleasure exhilarated by the high spirits of the young people in the house party Nigel & Kiffer & Richard (& several attractive young girls) – effervescent & full of sorties with Meredith.

After the return weekend at home [8–9 September] G & I took Nigel & odd furniture to his flat & stayed the night with Catherine [c. 12 September].

Collected Shush next morning & drove to Great Bardfield to introduce him to John Aldridge whose painting he admires in the hopes that he may become his Tutor at the Slade this coming beginning term. Arrived for lunch with the Aldridges. Lovely sunny day, brightening as we left London into peculiar East Anglian light. Shush took his work and photographs & we had a happy afternoon. I took Shush to catch a train from Braintree after tea. He was very impressed with John's work & the beauty of their home. (G complained of all over pain in chest – sounded muscular & we thought he might have taken a muscular cold gardening on the previous Monday.) We had an interesting evening with them – & slept well. Asked John if we could save our pennies & one day buy a lovely painting of a cornfield which G greatly loved.

Set off after breakfast [Friday 14 September?] in bright sunshine to go north into Suffolk to lunch with the Brookes & arrange with them to help Arthur Bliss's daughter & husband. So enjoyed driving through golden still uncut cornfields. Warm welcome from the Brookes – Justin ruddy & alive as ever full of enthusiasm – took G to see his fruiting apricots. Started for London after lunch. Stopped & lay resting in a cornfield – in warm sun – G slept as I read to him. (Still in pain). Collected Nigel at the flat, having painted his landing a heavenly blue & set off for home into a fine evening sky – Kiffer welcomed us home – G in more acute pain. Took dope & went soon to bed.

Saturday Sept [15th]. G woke still in pain, and I later diagnosed a rash on his chest as shingles. Tom off duty, but rang up partner & found the only thing was 2 Veganin every four hours. Tom came Sunday morning [16 September] & confirmed it. G still about though in pain. Urged him to lie down if it helped ease it.

Monday [17 Sept] – Pain very acute. Tom brought other dope. G got up to tea to welcome Sumsions on their way home from Brighton – took Physeptone to ease it. Happy tea in sittingroom sunshine. John Russell came in later. The boys had returned to London that day. Returned to bed & Tom came with morphia night & morning which is a comforting drug without ill effects & gave G relief.

Just as we were hoping we were through the worst of the shingles & complications another rash that Friday [21 September] appeared. Tom diagnosed chicken pox – this didn't bring any extra discomfort except later irritation.

Boys home for the weekend. Kiffer took the first rehearsal of the string players & did very well. They greatly entertained G playing thro' a salon piece for cello & violin (sent by Cedric Davie) on Sunday.

Off back to London with a rush & a swirl on Monday morning [24 September]. G's temperature normal for first time & we hoped that the worst was over. Had a Pilsner & some salmon & peas for lunch – noticed muddled thinking in dictating letter to Lady Ponsonby. Later John Russell came & I took him up to see G from the doorway. I was surprised G was not more interested & was alarmed at his lack of mental co-ordination – took John down & gave him some beer. Rang Tom immediately & he came straight from the garden. G still detached & somnolent. Tom gave him thorough examination for reflexes. Felt he wd like to contact Dr Calendar in Oxford in the absence of Witts. Tried to catch her all that evening but she wasn't available. Came again at ten for usual morphia.

Tuesday [25 September]. Tom as usual in the morning, found G very drowsy after the exertions of bathing. He brought Dr Budenoch over in the afternoon. G withdrawn & not interested. He took blood test & chicken-pox sample, & later reported the blood to be in an even better condition. Tom still worried. Despite usual morphia G had a very restless night with the obvious irritation of the chicken-pox which was very profuse. I fell off to sleep once or twice & was unable to prevent him lacerating his underarm. Couldn't leave him for a moment & had great difficulty in getting him cleaned & changed for Tom, & knew I cd no longer deal with him.

[Wednesday 26 September] Tom saw immediately that he cd also no longer be responsible & ordered an ambulance to take him to Oxford. Didn't give him the usual morphia & I found it very difficult to keep him comfortable – & had to give him Physeptone. He was mostly oblivious and I told him we were going to Oxford in case he was perturbed. He did just say 'oh no' but on reasoning with him seemed content & withdrawn. Jack & I & the two ambulance attendants carried him down. He was slightly surprised at the female (who was immense) but courteous in acknowledgement. His temp went down during the drive & I was able to keep him contented. He even remarked on interior decoration & asked once where we had got to – but was withdrawn & not really connected. Seemed contented & comfortable once in the hospital bed – & to accept everything without any reaction. Drs obviously puzzled with his condition. I left him without him knowing & quite withdrawn – & felt comforted by knowing he was being made as comfortable as was possible. Made arrangements for him to listen in to his cello concerto shd consciousness clear – but though he was co-operative & even talked to the nurses later he made no reference to it & was not connected. The nerve specialist didn't find anything beyond encephalitis as the cause of the brain inflammation & the comatose condition descended that night & they felt his condition serious next morning [Thursday 27 September]. I went over after lunch & found him taking cortisone & orange of glucose. The Drs were alarmed at a short convulsion he had had in the night. He was more aware when I was there & obviously co-operating in taking nourishment – and as I sat & talked to him, I became quite contented even happy in feeling all was well with him – (possibly the awareness of the end of his suffering). I stayed with him until the evening & shortly after I left he had another convulsion & died.

The shadow has fallen.

CHAPTER 12

Afterwards

Gerald died while Joy was driving home late that evening, and she knew what it must be when she was told that Tom Scott had a message for her. She phoned Nigel in London, who went round to see Kiffer; the two sons agreed to meet at Paddington first thing the following morning, and arrived back at Ashmansworth for a weekend shockingly different from the 'rush & . . . swirl' of the previous one. Shock was the only word that can have meant anything to all those who were then told the news. Laurence Whistler, a neighbour of the Milfords and a new Finzi friend from earlier in the year (Gerald admired his poetry and had started a setting of 'The quick and the dead' in the 1940s), was passing by on his way home to Lyme Regis, and phoned early to ask whether he might drop in, only to be told by Joy, 'Gerald died last night' (C. Finzi 1992: 47). Many heard of Gerald's death over the radio on the 9 o'clock news; Kirstie Milford returned home that evening to find Robin in tears, and Iris Lemare wrote to tell Joy of 'that awful breakfast in London (where I was) and the news starting by the explosion of the latest Atom Bomb (that Gerry would have hated so much) and ending with this other complete Bombshell' (19561002a). The Vaughan Williamses were on holiday in Majorca, and Gil Jenkins despatched a special messenger to them by air with a letter lest they should hear the news first in the papers. The following day they both wrote to Joy, Ursula summoning something of healing creativity:

We were going out today – & we sat in a remote hermitage high on a mountain with the island & the sea below us in a pale blue haze, & Ralph dictated the letter he is sending to the Times. It all seems very fitting, & there were swallows – perhaps some of yours, on their way south.

Nothing counts much just now, but when you want us, we are here. (19560929b)

Letters of sympathy and tribute to them both poured into Church Farm. All make poignant but inspiriting reading in their thankfulness for a good life. Graham Hutton, who had known Gerald longer than most of his and Joy's friends, spoke true when he said, 'For Gerald one cannot feel sad, since he was always so interested in life and people, and he had a full if short life. Thank God he did not remain a cripple or invalid . . . he has come and gone, and all the grief must go for you' (19560928a). From the other side of the world, in Australia, Priscilla Kennedy, who had occasionally played with the Newbury String Players, wrote, 'I have never known anyone with such vitality' (19561109b). Clearly everyone had come away from his presence with a slightly different trophy of enlightenment, as they told Joy. 'Unlike most composers his view was not bounded by his own creative world,' wrote Anthony Lewis (19560930f); Reynolds Stone's wife Janet could 'never forget the sound of his wonderful reading voice hour after hour as you drew one of [the children] – & his absolute pride & faith in you' (19560929c); Meredith Davies felt 'You can judge a man by his family, and I think Gerald could have been wonderfully proud of his' (19560928n); Albi Rosenthal remembered his 'luminous personality' with its 'irresistible attraction' (19560928o); Rutland Boughton, after reading about his illness in a letter from Joy, wrote a second time to say, 'What we have now learned of Gerald gives us new faith in the courage and essential goodness of human nature' (19561019); Rann Hokanson, hearing of Gerald's death months later from Myra Hess in San Francisco, told Joy, 'Of all the creative artists I have ever known, he was one of the least self-centered and most lovable' (19570430). Gilbert Spencer quoted 'This upright man' (195609–11?).

Sadder were the two letters congratulating Gerald on the Cello Concerto broadcast the night before he died. He never read Bliss's final encomium, 'It bears the unmistakable stamp of greatness' (19560927a). When Bliss wrote again the following day it was to tell Joy that she and Gerald had been 'entirely special' for him and Trudy. 'Gerald's value – his music, his integrity, his courage, his own particular view of what was important made me love him dearly. The world of your own that you both had made together was like nothing else in our lives' (19560928j). Rubbra offered to help put the manuscripts in order, but the job was unquestionably Ferguson's, and over the ensuing years he undertook it with devotion, expertise and aplomb, assisted by Joy and Christopher. Before the end of October he had completed a typescript catalogue of works; preparation of posthumous publications followed, including the 26 finished songs grouped by the editors into the Hardy sets *I Said to Love* and *Till Earth Outwears*, published in 1958, and two volumes to various poets, *Oh Fair to See* and *To a Poet*, issued in 1965–6. Alongside them appeared the remaining editions for which Gerald had been responsible – Gurney Volume 4, the Boyce *magnum opus*, and a residue of Bond and Mudge.

There was no funeral service, and Gerald was cremated on 2 October. Joy kept his ashes until 1973, when she scattered them on May Hill with those of her sister; there Gerald had spent childhood holidays and first become familiar with the West Country apple varieties, which in true Hardy fashion he might now help infinitesimally to nurture.

More than one proposal was made about a biography. Delighted with Simona Pakenham's study of himself which appeared in 1957, Vaughan Williams suggested Finzi as the subject of her next book. The Faith Press wrote to Joy around the same time expressing interest in a Finzi study and mentioning Percy Young as a possible author. Other arrangements had already been made, however, for at the Cheltenham Festival in July 1956, amid the increasingly uncongenial critical atmosphere surrounding new British music, the Finzis had found that 'perhaps the nicest thing about all critics on this occasion was the pleasure of meeting little Diana McVeagh. We were charmed by her bright personality – A great character for one so apparently demure & young' (J. Finzi 19560716–20). Gerald had read and admired her book on Elgar when it appeared in 1955 and asked her to consider doing one on Parry. She told him she wanted to move away from Britain for her next project and in any case would not be happy writing about a composer most of whose music she was unable to hear in performance. But within two or three weeks of Gerald's death Joy had asked her to write his life-and-works instead and she had agreed. It has not yet appeared.

A composer's reputation often declines rapidly after his or her death, but Finzi's was helped by his creative lifestyle, in that he had left behind a number of late or revised works, unperformed and unpublished and of a nature such that plenty of friends would want to hear them, plus a family glad to have them edited and released. It was sad in a way that during his lifetime, at least since his reputation had been established, he had not believed in holding soirées for a first hearing of his own music, for Church Farm was the perfect place and his songs the perfect material for them. It must have seemed strange when the first such event occurred in his posthumous absence, on 24 July 1957, and the songs comprising *Oh Fair to See* and *Till Earth Outwears* were performed – twice, before and after supper – by Wilfred Brown and Herbert Sumsion (Ferguson was on tour in South Africa). Blunden was there, to hear 'To Joy' and 'Harvest', and so was Sylvia Townsend Warner, who with her partner Valentine Ackland had met the Finzis in Dorset in August 1955 and had been greatly struck by the charm and appearance of 'Tiber-eyed', Italianate Gerald with his 'sturdy upright carriage, and . . . round green eyes' (ibid.: 218–19). Navarro, Milford and Laurence Whistler were also present, and Nigel's twenty-first birthday celebrations were beginning.

Earlier, at the Victoria and Albert Museum on 27 January, *I Said to Love* and the Eclogue had been premièred at a Finzi memorial concert in the Chamber Music Society's Museum Gallery Concerts series, the former by John Carol Case and Howard Ferguson, the latter by Kathleen Long (who had played the Grand Fantasia as long ago as 1929) and the Kalmar Orchestra (including both Christopher and Nigel on this occasion) conducted by John Russell. Later in the year Christopher Finzi launched the Prelude for strings with the NSP at Stockcross (27 April), and on 11 December, once Ferguson had had time to complete its orchestration, Manchester saw the first performance of *The Fall of the Leaf* – surely a melancholy occasion, for this deeply flawed work was no substitute for the centenary commission the Hallé should have had. Both works were published in 1958, and *To a Poet* was given its first performance in 1959, by John Carol Case and Ferguson at a Macnaghten concert on 20 February in London, the first public hearing of *Till Earth Outwears* having preceded it a year earlier, on 21 February 1958, given by Brown and Ferguson at the Arts Council offices in St James's Square, London, where *Oh Fair to See* was also publicly premièred, though not until 8 November 1965.

By this time, nearly a decade after his death and with Vaughan Williams long dead too, Finzi's reputation was having to fight for survival along with that of his whole generation, and even Elgar was nationally sidelined in the harshly modernistic and international climate of the 1960s led from the top by William Glock at the BBC. Though

Boosey & Hawkes were loyal enough to Finzi's published output and consolidated it when they eventually took over his early pieces from OUP, there can have been very few performances of works such as the Cello Concerto and *Intimations of Immortality* during this decade, and in the early 1970s, as an undergraduate at Cambridge, the author remembers picking a score of *Intimations* off the departmental library shelves, expecting never to hear it even on the radio.

But with the arrival of the mono and then the stereo LP from the late 1950s onwards, recordings were beginning to act as a lifeline between unfashionable composer and unfashionable public. Even the dreadful old British Council one of *Dies natalis* on 78s must have helped 'the affection which an individual may retain after his departure' to begin to bear fruit, a century or two earlier than Finzi's theory of history would have it, when *Dies* became a GCE A-level set work in 1960–1. Then in 1964 HMV issued the translucent, definitive perform-ance of *Dies natalis* on disc, given by Wilfred Brown and the English Chamber Orchestra conducted by Christopher Finzi, whose bio-graphical sleeve note on his father was almost as important as the recording itself in being the first piece of writing to reach beyond the readership of trade and scholarly journals and tell the world some-thing about the remarkable man behind the music. Soon other recordings followed, though initially at the prompting (and from the pocket) of enthusiasts rather than the taste-dictating big companies, and royalties accrued.

This the remarkable woman behind the remarkable man lived to see and influence. Joy, as one would expect, remained outwardly a tower of strength after Gerald's death. She did not grieve in front of others, and wasted no time in going where he would not have followed, on holiday to Italy in the spring of 1957. Inwardly she never fully recovered from the loneliness that had descended. For a while it looked as though she might marry Fraser Darling, whose wife Avril Morley had died of cancer around the same time as Gerald; but he had three children, and it was too soon for her, though not for him (he married the children's nanny). Perhaps the eventual renaissance of Gerald's reputation hin-dered her from moving on; 'I really cannot dismiss my marriage to G – it seems to continue unspoken,' she wrote in 1977 when she came to burn his wooden-framed blotting pad (J. Finzi 197709). Earlier, it had taken her a decade to exorcise his ghost from the Ashmansworth book room and use it herself. When she did so she wrote him a letter:

My dear – a gale is blowing hard from the south – the kind that when it rarely blows from that quarter forces rain through the bookroom window . . . The new oil stove, which continually breathes out warmth fills this room for the first time with an enfolding gentle heat so that the books no longer smell or register their damp on the window glass in the morning, is hiccuping with the wind . . .

Since this room has become warm I have returned from following the sun in the dining room & sitting room & now have my writing and papers here – surrounded by these almost audible shelves – which nourished you in your isolated youth & which enfold me in my declining age. I'm not yet certain of their destination & to whom they will continue to minister – that will come. Ceddie's excited voice from St Andrews the other morning to tell me they had got the money to buy the 18th century music library. This wd seem the right continuation for the work you started & the core on which he can build and extend his department. Things move inexplicably – threaded to unseen impulse & I'm beginning to emerge from the dark shadow which fell on me in 1956. I strangely feel beginnings – a new born strengthening confidence – tentative & easily abashed – but there. (J. Finzi 19660225)

It must have been difficult to know what to do with Gerald's collections, for however much she added to the book room – and she did add a great deal of poetry – it was his personal library, not hers, and she eventually realised, wisely, that she did not want to embrace the declining age that being enfolded by the books would precipitate. Church Farm in any case saw radical change as Christopher married Hilary du Pré (Jacqueline's sister) in 1961, started a family, ceased to be a professional cellist, took up chicken farming, and eventually divided the house, which he had extended, for the use of several families in a kind of commune in the 1970s mould. Not without anguish, Joy decided it was time to move. 'I always felt [the house] was like an ark,' she wrote to Alice Sumsion in September 1974, 'and during the war it was! – and now again, at a time of increasing pressures, it has filled up with strangers.' If anything, what she wanted to hold on to was not Church Farm but Nigel, perhaps because living overseas he was so far away. She moved temporarily to a delightful old cottage north of Newbury in 1974 and eventually to an even lovelier one, Bushey Leaze, where her hospitality towards the younger generation became legendary (see C. Finzi 1992). The books went to Reading, where she made sure their new surroundings were not a mausoleum by establishing an annual poetry seminar with the support of the University Librarian, James

Thompson. Most of Gerald's scores were given to Reading University's Music Department, while the shelves at Ashmansworth filled up again with some of Vaughan Williams's that Christopher had inherited. Joy's own reputation as an artist never blossomed further but never waned either, as her sketches of Bliss and Vaughan Williams were reproduced on the *Musical Times* front covers celebrating the two men's anniversaries in 1971 and 1972 before their more frequent circulation among Finzi *aficionados* from the 1980s onwards. She published a book of verse, *A Point of Departure* (1967), very much as a vehicle for Richard Shirley Smith's wood engravings. Poetry was not her strongest suit, though 'Last lullaby' in *A Point of Departure* reads as a touching epitaph for Gerald and the first poem in the book is addressed to him; another is 'For Ivor Gurney'.

Blunden also wrote a poem in Gerald's memory, 'For a musician's monument', published in *A Hong Kong House* (1962), one of the first of a growing number of tributes to Finzi in literature, visual art and music. The most recent is Martyn Wade's striking radio play, *Before and After Summer*. Others have come from fellow-composers. 'Finzi's rest' by Howells (see Chapter 3) was published in *Howells' Clavichord* in 1961. An organ piece by Ian Parrott, 'Hands across the years (In memoriam Gerald Finzi)' (1983), is a set of variations on the slow movement of the Cello Concerto and links its rapt D major secondary-seventh chord just before the end with the identical one that opens the slow movement of Tchaikovsky's Serenade for Strings, perhaps more cannily than he knew. Tony Scott, who in later life has had cause to say a number of forceful things to Love, based his fiery 'Metamorphoses on themes by Gerald Finzi', another 1980s organ piece, on motifs from that song and 'My lovely one'. Yet another organ work, an undated one by John Hall, is entitled Five Short Pieces, Op. 71, on Themes by Finzi; the themes are from the Interlude. More suggestive than all these is Rubbra's Seventh Symphony, which he was composing at the time of Finzi's death. Should one hear his tribute to a noble life in the tragic yet restrained and beautiful grandeur of its Passacaglia? This is one of Rubbra's finest achievements, and the temptation to interpret it thus arises because in the preceding scherzo there seems to be a subliminal reference to *Intimations of Immortality* (ex. 12.1.a and b), the Finzi concordance being the orchestral welling-up that follows the line 'The things which I have seen I now can see no more'.

Gerald had left provision in his will for the 're-issue or furtherance

EX. 12.1.a (Finzi)

EX. 12.1.b (Rubbra)

in any way of my musical works' at the discretion of his executors, and he envisaged three-year bursaries to 'Musical Composers of English birth above twenty four years of age preferably but not necessarily with domestic ties' should his own issue not attain vested interest in the estate. Burgeoning descendants notwithstanding, in 1969 the Finzi Trust was formed, and it helped plan and finance the methodical coverage of his output on record, initially with Lyrita Recorded Edition, which issued all the Hardy song sets between 1968 and 1971, sung by John Carol Case, Robert Tear and Neil Jenkins and played by Ferguson, and went on to tackle *Intimations* in 1975 with Vernon Handley and most of the instrumental works by the end of the decade, under Boult and Handley, including the Cello Concerto played by Yo-Yo Ma in his first commercial recording. Lyrita was joined by Argo and Hyperion, and Handley by Richard Hickox, as Finzi promoters as the 1980s approached. By this time it should have become clear to the public, as it undoubtedly was to the Trust, that nothing succeeds like success, but this nevertheless needed to be pointed out by Lewis Foreman in an important *Musical Times* article (1980) entitled 'Reputations . . . bought or made?' that drew attention to the astute reinvestment of composers' royalties in recordings, publications and publicity that in turn would bring in more royalties; he cited the Finzi Trust as exemplary in this respect.

The implication of Foreman's article was that it was no longer possible, if indeed it ever had been, to measure a composer's value in terms of their critical standing, because market forces had overtaken critical authority as creators of taste. This was a somewhat different situation from the Britten 'racket' of thirty-five years earlier, because then critical consensus – Finzi considered it hysteria – had created the market. Now criticism, in any case no longer so obviously in the hands of an establishment élite, was largely irrelevant.

Not everyone was happy with the way things were going, the Sumsion family for instance rather disapproving of the steps towards the heritage industry and all its merchandising that Finzi and his reputation took with the first Summer Weekend of English Music at Ellesmere College in 1981 and the founding of the Finzi Trust Friends the following year. The Ellesmere weekend's use of Lambert's silhouette in a roundel in white on the Wedgwood blue programme book was a brilliant marketing ploy but proved their point. True, the Trust and the Friends, blessed with two or three of the liveliest young music administrators in Britain at the helm, were quick to sponsor competitions for performers and composers and commission new British works as well as rescue older ones from neglect, not all of them by acquaintances or kindred spirits of Finzi, as they gradually worked outwards in their remit over the course of the remaining three summer weekends, held triennially until 1990. This has been a service to British music overall; nor would one wish away the associated commissions and tributes from the other arts – the Finzi Bowl, now in the Ashmolean Museum, engraved on glass by Laurence Whistler and his son Simon, Whistler's window to English music in Ashmansworth Church porch (1976), with lettering by Ann Hechle, his memorial pane to Butterworth at Radley College, unveiled under the auspices of the Friends prior to the 1987 Summer Weekend there, and Reynolds Stone's Finzi memorial stone in Ashmansworth churchyard. But for all the broad church of younger performers and composers assisted by the Trust or independently discovering and reinterpreting Finzi's music – Raphael Wallfisch, Stephen Varcoe, Nicholas Daniel, Michael Collins, Anne Dawson and Paul Spicer (founder and conductor of the Finzi Singers) outstanding among the performers – it cannot be denied that 'Finzi and his friends', as the title of one of the recordings puts it, have recreated something of the cosy myth that was his during the Three Choirs years (and it is at that festival that they meet annually). Until her decline at the end of the 1980s (she died in June 1991), Joy presided over the new, posthumous artistic household as graciously but formidably as ever she did at Ashmansworth and in Gloucester during Gerald's lifetime, and must have felt triumphant if bemused at its farther-flung manifestations in the USA, where Philip Brunelle launched the First Finzi Festival of America in Minneapolis in May 1990 and, thanks to the Finzi Friends of America, Michael Dukakis proclaimed Sunday, 31 January 1988 to be 'Gerald Finzi Day' in the Commonwealth of Massachusetts and urged his citizens to 'take cognizance of this event and to participate fittingly in its observance'. Did it ever occur to Joy that by this stage the myth of the minor composer was getting out of hand? What it needed was what it got at the end-of-festival party in Minneapolis, when Percy Young brilliantly lampooned the whole Finzi industry with his impromptu biography of Harry Gill.

We have to ask, therefore, whether Finzi's posthumous career has inflated his reputation, still more whether it has circumscribed it. The spectre of inflation cannot be gainsaid when one considers that Finzi died only a year younger than Beethoven, eight years younger than Britten, yet left an output a fraction of theirs in size and scope. One allows for his having been a late developer. In this he seems to have taken comfort in being similar to Vaughan Williams, who likewise slowly but tenaciously took by the horns a discipline for which he had little natural aptitude, perhaps because it was one of the few peaks not yet conquered by an illustrious family. Nevertheless, by the age of fifty-five Vaughan Williams had given the world his first three symphonies, *Flos campi*, the Tallis Fantasia, two operas, *Job* (in sketch) and a host of minor and functional pieces in addition to those parts of his output that could be set alongside Finzi's. He had also made his mark in London (for instance, as a professional choral conductor), studied abroad with two of the leading continental composers, committed himself institutionally to teaching young composers, started and continued his own music festival, collected and arranged countless folksongs, worked at some length in the theatre, seen traumatic active service in the First World War and spent two years editing a standard hymnal. To almost all such manifestations of the rough-and-tumble of musical citizenship Finzi by contrast said a firm no. His fastidiousness precluded it.

Fastidiousness is the last quality one would apply to Vaughan Williams, and he probably envied it in Finzi, just as he had envied, perhaps worshipped it in Butterworth, a friend whose early loss was probably never made wholly good but whose role as musical godson and critical confidant must have been at least partly taken over by Finzi from the 1930s onwards. Yet fastidiousness alone would never have made him say to Finzi, when he asked him to replace R. O. Morris as one of his literary executors in 1949: 'Perhaps you will like to know . . . that I am leaving you Beethoven's tuning fork which was left to me by Gustav Holst to be passed on to anyone I considered worthy' (19490605). Finzi died before Vaughan Williams, of course, but no-one else merited the tuning fork, and it is now in the British Museum.

It was not the Finzi of ruminative miniatures, the Classic FM Finzi of Eclogues and Preludes and Elegies and Romances and Rhapsodies, of Friends' newsletters and Three Choirs lunches and songs sung winsomely by ex-lay clerks, who deserved Beethoven's tuning fork. Nor was it the young man whose music still sounded like that of his hero, who was not one for male flattery. It was, rather, the extraordinary overall creative *will* of his younger friend that surely brooked no denial in the eyes of Vaughan Williams and so many of those who came into contact with Finzi.

As Finzi was well aware, only children normally show that will in its purest form, and in his determination to celebrate and hold on to it, it became the most natural thing in the world – his world – that he should turn to Wordsworth and Traherne. Yet before he could build that world of ideas and affinities, it necessitated rejecting almost everything around him in his early years. It was a violent action of disillusionment that must have left huge scars, this determination to do things his way rather than by example, and doubtless the following passage from Traherne's *Centuries of Meditations* rang true when he read it a decade or more later:

The first light which shined in my infancy in its primitive and innocent clarity was totally eclipsed: insomuch that I was fain to learn all again. If you ask me how it was eclipsed? Truly by the customs and manners of men, which like contrary winds blew it out; by an innumerable company of other objects: rude,

493

vulgar, and worthless . . . finally by the evil influence of a bad education that did not foster and cherish it. All men's thoughts were about other matters; they all prized new things which I did not dream of. I was a stranger and unacquainted with them . . . ambitious also, and desirous to approve myself unto them. And finding no one syllable in any man's mouth of those things, by degrees they vanished . . . (Bradford 1991: 229–30)

But *why* did he have to reject his exemplars?

Finzi is full of contradictions. He emphasised environment above all things, yet it was his own early environment that he refused to acknowledge. He lived next door to Frederic Cowen for the first twelve years of his life but never once mentioned him afterwards; in view of this, and Cowen's expensive lifestyle in one of the most fashionable streets in London and knighthood while the Finzis were still his neighbours, Gerald's story about his uncle trying to persuade him that as a composer he would be poor makes no sense. His mother being a composer too is another reason to doubt the assumption that for him to choose to be a composer at the age of ten or eleven was a sign of radical independence. It was the most natural thing in the world, and one has to ask instead what phenomenon of arrested development prevented him from becoming the fluent young musician both parents, not to mention his music-publishing uncle, would have encouraged and understood.

Why did he fail to emulate them all, and what made him spurn the very pedigree and security that gave him the strength and chutzpah to do so? How are we to understand the Gerald Finzi whose mother's family consorted with the Rothschilds, whose father's earned the encyclopaedia entry 'noble Italian Jewish family' detailing ancestors back to the Middle Ages, and whose continental intertwinings evidently took in the likes of Garibaldi? How could his father work within earshot of the Bevis Marks synagogue and turn his back on it, his whole family live virtually in the same road, at the very pinnacle of London Jewry's standing, and not be utterly imbued with Sephardi culture, its customs, constraints, social rituals, even its music? It is difficult to believe that these ceased to have meaning for Gerald's parents, impossible to accept that he himself was not massively influenced by them.

Something must have gone disastrously wrong in his childhood for him to have shut the door so spectacularly on it all. Was there something that happened, some circumstance that marked him off from his brothers and sister? Age alone surely cannot have done so. They were all equally prey to xenophobia or anti-Semitism, and to the trauma of their father's cancer; Edgar was less than three years older than Gerald, and he remained a member of the Lauderdale Road congregation at the time of his death, as the synagogue's war memorial testifies to anyone who walks down Sutherland Avenue in Maida Vale. In any case, if Gerald always felt a stranger among his sister and brothers, and prized family so little, why did he suffer from such personal insecurity and set such great store by his own parenthood and homemaking? Did he, perhaps, cement his family feelings only after some massive argument with his uncles about his career? Did he even forfeit some of his inheritance as a result of such a confrontation? It is not easy to see where all the family wealth went to, and whatever passed between Finzi and his guardians, he had not forgotten it thirty years later, when he set the following as an exam question for the music students at St Andrews University: 'An imaginary Uncle, who strongly disapproves of the idea that you should take up music as a profession, writes you his reasons. Give his letter in not more than 250 words' (19520129).

None of it yet adds up, and there are so many things we do not and may never know, whether or not he suppressed them, that we can only guess at the nature, size and timing of the event or perception that ruptured his childhood identity. What we can be absolutely sure of is that it was irrevocable, a pivot on which his entire subsequent self hinged. Here, surely, is the root of his affinity with Hardy, from whom in so many ways he was utterly different. What Hardy celebrated in the structure of both his life and his poetry was not just the gradual changes that time wreaks but the brutal, often sadistic suddenness of acknowledgement that is humankind's way of perceiving them and to which a desperate defiance to have nothing more to do with the old or the first cause is anger's reaction. Hence his shutting the door on the nineteenth century and his novels, in a passionate yet never wavering career move that led him to poetry instead. Hence the treatment of Emma up to her death. Hence the abjuring of Love, the utterly callous leaving to her fate of Amabel as he 'fling[s] across the gate' a farewell little short of a curse. Hence those 'before and after' structures, those pivoted forms, that we have traced in the Hardy poems Finzi sets and the music he matches them with.

But do we really know the truth? Did Finzi really know it? If only a provisional estimate of this man, his music, this curious phenomenon in twentieth-century British musical history, is possible, we are left with

495

someone who, for all his charm and attraction and containedness and elegiac sweetness and reassuring Englishness is at bottom a cultural enigma. How well did he understand himself? How are we to interpret those pursed lips in the photographs, that incessant earnest vitality, that blurted acknowledgement that his wife-to-be was *not* like Harriet Cohen, that avoidance of the word 'Jewish' in his stylistic analysis of Bloch, the Jewish composer *par excellence*? It is time to stop hearing him as he heard himself and take a deeper sounding, a longer view. The myth has run its course and needs replacing, though it is extraordinarily difficult for us to approach his music, indeed any music, with an inno-cent ear. The first bar of ex. 12.2, for instance (from the slow movement of the Cello Concerto, but it might almost be from *Fiddler on the Roof*), is about as far from agreed notions of musical Englishness as the second is representative of them. But at the same time they fuse effortlessly into an elegiac rumination of great beauty, and whatever else we need to adjust in our approach to Finzi, we can continue to feel the sense of *loss* he conveyed. Had he been a greater composer like Mahler he might have found ways of expressing this more overtly in his music, indeed in his life, since for all the ecstasy of *Dies natalis* about the making of the child there is no corresponding facing up to the pain and struggle about the making of the man in Finzi's creative testimony. Perhaps he did begin to express his more subliminal self in his later works, not least in the Cello Concerto. One might even speculate as to whether the fact that so many of his songs are for baritone involves an unconscious attempt to recapture his father's voice.

One thing is certain: his identity, if it did ever get anywhere near greatness, was not the watertight unitary one he would have himself and us believe, but, as with us all, a multiple one, and it took in

EX. 12.2

496

everything. At that fundamental level he was intensely English and intensely Jewish, perhaps also intensely Christian as well as intensely agnostic, dogmatic as well as liberal, puritan as well as free. That is why *In terra pax* contains the best and the most of him, for it delves right to the heart of our shared cultural myths, locating the pastoral in those fields near Bethlehem as well as on a Gloucestershire hilltop, speaking words of sorrowful comfort but facing an empty universe. Humankind in its deepest, loneliest moments has stood peering into that darkness hearkening for a sign. Finzi, in rejecting the comfort of his background, must have known loneliness as great as any. Perhaps there was some curious touch of destiny visited upon him in early life, some compulsion to leave home and be a prophet, that never had time to be fulfilled and that we do not yet understand because it deposited only unconnected signs. The absent whole is worth continuing to look for, though we shall not find it in a tea tent on the lawn of a cathedral close, or at the mezuza-clad porches of St John's Wood, or in Mrs Finzi's or Sir Frederic Cowen's parlour, or on the Ridgeway, or in the kitchen at Ashmansworth, or even in Hardy's poetry; but if we can somehow find a way of putting all these things together, we may begin to grasp the potential of Gerald Finzi's mind, only part of which ever found its way out in the music he left behind, for other parts had been so tightly locked that he could not turn the key.

APPENDIX *Love's Labour's Lost*

Act/scene	Item	BBC Home Service radio production (16 Dec 1946)	Songs as performed (Wigmore Hall, 7 July 1947) and published (1948)	Suite as initially extracted (order of movements uncertain—as found in Bodl MS Mus.c390, ff.105-119) (√= Cheltenham Festival concert performance, 20 July 1952)	Appendices to Suite (Bodl MS Mus.c390, ff. 120-31) I: Masque music (M) II: Fanfares (F) and III: Various (V) (and additions for Chalkhill Park theatre prod", 21-4 June 1953)	Suite as published and recorded {with sectional cues for NI 5101} (=BBC radio broadcast, 26 July 1955)
	[Narrator]	No 15 (bb.1-6)				
	Introduction	No 1 (11 bars)		No 1/i (11 bars), 1/iii (8 bars) and 1/v (9-10 bars) √		No 1[Introduction]B {0'35"}, B, {1'44"}, B₂ {3'25"}
V/i (or else-where)	Lords' 'signature' fanfares:				(omitted from prod"):	[not in hire score]
	Longaville ('bankrout quite the wits')				F1 (4 bars)	
	Dumaine ('living in philosophy')				F1a (4 bars)	
	Berowne ('the last that will last keep his oath')				F1b (4 bars)	
I/i	Entry of Costard etc	No 2 (6 bars)			V2: Costard music (6 bars)	No 6[Quodlibet (Clowns)]B {0'12"} (21 bars), coda {1'48"} (8 bars)
I/i	End of scene	No 3 (=no 1, last 6 bars)				
I/i-I/ii	Entr'acte: Armado	No 4 (8 bars)		No 1/ii (7-8 bars) √		No 1C {1'20"}
I/ii	'If she be made of white and red'		2. Songs for Moth (a)	√		
I/ii	Entry of Costard	No 2				
I/ii	Exit of Costard	No 2				
I/ii-II/i	Entr'acte: Princess	No 5 (18 bars)		No 1/iv (21-22 bars) √		No 1D {2'17"}
II/i	Entry of Princess			No 6: Nocturne (29 bars)	II, F2: Flourish for the Princess (22 bars)	No 3[Nocturne]B {0'35"}
III/i	Armado (song intro.)	No 6 (=no 4) (3 bars)				No 1A
III/i	Song: 'False Concoline!'	No 7	2. Songs for Moth (b)	No 5/ii (17 bars) [part of Vignette: Moth] √		No 2['Moth']B {0'40"}

Act/scene	Item	Radio production	Songs	Suite as initially extracted	Appendices to Suite	Suite as published and recorded
III/i-	Entr'acte	No 9 (21 bars)				No 6C {1'01"} (25 bars)
IV/i	Entr'acte			?√ <-------	-------	No 10[Finale]D {1'34"} (22 bars)
IV/i	'Thou canst not hit it' (lines 127-30)				V1: Song and dance (21 bars)	[not in hire score]
IV/ii	Hunting music 1	No 10 (17 bars)				No 4: The hunt (145 bars)
IV/ii-	Entr'acte: Hunting music 2	No 11 (6 bars)			< - - - - - - - -	
IV/iii	King's poem	No 12 (34 bars)		No 2: Three Soliloquies I (34 bars)√		No 7: Soliloquy I
IV/iii	Longaville's sonnet	No 13 (17 bars)		No 3: Three Soliloquies II (17 bars)√		No 8: Soliloquy II
IV/iii	Dumaine's 'sonnet'	No 14 (16 bars)		No 4: Three Soliloquies III (27 bars)√		No 9: Soliloquy III
IV/iii	Entry of Costard	(cut)				
IV/iii	Exit of Costard	(rhythm notated in script)				
IV/iii-V/i	Entr'acte	No 15 (23 bars)		?√ <------		No 10C {0'56"}, C1 {2'47"}
V/i-V/ii	Entr'acte	No 16 (13 bars)			V2a: Dull's hey	No 6D {1'27"}
V/ii	Dance ('blackamoors')	No 17 (cut?) (11 bars)		?√ <------	- - - - - - -	No 10A (Entry of the Russians)
V/ii	cue: 'All hail, the richest beauties'	No 18 (cut) (6 bars)				
V/ii	Exit of Moth	No 19 (3 bars)		No 5/i (17 bars) and iii (15 bars): Vignette: Moth√		No 2A, A1
V/ii	Background to dance	No 20 (32 bars)		No 7: Dance (95 bars)√		No 5: Dance
V/ii				?√ <------	- - - - - - -	No 10B (Dance of the 'mess of Russians') {0'24"} (14 bars), B1 {1'29"}, B2 {2'25"}, B3 {3'21"}
V/ii	Re-entry of King	No 18 (6 bars)				
V/ii	Entry of Costard	(rhythm notated in script)				
V/ii	'Pompey' fanfares	No 21 (2 bars)			M1	
		No 21a (2 bars)			M1a	
		No 21b (2 bars)			M1b	
		No 21c (4 bars)			M1c	

Act/scene	Item	Radio production	Songs	Suite as initially extracted	Appendices to Suite	Suite as published and recorded
V/ii	Nathaniel as Alexander	No 22 (7 bars)			M2	No 6A, A₁ {0'49"}
V/ii	'Judas Maccabeus/Hercules' fanfare	No 23 (11 bars)			M3	
V/ii	Moth as Hercules strangling serpents				M4 (7 bars)	
V/ii	Exit of Moth	X (=no 19)			M4a (3 bars)	
V/ii	Holofernes				M4b (=M3) (3 bars)	
V/ii	'Hector' fanfare	No 24 (4 bars)			M5 (4 bars)	
		No 24a (2-bar alternative crossed out)			M5a (5 bars)	
V/ii	Entry of Marcade	No 25 (6 bars)				No 3A (11 bars)
V/ii	Introductions to songs	No 26	[incorporated below]			
		No 26a				
		No 26b				
		No 26c				
V/ii	Song: 'When daisies pied'	27	1. Songs of Hiems and Ver (a)	✓		
V/ii	Song: 'When icicles hang by the wall'	28	1. Songs of Hiems and Ver (b)	✓		

Bibliography

See the separate index for letters. R. denotes a reprinted or revised edition and is the one to which page references apply.

Amis, J., *Amiscellany: my life, my music* (London and Boston, 1985)

Anderson, W. R., *New Works by Modern British Composers: Third Series: a description* (London, 1928)

Anon, *The Magnet: the magazine of Mount Arlington*, Hindhead, Surrey iv/1 (1915), 4

Anon, 'Practice recitals and invitation concerts', *RAM Club Magazine* 93 (1932), 40–1

Anon [and C. S. G., G. A.], obituary tributes to Detmar Blow, *The Times*, 8, 9, 11, 18, 21 February 1939, 16, 19, 14, 14, 16 [anon 1939a]

Anon, obituary of Detmar Blow, *Journal of the Royal Institute of British Architects,* Third Series xlvi (1939), 571 [anon 1939b]

Anon, 'MTA composer of the year: Gerald Finzi', *Music Teacher and Piano Student* xxxiv (1955), 597

Anon, 'Mr Gerald Finzi: a sensitive composer', obituary, *The Times*, 28 September 1956, 13. Reprinted in *Finzi Trust Friends Newsletter* xii[*recte xiii*]/1 (1995), [4].

Anon, *Who Was Who VIII: 1981–1990* (London, 1991)

Anon, ed. *Twentieth Century Composers, Part One: The Music Manuscripts of Sir Michael Tippett, Sir Arthur Bliss and Gerald Finzi: a listing and guide to the Research Publications collection* (Reading, 1992)

Anon, obituary of Iris Lemare, *The Times*, 8 May 1997, 16

Anon, ed., *Downe House Scrapbook: 1907–1957* (privately printed, n.d.)

Ashbee, C. R., *Craftsmanship in Competitive Industry: being a record of the workshops of the Guild of Handicraft, and some deductions from their twenty-one years' experience* (Campden and London, 1908)

Aslet, C., *The Last Country Houses* (New Haven and London, 1982)

– and Powers, A., *The National Trust Book of the English House* (New York and Harmondsworth, 1985)

Avery, K., 'Finzi, Gerald', in *Grove's Dictionary of Music and Musicians*, ed. E. Blom (London, 1954), III, 135–7

Bairstow, E. C., *Counterpoint and Harmony* (London, 1937, 2/1945)

– and Greene, H. P., *Singing Learned from Speech: a primer for teachers and students* (London, 1946)

Banfield, S., 'The Immortality Odes of Finzi and Somervell', *Musical Times* cxvi (1975), 527–31

– *Sensibility and English Song: critical studies of the early twentieth century* (2 vols, Cambridge, 1985)

– sleeve note to recording of music by Vaughan Williams (EMI 7 49745, 1988)

– sleeve note to recording of music by Finzi (EMI 7 49913 2, 1989)

– 'Finzi and Wordsworth', *Finzi Trust Friends Newsletter* x/2 (1992), [2–10]

– 'England, 1918–45', in *Man & Music. Modern Times: from World War I to the present*, ed. R. P. Morgan (London, 1993), 180–205

– ed., *Music in Britain: The Twentieth Century* (Oxford, 1995)

Barsham, E., 'Parry's manuscripts: a rediscovery', *Musical Times* ci (1960), 86–7

Bate, J., *Romantic Ecology: Wordsworth and the environmental tradition* (London, 1991)

Batkin, M., 'Alfred and Louise Powell', in Greensted 1993, 92–109

Bebbington, G., *Street Names of London* (London, 1972)

Beechey, G., 'The church music of Gerald Finzi', *Musical Times* cxviii (1977), 667–70

Bendle, P., conversation with the author (5 August 1996)

Bennett, J., personal communications with the author (1991)

Bhabba, H., 'Of mimicry and man: the ambivalence of colonial discourse', *October* xxviii (1984), 126–8

Bliss, A. [and Scott, A.], 'Gerald Finzi – an appreciation', *Tempo* 42 (1956–7), 5–6

Bliss, A., *As I Remember* (London, 1970)

Blow, S., 'Blow-by-blow account of a duke's desertion', *The Spectator* cclvi (25 January 1986), 22–3

Blunden, E., ed., *Poems of Ivor Gurney* (London, 1954)

Boden, A., *F. W. Harvey: soldier, poet* (Gloucester, 1988)

– *Three Choirs: a history of the Festival* (Stroud, 1992)

Boult, A. C., *My Own Trumpet* (London, 1973)

Bourne, G. [Sturt, G.], *William Smith, Potter and Farmer: 1790–1858* (London, 1919)

Boyd, C. M., 'Gerald Finzi and the solo song', *Tempo* 33 (1954), 15–18

Boyes, G., *The Imagined Village: culture, ideology and the English Folk Revival* (Manchester and New York, 1993)

Bradford, A., ed., *Thomas Traherne: selected poems and prose* (London, 1991)

Brett, P., 'Are you musical?', *Musical Times* cxxxv (1994), 370–6

– letter to the author (1996)

Bunting, C., conversation with the author (24 July 1997)

Burn, A., ed., *Summer Weekend of English Music: Oxford 20–22 July 1984*, programme book (Liverpool, 1984) [Burn 1984a]

– sleeve note to 'A recital of English songs', Hyperion recording A66103, 1984) [Burn 1984b]

– conversations with Joy Finzi (tape recordings, 1984) [Burn 1984c]

– ed., *Summer Weekend of English Music: 16–19 July 1987 Radley College Abingdon*, programme book (Liverpool, 1987) [Burn 1987a]

– 'Quiet composure', *Country Life* clxxxi (1987), 118–19 [Burn 1987b]

– sleeve note to recording of music by Moeran and Finzi (EMI 7 49912 2, 1988)

– 'Introduction', *Gerald Finzi*, catalogue of works (Boosey & Hawkes, London, 1994), 4

– and McVeagh, D., eds, *Gerald Finzi: twenty-fifth anniversary celebration: Ellesmere College Weekend 17–19 July 1981*, programme book (Liverpool, 1981)

– and Rees, H., eds, *Summer Festival of British Music 1990: Radley College, Abingdon 11–15 July 1990*, programme book (Liverpool, 1990)

Burroughs, E. J. R., *Unity in Diversity: the short life of the United Oxford Hospitals* (Oxford, privately printed, 1978)

Cassuto, U., 'Finzi, Felice', 'Finzi, Giuseppe', 'Finzi, Moses', in *The Jewish Encyclopedia*, ed. I. Singer (New York and London, 1903) 390–1

Campbell, M., *Dolmetsch: the man and his work* (London, 1975)

Cannadine, D., *G. M. Trevelyan: a life in history* (London, 1992)

Cantwell, J. D., *The Second World War: a guide to documents in the Public Record Office* (London, HMSO, 1972, R.1993)

Carlisle, M. R., *Gerald Finzi: A Performance Analysis of 'A Young Man's Exhortation' and 'Till Earth Outwears', Two Works for High Voice and Piano to Poems by Thomas Hardy* (DMA dissertation, University of Texas, Austin, 1991)

Carol Case, J., conversation with the author (4 August 1996)

Carpenter, H., *Benjamin Britten: a biography* (London, 1992)

Carr-Saunders, A. M. and Wilson, P. A., *The Professions* (Oxford, 1933)

Cartwright, G., conversation with the author (8 March 1997)

Cesarini, D., ed., *The Making of Modern Anglo-Jewry* (Oxford, 1990)

Cesarini, D., 'The transformation of communal authority in Anglo Jewry, 1914–1940', in Cesarini 1990, 115–40

Cheyette, B., 'The other self: Anglo-Jewish fiction and the representation of Jews in England, 1875–1905', in Cesarani 1990, 97–111

Clark, L., ed., *Poems of Ivor Gurney, 1890–1937* (London, 1973)

Cline, E., 'The composer's use of words: the language and music of Gerald Finzi', *British Music* xiv (1992), 8–24

Clinton-Baddeley, V. C., *Words for Music* (Cambridge, 1941)

Cobbe, H., 'The correspondence of Gerald Finzi and Ralph Vaughan Williams', *Finzi Trust Friends Newsletter* x/1 (1992), [9–14]

Cole, H., 'Vision of innocent England: celebrating Gerald Finzi', *Country Life* clxx (1981), 575

Colles, H. C. and Ferguson, H., 'Morris, R(eginald) O(wen)', in *The New Grove Dictionary of Music and Musicians*, ed. S. Sadie (London and New York, 1980), XII, 591–2

Comino, M., *Gimson and the Barnsleys: 'wonderful furniture of a commonplace kind'* (London, 1980, R.1991)

Cook, J., *Towards a Performing Version of the Finzi Piano Concerto* (BA Hons dissertation, Oxford University, 1994)

Cooper, I., *The Orchestral and Chamber Works of Gerald Finzi* (M.Litt. dissertation, University of Bristol, 1985)

Copley, I., *Robin Milford* (London, 1984)

Core, P., *Camp: the lie that tells the truth* (New York, 1984)

Couperin, F., ed. Gilbert, K., 'Preface', *Quatriéme Livre de piéces de Clavecin* (Paris, 1730, R.1970), ix–x

Craggs, S., *Arthur Bliss: a bio-bibliography* (New York, Westport, CT and London, 1988)

– *John Ireland: a catalogue, discography, and bibliography* (Oxford, 1993)

Crispi, F., *I Mille* (Milan, 1911)

Crowest, F. J., ed, *English Music [1604–1904]: being the lectures given at the Music Loan Exhibition of the Worshipful Company of Musicians, held at Fishmongers' Hall, London Bridge, June–July, 1904* (London and New York, 1906)

Crum, M., 'Working papers of twentieth-century British composers', *Bodleian Library Record* viii (1968), 101–3

Crutchfield, J. E., *A Conductor's Analysis of Gerald Finzi's 'Intimations of Immortality'; 'Lo, the Full, Final Sacrifice'; and 'Magnificat'* (DMA dissertation, Southern Baptist Theological Seminary, 1994)

Cutts, V., letter to the author (1991)

Dale Roberts, J., 'Recalling Finzi', in Burn and Rees 1990, 19

Dale Roberts, J., conversation with the author (7 November 1996)

Darley, G., *Villages of Vision* (London, 1975)

Davey, P., *Arts and Crafts Architecture* (London [and USA as *Architecture of the Arts and Crafts Movement*], 1980, R.1995)

Denning, L. A., *A Discussion and Analysis of Songs for the Tenor Voice Composed by Gerald Finzi With Texts by Thomas Hardy* (DMA dissertation, University of Miami, 1995)

Dibble, J., *C. Hubert H. Parry: his life and music* (Oxford, 1992)

Dickinson, P., *The Music of Lennox Berkeley* (London, 1988)

Dingley, P., *The Finzi Book Room at the University of Reading: a catalogue* (Reading, 1981)

Dolan, S., 'Upsetting the apple cart', *The Independent,* 12 October 1990, 28

Doyle, B., *English & Englishness* (London and New York, 1989)

Dressler, J. C., *Gerald Finzi: a bio-bibliography* (Westport, CT and London, 1997)

Dyson, R., conversation with the author (20 August 1996)

Eaton, S., letter to Joy Finzi, *Finzi Trust Friends Newsletter* iv/1 (1986), [13–14]

Ehrlich, C., *Harmonious Alliance: a history of the Performing Right Society* (Oxford, 1989)

Elbogen, I., 'Finzi', in *The Jewish Encyclopedia,* ed. I. Singer (New York and London, 1903), V, 389–90

Elliston, S., letter to the author (1991)

Ely, P., ' "A combination of Don Quixote and D'Artagnon": John Haines on Ivor Gurney', *The Ivor Gurney Society Journal* i (1995), 59–68

Emden, P. H., *Jews of Britain: a series of biographies* (1944)

Evans, P., 'Instrumental music I', in Banfield 1995, 179–277

Fawkes, R., 'Just an ordinary man', *Classical Music,* 12 August 1995, 25

Ferguson, H., 'Gerald Finzi (1901–1956)', *Music and Letters* xxxviii (1957), 130–35 [Ferguson 1957a]

– 'Gerald Finzi', *Canon* xi (1957), 111–12 [Ferguson 1957b]

– 'Gerald Finzi (1901–1956)', *Hallé* 100 (1957), 8–11 [Ferguson 1957c]

– sleeve note to recording of songs by Finzi (Lyrita SRCS 38, 1968)

– sleeve note to recording of songs by Finzi (Lyrita SRCS 51, 1971)

– conversations with the author (1974–96)

– letter to Philip Thomas (14 March 1984)

– letters to the author (1985–96)

– 'People, events and influences', in Ridout 1989, 7–15

– 'Meetings with Vaughan Williams', in Burn and Rees 1990, 12–13

– and Navarro, D. de, eds, *J. M. de Navarro: Collected Poems* (Cambridge, privately printed, 1980)

Finberg, J., *The Cotswolds* (*The Regions of Britain*) (London, 1977)

Finzi, C., sleeve note to recording of music by Finzi (World Record Club, SCM 50, 1964)

- personal communications with the author (1990–96)
- ed., *Joy Finzi 1907–1991: tributes from her friends* (privately printed, 1992)

Finzi, G., review of Maud Karpeles: *Folk-Songs from Newfoundland, Journal of the Folk Dance and Song Society* i (1935), 157

- handwritten note accompanying posthumous sketch by Joy Finzi of Lilian Annie Black (1939)
- *Absalom's Place: catalogue of works* (typescript, July 1941, R. June 1951), in J. Finzi n.d.
- 'Critic on the air', BBC 3rd Programme talk (typescript, 1 April 1948)
- 'Obituary: R. O. Morris', *The RCM Magazine* xlv/2 (1949), 54–6 [G. Finzi 1949a]
- 'Hubert Parry, a revaluation', *Making Music* 10 (1949), 4–8 [G. Finzi 1949b]
- 'Introduction', *John Stanley: Concerto No. 3 in G* (London, 1949) [G. Finzi 1949c]
- 'Environment and music', *Mercury* 7 (1950), 25–7 [G. Finzi 1950a]
- 'Words and music', guest page, *Oxford Guardian*, 5 October 1950, 13 [G. Finzi 1950b]
- 'John Stanley (1713[*sic*]–1786)', *Proceedings of the Royal Musical Association* lxxvii (1950–1), 63–75
- 'Music and the amateur', book review, *Making Music* 17 (1951), 13–14
- 'Vaughan Williams – the roots and the tree', *Philharmonic Post* vi/6 (1952), 64–5, 71
- 'John Stanley', *Tempo* 27 (1953), 21–7 [G. Finzi 1953a]
- 'Leith Hill Festival' (typescript, 14 April 1953) [G. Finzi 1953b]
- Preface, *Charles Wesley: Easy String Quartets* (London, 1953) [G. Finzi 1953c]
- 'Herbert Howells', *Musical Times* xcv (1954), 180–83 [G. Finzi 1954a]
- '[Marion Scott] as guardian of genius (Ivor Gurney's work)', Society of Women Musicians conference (typescript, 25 June 1954); printed in Marion Scott commemorative programme, 8–11 [G. Finzi 1954b]
- Preface, *Richard Mudge: Concerto No. 4 in D minor for string orchestra and continuo* (London, 1954) [G. Finzi 1954c]
- Preface, *John Garth: Concerto No. 2 in B flat major for violoncello solo, string orchestra, and continuo (ad lib)* (London, 1954) [G. Finzi 1954d]
- 'The composer's use of words': [three] Crees Lectures, RCM (typescript, 1955)
- 'Music for *Love's Labour's Lost*', introduction to orchestral suite (Boosey & Hawkes hire score, London, ?1955)
- Preface, *Charles Wesley: Concerto No. 4 in C major [for keyboard]* (London, 1956)

– Preface, *Capel Bond: Concerto No. 6 in B♭ for bassoon, string orchestra and continuo* (London, 1957) [G. Finzi 1957a]

– Preface and critical apparatus, *William Boyce: Overtures* (Musica Britannica xiii, London, 1957), xiii–xxvii, 163–4 [G. Finzi 1957b]

Finzi, J. A., Layman, Clark 1975–6. Unpublished records drawing on research undertaken on behalf of the firm by Miss D. C. Stockhausen (employee), David Carrington (*Jewish Chronicle*), Claudio Vita Finzi (University College, London), Geoffrey Langley (Avon County Reference Librarian) and R. N. Carvalho, and on information in *Ievreiskaia Enziklopedia* xv (St Petersburg, 1913)

Finzi, J., personal journal (1936–56)

– 'For Diana McVeagh', reminiscences of Gerald Finzi (typescript, 1950s?)

– 'Gerald Finzi – composer – 1901–1956', introduction to the Finzi Book Room, Reading University Library (typescript, 1973)

– conversations with the author (28 March and 28 October 1974)

– letters to the author (1974–85)

– 'Introduction' to S. Banfield: *The Hardy Songs by Gerald Finzi* (typescript, 1975)

– Finzi Trust Friends talk and notes (typescript, Christmas 1982)

– 'In that place', in Burn 1984a, 2

– 'Exhibition of portrait drawings by Joy Finzi', in Burn 1987a, 45 [J. Finzi 1987a]

– *In That Place: the portrait drawings of Joy Finzi* (Marlborough, 1987) [J. Finzi 1987b]

– *Absalom's Place* scrapbook (n.d.) (see G. Finzi 1941, R.1951)

Finzi, N., conversation with the author (8 August 1996)

Foreman, L., 'Reputations . . . bought or made?', *Musical Times* cxxi (1980), 27

– *From Parry to Britten: British music in letters 1900–1945* (London, 1987)

– personal communication (1996)

Forster, E. M., *Maurice* (London, 1971)

Fortis, U., *Jews and Synagogues* (Venice, 1973)

Foss, H., *Music in My Time* (London, 1933)

Foster, M., 'The Hussey legacy', *Finzi Trust Friends Newsletter* xi/2 (1993), [11–13]

Francis, A., sleeve note to recording of music by Finzi and Stanford (Hyperion A66001, 1980)

Frankel, B., 'His music caught the meaning of words', *Music and Musicians* v (December 1956), 15, 35

French, J. H., *The Choral Odes of Gerald Finzi (England)* (DMA dissertation, University of Cincinnati, 1995)

Fussell, P., *The Great War and Modern Memory* (London, Oxford and New York, 1975)

Gartner, L. P., *The Jewish Immigrant in England, 1870–1914* (London 1960, R.1973)

Gaunt, W., *The Pre-Raphaelite Tragedy* (London, 1942, R.1975)

– *The Aesthetic Adventure* (London, 1945, R.1975)

Gay, J. D., *The Geography of Religion in England* (London, 1971)

Germany, jr, S. R., *The Solo Vocal Collections of Gerald R. Finzi Suitable for Performance by the High Male Voice* (DMA dissertation, University of North Texas, 1993)

Gilman, S., *Jewish Self-Hatred: anti-Semitism and the hidden language of the Jews* (Baltimore, 1986)

Gilbert, M., *Jewish History Atlas* (London, 1969, R.1992)

Gillespie, N., 'The text of Stanley's "Teraminta" ', *Music and Letters* lxiv (1983), 218–24

Gooch, B. N. S. and Thatcher, D., *Musical Settings of Late Victorian and Modern British Literature: a catalogue* (New York and London, 1976)

– *A Shakespeare Music Catalogue* (5 vols, Oxford, 1991)

Grainger, P., letter to Roger Quilter, 8 October 1947 (Library of Congress, Washington, DC)

Graves, R., and Hodge, A., *The Long Week-End: a social history of Great Britain 1918–1939* (London, 1940, R.Harmondsworth, 1971)

Greene, H. P., Scott, M. M., Squire, J. C., de la Mare, W., Blunden, E., Vaughan Williams, R. and Howells, H., 'Ivor Gurney, the man . . . the poet . . . the musician', *Music and Letters* xix (1938), 1–17

Greensted, M. *et al, The Arts and Crafts Movement in the Cotswolds* (Stroud, 1993)

Grogan, C., 'Gerald Finzi (1901–56): an annotated bibliography' (typescript, 1992)

– 'Elgar, Streatfeild and The Pilgrim's Progress', in *Edward Elgar: music and literature*, ed. R. Monk (Aldershot, 1993)

Grover, R. S., *The Music of Edmund Rubbra* (Aldershot, 1993)

Gurney Archive, Gloucester Library

Hamm, C., 'Technology and music: the effect of the phonograph', in C. Hamm, B. Nettl and R. Byrnside, *Contemporary Music and Music Cultures* (Englewood Cliffs, NJ, 1975), 253–70

Handford, M., *Sounds Unlikely: six hundred years of music in Birmingham* (Birmingham, 1992)

Hansler, G., *Stylistic Trends and Characteristics in the Choral Music of Five Twentieth-Century English Composers: Benjamin Britten, Gerald Finzi, Constant Lambert, Michael Tippett, and William Walton* (Ph.D. dissertation, NY State University, 1957)

[Hardy, T.] ed. M. Millgate, *The Life and Work of Thomas Hardy* (London, 1928–30, R.1984)

Harker, D., *Fakesong: the manufacture of British 'folksong' 1700 to the present day* (Milton Keynes and Philadelphia, 1985)

Harman, C., ed., *The Diaries of Sylvia Townsend Warner* (London, 1994)

Haskell, H., 'The revival of early music', in Banfield 1995, 519–29

Havergal, H., 'Finzi, Gerald Raphael (1901–1956)', *Dictionary of National Biography 1951–1960* (London, 1971), 357–8

Hencke, D., 'Food on the rack', *Guardian*, 3 November 1989, 25

Henriques, R., *Marcus Samuel* (London, 1960)

Herbert, T., ed., *Bands: the brass band movement in the 19th and 20th centuries* (Milton Keynes and Philadelphia, 1991)

Heyman, B., *Samuel Barber: the composer and his music* (New York, 1992)

Hibberd, D., personal communication with the author (1993)

Highfield, J., *Gerald Finzi: the man and the music* (GRSM dissertation, RAM, 1978)

Hold, T., ' "Checkless griff", or Thomas Hardy and the songwriters', *Musical Times* cxxxi (1990), 309–10

Holman, P., sleeve note to John Stanley: *Six Concertos in Seven Parts, Op. 2* (Hyperion recording A66338, 1989), 4–5

– sleeve note to Capel Bond: *Six Concertos in Seven Parts* (Hyperion recording A66467, 1992), 4–6

Holst, I., *Gustav Holst* (London, New York and Toronto, 1938)

– *The Music of Gustav Holst* (London, 1951)

Holt, R., *Sport and the British: a modern history* (Oxford, 1989)

Howells, H., conversation with the author (13 March 1974)

Howells, U., conversation with the author (15 September 1996)

Howes, F., 'Recent work in folk-music', *Proceedings of the Musical Association* lxiv (1938), 39–69

[–] 'A poet's musician: the works of Gerald Finzi', *The Times*, 5 October 1956, 3

– *The English Musical Renaissance* (London, 1966)

Howkins, A., 'The discovery of rural England', in *Englishness: politics and culture 1880–1920*, ed. R. Colls and P. Dodd (London, New York and Sydney, 1986), 62–88

Hull, R., ' "What now?" ', in *British Music of Our Time*, ed. A. L. Bacharach (Harmondsworth and New York, 1946), 219–34

Hulme, D. R., *A Study of the English Art-Song Between the World Wars* (MA dissertation, University College of Wales, Aberystwyth, 1975)

Hurd, M., *The Ordeal of Ivor Gurney* (Oxford, 1978)

– 'Finzi and Gurney', in Burn and McVeagh 1981, 4 [Hurd 1981a]

- 'Building a library: the music of Gerald Finzi', radio script (BBC Radio 3, 10 October 1981) [Hurd 1981b]

Hussey, W., *Patron of Art: the revival of a great tradition among modern artists* (London, 1985)

Hutchings, A., 'Music in Britain, 1918–1960', in *The New Oxford History of Music, Vol X (The Modern Age: 1890–1960)*, ed. M. Cooper (London, 1974), 539

Hutton, G. and Smith, E., *English Parish Churches* (London, 1952, R.1976 with O. Cook)

Hyamson, A. M., *The Sephardim of England* (London, 1951)

Jackson, F., *Blessed City: the life and works of Edward C. Bairstow 1874–1946* (York, 1996)

Jacobs, A., *Henry J. Wood: maker of the Proms* (London, 1994)

Johnson, G., 'Voice and piano', in *The Britten Companion,* ed. C. Palmer (London, 1984), 286–307

Diack Johnstone, H., 'Music in the home I', in Johnstone and Fiske 1990, 159–201

- and Fiske, R., eds, *Music in Britain: The Eighteenth Century* (Oxford, 1990)

Jusserand, J. J., trans. Smith, L. T., *English Wayfaring Life in the Middle Ages (XIVth Century)* (London, 1884, R.1891)

Kavanagh, P. J., ed., *Collected Poems of Ivor Gurney* (Oxford and New York, 1982)

Kemp, I., *Tippett: the composer and his music* (London, 1984)

Kennedy, M., *The Works of Ralph Vaughan Williams* (London, 1964, R.Oxford, 1980)

- *A Catalogue of the Works of Ralph Vaughan Williams* (London, 1982)
- *Portrait of Walton* (Oxford and New York, 1989)

Kenyon, N., *The BBC Symphony Orchestra: the first fifty years 1930–1980* (London, 1981)

Kershaw, D., 'Film and television music', in Banfield 1995, 125–44

Keston, D., *Two Gentlemen from Wessex: the relationship of Thomas Hardy's poetry to Gerald Finzi's music* (M.Sc. dissertation, Bemidji State University, Minnesota, 1981)

Kildea, P. F., *Selling Britten: a social and economic history* (D.Phil. dissertation, Oxford University, 1996)

King, T., conversation with the author (13 March 1997)

W. M. L., 'Obituary notices: N. S. Finzi, MB, DMRE, FFR, FACR', *British Medical Journal,* 20 April 1968, 181

Lace, I., 'Elgar and other British composers in Sussex: II', *BMS News* 69 (1996), 202–4

Lambert, C., *Music Ho! a study of music in decline* (London, 1934)

Lambourne, L., *Utopian Craftsmen: the Arts and Crafts movement from the Cotswolds to Chicago* (London, 1980)

le Fleming, C., *Journey into Music (by the Slow Train): an autobiography* (Bristol, 1982)

Leach, K., *Finzi's Early Development as a Songwriter: a study of the song sketches, Bodleian Library MSS Mus.b.33–34* (B.Mus. Hons dissertation, Royal Holloway College, 1991)

Lee, E. Markham, 'The student-interpreter: Gerald Finzi: "A Young Man's Exhortation" ', *Musical Opinion* lxii/734 (1938), 118–19

Leighton, K., 'Memories of Gerald Finzi', *Finzi Trust Friends Newsletter* vi/1 (1988), [5–6]

Lemare, I., conversation with the author (4 August 1996)

Liley, S., *Gerald Finzi 1901–1956, Musical Poet: a critical study of his songs for solo voice and piano* (M.Mus. dissertation, University of Liverpool, 1988)

Lloyd, S., *Sir Dan Godfrey: champion of British composers* (London, 1995)
– 'Vaughan Williams's A London Symphony: the original version and early revisions, performances and recordings' (typescript, 1996) [Lloyd 1996a]
– letter to the author (1996) [Lloyd 1996b]

Long, N. G., 'The songs of Gerald Finzi', *Tempo* 17 (1946), 7–10

Lowerson, J., *Sport and the English Middle Classes: 1870–1914* (Manchester and New York, 1993)

Lutyens, E., *A Goldfish Bowl* (London, 1972)

McBurney, G., 'Orchestral music', in Ridout 1989, 38–53

McCoy, J. M., *The Choral Music of Gerald Finzi: a study of textual/musical relationships* (DMA dissertation, University of Texas, Austin, 1982)

McCray, J. E., *The British Magnificat in the Twentieth Century* (Ph.D. dissertation, University of Iowa, 1968)

MacDonald, C., 'The English spirit', *The Listener* civ (1980), 347–8

MacDonald, R. H., ed., *William Drummond of Hawthornden: poems and prose* (Edinburgh and London, 1976)

McGuinness, R. and Johnstone, H. Diack, 'Concert life in England I', in Johnstone and Fiske 1990, 31–95

McVeagh, D., sleeve note to recording of Finzi: *Intimations of Immortality* (Lyrita SRCS 75, 1975)
– sleeve note to recording of music by Finzi (Lyrita SRCS 92, 1977)
– sleeve note to recording of music by Finzi (Lyrita SRCS 84, 1978)
– sleeve note to recording of music by Finzi (Argo ZRG 896, 1979) [McVeagh 1979a]
– sleeve note to recording of music by Finzi (Lyrita SRCS 93, 1979) [McVeagh 1979b]

- sleeve note to recording of music by Finzi (Argo ZRG 909, 1979) [McVeagh 1979c]
- sleeve note to recording of Finzi: Cello Concerto (Lyrita SRCS 112, 1979) [McVeagh 1979d]
- 'Finzi, Gerald (Raphael)', in *The New Grove Dictionary of Music and Musicians*, ed. S. Sadie (London and New York, 1980), VI, 594–6 [McVeagh 1980a]
- 'Foreword', *Gerald Finzi*, catalogue of works (Boosey & Hawkes, London, 1980), 3 [McVeagh 1980b]
- 'Composers of our time: Gerald Finzi', *Records and Recording* xxiii/4 (1980), 30–33 [McVeagh 1980c]
- 'Finzi and Bairstow', in Burn and McVeagh 1981, 13 [McVeagh 1981a]
- 'Songs by Finzi and his friends', sleeve note to Hyperion recording A66015 (1981) [McVeagh 1981b]
- 'A Finzi discography', *Tempo* 136 (1981), 19–22
- sleeve note to recording of songs by Finzi (Hyperion A66161/2, 1985)
- sleeve note to recording of music by Finzi and Leighton (Chandos CHAN 8471, 1986)
- sleeve note to recording of instrumental music by Finzi (Nimbus NI5101, 1987)

Marsack, R., ed., *Edmund Blunden: Selected Poems* (Manchester, 1982, R.1993)

Matthews, D., 'Chamber music', in Ridout 1989, 27–37

Mellers, W., *Vaughan Williams and the Vision of Albion* (London, 1989)

Mil[ano], A., 'Finzi', in *Encyclopaedia Judaica*, ed. C. Roth (New York and Jerusalem, 1972), VI, 1300–1

Millgate, M., *Thomas Hardy: a biography* (Oxford and New York, 1985)

Mitchell, D., 'The music of Gerald Finzi', concert review, *Musical Times* xcv (1954), 490–1

- and Reed, P., ed., *Letters from a Life: selected letters and diaries of Benjamin Britten* (2 vols, London, 1991)

Morgan, J. and Richards, A., *The Book of Apples* (London, 1993)

Morris, R. O., 'Hubert Parry', *Music and Letters* i (1920), 94–103

- *Contrapuntal Technique in the Sixteenth Century* (Oxford, 1922)
- *Foundations of Practical Harmony & Counterpoint* (London, 1925)
- *Figured Harmony at the Keyboard* (London, 1931)

Mosse, W. E., ed., *Second Chance: two centuries of German-speaking Jews in the United Kingdom* (Tübingen, 1991)

Motion, A., *The Poetry of Edward Thomas* (London, 1991)

Münz, S., 'Finzi, Giuseppe', in *The Jewish Encyclopedia*, ed. I. Singer (New York and London, 1903), V, 390

Musgrave, M., *The Musical Life of the Crystal Palace* (Cambridge, 1995)

Nairn, I. and Pevsner, N., *The Buildings of England: Sussex* (Harmondsworth, 1965)

Naylor, G., *The Arts and Crafts Movement: a study of its sources, ideals and influence on design theory* (London, 1971)

Newman, E., 'Words and music', *Sunday Times*, 15, 22, 29 July 1945, 2, 2, 2

Niederbrach, D. W., *The Songs of Gerald Finzi: an analytical and critical examination* (DMA dissertation, University of Iowa, 1977)

Nochlin, L. and Garb, T., eds, *The Jew in the Text: modernity and the construction of identity* (London, 1995)

Notley, M., letter to the author (1991)

O'Connor, P., 'Music for the stage', in Banfield 1995, 107–24

Officer, A., 'Who was Ernest Farrar?', in *British Music Week: programme book of artistic events*, ed S. Banfield and T. Blacker (Keele University, 1984), 24–9. Reprinted in *British Music Society Journal* vii (1985), 1–10.

Orsi, P., *Cavour and the Making of Modern Italy: 1810–1861* (London, 1914)

Ottaway, H., 'The Three Choirs at Gloucester', *Musical Opinion* lxxx/950 (November 1956), 79–83

Ousby, I., ed., *The Cambridge Guide to Literature in English* (Cambridge, 1988)

Pakenham, S., conversation with the author (7 August 1996)

Palmer, C., *Herbert Howells: a centenary celebration* (London, 1992)

Parker, B. B., 'Textual–musical relationships in selected songs of Gerald Finzi', *NATS Bulletin* xxx (1974), 10–19

Parker, K., 'Finzi, *Requiem da camera* [etc]', review, *Finzi Trust Friends Newsletter* x/1 (1992), [21]

Pevsner, N., *The Buildings of England: London, except the Cities of London and Westminster* (Harmondsworth, 1952)

– *The Buildings of England: Leicestershire and Rutland* (Harmondsworth, 1960)

– and Lloyd, D., *The Buildings of England: Hampshire and the Isle of Wight* (Harmondsworth, 1967)

Pierce, E. A., *A Videocassette Analysis and Performance of Song Cycles by Ralph Vaughan Williams, Gerald Finzi and Ivor Gurney With Short Commentary on Each* (DMA dissertation, Eastman School of Music, 1975)

Pitfield, T., 'Dropped names: a nonagenarian composer's memorabilia', *British Music* xvii (1995), 7–19

Pollins, H., *Economic History of the Jews in England* (East Brunswick, NJ, London and Toronto, 1982)

Popkin, J. M., *The Finzi Bowl* (Oxford, 1986)

Popplewell, C., 'Church Farm, Ashmansworth', *Finzi Trust Friends Newsletter* xii[recte xiii]/1 (1995), [1–3]

Powers, A., 'Harmonious mansions: two composers' houses of the 1930s', *Country Life* clxxviii (1985), 559–63

Prictor, M. J., 'The poems of Thomas Hardy as song', *Context* 6 (1993–4), 34–42

– *'His Own Sweet Way': a study of the critical reception of the works of Gerald Finzi (1901–1956)* (M.Mus. dissertation, University of Melbourne, 1996)

Ray, D. B., *Ivor Gurney (1890–1937): his life and works* (MA dissertation, California State University, Long Beach, 1980)

Redlich, H., 'Finzi, Gerald', in *Die Musik in Geschichte und Gegenwart*, ed. F. Blume (Kassel and Basle, 1955), IV, 246–7

Renouf, D., *Thomas Hardy and the English Musical Renaissance* (Ph.D. dissertation, Trent Polytechnic, Nottingham, 1986)

Ridout, A., ed., *The Music of Howard Ferguson* (London, 1989)

Robinson, K. E., *A Critical Study of Word/Music Correspondences in the Choral Works of Gerald Finzi* (Ph.D. dissertation, Northwestern University, 1994)

R[ose?], B[ernard] W. G., obituary tribute to Gerald Finzi, *The Times*, 10 October 1956, 13. Reprinted in *Finzi Trust Friends Newsletter* xii[*recte* xiii]/1 (1995), [5].

Roth, C., *The Great Synagogue, London, 1690–1940* (London, 1950)

Rubbra, E. [Duncan-], 'The younger English composers: VI – Gerald Finzi', *Monthly Musical Record* lix (1929), 193–4

– 'Gustav Holst, some technical characteristics', *Monthly Musical Record* lxii (1932), 52–9. Reprinted in *Gustav Holst: collected essays*, ed. S. Lloyd and E. Rubbra (London, 1974), 29–39.

– with Spencer, G., Russell, J. and W[alker], A., 'Mr Gerald Finzi: wide sympathies', *The Times*, 12 October 1956, 13. Reprinted in *Finzi Trust Friends Newsletter* xii[*recte* xiii]/1 (1995), [5–6].

– 'Finzi and Edmund Rubbra', in Burn and McVeagh 1981, 16

Russell, J., 'Gerald Finzi – an English composer', *Tempo* 33 (1954), 9–15

– 'Gerald Finzi', *Musical Times* xcvii (1956), 630–1

– 'Gerald Finzi (1901–1956)', *Making Music* 33 (1957), 7–9

Sadie, S., 'Music in the home II', in Johnstone and Fiske 1990, 313–54

Sands, M., *Invitation to Ranelagh, 1742–1803* (London, 1946)

– 'The problem of "Teraminta" ', *Music and Letters* xxxiii (1952), 217–22

Sayers, D. L., 'The Beatrician vision in Dante and other poets', *Nottingham Mediaeval Studies* ii (1958), 3–23

Schaarwächter, J., *Die britische Sinfonie 1914–1945* (Cologne, 1995)

Schubert, D. T., *The Relationship of Text and Music in Gerald Finzi's Song Set: 'I Said to Love'* (DMA dissertation, University of Oklahoma, 1993)

Scott, A., conversation with the author (5 August 1996)

Scott, D., 'The "jazz age" ', in Banfield 1995, 57–78

Scott, M. M., 'Chamber music of the month', *Musical Times* lxxvii (1936), 455–7

– 'Preface', *Ivor Gurney: A First [and Second] Volume of Ten Songs* (London, 1938)

– 'Postscript. July 1950', *Ivor Gurney: A Third Volume of Ten Songs* (London, 1952)

– 'Howells's Piano Quartet', in Burn and Rees 1990, 12

Seeley, R., letter to the author (1991)

Service, A., *Edwardian Architecture: a handbook to building design in Britain 1890–1914* (London, 1977)

Shuttleworth, A., 'Memories of Gerald Finzi, his music, home, family and the Newbury String Players 1945–56', *Finzi Trust Friends Newsletter* xii[*recte* xiii]/1 (1995), [9–10]

Sitwell, O., 'Ada Leverson', *Noble Essences* (London, 1950), 127–62

Slobin, M. *et al*, 'Jewish–American music', in *The New Grove Dictionary of American Music*, ed. S. Sadie and H. Wiley Hitchcock (London and New York, 1986), II, 569–73

Smith, B., *Peter Warlock: the life of Philip Heseltine* (Oxford and New York, 1994)

Spearing, R., *H. H.: a tribute to Herbert Howells on his eightieth birthday* (London, 1972)

Spicer, P., sleeve note to recording of music by Howells (Hyperion A66610, 1992), 3–7

Spieth-Weissenbacher, C., 'Geoffroy-Dechaume, Antoine', in *The New Grove Dictionary of Music and Musicians*, ed. S. Sadie (London and New York, 1980), VII, 240

Stansky, P., *Redesigning the World: William Morris, the 1880s, and the Arts and Crafts* (Princeton, NJ, 1985)

Steiner, G. *et al*, *The Critical Moment* (London, 1964)

Stradling, R. and Hughes, M., *The English Musical Renaissance 1860–1940: construction and deconstruction* (London and New York, 1993)

Stunt, C., *Thomas Hardy and Gerald Finzi: an improbable partnership* (BA Special Hons dissertation, University of Bristol, 1996)

Sumsion, J., conversation with the author (6 August 1996)

Tann, J., *Gloucestershire Woollen Mills* (Newton Abbot, 1967)

Taylor, A. J. P., *English History: 1914–1945* (Oxford, 1965, R. Harmondsworth, 1970)

Taylor, D., *Hardy's Poetry, 1860–1928* (Basingstoke and London, 1981, R.1989)

– *Hardy's Metres and Victorian Prosody* (Oxford, 1988)

Theyer, O., conversation with the author (9 August 1996)

515

Thomas, P., private collection of manuscript sketches and other material by Gerald Finzi (n.d.)

- 'Children's songs, Op.1', in Burn and Rees 1990, 28 [Thomas 1990a]

- 'Requiem da camera', Finzi Trust Friends Newsletter viii/2 (1990), [14–15] [Thomas 1990b]

Thornton, R. K. R., ed., Ivor Gurney: Collected Letters (Ashington and Manchester, 1991)

Thornton, R. K. R. and Walter, G., Ivor Gurney: towards a bibliography (Birmingham, 1996)

Thorpe Davie, C., 'Introduction', Catalogue of the Finzi Collection (St Andrews University Library, 1982), iii–iv

Tobin, J. R., 'Living British composers, 6: Gerald Finzi', Pictorial Education (March 1954), 14

Toynbee, H., Heather Toynbee Pamphlets (unpublished, Surrey Heath Museum, Camberley, n.d.)

Trend, M., The Music Makers: heirs and rebels of the English musical renaissance: Edward Elgar to Benjamin Britten (London, 1985)

Trevelyan, G. M., Garibaldi and the Thousand (London, 1909)

Turner, D., Gerald Finzi's Songs: the context of the unpublished and fragmentary works (BA Hons dissertation, Oxford University, 1987)

Urrows, D., 'Gerald Finzi and his sacred choral music', The American Organist (July 1990), 82

Vaughan Williams, R., Bliss, A. and H[utton], G., 'Mr Gerald Finzi: a many-sided man', obituary, The Times, 3 October 1956, 13. Reprinted in Finzi Trust Friends Newsletter xii[recte xiii]/1 (1995), [6–7].

Vaughan Williams, U., RVW: a biography of Ralph Vaughan Williams (London, 1964)

- 'For art and artists', obituary of Joy Finzi, Guardian, 19 June 1991, 37

- conversation with the author (7 August 1996)

Verey, D., Gloucestershire: The Cotswolds (The Buildings of England, ed. N. Pevsner) (Harmondsworth, 1970)

Viotti, A., Garibaldi: the revolutionary and his men (Poole, 1979)

Vogel, D. E., A Recital of Selected Songs for the Low Male Voice Composed by Gerald Finzi Using the Poetry of Thomas Hardy (Ed.D. dissertation, Columbia University, 1967)

Wade, M., Before and After Summer, radio play (BBC Radio 3, 20 August 1995)

Walker, A., 'Gerald Finzi (1901–1956)', Tempo 52 (1959), 6–10

Webb, B., Edmund Blunden: a biography (New Haven and London, 1990)

Weber, C. J., 'Thomas Hardy music: with a bibliography', Music and Letters xxi (1940), 172–8

Werner, A., trans., *Autobiography of Giuseppe Garibaldi* (2 vols, London, 1889)

W[estrup], J. A., 'Finzi, Gerald', in *Grove's Dictionary of Music and Musicians*, supplementary volume, ed. H. C. Colles (London, 1940), 219

Whitehorn, M., *The Whitehorns in Five Centuries: to our parents on their Golden Wedding anniversary: 27th July 1971 (with family trees by John Whitehorn)*

Whitehorn, M., *Roy Whitehorn: 'A servant of the Word': 1891–1976* (1991)

Wiener, M. J., *English Culture and the Decline of the Industrial Spirit 1850–1980* (Cambridge, 1981)

Willey, E. L., 'British clarinet concertos', *The Clarinet* xii (1985), 15–16

Williams, A. Glyn, 'Stanley, Smith and "Teraminta" ', *Music and Letters* lx (1979), 312–15

Williams, R., *The Country and the City* (London, 1973)

Woodcock, G., ed., *William Cobbett: Rural Rides* (Harmondsworth, 1967)

Wyndham, V., *The Sphinx and Her Circle: a biographical sketch of Ada Leverson (1862–1933)* (London, 1963)

Young, P. M., *Alice Elgar: enigma of a Victorian lady* (London, 1978)

– *George Grove: a biography* (London, 1980)

Index of letters

(*indicates letters from Finzi; all others are to him)

Most of the letters listed below – largely in the form of photocopies, since the originals were destroyed by fire – are in the Bodleian Library, Oxford. The exceptions are as follows. The BBC correspondence (possibly more extensive than listed here) is at the BBC Written Archives Centre, Caversham Park, Reading; Finzi's letters to Herrmann are in the Bernard Herrmann Archive at the University of California, Santa Barbara; the Finzi–Thorpe Davie letters are in the University of St Andrews Library; three of Finzi's letters, and Joy's letter, to Iris Lemare, are with her estate, the others in the British Library or missing; his letters to Lady Ponsonby are at Shulbrede Priory; those to Marion Scott and to and from Ronald Gurney are in the Gurney Archive, Gloucester Library, along with other Gurney-related letters to Finzi given in square brackets below. Those from Marion Scott are missing, as are those to and from the Sumsions.

Doubtless many more letters to and from Finzi are still in existence. The author would be pleased to know of any that can be located.

19280312 Milford
19280315 Ferguson
19280319 Ferguson
19280321 Jacob
19280322 Milford*
19280323 Ferguson
19280326 Ferguson
19280330 Blow
192804? Ferguson
19280401–17? Strawson
19280405 Blow
19280406 Ferguson
19280409/10? Ferguson*
19280413 Ferguson
19280418 Strawson
19280422 Ferguson*
19280423 Ferguson
19280424 Blow
19280426 Ferguson
19280430a Bliss
19280430b Ferguson*
19280501 Strawson*
19280502? Bliss
19280503 Blow
19280506 Ferguson
19280507a Ferguson*
19280507b Morris
19280510 Blow
19280513 Ferguson
19280514 Ferguson*
19280515 Ferguson
19280516 Strawson*
19280518 Ferguson*
19280519 Ferguson
19280520 Erlebach
19280521 Strawson*
19280526a Strawson*
19280526b Erlebach
19280527 Ferguson
19280528 Villiers
19280611 Ferguson
19280612 Morris
19280614 Ferguson
19280615a Morris
19280615b Ferguson*
19280617a Morris
19280617b Ferguson
19280624 Ferguson
19280626 Blow
19280629 Morris
192807? Strawson*
19280705 Ferguson
19280713 Ferguson
19280714a Ferguson*
19280714b Ferguson*
19280715 Bairstow

19280730 Ferguson
19280801–03? Strawson*
19280808a Kaye
19280808b Morris
19280813 Morris
19280815 VW
19280817 Ferguson
19280821 Morris
19280822 Morris
19280825 Rubbra
19280830 Ferguson
19280831a Morris
19280831b Morris
19280903 Ferguson*
19280911 Blow
19280912 Jacob
19280918 Ferguson
19280924 Ferguson
19280925 Ferguson
19280927 Ferguson
19281003 Bliss
19281o? Morris
19281005? Morris
19281006 Rubbra
19281007 Jacob
19281009 Ferguson
19281010 Jacob
19281012 Rubbra
19281020 Ferguson*
19281025 Morris
19281026 Ferguson
19281030 Ferguson
19281101 Ferguson
19281103 Ferguson
19281122 Ferguson
19281130a Ferguson
19281130b Ferguson
19281202 Bliss
19281206 Bliss
19281207 Morris
19281213 Jacob
19281226 Bairstow
192812? Ferguson*
192812 Ferguson*
19281222 Villiers
19281223? Blow
19281223 Ferguson
19281228? Ferguson*
19281230 Ferguson
19290102 Ferguson*
19290111 Ferguson
19290114 Ferguson
19290204a Ferguson
19290204b Morris
19290226 Morris
19290228 Blow

19290403 Howells
19290409 Morris
19290421 Ferguson
19290422 Rubbra
19290423/24 Ferguson*
19290426 Rubbra
19290505 Ferguson
19290512? Morris
19290526 Rubbra
19290531 Morris
19290601 Ferguson*
19290605 Morris
19290610 Ferguson
19290615 Ferguson
19290617a Bliss
19290617b Villiers
19290630 Rubbra
19290709? Morris
192907? Morris
19290723 Ferguson*
19290726 Ferguson
192907–08?a Morris
192907–08?b Morris
192907–08?c Morris
19290802a Ferguson*
19290802b Ferguson
192908 Ferguson*
19290808? Bliss
19290809 Morris
19290815 Ferguson*
19290824/31? Morris
19290827? Morris
19290901 Ferguson
19290906 Ferguson
19290907 Gollancz/
Strawson
19290901–07? Lambert
19290901–12 Ferguson*
19290912 Strawson*
19290913 Morris
19290920 Ferguson
192909–1930? Bliss
19291002 Howells
19291017? Bliss
192910? Ferguson
19291020 Morris
19291023 Ferguson
19291105 Kaye
19291120a Bliss
19291120b Rubbra
19291122 Bliss
19291123 Lambert
19291128 Ferguson
19291222 Bairstow
19291231? Lambert
1929? Ferguson*

19320922 VW
19320924 Demuth
19321002? Lambert
19321014 Ferguson
19321017a Busch
19321017b Holst
19321018? Busch
19321103 Ferguson
19321104 Lambert
19321105 Busch
19321107? Lambert
19321115 Ferguson
19321125 Britten
19321127 Samuel
193212? Lambert
19321202 VW
19321204 Ferguson*
19321215 Ferguson
19321219 Bliss
19321224 Ferguson*
19330101 Ferguson
19330106 Lambert
19330108 Ferguson*
19330112 Busch
19330113 Lambert
19330116 Holst
19330117 Busch
19330118 Ferguson
19330123 Busch
19330203 Howells
19330204? Ferguson
19330205 Rubbra
19330206 Ferguson
19330219 Rubbra
19330223 VW
19330227 Ferguson
19330308 Ferguson
19330315 Britten
19330317 Busch
19330319 William Bliss
19330319–22? Lambert
19330323 Rubbra
19330325 Holst
19330330? Holst
19330330 Ferguson
19330401 Ferguson
19330413 Ferguson*
19330417 Ferguson
19330418 Dummett
19330419 Ferguson*
19330421 Ferguson*
19330422 Ferguson
193305?a VW
193305?b VW
193305–08? Lambert
193305/04? Ferguson [*Joy]

19330515 Hutton
19330517 Ferguson
19330531 Ferguson
19330601 Ferguson*
19330604a Rubbra
19330604b Ferguson
19330608? Bliss
19330611 Rubbra
19330621 Ferguson*
19330629 Coates
19330707 VW
19330712 Thorpe Davie*
19330713? Thorpe Davie*
19330714 Ferguson*
19330714–16? Thorpe
Davie*
19330716 Ferguson*
19330717 Coates
19330725 Hichens
193307? VW
19330804 VW
19330808 Morris
19330812 Morris
19330817 Ferguson*
19330818 Coates
19330819 Ferguson
19330821 Coates
19330823 Ferguson*
193309? Ferguson*
19330921 Morris
193309/10? Ferguson*
19331030 Morris
19331031 Holst
19331122 Coates
193311? Ferguson*
193311–12? Ferguson*
19331206/13/20? Holst
19331208 Plunket Greene
19331208? Thorpe Davie*
19331211? Drew
19331213 Busch
193312? Thorpe Davie*
19340106 Wilson
19340118 Ferguson*
19340120 Holst
19340122 VW
19340402 Ferguson
19340403/04 Ferguson*
19340404 Curwen
19340417 Thorpe Davie*
19340428 Ferguson
19340430 Ferguson*
1934? VW
19340508a Bliss
19340510? Bliss
19340508b VW

193405 Ferguson*
193405/06 Ferguson*
19340624 [Holst]
19340626 [Holst]
19340713? Morris
19340714–18? Ferguson
19340721 Ferguson*
19340725 Ferguson
19340817 Ferguson
19340817+ Ferguson*
19340821 Ferguson*
19340825 Ferguson*
19340912 Rubbra
19340913 Ferguson
19340915 Ferguson*
19340921 Rubbra
19341002 Ferguson
19341007 Ferguson*
19341010 Ferguson
19341031 Rubbra
19341207 Kennedy Scott
19341229 Ferguson*
1935–9? Macnaghten*
19350118 Rubbra
19350213 Thorpe Davie*
19350214? VW
19350303 VW
19350331 Marion Scott*
19350405 VW
19350410 Rubbra
19350413a Ferguson*
19350413b Marion Scott*
19350414 VW*
19350417 VW
19350424 Marion Scott*
19350502 Ferguson*
19350513 Ferguson*
19350516 Ferguson
19350601 Ferguson
193506?a Ferguson*
193506?b Ferguson*
19350606 Ferguson*
19350608 VW
19350613 Plunket Greene
19350614 Marion Scott*
19350618 Curwen
19350629 Rubbra
193507 Thorpe Davie*
19350704 VW
19350707? Bliss
193507–08 Marion Scott
[*Joy]
19350801 Ferguson*
19350802 Ferguson
19350812 Thorpe Davie*
19350813 Ferguson*

19370421b Rubbra
19370421c Marion Scott*
19370422 Ferguson
19370423a Ferguson*
19370423b Ferguson
19370502 Haines*
19370503 Rubbra
19370509 Navarro
19370510 Howells
19370511? VW
19370512 Marion Scott*
19370513 Howells
19370514 VW
19370515 Marion Scott*
19370530 Ferguson*
193705? VW
19370605 Navarro
19370605 Marion Scott*
19370607 Ferguson*
19370608 Navarro*
19370610a Navarro
19370610b Ferguson
19370616 Mullen
19370621 Ferguson
19370623 Ferguson
19370701a Ferguson
19370701b Marion Scott*
19370702 Ferguson*
19370705 Haines*
19370706 Marion Scott*
19370708 VW
19370711 Navarro
19370712 Ferguson
19370713 Haines*
19370721a Navarro*
19370721b Ferguson*
19370722a Ferguson
19370722b Marion Scott*
19370723 Navarro
19370725 VW
19370727 Navarro*
19370728a Blunden*
19370728b VW
19370728c Haines*
19370729 Navarro
19370731? Bliss
19370731 Navarro*
193707/08? Ferguson*
19370803 Navarro
19370808a Navarro*
19370808b Ferguson*
19370810a Rubbra
19370810b Busch*
19370813a Navarro
19370813b Ferguson
19370814a Navarro*

19370814b Marion Scott*
19370815 Ferguson*
19370817a Rubbra
19370817b Marion Scott*
19370830 Marion Scott*
19370831 Haines*
19370903? Navarro*
19370912a Navarro*
19370912b Ferguson*
19370914a Navarro*
19370914b Kennedy Scott
19370914c Ferguson*
19370915 Marion Scott*
19370916 Ferguson
19370919 Navarro
19370922 Blunden
19370923a Navarro*
19370923b Blunden*
19370927 Ferguson*
19370928a Ferguson*
19370928b Navarro
19370929 Ferguson
19370930? Navarro
19370930 Ferguson*
19371001 Navarro*
19371004 Ferguson
19371005 Navarro
19371006 Ferguson*
19371008 Navarro*
19371013 Rubbra
19371021 Ferguson
19371027 Navarro*
19371101 Navarro
19371109 Rubbra
19371117 Ferguson*
19371120 Ferguson
19371123 Ferguson
19371124a Rubbra
19371124b Ferguson
19371124c Marion Scott*
19371204 Ferguson
19371206 Navarro
19371207a Navarro*
19371207b Ferguson*
19371214 Navarro
19371218a Ferguson*
19371218b Haines*
19371228 Marion Scott*
19371229 Haines*
19371230? Navarro [*Joy]
19371231 Navarro
1937? Marion Scott*
19380101a Ferguson*
19380101b Marion Scott*
19380104 Marion Scott
19380105 Ferguson

19380108 Haines*
19380111 Ferguson
19380115 Ferguson*
19380116 Ferguson
19380118 Ferguson
19380123 Howells
19380126 Navarro
19380130 Navarro*
19380131 Navarro
19380201 Navarro
19380202 Ferguson*
19380207 Navarro
19380208 Marion Scott*
19380209? Navarro
19380210 Navarro
19380212a Navarro*
19380212b Busch
19380212c Marion Scott*
19380214a Ferguson
19380214b Busch*
19380215 Navarro
19380216 Busch
19380217a Ferguson*
19380217b Marion Scott*
19380219a Navarro*
19380219b I Holst
19380223 Ferguson*
19380227 Ferguson
19380301a Navarro*
19380301b Ferguson*
19380302 Busch*
19380305 Navarro [*Joy]
19380307 Navarro
19380311 Busch
19380312 Busch*
19380315 Busch
19380316 Busch*
19380318 Harland
19380325a Pyke
19380325b Busch
19380325c Busch*
19380327 Navarro
19380402 Navarro*
19380403 Howells
19380409 Navarro
19380421a Rubbra
19380421b Marion Scott*
19380427 Busch
19380502 Rubbra
19380504 Navarro*
19380509 Navarro
19380510 Navarro*
19380511 Rubbra
19380518 Milford
19380519 Milford*
19380528 Navarro*

19390725 Busch
19390731 Rubbra
193907?28? Milford
19390731 Milford
19390802a Rubbra
19390802b Ferguson
19390803 Busch
19390816 Blom
19390821 Busch
19390823? VW
19390825 Marion Scott*
19390829 Busch
19390901 Milford
19390902 Ferguson
19390903 Bairstow
19390904a Milford*
19390904b Marion Scott*
19390905 Rubbra
19390906 Milford
19390911 Navarro*
19390912a Navarro
19390912b Busch
19390913 Navarro
19390915a VW
19390915b Calvocoressi
19390917 Busch*
19390921a Navarro
19390921b Navarro
19390929 Kennedy Scott
19390930 Rubbra
193909/10? Milford
19391006 Ferguson
19391008 Bairstow
19391013 Milford
19391015 Ferguson
19391018 Milford*
19391021 Milford
19391023 Milford*
19391025 Ferguson
19391026 Milford
19391028 Navarro*
19391029 Navarro
19391101 Navarro*
19391107a Busch
19391107b Ferguson
1939?b Milford
19391110 Busch*
19391119 Busch
19391120 Milford*
19391126 Milford
19391126+ Milford
19391203 Haines*
19391207 Haines*
19391211a Milford
19391211b Ferguson*
19391216 Ferguson*

19391219a Busch
19391219b Ferguson
19391221 Navarro*
19391227 Rubbra
19391228 Milford*
19391230 Scott
1939 ?
19400101a Scott*
19400101b Blow
19400101c VW
19400102a Navarro*
19400102b Milford
19400110 Busch
19400111 Milford*
19400116 Ferguson
19400117? Milford
19400124 Busch
19400127a VW
19400127b Milford*
19400129a Scott*
19400129b Rubbra
19400201 Miles
19400204 Ferguson
19400205 Ferguson*
19400207a Navarro*
19400207b Ferguson
19400209 Navarro
19400211 Busch
19400217 Rubbra
19400220 Ferguson*
19400226 Rubbra
19400306 Rubbra
19400307 Navarro*
19400309 Navarro
19400311 Navarro
19400313 Ferguson*
19400317 Busch
19400320 Navarro*
19400321 Busch
19400327a Rubbra
19400327b Navarro
19400328a Milford
19400328b Ferguson
19400329a Milford
19400329b Peake
19400402 Milford*
19400403a Busch
19400403b Milford
19400405 Ferguson
19400408 Scott
194004 VW
19400413 Peake
19400414? Scott*
19400416 Navarro
19400418 Milford
19400420 Milford

19400401–20 Milford*
19400421 Navarro*
19400425a Navarro*
19400425b Ferguson
19400425c Milford*
19400425d Ferguson
19400509 Rubbra
19400516a Scott
19400516b Howells
19400520 Milford
19400521 Howells*
19400529 Milford*
19400530? Brooke*
1940?a Milford
1940?b Milford
19400602 Busch
19400606a Navarro
19400606b Ferguson
19400607a Navarro*
19400607b Ferguson*
19400616 Ferguson*
19400617 Busch*
19400710 Rubbra
19400711 Ferguson
19400713 Ferguson*
19400720 Ferguson
19400723a Scott*
19400723b Busch
19400727 Ferguson*
19400728+? Scott*
19400730a Rubbra
19400730b Howells
19400802 Ferguson*
19400804a Scott
19400804b Milford
19400805 Navarro
19400806 Ferguson
19400807 Rubbra
19400812 Rubbra
19400813 Ferguson*
19400814 Rubbra
19400816 Rubbra
19400818 Ferguson
19400819a Scott*
19400819b Ferguson*
19400828 Ferguson
19400830 Ferguson*
19400901 Scott
19400906? Ferguson*
19400907 Milford
19400908 Ferguson*
19400910 Milford*
19400911 Ferguson*
19400912 Navarro
19400914? Navarro*
19400916 Busch

19420214 Milford
19420217? Milford
19420218 Milford*
194202–03? Ferguson*
19420302 Tippett
19420303 Busch
19420306 Busch*
19420327 BBC/Chapman
19420330 Bliss
19420406 Busch
19420409a Busch*
19420409b Scott
19420411 Navarro*
19420414 Scott*
194204–05? Joy Finzi
19420422 Ferguson
19420426 VW
19420430 Milford*
1942? Milford
19420503 Milford
19420505a VW
19420505b BBC/Bliss*
19420513 Busch
19420515 Navarro*
19420518 Ferguson*
19420520 Ferguson
19420521 VW
19420523 Howells
19420524 Ferguson*
19420529 Marion Scott*
194205?a Joy Finzi
194205?b VW
19420603a VW
19420603b Howells*
19420604 Scott
19420606 Busch
19420607 Milford
194206? Milford
19420604 Navarro
19420615 Navarro
19420616 Busch*
19420617 Navarro*
19420618 Navarro
19420629 Busch
19420706–09? Joy Finzi
19420807 Busch*
19420815 Ferguson
19420816 Scott
19420821 BBC/Bliss*
194208–09? Milford
19420902 VW
19420908 Navarro*
19420918 Ferguson
19420920 Navarro
19420921 Rubbra
19420923 Scott

194209? VW
19421006a Scott
19421006b BBC/Bliss
19421006c Navarro
19421009a Busch*
19421009b BBC/Bliss*
19421012a Scott
19421012b Ferguson*
19421013a Navarro*
19421013b VW
19421012–18? Shaw
19421018? Navarro
19421018a Navarro
19421018b Ferguson
19421019a Rubbra
19421019b Busch
19421020 Scott
19421022 Milford
19421101? Rubbra
19421104 Ferguson*
19421107 Ferguson
19421108 Busch
19421113 Milford
19421114 Morris
19421116 Busch
19421/12? Milford
19421204 VW
19421208 Busch
19421231 Rubbra
1942 Rothenstein
19430107 Rubbra
19430117a Ferguson*
19430117b Busch
19430117c VW
19430122 Busch*
19430131 Scott
194302? Milford
19430218 Milford
19430314a Milford*
19430314b Busch
19430318 Milford
19430319–31? Milford
19430406 Rubbra
19430410? Wood
19430414 Blow
19430426 Scott
19430505 Milford
19430507 Rubbra
19430518 VW
19430531 Busch
194305–06 VW
19430601 Busch*
19430602 Milford
19430603 Milford*
19430614? Ferguson*
19430615 Ferguson

194306? Ferguson [*Joy]
19430627 Ferguson
19430628 Ferguson*
19430704 Rubbra
19430712 Howells*
19430720 Busch
19430802 UVW
19430812 Milford*
19430816 Rubbra
19430822 VW
19430903 Scott
19430906? Scott*
19430917a VW
19430917b Scott
19430923/30/1007/14 Scott*
19431016 Scott
19431020 Scott*
19431021a BBC/Clifford
19431021b Rubbra
19431112 Herrmann
19431126 Scott
19431129? Scott*
19431206 Hutchings
19431215 Navarro
19431217 Ferguson*
19431218 Milford
19431219 Scott [*Lizzie]
19431220 Rubbra
19431221 Scott*
19431222? Milford
19431223 VW
19431224 Howells
19431227 Howells*
19431231a Busch*
19431231b Milford*
19440102 Scott
19440105 Scott*
19440109 Scott*
194401–04? Scott*
194402? Joy Finzi
19440313 Busch
19440328 Milford*
19440331 Milford
19440406a Scott
19440406b Milford*
19440410 Busch
19440414 Scott*
19440420 Ferguson
19440425 Ferguson
19440429 Busch
194404?a Scott*
194404?b Milford
19440512 Scott*
19440525? Milford
19440526 van Wyk

19460505 VW
19460501+? Milford
19460507 Milford
19460518a Milford*
19460518b Thorpe Davie*
19460523 Milford
19460529 Milford
19460530 Milford*
19460603a Rubbra
19460603b Milford
19460606 Hussey W
19460609 Rubbra
19460612 Hussey W
19460621 Milford
19460622 Thorpe Davie*
19460623 Rubbra
19460703 Long
19460707 Scott*
19460712 Hussey D
19460715 Rubbra
19460716 van Wyk
19460719 Navarro*
19460721 Thorpe Davie*
19460722 Milford*
19460725 Milford
19460801 Milford
19460821 Thorpe Davie*
19460824 Navarro*
19460829 Ferguson
19460901 Milford*
19460903 Shore
19460904 Milford
19460908 Milford
19460912a Milford*
19460912b Ferguson
19460915 Milford*
19460916a Scott*
19460916b Milford
19460916? Hussey W
19460917a Scott
19460917b Rubbra
19460918a Wyton
19460918b VW
19460920? Milford
19460923 Hussey W
19460925 VW
19460926 Scott*
19460927a Wyton
19460927b VW
19460929 Scott
19460929? Scott*
19460930a le Fleming*
19460930b Ferguson
19461003 Eric Greene
19461008a Hull
19461008b VW

19461016a Scott*
19461016b Ferguson
19461021 Milford
19461025a Logan
19461025b Scott*
19461027 Milford
19461031 Milford*
19461103a Rubbra
19461103b Milford
19461106 Ferguson
19461111a Wyton
19461111b Thorpe Davie*
19461112 Milford
19461116? Thorpe Davie*
19461117 Thorpe Davie*
19461119 Thorpe Davie*
19461123a le Fleming*
19461123b Thorpe Davie*
19461127a Thorpe Davie*
19461127b Scott*
19461130 Milford
19461202 Ferguson
19461204 Ferguson
19461206 Ferguson
19461209 Thorpe Davie*
19461 2? Milford
19461214 Rubbra
19461217 Thorpe Davie*
19461218 Milford
19461219 Thorpe Davie*
19461220 Demuth
19461221 Scott*
19461222a Milford*
19461222b Wyton
19461223? Thorpe Davie*
19461225 Ferguson
19461226 Milford
19461229 Haines*
19461231a Rubbra
19461231b Milford
19470102 Sands*
19470106 Thorpe Davie*
19470108 Navarro*
19470113 Ferguson
19470116 Croker-Fox*
19470118 Navarro*
19470121 Morris
19470122 Macdonald
19470123 Scott
19470124 Scott*
19470127a Milford
19470127b Thorpe Davie*
19470129 Rubbra
19470202a Ferguson
19470202b Thorpe Davie*
19470210 Milford

19470212 Rubbra
19470213 Milford*
19470215 Howells*
19470220 Hussey W
19470222 Sands*
194702–03 VW
19470302 Milford
19470304 Hussey W
19470315 Milford
19470318 Sands*
19470319 Rubbra
19470319+ Sands
19470321 Milford*
19470325 Milford
19470327a Howells
19470327b Milford*
19470331a Navarro*
19470331b Ferguson
19470331c Milford
19470403 Redman
19470405 Milford
19470407 Ferguson
19470410 Rubbra
19470411 Ferguson
19470415 Ferguson
19470419 Douglas Fox
19470421 Ferguson
19470428 Milford
19470429 Rubbra
19470430 VW
19470503 Rubbra
19470504? Sands*
19470504a Sands*
19470504b Milford*
19470505 Ferguson
19470506 Thorpe Davie*
19470513a VW
19470513b Sands*
19470505–20 Milford
19470520 Milford
19470521 Milford*
19470522 Marion Scott*
19470523 Milford
19470525 Milford*
19470526+? Milford
194706 Thorpe Davie*
19470604 Marion Scott*
19470605 Milford*
19470606? le Fleming*
19470608 Wyton
19470616 Rubbra
19470617 Blunden*
19470618 Ponsonby*
19470619 VW
19470622 Sands*
19470624 Ponsonby*

19480822 Ponsonby*
19480825a Rubbra
19480825b Milford
19480904 Ferguson
19480908 Edmunds
19480910 Milford
19480912 Navarro*
19480917 Milford*
19480919 Juler*
19480920 Thorpe Davie*
19480921 Juler*
19480930 Blunden*
19481002a Ferguson
19481002b Thurston*
19481003 Thorpe Davie*
19481006 Milford*
19481007 Rubbra
19481008 Wyton
19481009 Milford
194810? Thorpe Davie*
19481014 Milford*
19481016 Ferguson
19481019 Navarro
19481024 Thorpe Davie*
19481025? Thorpe Davie*
19481030 Ponsonby*
19481031a Scott
19481031b Ferguson
19481104 Ponsonby*
19481107 Thorpe Davie*
19481124 Thorpe Davie*
19481127 Ferguson
19481128 Blunden
19481207 Ponsonby*
19481209 Thorpe Davie*
19481211a Rubbra
19481211b VW
19481212 Tom Scott
19481214 Scott
194812? Thorpe Davie*
19481216 Ponsonby*
19481217 BBC/Lowe
19481220 BBC/Lowe*
19481223 [Morris]
19481229 Milford
19481230 VW
1948/49 VW
194901 [Morris]
1949? Morris
19490102 Milford*
19490104a Haines*
19490104b Ferguson
19490106 VW
19490110 Thorpe Davie*
19490121 Thorpe Davie*
19490203 Rubbra

19490215 Scott*
19490221 Thorpe Davie*
19490307 Chissell
19490328 Chissell
19490330 VW
19490331 Scott*
19490416 Thorpe Davie*
19490421 Thorpe Davie*
19490424 Ferguson
19490502 Scott*
19490503 Ferguson
19490510 Ferguson
19490517 Ferguson
19490525 Milford
19490527 Ferguson
19490528/06? Milford*
19490528 Milford*
19490530 Thorpe Davie*
19490601 Milford
19490605 VW
19490607 Navarro*
19490608 VW
19490615? Milford*
19490618 Rubbra
19490622 VW
19490624 Levi
19490703 Thorpe Davie*
19490704 Rubbra
19490706 VW
19490712 Rose
19490714 VW
19490717 Ferguson
19490720 Alwyn
19490724 Thurston*
19490812 BBC/Irwin*
19490813 Thurston*
19490819 Rubbra
19490822 Blunden*
19490823 Ferguson
194908? Thurston*
194909? Thorpe Davie*
19490909a Blunden
19490909b VW
19490911 VW
19490912 Havergal
19490915 Thurston*
19490917 Milford*
19490918a Navarro*
19490918b Howells*
19490921a Thorpe Davie*
19490921b Thurston*
19490922 Howells
19490924a Scott*
19490924b Thurston*
19490927 Arts Council
19491004 Milford*

19491009? Thorpe Davie*
19491010 Milford
19491014 Ferguson
19491017a Scott
19491017b Ferguson
19491018 VW
19491106? VW
19491110 VW[*]
19491112 Milford
19491118 Benjamin
19491129 Alwyn
194911? UVW*
19491218 Milford*
19491221 van Wyk
19491224? Thorpe Davie*
19491228a Ferguson
19491228b Alwyn
19491231 Atkins
194?06? VW
194?0620? VW
1940s–50s VW
19500101 Blunden*
19500109a Ferguson
19500109b Thorpe Davie*
19500123 Ferguson
19500126a Edmunds
19500126b Ferguson
19500201 VW
19500204 Milford
19500206 Ferguson
19500213 Cullen
19500215 Thorpe Davie*
19500219 Frankel
19500222 Rubbra
19500307? Thorpe Davie*
19500317 Milford
19500318 Blunden
19500320? Thurston*
19500323 Dart
19500326 Thorpe Davie*
19500329 Plumptre
19500402/21? Thorpe
Davie*
19500409 Ponsonby*
19500412 Curwen
19500427 Ponsonby*
19500511 Ponsonby*
19500514 Wiren
19500518 Milford
19500519 Thorpe Davie*
19500522 Milford*
19500530 Croker-Fox*
19500602? Willcocks
19500603 VW
19500605 Ferguson
19500612 Ponsonby*

19510905? Milford
19510908a Thorpe Davie*
19510908b Marion Scott*
19510914 Ferguson
19510917 Thorpe Davie*
19510923 Atkins
19511001a Blunden
19511001b Thorpe Davie*
19511002 Blunden*
19511005a Ferguson
19511005b Buckland
19511007 Scott
19511008 Rubbra
19511009 Milford
19511012a Milford*
19511012b Scott
19511018 Howells*
19511022 Blunden*
19511027 Thorpe Davie*
19511028 Howells
195110? Thorpe Davie*
195110a Thorpe Davie*
195110b Thorpe Davie*
19511102a Milford
19511102b Thorpe Davie*
19511103 Ferguson
19511107 Milford*
19511112 Blunden*
19511113 Blunden
19511114 VW
19511115 le Fleming*
19511117 Thorpe Davie*
19511118 Howells
19511118 Brown
19511125 Ferguson
19511126a Milford
19511126b Blunden
19511126c Brown
19511128a Blunden*
19511128b VW
195112 Haines*
19511201 Blunden
19511203 Blunden
19511204 Howells
19511206 Buckland
19511208 Rubbra
19511209 Thorpe Davie*
19511212 VW
19511216a Buckland
19511216b Buckland
19511218 VW
19511220 Thorpe Davie*
19511223 Navarro*
19511227 VW
19511227–30? Croker-Fox
[*Joy]

19511229 Milford
19511231 Scott*
195201 Navarro [*Joy]
19520102 Bliss
19520104 Ferguson
19520107 Scott
19520109a Scott
19520109b VW
19520110 Rubbra
19520111 Scott*
19520123 Thorpe Davie*
19520126 Blunden*
19520129 Thorpe Davie*
19520131 Pizzey
19520131? Thorpe Davie*
195202 Thorpe Davie*
19520212 Thorpe Davie*
19520220 Scott
19520221 Ferguson
19520222 Scott*
19520226 Ferguson
19520305 Ferguson
19520308 Fergsuon
19520312a Rubbra
19520312b VW
19520317 Milford
19520323 Thorpe Davie*
19520324 Rubbra
19520403 BBC/Lowe
19520406? Scott*
19520412 Thurston*
19520415 Cannon
19520416 VW
19520427 Thorpe Davie*
19520430 Thorpe Davie*
19520504 Thorpe Davie*
19520511 Blunden
19520512 Rubbra
19520512–? Blunden [*Joy]
19520513 Milford
19520519 Blunden
19520520 Thorpe Davie*
19520522a Scott
19520522b VW
19520523 Ponsonby*
19520524 BBC/Ferguson
19520526 Rubbra
19520602 Cannon
19520603 Henderson/B&H
195206? Thorpe Davie
[*Joy]
19520613 Thorpe Davie*
19520615 Scott
19520620 Ferguson
19520622 Milford
19520622? Scott*

19520630a Brown
19520630b Marion Scott*
19520708a Powell
19520708b Blunden
19520701–29? Scott*
19520711 Blunden*
19520712 Rubbra
19520714 Blunden
19520717? Blunden*
19520718 Rubbra
19520719 Thorpe Davie*
19520720? Ponsonby*
19520721 Ferguson
19520722 Herrmann
19520723 Blunden
19520724 Blunden*
19520726 Powell
19520729 Marion Scott*
19520730 Scott
195207? Kelly
195208? Kelly
19520803? Scott*
19520804 Thorpe Davie*
19520809 Shiner
19520811 Rubbra
19520822a B&H
19520822b Ferguson
19520823 Scott*
195207+ Scott*
195208–09? Thorpe Davie*
19520901 Ferguson
19520906 Milford*
19520907 Cannon
19520910a Milford*
19520910b Ferguson
19520913 Milford
19520916 Blunden
19520917 Kelly*
19520921 Blow
19520922 Scott
19520923 Thorpe Davie*
19520926 Cannon
19520930 Ferguson
19521001? Thorpe Davie*
19521002 Blunden
19521003 Thorpe Davie*
19521004 Marion Scott*
19521006 Milford
19521007 Roth/B&H
19521009 Hinrichsen
19521014a Hinrichsen
19521014b VW
19521014c Thorpe Davie*
19521014d VW*
19521015a Hinrichsen
19521015b Howells*

19531128b Rubbra
19531130a Milford
19531130b Thorpe Davie*
1953? Scott*
19531201 Thorpe Davie*
19531201–09? Thorpe Davie*
19531202 Ferguson
19531205a Ferguson
19531205b Thorpe Davie*
19531207 Milford
19531212 Blunden*
19531218 Ferguson
19531223 Thorpe Davie*
19531226 Milford
19531231 [Gurney]
195312? Milford
1953–5? UVW
19540101 Haines*
19540102a Ferguson
19540102b Ponsonby*
19540105 [Gurney]
19540107a Milford
19540107b Blunden*
19540110 Rubbra
19540112 [Gurney]
19540115a Milford
19540115b [Gurney]
19540119 [Gurney]
19540126 Blunden
19540127 [Gurney]
19540128 Howells
19540130a Milford
19540130b Ponsonby*
19540201a Thorpe Davie*
19540201b [Gurney]
195402? VW
195402 Thorpe Davie*
19540202 de Peyer
19540203 [Gurney]
19540215 [Gurney]
19540219a [Gurney]
19540219b [Gurney]
19540220 Ferguson
19540221? Blunden*
19540222 [Gurney]
19540223 [Gurney]
19540225 Gurney*
19540227 Gurney
19540302 Gurney*
19540303 Ponsonby*
19540304 Ponsonby*
19540305a Howells*
19540305b [Gurney]
19540309 Howells
19540310 Blunden

19540313a Ferguson
19540313b Thorpe Davie*
19540322a Ferguson
19540322b Blunden*
19540325 Milford*
19540327 Milford
19540328 Teed
19540313? Thorpe Davie*
195403 Thorpe Davie*
19540402a Howells*
19540402b Blunden
19540402c Gurney*
19540403 Thorpe Davie*
19540405 [Gurney]
19540408 [Gurney]
19540409 Gurney
19540411 Howells
19540412 [Gurney]
19540420 Thorpe Davie*
19540422 Ferguson
19540424 Rubbra
19540428 Thorpe Davie*
19540506 Teed
19540508 Blunden*
19540510 Thorpe Davie*
195405? Thorpe Davie*
19540517 Ponsonby*
19540526 Rubbra
19540609 Teed
19540611a Blunden*
19540611b Thorpe Davie*
19540611c Thorpe Davie*
19540612a Ferguson
19540612b Thorpe Davie*
19540613 Milford*
19540616 [Gurney]
19540617 Blunden
19540618? Thorpe Davie*
19540619a Milford
19540619b BBC/VW
19540621 Milford*
19540621+ Milford
19540622a Teed
19540622b Ponsonby*
19540625 Thorpe Davie*
19540627 Thorpe Davie*
19540630 Milford
1954/48?07 Lord Chamberlain*
19540701 Croker-Fox*
19540705 Thorpe Davie*
195407? Thorpe Davie*
19540707 Howells
19540709a Rubbra
19540709b Howells
19540709c Bliss

19540709d Ferguson
19540711 Howells*
19540712 Frankel
19540713 Gurney
19540714a Teed
19540714b Thorpe Davie*
19540714c [Gurney]
19540714? Gurney*
19540715a Milford
19540715b Rubbra
19540716a Clark*
19540716b [Gurney]
19540719a Ferguson
19540719b Gurney
19540720 Milford
19540729 Ponsonby*
19540731 Ferguson
19540731? Ponsonby*
195408? Thorpe Davie*
19540803a Milford
19540803b [Gurney]
19540805 Clark*
19540806 [Gurney]
19540807 Thorpe Davie*
19540809 Clark
19540811? Croker-Fox*
19540814 Rubbra
19540816? Milford
19540818 Thorpe Davie*
19540822 Hutton
19540905 Clark
19540907a Parrott
19540907b Ferguson
19540910 Howells*
19540911 Barbirolli
19540913 Thorpe Davie*
19540914a Milford
19540914b Ferguson
19540916 Rubbra
19540919a Clark*
19540919b Thorpe Davie*
19540920 Parrott
19540923 Howells
19540930 Ferguson
19541002 Gurney
19541003 Thorpe Davie*
19541003? Blunden*
19541004 Ferguson
19541006 Parrott
19541007 Ferguson
19541008 Milford
19541009 Thorpe Davie*
19541011 Rubbra
19541012? Milford
19541014 Bliss
19541015a Blunden

19560221 Ferguson
19560224 Michael Wilson
19560302a Navarro*
19560302b Thorpe Davie*
19560306a Rubbra
19560306b Thorpe Davie*
19560301–19 Milford
19560312 Cannon
19560317 Rubbra
19560320 Milford*
19560320? Thorpe Davie*
19560321a Cannon
19560321b Barbirolli
19560322 Milford
19560323 Rubbra
19560327 Milner*
19560330 Blunden
1956? Milford
19560403 Milford
195603/04? Milford
19560413 VW
19560427a Williamson
19560427b Ferguson
19560429 Howells
19560430 Howells*
19560505 [Macnaghten]*
19560507a Rubbra
19560507b Howells
19560509 Ponsonby*
19560514 Ferguson
19560516 Thorpe Davie*
19560517 Ponsonby*
19560523 Howells*
19560524 Blunden*
19560528a Milford
19560528b Milford*
19560528c Howells
19560531 VW
19560601 Milford*
19560603 Thorpe Davie*
19560605 Thorpe Davie*
19560607 Thorpe Davie*
19560608? Thorpe Davie*
19560611 Milford
19560615 Thorpe Davie*
19560616a Milford
19560616b Navarro*
19560628a VW
19560628b Thorpe Davie*
19560701a Stone
19560701b Thorpe Davie*
19560702 Rubbra
19560703 Barbirolli
19560704 Ferguson
19560707 Blunden*
19560723a Milford

19560723b Rubbra*
19560725 Rubbra
19560731 Rubbra
19560805 Milner*
19560809 Casals
19560810a Ferguson
19560810b Thorpe Davie*
19560811 Thorpe Davie*
19560812 Milner*
19560813 Milford
19560822 Blunden*
19560823 Barbirolli
19560829 Whistler
19560910 Thorpe Davie*
19560912/05? Milford
19560915 Thorpe Davie*
19560915/08? Milford
19560916 Howells
19560918 Howells*
19560919 Thorpe Davie*
19560920a Ferguson
19560920b Thorpe Davie*

posthumous
19560927a Bliss
19560927b Stewart
19560928a Hutton
19560928b Howells
19560928c Milford
19560928d Kirstie Milford
19560928e Brown
19560928f Eaton
19560928g Rose
19560928h Suddaby
19560928i Bullock
19560928j Bliss
19560928k Trudy Bliss
19560928l VW [*Joy]
19560928m Kitty Stewart
Thomson
19560928n Meredith Davies
19560928o Albi Rosenthal
19560928p Boughton
19560928q Aldridge
19560928r Beryl and David
Alexander
19560928s Bunting
19560928t Mary Tregenza
19560928u Thomas
Armstrong
19560928v Latham
19560929a VW
19560929b UVW
19560929c Janet Stone
19560929d Hubert Byard

19560929e Julius Harrison
19560930a Frankel
19560930b Jacob
19560930c Barbirolli
19560930d Wilson
19560930e Maconchy
19560930f Anthony Lewis
195609–11? Gilbert Spencer
19561001a Luty Warr-
Cornish (née Blow)
19561001b Jill Day Lewis
19561001c Helen Robinson
19561002a Lemare
19561002b Rubbra
19561002c Hull
19561003a Jackson
19561003b Ian Davie
19561004a Eurich
19561004b Ward Clarke
19561006 Blunden
19561007 Charles Oman
19561009 Wyton
19561010a Claire Blunden
19561010b Scott
19561012 Cannon
19561014 Lemare [*Joy]
19561017 McVeagh (to
Ferguson)
19561018 Boult
19561019 Boughton
19561022 Milford
19561029 Antoinette
Rubbra
19561102 McVeagh
19561109a Olive Farrar (to
Katie)
19561109b Kennedy
19561114 Olive Farrar (to
Katie)
19561204 Olive Farrar (to
Katie)
19561207 Lambert (Mrs)
19570102 Herrmann
19570113 Olive Farrar
19570128 Howells
19570129 Ferguson
19570201 Katie
19570203 McVeagh
19570208 Ferguson [*Joy]
19570212a Ponsonby
19570212b Herrmann
[*Joy]
19570307 McVeagh
19570430 Hokanson
19570505 Ian Davie
19570514 Scott

Opus Numbers

(All designations, including blanks and projections into which posthumous works could be neatly fitted, were Finzi's own.)

1 Ten Children's Songs
2 *By Footpath and Stile*
3 English Pastorals and Elegies
   A Severn Rhapsody
   Requiem da camera
4 Psalms for unaccompanied SATB
5 Three Short Elegies
6 Introit
7 *New Year Music*
8 *Dies natalis*
9 *Farewell to Arms*
10 Eclogue
11 Romance
12 Two Sonnets by John Milton
13a *To a Poet*
  b *Oh Fair to See*
14 *A Young Man's Exhortation*
15 *Earth and Air and Rain*
16 *Before and After Summer*
17 Seven Poems of Robert Bridges
18 *Let Us Garlands Bring*
19a *Till Earth Outwears*
  b *I Said to Love*
20 *The Fall of the Leaf*
21 Interlude
22 Oboe Quintet/[Elegy]
23 Five Bagatelles
24 Prelude and Fugue
25 String Trio/[Prelude for strings]
26 'Lo, the full, final sacrifice'
27 Three Anthems
   'My lovely one'
   'God is gone up'
   'Welcome sweet and sacred feast'

Index of works

Index of settings

Jones, William (1746–94), from the Arabic (or Samuel Rogers): 'On parent knees'

Kerr, William: 'In memoriam DOM'

Knevet, Ralph (1600–71): Introduction (*Farewell to Arms*)

Lamb, Charles (1775–1834): 'The old familiar faces'

Lucas, F. L. (1894–1967): 'June on Castle Hill'

Macleod, Fiona (1855–1905): 'The reed player'; 'The twilit waters'

Masefield, John (1878–1967): 'From "August, 1914" '; *The Tragedy of Nan*

Milton, John (1608–74): Two Sonnets

Peele, George (?1558–?97): Aria ('His golden locks')

Pellow, J. D. C.: 'After London'

Raleigh, Walter (?1552–1618): 'Epitaph'

Rogers, Samuel *see* Jones, William

Rossetti, Christina (1830–94): 'Before the paling of the stars'; 'Oh fair to see'; Ten Children's Songs

Shakespeare, William (1564–1616): *Let Us Garlands Bring*; *Love's Labour's Lost* (including Songs for Moth, Songs of Heims and Ver)

Shanks, Edward (1892–1953): 'As I lay in the early sun'

Stevenson, Robert Louis (1850–94): 'Time to rise'

Taylor, Edward (?1645–1729): 'God is gone up'; 'My lovely one'

Thomas, Edward (1878–1917): 'Tall nettles'

Traherne, Thomas (?1638–74): *Dies natalis*; 'Intrada'; 'News'; 'The preparative'; 'The recovery'; 'The world'

Udall, Nicholas (1505–56): *Ralph Roister Doister*

Vaughan, Henry (1622–95): 'The brightness of this day'; 'Death (Dialogue between the Body and Soul)'; 'My God and King'; 'They are all gone'; 'Up to those bright and gladsome hills'; 'Welcome sweet and sacred feast'

Whistler, Laurence (*b*1912): 'The quick and the dead'

Wood, Ursula (*b*1911): 'Muses and Graces'

Wordsworth, William (1770–1850): *Intimations of Immortality*

General index

Abercrombie, Lascelles 67
Abraham, Harriette 5
Abrahams, Harold 26–7
Ackland, Valentine 486
Adcock, Mr 410–11
Adler, Guido 188
Albania 269
Aldbourne 166, 216–19,
    221–3, 225, 227, 237,
    241, 270, 420; Beech
    Knoll 216, 218, 235, 240
Aldbourne Band 168–9, 430
Aldridge, John 480
Alexander, Samuel 268
All Smith Choir 436
Allen, Hugh 86
Alston, Audrey 14
Ambrose, Bert 103
America, United States of 8,
    100, 110–12, 115, 131,
    162–3, 172, 225, 274,
    279, 319, 361, 369, 492;
    Americans 435; Broadway
    295, 335; California 398,
    484; CBS 319; Curtis
    Institute 99, 134;
    Hollywood 295, 374, 381,
    458; musicals 103, 334;
    New York 110, 226;
    Philadelphia 99, 110, 113,
    117; Smith College 435;
    Tin Pan Alley 418;
    University of California at
    Berkeley 277; Vassar
    College 44, 435–6

Amhurst Glee Club 436
Amis, John 314, 319, 430–1
Anderson, Mary 226, 300
Andriessen, Hendrik:
    Variations on a Theme by
    Couperin 286
Anglican chant 129–30
Aquinas, St Thomas 327–30,
    443
Architectural Association
    235
Armstrong, John 119, 171
Arne, Thomas 345, 406–8;
    keyboard concertos 393,
    405–7, songs 408; trio
    sonatas 414
Arnold, Malcolm 295, 327,
    335, 449; Clarinet
    Concerto 361
Arnold, Samuel 371
Arts and Crafts movement
    60–98, 117, 130, 140,
    240, 313, 335
Arts Council 283, 323, 432,
    439–40, 486
Ashbee, C. R. 71–2, 81, 117
Ashmansworth 236–7, 250,
    262, 270, 284, 312, 317,
    398, 421; Church Farm 9,
    65, 75, 77–8, 79, 128,
    165, 177, 217, 222, 226,
    235–41, 256, 269–71, 299,
    308, 314, 319, 343, 352,
    369–70, 391, 400, 412,
    421, 430, 435–6, 440,

445, 452, 459–61, 483–4,
    486–9, 492, 497; Doiley
    Bottom 273; St James's
    Church 282, 284–5, 455,
    491
Ashmore, Lawrence 285–6
Atkins, Ivor 324, 370
Auden, W. H. 161
Ault, Norman 310
Austin, William 429
Australia 22, 484;
    Aborigines 266–7; and
    New Zealand 319
Austria 173, 259, 263, 268;
    see also Germany;
    Viennese School, Second
Avison, Charles 408, 410

Bach, Johann Christian
    406–7
Bach, Johann Sebastian 122,
    131–8, 163, 213, 228,
    242, 284–5, 296, 304,
    322, 389, 401–2, 406–7,
    450, 458; 'Air on the G
    string' 136; Brandenburg
    Concertos 132, 406;
    Cantata 140 (Wachet auf)
    136, 401; cantatas 404;
    'Christe, du Lamm
    Gottes' 135; Chromatic
    Fantasia 157; concertos
    with strings 404, 406;
    Fantasia and Fugue in C
    minor for organ 132;

Fisher family 100
Flaherty, Robert 175
Flecker, James Elroy 51,
 290–1
Flemish art 108
Flood, W. H. Grattan 408
Foreman, Lewis 490–1
Forster, E. M. 72
Foss, Hubert 204–5, 295,
 395
Fox, Douglas 400
Fox Strangways, A. H. 393
France 12–13, 22, 173, 261,
 273; Chartres 172;
 Dunkirk 273; Huguenots
 267; musical style 336,
 339, 447; neoclassicism
 105; Paris 13, 69, 268,
 273; song 418; University
 of Paris 6
Franck, César 112
Franco-Russian aesthetic
 104–5
Frankel, Benjamin 375, 423,
 453–4
Frankel family 259
Fraser Darling, Frank 452,
 487
Freeman, John 50–2
Fricker, Peter Racine 472
Frost, Robert 67

Gardiner, Henry Balfour 53,
 227
Garibaldi, Giuseppe 4, 7,
 494
Garland for the Queen, A
 439–40, 442–3
Garth, John 410, 412
GCE examinations 487
Geer, Harold 44
Geoffroy-Dechaume,
 Charlôt 69–70
Georgian poetry 48, 61, 66,
 72, 88, 94, 342
Georgian period 392–3;
 composers 404; survival
 131, 412; neo-Georgian
 architecture 240
German, Edward 295, 335,

389; Merrie England 10;
 Nell Gwynn 469
Germany 7, 8, 12–14, 101,
 107, 162, 173, 231,
 258–68, 317; Anschluss of
 Austria 259; Austro-
 German tradition 104,
 372–3; cultural identity
 388; Hamburg 6; Hanover
 7; language 417; Leipzig
 14; Mannheim
 School 407; Munich
 crisis 173, 237, 239, 253,
 259–60; musical style
 288; nationality 23, 25;
 Nazis 232, 257–69; north
 German school 407; opera
 334; Pan-German
 customs Anschluss 173;
 Swinemünde 263; see also
 Czechoslovakia:
 Sudetenland; Hitler, Adolf
Gershwin, George 129
Gibbons, Orlando 151, 345
Gibbs, Cecil Armstrong
 54–5, 234; 'As I lay in the
 early sun' 47–8
Gibson, W. W. 67; Whin 88
Gilbert and Sullivan 23, 26;
 Utopia Limited 206
Gill, Harry 492
Gilmour, Kay (Katie) née
 Finzi 10–12, 21, 22, 24,
 352, 494–5
Gimson, Ernest 68, 71, 240,
 313
Glock, William 486
Gloucester and
 Gloucestershire 60–1, 67,
 99, 114, 324–5, 371, 388,
 399, 410, 452, 478–80,
 492, 497; Cathedral 222,
 480; Chosen Hill 60–3, 68,
 95–6, 454, 479, 497;
 Churchdown 60–1, 112;
 Hucclecote 61; Library
 399; Longford 61; May
 Hill 485; Twigworth 62,
 397; Upleadon 479–80;

see also Painswick; Three
 Choirs Festival
Gloucester Journal 398
Glover, Cedric 368
Glyndebourne 223
Godfrey, Dan 86, 115, 171
Godfrey, Peter 479
Godfrey, Sheila 479
Goebbels, Joseph 263, 267
Goering, Hermann 267
Goethe, Johann Wolfgang
 von 285, 388
Goldberg, Johann Gottlieb
 190
Goldsbrough Orchestra 459
Gollancz Ltd, Victor 270
Gomperts, Barbara 176
Goodwin, Felix 397
Goodwin & Tabb 406
Goossens, Eugene 62, 95,
 104; operas 334
Goossens, Léon 95,
 199–201, 234, 286
Goulden, Leila 169
Grainger, Percy 336, 392;
 'Country gardens' 69
Graves, Robert 51–3
Gray, George 19
Greco, El 369
Greek folksong settings 392
Greek National Committee
 for Broadcasting 392
Greene, Eric 286, 310,
 319–21, 324–5, 370–1
Greene, Harry Plunket 32,
 206, 393; Singing
 Learned from Speech 34–7
Greene, Maurice 408
Greenwood, Michael 333,
 339
Grieg, Edvard 268
Griller Quartet 170
Grinke, Frederick 286, 480;
 Grinke Trio 249
Grove, George 392
Groves, Charles 139, 141,
 310
Grynspan, Herschel 268
Guild of Handicraft 71, 117,
 209

evening-watch' 85; Four
Songs for Voice and
Violin 128; Fugal
Concerto 131; Fugal
Overture 131; Hardy
settings 53; Humbert
Wolfe songs 143, 155,
204, 354; *Hymn of Jesus*
82; *A Moorside Suite* 168;
operas 334; *The Perfect
Fool* 105; *The Planets* 32,
105, 475; *St Paul's Suite*
283–4; *Sāvitri* 50; Seven
Part-Songs 194
Holst, Henry 115, 286
Holst, Imogen 131; Oboe
Quintet 199
Honegger, Arthur 106
Hong Kong 398, 478;
University of 343
Hope, May 283
Hopkins, Antony 319
Hopkins, Gerard Manley
192
Horace 177, 216
Housman, A. E. 41, 54, 238,
417, 476; *A Shropshire
Lad* 146
Howard, Leslie 273
Howard-Jones, Evlyn 104,
111
Howe, Mira 295
Howells, Dorothy *née* Dawe
62–3
Howells, Herbert 25, 39, 54,
61–6, 100, 116, 121,
167–8, 231, 276, 303,
322, 327, 342, 389–90,
393–4, 396–7, 399, 418,
442, 451–3, 479; Clarinet
Quintet 365; Concerto for
Strings 66, 255; Elegy 65;
'Finzi's rest' 65, 489; 'Here
is the little door' 189;
Howells' Clavichord 489;
Hymnus paradisi 65–6,
369, 371–2, 380, 479; *In
Green Ways* 167;
Lambert's Clavichord 66;
'Miss T.' 94; *Missa*

Sabrinensis 65; Piano
Quartet 61–2, 66; Second
Piano Concerto 64; 'A
spotless rose' 189; Third
Violin Sonata 66
Howells, Michael 65, 303,
394
Howells, Ursula 63, 303
Howes, Frank 59, 155–6,
318, 342, 344, 350, 361,
372, 409, 431, 442–3,
452, 460, 469
Hughes, Hugh 269
Hull, Percy 252–3
Hungary: Budapest 283
Hunt, Leigh 216
Hussey, Dyneley 320
Hussey, Walter 326–7, 331
Hutchings, Arthur 233, 320
Hutton, Graham 162–5,
168–9, 174, 390, 484
Huxley, Julian 265
Hyam, David 6
Hyam, Hyam 6
Hyam, Kate 6
Hyam, Simon 6
Hyam Brothers 6
Hyperion Records 490

Iliff, Noel 331–2
India 11, 178, 270
Ipswich 6
Ireland 312, 447; Aran Isles
175, 224–5; Belfast 109,
113; Northern Ireland
178, 463; *see also*
Scotland: Celtic
influence
Ireland, John 15, 104–5,
168, 170, 172, 244, 273,
442; Cello Sonata 170;
Julius Caesar 339; Piano
Sonata 301; Second
Violin Sonata 66
Irving, Ernest 336
Irving, Henry 335–6
Irwin, Robert 208, 294, 312,
354–5
ISCM 87, 107, 171
Italy 4, 261, 273, 417, 487;

Ferrara 4; language 417;
Leghorn 4, 6; music 206,
296; opera 334, 407;
Padua 4; Pisa 6; primitive
painters 107; renaissance
polyphony 129; singing
style 34, 418; *see also*
Mediterranean influence

Jacob, Gordon 100–1, 110,
139, 300, 460
Jacobson, Maurice 118
James, Ivor 14, 200
Janáček, Leo: Sinfonietta
155
Japan 265, 343, 352, 398
Jarnach, Philipp 106
jazz 103, 175, 187–8; stride
187–8
Jenkins, Cyril 189
Jenkins, Gilmour 279, 483
Jenkins, Mr 80
Jenkins, Neil 490
Jewson, Norman 71
Joachim, Joseph 268
John Lewis Partnership
Society 195
Johnson, Samuel 411
Jones, Philip 286
Jones, William 222
Jonson, Ben 33, 296, 334
Joubert, John 315
Joyce, James 470
Juler, Pauline 299–300, 360

Kalmar Orchestra 318, 486
Katin, Peter 453
Kaye, Walter 125, 233
Keats, John 155, 215–16
Keller, Hans 248
Kelly, Gerald 353
Kelmscott Manor 70–1
Kennedy, Priscilla 484
Kennedy Scott, Charles 171,
194–6, 321
Kennet and Avon Canal 166
Kent 285–6, 420;
Canterbury Cathedral 431;
Dartford 394; Knockholt
217
Kerr, W. H. 61, 67